History of the Settlement of Upper Canada (Ontario)

HISTORY

OF THE

Settlement of Upper Canada,

(ONTARIO,)

WITH SPECIAL REFERENCE TO

THE BAY QUINTÉ.

BY

WM. CANNIFF, M.D., M.R.C.S.E.,

PROFESSOR OF SURGERY UNIVERSITY VICTORIA COLLEGE, AUTHOR OF THE "PRINCIPLES OF SURGERY."

TORONTO:
DUDLEY & BURNS, PRINTERS, VICTORIA HALL.
1869.

TO

THE HONORABLE

SIR JOHN ALEXANDER MACDONALD, K.C.B., D.C.L., M.P.,

PREMIER OF THE DOMINION OF CANADA,

THIS VOLUME IS BY PERMISSION RESPECTFULLY DEDICATED,

AS

A RECOGNITION OF HIS ABILITIES AS A CANADIAN STATESMAN,

AND AS A TRIBUTE TO A LONG STANDING INHABITANT OF BAY QUINTE, WHO HAS GIVEN HIS TALENTS AND ENERGIES TO LAY A SURE FOUNDATION FOR "A GREAT NORTHERN NATION."

BY HIS RESPECTFUL ADMIRER,

WILLIAM CANNIFF.

PREFACE.

In the year 1861 a meeting was convened at the Education Office, Toronto, with the view of establishing an Historical Society for Upper Canada. The writer, as an Upper Canadian by birth, and deeply interested in his country with respect to the past as well as the future, was present. The result of that meeting was the appointment of a Committee to frame a Constitution and By-Laws, and take the necessary steps to organize the proposed Society, and to report three weeks thereafter

The Committee consisted of the Hon. Mr. Merritt, Rev. Dr. Ryerson, Col. Jarvis, Mr. DeGrassi, Mr. Merritt, J. J. Hodgins, Dr. Canniff and Mr. Coventry. For reasons unknown to the writer, this Committee never even met. The following year the writer received a printed circular respecting an "Historical Society of Upper Canada" which had been established at St. Catharines, of which Col. John Clarke, of Port Dalhousie, was President; Hon. Wm. H. Merritt, Vice-President, and George Coventry, of Cobourg, Secretary.

"HONORARY MEMBERS."

"Chief Justice Sir John Beverley Robinson, Bart.,
Colonel Jarvis, *Toronto*,
Doctor Canniff, "
Henry Eccles, Esq., Q.C.,
William H. Kittson, Esq., *Hamilton*,
Henry Ruttan, Esq., *Cobourg*,
The Venerable Lord Bishop of Toronto,
Alfio DeGrassi, Esq., *Toronto*,
J. P. Merritt, *St. Catharines*,
Thomas C. Keefer, Esq., *Yorkville*,
Hon. George S. Boulton, *Cobourg*,
David, Burn, Esq., *Cobourg*."

At the request of this Society the writer undertook to prepare a Paper upon the Settlement of the Bay Quinté. Having been induced to take up his abode for a time at Belleville, near which he was born, the writer availed himself of every opportunity he could create while engaged in his professional duties, during a period of five years, to collect facts pertaining to the subject. After some months of labor, he was advised by friends, in whose judgment he had confidence, to write a History of the Bay Quinté, for publication.

Acting upon this advice, he continued, with increased energy, to collect and elaborate material. In carrying out this object, he not only visited different sections of the country and many individuals, but consulted the libraries at Toronto and Ottawa, as well as availed himself of the private libraries of kind friends, especially Canniff Haight, Esq., of Picton. As the writer proceeded in his work, he found the subject assuming more extended proportions than he had anticipated. He found that, to write an account of the Settlement of the Bay Quinté, was to pen a history of the settlement of the Province. Finally, he has been induced to designate the work "A History of the Settlement of Upper Canada."

The labor, time and thought which has been given to the subject need not to be dwelt upon. Every effort has been made, consistent with professional duties, upon which the writer's family is dependent, to sift a mass of promiscuous material which has come under investigation, so that grains of truth alone might fill the measure which this volume represents.

Various sources of information have been duly indicated in the text; but there are a large number of individuals, from whom information has been obtained, whose names could not be recalled.

This work has been one of love as well as labor; yet time and again the writer would have relinquished it had it not been for the words of encouragement, volunteered by his friends.

The writer has explained the cause of his writing this volume. He now presents it to the reader—to Canadians—to the world. He loves his country so well, that he regrets an abler pen had not undertaken the task, that justice might be more fully done to the worthy.

Fault may be found because of repeated and earnest protests against the attitude, assumed by the United States: the comments made in respect to their history: the contrast drawn upon the subject of LIBERTY and FREEDOM. The writer offers no excuse. He has endeavored to adhere to truth. It is true these pages have been written during a period of great irritation to Canadians, from the hostile and aggressive spirit which the United States have displayed towards us; but a record has been made which, it is trusted, will stand the test of the closest examination.

As to the work, apart from its historical character, no remark is offered, except that the writer is perfectly conscious of errors and imperfections. Time has not been allowed to polish; and while the pages have been going through the press, other necessary duties have prevented that close and undivided attention which the work demanded. But subscribers to the volume were urgent in their requests to have the work without further delay. The reader is referred to a page of *Errata*.

A concluding chapter it has been found necessary to omit, in consequence of the size already attained. In this it was intended to discuss the future prospects of the Dominion. The writer has unbounded faith in the Confederation scheme. Before this scheme was initiated, the writer, in a lecture delivered to a Toronto audience, uttered those words. Pointing out the elements which constitute the fabric of a great nation, he remarked that he "loved to contemplate the future, when all the British American Provinces would be consolidated into a grand whole; when, from the summit of the Rocky Mountains, would be seen—to the East along the magnificent lakes and river to the Atlantic, and down the western slopes to the Pacific—the ceaseless industry of the Canadian beaver, and the evergreen Maple Leaf overshadowing the peaceful homes of Canada." The prospects now are far brighter than when those words were spoken; and notwithstanding the obstacles—an unpatriotic company of Englishmen, the unscrupulous designs of covetous Americans, and the apathy of the British Government—the belief is broad and strong that the dream of the future will be realized. There is life in the tree whose seed was planted eighty years ago, and as it has in the past continued to grow, so it will in the future.

In concluding these prefatory remarks, we desire to tender our thanks to all who have assisted us directly or indirectly, by supplying information, and by encouraging words. Particularly we thank those gentlemen who gave their names as subscribers, some of them voluntarily, years ago, before the work was fairly commenced; also the Hon. Lewis Wallbridge, for procuring for us, when Speaker, copies of manuscript in the Parliamentary Library, at Ottawa.

Finally, we express our obligations to the Publishers and Printers.

Toronto, 27th March, 1869.

[*Copy Right secured.*

CONTENTS.

A SKETCH OF FRANCO-CANADIAN HISTORY.

CHAPTER I.

CHAPTER II.

DIVISION I.

THE REBELLION OF 1776—THE THIRTEEN COLONIES.

CHAPTER III.

CHAPTER IV.

CHAPTER V.

CHAPTER VI.

CHAPTER X.

CHAPTER XI.

DIVISION II.

TRAVELING IN EARLY TIMES—ORIGINAL ROUTES.

CHAPTER XII.

CHAPTER XIII.

CHAPTER XIV.

DIVISION III.

THE LOYALISTS AS PIONEERS—THE ORIGINAL SURVEY.

CHAPTER XV.

CHAPTER XVI.

CHAPTER XVII.

DIVISION IV.

THE FIRST YEARS OF UPPER CANADA.

CHAPTER XVIII.

CHAPTER XIX.

CHAPTER XX.

CHAPTER XXI.

CHAPTER XXII.

DIVISION V.

THE EARLY CLERGYMEN AND CHURCHES.

CHAPTER XXV.

CHAPTER XXVI.

CHAPTER XXVII.

CHAPTER XXVIII.

CHAPTER XXIX.

CHAPTER XXX.

CHAPTER XXXI.

PAGE

CHAPTER XXXII.

CHAPTER XXXIII.

DIVISION VI.

EARLY EDUCATION IN UPPER CANADA.

CHAPTER XXXVII.

CHAPTER XXXVIII.

CHAPTER XXXIX.

CHAPTER XL.

CHAPTER XLI.

DIVISION VII.

THE TERRITORY OF UPPER CANADA—THE BAY QUINTE.

CHAPTER XLII.

CHAPTER XLIII.

CHAPTER XLIV.

CHAPTER XLV.

DIVISION VIII.

THE FIRST TEN TOWNSHIPS IN THE MIDLAND DISTRICT.

CHAPTER XLVI.

CHAPTER XLVII.

CHAPTER XLVIII.

CHAPTER XLIX.

CHAPTER L.

CHAPTER LI.

CHAPTER LII.

CHAPTER LIII.

CHAPTER LIV.

CHAPTER LV.

CHAPTER LVI.

DIVISION IX.

THE EARLY GOVERNMENT OF UPPER CANADA.

CHAPTER LVII.

CHAPTER LVIII.

CHAPTER LIX.

CHAPTER LX.

CHAPTER LXI.

DIVISION X.

THE EARLY MILITIA OF UPPER CANADA.

CHAPTER LXII.

CHAPTER LXIII.

CHAPTER LXIV.

DIVISION XI.

ADVANCE OF CIVILIZATION.

CHAPTER LXV.

CHAPTER LXVI.

CHAPTER LXVII.

CHAPTER LXVIII.

DIVISION XII.

THE UNITED EMPIRE LOYALISTS—THE FATHERS OF UPPER CANADA.

CHAPTER LXIX.

CHAPTER LXX.

CHAPTER LXXI.

APPENDIX.

ERRATA.

Page 29, 12th line from top, instead of "1859," read "1759."

Page 80, 4th line from botton, instead of "are equally," read "were equally."

Page 102, 16th line from bottom, instead of "removed to the town," read "to the fifth town."

Page 104, instead of "Hodgins," read "Hudgins."

Page 104, 16th line from top, instead of "1859," read "1809."

Page 130, 4th line, 2nd paragraph, instead of "South," read "North."

Page 138, heading of page should be "Voyaging."

Page 192, bottom line, instead of "dispersed," read "dispossessed."

Page 257, 19th line, "gloomy," read "glowing."

Page 288, 19th line, "glowing a picture," should have "of" following

Page 293, instead of "Wesleyanism," read "Wesleyans."

Page 371, 14th line, instead of "1815," read "1615."

Page 437, 10th line from bottom, instead of "Lawer," read "Lawyer."

Page 585, 15th line, after "Governor," read *they were generally*.

Page 596, 3rd line, after "often," read *inferior*.

HISTORY

OF

THE SETTLEMENT OF UPPER CANADA,

WITH SPECIAL REFERENCE TO THE BAY OF QUINTÉ.

CHAPTER I.

INTRODUCTION.

A SKETCH OF FRANCO-CANADIAN HISTORY.

Contents—Antiquarianism — Records of the Early Nations—Tradition — The Press—The Eastern World—The Western World—Importance of History—Columbus—Colonization—Canada—America—Cartier—French Canadian writers — Cartier's first visit — Huguenots — Cartier's second visit—Jean Francois—Sir George E. Cartier—Establishment of the Fur Trade—Champlain—Discovery of Lake Ontario—Bay of Quinté—Quebec founded—First fighting with Indians—First taking of Quebec by the British—Returned to France—The Recollets and Jesuits—Death of Champlain—Foundation of Montreal—Emigration from France—The Carignan Regiment— DeCourcelle —Proposal to found a Fort at Lake Ontario—Frontenac—Fort at Cataraqui —La Salle — Fort at Niagara — First vessel upon the Lakes — Its fate —Death of La Salle, the first settler of Upper Canada—Founder of Louisiana—Discoverer of the mouth of the Mississippi.

There exists, as one characteristic of the nineteenth century, an earnest desire on the part of many to recall, and, in mind, to live over the days and years that are past; and many there are who occupy more or less of their time in collecting the scattered relics of by-gone days—in searching among the faded records of departed years, to eagerly catch the golden sands of facts which cling to legendary tales, and to interpret the hieroglyphics which the foot-steps of time have well-nigh worn away. To this fact many a museum can bear ample testimony. The antiquarian enjoys intense satisfaction in his labors of research, and when he is rewarded by the discovery of something new, he is but stimulated to renewed exertion. In the old world rich fields have been, and are now being explored; and in the new laborers are not wanting.

Since the days when man first trod the virgin soil of this globe, he has ever been accustomed to preserve the more important events of his life, and, by tradition, to hand them down to his childrens' children; and likewise has it been with communities and nations. Every people who are known to have occupied a place upon the earth, have left some indication of their origin, and the part they played in the world's great drama. In recent days, facts pertaining to nations and particular individuals are preserved in all their amplitude, through the agency of the Press. But in former centuries, only a few symbols, perhaps rudely cut in solid stone, commemorated events of the most important kind. The historians of Eastern nations have had to look far back into the misty past, to learn the facts of their birth and infant days; while the dark days of barbarism hang as a thick veil to obstruct the view. The middle ages, like a destructive flood, swept away, to a great extent, the records previously in existence. But out of the *debris* has been exhumed many a precious relic; and the stone and the marble thus obtained, have supplied valuable material on which to base trustworthy history.

In recording the events which belong to the Western world—this broad American continent—the historian has far less of toil and research to undergo. It is true the native Indian, who once proudly ruled the vast extent of the new world, has a history yet undeveloped. An impenetrable cloud obscures the facts appertaining to his advent upon this continent. The nature of his origin is buried in the ocean of pre-historic time. But in reference to the occupation of America by Europeans, the subjugation and gradual extermination of the Indian, the life of the pioneer, the struggles for political independence, the rapid growth and development of nations; all these results, embraced within the space of a few centuries, are freely accessible to the American historian.

The importance of history cannot be questioned; the light it affords is always valuable, and, if studied aright, will supply the student with material by which he may qualify himself for any position in public life. In the following chapters it is intended to draw attention more particularly to the new world, and to examine a few pages in the history of North America.

In the absence of any data upon which to base statements relating to the aborigines, we may say the history of the new world begins with the memorable and enterprising adventures of Christopher Columbus, in 1492; although there is evidence that

America had been previously visited by the people of Northern Europe, about the year 1000. The steady flow of emigrants which commenced a century later, from the old world to the new, of bold, energetic people, is a spectacle of grand import.

Almost every nation of Europe has contributed to the colonization of America. All, however, were not at first actuated by the same motives in braving the perils of the deep—then far greater than at the present day—and the dangers of the wilderness. The Spaniards were searching for the precious gold. The English desired to acquire territory;. the Dutch sought to extend their commerce; and the French, it is said, were, at first, intent only on converting the pagan Indians to Christianity.—(Garneau.) Space will not permit to trace the course of events in connection with the first settlements in America; the history of the several colonies, the bloody Indian wars, the contentions between the different colonizing people, the rebellions of the colonies and their achievement of independence. We shall mainly confine ourselves to those events which led to, and accompanied the settlement of Upper Canada.

Canada, the coast of which was first discovered by John Cabot, in 1497, is an honorable name, far more so than America. It has been a cause of complaint with some that the United States should appropriate to their exclusive use the name of America. But it is quite right they should enjoy it. It is after a superficial impostor, Amerigo Vespucci, who availed himself of the discoveries of Columbus, to vaunt himself into renown.

The word Canada is most probably derived from an Iroquois word, signifying Cabin. It has been stated on the authority of a Castilian tradition, that the word was of Spanish origin. The Spaniards, looking after gold, ascended the St. Lawrence, but failing to find the precious metal, exclaimed "Aca nada," (Here is nothing.) The natives hearing the land thus called, when Europeans again visited them, upon being asked the name of their country, replied "Canada," in imitation of the Spaniards. Again, Father Hennepin asserts that the Spaniards, upon leaving the land, gave it the appellation "El Cape di nada," (Cape nothing,) which in time became changed into Canada. But Charlevoix, in his "Histoire de la Nouvelle France," says that Canada is derived from the Iroquois word "Kannata," pronounced Canada, which signifies "love of cabins." Duponcion, in the "Transactions of the Philosophical Society of Philadelphia," founds his belief of the Indian origin of the name

Canada, on the fact that, in the translation of the Gospel by St. Matthew into the Mohawk tongue, by Brant, the word Canada is always made to signify a village. Taking the whole matter into consideration, there appears the best of reasons to conclude that Canada, a name now properly bestowed upon the Dominion, is of Indian origin, and signifies the country of a people who are accustomed to live in villages or permanent cabins, instead of in tents and constantly changing from one place to another.

The history of French Canada is one of unusual interest—from the time Jacques Cartier, in 1534, with two vessels of less than 60 tons burden each, and 122 men in all, entered for the first time the Gulf of St. Lawrence—up to the present day. It was not until the first decade of the 17th century, nearly a hundred years after Cartier first landed, that successful colonization by the French was accomplished. Nevertheless, Canada has as early a place among the colonies of America as New Netherlands or Virginia, which are the oldest States of the neighboring Union. Virginia was planted in 1608; New Netherlands (now New York,) was not settled until 1614. Prior to that, in 1609, Hudson had ascended the river now bearing his name, as far as the present site of Albany; but at the same time the intrepid Champlain was traversing the wilds of the more northern part of the territory to the south of Lake Ontario.

Although the history of New France is one of great interest, yet, in this local history, space can only be allowed to glance at the course of events in connection therewith. But French Canada is not in danger of suffering for want of historians to pen the events of her life. Already enthusiastic countrymen have done justice to the patriotism, valor and ability of the Franco-Canadian race. And, at the present time, earnest workers are in the field, searching among the records of the past, stowed away in Paris, with the view of making known all that can be learned of their sires. We find no fault with the intense love they bear to their language, their laws, their religion, their institutions generally. Such is characteristic of a high-spirited race; and, as common Canadians we rejoice to have so devoted a people to lay with us the foundation of our northern Dominion.

It has already been said that Jacques Cartier first landed in Canada in 1534. At this time the pent up millions of Europe, lying in a state of semi-bondage, were prepared to strike off the chains which had hitherto bound them, both in mind and body, to the select ones, who claimed that prerogative, as of Divine origin, and to avail themselves of the vast territory which Columbus had recovered from oblivion. Then was the future pregnant with events of the most startling nature—events fraught with interests of the most collossal magnitude. While America was to open up a new field for active labor, wherein all might pluck wealth, the art of printing, so soon to be in active operation, was to emancipate the mind, and cast broadly the seeds of universal liberty. Already was being broken the fallow ground, in the rich soil of which was to germinate the great truths of science.

In May, 1535, Cartier set out on his second voyage to the New World, in "La Grande Hermion," a vessel of 110 tons, accompanied by two other vessels of smaller size, with 110 men altogether. Reaching Labrador in July, he on St. Laurence Day entered St. John's River; and thus arose the name of St. Lawrence, afterward applied to the mighty river now bearing that name. Guided by two natives, Cartier ascended the St. Lawrence as far as the Isle d'Orleans, where he was received by the Indians in a friendly spirit. Cartier having determined to stay the winter, moored his vessels in the St. Charles River, with the Indian village of Stadaconé upon the heights above him. The same autumn he ascended with a small party to visit Hochelaga, now Montreal. Here he found a considerable village of fifty wooden dwellings, each fifty paces long, and twelve and fifteen broad. This village was fortified. An aged and withered chief accorded Cartier a distinguished reception; after which Cartier ascended to the top of the mountain, to which he gave the name Mont Real, or Royal Mount, a name subsequently given to the village which has become the commercial capital of the Dominion, and which is destined to rival even New York.

Cartier's stay in Canada during the winter was attended with much distress, and the loss by death of twenty-six of his men; while most of the rest were almost dying, being, it is related, saved by the medical skill of the natives. In the Spring he returned to France, carrying with him several Indians. It was five years later before another visit was made to Canada, owing to the civil and religious wars existing in France. It was the cruel laws enacted and put in force at this time in France that expatriated so many noble Huguenots who were dispersed throughout Great Britain, Ireland, and afterward America, the blood of whom yet flows in the veins of many of the descendents of the loyal refugees from the rebelling States of America. In the Summer of 1541

Cartier again set sail for the St. Lawrence. He was to have been accompanied by one Jean Francois de la Roque, a brave and faithful servant of the king, to whom had been conceded the privilege of raising a body of volunteers to form a permanent settlement upon the St. Lawrence. But unforseen difficulties prevented his sailing until the following year. In the meantime Cartier, to whom had been given command, with five ships, had, after a tedious passage, reached Canada, and ascended to Quebec. The intending colonizers immediately went ashore and commenced the work of clearing the land for cultivation. The winter was passed in safety, but in the spring, tired of waiting for the Governor, who ought to have followed him the year before, and discovering signs of hostility on the part of the savages, he determined to return to France. So he embarked all the men and set sail. Before he had reached the Atlantic, however, he met la Roque, with some two hundred more colonists, who desired Cartier to return, but he continued his course to France. Jean Francois landed safely at Quebec. In the autumn he sent home two vessels for provisions for the following year, while he prepared to undergo the severity of the coming winter, a season that brought severe trials, with the death of fifty of his men. The following year he set out with seventy men to seek fresh discoveries up the river, but he was unsuccessful. France, again immersed in war, paid no attention to the request for succor in the New World, but ordered Cartier to bring back the Governor, whose presence as a soldier was desired. With him returned all the colonists. Thus the attempt to establish a settlement upon the St. Lawrence failed, not, however, through any want of courage, or ability on the part of Cartier, the founder of Canada. The name thus immortalized and which disappeared from the history of Canada for many years, again occupies a place. And, Sir George Etienne Cartier, of to-day, although not a lineal descendent of the first Cartier, holds a position of distinction; and, as one who has assisted in effecting the Confederation of the provinces, his name will ever stand identified, as his great predecessor and namesake, with the history of our Canada.

In 1549, Jean Francois a second time, set out for Canada with his brother, and others, but they all perished on the way. This disaster prevented any further immediate attempt at settlement in Canada.

The commencement of the seventeenth century found France again in a state suitable to encourage colonial enterprize, and she, in common with other European nations was directing her attention to the yet unexplored New World. At this time one Pont-Gravé, a merchant of St. Malo, conceived the idea of establishing a fur trade between Canada and France; and to this end he connected himself with one Chauvin, a person of some influence at court, who succeeded in obtaining the appointment of governor to Canada, with a monopoly of the peltry traffic. These two adventurers, with a few men, set out for Canada, but arrived in a state of destitution. Chauvin died, while the others were preserved alive by the kindness of the natives. Chauvin was succeeded by De Chastes, Governor of Dieppe; and Captain Samuel Champlain, who had distinguished himself as a naval officer, was appointed to command an expedition about to proceed to the New World.

The name of Champlain is indelibly fixed upon the pages of Canadian history. It was he who traversed trackless forests, ascended the most rapid rivers, discovered the Lake of Ontario, by way of Bay Quinté, and gave his name to another lake. It was in 1603 that Champlain set out upon his voyage. He had but three small vessels, it is said, of no more than twelve or fifteen tons burden. He ascended as far as Sault St. Louis, and made careful observations. He prepared a chart, with which he returned to France. The king was well pleased with his report, and De Chaste having died, Governor de Monts succeeded him, to whom was granted, exclusively, the fur trade in Canada. But their operations were confined, at first, to Acadia, now Nova Scotia. In 1607 De Monts abandoned Acadia and directed his attention to Canada. Obtaining from the king a renewal of his privileges, he appointed Champlain his lieutenant, whom he despatched with two vessels. The party arrived at Stadaconé, on the 3rd of July. The party commenced clearing land where the lower town of Quebec now stands, and erected cabins in which to live. Having determined to make this the head-quarters of his establishment, he proceeded to build a fort. Thus was founded the ancient capital of Canada upon the Gibraltar of America. The powers granted to Champlain were ample, whereby he was enabled to maintain order and enforce law. During the well nigh one hundred years that had passed away since Cartier attempted to colonize, great changes, it would seem, had taken place among the Indians. Altogether different tribes occupied the Laurentian valley; and the former Indian villages of Stadoconé, and Hochelaga had been entirely destroyed, Champlain found the Indians of this place, the Algonquins, at enmity with other tribes to the west, the Iroquois. The Algonquins were glad to form an alliance with him against their long standing enemy. It suited the purpose of Champlain to thus ally himself; but the policy may well be questioned; at all events it inaugurated a long course of warfare between the French and the Iroquois, which only terminated when Canada became a British dependency. He, no doubt, was ignorant of the great power and superiority of the confederated five nations which formed the Iroquois people. The first encounter between Champlain and the Indians took place the 29th of July, 1609, by the lake which now bears his name, which had been known by the Indians as Lake Corlar. The Iroquois, who had never before seen the use of fire-arms, were naturally overwhelmed with surprise at this new mode of warfare, by which three of their chiefs were suddenly stricken to the earth; and they beat a hasty retreat, leaving their camp to the pillage of the enemy. The following year Champlain again set out with his Indian allies, and a second time drove them from the well contested field by the use of fire-arms. It was on this occasion he first met the Hurons, which were to become such fast allies, until almost exterminated. But the time came when the Iroquois, supplied with arms and trained to their use, by the Dutch, became better able to cope with the French. In 1612 Count de Soissons succeeded De Monts. Champlain, who was again engaged in war, was at the same time endeavoring to advance the peltry traffic, a trade that had many vicissitudes, owing to the changing opinions at home, and the uncertain support of merchants. He commenced the erection of a fort at Montreal, and formed an alliance with the Huron Indians.

In the year 1615, the Iroquois were collected near the foot of Lake Ontario, a body of water as yet unseen by Europeans. At the request of the Indians, it has been said Champlain set out to attack them, after having ascended the Ottawa. The course taken by him, and the disastrous result are given in connection with the discovery of the Bay Quinté. The year 1628 saw Canada, as well as the colony of Florida, pass under the power of the "Company of the Hundred Partners." The same year saw Quebec in a state of great distress, the inhabitants almost starving, and a fleet of British war vessels at the entrance of the St. Lawrence demanding the surrender of the fort. War was then existing between England and France, arising out of the intestine war of France, between the Huguenots and the Catholics, which had resulted in the subjugation of the former, many of whom had sought refuge in England and entered her service. Two of the vessels now threatening French Canada were commanded by Huguenots, one Captain Michel; the other David Kertk. The latter demanded the surrender of Quebec, but Champlain concealed the great straits to which he was reduced and bravely withstood the famine and cold through the long winter, in the hopes of relief in the spring, which was destined never to reach him. Instead of relief, the spring brought three vessels of war, commanded by Kertk's, two brothers, Louis and Thomas. The demand to surrender could no longer be refused, and upon the 29th July, 1618, the English took possession of Quebec. Louis Kertk became Governor, while Champlain accompanied Thomas Kertk to Europe. Quebec remained in British possession until the treaty of St. German-en-Laye, signed 29th March 1632, by which England renounced all claims upon New France.

Quebec was governed by Louis Kertk during the three years it was in possession of England, and he returned it to the French, it was alleged, a heap of ruins. On the ensuing year, the "Hundred Partners" resumed their sway, and Champlain was re-appointed Governor, who came with much pomp and took possession of Fort St. Louis with the beating of drums. Hereafter emigration from France was accelerated. Even some of the higher classes sought in Canada, repose from the troubles incident to religious and domestic war, although Catholics. The Jesuits were now superseding the order of Recollets, and were earnestly seeking to convert the Hurons; and at the same to secure their trusty allegiance. For two years prosperity continued to smile upon the province, and in 1635 the Jesuits laid the foundation stone of the College of Quebec. But the same year took from New France its chief and its greatest friend. Champlain died on Christmas day in Quebec, after "thirty years of untiring efforts to establish and extend the French possessions in America." This great discoverer, and founder of Quebec left no children, his wife remained in Canada four years, when she returned to France.

Following the death of Champlain was the terrible onslaught by the Iroquois upon the Hurons, whom they entirely destroyed as a nation, leaving but a remnant under the protection of the French. In 1642 M. de Maisonneuve laid the foundation of Montreal, the village consisting of a few buildings with wooden palisades, was then called "Ville-Marie." Maisonneuve gathered here the converted Indians to teach them the art of civilization.

The successor to Champlain was M. de Chateaufort: but we cannot continue to even sketch the history of the several Governors, and the successive steps in Canadian development only so far as they bear upon our subject.

In 1663 the population along the St. Lawrence numbered to between 2,000 and 2,500. In 1665 the number was increased by emigration, and by the arrival of the Carignan regiment, a veteran body of men who became permanent settlers, and who aided much in controlling the Indians and maintaining the power of the French. The same year live stock was introduced, and horses for the first time were seen in Canada. About this time commenced, in earnest, the struggle between England and France for the supremacy of the fur trade. The viceroy, M. de Tracy, began to erect regular forts upon the Richeleu. In 1671 there was a rendezvous of Indian Chiefs at Sault St. Marie, and through the influence of Father Allouez, the several tribes consented to become subjects of France. In the same year M. de Courcelles, now Governor, in pursuance of the attempt to govern the fur trade, conceived the idea of planting a fort at the foot of Lake Ontario. But he left before the work had commenced, and was succeeded by Louis de Buade, *Conte de* Frontenac, after whom the fort, subsequently erected, was called.

As the founder of the first settlement in Upper Canada, whose name is now so familiar, as belonging to a County, we may make space to say of Frontenac, that he was a gentleman of good birth, and had gained great distinction, having attained to the rank of Brigadier-General. He was somewhat proud and haughty, but condescending to his inferiors. His instructions from his master, the King, on coming to the Canada, were to secure the aggrandizement of France. Imigration in large numbers from France having been forbidden, he was to seek the increase of numbers in New France by stimulating early marriages. And to this day, the rate of increase by birth, among the French, is considerably greater than with the Anglo-Saxon.

He was to foster agriculture, the raising of stock, to increase the fishing operations, and the trade abroad; and he was instructed to take measures to construct a highway between Canada and Acadia, a plan which is only now about to be accomplished in the Intercolonial Railroad. Frontenac, likewise received very explicit instructions as to his procedure towards the Jesuits and Recollects; and he was charged " to administer justice with the strictest impartiality." The Colony being at peace, Frontenac's principal difficulty was in dealing with the Church, and he found it necessary to take high-handed steps to bring the Clergy into subjection to the State. There had been for years a struggle with respect to the liquor traffic among the Indians; the Bishops being opposed to it, while the Governor favored it for the purpose of furthering the trade in furs. The dissentions between parties became so great, and representations to the home authorities became so frequent and vexatious that Frontenac and the Intendant were both recalled in 1682. But during the incumbency of Frontenac, explorations had continued in the west, and the fort at Cataraqui had been fully established; and the Mississippi had been discovered by Pére Marquette and M. Joliet, in 1673. That same year Frontenac set out 29th of June, from Montreal, with an expedition for Cataraqui, arriving there 12th July. There was at this time one Robert Cavalier de la Salle, a native of Rouen, who had come to Canada when a young man, full of a project for securing a road by a northwestern passage to China. He was a man of ability and energy, but without means. But he managed to obtain the favorable notice of Governor Frontenac, who regarded him as a man after his own heart.

In the time of de Courcelles he opened a trading post near Montreal, now Lachine, so called from La Salle's belief that a pathway to China would be found thence across the Continent by the waters of the Ottawa or Upper Lakes. The discovery of the Mississippi caused no little sensation in Canada; and La Salle lost no time in asking permission and assistance to continue the western explorations, declaring his belief that the upper waters of the Mississippi would, if followed to there source, lead to the Pacific Ocean. He consequently submitted a petition for a certain grant of land at Cataraqui to the king, Louis X. (See under history of Kingston.)

Thus it seems that La Salle, a name greatly distinguished in connection with the discovery of the mouth of the Mississippi, stands connected very intimately with the foundation of Kingston. For him a Seigniory was here erected, and from this point he went forth on his eventful voyage. He was a man of much energy and lost no time in setting out. His boats laden with goods, and likewise with material for constructing a brigantine, and a fort, set sail for the Niagara River. The first steps La Salle prepared to take was to erect a second fort at Niagara, and then to build his vessel upon the waters of Lake Erie.

The construction of the defensive work of the fort, however, suited not the views of the Indians, so he satisfied himself with a palisaded storehouse. In the winter the vessel was commenced, six miles above the Falls. By the middle of summer it was ready to be launched, which was done with a salute of cannon, and the chanting of a Te deum, amid great rejoicing. There was also great demonstration among the Indians, who designated the French "Otkou," or "men of a contriving mind." The vessel was named *Griffon*, and on the 7th August, 1679. with seven guns, and small arms, and loaded with goods she entered Lake Erie. A few day's sail and Detroit, or the strait was reached; and on the 23rd August, she was cutting the waters of Lake Huron. In five days Michilmicinac was gained; then the voyageur proceeded to the western shore of Michigan, where he cast anchor. The wonder of the Aborigines, as they witnessed this mounted craft, and heard the thunder tones of the cannon, may be conceived. But this first vessel upon the western lakes, which had at first so prosperous a voyage, was doomed to early destruction. Men of enterprise and success invariably have to encounter enemies born of incapacity and jealousy, who in the absence of the victim, may sow the seeds of evil. La Salle had not a few of such enemies, it would seem, to encounter. After his departure his creditors had seized his possessions, and he, as soon as he heard of it, loaded the *Griffon* with peltries and despatched her for Niagara. But the *Griffon* never reached Detroit, the waters of Lake Huron swallowed her up, and all on board. La Salle proceeded with thirty men to the lower end of Lake Michigan, and laid the foundation of another fort. He then continued westward to the Illinois River, and formed still another fort. But this chain of forts thus established by La Salle, was not destined to accomplish the great end aimed at. Among the opponents of La Salle, were not only those jealous of his success, but likewise rival merchants, who were ill pleased to see the fur trade monopolized by one; and then, there was the growing trade by the English. These many obstacles and the loss of his vessel with its cargo, and of a second one, in the Gulph of St. Lawrence, about this time, valued at £22,000, had the effect of seriously crippling him; yet his was a nature not easily overcome. Leaving Father Hennepin to explore the Illinois River and the Upper Mississippi, he set out March 2nd, 1680, for Montreal, accompanied by four whites and an Indian guide.

Two years later and the indomitable La Salle, nothing daunted, who had compounded with his creditors, and suffered repeated disappointments, is found traversing the forest, for the Mississippi, to descend that stream to its mouth. He reached the Mississippi, 6th Feburary, 1682. Descending the stream he stopped at the mouth of the Ohio to erect a fort. He then continued his easy course down the Father of rivers, and reached its mouth on the 5th April, and took formal possession of the territory in the name of the king, calling the place after him, Louisiana. The glory thus won by La Salle, was not to be crowned with the success, financially, that ought to have followed. At this juncture Governor Frontenac, seemingly the only friend La Salle had, was called home to be followed by M. de la Barre. A continuation of the persecutions and misrepresentations of his conduct, led to the sequestration of Fort Frontenac, as well as Fort St. Louis, and in the following year he was called upon to defend himself at court, which he was able to do. The result was an order to reinstate the founder of Louisiana on his return, in Fort Frontenac, and to repair all damages which his property had sustained in that locality.

La Salle was graciously received by the king on account of his discovery of the mouth of the Mississippi, and was commissioned to begin a colonization of Louisiana. The same unfortunate luck continued to attend him. He sailed July 24th, 1684, from La Rochelle with two ships of war and two other vessels, having some 500 persons in all. The fleet was commanded by M. de Beaujeu. Between the commander and La Salle, a misunderstanding arose which ended in decided aversion. One of the ships was captured by the Spaniards, and the others overpassed the mouth of the Mississippi by many leagues. The commander instead of assisting to carry out La Salle's object, did all he could to thwart him. One of the vessels was run upon the reefs and lost. Finally Beaujeu left La Salle with his people upon a desert shore without provision, and put out to sea. Although 120 leagues distant from the Mississippi, in Texas, La Salle set some of his people to cultivate the land, and began to construct a fort. But the craftsmen were deficient. The seed sown did not grow, the savages became troublesome, and one evil after another rapidly succeeded until his men were mostly all dead. As a last resort La Salle determined to set out for Canada to proceed to France. It was early spring and the indomitable discoverer found but slow progress; at last some of those accompanying him, mutinied together and resorted to force, during which La Salle was mortally wounded. Thus perished the discoverer of the mouth of the Mississippi, the founder of Louisiana, as well as the first land owner of Upper Canada. It is worthy of note here how great was the territory of France in America at this time. It was a vast region, embracing within its limits the Hudson's Bay territory, Acadia, Canada, a great part of Maine, portions of the States of Vermont and New York, with the whole of the valley of the Mississippi. And a great portion of this ought, to-day, to form part of Canada, some of which would, were it not for the indifference, or stupidity of English commissioners, and the contemptible trickery of Americans, such as the act of concealing the fact of the existence of a certain map by Daniel Webster, which would prove adverse to his pretentions.

It has been deemed appropriate to follow La Salle in his steps, not alone because he was the first settler in Upper Canada, who held land property; but because we learn of the way in which the French, originally struggling to gain a footing in the Lower St. Lawrence, gradually extended westward, carrying in one hand the Cross, and with the other, planting forts for the purpose of trade, and erecting such defences as the uncertain character of the natives rendered necessary. We learn how it came, that fort after fort, whose ruins may yet be traced across the continent, were planted along a route which commenced at the mouth of the mighty St. Lawrence, extended along the western lakes, and then turning southward terminated at the mouth of the majestic Mississippi.

INTRODUCTION.

(CONTINUED.)

CHAPTER II.

Contents :—Cataraqui fort strengthened—Kente Indians seized and carried captive to France—Massacre of Lachine—Commencing struggle between New England and New France—Siege of Quebec by Sir Wm. Phipps—Destruction of Fort Cataraqui—Its re-erection—Treaty of Ryswick—Death of Frontenac—Iroquois in England—Another attempt to capture Quebec—Decline of French power—Population of Canada and of New England—Continuation of the contest for the fur trade—Taking of Fort Louisburg—Col. Washington, dishonorable conduct—Inconsistency of Dr. Franklin—Commencement of seven years' war—Close of first year—Montcalm—His presentiment—Taking of Fort Oswego—Of Fort William Henry—fearful massacre—The state of Canada—Wolfe appears—Taking of Frontenac—Duquesne—Apathy of France—The spring of 1759—Reduced state of Canada—The overthrow of French power in America—The result—Union of elements—The capture of Quebec—Wolfe—Death of Montcalm—Fort Niagara—Johnson—Effort to retake Quebec—Wreck of the French army—Capitulation at Montreal—Population—The first British Governor of Canada—The Canadians as British subjects—The result of French enterprise—Rebellion.

In 1685 Marquis DeNonville became Governor, and brought with him to Canada 600 regular troops. The Iroquois had become allies of the English, with whom they preferred to trade. DeNonville ascended to Cataraqui with two thousand men. Arrived at Cataraqui, he tried, by gentle means at first, to obtain certain terms from them, but the Iroquois were insolent, being supported by the English traders. DeNonville wrote to Paris for more troops, and, in the mean time, proceeded to accumulate stores at Cataraqui, and to strengthen the fort at Niagara. The King sent to Canada, in 1687, 800 soldiers, to assist in subduing the Iroquois. DeNonville becoming bold, and in his increased strength, pursued a course of trickery which has been branded by all writers as antichristian, and more savage than anything pertaining to the savages (so-called) of America. Pére Lamberville, a missionary among the Iroquois, caused a certain number of chiefs to congregate at Fort Frontenac, to confer with the governor, and when they were within the precincts of the fort they were seized and carried captive in chains, even to France, and there sent to the galleys. Draper says that these were Indians of the tribes called Ganneyouses and Kentes, and that about 40 or 50 men, and 80 women and children were seized, who were forwarded to France. The attitude of the Indians under such trying circumstances, towards the missionary among them, stands out in prominent contrast to the vile conduct of the French governor. The missionary, summoned by the chief, was thus addressed: "We have every right to treat thee as our foe, but we have not the inclination to do so. We know thy nature too well; thine heart has had no share in causing the wrong that has been done to us. We are not so unjust as to punish thee for a crime that thou abhorrest as much as we." Then the aged chief informed him that the young men of the tribe might not feel so lenient, and that he must leave, at the same time causing him to be conducted by a safe path from their midst.

For a time DeNonville somewhat curbed the Iroquois; but in the end he failed completely to hold the ground which had previously been acquired. For four years he continued to govern; matters continually growing worse, until, in the spring of 1689, 1,400 Iroquois made an onslaught on the island of Montreal. The inhabitants, in the depth of sleep, knew nothing of their danger, until the fearful whoop and the bloody tomahawk and scalping knife were already at work. The butchery was most fearful; the cruelties to women and children most revolting. Besides those instantly killed, 200 were burnt alive, and others died under prolonged torture. This was called the massacre of Lachine. The governor was paralyzed, and no step was taken to redress the great evil.

It was under such circumstances that he was recalled, and superseded by De Frontenac, who had again been requested to become governor. Frontenac landed at Quebec on the 18th October, 1689, and was received with every demonstration of joy.

Frontenac entered upon his duties shortly before the renewal of hostilities between England and France. All of Protestant Europe, indeed, were enlisted in the war which had, to a great extent, arisen from the cruel course pursued by France towards the Huguenots. Frontenac, whose master foresaw the war, which was declared in the following year, brought with him full instructions to prepare for a vigorous warfare all along the frontier of New France, even to the Hudson Bay territory. By this time the English settlements upon the Atlantic coast had attained to no inconsiderable strength, and were already engaging in trade by water, as well as with the Indians in peltries; and already it had become a question of conquest by New England or by New France. The present juncture seemed one favorable for bold measures on the part of the Anglo-Americans. They had rapidly advanced in material strength, while the French had rather declined, owing to the want of immigration and to the frequent destructive incursions of the Iroquois. The declaration of war between England and France, in June, 1689, saw the colonists prepared to contest the ground for supremacy, and monopoly of the fur trade. The French, notwithstanding their limited numerical strength, hesitated not to enter the field, and made up their want of numbers by superior and determined bravery. Before De Frontenac had arrived, everything was going on badly with the Canadians. M. DeNonville had, before his departure, instructed Senor de Valreuve, commandant at Cataraqui, to blow up the fort, which had been accordingly done; and the country abandoned to the Indians, who now ranged the country, to the very entrance of Montreal. But Frontenac determined to take bold and active measures to carry the war into the enemies country, notwithstanding the odds against the French. Organized plans of attack, at different points, were arranged, one of which, in its carrying out, was quite as cruel and barbarous as the Lachine massacre, which it was intended, as afterwards stated, it should revenge. A party of French and Indians were led in the direction of Albany. On their way, one night, about eleven o'clock, they attacked the sleeping town of Schenectady, and put the defenceless inhabitants to the sword. Those acts cannot be justified in Europeans, and show the fearful spirit of barbarity which reigned in those early days of America. The effect produced by the bands of raiders that swept over the British colonies along the frontier, and here and there, into the very interior, was salutary to the French interests, and the spring saw the French flag much more respected by the Indians than it had lately been: yet the Iroquois earnestly and boldly strove to carry death to the door of every Canadian hamlet. The energetic measures adopted by Frontenac frustrated all their attempts; yet it was unsafe for the husbandman to go to the field, so that famine began to appear. The spring of 1691 saw, however, instead of a repeated invasion of New England, extensive preparations in the latter country to invade Canada. Sir William Phipps was preparing to sail from Boston, with a squadron, to capture Quebec, and General Winthrop, with forces from Connecticut and New York, was mustering his militia, to invade by land. The latter marched to, and encamped upon, the banks of

Lake George, where he waited for the appearance of Phipps, by the St. Lawrence; but, in the meantime, disease attacked his troops, and he was obliged to retrace his steps to Albany. Scarcely had Winthrop departed when the fleet under Phipps entered the waters of the St. Lawrence, and ascended, to invest the City of Quebec, appearing in sight on the 16th of October. Phipps demanded a surrender; but Frontenac, although with an inferior garrison and but few troops, gave a spirited refusal; and ultimately, before the close of the month, Phipps found it expedient to retire. Thus terminated the first siege of Quebec.

The ensuing four years presented one continuous scene of border warfare. While hostilities in Europe were exhausting the resources of France, Canada, under Frontenac, was more than holding its own. The British Americans vainly tried again to besiege Quebec, making an attack by land; but each attempt was attended with disaster. Frontenac, recognizing the importance of Cataraqui as a place of defence, sent 700 men to re-erect the fort. In this he was opposed by the Intendant, M. de Champigny, and even by the home government; but he had the work completed in 1695, before orders came to abstain from erecting it. Frontenac had submitted a report giving the reasons why the fort should exist, namely: in time of peace for trade, and to repair hatchets and arms; and in time of war to afford a place of retreat, and to give succor and provisions; also a place to organize expeditions against the Iroquois, and to receive the sick and wounded on returning from expeditions. On the other hand, De Champigny reported that the trade would not be much in time of peace, as the Iroquois would prefer to deal with the English, who would give more; that the Indian should carry the beaver skin to the French, not the French go for it; that the fort was out of the direct course of trade, some thirty or forty leagues; that the force necessary to carry provisions would at any time be capable of proceeding against the enemy. It would be better to take a more southerly course from Montreal into the enemy's country, while Cataraqui is situated upon the opposite side of the lake; that it was an unfit place for sick and wounded, being "very unhealthy, eighty-seven having died there in one year, out of the hundred who composed the garrison." "The swamp poisons the garrison," which is so situated that it affords no protection except to the men within it, who might as well be in a prison. He counselled that the fort should be abandoned, as it was useless and expensive. Frontenac, however, having erected the fort, garrisoned it with 48 soldiers. The expense of re-establishing the fort and supplying the necessary provisions cost some £700. At this juncture the French had entertained the idea of calling in the outposts along the western lakes and upon the Mississippi, but it was represented that to do so was to open the way for the exclusive trade of the Indians with the English. But Frontenac advised no such measures. He, by his determined bravery, succeeded in bringing the Iroquois to respect the French name, and he often carried fire and death into their very country. When the war terminated, the old boundaries of the Provinces had been fully re-established, and honors were conferred upon the governor by his royal master. In 1697 the war terminated by the treaty of Ryswick, signed September 11, by which the French were to restore all places taken from the British in America; and it was stipulated that a commission should be appointed to determine the respective boundaries of the Provinces.

In the year 1698, on the 28th November, Count de Frontenac died, aged 77, much beloved by the Canadians, after having raised New France from a low condition to a high state of material advancement. But against him was too truly said that he encouraged the dreadful traffic of liquor among the Indians, in order that advantageous trading, in which the governor allowed himself to meddle, might be carried on.

On 26th May, 1703, M. de Callière, who had been the successor of Frontenac, died, and the governor of Montreal, who was the Marquis de Vaudreuil, was nominated as successor.

This appointment, made at the instance of the colonists, was conferred with hesitancy, the reason being that his Countess was a native-born Canadian! Not only in that day but in later days, and under other circumstances, we have seen the belief obtaining that natives of Canada must, from the nature of their birth-place, lack those qualifications for distinguished positions with which those from home are supposed to be so eminently endowed.

The British Colonists by this time began to entertain desires to conquer Canada, and steps were taken to accomplish the taking of Quebec. Among those who took an active part, by raising provincial troops,-and in visiting England to obtain assistance, was General Nicholson, whose descendants to this day live in the vicinity of the Bay Quinté, and in the Lower Provinces. In 1710 he visited England, in company with five Iroquois chiefs, who were presented to Queen Anne, and who received distinguished attention, being conveyed to the palace in royal coaches. It was following this that the Queen presented those interesting pieces of Communion plate to the five nations, part of which may be seen at Tyendinagua, and part at the Grand River. A futile attempt was made by Nicholson, with a fleet under Admiral Walker, in 1711, to take Quebec. The whole enterprise not only failed but was attended with great disaster. General Nicholson, with his army at Lake Champlain, had to give up his desire to capture Montreal and Quebec.

On March 30, 1713, was signed the treaty of Utrecht. In this treaty abridgement of French territory in America was effected. Acadia, Hudson's Bay territory and Newfoundland were ceded to Britain. French power was on the decline both in America, and Europe. Vainly the French tried to regain what they had lost in Newfoundland and Acadia, by founding an establishment at Cape Breton, and in the foundation of the historic fort of Louisburg.

In 1714 Governor Vaudreuil went to France, where he remained until September, 1716. He then returned to Canada, and set about improving the state of affairs generally. Quebec, at the present day such an impregnable fortress, was not, in any respect, regularly fortified before the beginning of this century. To the natural strength of the place was first added artificial aid, in 1702. To this again were added, in 1712, other defences, and in 1720, by the approval of the home government, the fortification was systematically proceeded with. At this time the colony was divided into three distinct governments, those of Quebec, Three Rivers, and Montreal; and the whole was sub-dividided into eighty-two parishes. The whole population was estimated at 25,000; whilst at the same time the British colonies had 60,000 males able to bear arms. The governor, aware of this, already began to fear a successful invasion of Canada.

M. de Vaudreuil died October 10, 1725, having been governor twenty-one years. He was succeeded by the Marquis de Beauharnois, who arrived at Quebec in 1726. The contest for the supremacy of the fur trade continued. The British seeing the advantage of the line of forts held by the French determined to erect a fort also, and selected the mouth of the Oswego for its site. As an offset to this aggression on the part of the British, against which the French vainly protested, the French fort at the mouth of the Niagara was erected, with defences; and orders were given that a stone fort should replace the one originally constructed of wood, at

Cataraqui. In 1731, Fort Frederick was also erected, at Crown Point, on Lake Champlain. This year, Varrennes, Sieur de la Vérendrye, urged by the governor, set about to discover a route to the Pacific ocean; but he only reached the foot of the Rocky Mountains, being the first white man to discover them. About this time the fort at Toronto (Lake) is, for the first time, referred to. For more than a decade the strife for the peltry traffic continued to be waged, yet without any actual warfare. It was seen by all that peace could not continue, and New England and New France were all the time anticipating the conflict. In 1745 war broke out in Europe, and immediately extended to America. It will be remembered that the French were dispossessed of Acadia, but had subsequently erected a fort upon Cape Breton, Louisburg. From this naval stronghold they were able to send privateers and men-of-war. The English, in the meantime, seeing this evil, and that this was a protection to the only entrance to French territory, determined to possess it promptly, if it were possible. To carry out this project, which originated with Governor Shirley, of Massachusetts, 4,000 militia, levied in Mass., New Hampshire, Maine, and Connecticut, under Colonel Pepperel, sailed from Boston in March. The attack upon this strong fort was so well planned and carried out, that full success was the result. Admiral Warren arrived with ships to give assistance, and captured a French ship of 64 guns, with 560 soldiers and supplies. Already the Anglo-Americans were beginning to display the energy (derived from an energetic race) which was to overturn British domination in the Atlantic States. But in the first place it was necessary that England should extinguish French power. The brilliant nature of the attack and taking of Fort Louisburg was recognized by the granting of baronetcies to Governor Shirley and Colonel Pepperel. This success hastened the determination to conquer Canada—a desire already existing in the hearts of the Anglo-Americans; and Governor Shirley applied to the British government for regulars and a fleet for that purpose. Meanwhile, a fleet, with several thousand troops, sailed from France, with a view of re-taking Cape Breton and Acadia; but tempest and disease destroyed the force, until it was no longer able to invade.

From the year 1745 border warfare continually blazed along the frontier. The French, with their savage allies, carried the scalping-knife and the torch into the British settlements, captured Fort Massachusetts and Fort Bridgman, and gained other victories, and the luckless settlers had to seek safety in the more largely-settled parts of the country.

Again came temporary peace to the colonists. In 1748, upon the 7th of October, the treaty was signed at Aix-la-Chapelles, by the terms of which Cape Breton reverted to the French. This treaty was, however, but a lull in the struggle in America, which was destined to end in conquest.

The French continued to strengthen their outposts. Detroit was garrisoned, and forts of stone were built at Green Bay, Toronto, and La Presentation. In 1756, Fort Duquesne, at Pittsburgh, was established. It was in this year that Washington first came before the public as an actor. He led a considerable force to the west, with the view of destroying Fort Duquesne, and encountored a small body of French. The man who subsequently became a hero by concurring events, as well as by his own energy, did not, on this occasion—if we may credit history—act a very honorable part. Informed of the camping ground of the enemy, he marched all night, to attack them in the morning. Junonville, the commander, when aware of the proximity of Washington, made known to him by a trumpeter that he had a letter to deliver, and when Junonville had begun to read his letter firing was suddenly re-commenced. The painters of Washington's character have tried to cover this stain; but unbiassed recorders think he was by no means blameless. But Washington's humiliation rapidly followed this unmanly procedure.. The main force of the French, hearing of the massacre by Washington, advanced to revenge it; and, attacking him in his own chosen position, succeeded, after ten hours' fighting with muskets alone, against cannon, in driving Washington from his position, and compelled him to make an inglorious retreat.

At the beginning of 1755, England sent out additional soldiers and means of war, and appointed General Braddock, who had distinguished himself as a soldier, to act as military chief.

At this time, "Dr. Franklin estimated the whole English provincials at a total of 1,200,000; whilst the whole number of people in Canada, Cape Breton, Louisiana, &c., was under 80,000 souls."—(*Garneau*). At the same time France was weak, by the presence of an indolent King, who allowed himself and kingdom to be governed by a courtesan, Madame de Pompadour. Religious dissensions and stagnation of trade, all contributed to place France in but a poor position to engage in war. Great Britain, on the contrary, was in all respects prosperous. At such a favorable time it was that the Anglo-

Americans urged the mother country to carry on, with the utmost rigor, a war for the subjugation of Canada. Franklin, as astute a politician as clever in science, was their principal mouthpiece. He who, twenty-five years thereafter, repaired to Paris, to arouse the public feeling of France and entire Europe against Britain; the same who came to Canada to revolutionize it in 1776, was, in 1754, the greatest promoter of the coming invasion of the French possessions in North America. "There need never be permanent repose expected for our thirteen colonies," urged he, "so long as the French are masters of Canada." Thus was inaugurated what is known as the seven years' war.

The respective combatants marshalled their forces for the conflict. The French, nothing daunted, took energetic measures to repel the foe, and strike blows here and there, as opportunity afforded. A force was sent to take Fort Oswego from the English, while Johnson, a name to be mentioned hereafter, was despatched to attack Fort Frederick. The first great battle was fought in the Ohio valley, by General Braddock. Here the French gained a signal victory, with but a few men, and utterly put to rout their enemy. At Fort Edward, the French, under General Dieskau, were less successful in an encounter with Johnson, the French commander being taken prisoner.

The close of the first year saw Forts Frederick, Niagara and Duquesne, still in the hands of the French, while bands of savages and Canadians traversed the British settlements, massacreing and burning all before them.

The ensuing year witnessed more elaborate arrangements to continue the war. France sent to Canada soldiers, provisions, war material and money; and, also, the Marquis de Montcalm was selected to take charge of the army. Montcalm had seen service, and with him came other officers likewise experienced.

Proceeding to Montreal, he conferred with the Governor, and it was determined to form two principal camps, one at Ticonderoga, the other at Frontenac, and a battalion was despatched to Niagara.

The British, at the same time, made extensive preparations, both in the colonies and at home, and the Earl of London was appointed generalissimo.

It is a remarkable fact that Montcalm had from the first a fatal presentiment as to the issue of the war; yet he, all the same, took every step that prudence and energy directed, to secure the success of his army. There was also a coolness between him and the Governor, who manifested a determination and energy worthy of him. It was determined that fresh attempts should be made to possess Fort Oswego, and General Montcalm arrived at Frontenac for that purpose on the 29th of July. Upon the 11th August they reached Oswego and invested the Fort, which was obliged to surrender on the 14th, the commander, Colonel Mercer, having been killed. The Fort was razed to the ground. The Canadians then withdrew to their homes carrying the prisoners of war, and the guns of the Fort, and provisions with them. This was the principal event of this year. The winter saw the Canadians suffer from famine and small-pox. During the winter 1757-8, there was continued hostility, and in the following year Montcalm succeeded in taking Fort William Henry, after a siege of four days. Colonel Munroe commanded the Fort, and he trusted for support to General Webb, who failed to afford it, but instead sent a message to Munroe to retire, which note fell into the hands of Montcalm. Munroe on the morning of the 9th, displayed his flag of truce The events of this capitulation have ever been held in remembrance, because of the fearful massacre which the Indians made of the English, who had surrendered, and who marched out without their arms, in full confidence in the integrity of the victorious besiegers. Stern history has cast no little blame upon Montcalm, for at least remissness of duty; and the pen of historic fiction has found it a fruitful theme with which to weave a story, and record thrilling events.

The ensuing winter was one of great privation to the Canadians, the harvest had failed; and everything began to look dark indeed for the devoted French; yet four years of war had given all the advantage to their arms. The continued ill-success of the British, caused them to raise increased numbers of men, so that by numerical force they might overwhelm the French. In the spring of 1758, 80,000 British combatants were ready to march. While such was the condition and war-like spirit which obtained upon the British side, a far different state of affairs existed with the French. Success had so far attended the gallant feats undertaken by them, All along the lengthened border the foe had been defeated, or had gained but scant victory. Again, the Iroquois nation, impressed with the success thus obtained by the French, and gratified to have the Fort of Oswego, always unpleasent to them, destroyed, seemed inclined to take sides with them, certainly did not favor the English. But, when so much has been said the extent of French power in America has been stated. Canada was no longer receiving support from France. The colonists had been weakened by continual warfare and repeated crop-failures.

But undeterred by the dark clouds that continued to thicken, the Canadians buckled on their armor to fight till the very last. Says Montcalm to the Minister at home, "We shall fight and we shall bury ourselves, if need be, under the ruins of the colony." Again the tide of war ebbed and flowed with fearful power. Carillon was made red with British blood, as vain endeavors were made to capture that French strong hold. Against Louisburg, Cape Breton, Carillon, Lake Champlain, and Duquesne in the Ohio Valley, the English arrayed their fleets and armies. In the attack now made upon Louisburg, for the first time appears the name of Wolfe, who distinguished himself by scaling a rock, with a hundred men, which had hitherto been regarded unaccessable. After a spirited defence, the French surrendered the Fort, a perfect wreck, July 26. About this time Cape Breton passed into British hands, and thus was opened to the English, the Fort of Quebec.

In the mean time the attack upon Fort Carillon by General Abercromby, with a strong army, had proved a complete failure. The French, although few, desperately met the repeated assaults made during half a day, and Abercromby, cut up and ashamed, was forced to relinquish the matter. This battle was fought July 8th, in which 3,600 men struggled successfully for six hours against 15,000 picked soldiers. (*Garneau*). De Lévis, who had been in command at Fort Frontenac, was called by Montcalm to take part in the defence of Carillon. This left Fort Frontenac comparatively weak, and Abercromby, having learned the fact, despatched Colonel Bradstreet, who had taken an active part in the battle, to capture the Fort. Bradstreet set out with 3,000 men, 11 guns and mortars. The invading force reached its destination August 25. The Fort had been left with 70 men under the command of M. de Noyan, notwithstanding, the Fort was bravely defended for a time. "The victors captured many cannons, quantities of small arms, boats of provisions and nine newly armed barques,—part of the trophies brought from Oswego when captured. After loading his barges to the waters-edge, Bradstreet released his prisoners on parole, burnt the Fort, also seven of the barks, and returned to his country." (*Garneau.*) This was a severe blow to the struggling Canadians. The Governor had ordered the farmers from the field, and all the savages he could command, to march to the assistance of Fort Frontenac; but when the party reached Fort Présentation, (Ogdensburg), it was learned that Frontenac was already destroyed. To add to the misfortune of the French, the same autumn, General

Forbes, notwithstanding a part of his force had been previously defeated, secured the destruction of Fort Duquesne on the Ohio. This closed the engagements for the year 1748, and everything looked for the French, most discouraging. The winter was spent by the English in preparing for a still more determined continuation of the war; while the French wasted their energies in domestic dissention. The Governor M. de Vandreuil and Montcalm ceased not to quarrel, and to charge each other with incompetency, and even crimes. At the same time the means of the country was absorbed by unpatriotic merchants, who availed themselves of the circumstances of the country to amass fortunes by illegal traffic in furs with the Indians.

The Government at home, although informed by Montcalm that Canada would be conquered if help were not sent, took no step to assist the devoted Colonists, who, although disheartened were not disposed to surrender allegiance to their native country, even when all but forsaken. The spring of 1759 beheld them standing to their arms with calm determination, awaiting the onset of the foe. The British as in previous years prepared to invade Canada simultaneously at three different points. There was no fortress in the Lower St. Lawrence to obstruct their advance by water, so Quebec was the point at which, to the east, the attack would be made. A corps of 10,000 men commanded by General Wolfe, who we have seen, distinguished himself at the taking of Louisburg, prepared to ascend the St. Lawrence to invest the capital. Another force 12,000 strong under General Amherst, a name we shall have to speak of hereafter, was to pass by Lake Champlain to descend the Richeleu and to join Wolfe at Quebec. And a third force, under General Prideaux, with savages under Sir William Johnson, were to possess Fort Niagara,and then descend to the capture of Montreal. Opposed to the numerous and well appointed armies of invasion, there was, according to Garneau, all in all of Frenchmen, between the ages of 16 and 60, capable of bearing arms, but a little over 15,000. In the early spring, one M. de Corbiere, ascended with the view of rebuilding Fort Frontenac. 300 men were also sent to repair and defend Niagara. But it soon was deemed expedient to recall them and to concentrate their forces. Every man from even the more remote parts, presented himself to the nearest place of rendezvous. In the latter part of May, word came that the enemies ships were coming.

The events connected with the overthrow of French supremacy in Canada cannot fail to impress the student of Canadian history.

The capture of Quebec, and, as an inevitable result, the conquest of Canada are events of great interest; but the space cannot be allowed here to more than refer to the thrilling scenes of valor displayed by the victors and the vanquished. As Canadians of British origin we recognize the event as one not to be deplored, however Franco-Canadians may regard the question. The conquest of Canada, was to add a new element to that of the British American which was destined to grow, and to act no mean part in respect to British interests in America, and we believe, ultimately to completely amalgamate with a portion of the older elements, and thus to beget a race, under Confederation, none the less noble, none the less stable, and none the less glorious, than that race (a prototype of this)—the Original Anglo-Saxon derived from the Norman, who came to England with William the Conqueror, as well as the Saxon elements.

More than a hundred years have passed away since the fall of Quebec. The centenary anniversary of the event has been celebrated with an amount of enthusiasm which probably Quebec never witnessed before. Since the American Revolution, when the French Canadians fought by the side of the American Loyalist to defend Quebec, the former have ceased to be a conquered people—Sequestrated from France, they have escaped all the horrors which have since swept over that people, while they have retained their language, religion, and laws. A hundred years has eradicated or rather changed all the feelings which burned so fervently in the French Canadian heart, except their love of Canada; and they have joined heartily with the Anglo-Saxon to erect a joint monument which commemorates at once the heroism of Wolfe, and the gallantry of Montcalm.

Although the forces invading under Wolfe, exceeded in number those who defended the citadel, yet, the greatest heroism was displayed in its taking. The British fleet of "20 ships of the line with frigates and smaller war vessels," and transports, reached the Isle of Orleans, June 25, where the land force disembarked and proceeded deliberately te invest the stronghold, finding a more difficult task than had been expected. Repeated attempts and assaults were made with the result of showing Wolfe how strong was the position his youthful ardor would fain secure. Not alone was he baffled thus, but a severe illness prostrated him to death's door, whose portals were so soon to be opened to him, by another means. In his moments of discouragement he had written home in a spirit not calculated to afford hope. The plan which resulted in success, it is said was suggested by his three faithful Generals, Monkton, Townshend and Murray.

The night before the 13th of September, 1759, the day upon which Wolfe was to win imperishable laurels, and to lay down his life, he felt a presentiment that his end was near, and carefully arranged all his worldly affairs. On the evening of the 12th he invited Captain John Davis (afterwards Admiral, Earl St. Vincent), of the *Porcupine* sloop of war, to spend an hour or two on board the *Sutherland*." Wolfe, in the course of their conversation, said that he knew he should not survive the morrow ; and when they were about to separate, he took from his bosom the picture of Louther and delivered it into the hands of his friend, whom he requested, should his foreboding be fulfilled, to restore the pledge to the lady on his arrival in England."

Having previously made disposition of his forces to prepare the way for the final attack, and, as well in some instances, to deceive the enemy as to his intentions, Wolfe finally, at one o'clock, upon the morning of the 13th September, set out in flat bottomed boats to make his landing at Fuller's Cove, thereafter to be called after himself. The night was dark, and other circumstances being favorable the landing was safely effected, the heights ascended, and at the break of day Montcalm learned with the utmost astonishment that the enemy was upon the heights of Abraham in battle array. Montcalm hastened to drive away the venturesome foe, but this was not to be accomplished; a few hours brought a realization of his early presentiment. After a spirited struggle the French were to be seen running, the announcement of which made Wolfe die happy; and, Montcalm was wounded unto death. He died on the 14th. The defeat of Montcalm secured the capture of Quebec, yet it was not until the 18th September that the city surrendered, and French writers would make it appear that even then it were not necessary.

The command of the French army after the death of Montcalm devolved upon Gen. de Lévis, who had been absent up the St. Lawrence. He returned to Montreal only in time to hear of Montcalm's defeat. He hastened to the rescue of the beleaguered city, but he reached the vicinity, not until Quebec had passed into the hands of the British.

During the time these exciting scenes had been transpiring at Quebec, Gen. Amherst had been confronting Boulamaque, upon the shores of Lake Champlain; whom he had compelled to return, and to destroy Fort Frederick and to retire to Isle Aux Nois. In the west, at Niagara Gen. Prideaux and Sir Wm. Johnson had been successful in taking the Fort from Pouchot. By this, Lake Ontario with its northern shore, as well as the region of the Bay of Quinté came into the possession of the British.

The expedition to capture Fort Niagara, taken at the urgent request of the Governor of New York, was under the command of General Prideaux. The attacking party landed at Four Mile Creek almost four miles east of the Fort, on the 6th July, 1859. Fort Niagara was garrisoned by 486 men according to Pouchot, the French commander, but according to English statements 600. General Prideaux forces numbered, according to Capt. de Lancy, 1,200, and 1,000 Indians, as said by Sir William Johnson. Pouchot discovered their approach the following day. "He despatched couriers to Presque Isle, to Fort Machault, at the mouth of French Creek, Pa., and to the commander of the Fort at the "Carrying Place" for assistance. Reinforcements were sent, numbering about 600 French, and 100 Indians. They resembled when passing down the rapids, "a floating island, so black was the river with batteaux and canoes." They landed a few miles above the falls and proceeded to Lewiston and thence to relieve Pouchot. In the mean time the siege had been pressed with vigor. Prideaux, the English General, had been killed and the command had devolved on Sir W. Johnson. The English learned of the approach of the reinforcements, and Captain James de Lancy was despatched to a position in ambuscade above the present site of Youngstown. The French discovering the English in ambush, made an impetuous attack upon them, but the English withstood the assault, and eventually turned the tide against the enemy, who were put to flight, 200 being killed, and 100 taken prisoners. Pouchot learned of the disaster about two o'clock; and, two hours after Sir W. Johnson demanded a surrender. That same evening, or on the following morning he complied; but he has stated that he would not have done so had it not been for the mutiny of the Germans who formed a part of the garrison. On the 26th the garrison left the fort to be transported to New York. Thus was the power of the French broken in the west, and the English became masters of the key to the North-west.

The following spring Gen. de Lévis determined to make an effort to retake Quebec, and upon the 28th of April, the plains of Abraham were again red with blood, and the British, under Gen. Murray, were compelled to seek safety within the walls of the city, where they were besieged until the 9th, when a British frigate arrived and gave succor.

On the 14th July Gen. Murray, with a large sailing force, commenced the ascent of the St. Lawrence. At the same time Gen. Amherst, with a considerable force was commencing a descent from Oswego. The two were thus advancing toward Montreal, each subduing on the way such forts and garrisons as were deemed of sufficient importance. By the first of September, the city of the Royal Mountain, containing the wreck of the French army was encompassed on either hand. The Governor, upon the night of the 6th, held a council of war, at which it was determined to capitulate. The celebrated a^t was signed on the 8th September, 1760, and the same day the English took possession of the city. Thus Canada passed into the possession of the British. The terms of capitulation were more favorable to the French than they had any reason to expect, and those terms have ever been fulfilled.

The Governor, Gen. de Lévis, the officers, and a large number of men, women and children returned to France. At the time of the taking of Montreal, there remained at Detroit some three or four hundred families. This Fort and others around the lakes yet held by the French were surrendered to Major Rogers, a person again to be spoken of. The population according to the Governor, left of French origin, was 70,000.

The Canadians who did not return to France repaired to their homes and renewed their peaceful avocations.

The first British Governor, Sir Jeffry Amherst, entered upon his functions 1763.

We have now very cursorily indeed, noticed the history of the French Canadians up to the time they became British subjects. We have seen they did not willingly become such; yet scarcely fifteen years were to pass away before their loyalty to the British flag was to be tested; not indeed to decide whether they should again become a part of France, rather than remain British, but whether their condition as British subjects was so intolerable that they should seek other protection of a foreign origin.

We shall see that although promises were held out of great political advantage they preferred to remain as they were. There remained in the hearts of the Canadian French, not so much a dislike to England as a detestation to the New Englander. Hence it was that when the rebel banner was unfurled in 1776, with the declaration of American Independence upon it, no Canadian rallied around it. Although commissioners from the rebel congress visited them with honied words and fair promises, they received no friendly welcome. The Canadians regarded their old enemies as enemies still, and they turned their backs upon the revolting provinces and their faces toward old England for protection. The commissioners to the Canadians, composed of Dr. Benj. Franklin, Samuel Chase and Charles Carrol, with his brother, a Jesuit Priest were appointed to this mission, on the 15th February, 1776. The same Franklin who now offered the French "freedom," had urged upon the British in 1753 the expediency of reducing Canada!!

For a century and a half France endeavored in vain to erect a power in America; but shall we say that it was all in vain?

The monument although broken, so far as France is concerned yet stands a lasting memorial of French energy, of religious fervor, stern determination, and indomitable valor. And, when the wave of revolution passed ovar the thirteen British Colonies, the column was conspicuous enough to be seen by refugees; the protection Canada offered was sufficient for the homeless families of U. E. Loyalists. Canada was a sacred spot, although French. It constituted a nucleus, around which collected those who preferred order to rebellion. Those who had fought as opponents at Duquesne, at Niagara, at Frontenac, at Tyconderoga, and upon the Plains of Abraham, were joined together. The heel, which had assisted to crush the Canadian French, now sought and found a resting place among those who had been overcome. Thus was to be laid the foundation of the Dominion of Canada, whose future is to be great. Stretching from seaboard to seaboard, it is destined to become, ere it has reached the present age of the United States, the Russia of America, with the purest principles of government the world has ever known.

We now approach the period of time when another element of discord was to appear among the races which inhabited America. Bloody Indian wars had in the past swept back and forth across the woody land. Rival colonizers had resorted to strife, to extend territorial power. European weapons had been transported to wage wars of extermination. Conquest and subjugation of Indians and rivals had been witnessed; but now Rebellion, a term that has received fresh significance in the late civil war in the United States, was to be initiated. The British blood and money which had been lavishly spent for the Anglo-Americans, had only prepared those colonists to seek other advantages. The Indians held in subjection, the French conquered, the mother country itself must now be coerced to give full rein to the spoiled and wayward offspring.

DIVISION I.

THE REBELLION OF 1776—THE THIRTEEN COLONIES.

CHAPTER III.

Contents:—First American Rebellion—Independence—Traitors made Heroes—Loyalists driven away to found another Colony—The responsibility of rebelling—Treatment of the Loyalists—The several Colonies—The first Englishman in America—Receives £10—English Colonisation—Virginia—Convicts—Extent of Virginia—First Governor—Virginians not willing to rebel—Quota supplied to the rebel army—New York—Hudson—The Dutch—New Netherlands—Price of New Amsterdam (New York)—First Legislative Assembly—Not quick to rebel—Quota of rebel troops—Gave many settlers to Upper Canada—New Jersey—Its settlement—A battle ground—Gave rebel troops; also loyal troops—Furnished settlers to Upper Canada—Massachusetts—Captain Smith—New England Puritans—The "Mayflower"—First Governor—Cruel treatment of Indians—Massachusetts takes the lead in rebelling—Troops—Loyalists—New Hampshire—Troops—Delaware—Settlement—Quota of rebel troops—Connecticut—Education—Troops—Roman Catholics—Toleration—Rhode Island—Providence—Inconsistency of the Puritans—Roger Williams—North Carolina—Inhabitants—South Carolina—Many loyalists—Pennsylvania—William Penn—Conduct toward Indians—The people opposed to rebellion—Georgia—Oglethorpe—Policy of England—New England.

In the introductory chapters a brief sketch has been given of the settlement of America. We now approach the important events which belong to the first great American rebellion, which culminated in the Declaration of Independence by the thirteen British American Colonies, and terminated in the recognition of their independence by the parent State. The rebellion had resulted in a revolution, and traitors were made heroes!

It forms a part of the present undertaking to record some of the facts relative to the steps by which the now powerful United States were, as a whole, ushered into the arena of nations, and by which a large class of Americans, true to their British allegiance, were compelled to leave their native country to found another colony in the northern wilderness. To be justified in rebelling against the constituted authorities there must be the most cogent reasons; to take up arms against the State—to initiate a civil war, is assuming the most fearful consequences.

To present even a brief account of the circumstances which led to the settlement of Upper Canada, it becomes necessary to dwell for a time upon the great rebellion of 1776, the result of which was adverse to those Americans who adhered to the old flag under which they had been born, had come to the new world, and had prospered; a rebellion which was attended and followed by persecution and violence, imprisonment and confiscation, banishment, and, too often, death; which caused a stream of refugee loyalists to set in toward the wilderness of Canada.

At the time of the rebellion of the English colonists in America, they consisted of thirteen provinces. Massachusetts, with her colony of Maine, New Hampshire, Rhode Island, Connecticut, New York, New Jersey, Pennsylvania, Delaware, Maryland, Virginia, North Carolina, South Carolina, and Georgia. It may be well to briefly notice these several states, and the part each took in the war for Independence.

The first Englishman to set foot upon the continent of America was John Cabot, who discovered Newfoundland, and probably the adjacent mainland, June 4, 1497. The event is noticed in the Privy Purse expenditure thus: "1497, Aug. 10—To hym that found the new Isle, £10," which seems to have been a grant for his services.

VIRGINIA.

In the year 1578, Sir H. Gilbert endeavoured to establish a settlement at the mouth of the Roanoke. Failing in his undertaking, his half brother, Sir Walter Raleigh, made a similar effort the following year, which likewise failed. It was Sir Walter Raleigh who gave the name to Virginia, in honor of Elizabeth, the virgin Queen. A third and successful effort was made to colónize in 1607–8, at Jamestown. This dates the commencement of English colonization of America. Some time later, America was looked upon as a country quite beyond the pale of civilization, even as Botany Bay was at a still later period; and in the year 1621, the British Government transported to Virginia 100 convicts. But notwithstanding, "Virginia," to use the words of Morse's Geography, "the birth-place of Washington, has given six Presidents to the Union."

The colony of Virginia was originally indefinite in its boundary; and, judging from old maps, it would seem to have included all of North America. But a map dated 1614 shows the more northern part as New England. The first Governor of Virginia entered upon his duties in 1619.

This State was by no means quick to sever the connection with the mother country. Many of her sons stood up for the crown, and very many families became refugees. Washington said of Virginia, in a letter, that "the people of Virginia will come reluctantly into the idea of independence." But in time, by the specious representations of Washington and others, the State produced a certain number of rebels. The quota demanded by the rebel congress was 48,522. She supplied, in 1776, 6,181; and afterwards 20,491.

NEW YORK.

In the year 1609 Hendrick Hudson, an Englishman, in the employ of Holland, first explored the great river running through New York State, which now bears his name. He, on behalf of the Dutch took possession of the country. Settlement first took place in 1614, and by 1620, a considerable colony was planted. The island of Manhatten, where now stands New York City, was honestly purchased of the Indians for twenty-four dollars. The village thus founded was called New Amsterdam, and the colony was designated New Netherlands.

Having been taken by the English in 1674, the name of the territory was changed to New York, after James, Duke of York, brother to Charles II. The first Legislative Assembly for this Province, met in New York, 17th October, 1683, just one hundred years before Upper Canada began to be settled.

The State of New York was not among the foremost in rebelling. The Dutch element which prevailed, was not given to change. Some of the most exciting events and battles of the war were enacted in this State. Right royally did the people take up arms against the rebels and drive Washington from Manhatten. Battalions and regiments were repeatedly raised and organized in this State. The valleys of the Mohawk and Hudson became historic grounds. Here was witnessed the ignoble failure of Burgoyne's Campaign, which was the commencement of the decline of British power; and the City of New York was the last ground of the States occupied by British troops, until the war of 1813. New York furnished troops for the rebel cause, in 1775, 2,075; in 1776, 3,629; and subsequently 12,077.

Of all the States, New York gave the largest number of pioneers to Upper Canada.

NEW JERSEY.

New Jersey was settled in 1620 by the Dutch and Swedes. Having been taken by the English, it was given by Charles II. to the Duke of York. Retaken by the Dutch in 1673, it was bought by Wm. Penn and his friends. At one time it was divided into East Jersey and West Jersey, East Jersey belonging to Penn. In 1702 the two Jersies were united under one government, and received the name of *New Jersey.*

Upon the grounds of this State were fought some of the most decisive battles of the war.

Of the Rebel troops Jersey supplied in 1676, 3,193. The quota required afterwards was 11,396—of which she granted 7,534. But Jersey also gave a large number of Royal troops.

New Jersey furnished a good many settlers to Upper Canada, of whom one of the most distinguished is the Ryerson family. Many of the settlers along the bay retain interesting traditions of their Jersey ancestry.

MASSACHUSETTS.

The territory of this State was originally discovered by the Cabots in 1497, and visited by Capt. John Smith in 1614, by whom it was said to have been named New England. It consisted of the present States of Maine, New Hampshire, Vermont, Rhode Island, Connecticut, and Massachusetts. In 1620, upon 22nd December, the Puritan Fathers landed upon the Plymouth Rock, some 30 miles from Boston, and planted the first of the New England States. The "Mayflower," by which they had traversed the Atlantic was only 180 tons burden. She sailed from Southhampton with 102 emigrants. Half of this number died from cold and hardship the first year. They selected for their first Elder one John Carner, who as chief officer had great control. He has consequently been called the first Governor of New England. The territory had been granted by James I. to the "Plymouth Company." Although the

Puritans had left their homes because they did not enjoy their rights, they forgot the Golden Rule in their forest homes. They failed to remember that the Indian had rights. The untutored native thought he had a right to the soil, and as the Puritans, unlike Penn, were unwilling to recognize his rights, but undertook to appropriate the territory, there ensued bloody Indian wars. The Puritan revenged himself, and the native retalliated. So, for many years border massacres were common and terrible.

Massachusetts with the other New England States, took the lead in rebellion, and by great pains succeeded in indoctrinating the midland and Southern States. The first blood of the rebellion was shed in this State, at Lexington and Bunker Hill. The State supplied troops in 1775, 16,444; in 1776, 13,372. The quota subsequently required was 52,728, of which 38,091 was furnished.

But Massachusetts had not a few true-hearted loyalists of whom a considerable number became settlers in Upper Canada. At the evacuation of Boston "1,100 retreated in a body with the Royal army. Altogether there left Massachusetts at least 2,000 United Empire Loyalists." The Colony of Maine also had a good many adherents of the crown—(*Sabine.*)

NEW HAMPSHIRE.

This Province was first colonized by emigrants from Hampshire, England, in 1623. Subsequently it was peopled by English from other parts, and by Scotch.

New Hampshire supplied in 1775, 2,824 troops; in 1776, 3,012. Her quota was 10.194. Granted 6,653. We are at the same time assured by Sabine that New Hampshire had many and powerful opponents of rebellion.

DELAWARE.

Delaware was originally settled by Swedes and Finlanders in 1627. Became a part of New Netherlands in 1655, and in 1664 fell to the English. It was included in the grant of Wm. Penn in 1682. In 1701 it was erected into a colony for legislative purposes.

She supplied rebel troops in 1776, 609. Her quota fixed was 3,974. Supplied 1,778.

CONNECTICUT.

Connecticut was first occupied by emigrants in 1631. The Charter was granted by Charles II., which continued in existence until 1818, when it was superseded by the existing constitution. Connecticut "has uniformily been a nursery of educated men of every class" for the Union. And, it may be added, a number found their way to Upper Canada, as school teachers, subsequent to the Revolution. And there was a certain number of the people of Connecticut among the Loyalists. Sabine says a good many.

This State furnished for the rebel war in 1775, 4,507; in 1776, 6,390. The quota fixed was 28,336, of which was given 21,142.

MARYLAND.

Maryland was granted to the second Lord Baltimore, a Roman Catholic, by Queen Mary, in 1632 or 4. He colonized the Province with a company of Co-religionists of the higher class of English gentry. It was named after the English Queen, Henrietta Maria. "In 1649, it was made, as has been well said, 'a land of sanctuary,' by the toleration of all religious denominations, but the Puritans, expelled from Virginia, made great trouble in the Colony."

The State supplied troops in 1776, 637. Quota fixed by congress 26,608, of which she supplied 13,275.

RHODE ISLAND.

Massachusetts, planted by Puritans, who came to secure liberty of conscience, would not allow certain individuals in their midst to enjoy like religious liberty, and hence the foundation of Rhode Island. Providence, its original name, was thus significantly called, because here the Baptists, under Roger Williams (oppressed by the Puritans of Plymouth), found a *providential* asylum. This was in 1636. In how short a time (16 years) had the oppressed learned to act oppressively!

A charter was granted to Roger Williams in 1642. The government continued to exist under this charter until 1842, a period of 200 years.

Rhode Island gave troops to the number of 1,193 in 1775, and 798 in 1776. Quota demanded, 5,694; furnished 3,917.

NORTH CAROLINA.

This colony was planted in 1653 by the older colony of Virginia The colony at first included both North and South Carolina, which continued until 1693, when the south part was erected into a separate colony, under the name of South Carolina. The inhabitants of North Carolina consisted, in part, of refugees from England at the overthrow of the Stuarts. These mainly remained loyal to the crown, and were destined to again become refugees. At the commencement of the rebellion the people of this colony were about equally divided between the adherents of the crown, and the rebels. The loyalists were a devoted band. At the same time, the rebels—at least some of them—took extreme steps. They formally demanded a separation from Great Britain in May, 1775, fourteen months before the 4th July declaration of 1776. The State provided, in 1776, 1,134 rebel troops. The quota asked for was 23,994, but only 6,129 was granted.

SOUTH CAROLINA.

South Carolina was first settled in 1670.

"The great body of the people were emigrants from Switzerland, Germany, France, Great Britain, and the northern colonies of America, and their descendants, and were opposed to a separation from the mother country;" yet South Carolina furnished troops for the rebellion, in 1776, to the number of 2,069. Subsequently she gave 4,348; although her quota, as fixed by Congress, was 16,932.

In this colony were many who could not see the justice of a rebellion. Yankee descendants may say they "bowed their necks to the yoke of colonial vassalage," but it was a wise spirit of conservatism which is expressed in the desire to "look before you leap." "Persons who had refused to enlist under the whig banner, flocked to the royal standard by hundreds." "Sir Henry Clinton informed the British Government that the whole State had submitted to the royal arms." This general attachment to the British crown made the rebels vindictive and bloodthirsty, and they sought to drive away the loyal and peacable by a vengeful shedding of blood. Consequently, the tories retaliated, and Chief Justice Marshall said, "the whigs seem determined to extirpate the tories, and the tories the whigs; some thousands have fallen in this way in this quarter." "Being almost equally divided, reciprocal injuries had gradually sharpened their resentment against each other, and had armed neighbour against neighbour, until it became a war of extermination." Now, it is submitted that rebellion can hardly be justified when the people are so equally divided. Sabine remarks that "after the fall of Charleston, and until the peace, the tories were in the ascendant."

PENNSYLVANIA.

This splendid colony was granted to William Penn, the Quaker and philanthrophist, who was the son of Sir William Penn, an eminent English admiral. Sir William held a claim against the British government for £16,000; and, some time after his death, his son having his attention directed to the new world, obtained, in lieu of that amount, the grant of land now forming this State. The charter was granted by Charles II. in 1681. Penn sought the new world to escape the persecutions inflicted upon him at home. This he had brought upon himself, by freely expressing his decided sectarian views, and by writings, disseminating the teachings of George Fox, also by attacking the Established Church. He was repeatedly imprisoned in the Tower. and even in Newgate for six months. Penn, on procuring the grant of land, determined to make it "a home for his co-religionists, where they might preach and practice their convictions in unmolested peace." To the territory he gave the name of Sylvania; but afterwards King Charles insisted that Penn should be prefixed, making it Pennsylvania. Penn sailed from England, with several friends, in August, 1682. On reaching America he found that some Swedes amd Finns had settled along the banks of the Delaware. Although Penn had a charter by which he could possess the land, yet, as an European, he did not forget the original and rightful owners of the soil. Penn's conduct in this respect stands out in striking contrast to the course pursued by the Puritans. It was on the 30th November, 1682, that William Penn held his famous interview with the Indian tribes, when he effected a straightforward treaty with them, never to be broken or disturbed, so that he secured perpetual peace and respect. By this humane course with the Indians, and by encouraging emigration of all classes, securing to them the fullest liberty of conscience by a wise constitution, he succeeded, with his co-religionists, in building up a most flourishing colony. Subsequently the population was enlarged by numerous accessions from Scotland and Germany.

The government of Pennsylvania was proprietary, and continued such until the revolution swept away the charter, and made the children of William Penn outcasts from the land they and their fathers had made fertile. At the time of the revolution, John Penn, son of Richard Penn, who was the grandson of William Penn, was the Governor of the colony. He, with the masses of the people in the middle States, was opposed to the rebellion. It is said there were thousands of loyalists in this State who desired and offered to serve the crown, but whose services were lost through bungling by those in office. Yet the State gave troops to the rebel cause; 400 in 1775, and in the following year 5,519. The quota allotted was 40,416; granted, 19,689.

GEORGIA.

This was the last of the thirteen colonies established. The founder was Oglethorpe, who effected a settlement in 1773, and who lived to see the colony a State. The colonists landed at Charleston in January, 1733.

When the rebellion broke out, this colony was "justly regarded as highly loyal." She refused to send delegates to the first rebel congress; "and that she was represented in the second was owing to the zeal of a native of Connecticut, Dr. Seymour Hall. It required time and labour to organize a party of 'liberty men' to complete the Confederacy." The number of troops supplied in 1775 was 350; the quota was fixed at 3,974, and there was supplied 2,328.

The history of England between the periods when Virginia and Georgia, the oldest and youngest of the colonies that rebelled, were founded, was one of turmoil and strife, of religious contentions and civil war; and the colonists cast off during this hundred years carried with them, across the Atlantic, heartfelt bitterness, and many of them no little passion for evil. Notwithstanding, we have seen that the Southern States, with Pennsylvania and New York, did not seek to divide their connection with the parent State. It was generally admitted that the policy of England towards them "had been mild—perhaps liberal." But, as we have seen, New England, with a few malcontents in other states—envious office-seekers, managed to disseminate the principles of rebellion—principles that New England has quite forgotten in her treatment of the South.

NEW ENGLAND.

Of the aforementioned colonies, they all had received and had secured to them by charter, from an indulgent mother country, governments of the most liberal nature. Civil and religious liberty were fully enjoyed. Says Mr. Sabine: "Virtually, republican charters; subject only to the appointment of a governor on the part of the Crown. Every colony was, practically, a State within itself; and it is a suggestive fact that the very earliest assertion of legislative superiority on the part of the mother country only operated negatively, by forbidding every colony to make laws repugnant to those of England."

Certain of the British colonies were, together, called "New England," and since the Independence they are known as the New England States. They consist of New Hampshire, Vermont, Massachusetts, Rhode Island, Connecticut, and Maine, which was then a colony of Massachusetts. This region was granted by James I. to the Plymouth Company in 1606. It was called North Virginia, but it was changed some years later, before it was actually settled. It was the people of these States to whom the term "Yankee" was originally applied; and now, in the United States, this epithet is used solely in reference to these States; but in Canada and England the word is applied very generally to all Americans. The origin of the word Yankee is probably traceable to the Indian appellation "*Yengee*," for English, or *Anglais*, after the French.

CHAPTER IV.

CONTENTS:—American Writers—Sabine—Loyalists had no time to waste—Independence not sought at first—Adams—Franklin—Jay—Jefferson—Washington—Madison—The British Government—Ingratitude of the Colonists—Taxation — Smugglers — Crown Officers — Persistance—Superciliousness—Contest between Old England and New England.

It is most refreshing to one who has been accustomed to see American school books, and even religious American tracts thickly strewn with the most fulsome self-praise, and wordy accounts of British tyranny, and of American purity and valor; to read the speeches, and listen to 4th of July orators, who, with distorted history and hifalutin panegyrics, have not ceased to wrap their country in a blazing sheet of glory. After suffering all this, *ad nauseum*, it is most agreeable to read the writings of one American author upon the subject of their Independence, who can do some justice to the Loyalists. Reference is made to Lorenzo Sabine, the author of "Royalists of the American Revolution." Considering the prejudices which exist throughout the United States against every thing British, and the over-weening vanity of the people in respect to the success which crowned their efforts to dismember the British Empire; it is a matter for grateful recognition that a native of New England should take up his pen to write redeeming words on behalf of the Loyalists whom they had been taught to stigmatize, to be read by his fellow countrymen. Living upon the borders, beyond which he could see the settled refugees working out their destiny, under adverse circumstances, and laying the foundation of a nation, he took up his pen, while the Upper Canadians were yet struggling with the forest, and without time to gather up the records of their wrongs, their losses, their persecutions, and more than all, the malicious charges against them; and hurl them back at their traducers. On behalf of those who will accept the writer as a representative of the United Empire Loyalists, he thanks Lorenzo Sabine, for what he has said. He has said nothing but the substantial truth in our favor, and in saying that, he has said very much. In his prefatory remarks, after referring to their deficiency of knowledge of the "Tories" he says. "The reason is obvious. Men who, like the Loyalists, separate themselves from their friends and kindred, who are driven from their homes, who surrender the hopes and expectations of life, and who become outlaws, wanderers, and exiles,—such men leave few memorials behind them. Their papers are scattered and lost, and their very names pass from human recollections."

Before considering the question, whether the American colonies were justified in taking an extreme step; it is most necessary to state that, at the first there were but an insignificant number of the colonists who held the belief that armed rebellion was demanded. Even among those who, with no mild-toned language denounced the mother country for enacting laws oppressive to the commerce and industry of the Americans, no one was found to advocate separation; on the contrary to use the words of Sabine " The denial that independence was the final object, was constant and general. To obtain concessions and preserve the connection with England, was affirmed everywhere; and John Adams, years after the peace, went further than this, for he said '*There was not a moment during the Revolution, when I would not have given everything I possessed for a restoration to the state of things before the contest began, provided we could have had a sufficient security for its continuance.*' Again, Franklin's testimony, a few days before the affair at Lexington, was, that he had "more than once travelled from one end of the continent to the other, and kept a variety of company, eating, drinking, and conversing with them freely, and never *had heard in any conversation from any person drunk or sober, the least expression of a wish for separation, or a hint that such a thing would be advantageous to America.*" Mr. Jay is quite as explicit. "During the course of my life and until the second petition of Congress in 1775, *I never did hear an American of any class, of any description, express a wish for the independence of the colonies.* It has always, and still is, my opinion and belief, that our country was prompted and impelled to independence by *necessity*, and not by *choice*." Says Mr. Jefferson, "What, eastward of New York, might have been the dispositions toward England before the commencement of hostilities, I know not, but *before that* I never heard a whisper of a disposition to separate from Great Britain, *and after that, its possibility was* contemplated with affliction by all," Washington, in 1774, sustained these declarations, and, in the "Fairfax County Resolves" it was complained, that "*malevolent falsehoods*" were propagated by the ministry to prejudice the mind of the king; *particularly* that there is an intention in the American colonies to *set up for independent States;* and Washington expressed a wish that the "dispute might be left to posterity to determine." Mr. Madison was not in public life until May, 1776, but he says, "It has always been my impression, that a *re-establishment of the colonial relations* to the *parent country, as they were previous to the controversy*, was the real object of *every* class of the people, till the despair of obtaining it."

The testimony of these Fathers of the Republic, cannot be impeached; and, we must, therefore, seek for the cause of the rebellion in some other place. We have seen how the British colonies were planted. In connection with them, two leading influences may be discovered constantly at work, one of a personal nature; the other referring to the State. Individuals would not sever the ties of homeship and brave the wide ocean, to expose themselves to the varied dangers of the wilderness, did they not have good reason to expect due returns. The Government would not afford ships and means to send her sons to distant shores, unless the colony would become serviceable to the parent State. The British Government had enabled many a hardy son to lay the foundation for substantial wealth. More than all, the colonies of America had been assisted to put under their feet their French rival. For their benefit the Crown expected, and undertook to enforce some tribute. But the colonists would not recognize the right of the Crown to tax them for their labor. For all the British Government had done for the colonies, for all the money spent, she required that the colonists should be taxed. Laws were enacted, and officers and revenue collectors appointed to enforce the laws. It was required that these colonies should not trade, without certain restrictions, with foreign nations; but the merchants of Massachusetts, having tasted the sweets of unrestricted trade, were unwilling to pay revenue to the Crown, although trading under the protection of the British flag. And so it came that when royal collectors of customs were sent out; when men of war coasted the shores of Massachusetts to prevent smuggling, by Hancock and others, there was no disposition to submit to Imperial taxation. For years the law relating to revenue had been a dead letter almost, the smugglers having used hush money. But at last Government determined to put down illicit trade. It is true the colonies did not object without a special plea, which was "no taxation without representation." But the real points at issue were, whether contraband commerce should continue and increase, or the Crown receive the dues demanded by law. "Nine-tenths probably, of all the tea, wine, fruit, sugar, and molasses, consumed in the colonies were smuggled. To put this down was the determined purpose of the ministry. The commanders of the ships of war on the American station were accordingly commissioned as officers of the customs; and, to quicken their zeal, they were to share in the proceeds of the confiscations; the courts to decide upon the lawfulness of seizures, were to be composed of a single judge, without a jury, whose emoluments were to be derived from his own condemnations; the Governors of the colonies and the military officers were to be rewarded for their activity by swearing also, either in the property condemned, or in the penalties annexed to the interdicted trade." And was not the Crown correct in enforcing laws intended for the public weal? Had hostile fleets approached Boston harbour to invade, instead of smuggling crafts, freighted with luxuries, would not the colonist have called loudly for Imperial help to protect? But if the Government had the best of rights to enforce the laws, it certainly displayed much want of judgment in the mode adopted to carry out its demands. The foregoing, from Sabine, recalls to us at once the cause why resistance was strenuously made. The mode of paying their Crown officers was well calculated to kindle feelings of the most determined opposition on the part of the illicit traders, such as John Hancock, John Langdon, Samuel Adams, William Whipple, George Clymer, Stephen Hopkins, Francis Louis, Philip Livingston, Eldridge Gerry, Joseph Hewes, George Taylor, Roger Sherman, Button Gurnett, and Robert Morris, all signers of the declaration of independence,—all smugglers!

And thus it came about. The Crown was determined to exact taxes, and ignorant of the feelings of the colonists; and the colonists, grown rich by unrestricted trade—by smuggling, entered into a contract, which was only to end in dismemberment of the British Empire. Side issues were raised, cries of oppression shouted, the love of liberty invoked and epithets bandied; but they were only for effect, to inflame the public mind, of which there was much wavering. Of course, there were other things which assisted to ripen rebellion, at least were so represented, that they added to the growing discontent. Colonies, when they have become developed by age, and powerful by local circumstances, will naturally lose the interest which animates the subject at home. It is in the nature of things that the love of country should gradually change from the old home to the new. The inhabitants of the colonies were in many cases but descendants of European nations, who could not be expected to retain the warmest attachment to the parent country. The tide of war had changed the allegiance of many a one. The heterogeneous whole could not be called English, and hence it was more easy to cast aside the noble feeling called patriotism. Then there were jealousies of the Crown officers, and everything undertaken by the home government, having the appearance of change, was promptly suspected as being intended to degrade them. The exclusiveness of the regular army and superciliousness to the provincial troops, during the French war, caused many a sting, and the thought of insult to the provincial officer remained to rankle and fester in the mind of many a military aspirant. The proposal to introduce Episcopal Bishops, to give precedence to the Established Church, had its effect upon many, yet many of the non-conformists were equally loyal.

The contest was originally between New England and Old England. While the Middle and Southern States were for peace, or moderate measures, the north sedulously worked to stir up strife by disseminating specious statements and spreading abroad partisan sentiments. Massachusetts took the lead. Founded by Puritans, (who, themselves were the most intolerant bigots and became the greatest persecutors America has seen,) these States possessed the proper elements with which to kindle discontent.

Thus we have learned that independence was not the primary object of revolt, and we have seen that the leaders in rebellion were principally New Englanders, and were actuated mainly by mercenary motives, unbounded selfishness and bigotry.

CHAPTER V.

Contents:—The signers of the Declaration of Independence—Their nativity—Injustice of American writers for 80 years—Cast back mis-statements—The whigs had been U. E. Loyalists—Hancock—Office-seekers—Malcontents stir up strife—What the fathers of the Republic fought for—Rebel committees—Black mail—Otis, John Adams, Warren, Washington, Henry, Franklin—What caused them to rebel—What the American revolutionary heroes actually were—Cruelty, during and after the war—No freedom—The political mistake of the rebels in alienating the loyalists—The consequence—Motives of the loyalists—False charges—Conscientious conservatives—Rebellion not warranted—Attachment to the old flag—Loyalists driven away—*Suppressio veri*—Want of noble spirit towards the South—Effects—Comparison between loyalists and rebels—Education—Religion—The neutral—The professions.

Of the fifty-six signers of the Declaration of Independence nine were born in Massachusetts, seven in Virginia, six in Maryland, five in Connecticut, four in New Jersey, four in Pennsylvania, four in South Carolina, three in New York, three in Delaware, two in Rhode Island, one in Maine, three in Ireland, two in England, two in Scotland, and one in Wales. Of these twenty-one were attornies; ten merchants; four physicians; three farmers; one clergyman; one printer; and ten men of fortune.

THE MOTIVES.

But let us more carefully consider the motives in connection with the rebellion of '76. So assiduously have our fathers, the U. E. Loyalists, been branded by most American writers as altogether base, that it becomes us to cast back the mis-statements—to tear away the specious covering of the American revolutionary heroes, and throw the sunlight of truth upon their character, and dispel the false, foul stigma, which the utterances of eighty years have essayed to fasten upon the noble band of Loyalists.

Up to 1776, the whigs as well as the tories were United Empire Loyalists; and it was only when the king's forces required taxes; when the colonists were requested no longer to smuggle; when they could not dispossess the tories of the power and emoluments of office—it was only then that the Declaration of Independence was signed by those more particularly interested. John Hancock, whose name stands first upon the document, in such bold characters, had been a successful smuggler, whereby he had acquired his millions, and no wonder he staked his thousands on the issue. Evidence is not wanting to show that many of the leaders of the rebellion, had they been holders of office, would have been as true to the British Crown as were those whom they envied. Every man who took part on the rébel side has been written a hero; but it is asking too much to request us to believe that all the holders of office were base, and lost to the feelings of natural independence and patriotism; more especially when a large proportion of them were, admittedly, educated and religious men; while, on the contrary, the rebels alone were actuated by patriotism and the nobler feelings of manhood. Apart from the merits or demerits of their cause, it must be admitted that the circumstances of the times force upon us the thought that a comparatively few needy office-seekers, or lookers-after other favors from the Crown, not being able to obtain the loaves and fishes, began to stir up strife. A few, possessed of sufficient education, by the aid of the wealthy contraband traders, were enabled, by popular sensational speeches and inflammatory pamphlets, to arouse the feelings of the uneducated; and, finally, to create such a current of political hatred to the Crown that it could not be stayed, and which swept away the ties that naturally attached them to Great Britain.

We may easily imagine the surprise which many experienced in after days, when the war had ended and their independence was acknowledged, to find themselves heroes, and their names commemorated as fathers of their country; whereas they had fought only for money or plunder, or smuggled goods, or because they had not office. In not a few cases it is such whose names have served for the high-sounding fourth of July orators; for the buncombe speechifier and the flippant editor, to base their eulogistic memoriams. Undoubtedly there are a few entitled to the place they occupy in the temple of fame; but the vast majority seem to have been actuated by mercenary motives. We have authenticated cases where prominent individuals took sides with the rebels because they were disappointed in obtaining office; and innumerable instances where wealthy persons were arrested, ostensibly on suspicion, and compelled to pay large fines, and then set at liberty. No feudal tyrant of Europe in the olden times enforced black mail from the traveller with less compunction than rebel "committees" exacted money from wealthy individuals who desired simply to remain neutral.

It has been said that Otis, a name revered by the Americans, actually avowed that he "would set Massachusetts in a flame, though he should perish in the fire." For what? Not because he wanted liberty, but because his father was not appointed to a vacant judgeship! It is alleged that John Adams was at a loss which side to take, and finally became a rebel because he was refused a commission in the peace! It is said that Joseph Warren was a broken-down man, and sought, amid the turmoil of civic strife, to better his condition. And the immortal Washington, it is related, and has never been successfully contradicted, was soured against the mother county because he was not retained in the British army in reward for his services in the French war. Again, Richard Henry was disappointed in not receiving the office of stamp distributor, which he solicited. Franklin was vexed because of opposition to his great land projects and plans of settlement on the Ohio. Indeed it is averred that mostly all the prominent whigs who sided with the rebels were young men, with nothing to lose and everything to gain by political changes and civil war. Thus it will be seen that the so-called American revolutionary heroes have not altogether clean hands, however much they may have been washed by their descendants. The clothing placed upon them may conceal the dirt and dross and blood, but they are indelibly there.

It is not alone the motives which constituted the mainsprings of the rebels' action that we place in the balance, but their conduct towards those who differed from them. Individual instances of cruelty we shall have occasion to introduce; but it may here be said that it was the tories who acted as the conservators of peace against a mobocracy, and consequently were made to suffer great afflictions. It was because of this they were forced away to live and die as aliens to the land of their birth. The tories were Americans as well as the whigs; and when at last Great Britain ceased to try to coerce the colonies, and their independence was secured, then a nobler spirit should have obtained among the conquerors, and no one, because he had conscientiously been a conservative, should have been treated with opprobrium. It always becomes the victorious to be generous; and we, with all respect to many American friends, submit that, had patriotism alone actuated the revolutionary party, the American loyalists would have been invited to join with the whigs in erecting a mighty nation. Had *freedom*, indeed, been the watchword then, as it has flauntingly been since, it would have been conceded that the tory had a right to his opinion as well as the whig to his. Do the Americans descant upon the wisdom and far-seeing policy of those who signed the Declaration of Independence and framed the constitution of the Union? Monroe, we doubt not, had a different opinion when he begot the doctrine "America for the Americans." Had the U. E. Loyalists been treated honorably; had they been allowed but their rights; had they not been driven away; then the name *British American* would forever have passed away; and instead of a belt of British provinces on their north, to constitute a ceaseless cause of misunderstanding with England, the star-spangled banner would, doubtless, long ago, have peacefully floated over all our land. Looking at the subject from this (an American) stand-point, we see that a shortsighted policy—a vindictive feeling, a covetous desire for the property of the tories—controlled the movements of the hour; and when the terms of peace were signed the birthright of the American tory was signed away, and he became forever an alien. But, as we shall see, he, in consequence, became the founder of a Province which, like a rock, has resisted, and ever will resist, the northward extension of the United States.

MOTIVES OF THE LOYALISTS.

Whatever may have been the incentives to rebellion, yielded to by those who revolted, there cannot rest upon the mind of the honest reader of unbiassed history a doubt as to the motives of the loyalists. The home-spun eulogists of the United States revolutionary soldiers have never ceased to dwell upon the principles which fired the breasts of the patriots, and nerved their arms to deeds of daring and successful warfare; all the time observing silence respecting the bravery of those who, from the same walks of life, engaged in the strife as the determined antagonists to rebellion. They have again and again charged upon the "king's men" that it was because they were servants of the Crown and feeders at the government stall that loyalty was assumed and fought for. But facts, when allowed to stand out uncovered by the cant of liberatists, declare, in words that may not be gainsayed, that there were a vast number who held no appointment under the Crown, yet who, from first to last, were true—naturally true—to their king and country. The great mass were essentially conservatives, called "tories." They held the opinion that to rebel was not only unnecessary but wrong. They believed that the evils of which the colonists had just reason to complain were not so great as to justify the extreme step taken by the signers of the Declaration of Independence; that any injustice existing was but temporary and would, when properly and calmly represented to the home government, be remedied; that to convulse the colonies in war was an unjustifiably harsh procedure; and, entertaining such a belief, it is submitted that they were noble indeed in standing up for peace—for more moderate measures. Moreover, not unlikely, many were impressed with the view that the disaffected were laboring under an erroneous idea of oppression; that the training incident to pioneer life, the previous wars with the French Canadians, the constant contentions with the Indians, had begotten false views of their rights, and made them too quick to discover supposed wrongs. Candidly impressed with such thoughts, they could not be otherwise than true to the natural instincts of their heart, and refuse to take part, or acquiesce in throwing overboard the government of England, and so become aliens to the flag under which they were born and had lived, and for which they had fought. Not many may cast aside their feelings of nationality; not many can forget the land of their birth; not a large number will bury the associations of a life-time without the most potent causes. And, doubtless, the Anglo-American who faithfully adhered to the old flag possessed all the ardor of a lofty patriotism. But the American writer has forgotten all this. In the broad sunlight of national success he has not discovered the sacred longings of the U.E. Loyalists for the Union Jack. Looking at the events of '76 by the lurid glare of civil war, his eyes are blinded to the fact that a noble band, possessing equal rights with the rebels, loved England, notwithstanding all her faults, and for that love sacrificed their all of worldly goods. The citizens of the United States would prefer to have it said in history that the U. E. Loyalists, in every instance, voluntarily left their homes during the war, or at its close. The loyalists are thereby, no doubt, made to appear more devotedly attached to the British Crown. But it is right to have it distinctly stated that American writers mostly make themselves guilty of *suppressio veri*. The latest instance of this is seen in a report to the Hon. Hugh McCullough, Secretary of the Treasury, prepared by E. H. Derby, Commissioner of the Treasury Department, dated January 1st, 1866, who, in remarking upon the British Colonial policy from 1776 down to 1830, takes occasion to say that, "at first there was little fellowship between the United States and the Provincialists, many of whom were descended from the loyalists who *followed* the British troops from our shores." The fact is, however, that many of them were driven away. The tories were not loyal without sense; and when the fortune of war had turned against them, they would, in great numbers, have made the best of their changed condition, and have lived to become true citizens of the new-born nation. But this was not to be. The loyalists were to be made feel that they were outcasts. It is the same ignoble and unstatesmanlike course which is now being pursued toward the subdued South. They must needs be made to know they are rebels. It is a shortsighted policy, even as the former was. The former led to the establishment of a nation to their north, which will stand, even after the Union lies in fragments; the latter fosters a feeling of alienation, which will speak upon the first opportunity, in the thunder tones of war.

If a comparison is instituted between the rebels of 1776, and those who were conservators of peace, the contrast is found to be very great. It is charged against the loyalists that all office-holders were tories; but is this more worthy of remark than the fact that many became rebels because they could not obtain office. Nay, the latter is infinitely more heinous in its nature. If we look at the two parties, with respect to education and, it may be added, religion, it is found that the great bulk of the educated and refined, the religious classes, especially the clergy, the leading lawyers, the most prominent medical men, were all loyalists. It was not because they were office-holders, it was because they possessed a moral and elevated mind, educated to a correct standard. Then, again, there was a large class of citizens who loved retirement, and who begged to be allowed to remain neutral, but who were actually compelled to take sides with the rebels or be driven away.

The peaceably inclined, who looked for guidance to their spiritual instructors, generally beheld them, if not actually advocating the interests of the crown, at least setting an example against rebellion, and they were thus strengthened in their feelings of loyalty, or determination to remain neutral. The flame of patriotism was kept aglow in many a heart by the earnest prayer of the gospel minister. Says Sabine: "From what has now been said it is evident that a very considerable proportion of the professional and editorial intelligence and talents of the thirteen colonies was arrayed against the popular movement." Again: "a large number of the clergy were United Empire Loyalists." Also, "the giants of the law were nearly all loyalists." The physicians were mostly tories, but were, as a general thing, not molested. "A few were banished; others became surgeons in the army."

CHAPTER VI.

Contents:—Republicanism—The lesson of the first rebellion—The late civil war—The Loyalists; their losses and hardships—Ignored by Americans—Unrecorded—The world kept in ignorance—American glory—Englishmen—Question of Colonial treatment—The reason why Great Britain failed to subdue the rebellion—Character of the rebel bravery—The great result—Liberty in England and United States contrasted—Slavery—The result to U. E. Loyalists—Burgoyne—Mobocracy—Treatment from "Sons of Liberty"—Old men, women and children—Instances of cruelty—Brutality—Rapacity—Torture—The lower classes—"Swamp Law"—Fiendish cruelty—Worse than Butler's Rangers—Seward and the Fenians—Infamous falsification—Close of the war—Recognition of independence by Great Britain—Crushed hopes of the Loyalists—In New York—Their conduct—Evacuation day—The position of the Loyalists—Confiscation—"Attainting"—Seizing estates—Paine—Commissioners at Paris—British Ministry—Loyalists' petition—King's speech—Division of claimants—Six classes—The number—Tardy justice—Noble conduct of South Carolina—Impostors—Loyalists in Lower Canada—Proclamation—The soldiers' families—Journeyings—Meeting of families.

THE RESULT.

Almost a hundred years have passed away since the war-cloud arose which swept away thirteen of Britain's colonies upon the uncertain and tempest-tossed ocean of Republicanism. That storm is long since stilled, as well as the hearts of those who took part therein.

While the statesman and politician may, with advantage, study the lesson then read, and which has been but lately annotated by the United States civil war, by the determined subjection of eight millions of Southerners, who desired freedom to establish a new government, let it be our humble occupation to record some of the immediate individual results of that great tempest, of which American writers, with but few exceptions, have never spoken fairly. Writers among them are not wanting to give lively pen pictures of their revolutionary heroes; not only forgetting the sufferings of the loyalists—the devoted ones, who gave up all—property, homes, friends, all the associations of a birth-place, rather than bow the knee to Baal; but who have wilfully misrepresented them; have charged them with crimes, at once atrocious and unfounded. The sufferings, the losses, the hardships, incident to pioneer life, with the noble purposes and undeviating loyalty of the British American tories, have never been fully related—never engaged the pen of the faithful historian. American writers, on the contrary, have recorded in glowing colors the deeds and actions of the "fathers of the Republic." To this no objection can be made; but may we not charge those historians with uncharitableness, with unnecessary neglect of the claims of the loyalists to pure motives, with ignoring their brave deeds, their devoted suffer ings, and with unduly ascribing to the "king's men" motives base and cruel. But the sufferings of the U. E. Loyalists are unrecorded. The world has rarely been told that they were persecuted, their homes pillaged, their persons maltreated, their valuables seized, their houses made desolate, their real estate taken from them, without legal proceedings. The world has been so flooded with the writings of Americans, describing their own excellencies and eulogizing their own cause, that no space has been found to do simple justice to the noble ones who preferred British rule to the uncertain and untried. Indeed, so strongly and for so long a time has the current been flowing to swell the ocean of American glory, that hardly a voice or pen is found doing service for the unfortunate loyalists, who chose to endure a little rather than rush into the vortex of rebellious strife. Even Englishmen have so long listened to one-sided statements, that no one of them can be found to say a word for the old tory party of America. Hence it is that the U. E. Loyalists are very imperfectly known; their history unwritten, their tales of sorrow unattended to, their noble doings unsung. Had there been a hand to guide a describing pen,—to picture the doings, the sufferings, the self-denying heroism of the loyal barty; to recount the motives underlying all they did; and had there boen ears as willing to listen, and eyes to read, and hearts to receive the facts as those of a contrary nature have obtained, then a far different impression would have been made, and fixed upon the world.

That the British Government was right or wise in its treatment of the American colonies we now have every reason to doubt. At the same time, that England might have subdued that rebellion, had she put forth her undivided strength, there is but little reason to question. Had she not been engaged in a formidable war with France; or even with that, had her statesmen acquired a correct knowledge of America as to topography, and as to the feelings and wishes of the people and their just complaints; or had able generals been entrusted with the command of the armies, instead of incompetent favorites; or had a little diplomacy been practiced, and the ringleaders of the whig faction—often hungry agitators—been conciliated by office; in either event the rebellion might have been nipped in the bud, or easily overcome. The American Republic owes its independence to the circumstances in which Great Britain was then placed, and the incapacity of a few of the British Generals, rather than to superior bravery, extraordinary military talent, or any high-toned longing for liberty. No doubt many of the rebelling party were brave; but it was often the bravery of the guerilla, or the desperate adventurer.

Of the great result—the recognition of the independence of the rebelling provinces by the mother country—we design not to speak at length. It will always remain a question, whether it would not have been better for the States themselves, and the world at large, if they had remained a part of the British Empire. That the evils of which they complained would, in due time, have been removed, upon proper representation, there is no substantial reason to doubt. That the principles of true freedom would have advanced and spread quite as rapidly, and that, to-day, liberty, in the broadest sense, would have reigned in the world fully as triumphant, the whole history of England and the United States sufficiently attest. It was many long years after Britain had struck off the chains of slavery before the United States reached the same point; and then only because it became a "military necessity." Looking at the two nations to-day, and judging by the utterances of the two respective people, whether enunciated in the halls of legislature, by the head of the nation, by the bar, in the pulpit, by the press, or from the platform; or if we be guided by the public deeds of each, it is submitted that the more genuine ring of the metal sounds from beneath the wide-spreading banner of old England.

The effect of the successful rebellion, to which it is intended to refer, has reference to the United Empire Loyalists of America. And first, the effect upon them during the war.

The defeat of Burgoyne was the first event which immediately led to severe disaster of the loyalists. This general, with more assurance than foresight, and perhaps more courage than military skill, succeeded, not only in leading his army to destruction, but in placing the friendly inhabitants on his route in such a position that no mercy was subsequently extended to them by the ruthless rebels. When he surrendered, instead of securing for them immunity from any harm, he entirely neglected their interests; notwithstanding they had supplied his troops with provision. The relentless conduct of the rebels in arms and the whig government was bloodthirsty and vindictive. Their hate towards those who would not take sides with them, whether in arms for the Crown or not, was barbarous. Persons suspected of sympathy with the tories were subjects of continued molestation. Mobocracy reigned. Vagabond bodies of men were sent abroad to range the country, to lay waste and destroy the property of the loyalists, imprison the suspected, and seize the goods of the unprotected. Tarring and feathering was of common occurrence. Massachusetts especially gained a name for cruelty far exceeding any which has been applied to the Indians, with all their barbarism. There was a villainous band who called themselves the "Sons of Liberty," who carried fire and sword—not against an open enemy in the light of day, but to peaceful firesides in the darkness of night. Their victims were the old men, the women and children, and the defenceless. Old men and children were driven to the woods for shelter, or placed in a closed room, and, with chimney stopped, smoked to suffocation. Females were subject to insult and the most fiendish treatment. Dwellings were fired at night, and their occupants left houseless, and exposed to the inclemency of the weather.

Suspected persons were arrested and put to terrible torture, such as attaching a rope to the neck and hauling the individual through the water till insensible ; or suspending him to a tree till life was almost gone. This was frequently done with the object of extracting information as to the whereabouts of a father or a brother, or as to the place where money and valuables were concealed. The tales of cruelty the writer has heard related concerning the treatment the loyal party were exposed to, would harrow up the soul of any one possessing feelings of pity and commiseration.

The loyalists who immediately suffered, that is, while the war was in progress, were many. Military forts were established here and there, to which many fled precipitately from the several States.

It is a matter of extreme astonishment how men who set up the standard of revolt under the sacred name of liberty, could so far ignore the firinciples of liberty in the treatment of innocent old men, women and children, as we find stated by honest witnesses. The darkest tales of savage dealing come to us from our fathers. Families, whose sole offence consisted in being unwilling to rebel, and in being desirous to remain faithfully neutral, were the objects of the rapacious prey of a brutal soldiery. Their substance when not available for the rebel horde, was scattered to the winds. Devouring fire was cast into peaceful homes. How gross the hypocracy, how base the motives that actuated very many of the adventurers in rebellion. The most hellish means were adopted at times, to force away persons of property, that the so-called "Sons of Liberty" might enjoy their substance and homes. Attending these scenes of desolation and refined crulty, their imprisonments and torture, were incidents of thrilling interest, of fearful suffering, of hairbreadth escapes, of forlorn rescues.

The lower classes of those who rebelled were men of bold and lawless nature: whether we pass along the shores of New England, among the fishermen, or travel thorough the woods of Maine and New Hampshire, and become acquainted with woodmen of the forest, or as they were called "Loggers and Sawyers." The spirit that animated the merchants of Boston and Salem, in their extended operations of smuggling, lived, also, in the reckless fishermen and woodmen; and for years before the rebellion really commenced they had been resisting, even by physical force, the revenue officers, who were often expelled from the woods by what was called "swamp law." Men with such nature, finding that their lawlessness had become popular, and that steps were being taken to resist the government on a general plan, were not slow to act their part. One result of the rebellion was a determined and systematic course of retaliation upon those who had recognized the majesty of the law. A continued and uncompromising persecution was entered upon toward them.

No history can parallel the deeds of atrocity enacted by the villanious "Liberty men." Said an old lady, on the verge of the grave, and with voice tremulous in remembrance of fiendish acts she had witnessed. "The Rebels, on one occasion entered a house and stripped it of everything, even the bed on which lay a woman on the point of confinement. But a single sheet was left to cover the woman upon a winters night, who, before morning became a mother." In 1776, there arrived at Fort George, in a starving state, Mrs. Nellis, Mrs. Secord, Mrs. Young, Mrs. Buck and Mrs. Bonnar, with thirty-one children, whom the circumstances of the rebellion had driven away. Talk about the cruelty of Indians and of Tory oppression. The unprincipled rebels did well to try to hide their ignominious deeds behind the fabrications respecting the doings of Butler's Rangers, and the noble-minded Brant. May we not cease to wonder that the descendents of the rebels in the year 1866, endeavour to hound on a pack of thieves and murderers to possess themselves of the homes our fathers sought out for us. The self-applauding writers of the revolutionary war, found it convenient to forget the doings of the "Sons of Liberty" and of Sullivan, while they laid to the charge of Butler's Rangers and the Indians, acts of inhumanity (which we are informed on good authority are unfounded, Butler having never abused woman or child.) In the same manner, Secretary Seward found it desirable to falsify dates, by saying the Fenians invaded Canada on the 6th of June, that it might appear he had vindicated promptly their neutrality laws;" whereas they actually crossed, and engaged in battle, on the morning of the 2nd. But as time will fully bring out the facts connected with the first American rebellion, and place them face to face with one-sided history, so will faithful history record the whole truth of the infamous invasion of our country by a band of American citizens with United States arms in their hands. Those deeds of blood, enacted by men under the hypocritical cry of liberty have not been forgotten by the United Empire Loyalists, but have been handed down to us, to place on record against the cruel actors.

Hostilities ceased 19th April, 1783, and on the 20th September, the independence of the United States was acknowledged.

The recognition of independence by Great Britain, was the death knell to the cherished hopes of the loyalists. Many had escaped into the provinces, and many were in the army, and not a few were in England. Although the majority of them had been driven away, a few still remained in those places, yet held by the British forces, as New York. "When the news of peace became known, the city presented a scene of distress not easily described. Adherents to the Crown, who were in the army, tore the lappels from their coats and stamped them under their feet, and exclaimed that they were ruined; others cried out they had sacrificed everything to prove their loyalty, and were now left to shift for themselves, without the friendship of their king or country. Previous to the evacuation, and in September, upwards of 12,000 men, women, and chidren, embarked at the city, at Long and Staten Islands, for Nova Scotia and the Bahamas," and for Canada. "Some of these victims to civil war tried to make merry at their doom, by saying they were bound to a lovely country, where there are nine months winter and three months cold weather every year, while others, in their desperation tore down their houses, and had they not been prevented, would have carried off the bricks of which they were built." The British had possessed New York since 15th September, 1776, and on the 25th November, 1783, yielded it up to the Americans. This is "Evacuation day."

When Cornwallis surrendered he vainly tried to obtain a promise of protection for the Loyal Americans, who, in part, formed his army. Failing in this, he sent an armed vessel away with a large number.

At this time, beside the many who had become refugees, there were some loyalists scattered through the States. Many of these remained in the now Independent States, and many of them would have returned, to become faithful citizens under the new order of things, had they been allowed so to do. But the young Republic knew not how to be magnanimous to those whom the fortunes of war had left in great distress—whom they had conquered, and the United Empire Loyalists were made aliens from their native homes. Their property must be confiscated, and many being large land owners, rich prizes were thus secured. While the conflict continued to rage there was some excuse, but when war had ceased, and everything had been accomplished that the most craving rebel could wish, it was a ruthless, an ungenerous, nay, a base proceeding on the part of the revolutionists, to force away their very brethren, often related by the ties of consanguinity. But it was a spirit as unprincipled as this, which instigated the rebellion, and which characterized the vast majority of those who fought under the sacred name of liberty, and such was the spirit of the conquerors.

The successful rebels determined to possess themselves of the lands and property of the loyalists, even in violation of treaty. The action of Congress was sufficiently high-handed and wanting in generosity; but the proceedings of the State Legislatures, with a few exceptions, were execrable—characterized by ignoble and vindictive passion.

The Legislatures of each state took early steps to punish the adherents of Britain, to dispossess them of their property, and to banish them. Massachusetts took the lead in dealing severely against the loyalists. A rebel magistrates' warrant was sufficient to banish one. Hundreds of Massachusetts Loyalists were prohibited from returning on penalty of imprisonment and even death. And the other States were active in "attainting" and confiscating, often without the form of trial. Each State carried on its function as a government, and trials ought to have been granted, in common justice to every one. But the Whigs were intolerent, hot-headed, malevolent, unforgiving. It has been said that "if it be conceded that rebellion against England was right, then every step necessary to success was justifiable. If we grant all this there remains the fact that after success had crowned rebellion, persecution and confiscation continued. New York, on the 12th May, 1784, passed "An act for the speedy sale of the confiscated and forfeited estates within the States." The powers consisted in the appointment of "commissioners of forfeitures." Among those who lost their land was one Davoe. He had 300 acres near New York, twenty miles, which was confiscated and given to the notorious Tom Paine, the infidel, whose extreme liberal views expressed in his work, "Common Sense," made him the friend of Washington, and revolutionists generally. Paine, after taking part in the French Revolutions, came, in 1802, to his place in New York, where he enjoyed the loyalists' confiscated property until his death, 8th June, 1809.

In the terms of peace signed at Paris, there was no security effected for the losses sustained by the American Loyalists.

As Burgoyne at his inglorious surrender at Saratoga, thought not of the innocent inhabitants of the Mohawk and Hudson, who had indentified themselves with the loyal cause, and supplied his troops with provisions, and left them to the merciless "Sons of Liberty," to be despoiled of their all, and exposed to fearful cruelty, so at the last, when the British Government relinquished the attempt to subdue rebellion, the American Loyalists were of remote consideration. We can gather now but the outlines of this great wrong done unto noble men. The particulars are buried in the wreck of fortune, and of happiness, respecting all worldly matters. The after life of the loyalists was of too earnest a nature to allow time to place on record the sufferings, and the wanderings of the disinherited. The lost cause did not stimulate men to draw upon imagination, such as may be found in gaudy-hued descriptions of American revolutionary heroes, male and female. But there is sufficient of facts recorded, and engraven by the iron pen of extreme anguish upon hearts, that were of flesh, to stamp the persecutors with infamy, and mark the refugees, that clustered around the border forts, and found homes at Sorel, Lachine, and Montreal, with the highest attributes of patriotism and love of country.

The conduct of the ministry, and the commissioners at Paris is open to the severest censure. They left the claims of the loyalists to be decided by the American Congress. We may allow them the credit of having held the belief, that this body would be actuated by a feeling of justice and right, but the error was a grave one, the wrong grievous and hard to be endured. In pursuing this course, the British ministry did not escape condemnation by members of Parliament, and a feeling of sympathy was evoked that led to a tardy dispensing of justice. Lord North said "that never were the honor, the principles, the policy of a nation, so grossly abused as in the desertion of those men, who are now exposed to every punishment that desertion and poverty can inflict, because they were not rebels." Mr. Sheridan "execrated the treatment of those unfortunate men, who, without the least notice taken of their civil and religious rights, were handed over as subjects to a power that would not fail to take vengence on them for their zeal and attachment to the religion and government of the mother country," "and he called it a crime to deliver them over to confiscation, tyranny, resentment and oppression." Lord Loughborough said that "in ancient nor modern history had there been so shameful a desertion of men who had sacrificed all to their duty and to their reliance upon British faith." Others, in terms of equal severity, denounced the ministry in Parliament for their neglect. The ministry admitted it all, but excused themselves by the plea that "a part must be wounded, that the whole of the empire may not perish"—that they "had but the alternative, either to accept the terms proposed, or continue the war."

"A number of loyalists in England, came to the United States to claim restitution of their estates, but their applications were unheeded," except to imprison, and banish them.

The treaty of peace signed, without any provision for the suffering loyalists, they at once took steps to petition the Imperial Parliament for justice. "They organized an agency, and appointed a Committee, composed of one delegate, or agent from each of the thirteen States, to enlighten the British public." "At the opening of Parliament the King, in his speech from the throne, alluded to the 'American sufferers' and trusted generous attention would be shewn to them.'" An act was consequently passed creating a "Board of Commissioners" to examine the claims preferred. The claimants were divided into six classes.

"*First Class.*—Those who had rendered service to Great Britain."

"*Second Class.*—Those who had borne arms for Great Britain.

"*Third Class.*—Uniform Loyalists."

"*Fourth Class.*—Loyal British subjects residents in Great Britain."

"*Fifth Class*—Loyalists who had taken oaths to the American States, but afterward joined the British."

"*Sixth Class.*—Loyalists who had borne arms for the American States, and afterwards joined the British navy or army."

The claimants had to state in writing, and specifically the nature of their losses. Great and unnecessary caution was observed by the Board. The rigid rules of examinations caused much dissatisfaction and gave the Board the name of "Inquisition."

The 26th of March, 1784, was the latest period for presenting claims, which was allowed, and on or before that day, the number of claimants was two thousand and sixty-three. A "second report which was made in December of the same year, shows that one hundred and twenty-eight additional cases had been disposed of." In May and July 1865, one hundred and twenty-two cases more were disposed of. In April 1786, one hundred and forty more were attended to. The commissioners proceeded with their investigations during the years 1786 and 1787." "Meantime" and to her honor be it said "South Carolina had restored the estates of several of her loyalists."

Years passed away before the commissioners had decided upon all the claims, and great and loud was the complaint made by the claimants. The press was invoked to secure a more prompt concession of justice, pamphlets were published on their behalf, and one printed in 1788, five years after the peace, contained the following: "It is well that this delay of justice has produced the most melancholy and shocking events. A number of the sufferers have been driven by it into insanity, and become their own destroyers, leaving behind them their helpless widows and orphans to subsist upon the cold charity of strangers. Others have been sent to cultivate a wilderness for their subsistance, without having the means, and compelled through want, to throw themselves on the mercy of the American States, and the charity of their former friends, to support the life which might have been made comfortable by the money long since due from the British Government, and many others, with their families are barely subsisting upon a temporary allowance from government, a mere pittance when compared with the sum due them."

The total number of claimants was 5,072, of whom 924 withdrew or failed to make good the claim. The sum of money allowed was £3,294,452. We have seen there was, in addition, given to the widows and orphans, between 20,000 and 30,000 pounds.

There is no doubt that a certain number of the claimants were imposters, while many asked remuneration above what their losses had actually been, and this caused the commissioners to examine more closely the claims proffered. But it is submitted that they ought, in dealing with the money already granted by a considerate Parliament, to have loaned on the side of clemency.

At the close of the contest there were a large number of Refugees in Lower Canada, especially at Fort St. John, about twenty-nine miles from Montreal. In the main these were American born, and principally from the New England States; yet there were representatives from England, Ireland, Scotland and Germany. Besides the Refugees, there were several Provincial Corps, which were no longer to be retained in the service, but to be disbanded. Of these there was the 84th, often called Johnson's regiment, this was 800 strong, mostly Dutch, from the Mohawk, and Hudson, descendants of the old stock. This regiment consisted of two corps, one under Major Jessup, stationed at St. John's, and the other under Rogers, a part of which at least, was stationed at Fort Oswego, Jessups corps became the first pioneers upon the St. Lawrence, and Rogers among the first along the Bay of Quinté. Both settled in 1784. There were other troops stationed at St. John's, and likewise not a few who had discharged irregular, but important duties, as scouts, and in other ways.

It has been generally estimated that at the close of the struggle, and as a result, there were distributed of American Loyalists upon the shores of Canada, about 10,000. At the first, most of these were in Lower Canada, but there were likewise a few at the frontier forts upon the Upper waters, and a few detached squatters. Then, "there was not a single tree cut from the (present) Lower Province line to Kingston, 150 miles; and at Kingston there were but a few surrounding huts; and from thence all around Lake Ontario and Lake Erie, with the exception of a few Indian huts on some desolate spot of hunting ground, all was a dense wilderness." (Ex Sheriff Sherwood.)

"A proclamation was issued," says Croil in his history of Dundas, "that all who wished to continue their allegiance to Britain, should peaceably rendezvous at certain points on the frontiers. These were, Sackets Harbour, Carleton Island, Oswego and Niagara, on the Upper Canada confines; and Isle Aux Nois, on the borders of Lower Canada. Jessup's Corps was stationed at Isle Aux Nois, and late in the autumn of 1783, the soldiers were joined by their wives and little ones, who had wandered the weary way on foot, to Whitehall, through swamps and forest,—beset with difficulties, dangers, and privations innumerable. The soldiers met them there with boats, and conveyed them the rest of their journey by water, through Lake Champlain. Imagination fails us when we attempt to form an idea of the emotions that filled their hearts, as families, that had formerly lived happily together, surrounded with peace and plenty, and had been separated by the rude hand of war, now met each others embrace, in circumstances of abject poverty. A boisterous passage was before them, in open boats, exposed to the rigors of the season—a dreary prospect of the coming winter, to be spent in pent up barracks, and a certainty should they be spared, of undergoing a lifetime of such hardships, toil and privation, as are inseperable from the settlement of a new country." As soon as the journey was accomplished, the soldiers and their families, were embarked in boats, sent down to Richelieu to Sorel, thence to Montreal, and on to Cornwall, by the laborious and tedious route of the St. Lawrence. (See settlement of Ernest town.)

CHAPTER VII.

Contents:—A spirit of strife—The French war—British American Troops—Former comrades opposed—Number of U. E. Loyalists in the field—General Burgoyne—Defeat—First reverse of British arms—The campaign—Colonel St. Leger—Fort Stanwix—Colonel Baume—Battle of Bennington—General Herkimer—Gates—Schuyler—Braemar Heights—Saratoga—Surrender—The result upon the people—Sir John Johnson—Sir William—Sketch—Indian Chief—Laced coat—Indian's dream—It comes to pass—Sir William dreams—It also comes to pass—Too hard a dream—Sir John—Attempt to arrest—Escape—Starving—Royal Greens—Johnson's losses—Living in Canada—Death—Principal Corps of Royalists—King's Rangers—Queen's Rangers—Major Rogers—Simcoe—The Rangers in Upper Canada—Disbanded—The Hessians.

The seven years' war between Canada and New England, in which a large number of the Colonists were engagod, had created not a few officers of military worth and talent, while a spirit of strife and contention had been engendered among the people generally. The Colonial war, carried on with so much determination, was stimulated, not so much by the English nation at home as by New Englanders. It was they who were chiefly interested in the overthrow of French power in Canada. While money and men had been freely granted by the Imperial Government, the several colonies had also freely contributed. They "furnished in that war quite twenty-eight thousand men, in more than one of the campaigns, and every year to the extent of their ability." "On the ocean, full twelve thousand seamen were enlisted in the Royal Navy and in the Colonial Privateers." In this manner had been formed a taste for military life, which waited to be gratified, or sought for food. When, therefore, the unsavory acts of England wounded the Colonial vanity, and demagogues traversed the country to embitter the feelings of the mass against the king, the hot-headed were not slow to advise an appeal to arms. At the same time, the loyal in heart, the conservators of Imperial interest, viewing with wonder and alarm the manifestation of fratricidal war—of rebellion, felt it their duty to take up arms against the unprincipled (and often dishonest) agitators, and endeavor to crush out the spirit of revolt. And thus it came, that very many who had fought side by side at Ticonderago, Crown Point, Du Quesne, Niagara, Oswego, Frontenac, Montreal, and around Quebec, under a common flag, were now to be arrayed in hostile bands. Not state against state, nor yet merely neighbor against neighbor, but brother against brother, and father against son! Civil war, of all wars, is the most terrible: in addition to the horrors of the battle-field, there is an upheaving of the very foundation of society. All the feelings of brotherhood, of christian love, are paralyzed, and the demon of destruction and cruelty is successfully invoked.

Behold, then, the British Americans divided into two parties; each buckling on the armor to protect from the other, and sharpening the weapons of warfare to encounter his kindred foe. The contest of 1776–'83 is most generally looked upon as one between the English and Americans; but in reality it was, at first—so far as fighting went—between the conservative and rebel Americans. In an address to the king, presented by the loyalists in 1779, it is stated that the number of native Americans in his service exceeded those enlisted by Congress. Another address, in 1782, says that "there are more men in his Majesty's provincial regiments than there is in the continental service." Sabine says that "there were 25,000, at the lowest computation." If such be the case, the question may well be asked, how came it that the rebels succeeded? Looking at the matter from our distant stand-point, through the light of events we find recorded, there seems but one conclusion at which we may arrive, namely, that the disaster to the British arms was due—altogether due—to the incapacity of certain of the generals to whom was intrusted the Imperial interests in America.

THE COMBATANTS—BURGOYNE.

The most notable instance of mistaken generalship was that of Burgoyne. His campaign in the summer of 1777, and the final overthrow of his army and surrender at Saratoga, will engage our particular attention; inasmuch as it was the first decided reverse to the British arms, and by giving courage to the rebels, assisted much to further their cause. Thereby their faith was strengthened, and the number of rebels increased from no inconsiderable class, who waited to join the strongest party. Again, the scene of this campaign was close to the borders of Canada, and there followed a speedy escape of the first refugees from the Mohawk valley and the Upper Hudson to the friendly shores of the St. Lawrence.

A year had elapsed since the Declaration of Independence, and England had sent troops to America, with the view of assisting the forces there to subdue the malcontents. In the early part of July, Burgoyne set out from Lower Canada with about 8,500 soldiers, 500 Indians, and 150 Canadians, intending to traverse the country to Albany, possessing himself of all rebel strongholds on the way, and thence descend along the river Hudson, to New York, to form a junction with General Howe, that city having been captured from the rebels the 15th September previous. Passing by way of Lake Champlain, he encountered the enemy on the 6th July, and captured Ticonderoga and Mount Independence, with 128 cannon, several armed vessels, a quantity of baggage, ammunition and provisions. "This easy conquest inflamed his imagination." The first step towards the defeat of his army was the unsuccessful attempt of Colonel St. Leger, with 800 men, who ascended the St. Lawrence to Oswego, and thence up the river, to take Fort Stanwix (Rome), intending to descend the Mohawk and join Burgoyne with his main force, as he entered the head of the valley of the Hudson. Colonel St. Leger arrived at Fort Stanwix on the 3rd August, 1777. For a time he was the winner; but for some reason, it is said that the Indians suddenly left him, and his troops, seized with a panic, fled. In the meantime, General Burgoyne was pursuing his way, having driven General Schuyler from Lake St. George to the mouth of the Mohawk river.

Burgoyne, flushed with this renewed success, after his late cap-

5

ture of Ticonderoga and Mount Independence, vainly supposed he could advance steadily down the Hudson. He sent a body of men, 500 strong, under Colonel Baume, into the interior, eastward, with the view of encouraging the inhabitants to continued loyalty, and of arresting the machinations of the rebels. Near Bennington the rebels had an important post, with magazines, and a large force under General Stark. Baume, ignorant of their strength, rushed headlong against the enemy. Nothing daunted, he led on his 500 brave men. For two hours he contended with the unequal foe, when his troops were almost annihilated, and he fell from his horse, mortally wounded. But few escaped to tell the tale. Meanwhile, Burgoyne, apprised of the danger surrounding Baume, had sent assistance under Colonel Breynan. Unfortunately, they had not much ammunition, and, after fighting until all was exhausted, they had to flee. These three reverses paved the way for the final overthrow of Burgoyne. He was still marching forward, bent on reaching Albany, to accomplish the object of the campaign—a juncture with the army of General Howe. But now in his rear, to the west, instead of Colonel St. Leger descending the Mohawk, was General Herkimer, who had dispersed St. Leger's force; and to the east was General Stark, flushed with his victories over Baume and Breynan. Burgoyne met Gates at last on Braemar heights, and again, and for the last time, led his troops on to victory, although the contest was well sustained. General Schuyler had intrenched his forces at the mouth of the Mohawk, and Burgoyne, having waited until his provision was exhausted, at last resolved to make an assault. It was bravely made, but without success; and before night-fall the army was retreating. Night, instead of enabling them to regain their spirits and renew their ardor, only brought the intelligence of the defeats previously sustained at Stanwix and Bennington. This was the 7th October. Flight now was the only possible chance for safety. The tents were left standing; his sick and wounded forsaken. But the enemy now surrounded him; the places he had taken were already re-taken; and upon the 10th of the month he found himself helpless upon the fields of Saratoga, where he surrendered. The whole of the men were sent to Boston and other places south, there to languish in prison.

Thus it came that the inhabitants in this section of the country came under the power of the rebels, and those who had adhered to the loyal side were mercilessly driven away at the point of the bayonet. The writer has heard too many accounts of the extreme cruelty practised at this time to doubt that such took place, or question the fiendish nature of the acts practised by the successful rebels against, not foes in arms, but the helpless. Many thus driven away (and these were the first refugees who entered Canada) suffered great hardships all through the winter. Most of the men entered the ranks subsequently, while not a few, from their knowledge of the country, undertook the trying and venturesome engagement of spies. The families gathered around the forts upon the borders had to live upon the fare supplied by the commissariat of the army. A large number were collected at Mishish; and the story goes that a Frenchman, whose duty it was to deal out the supplies, did so with much of bad conduct and cruel treatment.

SIR JOHN JOHNSON.

Among the officers who served with General Burgoyne was Sir John Johnson, who had been the first to suffer persecution, the first to become a refugee, and who became a principal pioneer in Upper Canada.

"His father, Sir William Johnson, was a native of Ireland, of whom it was said, in 1755, that he had long resided upon the Mohawk river, in the western part of New York, where he had acquired a considerable estate, and was universally beloved, not only by the inhabitants but also by the neighboring Indians, whose language he had learned and whose affections he had gained, by his humanity and affability. This led to his appointment as agent for Indian affairs, on the part of Great Britain, and he was said to be 'the soul of all their transactions with the savages.'"

Of Sir William's talents and shrewdness in dealing with the likewise shrewd Indian, the following is found in Sabine: "Allen relates that on his receiving from England some finely-laced clothes, the Mohawk chief became possessed with the desire of equalling the baronet in the splendor of his apparel, and, with a demure face, pretended to have dreamed that Sir William had presented him with a suit of the decorated garments. As the solemn hint could not be mistaken or avoided, the Indian monarch was gratified, and went away, highly pleased with the success of his device. But alas for Hendrick's shortsighted sagacity! In a few days Sir William, in turn, had a dream, to the effect that the chief had given him several thousand acres of land. 'The land is yours,' said Hendrick, 'but now, Sir William, 'I never dream with you again, you dream too hard for me.'"

At the breaking out of the revolutionary war, Sir John, who had succeeded to his father's title, appears, also, to have inherited his influence with the Indians, and to have exerted that influence to the utmost in favor of the Royal cause. By this means he rendered himself particularly obnoxious to the continentals, as the Americans were then called. Accordingly, in 1776, Colonel Dayton, with part of his regiment, was sent to arrest him, and thus put it out of his power to do further mischief. Receiving timely notice of this from his tory friends at Albany, he hastily assembled a large number of his tenants and others, and made preparations for a retreat, which he successfully accomplished.

"Avoiding the route by Lake Champlain, from fear of falling into the hands of the enemy, who were supposed to be assembled in that direction, he struck deep into the woods, by way of the head waters of the Hudson, and descended the Raquette river, to its confluence with the St. Lawrence, and thence crossed over to Canada. Their provision failed soon after they had left their homes. Weary and foot-sore, numbers of them sank by the way, and had to be left behind, but were shortly afterwards relieved by a party of Indians, who were sent from Caughnawaga in search of them. After nineteen days of hardship, which have had few parallels in our history, they reached Montreal. So hasty was their flight, that the family papers were buried in the garden, and nothing taken with them but such articles as were of prime necessity." Soon after his arrival at Montreal he was "commissioned a colonel, and raised two battalions of loyalists, who bore the designation of the Royal Greens. From the time of organizing this corps, he became one of the most active, and one of the bitterest foes that the whigs encountered during the contest. So true is it, as was said by the wise man of Israel, that 'a brother offended is harder to be won than a strong city, and their contentions are like the bars of a castle.' Sir John was in several regular and fairly conducted battles. He invested Fort Stanwix in 1777, and defeated the brave General Herkimer; and in 1780 was defeated himself by General Van Rensselaer, at Fox's Mills."

The result of his adherence to the Crown was, that his extensive family estates upon the Mohawk were confiscated; but at the close of the war he received large grants of land in various parts of Canada, beside a considerable sum of money. He continued to be Superintendent of Indian affairs, and resided in Montreal until his death, in 1822.

THE LOYAL COMBATANTS.

The following are the principal corps and regiments of loyalists who took part in the war against the rebels, and who were mainly Americans:

"The King's Rangers; the Royal Fencible Americans; the Queen's Rangers; the New York Volunteers; the King's American regiment; the Prince of Wales' American Volunteers; the Maryland Loyalists; De Lancey's Battalions; the Second American regiment; the King's Rangers, Carolina; the South Carolina Royalists; the North Carolina Highland Regiment; the King's American Dragoons; the Loyal American Regiment; the American Legion; the New Jersey Volunteers; the British Legion; the Loyal Foresters; the Orange Rangers; the Pennsylvania Loyalists; the Guides and Pioneers; the North Carolina Volunteers; the Georgia Loyalists; the West Chester Volunteers. These corps were all commanded by colonels or lieutenant-colonels; and as De Lancey's battalions and the New Jersey Volunteers consisted each of three battalions, there were twenty-eight. To these, the Loyal New Englanders, the Associated Loyalists and Wentworth's Volunteers, remain to be added. Still further, Colonel Archibald Hamilton, of New York, commanded at one period seventeen companies of loyal Militia."

Respecting the officers and more prominent men of the corps, who settled in Canada, we have succeeded in collecting the following account.

THE QUEEN'S RANGERS.

This corps acted a very conspicuous part during the war. It was raised by Major Robert Rogers, of New Hampshire, son of James Rogers. He had served during the French war, with distinction, as commander of Rogers' Rangers, and was, "in 1776, appointed Governor of Michilimacinac. During the early part of the rebellion he was in the revolting states, probably acting as a spy, and was in correspondence with the rebel Congress, and with Washington himself. He was imprisoned at New York, but was released on parole, which, it is said, he broke (like General Scott in 1812), and accepted the commission of colonel in the British army, and proceeded to raise the corps mentioned." About 1777 "he went to England, and Simcoe succeeded him as commander of the Queen's Rangers."

Sabine, speaking of John Brown Lawrence, says he was imprisoned in the Burlington gaol, New Jersey, and that "Lieut.-Colonel John G. Simcoe, commander of the Queen's Rangers, was a fellow-prisoner, and when exchanged said, at parting, 'I shall never forget your kindness.' He did not: and when appointed Lieutenant-Governor of Upper Canada, he invited Mr. Lawrence to settle there," and, through the Governor, he acquired a large tract of land.

The Queen's Rangers were disbanded in 1802, having been associated with the events of the first government of Upper Canada, their colonel (Simcoe) having been the first Governor. A detachment of this regiment were stationed upon the banks of the Don, before there was a single white inhabitant where now stands Toronto.

FERGUSON'S RANGERS.

This corps formed a part of Burgoyne's army at the time of surrendering, and, "with other provincial prisoners, retired to Canada, by permission of Gates."

THE HESSIANS.

The British Government, during the course of the war, procured some foreign troops from one of the German Principalities upon the Rhine, mostly from Hesse-Hamburg. This foreign legion was under the command of General Baron de Reidesel, of their own country. It would seem from the testimony of their descendants in Marysburgh, that the British Government employed the men from the Government of the principality, and that the men did not voluntarily enter the service, but were impressed. These Hessians were drilled before leaving their country. They were composed of infantry, artillery, and a rifle company, "Green Yongers." They were embarked for Canada, by way of Portsmouth, and reached Quebec in time to join the British army, and meet the enemy at Stillwater. Conrad Bongard, of Marysburgh, informs us that his father was one of the company under General Reidesel. He was in the artillery, and accompanied Burgoyne in his eventful campaign; was at the battle of Tyconderoga; and, with the rest of the Hessian troops, was taken prisoner at Saratoga. They were taken down to Virginia, and there retained as prisoners of war for nearly two years. Being released on parole, many of them, with their General, were conveyed back to Germany; but some of them, having the alternative, preferred to remain in America, to share with the loyalists in grants of land. (See Marysburgh, where the Hessians settled). Conrad Bongard became the servant of Surveyor Holland, and was with him as he proceeded up the St. Lawrence, to survey. Bongard married a widow Carr, whose husband had been in the 24th regiment of Royal Fusiliers, and had died while the prisoners were retained in Virginia. He eventually settled in the fifth township, where he died, January, 1840, aged 89. His wife, Susan, died February, 1846, aged 98. Both were members of the Lutheran church. Mrs. B. was a native of Philadelphia.

The wife of the General, Baroness de Reidesel, has left an interesting record of the battles prior to Burgoyne's surrender.

CHAPTER. VIII.

CONTENTS.—Indian Names—The Five Tribes—The Sixth—Confederation—Government—Subdivisions—Origin—Hendrick—Death—Brant—Birth—Education—Married—Teaching—Christianity—Brant elected Chief—Commissioned a British Captain—Visits England—Returns—Leads his warriors to battle—Efforts of Rebels to seduce Brant to their cause—Attempted treachery of the Rebel Herchimer—Border warfare—Wyoming—Attempt to blacken the character of Brant—His noble conduct—Untruthful American History—The inhabitants of Wyoming—The Rebels first to blame—Cherry Valley—Van Schaick—Bloody orders—Terrible conduct of the Rebels, Helpless Indian families—Further deeds of blood and rapine by the rebel Sullivan—A month of horrible work—Attributes of cruelty more conspicuous in the Rebels than in the Indians—The New Englander—Conduct toward the Indians—Inconsistent—The "down trodden"—The Mohawks—Indian agriculture—Broken faith with the Indians—Noble conduct of Brant—After the war—His family—Death—Miss Molley—Indian usage—The character of the Mohawk—The six Indians as Canadians—Fidelity to the British—Receiving land—Bay Quinté—Grand River—Settling—Captain Isaac, Captain John—At present—Mohawk Counsel.

THE SIX NATIONS.

This once powerful Confederacy styled themselves Kan-ye-a-ke; also, they sometimes called themselves *Aganuschioni* or *Agnanuschioni*, which signifies *united* people. The French designated them Iroquois, from a peculiar sound of their speech. The English knew them as the *Five Nations*, and *Six Nations*, more generally by the latter term. The original five tribes that formed the Confederacy, were the Mohawks, Oneidas, Cayugas, Onondagas, and Senecas. Subsequently in 1712, the Tuscaroras came from the south, North Carolina, and made the sixth nation. But according to some authority, there were six nations before the Tuscaroras joined them. However, we learn from several sources, that up to 1712, the English, in speaking of them, referred to only five nations. The Oneidas seem, at one time, to have been omitted, and the Aucguagas inserted in their stead. The oldest members of the confederation were the Mohawks, Onondagas, and Senecas. The union of those three tribes took place prior to the occupation of America by the Europeans. The time at which the confederation of the five nations was formed is uncertain, but it is supposed to have been in the early part of the sixteenth century. The league binding them together was rather of a democratic nature.

Each tribe was represented in the great council of the nation by one principal sachem, with a number of associates.

They were always deliberate in their councils, considerate in their decisions, never infringing upon the rights of a minority, and dignified in their utterances. They were noted, not only as warriors, but as well for their agriculture, their laws, and their oratorical ability.

Each tribe was subdivided into classes, and each of these had a device or "totem," namely, the tortoise, the bear, the wolf, the beaver, the deer, the falcon, the plover, and the crane.

They were for hundreds of years the terror of the various Indian tribes peopling North America, and most of the time could at will, roam the wide expanse between the Hudson Bay and the Carolinas. Other tribes, too weak to oppose them, were from time to time completely exterminated. Of these was the Erie tribe, which had entirely disappeared by the year 1653. Of those who stubbornly resisted the Six Nations, were the Hurons, the Adirondacks, of the north, the Delawares, the Cherokees, and the Mohicans.

Smith, an historian of New York, says that in 1756 "Our Indians universally concur in the claim of all the lands not sold to the English, from the mouth of Sorel River, on the south side of Lakes Erie and Ontario, on both sides of the Ohio, till it falls into the Mississippi; and on the north side of those lakes, that whole territory between the Outawais River, and the Lake Huron, and even beyond the straits between that and Lake Erie."

"When the Dutch began the settlement of New York, all the Indians on Long Island, and the northern shore of the Sound, on the banks of the Connecticut, Hudson, Delaware, and Susquehannah rivers, were in subjection to the Five Nations," and in 1756, "a little tribe, settled at the Sugar-loaf Mountain, in Orange County, made a yearly payment of about £20 to the Mohawks."

Among the traditions of this people is one that they had a supernatural origin from the heart of a mountain, that they then migrated to the west, where they lived for a time by the sea shore.

Then, in time returned to the country of the lakes. A country now passed into the hands of the white man, who paid no just price. But the names of many places yet indicate the history of the ancient owners of the soil.

Among the Mohawks, in the beginning of the eighteenth century, was a chief known as Old King Hendrick, or Soi-euga-rah-ta, renowned for eloquence, bravery, and integrity. He was intimate with Sir William Johnson, and it was between them that the amusing contention of dreams occurred, that has been narrated.

In 1755, a battle was fought at Lake George, between the French, under Baron Dieskau, and the English, under Johnson, resulting in the defeat of the French. The French and English were supported by their respective allies. At this engagement Old King Hendrick, then seventy years old, but still full of energy and courage, was killed. Strangely enough it was at this battle that Brant, then only thirteen years old, first took part with his tribe in the contest. The mantle of Soieugarahta fell upon the youthful Thayendinagea.

Thayendinagea, or *Joseph Brant*, was born upon the banks of the Ohio, in the year 1742, while his tribe was on a visit to that region. According to Stone, his biographer, he was the son of "Tehowaghwengaraghkwin a full-blooded Mohawk, of the Wolf tribe."

After the battle at Lake George, Brant continued with his people under Johnson till the close of that bloody war. At its close, about 1760, Brant, with several other young Indians, was placed by Johnson at Moor School, Lebanon, Connecticut. After acquiring some knowledge of the rudiments of literature, he left the school to engage in active warfare with the Pontiacs and Ottawas. "In 1765, we find him married and settled in his own house at the Mohawk Valley. It is said he was not married, except in the Indian mode, until the winter of 1779, when at Niagara, seeing a Miss Moore, a captive, married, he was also thus married by Colonel John Butler, to a half-breed, the daughter of Colonel Croghan, by an Indian woman. Here he spent a quiet and peaceful life for some years, acting as interpreter in negotiations between his people and the whites, and lending his aid to the efforts of the missionaries who were engaged in the work of teaching and converting the Indians.

"Those who visited his house, spoke in high terms of his kindness and hospitality." Sir William Johnson died in 1774, and was succeeded by his son-in-law, Colonel George Johnson, as Indian agent, who appointed Brant his Secretary. The same year Johnson had to flee from the Mohawk, westward, to escape being captured by a band of rebels. He was accompanied by Brant and the principal warriors of the tribe. The rebels vainly tried to win the Indians to their side; but excepting a few Senecas, they preferred their long tried friends. The regular successor of Old King Hendrick, was "little Abraham." It is said he was well disposed to the Americans, probably through jealousy of Brant. At all events, Brant, by universal consent became the principal chief. He proceeded with the other chiefs, and a large body of Indian warriors to Montreal, where he was commissioned as a captain in the British army. "In the fall of 1775, he sailed for England to hold personal conference with the officers of government. He was an object of much curiosity at London, and attracted the attention of persons of high rank and great celebrity." Brant returned to America in the spring following, landed near New York, and made his way through his enemy's country to Canada. He placed himself at the head of his warriors, and led them on to many a victory. The first of which was at the battle of "the Cedars."

But the rebels did not cease endeavoring to seduce Brant to their cause. In June, 1777, General Herkimer of the rebel militia approached Brant's headquarters with a large force, ostensibly to treat on terms of equality. Brant had reason to suspect treachery, and consequently would not, for some time, meet Herkimer. After a week, however, he arranged to see General Herkimer, but every precaution was taken against treachery, and it appears that not without cause. Brant and Herkimer were old, and had been intimate friends. Brant took with him a guard of about forty warriors. It would seem that Herkimer's intention was to try and persuade Brant to come over to the rebels, and failing in this to have Brant assassinated as he was retiring. Says an American writer, Brownell, "We are sorry to record an instance of such unpardonable treachery as Herkimer is said to have planned at this juncture. One of his men, Joseph Waggoner, affirmed that the General privately exhorted him to arrange matters so that Brant and his three principal associates might be assassinated." Well does it become the Americans to talk about savage barbarity. Brant thwarted the intentions of his old friend by keeping his forty warriors within call. During all of the repeated attempts to get the Mohawks they never swerved, but reminded the rebels of their old treaties with England, and the ill-treatment their people had sustained at the hands of the colonists.

The head-quarters of Brant was at Oghkwaga, Owego, upon the Susquehanna. During the summer of 1777 while Burgoyne was advancing, the Mohawks under Brant rendered important service. In the attempt to capture Fort Stanwix, they took a prominent part. In the summer of 1778 the Indians, with Butler's Rangers were engaged principally in border warfare. It was during this season that the affair at Wyoming took place, which event has been so extravagantly made use of to blacken the character of the Indians and vilify the "tories." That Brant was not inhuman, but that he was noble, let recent American writers testify. Brownell says: "many an instance is recorded of his interference, even in the heat of conflict, to stay the hand uplifted against the feeble and helpless."

It was in the latter part of June that a descent was planned upon the settlements of Wyoming. Of this event, again we will let Brownell speak:—"It has been a commonly received opinion that Brant was the Chief under whom the Indian portion of the army was mustered, but it is now believed that he had as little share in this campaign as in many other scenes of blood long coupled with his name. There was no proof that he was present at any of the scenes that we are about to relate."

"No portion of the whole history of the revolution has been so distorted in the narration as that connected with the laying waste of the valley of Wyoming. No two accounts seem to agree, and historians have striven to out-do each other in the violence of their expressions of indignation, at cruelties and horrors which existed only in their imaginations, or which came to them embellished with all the exageration incident to reports arising amid scenes of excitement and bloodshed.

Wyoming had, for many years, been the scene of the bitterest hostility between the settlers under the Connecticut grant, and those from Pennsylvania. Although these warlike operations were upon a small scale, they were conducted with great vindictiveness and treachery. Blood was frequently shed, and as either party obtained the ascendency, small favor was shown to their opponents, who were generally driven from their homes in hopeless destitution. We cannot go into a history of these early transactions, and only mention them as explanatory of the feelings of savage animosity which were exhibited between neighbors, and even members of the same family, who had espoused opposite interests in the revolutionary contest." Such, be it noted, was the character of the inhabitants of Wyoming valley, who have been so long held up as innocent victims of Indian barbarity. By the above, we learn that prior to this, there had been contentions between the loyalists and rebels. The party who entered Wyoming to attack the Fort, were under Colonel John Butler, and was composed of some 300 British regulars and refugees, and 500 Indians. Now, it would seem that the depredation which was committed after Colonel Zebulon Butler, the rebel leader, had been defeated, and the Fort had capitulated, was to a great extent due to retaliatory steps taken by the loyalists who previously had been forced away, and had seen their homes committed to the flames. Such was the border warfare of those days. It was not Indian savagery, it was a species of fighting introduced by the "Sons of Liberty." And if we condemn such mode of fighting, let our condemnation rest first, and mainly upon those who initiated it. Not upon the Indians, for they were led by white men—not upon Brant, for he was not there—not so much npon the loyalists, for they had been driven away from their homes; but let it be upon those who introduced it.

The rebels were not slow to seek retribution for their losses at Wyoming. Aided by a party of Oneidas who lent themselves to the rebels, "Colonel Wm. Butler with a Pennsylvania regiment, entered the towns of Unadilla and Oghkwaga, and burned and destroyed the buildings, together with large stores of provisions intended for winter use." In turn, Walter Butler led a party of 700, a large number being Indians under Brant, to attack a fort at Cherry Valley which was "garrisoned by troops under Colonel Ichabod Alden." It will be seen that the Indians and loyalists did not enter an unprotected place to burn and destroy. They attacked a garrison of troops. But the Indians exasperated by the cruel procedure at Oghkwaga, became ungovernable, and about fifty men, women and children fell by the tomahawk. This was the retaliation which the Indian had been taught to regard as justifiable for the wrongs which had been inflicted upon his own tribe—his little ones; yet be it remembered, and later American writers admit it, that the commanders, Butler and Brant, did all they could to restrain the terrible doings of the exasperated men. "Specific instances are reported in which the Mohawk Chief interfered, and successfully, to avert the murderous tomahawk."

And now begins the bloody revenge which the rebels determined to inflict upon the Indians, without respect to tribes. In April, 1779, Colonel Van Schaick was despatched with a sufficient force for the purpose, with instructions "to lay waste the whole of their towns, to destroy all their cattle and property." "The Colonel obeyed his orders to the letter, and left nothing but blackened ruins behind him." It was merely a march of destruction, for the Indians were not there to oppose their steps. The villages and property that were destroyed belonged to the Onondagas, although they had not taken a decided stand with the loyalist party. It was enough that they were Indians, and would not join the rebels. But this was merely a prelude to what was preparing, in pursuance of a resolution of the rebel congress. The infamous duty of commanding this army of destruction, town destroyers the Indians called them, was entrusted to General Sullivan, whose nature was adequate to the requirements of the command.

On the 22nd August, 1779, five thousand men were concentrated at Tioga, upon the Susquehanna. The men were prepared for their uncivilized duty by promises of the territory over which they were about to sow blood and fire. The Indians had no adequate force to oppose their march westward over the Six Nations territory. Brant with his warriors, with the Butlers and Johnsons made a gallant resistance upon the banks of the Chemung, near the present town of Elmira. But, after suffering considerable loss, the vastly superior force compelled them to flee, and there remained nothing to arrest the devastating rebel army, and during the whole month of September they continued the work of despoliation.

It has been the custom of almost all American historians to give the Indians attributes of the most debasing character. At peace, unworthy the advantages of civilization; at war, treacherous and ferociously cruel. For this persistent and ungenerous procedure it is impossible to conceive any cause, unless to supply an excuse for the steady course of double-dealing the Americans have pursued toward the original owners of the soil, and provide a covering for the oft-repeated treachery practised toward the credulous Indian by the over-reaching new Englander. To the Mohawk Nation particularly, since they proved true allies of the British, have American writers found it agreeable to bestow a character noted for blood and rapine. Nothing can be more untrue than the character thus gratuitously portrayed, nothing more at variance with the essential nature of the Indian, when free from European intrigues, and the cursed fire-water. The aboriginal races of North America are not by nature, blood-thirsty above Europeans. That they are honest, just and true, capable of distinguishing between right and wrong, with a due appreciation of well-kept faith, is well attested by the conduct which has ever been observed by them toward, not alone the Pennsylvanians, but every man found to be a quaker. No instance can be found recorded throughout the long bloody wars of the Indians, where a hair of the head of a single man, woman or child of that denomination was injured by the Indian; and thus because the upright Penn never defrauded them. The Americans, while British colonists, with the exception alluded to, made themselves obnoxious to almost all Indian tribes. They never secured that hearty and faithful alliance that the French did. There seemed to be something in the air, especially of the New England States, which in a few generations blinded the eye, by which the golden rule is to be observed.

The Americans, who have ever set themselves up as the champions, *par excellence*, of liberty, to whom the "down-trodden of the old world" could look for sympathy, if not direct support, have signally failed to observe those lofty principles at home toward the natives of the soil, while they continued for eighty years to keep in chains the sable sons of Africa. They have found it convenient and plausible to prate about the political "tyranny of European despots;" but no nation of northern Europe has shown such disregard for the rights of their people as the United States have exhibited toward the original owners of the soil. Avarice has quite outgrown every principle of liberty that germinated ere they came to America. The frontier men, the land-jobber, the New England merchant, as well as the Southern Planter, have alike ignored true liberty in defrauding the Indian, in sending out slavers, and in cruel treatment of the slave. Then can we wonder that the noble-minded Indian, naturally true to his faith, should, when cheated, wronged,—cruelly wronged, with the ferocity natural to his race, visit the faithless with terrible retribution?

The unbiassed records of the past, speak in tones that cannot be hushed, of the more noble conduct of the natives, than of those who have sought to exterminate them. The Mohawks, although brave warriors, fought not for the mere love of it. They even at times strove to mediate between the French and New Englanders.

To the Mohawks, the American writer has especially bestowed

a name bloody and ignoble. And all because they listened not to their wily attempts to seduce them to join the rebels, but preferred to ally themselves with the British. No doubt the Indian had long before discriminated between the rule of British officers, and the selfish policy of local governments. And hence, we find, in every scrap of paper relating to the Mohawks, unfounded accounts of savage doings. But taking, as true, the darkest pages written by the Americans against the Six Nations, they present no parallel to the deeds of brutal vengeance enacted by the American army under Sullivan, when he traversed the fruitful country, so long the home of the Iroquois. Says an American writer: "When the army reached the Genesee Valley, all were surprised at the cultivation exhibited, by wide fields of corn, gardens well stocked, their cattle, houses, and other buildings, showing good design, with mechanical skill, and every kind of vegetable that could be conceived. Beautiful as was the scene in the eyes of the army, a few days changed it to utter desolation; neither house, nor garden, grain, fruit tree, or vegetable, was left unscathed."

Says Stone: "Forty Indian towns were destroyed. Corn gathered and ungathered, to the amount of 160,000 bushels, shared the same fate; their fruit trees were cut down; and the Indians were hunted like wild beasts, till neither house, nor fruit tree, nor field of corn, nor inhabitant, remained in the whole country." And the poor Indian women, and children, and old men, were thus left at the approaching winter to seek support at the British garrisons. Truly the rebels of '76 were brave and civilized!

Thirteen years after, one of the chiefs said to Washington, "Even to this day, when the name of the town-destroyer is heard, our women look behind them and turn pale, and our children cling close to the necks of their mother; our sachems and our warriors are men, who cannot be afraid, but their hearts are grieved with the fears of our women and children." Thus the brave Sullivan, with his thousand rebels, made war against old men, women and children, who were living in their rightful homes. This was fighting for liberty!

The blood of the Indian, as well as the slave, has risen up to reproach the American, and it required much of fresh blood to wash away the stains remaining from their deeds of cruelty and rapine, inflicted during their revolutionary war, under the name of liberty. The soldiers of Sullivan were stimulated in their evil work by promises of the land they were sent to despoil; and the close of the war saw them return to claim their promises, while the rightful owner was driven away. A certain portion of the Six Nations having received pledges from the United States Government for their welfare, remained to become subjects of the new nation. But excepting Washington himself, and General Schuyler, not one heeded their promises made to the Indian. The most unjust proceedings were begun and ruthlessly carried on by individuals, by companies, by legislators, by speculators, to steal every inch of land that belonged by all that is right, to the Senecas. How unlike the benignant and faithful conduct of the British Government in Canada.

Brant continued during the war to harass the enemy in every possible way; and in the following year, August, planned a terrible, but just retaliation for the work of Sullivan's horde. It was now the turn of the rebels to have their houses, provisions and crops, despoiled. But all the while "no barbarities were permitted upon the persons of defenceless women and children, but a large number of them were borne away into captivity." Again, in October, Johnson and Brant, with Corn Planter, a distinguished Seneca chief, invaded the Mohawk Valley. In this foray, the same conduct was observed toward women and children. On one occasion, Brant sent an Indian runner with an infant, that had been unintentionally carried from its mother with some captives, to restore it. Still, again the following year, the Indians under Brant, and the Royalists under Major Ross, were found over-running their old homes along the Mohawk and Schoharie. On this their last expedition, they were met by the rebels in force under Colonel Willet, with some Oneida warriors, and defeated them. Colonel Walter N. Butler, whom the rebels have so often tried to malign, was shot and scalped by an Oneida Indian, under the command of the rebel Willet.

We learn by the foregoing that the Iroquois were not only brave as warriors, but they had attained to a much higher position in the scale of being then other tribes inhabiting America. They were not ignorant of agriculture, nor indifferent to the blessings derived therefrom. The rich uplands of the country lying to the north of the Alleghanies, were made to contribute to their wants, as did the denizen of the forest. They are equally at home, whether upon the war path, the trail of the deer, or in the tilling of land. The plow of the Anglo-Saxon has not in seventy years completely effaced the evidences of their agricultural skill. And not less were their sachems noted for wisdom in council, and for eloquence. Not only corn, but beans and other cereals were cultivated, particularly by the Six Nations. Fruits and edibles, introdued by the Europeans, were propagated by the natives, and when the rebel Sullivan, in accordance with orders from Washington, swept over their country, large orchards of excellent fruit, as well as fields of grain, were met with and ruthlessly destroyed, as were the women and children, with their peaceful homes.

According to Rochefoucault, Brant's manners were half European; he was accompanied by two negro servants, and was, "in appearance, like an Englishman." Brant visited England in December 1785, and was treated with great consideration.

After the close of the war, Brant settled at Wellington Square, upon land conferred by the Crown, where he lived after the English mode. He died here 24th November, 1807. His wife, who never took to civilized life, after her husband's death, removed to the Grand River, and lived in her wigwam. Some of her children remained in the "commodious dwelling," and others accompanied her to the life of the wigwam. According to Weld, Brant had at one time thirty or forty negro slaves, which he kept in the greatest subjection. He also says that Brant's half pay as a captain, and his presents yearly received, amounted to £500.

His last days were made unhappy by a debased son, who, after threatening his father's life, was at last killed by him, in self defence, by a short sword which Brant wore at his side. Respecting another of his sons, the Kingston *Herald*, September 5th, 1832, says:

> "It is with unfeigned sorrow that we announce the death of CAPTAIN JOHN BRANT, Chief of the Six Nations Indians. He died of Cholera, at Brantford, on the 27th ult., after an illness of only six hours. Mr. Brant was the son of the celebrated Indian Chief, whose memory was unjustly assailed by Campbell the Poet, and for the vindication of which the subject of this notice some years ago purposely visited England. Possessing the education, feelings, and manners of a gentleman, he was beloved by all who had the pleasure of his acquaintance, and his death cannot fail to be deeply and very generally regretted."

We have spoken of the intimacy that existed between the Mohawks and Sir William Johnson, the Colonial Agent of England. This, be it remembered, was more than a hundred years ago, and great changes have taken place in the opinion of many with regard to certain irregularities of society. We cannot excuse the conduct of Sir William, when he had lost his European wife, in taking the sister of Brant, Miss Molly, without the form of matrimonial alliance; but we must concede every allowance for the times in which he lived. But while grave doubt may rest upon the moral principle displayed by him, we see no just reason to reflect in any way upon the Indian female. Miss Molly took up her abode with Sir William, and lived with him as a faithful spouse until he died. However, this must not be regarded as indicating depravity on the part of the simple-minded native. It must be remembered that the Indian's mode of marrying consists of but little more than the young squaw leaving the father's wigwam, and repairing to that of her future husband, and there is no reason to doubt that Miss Molly was ever other than a virtuous woman. And this belief is corroborated by the fact that four daughters, the issue of this alliance, were most respectably married.

Of the Six Nations, this tribe always stood foremost as brave and uncompromising adherents to the British Government, notwithstanding the utmost endeavors of the rebels to win them to their side. It becomes, consequently a duty, and a pleasing duty to refer more particularly to this race, a remnant of which yet lives upon the shore of the bay. Among the Mohawks are, however, remnants of some of the other tribes.

The tribe is so-called, after the river, upon whose banks they so long lived. They did not formerly acknowledge the title, but called themselves by a name which interpreted, means "just such a people as we ought to be." This name is not known, unless it may be Agniers, a name sometimes applied by the French.

This tribe was the oldest and most important of the Six Nations, and supplied the bravest warriors, and one of its chiefs was usually in command of the united warriors of all the tribes.

It must not be forgotten that the Mohawks, who came to Canada, and other tribes of the Six Nations, were to all intents, United Empire Loyalists. At the close of the struggle, we have seen elsewhere, that the commissioners at Paris, in their unseemly haste to contract terms of peace, forgot how much was due to the loyalists of America, and urged no special terms to ameliorate the condition of the many who had fought and lost all for the maintenance of British power. Likewise did they forgot the aboriginal natives who had equally suffered. The fact that these Indians were not even referred to, gave Brant a just cause of complaint, which he duly set forth in a memorial to the Imperial Government. But, as the British Government and nation subsequently strove to relieve the suffering condition of the refugees, so did they afford to the loyal sons of the forest every possible facility to make themselves comfortable. Indeed, the British officers in command, at the first, gave a pledge that all that they lost should be restored. The promise thus given by Sir Guy Carleton, was ratified by his successor, General Haldimand, in 1779, Captain General and Commander-in-Chief in Canada, and confirmed by Patent, under the Great Seal, January, 14, 1793, issued by Governor Simcoe.

At the close of the war, a portion of the Mohawks were temporarily residing on the American side of Niagara River, in the vicinity of the old landing place above the Fort. The Senecas, who seem to have been at this time more closely allied than other tribes to the Mohawks, offered to them a tract of land within the territory of the United States. But the Mohawks would not live in the United States. They declared they would "sink or swim with England."

Brant proceeded to Montreal to confer with Sir John Johnson, General Superintendent of Indian affairs. "The tract upon which the chief had fixed his attention, was situated upon the Bay de Quinté." General Haldimand, in accordance with this wish, purchased a tract of land upon the bay from the Mississaugas, and conveyed it to the Mohawks. Subsequently, when Brant returned to Niagara, the Senecas expressed their desire that their old and intimate friends, the Mohawks, should live nearer to them than upon the Bay de Quinté. Brant convened a council of the tribe to consider the matter, the result was, that he went a second time to Quebec to solicit a tract of land less remote from the Senecas. Haldimand granted this request, and the land, six miles square, upon the Grand River, was accordingly purchased from the Mississaugas, and given to them, forty miles off from the Senecas. The above facts are taken from Brant's MS. and History. We may infer from this fact, that the party who did come to the bay under Captain John, felt less attachment to the Senecas than the other portion of the tribe. The quantity of land on the bay originally granted was 92,700 acres; but a portion has been surrendered.

In the early part of the rebellion, the Mohawk families fled from their valley with precipitation. They mostly went to Lachine, where they remained three years. They then ascended the river in their canoes, and probably stayed a winter at Cataraqui, the winter of 1783-4. The whole tribe was under Brant. Second in command was Captain John, a cousin of Brant, and his senior in years.

In the spring, a portion of the tribe entered the Bay Quinté, and passed up to the present township of Tyendinaga. The majority, led by Brant, passed up along the south shore of Lake Ontario to Niagara.

THE MOHAWKS AS CANADIANS.

Descendants of the bravest of all the brave Indian warriors of America, we find them peaceable and in most respects imbibing the spirit of the day. Ever since the party settled on the bay, they have manifested no turbulent spirit, none of those wild attributes natural to the wild-woods Indian, toward their white neighbors. Among themselves there has been one occasion of disturbance. This arose from the quarrelsome nature of one Captain Isaac Hill. This Chief, with his people, formed a part of Brant's company that settled on the Grand River. After a few years, having disagreed with his nation, and become exceedingly disagreeable from his officious and selfish conduct, he removed to the bay, and united himself with Captain John's party, which received him. But he failed to live peaceably with them. Eventually the disagreement resulted in a serious hostile engagement between the two branches, who fought with tomahawks and knives. But one person was killed, a chief of Capain John's party, Powles Claus, who was stabbed in the abdomen. But subsequently Captain Isaac Hill became a worthy inhabitant. His house still standing, then considered large, was frequently open to the more festive, across the Bay in Sophiasburgh.

Out of the six hundred Indians, now living upon the Reserve, there is only one with pure Indian blood. His name is David Smart. It has been elsewhere stated, that the custom prevailed among the Mohawk nation, to maintain the number of the tribe, by taking captive a sufficient number to fill the vacancies caused by death of their people. The result was, that these captives marrying with Indians, they gradually underwent a change, and the original appearance of the Mohawk has lost its characteristic features. The circumstances of the Indians during the revolutionary war, and subsequently in settling in Canada, led to frequent unions between the white men of different nationalities and the Indian women. Therefore, at the present day there remains but little more than a trace of the primal Indian who lorded it, a hundred years ago, over no inconsiderable portion of the North American Continent.

When visiting the Indians, on our way, we met some eight or ten sleighs laden with them, returning from a funeral. We were much struck with the appearance of solid, farmer-like comfort which their horses and conveyances exhibited, as well as they themselves did in their half Canadian dress.

While drunkenness has prevailed among the older Indians, it is pleasing to know that the younger ones are far more regular in their habits. For this, much credit is due to the Christian oversight of their former and present pastors. They have 1800 acres of land. They number 630, and are increasing yearly.

The seal of the Mohawk Counsel may be seen with the Rev. Mr. Anderson. The armorial bearings consist of the wolf, the bear and the turtle. These animals, in the order here given, indicate, not tribes, nor families exactly, but rank. The wolf is the highest class, the bear next in rank, and the turtle the lowest grade.

CHAPTER IX.

Contents:—Individuals—Anderson—Bethune—Burwell—Butler—Canliff—Claus—Coffin—Doune—Jarvis—Jones—McDonald—McGill—McGilles—Merrit—Munday—Peters— Robinson—Singleton— Ross—McNab—Allen— Allison—Ashley —Bell —Burritt —Casey—Carscallion— Church—Clark—Crawford—Dame—Daly—Diamond.

INDIVIDUAL COMBATANTS.

The immediately following notices of the combatants who settled in Upper Canada are extracted from Sabine.

"At the beginning of the revolution, Samuel Anderson, of New York, went to Canada. He soon entered the service of the Crown, and was a captain under Sir John Johnson. In 1783 he settled near Cornwall, in Upper Canada, and received half-pay. He held several civil offices: those of Magistrate, Judge of a district court, and associate Justice of the Court of King's Bench, were among them. He continued to reside upon his estate near Cornwall, in Upper Canada, until his decease in 1836, at the age of one hundred and one. His property in New York was abandoned and lost."

"Joseph Anderson, lieutenant in the King's regiment, New York. At the peace he retired to Canada. He died near Cornwall, Canada West, in 1853, aged ninety. He drew half pay for a period of about seventy years. One of the last survivors of the United Empire Loyalists."

"John Bethune, of North Carolina, chaplain in the Loyal Militia. Taken prisoner in the battle at Cross Creek in 1776. Confined in Halifax gaol, but ordered finally to Philadelphia. After his release, his continued loyalty reduced him to great distress. He was appointed chaplain to the 84th regiment, and restored to comfort. At the peace he settled in Upper Canada, and died at Williamstown in that colony, in 1815, in his sixty-fifth year."

"James Burwell, of New Jersey, born at Rockaway, January 18, 1754. Our loyalist enlisted in his Majesty's service in the year 1776, at the age of twenty-two, and served seven years, and was present at the battle of Yorktown, when Lord Cornwallis surrendered, and was there slightly wounded."

"Came to Upper Canada in the year 1796, too late to obtain the King's bounty of family land, but was placed on the United Empire list, and received two hundred acres for himself and each of his children. He removed to the Talbot settlement in the year 1810. He died in the County of Elgin, Canada, July, 1853, aged ninety-nine years and five months."

"John Butler, of Tyron, now Montgomery county, New York. Before the war, Colonel Butler was in close official connection with Sir William, Sir John, and Colonel Guy Johnson, and followed their political fortunes. At the breaking out of hostilities he commanded a regiment of New York Militia, and entered at once into the military service of the Crown. During the war his wife was taken prisoner, and exchanged for the wife of the whig colonel, Campbell. Colonel John Butler was richly rewarded for his services. Succeeding (in part) to the agency of Indian affairs, long held by the Johnsons, he enjoyed, about the year 1796, a salary of £500 stg. per annum, and a pension, as a military officer, of £200 more. Previously, he had received a grant of 500 acres of land, and a similar provision for his children. His home, after the war, was in Upper Canada. He was attainted during the contest, and his property confiscated. He lived, before the revolution, in the present town of Mohawk."

"Joseph Canliff, in 1781 a lieutenant in the first battalion New Jersey Volunteers." This person is probably of the same lineage as the writer of this work, great confusion often existing with regard to the spelling of names in the early days of America.

"Daniel Claus. He married a daughter of Sir William Johnson, and served for a considerable time in the Indian Department of Canada, under his brother-in-law, Colonel Guy Johnson."

"William Claus, Deputy Superintendent General of Indian affairs, was his son."

Coffin—There were several of this name who took part in the war against the rebellion. Of these, the following are connected with Canadian history:

"Sir Thomas Aston Coffin, baronet, of Boston, son of William Coffin. He graduated at Harvard University in 1772. At one period of the rebellion he was private secretary to Sir Guy Carleton. In 1804 he was Secretary and Comptroller of Lower Canada." Afterwards Commissary General in the British army.

"Nathaniel Coffin, of Boston. After the revolution he settled in Upper Canada." Served in the war of 1812. "For a number of years was Adjutant-General of the Militia of Upper Canada. Died at Toronto in 1846, aged 80."

"John Coffin: was Assistant Commissary General in the British army, and died at Quebec in 1837, aged 78."

"Doane, of Bucks County, Pennsylvania. Of this family there were five brothers, namely: Moses, Joseph, Israel, Abraham, Mahlon. They were men of fine figures and address, elegant horsemen, great runners and leapers, and excellent at stratagems and escapes. Their father was respectable, and possessed a good estate. The sons themselves, prior to the war, were men of reputation, and proposed to remain neutral: but, harassed personally, their property sold by the whigs because they would not submit to the exactions of the time, the above-mentioned determined to wage a predatory warfare upon their persecutors, and to live in the open air, as they best could do. This plan they executed, to the terror of the country around, acting as spies to the royal army, and robbing and plundering continually; yet they spared the weak, the poor and the peaceful. They aimed at public property and at public men. Generally, their expeditions were on horseback. Sometimes the five went together, at others separately, with accomplices. Whoever of them was apprehended broke jail; whoever of them was assailed escaped. In a word, such was their course, that a reward of £300 was offered for the head of each.

"Ultimately, three were slain. Moses, after a desperate fight, was shot by his captor; and Abraham and Mahlon were hung at Philadelphia.

"Joseph, before the revolution, taught school. During the war, while on a marauding expedition, he was shot through the cheeks, fell from his horse, and was taken prisoner. He was committed to jail to await his trial, but escaped to New Jersey. A reward of $800 was offered for his apprehension, but without success. He resumed his former employment in New Jersey, and lived there, under an assumed name, nearly a year, but finally fled to Canada. Several years after the peace he returned to Pennsylvania, 'a poor, degraded, broken-down old man,' to claim a legacy of about £40, which he was allowed to recover, and to depart. In his youth he was distinguished for great physical activity."

The only separate mention of Israel is, that "in February, 1783, he was in jail; that he appealed to the Council of Pennsylvania to be released, on account of his own sufferings and the destitute condition of his family, and that his petition was dismissed."

"Stephen Jarvis, in 1782 was a lieutenant of cavalry in the South Carolina Royalists. He was in New Brunswick after the revolution, but went to Upper Canada, and died at Toronto, at the residence of the Rev. Dr. Phillips, 1840, aged eighty-four. During his service in the revolution he was in several actions."

"William Jarvis, an officer of cavalry in the Queen's Rangers. Wounded at the siege of Yorktown. At the peace he settled in Upper Canada, and became Secretary of that Province. He died at York in 1817. His widow, Hannah, a daughter of the Rev. Dr. Peters, of Hebron, Connecticut, died at Queenston, Upper Canada, 1845, aged eighty-three."

"David Jones was a captain in the royal service, and is supposed to 'have married the beautiful and good Jane McCrea, whose cruel death, in 1777, by the Indians, is universally known and lamented.' According to Lossing, he lived in Canada to an old age, having never married. Jane McCrea was the daughter of the Rev. James McCrea, of New Jersey, loyalist."

"Jonathan Jones, of New York, brother of Jane McCrea's lover. Late in 1776 he assisted in raising a company in Canada, and joined the British, in garrison, at Crown Point. Later in the war he was a captain, and served under General Frazer."

McDonald—There were a good many of this name who took part as combatants, of whom several settled in Canada.

Alexander McDonald was a major in a North Carolina regiment. "His wife was the celebrated Flora McDonald, who was so true and so devoted to the unfortunate Prince Charles Edward, the last Stuart, who sought the throne of England. They had emigrated to North Carolina, and when the rebellion broke out, he, with two sons, took up arms for the Crown."

Those who settled in Canada were "Donald McDonald, of New

York. He served under Sir John Johnson for seven years, and died at the Wolfe Island, Upper Canada, in 1839, aged 97."

"Allan McDonald, of Tryon, New York," was associated with Sir John Johnson in 1776. "He died at Three Rivers, Lower Canada, in 1822, quite aged."

"John McGill.—In 1782 he was an officer of infantry in the Queen's Rangers, and, at the close of the war, went to New Brunswick. He removed to Upper Canada, and became a person of note. He died at Toronto, in 1834, at the age of eighty-three. At the time of his decease he was a member of the Legislative Council of the Colony."

"Donald McGillis resided, at the beginning of the revolution, on the Mohawk river, New York. Embracing the royal side in the contest, he formed one of a 'determined band of young men' who attacked a whig post and, in the face of a superior force, cut down the flag-staff, and tore in strips the stars and stripes attached to it. Subsequently, he joined a grenadier company, called the Royal Yorkers, and performed efficient service throughout the war. He settled in Canada at the peace; and, entering the British service again in 1812, was commissioned as a captain in the Colonial corps, by Sir Isaac Brock. He died at River Raisin, Canada, in 1844, aged eighty years."

"Thomas Merrit, of New York, in 1782 was cornet of cavalry in the Queen's Rangers. He settled in Upper Canada, and held the offices of Sheriff of the District of Niagara and Surveyor of the King's Forests. He received half pay as a retired military officer. He died at St. Catharines, May, 1842, aged eighty-two."

"Nathaniel Munday, in 1782 was an officer in the Queen's Rangers. He was in New Brunswick after the revolution, and received half pay; but left that colony and, it is believed, went to Canada."

"John Peters, of Hebron, Connecticut; born in 1740. A most devoted loyalist. He went to Canada finally, and raised a corps, called the Queen's Loyal Rangers, of which Lord Dorchester gave him command, with the rank of lieutenant-colonel."

"Christopher Robinson, of Virginia, kinsman of Beverley. Entered William and Mary College with his cousin Robert; escaped with him to New York, and received a commission in the Loyal American regiment. Served at the South, and was wounded. At the peace he went to Nova Scotia, and received a grant of land at Wilmot.

He soon removed to Canada, where Governor Simcoe gave him the appointment of Deputy Surveyor-General of Crown Lands. His salary, half pay, and an estate of two thousand acres, placed him in circumstances of comfort. He was the father of several children, some of whom were educated in the mother-country. He died in Canada. His widow, Esther, daughter of Rev. John Sayre, of New Brunswick, died in 1827. His son, Beverley Robinson, who was born in 1791, was appointed Attorney-General of Upper Canada in 1818; Chief Justice in 1829; created a Baronet in 1854; and died in 1863."

"Singleton—A lieutenant in the 'Royal Greens,' was wounded in 1777, during the investment of Fort Stanwix." Probably Captain Singleton, who settled in Thurlow, Upper Canada, was the same person.

"Finley Ross, of New York, was a follower of Sir John Johnson to Canada in 1776. After the revolution he served in Europe, and was at Minden and Jena. He settled at Charlotteburgh, Upper Canada, where he died, in 1830, aged ninety."

"Allan McNab, a Lieutenant of cavalry in the Queen's Rangers, under Colonel Simcoe. During the war he received thirteen wounds. He accompanied his commander to Upper Canada, then a dense, unpeopled wilderness, where he settled. He was appointed Sergeant-at-arms of the House of Assembly of that Province, and held the office many years. His son, the late Sir Allan McNab, was a gentleman who filled many important offices in Upper Canada."

The Hamilton *Spectator*, speaking of the death of Sir A. N. McNab, says: "The Hon. Colonel Sir Allan Napier McNab, Bart., M.L.C., A. D. C., was born at Niagara in the year 1798, of Scotch extraction,—his grandfather, Major Robert McNab, of the 22nd regiment, or Black Watch, was Royal Forester in Scotland, and resided on a small property called Dundurn, at the head of Loch Earn. His father entered the army in her Hajesty's 7th regiment, and was subsequently promoted to a dragoon regiment. He was attached to the staff of General Simcoe during the revolutionary war; after its close he accompanied General Simcoe to this country. When the Americans attacked Toronto, Sir Allan, then a boy at school, was one of a number of boys selected as able to carry a musket; and after the authorities surrendered the city, he retreated with the army to Kingston, when through the instrumentality of Sir Roger Sheaff, a friend of his father's, he was rated as mid-shipman on board Sir James Yeo's ship, and accompanied the expeditions to Sackett's Harbor, Genesee, and other places on the American side of the lake. Finding promotions rather slow, he left the navy and joined the 100th regiment under Colonel Murray, and was with them when they re-occupied the Niagara frontier. He crossed with the advanced guard at the storming and taking of Fort Niagara. For his conduct in this affair he was honored with an ensigncy in the 49th regiment. He was with General Ryall at Erie, and crossed the river with him when Black Rock and Buffalo were burned, in retaliation for the destruction of Niagara, a few months previous. After the termination of this campaign, Sir Allan joined his regiment in Montreal, and shortly after marched with them to the attack of Plattsburg. On the morning of the attack he had the honor of commanding the advanced guard at the Saranac Bridge. At the reduction of the army in 1816 or 1817, he was placed on half-pay.

It is impossible at this time to give anything like a history of the disbanded soldiers who settled on the shores of the Bay and the St. Lawrence. There could not be allowed the space necessary to do justice to the character of each. But even if such were possible we are wanting in the essential matter of information. We propose, however, to insert the names of every one known to have been a loyal combatant, whether an officer or private, with such statements relative to his history as we possess. We shall not confine ourselves to this particular region of the Province, but include those who settled at Niagara, and in Lower Canada. And while we may not supply a complete account of any one, it is trusted that the instalment will not be unacceptable to the descendants of those to whom we refer. We shall arrange them alphabetically without reference to rank or station.

Captain Joseph Allen, formerly Captain Allen of New Jersey, held a commission in the British Army at New York for some time during the war. He owned extensive mill property, and was regarded as a very wealthy person. All his possessions were confiscated, and he in 1783, found his way, among other refugees, first to Sorel, where he stayed a winter, and finally to Upper Canada. His family consisted of two sons, John and Jonathan, and three daughters, Rachel, Ursula, and Elizabeth. Captain Allen was one of the first settlers in Adolphustown, and his descendants still live in the township, among whom are Parker Allen, Esq., J. D. Watson, Esq., and David McWherter, Esq. Captain Allen had extensive grants of land in Adolphustown, and in Marysburgh, and elsewhere; as well as his children. Jonathan Allen, succeeded his father upon the homestead, and was for many years an acceptable Justice of the Peace. His brother, Joseph Allen, moved to Marysburgh, and was a Captain of militia during the war of 1812. Captain Allen brought with him several slaves, "who followed his fortunes with peculiar attachment, even after their liberation."

We have seen that the rebellion led to the divisions of families. It was so with the Allison family of Haverstraw, New York. There were seven brothers, two sided with the rebels. One Benjamin, being a boy, was at home, while the other four took part with loyalists. One settled in New Brunswick, probably the Edward Allison Sabine speaks of, who had been captain in De Lancey's third battalion, and who received half-pay, and after whom *Mount Allison* is called.

Joseph Allison was living at Haverstraw, New York. He was for a time engaged in the navy yard at New York. At one time he and another entered the rebel camp, and after remaining a few days availed themselves of a dark night and carried off five excellent horses belonging to a troop of cavalry. They were pursued and barely escaped. Allison took these horses in return for the loss of his house and other property which the rebels had ruthlessly burned. He was at the battle of White Plains, and had narrow escapes, his comrade beside him was shot down, and his canteen belt cut in two by a ball. As he could not carry the canteen, he took time to empty that vessel of the rum which it contained.

His neighbors at Haverstraw were exceedingly vindictive against him. After several years, he visited there to see his aged mother, when a mob attempted to tar and feather him, and he had to hide in the woods all night. Allison came to Canada with Van Alstine, and drew lot 17, in Adolphustown. A strong, healthy and vigorous man, he contributed no little to the early settlement. Died upon his farm, aged eighty-eight. His wife's name was Mary Richmond, of a well-known quaker family. His descendants still occupy the old homestead, a most worthy family. Benjamin Allison, the youngest, came to Adolphustown in 1795.

William Ashley, sen., was born in the city of London, England, in the year 1749, and joined the army at an early age.

During the American Revolotionary war, he came out under General Howe, serving in all his campaigns until the close of the struggle. He had two brothers also in the army with him, one of whom returned to England, and the other settled somewhere in the

United States, the exact locality not now being known. General J. M. Ashley, Republican member of Congress from Ohio, is, so far as can be ascertained, a descendant of this brother.

After the termination of the war, William Ashley came to Canada, and first settled in the township of Loborough, county of Frontenac, where he married Margaret Buck, the daughter of a U. E. L., and one of the first settlers in this part of Canada. He resided here until about 1790, when he removed to Kingston, where he followed the employment of a butcher, and was the first butcher in Kingston, a fact he often mentioned in his old age. He built a house of red cedar logs, cut from the spot, which continued to stand until 1858, when it was taken down and a small brick building, the "Victoria Hotel," built on the site. When removed the logs were found in a perfectly sound condition, they having been covered with clapboards many years ago, which preserved them from the weather.

This house stood on Brock street, near the corner of Bagot street. At the time of its erection there were scarcely twenty residences in the place, and that part of the city now lying west of the City Hall was then covered with a dense forest of pine, cedar and ash. William Ashley lived to see this pass away and a flourishing city spring up. He died in 1835, leaving a family of ten children—Margaret, Mary, Elizabeth, William, John, James, Thomas, Henry, Adam and George: all of whom are now dead excepting Thomas, who resides near Toronto.

James also died in 1835, and Henry, who was the first gaoler in Picton, died in 1836, at the early age of thirty-one.

William Ashley, Jun., married Ann Gerollamy, daughter of an officer in the British army, serving through the Revolutionary War, and acting as Orderly in the war of 1812. He left Kingston in 1830, and resided until 1842 near the mouth of Black River, in the township of Marysburgh, and then returned, and continued to reside there, teaching, and filling various offices until his death, August 16, 1867.

The *British Whig* newspaper when recording his death, remarked, "Mr. Ashley was one of our oldest citizens, and has lived to witness many changes in his native place. He was born on the very spot where the *British Whig* office now stands." The last sentence is a mistake, he was not born in the city, but in the township of Loborough; although the building containing the *British Whig* office still belongs to the 'Ashley property' on Bagot Street."

John Ashley was gaolor in Kingston for a number of years when the gaol stood near the site of the present Post Office, and filled public situations from the time he was nineteen years of age until his death in 1858. He was a prominent member of the County Council for nearly twenty years, and was Colonel of the militia at the time of his death.

Adam and George Ashley both died in 1847.

William Bell—We shall have occasion to speak of William Bell in different places in these pages. He was born August 12, 1758, in County of Tyrone, Ireland.

At the time of the Revolutionary War he was a sergeant in the 53rd regiment of the line. Some time after the close of the war, he succeeded in procuring his discharge from the service, at Lachine, and came to Cataraqui, sometime in 1789. He was on intimate terms with John Ferguson, and, we believe, related by marriage. It was at Ferguson's solicitation that Bell came to the Bay. We have before us an old account book, by which we learn that Ferguson and Bell commenced trading on the front of Sidney in the latter part of 1789. They remained here in business until 1792. Subsequently Bell became school teacher to the Mohawks, and seems to have done business there in the way of trading, in 1799. In 1803 we find him settled in Thurlow. Ferguson, who was living at Kingston, had been appointed Colonel of the Hastings Militia, and Bell was selected by him to assist in organizing the body. He was commissioned captain in December 1798, Major in August 1800; and in 1809 Lieutenant-Colonel. Colonel Bell was well known as a public man in Thurlow. He was appointed to several offices—Magistrate, Coroner, and finally Colonel of the Hastings Battalion. As magistrate he took an active part in the doings of Thurlow and Belleville for many years. He was also an active person in connection with the agricultural societies, until a few years before his death, 1833. The papers left by Colonel Bell have been of great service to us. His wife's name was Rachel Hare, who died 1853, aged eighty-one.

Colonel Stephen Burritt took part in the war against the rebels, being seven years in the army, in Roger's Rangers. He settled upon the Rideau, the 9th of April, 1793. In the same year was born Colonel E. Burritt, who was the first child born of white parents north of the Rideau. This interesting fact was given to the writer by Colonel E. Burritt in 1867. Colonel Burritt is a cousin of the celebrated Learned Blacksmith.

Willet Casey was born in Rhode Island. His father was killed in battle during the war. At the close of the war he settled near Lake Champlain, upon what he supposed to be British territory, but finding such was not the case, and although he had made considerable clearing, he removed again. Turning his steps toward Upper Canada with his aged mother and wife, he reached in due time, the 4th township. The family, upon arriving, found shelter in a blacksmith's shop until a log hut could be built. Three months afterwards the old mother died. Willet Casey had a brother in a company of horsemen, who fought for the British. He remained in the States and went South. It is probably the descendants of this Casey, who took an active part in the late civil war in the United States.

The writer has seen the fine, erect old couple that came to Canada, when on the verge of eighty, and two nobler specimens of nature's nobility could not be imagined.

Luke Carscallion was an Irishman by birth, and had served in the British army; he had retired and emigrated to the American colonies prior to the rebellion. He desired to remain neutral, and take no part in the contest. The rebels, however, said to him that inasmuch as he was acquainted with military tactics he must come and assist them, or be regarded as a King's man. His reply was that he had fought for the king, and he would do it again, consequently an order was issued to arrest him; but when they came to take him he had secreted himself. The escape was a hurried one, and all his possessions were at the mercy of the rebels—land to the amount of 12,000 acres. They, disappointed in not catching him, took his young and tender son, and threatened to hang him if he would not reveal his father's place of concealment. The brave little fellow replied, hang away! and the cruel men under the name of liberty carried out their threat, and three times was he suspended until almost dead, yet he would not tell, and then when taken down one of the monsters actually kicked him.

Oliver Church was Lieutenant in the 84th regiment. He settled with the many other half-pay officers, on the front of Fredericksburgh, three miles west of Bath. He had three sons, and three daughters, who settled upon the Bay, but are now dead except one daughter. Lieutenant Church died in 1812, and his wife some years later. They were both very old when they died.

A grand-child of the old veteran, Mrs. H. of Belleville informs us that she has often heard about her grandfather having to crush grain by hand, and spending a week going to the Kingston mill.

Robert Clark, late of the Township of Ernest town, in the County of Addington, was born March 15, 1744 on Quaker Hill, Duchess County, Province of New York. He learned the trade of carpenter and millwright, of a Mr. Woolly. He left his family and joined the British standard in the revolutionary war, was in General Burgoyne's army, and was requested by the General that he and other Provincial volunteers, should leave the army and go to Canada, which place he reached after some weeks of great suffering and privation. The day after he left (October 17, 1777,) General Burgoyne capitulated, and surrendered his arms to the American Generals Gates and Arnold. Robert Clark subsequently served two years in his Majesty's Provincial Regiment, called the Loyal Rangers, commanded by Major Edward Jessup, and in Captain Sabastian Jones' company, and was discharged on the 24th December, 1783. He owned two farms in Duchess County, one of 100, the other of 150 acres, both of which were confiscated. He was employed by the government in 1782-3 to erect the Kingston mills, (then Cataraqui) preparatory to the settlement of the loyalists in that section of Upper Canada, at which time his family, consisting of his wife and three sons, arrived at Sorel in Lower Canada, where they all were afflicted with the small pox, and being entirely among strangers they were compelled to endure more than the usual amount of suffering incident to that disease, their natural protector being at a distance, and in the employ of the government, could not leave to administer to their necessity. In 1784, his family joined him at the mills, after having been separated by the vicissitudes of war for a space of seven years. In 1785 he removed with his family to lot No. 74, 1st concession Ernest town, in which year he was again employed by government to erect the Napanee mills. He was appointed Justice of the Peace for the district of Mecklenburgh, in July 1788, and a captain in the militia in 1809, and died 17th December, 1823.

John C. Clark was married to Rachel Storer, and had a family of ten sons and three daughters.

Captain Crawford, of the Rogers corps, settled on lot No. 1 of Fredericksburgh. Became a magistrate, and lived to be an old man, was also colonel of militia.

George Dame was the son of Theophilus Dame, evidently a veteran soldier, from the copy of his will now before us. He gave to his "son, George Dame, the one-half of my (his) real estate in Dover, England, to hold to him forever," also his wearing apparel, books, gold watch, gilt-headed cane, horses, sleigh and harness, and one hundred dollars." He bequeathed to his grandson, John Frederick Dame, his camp bedstead, and curtains and valence for carriage of camp bedstead, and his silver-mounted hanger. To his grandson Augustus Dame, his fusee, gorget, and small seal skin trunk. To another grandson he left his double-barrelled pistol. By reference to these items we learn that Theophilus Dame must have been a British officer of some standing.

His son, George Dame, followed in the footsteps of his father in pursuing the profession of arms. We have before us a document, dated 1765, which declares that "Ensign George Dame of the 8th or King's Own Regiment of foot, was admitted burgess of the Burgh of Dumfries, with liberty to him to exercise and enjoy the whole immunities and privileges thereof, &c." For some reason this commission in the 8th regiment was relinquished; but ten years later we find he has a commission from General Carleton, Major-General and Commander-in-chief of His Majesty's forces in the Province of Quebec, and upon the frontier thereof, appointing him "Ensign in the Royal Regiment of Highland Emigrants commanded by Lieutenant Colonel Commandant Allan McLean." "Given under my hand and seal at the Castle of Saint Lewis, in the city of Quebec, 21st of November, 1775." In 1779 he received a commission from Frederick Haldimand, Captain-General and Governor-in-Chief, &c., appointing him "Captain in a corps of Rangers raised to serve with the Indians during the rebellion, whereof John Butler, Esq., is Major Commandant".

After the close of the war, Captain Dame lived at Three Rivers, Lower Canada, where we find him acting as Returning Officer in 1792, Mured Clarke being Lieutenant Governor. He died at Three Rivers, April 16th, 1807.

An official paper before us sets forth that "Guy, Lord Dorchester, authorizes Frederick Dame, 'by beat of drum or otherwise,' forthwith to raise from amongst the inhabitants of Upper and Lower Canada, as many able-bodied men as will assist the completing of a company, to be commanded by Captain Richard Wilkinson. This company to be mainly provincial, and for the service of Canada, and to serve for the space of three years, or during the war. This order shall continue in force for twelve months." Dated at the Castle of St. Lewis, Quebec, 21st June, 1796. This is signed "DORCHESTER."

The same year, bearing date the 17th December, is a commission from Robert Prescott, Esq., Lieutenant-Governor, appointing Frederick Dame ensign to the second battalion Royal Canadian Volunteers.

In the year 1802 John Frederick Dame received his commission as Surveyor of Lands in Upper and Lower Canada, from Robert Shore Milnes, Lieutenant-Governor, upon the certificate of Joseph Bouchette, Esq., Deputy Surveyor-General. Up to this time it would seem he had been living at Three Rivers.

Allan Dame, a son of the aforementioned, is now residing in Marysburgh, not far from McDonald's Cove. He is now in the neighborhood of sixty: this is his native place. He is a fine specimen of an English Canadian farmer; and well he may be, being a descendant of a worthy stock, of English growth. He is married to the granddaughter of Colonel McDonald.

Daly—P. K. Daly, Esq., of Thurlow, has kindly furnished us with the following interesting account:

Captain Peter Daly, my grandfather, was the son of Capt. Daly, of an Irish regiment, that was stationed in New York for some years before the outbreak of the old revolutionary war, but was called home to Ireland before the commencement of hostilities; and finally fell a victim to that cruel code of honor which obliged a man to fight a duel.

At the earnest solicitation of a bachelor friend, of the name of Vroman, he had been induced to leave his son Peter behind. Mr. Vroman resided upon the banks of the Mohawk, where the city of Amsterdam now stands. He was a man of considerable wealth, all of which he promised to bestow upon his son, Peter Daly; a promise he would, in all probability, have kept, had circumstances permitted; but he was prevented by the stern realities of the times—those stern realities that tried men's souls, and called upon every man to declare himself. The subject of this sketch could not dishonor the blood that flowed in his veins, and, although but 16 years of age, he clung firmly to the old flag that, for "a thousand years had braved the battle and the breeze." He joined a company, and followed the destiny of his flag along the shores of Lake Champlain, where, in one night, he assisted in scaling three forts. He assisted in taking Fort Tyconderoga, and gradually fought or worked his way into Canada. The war closing, he, in company with other loyalists, came up the Bay of Quinté, and subsequently married and settled in the second concession of Ernest town, in the vicinity of the village of Bath, where, by cultivating his farm, and by industry, he secured a comfortable living.

He was remarked through life for his strictly honorable dealing, and his adherence to "the old flag." In religion he was a firm Presbyterian. From his old protector, Vroman, he never heard anything definite. He cared but little for the land that had driven him into exile, to dwell among the wild beasts of the unbroken forest.

It is supposed that Vroman, in his declining years, gave his property to some other favorite. Be that as it may, Peter Daly saw none of it, but came into this country naked, as it were; carved out of the forest his own fortune, and left a numerous and respected family. There are now only two of his sons living, Thomas and Charles, who live on the old farm, near Bath. His eldest daughter, Mrs. Aikens, is still living, in Sidney. My father, Philip, was the eldest. He died at Oak Shade, in Ernest town, in 1861, in the 71st year of his age. David, the next son, lived and died at Waterloo, near Kingston; and Lewis lived and died at Storrington. The first wife of Asal Rockwell, of Ernest town was a daughter of his. Jacob Shibly, Esq., ex M.P.P., married another daughter; and the late Joshua Boatte another. Their descendants are numerous.

John Diamond was born in Albany, with several brothers. An elder brother was drafted, but he tried to escape from a service that was distasteful to him; was concealed for some time, and upon a sick bed. The visits of the doctor led to suspicion, and the house was visited by rebels. Although he had been placed in a bed, and the clothes so arranged that, as was thought, his presence would not be detected, his breathing betrayed him. They at once required his father to give a bond for $1,200, that his son should not be removed while sick. He got well, and, some time after, again sought to escape, but was caught, and handcuffed to another. Being removed from one place to another, the two prisoners managed to knock their guard on the head, and ran for life through the woods, united together. One would sometimes run on one side of a sapling, and the other on the opposite side. At night they managed to rub their handcuffs off, and finally escaped to Canada. Of the other brothers, two were carried off by the rebels, and never more heard of. John was taken to the rebel army when old enough to do service; but he also escaped to Canada, and enlisted in Rogers' Battalion, with which he did service until the close of the war, when he settled with the company at Fredericksburgh.

John Diamond married Miss Loyst, a native of Philadelphia, whose ancestors were German. She acted no inferior part, for a woman, during the exciting times of the rebellion. They married in Lower Canada. They spent their first summer in Upper Canada, in clearing a little spot of land, and in the fall got a little grain in the ground. They slept, during the summer, under a tree, but erected a small hut before winter set in.

CHAPTER X.

CONTENTS.—Ferguson—Frazer—Gerollemy— Goldsmith— Harrison—Hodgins—Hicks—Howell—Hover—Hogle—Ham—Herkimer—Holt—Jones— Johnson—Ketcheson—Loyst— Myers—McArthur—Miller— Mordens— McDonald—McDonnell—McDonell—Ostrom—Peterson.

INDIVIDUAL COMBATANTS—CONTINUED.

Among the early and influential settlers upon the bay, was John Ferguson. It has been our good fortune to come into possession of a good many public and private letters penned by his hand, and invaluable information has thus been obtained. The following letter will inform the reader of the part he took in the service during the war. It is addressed to Mr. Augustus Jones.

KINGSTON, 22nd July, 1792.

DEAR SIR,—

Inclosed is my old application for the land on the carrying place, which I send agreeable to your desire. I need not attempt to explain it better, as you know so well what I want. I wish, if consistent, that land, 200 acres, Mrs. Ferguson is entitled to, might be joined to it. If I cannot get a grant of the carrying place, will you be so good as to let me know what terms it may be had on. I have it in my power to settle the place immediately, had I any security for it. I am certain Mr. Hamilton will interest himself for me, but I am loth to apply to him at present, as in all probability he has too much business to think of besides. hould it be asked how and where I served, I will mention the particulars. The 24th June, 1774, I was appointed, and acted as barrack-master until 24th March, 1778, when I was ordered to Carleton Island, being also commissary at the post. Thirteenth April, 1782, I was appointed barrack-master of Ontario, where I remained until ordered to Cataraqui in September, 1783, and acted as barrack-master for both posts, until 24th June, 1785, when I was obliged to relinquish it, having more business in the commissary's department than I could well manage, with the other appointment, occasioned by the increase of loyalists settling in this neighborhood. Twenty-fifth Feburary. 1778, my father then being commissary of Oswegotchie, delivered the stores to me, as he was unable to do the duty himself. He died 13th March, following, when I was appointed his successor.

The 13th April, I was ordered to Carleton Island to assist Mr. McLean in the transport business. In November, 1778, I was again sent to Oswegotchie, where I remained commissary of the post until 24th June, 1782, when I was sent to Ontario to take charge there, from thence I was sent to this place, 24th September, 1783, where I remained until a reformation took place in the commissary department, and I was on the 24th June, 1787, served like a great many others, sent about my business without any provision, after having spent my best days in His Majesty's service.

You see I was eleven years barrack-master, and nine years a commissary, I was also six years in the Commissary General's office at Montreal (a clerk,) during which time my father was permitted to do my duty as barrack-master. I will write you again by next opportunity.

Your very humble servant,

(Signed) JOHN FERGUSON.

Ensign Frazer, of the the 84th regiment settled at the point of Ernest town. Had three sons. His widow married Colonel Thompson.

The Cornwall *Freeholder*, notices the death of Mr. Frazer, of St. Andrew's, C. W., the discoverer of Frazer river, and of Mrs. Fraser, who departed this life a few hours afterwards. Mr. Frazer was one of the few survivors of the find old "Northwesters," and his name, as the first explorer of the golden stream which bears it, will be remembered with honor long after most of the provincial cotemporaries are forgotton. The *Freeholder* says: "Mr. Frazer was the youngest son of Mr. Simon Frazer, who emigrated to the State of New York, in 1773. He purchased land near Bennington; but upon the breaking out of the revolutionary war, he attached himself to the royal cause, and served as captain, at the battle of Bennington; where he was captured by the rebels. He died in Albany jail, about thirteen months afterwards, his end being hastened by the rigorous nature of the imprisonment. He was married to Isabella Grant, daughter of Daldregan, and had issue, four sons and five daughters. The widow, with her children, came to Canada after the peace of 1783. Simon Frazer, the elder, the father of the object of this notice, was the second son of William Frazer, the third of Kilbockie, who, by his wife, Margaret, daughter of John McDonell, ot Ardnabie, had nine sons:—1st. William, the fourth of Kilbockie: 2nd. Simon, who came to America, as we have seen; 3rd. John, who was captain in Wolf's army, shared in the honors of the capture of Quebec, and was subsequently, for many years, Chief Justice of the Montreal district; 4th. Archibald, who was Lieutenant in Frazer's regiment, under General Wolfe, was afterwards captain of the Glengarry Fencibles, and served in Ireland during the rebellion in '98; 5th. Peter, a doctor of medicine, who died in Spain; 6th. Alexander, who served as captain in General Caird's army, and died in India; 7th. Donald, a Lieutenant in the army, who was killed in battle in Germany; 8th. James, also a Lieutenant in the army, and one of the sufferers in the Black Hole of Calcutta, in 1756; 9th. Roderick, who died at sea."

Mr. J. B. Ashley, a native of Marysburgh, to whom much valuable information we possess is due, says: "My great grandfather, James Gerollamy, was but seventeen years of age when he joined General Clinton's army in 1779, and remained in the service until the virtual close of the war in 1782, when he came from New York to Quebec, and thence to Bath, where he settled, on what was until lately known, as the "Hichcock Farm." He afterwards removed to the town, and settled on lot No. 11, 1st concession, lake side. He received from government certain farming implements, the same as before mentioned. A part of them coming into the hands of my father, Augustus Ashley, of Marysburgh. The hatchet, I have often used when a young lad in my childish employments. It is now lost. The share and coulter belonging to the plough, remain among a collection of old iron in my father's woodshed until the present day. James Gerollamy, married Ann Dulmage, the daughter of Thomas Dulmage, who came with him to Canada and settled near him at Bath, in the second town, and subsequently moved to lot No. "D," at the head of South Bay, in the township of Marysburgh, where he died. The graves of himself and wife being still under a large maple tree, close to the site of his house.

James Gerollamy, and his two sons, James and John, served through the war of 1812, under General Provost, Brock and

Drummond. The old man holding the rank of Orderly, and his son James that of Lieutenant. The latter received a grant of 1000 acres of land for services as a "spy," he was one of the number who planned the successful attempts upon Oswego, Black Rock and Buffalo, and at the battle of Niagara, generally known as "Lundy's Lane." He fought in the company or regiment known as "Grenadiers," which, in their manœuvering were compelled to run and wallow over a field of corn with mud ankle deep.

The whole family were remarkable for large size, being over six feet in height,of great strength,and healthy,with robust constitutions The old gentleman was acknowledged the surest marksman in this section of the country, and his "fusil," was his constant companion. He died about ten years ago, aged about ninety-five years, being in full possession of his faculties until the last. I can well remember seeing him sauntering through the garden, bent with his weight of years, and leaning on his staff.

Thomas Goldsmith, a native of Ulster Co., Montgomery town, New York. He was engaged as a spy, and discharged important and successful duties, in carrying information from Gen. Burgoyne to Lord Cornwallis, and returning with despatches. He frequently passed the guards of the Continental army, and often was subjected to a close search, but succeeded in eluding detection. Goldsmith owned one thousand acres of land, on which was a flouring mill with two run of stones. Also, a sailing vessel launched, but not entirely finished, for the West India trade. The boat was sacrificed. The produce of his farm was paid for in Continentiel bills. The mallable iron of his mill was taken to make a chain to put across the Hudson to stop boats. His neighbors, the rebels, catching him one day from home, covered him and his horse and saddle, with a coat of tar and feathers. After the close of the war, he was compelled to part with his land to get away. It was sold for a mere trifle. He came into Canada in 1786, bringing with him some cattle, most of which died for want of something to eat. He was accompanied by David Conger, and reached Kingston, June 24. Settled at first in the fourth township; but soon after removed to Holliwell, where he received a grant of 400 acres of land, 1st. con., lot 9. Here he lived and died, aged ninety.

Sergeant Harrison was a native of Ireland, and served for many years in the fifty-third regiment. For some time during the revolutionary war, he was in the Quarter-master's store, and post office. He was altogether twenty-eight years in the service. At the close of the war, he settled in Marysburgh, with the first band, not connected with the Hessians, and was probably under Wright in the commissary department for the settlement. He settled on lot nine, east of the Rock.

William Hodgins was born on a small island, known as Ginn's Island, lying about three and a half miles from the Virginia shore, in Chesapeake bay, where his father, Lewis Hodgins, had a farm of two hundred acres. He joined the Royal army with his younger brother Lewis, in 1778, serving in the regiment known as the Queen's Rangers, under Lord Cornwallis; where he held the rank of sergeant, and his brother that of corporal. At the battle of Yorktown, he was wounded and taken prisoner, and his brother was killed. After his exchange he came to New Brunswick, and settled about thirty miles above Fredrickton, on the St. John's river, where he lived until 1859, when he removed to Canada. First settling in Adolphustown, near what is known now as Cole's Point. He joined the incorporated militia during the war of 1812, serving under Colonel McGill, and Colonel Shaw. He received the right to considerable land; but after the capture of York, now Toronto, by the Americans in 1813, and the consequent destruction of property, the documents pertaining to the same were burnt, and he could not, as a consequence, get his grant. Immediately after the war of 1812, he removed to Marysburg, where he remained until his death.

The above information is received from Mr. William Hodgins, son of the above mentioned William Hodgins, who is now an old man, he having served with his father in the war of 1812.

"It would have done you good to have heard the old gentleman, with his silver locks flowing in the wind, whitened with the frosts of four-score winters, as he descanted upon scenes and incidents in connection with the war, through which he served, and to have witnessed his eye twinkle with pride, when he referred to the loyalty of his honored parent."—(*Ashley.*)

Edward Hicks, who settled in Marysburgh, was placed in prison with his father. His father was taken out and hanged before his window upon an apple tree, (a piece of refined cruelty worthy a rebel cause). This aroused Edward to a state of desperation, who with manacled hands, paced his cell. To carry out his intention, he feigned illness, and frequently required the guard to accompany him to the outer yard. At night fall he went out accompanied by the guard. Watching the opportunity, he drew up his hands and struck a furious blow upon the head of the soldier with his hand-cuffs, which laid the man prostrate. Edward darted away to a stream which ran near by, and across which was a mill-dam and a slide. He rushed under this slide, and before a cry was raised, he concealed himself under the sheet of water. He could hear the din and tumult, as search was everywhere made through the night. Cold, wet, benumbed, hungry and hand-cuffed, he remained in his hiding place until the following night, thirty-six hours, when he crept out and escaped to the woods. After nine days of fasting he reached the British army. Edward Hicks did not forget the death of his father. He "fought the rebels in nine battles afterward, and still owes them grudge."

Joseph, Joshua and Edward, belonged to Butler's Rangers, and saw no little service. They were from Philadelphia, and left considerable property. They had granted them a large tract of land west of Niagara, where sprung up Hicks' settlement. Joseph Hicks afterwards settled on lot six, Marysburgh, west of the Rock.—(*Ashley.*)

Edward Hicks is represented as having been a very powerful man, often performing remarkable feats of strength, such as lifting barrels of flour and pork to his shoulders, and such like.

He went to Boston in 1778, in the character of a spy, and was detected by the Americans, and taken prisoner. He represented himself as a young man searching for his mother, who had removed to that section of the country; but it is supposed that his captors considered him as rather too smart looking a young man to be lost in any enterprise, he being of fine build, standing good six feet, and possessing an intelligent countenance, and at his trial, condemned him as a spy to be dealt with accordingly.—(*Ashley.*)

John Howell, a son of Richard Howell, from Wales, was born in New Jersey in 1753. When 24 years old he took up his residence at Johnstown, on the Mohawk river. At the commencement of hostilities, in 1776, he joined Sir John Johnson's 2nd battalion, and was raised to the position of serjeant-major. His name appears as such upon the battalion roll, now before the writer. He remained in the army during the war, doing duty at St. Johns, Coteau du lac, and at many other places. When his company was disbanded at Oswego, in 1782, he came immediately to Kingston, and thence to Fredericksburgh, where he settled upon his lot of 200 acres. By adhering to the loyal cause, Sergeant Howell suffered serious loss in real estate.

The pleasant town of Rome now stands upon the land which was his. His valuable property was not yielded up to the rapacious rebels without a legal effort to recover possession. The case was in court for many years, and Sergeant Howell spent $1,400 in vain efforts to recover. No doubt it was pre-judged before he spent his money. An event in Howell's life during the war is not without a touching interest. Before joining the regiment, he had courted and won the heart of a fair lady at Johnstown. While stationed at Coteau du lac he obtained permission during the winter, when hostilities were suspended, to go to Johnstown to obtain his bride. Guided by seven Indians, he set out to traverse a pathless wilderness, on snow-shoes. The wedding trip had its perils, and almost a fatal termination. On their return they lost their way in the interminable woods, and soon found themselves destitute of food. For days they were without anything to eat. One day they shot a squirrel, which, divided among them, was hardly a taste to each. The thongs of their shoes were roasted and eaten, to allay the pangs of hunger. At last they succeeded in shooting a deer, which had well nigh proved the death of some, from over-eating. Two of the men were left behind, but they subsequently came in.

Sergeant Howell's loss as a loyalist was great; but, so far as could be, it was made good by Government. He drew 1,200 acres of land as an officer, and the same quantity for his family. At an early date after his arrival at the Bay he was appointed Commissioner in the Peace; and subsequently he was made Colonel of the Prince Edward Militia.

Soon after settling in Fredericksburgh he built a windmill, probably the first mill built by an individual in the Province. He afterwards sold it to one Russell. The remains still mark the spot.

He finally settled in Sophiasburgh, while it was yet considered by the infant colony as the backwoods of the settlement. He was a man of liberal education for the times, and was conversant with the Dutch and French languages, and understood the Indian dialect. From his former connection with the Johnson settlement upon the Mohawk, and his close contiguity to the Mohawk Indians upon the Bay, he held a high place in their regard. He often visited them; and their chiefs as often paid him state visits. They often called upon him to settle their disputes, which he never failed to do by his sternness and kindness combined. His presence was sufficient to inspire awe amongst them when disposed to be troublesome, which was increased by his long sword which he would hang to his side.

Henry Hover was quite a boy when the rebellion was progressing, being about sixteen when the Declaration of Independence was signed. Living along the Hudson, near New York, he went out one day for the cows, when he was caught by some rebels and carried to Lancaster jail. After being in prison for some time he was released, and permitted to go to New York. He some time after, by some means, enlisted in Butler's Rangers, and set out, with four others (one his brother), to traverse the wide country on foot, from New York to Fort Niagara, the head-quarters of the company. Lying one night under the trees, they were suddenly attacked by a scouting party of rebels, by being fired upon. One was killed, and the rest taken prisoners. Henry Hover remained in prison, in chains, until the close of the war, nearly two years. The hardships and cruelties he endured were, indeed, terrible. When he was taken prisoner he had on a pair of linen trowsers; no others were ever given him; and when he was released these were hanging in shreds upon him. They had nothing to lie upon but the cold brick floor, two persons being chained together. Years after, a stranger called one day at Hover's in Adolphustown. Hover not being at home, the man wrote his name, "Greenway," the man to whom Henry had been chained for many a weary day and month in prison. Hover being released at the close of the war, reported himself at Niagara, and was discharged with the rest of his company. He received all his back pay, while in jail, and a grant of land at St. Davids; but his father, Casper Hover, a refugee, had settled in Adolphustown, having come in Major VanAlstine's corps. Henry wished to see his parents, from whom he had been so long separated, and sought a chance to go down from the Niagara frontier. He entered on board an old "hulk," an old French vessel coming down the lake, and so got to Kingston, which place he reached soon after VanAlstine's company had settled in the fourth Township. Henry set out from Kingston on foot, along the bay, through the woods. In time he arrived at the third township. He was misdirected across to Hay Bay. Following its shores, he met Holland's surveying party, who told him that he was astray, and put him on the correct track. Henry Hover determined to remain at the bay, and was included among the original settlers under VanAlstine, drawing land like the rest, being the only one who did not belong to that company. He sleeps from his warfare—from his long life of well-spent industry, in the "old U. E. burying ground," at the front, in Adolphustown.

Among those who fought the unequal battle of Bennington was

Captain Hogle, who was shot dead. He was a native of Vermont. He left a widow and three sons, who were yet young. They were under the necessity of leaving their valuable possessions and removing to Canada. They buried plate in the garden, which was never regained. At the expiration of the war they settled in Ernest town.

David Hartman—was present at the battle of Bennington, and was shot through the chest. Notwithstanding, he lived for many years. He settled in Ernest town.

John Ham, the founder of the Ham family of Canada, so well and so favorably known in different sections of the Province. He was born near Albany. His father was a native of Germany, although of English parentage. John Ham was a soldier during the war, and in one of several engagements; was wounded in the leg. The ball, lodging in the calf, was cut out, and, at the request of the suffering but brave hero, was shot back at the foe. He was one of the company who settled in Ernest town. He had a family of ten children, eight of them being sons, namely: John, Henry, Peter, George, Jacob, Philip, Benjamin, and Richard, all of whom lived and died in Canada.

The name of Herkimer is engraved upon the history of America, both in the United States and in Canada. "Colonel Hanjost Herkimer, or John Joost, was a son of Johan Jost Herkimer, one of the Palatines of the German Flats, New York, and a brother of the rebel general, Nicholas Herkimer." "His property was confiscated. He went to Canada, and died there before 1787."—(*Sabine.*) Prior to the war he had occupied several public offices. He served as an officer in Butler's Rangers. We find his name inserted for lot 24 of Kingston, on which now stands part of the city. His son Nicholas settled upon the Point now bearing the family name. He married a Purdy, and had several children. His end was a sad one, being murdered by a blacksmith, named Rogers, who escaped. A daughter was married to Captain Sadlier, another to an officer in the army, and a third to Mr. Wartman.

The old family place in New York State is yet indicated by the name of Herkimer County.

"William Johnson Holt was ensign in Ferguson's Rangers. This corps formed part of the army of Burgoyne at the time of his surrender, and, with other provincial prisoners, retired to Canada, by permission of Gates. The subject of this notice settled in Montreal, where he held the lucrative office of Inspector of Pot and Pearl Ashes, and received half pay for nearly fifty years. He died at Montreal, in 1826. By his first wife (Rush Stevens, of Pittsfield,

Massachusetts), he was the father of a large family of sons and daughters; by his second wife (Elizabeth Cuyler) he left no issue. His sixth son, Charles Adolphus, alone has surviving male children, of whom the eldest, Charles Gates Holt, is (1864) a distinguished counsellor-at-law, and a gentleman of the highest respectability, at Quebec. In February, 1864, he was appointed one of "Her Majesty's Counsel, learned in the law," and thus entitled to wear the "silk robe."

"John Jones, of Maine, captain in Rogers' Rangers. Being of a dark complexion, he was called 'Mahogany Jones.' Prior to the war he lived at or near Pownalborough, and was Surveyor of the Plymouth Company. As the troubles increased, the whigs accused him of secreting tea, and broke open his store. Next, they fastened him to a long rope, and dragged him through the water until he was nearly drowned. Finally, to put an end to his exertions against the popular cause, he was committed to jail in Boston. He escaped, went to Quebec in 1780, and received a commission in the Rangers. In Maine, again, before the peace, he annoyed his personal foes repeatedly. Among his feats was the capture of his 'old enemy,' General Charles Cushing, of Pownalborough. Jones, immediately after the peace, was at the Bay of Fundy, and interested in lands granted on that island to loyalists. In 1784 he resumed his business as surveyor, on the river St. Croix. At length, 'his toryism forgotten,' he removed to the Kennebec. He died at Augusta, Maine."

Captain William Johnson, of the King's Royal regiment, afterwards colonel of the Militia of Addington. Besides the celebrated Sir John Johnson's family, there were a large number of combatants and loyalists of this name, and mostly all of them were conspicuous for their gallant deeds in arms. Captain William Johnson settled some miles west of Kingston, on the front. Left one child, a daughter, who married McCoy. They removed to Toronto. It is said by Mr. Finkle that the first militia mustered in Upper Canada was by Col. William Johnson, at Finkle's tavern.

The name of Johnson has become somewhat famous in Canadian history. James Johnson, an Irishman, was a soldier in Rogers' Battalion. He came to Upper Canada with the first settlers of Ernest town, and was captain of the cattle-drivers that came at that time, or a year later. He got his location ticket at Carleton Island. He had a family of seven sons and six daughters. Six of the sons names were: Daniel, James, William, Matthew, Jacob, Andrew.

The last-mentioned supplies us with the above information. He is now upwards of one hundred years of age.—(See U. E. Loyalists).

William Ketcheson, of Sidney, who was born September, 1782, at Bedford, New York, says that his father, William Ketcheson, was a native of England, and came to America with his grandfather, his father being dead. They settled in South Carolina, and lived there until the rebellion broke out. William Ketcheson, sen., was then about seventeen years of age, and entered the British service as a dragoon, under Lord Cornwallis. He served during the war; took part in many engagements, and was wounded in the thigh. Shortly before the close of hostilities he was married to Mary Bull, daughter of John Bull, a loyalist. After the peace he went to Nova Scotia, and engaged in fishing for a while; lived in a shanty at a rock-bound place, called Portoon. A fire ran over the place, burning up mostly everything, and almost our informant, who was then only about 18 months old. He and his mother were put on board a boat and taken to New York. The father remained to settle his affairs at Nova Scotia, and then came on into Canada, alone, in 1786. He worked a farm on shares, in the third township, belonging to John Miller. Raked in the grain; went for his family, and then subsequently worked Spence's farm on shares for many years. Finally moved to Sidney, in 1800, and settled in the fifth concession.

"John Waltermeyer a tory partisan leader. He was noted for enterprise and daring, but not for cruelty or ferocity. In 1781, at the head of a band of Tories, Indians, and Canadians, he attempted to carry off General Schuyler, whose abode at that time was in the suburbs of Albany. The party entered the dwelling, commenced packing up the plate, and a search for the General. But that gentleman opened a window, and, as if speaking to an armed force of his own, called out,—"Come on, my brave fellows; surround the house, and secure the villians who are plundering." The happy stratagem caused Waltermeyer and his followers to betake themselves to flight."

The foregoing statement is taken from Sabine, we shall now give information derived from Captain Myer's descendants, and others who knew him well. It is without doubt correct.

Captain Myer's father and brother identified themselves with the rebel party, and we have heard it stated that he was at first, a rebel also, but not receiving promotion as he expected, forsook the cause, and upon the offer of a captaincy in the British forces allied himself to them. That this was the pure invention of his enemies is sufficiently plain. At the beginning of the rebellion Captain Myers, with his father, was a farmer in the vicinity of Albany, and could have had no reason for promotion. As to the captaincy, we find that he did not receive it until 1782, when the war had virtually closed, as the following shows:

Frederick Haldimand, Captain-General and Governor-in-Chief of the Province of Quebec and territories depending thereon, &c., &c., &c. General and Commander-in-Chief of His Majesty's forces in said Province and territories thereof, &c., &c., &c.

TO JOHN WALTER MYERS, ESQ.:

By Virtue of the power and authority in me vested, I do hereby constitute, appoint you to be *captain* in the corps of Loyal Rangers whereof Edward Jessup, Esq., is Major-Commandant. You are therefore carefully and diligently to discharge the duty of *captain* by exercising and well disciplining both the inferior officers and soldiers of the corps, and I do hereby command them to obey you as their *captain*, and you are to observe and follow such orders and directions as you shall from time to time receive from me your Major, Major-Commandant, or any other of your superior officers, according to the rules and discipline of war. In pursuance of the trust hereby reposed in you. *Given* under my hand and seal at Arms, at the Castle of *St. Louis, at Quebec*, this thirtieth day of May, one thousand seven hundred and eighty-two, and in the twenty-second year of the reign of our Sovereign, Lord George the Third, by the Grace of God, Great Britain, France and Ireland, King Defender of the Faith, and soforth.

(Signed) FRED. HALDIMAND.

By His Excellency's Command,

R. MATHEWS.

It is true that during the war he made the attempt to take General Schuyler a prisoner. He went with ten men to Albany for the purpose of seizing the General, and carrying him away captive. On entering the yard at night, they looked through the window and saw the object of the expedition, but when they had entered the house he could no where be found, although search was made from cellar to garret. But in the garret were a number of puncheons turned up side down. Some of them were examined, but not all. After the war had closed, the Governor called on Myers and told him that had he turned over the other punch.

eons he would have found him. A faithful female slave had placed him there. The men with Myers had instruction to touch none of the Governor's property, after leaving the place, however, he found one of the men in possession of a silver cup. This was sent back to the Governor afterward.

During the war, Myers on one occasion, perhaps when he was returning from his attempt to take Schuyler, was nearly starved to death. He had with him a favorite dog, which became sick for want of food. He carried the dog for days, not knowing but he would have to kill him for food. But they all got safely out of it, and he retained the dog for many a day, and on one occasion he showed him to Schuyler. After the war Captain Myers enjoyed a pension of 5s. 6d. a day. He lived in Lower Canada two years. A certificate of Masonry informs us that he was in Quebec in 1780. He frequently carried despatches to New York, in the first years of the war; upon one occasion he was in a friend's house when the rebels came up, he jumped out of the back window and ran to the woods, he was seen, and persons on horseback came rapidly to the woods, and tied their horses, to pursue him on foot, which they hastily did; Myers had, however, hidden himself close by, and when they had fairly entered the woods in pursuit of him, he jumped up and deliberately selected the best horse, upon which he mounted, and so made an easy escape to New York.

He came up the bay at an early date, and it would seem squatted on the front of the ninth town before it was surveyed. He then moved up to Sidney where he lived until 1790, when he returned to the Moira River.

Captain Myers was a bold man, with limited education, but honest, and, like many others of the Dutch Loyalits, given to great hospitality. He was a pioneer in mill building, in trading, and in sailing batteaux and schooners, up and down the bay.

Charles McArthur, a native of Scotland, came to America before the rebellion, and settled upon the Mohawk River. Took part in the war, in Burgoyne's army. Lived for some time at Oswegotchie, when he removed to head of the bay. There were living then west of the Trent River only the following families: Peter Huffman, Donald McDonell, John Bleeker, Esq., and John McArthur. A daughter of Charles McArthur still lives at Belleville, having been born at Oswegotchie, now aged 78, (Mrs. Maybee.)

Ensign Miller, of Jessup's corps, was a native of Duchess

County. He had a brother an ensign, who lived and died at Montreal. Settled in Fredericksburgh, adjacent Adolphustown; drew in all 2,000 acres of land, in different places. Died 1805, aged forty-seven. Another brother came to the Province the year after the U. E. list had closed. He was the father of Rev. Gilbert Miller of Picton, and died at the age of ninety. Mr. G. Miller informs us that two great uncles, named Ogden, were with the British troops at the taking of Fort Frontenac.

All of this name (Ogden) are supposed to be related. They were, it is thought, of Welsh origin. One of that name settled upon the Delaware River previous to the rebellion. It is not quite certain whether this first Ogden died by the banks of the Delaware, or as is thought came to the Bay Quinté. He had three sons, one of whom died before their removal, leaving four sons. They, with their uncles, came at a very early date to Hamilton, but the four nephews removed to the Bay Quinté about 1790. Their names were James, John, Joseph and Richard. The numerous body living around the bay of this name, have all sprung from these four brothers. (Marshal R. Morden.)

Mr. James Morden was a private in His Majesty's Provincial Regiment, King's Royal of New York, Sir J. Johnson Commander. Discharged 1785 at Montreal, at the age of twenty, having served three years.

Colonel McDonald, as he was subsequently called, as an officer of militia, served under Sir John Johnson. He was one of the first settlers of the fifth township at the Bay Quinté. He landed first in the cove bearing his name, near Mount Pleasant, 1784. We have stood upon the spot where he first set foot upon the land, and pitched his tent. This cove is marked upon some of the old maps as Grog Bay, but in reality, Grog Bay was a small inlet from the cove. Colonel McDonald lived to be eighty-five years old. He drew large quantities of land, besides receiving many other favors from government. He left but one offspring, a daughter, who married a native of France named Prinyea, whose descendants are worthy inhabitants of the place.

We find the following newspaper record: "Died on the 3rd October, 1815, Sergeant Alexander McDonald, in his 78th year. This worthy veteran enlisted in 1757 in the 78th or Frazer's regiment, in which he served at the taking of Louisburg and Quebec. In 1763 he was drafted into the 60th, and served in the active campaigns during the American war, under the late General Provost, in Carolina and Georgia. In 1799 he was drafted from the 60th into the 41st regiment, in which he served till August 1811, when he was discharged, after a faithful service of fifty-five years."

The Canadian *Courant* spoke of J. McDonnell, as follows:—"The subject of this memoir was born in Glengary, in the Highlands of Scotland, about the year 1750. His father was principal tackman on the estate. The spirit of emigration prevailed very much in Scotland, and particularly in the Highlands, a little before the commencement of the American war. The father of Mr. R. McDonnell partaking of the feelings of his clan, and anticipating many advantages in this new world, accompanied a considerable emigration from Glengary estate, of which he was one of the principal leaders. Mr. R. McDonnell landed at New York with his father, and a number of the same name, in 1773, but the disputes between Great Britain and the colonies having assumed a very serious appearance, it was thought prudent to send him into Canada. Being designed for commerce, he was placed in a counting house, but the war breaking out, the spirit of his ancestors burst forth with an ardor which could not be restrained. He joined the Royal Standard, and was immediately appointed to an ensigncy, in the 84th regiment. In this subordinate situation he did not fail to distinguish himself by his bravery and good conduct, and on one singular and trying occasion he exhibited the greatest intrepidity and coolness. He was advanced to the command of a company in Butler's Rangers. Many of your readers still remember that the services required by this regiment were of the most arduous kind. They were sent out on scouting parties, and employed in picking up intelligence, and in harrassing the back settlements of the enemy. As their marches lay through pathless forests, they were frequently reduced to the greatest necessities, nor had they even, while on service, any of those comforts which are so common in regular camps. In the many expeditions and contests in which this regiment was engaged, during the war, Captain McDonnell bore a distinguished part, but the great hardships which he had to surmount, undermined a constitution naturally excellent, and entailed upon him a severe rheumatism which embittered the remaining part of his life.

During some time he acted as Pay-master of the regiment, and by his own care and attention he found himself at the end of the war in the possession of a small independence. This he considered equally the property of his father, brothers and sisters as his own, and proved by his generosity that his filial love and brotherly affection were equal to his other virtues. In 1794 when it was thought proper to levy a regiment in this country to remedy the great desertion which attended regiments from Europe, he raised a company.

"In 1795 he was promoted to the majority, and the regiment having been divided into two battalions, he became Lieutenant-Colonel of the 2nd, in 1796.

"He commanded at Niagara during the building of Fort George, and in 1802 he again retired on half-pay, the Royal Canadian Regiments having been most injudiciously reduced during the continuance of the ephemeral peace of Amiens. While at Fort George he married Miss Yates, a lady from the States, whose amiable and obliging manners gained the esteem of all who had the honor of her acquaintance. By this lady, in whom the Colonel enjoyed all that has to be wished in a companion and friend, he has a son, a promising boy, who, it is to be hoped, will inherit the virtues of his father. The Colonel's active benevolence was known to all, and experienced by many of his friends.

"There was something so generous, so noble in his manner of doing a kindness of this sort, as to give it a double value.

"In 1807 he was appointed Paymaster to the 10th Royal Veteran Battalion, a situation certainly far below his merits—but his circumstances, which, owing to his generous disposition, were by no means affluent, induced him to accept it.

"He had been exceedingly infirm for many years, and perhaps the severe climate at Quebec was too much for his weak constitution. Certain it is that this city has been fatal to several respectable characters from the Upper Province. He caught a severe cold in the beginning of November, 1809, accompanied with a violent cough and expectoration; he was not, indeed, thought dangerously ill, till within a short time of his death, but his feeble constitution could not support the cough, and he expired on the twenty-first.

"Such are the scanty materials which I have been able to collect respecting the life of a most excellent officer and honorable man, who became dearer to his friends and acquaintances the longer he was known to them.

"He was rather below the middle size, of a fair complexion, and in his youth, uncommonly strong and active. For some time past his appearance was totally altered; insomuch that those who had not seen him for many years, could not recognize a single feature of the swift and intrepid captain of the Rangers.

An acute disease made it frequently painful for him to move a limb, even for days and weeks together, but though his body suffered, his mind was active and benevolent, and his anxiety to promote the interests of his friends ceased only with his life."

Among those who took part in the unequal engagement at Bennington, was Alexander Nicholson, a Scotchman, who came to America shortly before the war broke out. He enlisted as a private under Burgoyne; but before the close of the war, received a commission. He was one of a company which was all but annihilated at Bennington. He stood by his Colonel when that officer was shot from his horse. Vainly trying to get him re-horsed, that officer told him it was no use, that he had better flee. The day being evidently lost, he proceeded to escape as best he could. With his arm wounded, he managed to escape through a field of corn to the woods. Coming to a river, he was arrested by an Indian upon the opposite bank, who, mistaking him for a rebel, fired at him. The Indian being undeceived, he forded the river. Making good his escape, he, with many others, wandered for days, or rather for nights, hiding by day, as scouts were ranging the woods to hunt out the tories. There were, however, friends who assisted to conceal them, as well as to furnish them with food. He often spoke of his sufferings at that fearful time; lying upon the cold ground without covering, and sleeping, to wake with the hair frozen to the bare ground. Subsequently Nicholson was attached to Rogers corp's. He settled in Fredericksburgh, at the close of hostilities, and subsequently removed in 1809, to the township of Thurlow.

Ostrom was engaged to carry despatches through the enemy's line. On one occasion he had the despatch in a silver bullet, which he put in his mouth. Having reason to believe he would be diligently examined, he took it from his mouth as he would a quid of tobacco, threw it in the fire and thus escaped.

Nicholas Peterson, with his three sons, Nicholas, Paul and Christopher, were living near New York, and took a part in the war.

They assisted in fighting one of the most remarkable battles of the revolution. It took place on the west side of the North River, opposite the city of New York, when seventy-five British Militiamen resisted an attack made by 5,500 rebels, for several hours.

The British had a Block House, made of logs, with a hollow excavation behind, and in this hollow they loaded their guns, and would then step forward and discharge them at the enemy. Only three of the British were slain ; the rebels lost many. These Petersons lost everything of any importance, when they left New York. Some of their valuables they buried to preserve them from the enemy, and the rest they left to their use.

Nicholas and Paul settled on lots No. 12 and 13, in the first concession of Adolphustown, south of Hay bay.

CHAPTER XI.

CONTENTS.—Rogers' family—Ryerson—Redner—Sherwood—Taylor—Van Dusen —Williamburgh — Wright — Wilkins — Young — Officers who settled in Niagara District.

Under Queen's Rangers will be found some account of Major Rogers, derived from Sabine. We here give further information, procured from Robert D. Rogers, Esq., and Dr. Armstrong, of Rochester, New York, who is a native of Fredericksburgh, and who, for many years, practised his profession in Picton and Kingston.

Robert D. Rogers, of Ashburnham, writes : " My grandfather, James Rogers, settled first in Vermont, and had several large tracts of land there, he, and his brothers were officers in the Queen's Rangers, of which his brother Robert was the chief officer; they were employed in the wars of the French and Indians, until the taking of Quebec by the British, after which the said Robert Rogers was ordered by General Amherst to proceed westward and take possession of all the forts and places held by the French, as far west as Detroit and Michilimicinac, which he did in the fall of 1760; and he afterwards went to England, where he published a journal kept by him during the French and Indian wars, and up to 1761, which was published in London 1765. He also wrote another book, giving a description of all the North American Colonies. My grandfather continued to reside in Vermont, until the time of the revolution, when he joined the British army, and after peace was proclaimed, settled near the East Lake in Prince Edward. I have heard that he was buried in Fredericksburgh, but do not know the place. My father represented Prince Edward in the first Parliament of Upper Canada, of which he was a member for twenty-six years."

From Dr. Armstrong, we learn that "Major Rogers was born in Londonderry, New Hampshire, about the year 1728. His wife was the daughter of the Rev. David McGregor, pastor of the Presbyterian church, Londonderry, of which his father, the Rev. James McGregor, formerly of Londonderry, Ireland, was the founder, April 12, 1719. Major Rogers was the father of three sons and three daughters. He removed with his family to Vermont, where he had become the proprietor of a large tract of land. Here he lived until the breaking out of the rebellion, (see Queen's Rangers.) After the conclusion of the war, Major Rogers, abandoning his property in Vermont, much of which had been destroyed, his herds of cattle driven off and appropriated to their own use by his neighbors, removed with his family to Canada and settled in Fredericksburgh. That he had been there previously and explored the country, and that he had taken with him a corps of soldiers, is altogether probable, for I well remember to have seen in my earliest boyhood, evidences of previous military strife, such as numerous broken guns, swords, and other worn-out weapons. At Fredericksburg, Major Rogers erected, as he had done before at Londonderry, Vermont, the first frame house in the township. How long he remained here I am unable to say, but probably several years. My own birth-place, August 29, 1789, was in a little village one or two miles below his residence, and as I was one of his legatees, he probably remained there for some time after that event. I find no record of his death, but it probably took place about the year 1792. He was buried in Fredericksburgh, as were his widow and eldest daughter (my mother), 1793. His eldest son James, returned to Vermont and recovered a considerable portion of the land in Londonderry. He afterward, in 1819, removed with his family to Haldimand, where he died several years ago. His second son, David McGregor, familiarly known also as "Major Rogers," remained in Canada up to the time of his death, about 1823. While quite a young man, he was elected a member of the first Parliament of Upper Canada. He then resided at Little Lake in the township of Hallowell. He afterwards removed to Cramahe, where I found him in 1803, engaged as a merchant, holding the office of clerk of the Peace, clerk of the District Court, and Registrar of Deeds, besides being a member of

Parliament, and carrying on a farm. His name is pretty closely identified with the early history of Upper Canada. He was a man of great energy of character and sound judgment, was highly respected and esteemed, and died greatly lamented. After remaining in Fredericksburgh several years, the family of the late Major (James) Rogers removed to the "Little Lake," so called. This was the scene of my earliest recollections. In the same neighborhood had resided Mr. Peters, and his family. He was a native of New England, remained loyal to the Crown, became an officer in the Queen's Rangers, and was amoug the early refugees to Canada. He afterwards became sheriff of Newcastle, having removed from the Little Lake, first to the Carrying Place, and afterwards to Cramahe, about the year 1804, where he died many years ago.

Joseph Ryerson, of New Jersey, one of the five hundred and fifty volunteers who went to Charleston, South Carolina. For his good conduct in bearing despatches one hundred and ninety-six miles into the interior, he was promoted to a Lieutenancy in the Prince of Wales' Volunteers. Subsequently he was engaged in six battles, and once wounded. At the peace he went to New Brunswick, thence to Canada, where he settled and became a Colonel in the militia. In the war of 1812, he and his three sons were in arms against the United States. He died near Victoria, Upper Canada, in 1854, aged ninety-four, one of the last of the "old United Empire Loyalists"—(*Sabine.*)

One of Captain Ryerson's old comrades, Peter Redner, of the bay, says, he was "a man of daring intrepidity, and a great favorite in his company." He often related an instance when Captain Ryerson, commanding a scouting party, for which peculiar service he was eminently fitted, ventured to crawl up to a tent of American officers, and discovering one standing in the door who saw him, he walked boldly up, thus lessening suspicion, and drawing his bayonet immediately ran him through the body, and escaped before his companions had sufficiently recovered from the shock to give pursuit. He represented Captain Ryerson as being one of the most determined men he ever knew, with the service of his country uppermost in his mind, he often exposed himself to great danger to accomplish his desires.

Samuel Ryerson, of New Jersey, brother of Joseph, joined the Royal Standard, and received a commission as captain in the Third Battalion of New Jersey Volunteers; went to New Brunswick at the peace, thence to Canada, where he settled,

Peter Redner, a native of New Jersey, was connected with the service for some time. He was in the same division as Captain Ryerson, and during his subsequent life was always delighted to tell of the incidents in connection with the several campaigns through which he passed, especially such as related to "his friend Ryerson," to whom he was much attached.

At the close of the war he went to Nova Scotia, where he drew land; but not liking the place, he disposed of his land and came to Canada. He purchased lot ninety-four in Ameliasburgh for a small consideration, from William Fox, a United Empire Loyalist, of Pennsylvania, who had drawn it.—(*Ashley.*)

Walter Ross—He arrived, an emigrant from Scotland, at Quebec, the night before the fall of Montgomery. He, with others from the ship, immediately took up arms, and assisted. to repulse the enemy in a most distinguished manner. He subsequntly lived with Major Frazer, and became so great a favorite that the Major assisted him to an ensigncy. After the close of the war he married Miss Williams, of Ernest town, and settled in Marysburgh, on the lake shore.

The Ruttans were descendants of the Huguenots. Says Sheriff Ruttan: "My grandfather emigrated to America about the time of Sir William Johnson, Bart., in 1734, and settled at a town called New Rochelle, in Westchester county, New York. This town, or tract of land, was purchased in 1689, expressly for a Huguenot settlement, by Jacob Leister, Commissioner of the Admiralty, under Governor Dongan of New York. It soon increased, and in 1700 had a vast number of militia officers, loyal to the backbone. To this settlement my grandfather repaired soon after his arrival. My father and uncle Peter were born here about 1757, and 1759. Both entered the army in the 3rd battalion of Jersey volunteers, one as Lieutenant, the other as Captain. This was about the year 1778. In the year 1778, my uncle Peter accompanied Brant from New York to Western Canada, on a tour of observation, being a great favorite, so much so that he named his son Joseph Brant Ruttan, as a token of his friendship. As a further token of his esteem, Brant, at parting, presented him with a handsome brace of pistols, which he valued highly. At his decease, they came into my possession. My father and uncle had grants of 1200 acres of land each, at Adolphustown, in the Midland District, this was in 1783 or 1784."

Sheriff Ruttan, when a child, met with a slight accident which probably turned the current of his life from one of comparative obscurity to notoriety. Henry Ruttan went out with his brother one spring morning to tap trees for sugar making. Accidentally two of Henry's fingers were severed from his hand by an untoward stroke of the sharp axe. This loss led his father to send him to school, as he could not perform manual labor. Respecting his education, the reader is referred to the division on "Early Education." With the education obtained in Adolphustown, he went to Kingston and was apprenticed with John Kerby, a successful merchant. By industry as well as talent, Henry advanced to be a partner, and was entrusted to open a store in the "new township" near Grafton, in Newcastle. Subsequently, he distinguished himself as a soldier, in 1812, then as a member of Parliament, as Speaker, and for a long time as Sheriff. Latterly his name is associated with inventions for ventilation of buildings and cars.

Captain Schermerhorn was among the first settlers upon the bay Quinté. Respecting the nature of his services during the war we have no record, nor have we learned in what regiment he served; but most probably in Johnson's. The writer has in his possession a portion of an epaulet which belonged to this officer. He drew large quantities of land in the western part of the Province, as well as a lot in Fredericksburgh. He died in 1788 when on a visit to Montreal to procure his half-pay. His widow and eldest son died soon after. His youngest son, John, settled on lot 95, 9th concession Ameliasburg.—(*J. B. Ashley.*)

"Colonel Spencer" was an officer in Roger's Battalion, settled on lot 9, 1st concession Fredericksburgh additional. He died shortly after the commencement of the war of 1812, having been Colonel of the militia, and active in preparing to meet the foe. He was buried, with military honors, upon his own farm.

His brother Augustus was an ensign, and settled at East Lake, on half-pay. His wife, Sarah Conger, lived to be ninety-four years old.

In the former part of last century there were born three brothers, Seth, Thomas, and Adiel Sherwood, in old Stratford, in the Province of Connecticut. The three brothers removed, 1743, to New York State, five miles north of Fort Edward, within a short distance of the spot where Burgoyne surrendered. At the commencement of the rebellion, Seth and Adiel identified themselves with the rebel party, becoming officers in the army, while Thomas adhered to his Sovereign. It was probably after the defeat of Burgoyne, when he proceeded to St. John, Lower Canada, and was subsequently employed by the British Government on secret service in the revolting State. His knowledge of the country enabled him to bring from the territory of the enemy not a few who were desirous of serving in the British army. In 1779 his family removed to St. Johns, and he received an appointment as subaltern in Major Jessup's corps.

At the close of the war, Thomas Sherwood came with his corps to the St. Lawrence, and became the first actual settler in the county of Leeds. He was well known as an active public man, "he was ever ready to give assistance and instructions to the new comers." He also assisted in the first survey of that part. He was among the first magistrates. He lived on his farm forty-two years, and died, aged 81, in peace.

Adiel Sherwood, from whom we receive the foregoing facts, was the son of Thomas, and was born at the homestead in New York State, 16th May, 1779, shortly before the family left for Canada. He says: "I remained with the family at St. Johns until May, 1784, when we came in the very first brigade of batteaux to the Upper Province, where my father pitched his tent, about three miles below Brockville, so that I may say I saw the first tree cut, and the first hill of corn and potatoes planted by an actual settler." Mr. Adiel Sherwood at an early date, 1796, was appointed an ensign in the first regiment of Leeds Militia. He was promoted from time to time until he became Colonel. He was commissioned a Magistrate, Clerk of the Peace, Commissioner of Land Board, and finally Sheriff for the district of Johnstown. He was connected with the militia fifty years, when he retired on full rank. Was Treasurer of the District twenty-five years, and Sheriff thirty-five. Mr. Sherwood still lives, an active, genial, and christian-minded gentleman, and we take this occasion to express our feelings of gratitude for his assistance and sympathy in this our undertaking.

There were a good many of the name of Taylor among the loyalists residing at Boston, New York, and New Jersey. They were all in the higher walks of life, and some filled high public stations. One family, consisting at the time of the rebellion, of a mother and three sons, has a tragic and deeply interesting history. For many of the particulars I am indebted to Sheriff George Taylor, of Belleville, a descendant of the youngest of the brothers.

Sheriff Taylor's father was named John, and was born upon the banks of the Hudson, of Scotch parents. He was fourteen years old when the rebellion broke out. His two brothers were officers in the British army, and were employed in the hazardous duties of spies. The only knowledge he has of his uncles, is that they were both caught at different times, one upon one side of the Hudson and the other the opposite side; both were convicted and executed by hanging, one upon the limb of an apple tree, the other of an oak. John Taylor was at home with his mother upon the farm, at Kinderhook. But one day he was carried off while from the house, by a press gang, to Burgoyne's army. He continued in the army for seven years, until the end of the war, when he was discharged. During this time he was in numerous engagements, and received three wounds at least, one a sabre wound, and a ball wound in the arm. It is stated on good authority, (Petrie) that he once carried a despatch from Quebec to Nova Scotia, following the Bay of Fundy. His mother in the meantime was ignorant of his whereabouts, and held the belief that he was dead, or carried off by the Indians. At the expiration of the war he went to New Brunswick by some means, subsequently he undertook to walk on snowshoes, with three others, from St. Johns to Sorel, which he accomplished, while the three others died on the way; he saved his life by killing and eating his dog. He procured his discharge at Sorel. In 1783 he came up the St. Lawrence to Cataraqui, and thence walked up the bay as far as the mouth of the Moria River, occompanied by one William McMullen. Ascending the Moria he chose the land, where is now the 4th concession of Thurlow, the "Holstead farm." He lived here a few months, but the Indians drove him away, declaring the river belonged to them. He then bought lot No. 5, at the front, of Captain Singleton, property which yet bears his name. John Taylor married the daughter of a U. E. Loyalist by the name of Russell.

Two or three years after he came to Thurlow, he visited his old home at Kinderhook, to see his mother, who knew not he was alive. She accompanied him back to Canada, although hard on ninety years old. She did not live long in her new home.

Two intimate comrades of John Taylor in the army, were Merritt and Soles, father of D. B. Soles, formerly of Belleville.

Respecting the brothers of John Taylor, the following appeared in the Hastings *Chronicle* of Belleville, 13th November, 1861.

"A Spy of the Revolution.—In the year 1776, when Governor Clinton resided in Albany, there came a stranger to his house one cold wintry morning, soon after the family had breakfasted.

He was welcomed by the household, and hospitably entertained. A breakfast was ordered, and the Governor, with his wife and daughter employed in knitting, was sitting before the fire, and entered into conversation with him about the affairs of the country, which naturally led to the enquiry of what was his occupation. The caution and hesitancy with which the stranger spoke, aroused the keen-sighted Clinton. He communicated his suspicion to his wife and daughter, who closely watched his every word and action. Unconscious of this, but finding that he had fallen among enemies, the stranger was seen to take something from his pocket and swallow it. Meantime Madam Clinton, with the ready tact of a woman of those troublesome times, went quietly into the kitchen, and ordered hot coffee to be immediately made, and added to it a strong dose of tartar emetic. The stranger, delighted with the smoking beverage, partook freely of it, and Mrs. Clinton soon had the satisfaction of seeing it produce the desired result. From scripture out of his own mouth was he condemned. A siver bullet appeared, which upon examination was unscrewed and found to contain an important despatch from Burgoyne. He was tried, condemned and executed, and the bullet is still preserved in the family."

"The foregoing article we clip from the Boston *Free Flag* of the 2nd November, 1861, this, there is reason to infer, is a special reference to a relative of one of the oldest families in this part of Canada. John Taylor in his life time, well known to the first inhabitants of Belleville, had two brothers employed upon secret service for the British Government during the American revolutionary war, their names were Neil and Daniel. At different times they were each apprehended and suffered the severe penalty of the law. A tradition of the Taylor family of this place, agrees in all particulars with the above article, and points to one of the Taylor brothers as the person therein alluded to."

Sabine says that "Daniel Taylor in 1777, was dispatched by Sir Henry Clinton to Burgoyne, with intelligence of the capture of Fort Montgomery, and was taken on his way by the whigs as a spy. Finding himself in danger, he turned aside, took a small silver ball or bullet from his pocket and swallowed it. The act was seen, and General George Clinton, into whose hands he had fallen, ordered a severe dose of emetic tartar to be adminis- tered, which caused him to discharge the bullet. On being unscrewed, the silver bullet was found to contain a letter from the one British General to the other, which ran as follows:

FORT MONTGOMERY, October 2, 1777.

Nous voici—and nothing between us but Gates. I sincerely hope this little success of ours may facilitate your operations. In answer to your letter of 28th of September, by C. C., I shall only say, I cannot presume to order, or even advise, for reasons obvious. I heartily wish you success.

Faithfully yours,

H. CLINTON.

To General Burgoyne.

Taylor was tried, convicted, and executed, shortly after his detection."

Conrad VanDusen was a native of Duchess County, N. Y., born 23rd April, 1751. His father was Robert VanDusen. At the commencement af the rebellion he was in business as a tailor, in New York City. He served during the whole of the war, seven years, in Butler's Rangers. During this time, his wife, who was also from Duchess County, formerly a Miss Coon, carried on the tailoring business in New York, and succeeded in saving fifty-three guineas. On leaving for Canada with VanAlstine, they brought with them two large boxes of clothing. They also had some jewellry.

During the war VanDusen was sometimes employed upon secret service, and upon one occasion was caught, and condemned to be hanged. Upon leaving the room in which he had been tried, he managed to convey to a woman present, whose earnest demeanor led him to believe she was friendly, a gold ring, a keep-sake of his wife. By some means VanDusen escaped, having concealed himself in a swamp under water, with his face only above water, and in after years he was surprised and rejoiced to receive by letter the identical ring, which had been sent to him by the woman into whose hands he had so adroitly placed it. She had directed the letter to Cataraqui.

The close of the war found VanDusen at New York, and he joined VanAlstine's band of refugees, and settled in Adolphustown. Subsequently he removed to Marysburgh, lot No. 9, where he died, aged seventy-six years and seven months. He lies buried in the U. E. burying ground, Adolphustown.

Frederick Frank Williamsburgh, at the time of the war lived upon the Susquehanna, and owned a thousand acres of land. He was a sickly man. His family consisted of a son eleven years old, and three daughters. One day he went some distance to a mill, taking his children with him, and leaving his wife and mother at home. That day the rebels made a raid, and he was taken prisoner from his children on the road; and coming to his barn, it, with all his grain was burned up. His wife and old mother sought safety in the woods, and the house was stripped of everything. The children arriving home without their father, found no mother, or grandmother, only the smoking ruins of the barn and the dismantled house. Frightened almost to death, and expecting to be killed before mor-n ing, they lay down on the floor. About midnight came a knock at the door, after a time they summoned sufficient courage to ask who was there, when it was found to be neighbor who had been hunted in the woods for three days and who was almost starved. He was admitted, and having slept for a short time, he proceeded to prepare a raft upon the river; upon this he placed some flour he had concealed in the woods, and the children, with himself, and floated down the river. But the morning brought the enemy, and they were taken. The children were conveyed to a place where they found their mother; but the father having been thrown into a prison, in three months his weak constitution succumbed to the cruelty of his prison house.

The family found their way to Lower Canada, after a time, living upon the rations dealt out from day to day from the commissariat department. They, after a time, went to Montreal, and one son, when twelve year old, enlisted. For a time he acted as tailor to the regiment, but subsequently became a favorite with the Colonel and was promoted. The descendants of this William Williamsburgh now live in Belleville.

Sergeant Daniel Wright was born in the city of London, 1741. He was sergeant in the 74th regiment. Sergeant Wright was present at the battle before Quebec, when Montgomery was killed. He settled in Marysburgh in 1784. He was commissary officer for the fifth township, and was subsequently appointed magistrate and then registrar, which office he held for upwards of thirty years. Was Lieut. Colonel in the Prince Edward Militia. "Old Squire Wright" was a man of education and gentlemanly deportment, strictly religious, and noted for his urbanity; he obtained the soubriquet of "Squire civil." It is said he was never known to smile. Unlike other retired officers, it is said, he did not seek to acquire extensive tracts of land. Died April, 1828, aged eighty-seven.

The following is from the Kingston *Chronicle*: "Died at the Carrying Place, 27th February, 1836, Robert Wilkins, Esq., in the ninety-fourth year of his age. He entered the army at the early age of seventeen, in the 17th Light Dragoons, then commanded by the late Colonel Hale. Soon after he joined the regiment it was ordered to Scotland. There it did not long remain; the "Whiteboy" conspiracy had been formed in Ireland. From Ireland he sailed with the same distinguished regiment for the British American Colonies, then raising the standard of revolt, landed at Boston, and a few days after bore a conspicuous part in the battle of Bunker's Hill, on which occasion he had two horses shot under him. He was present at most of the engagements in the northern colonies. At the battle of White Plains, he was one of the forlorn hope, where he received a severe contusion on the breast, and lost the thumb of his right hand. After recovering from his wounds, he retired from the army, and entered into mercantile pursuits in the city of New York. There he carried on a prosperous business until peace was concluded; but when that city was evacuated by the British troops (in 1783) he was too strongly attached to his king to remain behind. He then accompanied them to Shelburne, Nova Scotia. In the improvements of that luckless place, he expended a large sum of money, but finding that the place would not succeed, he left, and in 1789, returned to his native country, from which, three years after, he was induced to follow Governor Simcoe to this colony, just after it had received its constitution, and became a distinct government. From that time he remained in Upper Canada, and most of the time at this place. Of Christian doctrine and Christian duty, he had a much deeper sense than was obvious to occasional visitors. His hospitality was proverbial, and never under his roof was the poor refused food or shelter. His remains were followed to the church, and thence to the house appointed for all living, by not less than 300 of his friends and neighbors."

For an account of the son of the above, see notices of U. E. Loyalists.

Col. H. Young—His father was a native of Nottingham, England, and came to New York when eighteen years old, and settled at Jamaica, Long Island. He was a gunsmith by trade. Subsequently he removed to Husack, northern New York. He had four sons, George, Henry, William, John, and two daughters. His second son Henry, was born at Jamaica, 10th March, 1737. At the age of eighteen he joined the British army, as a volunteer. He was present at the battle of Tyconderoga, under General Abercrombie. He was also with the army under General Amherst, which went from Albany to Montreal, to join the army from Quebec, under General Murray. Continued in the army until 1761, when he returned home, married a Miss Campman, and lived in peace until the rebellion broke out. He again joined the British army as a private, and was at the battle of Bennington, but he so distinguished himself that he was promoted to an ensigncy in the King's Royal Regiment, of New York. During the war he took part in seventeen battles, but escaped with one wound in the hand. In the year 1780, he was sent with Major Ross to Carleton Island. For three years he was at this place, or Oswego. In 1783 he was discharged on half pay, and received grants of land—3,000 acres, with the privilege of selecting the place. Immediately after his release he set out, sometime during the summer or autumn of 1783, to prospect for land. In a small canoe, he, with a brother officer, named, it is said, McCarty, proceeded up the bay Quinté, and into Picton bay to its head, thence to East Lake. Having decided to take land here, he left his son during the winter. In the following spring 1784, he brought his family from St. Johns, where they had been staying. (See settlement of Prince Edward). Colonel Young died at East Lake. 3rd December, 1820, aged eighty-three years and nine months.

Daniel Young was in the Engineer Department during the latter part of the revolutionary war. He died at East Lake, 30th September, 1850, aged eighty-five.

Henry Young was Lieutenant of Militia in the war of 1812. Went to Kingston on duty, where he died, latter part of December, 1812.

Among the first settlers of the Upper Province, especially upon the St. Lawrence, and who took part in the war, may be mentioned, Captain Thomas Frazer, Captain William Frazer, Lieutenant Solomon Snider, Lieutenant Gideon Adams, Captain Simon Covelle, Captain Drummond, Ensign Dulmage, Ensign Sampson, Lieutenant Farrand, Captain Amberson, Lieutenant McLean, Lieutenant James Campbell, Lieutenant Alexander Campbell, Sergeant Benoni Wiltsie, Ensign E. Bolton, Captain Justus Sherwood, Captain John Jones, Lieutenant James Breakenridge, of Roger's corps.

Colonel Clarke, of Dalhousie, gives a "list of half pay officers who settled in the Niagara District after the rebellion of the colonies:"

Colonel John Butler, originator of Butler's Rangers, an Irishman, a connection of Lord Osmore; Captain Andrew Brant,

Butler's Rangers; Captain B. Fry, Captain P. Hare, Captain Thos. Butler, Captain Aaron Brant, Captain P. Paulding, Captain John Ball, Captain P. Ball, Captain P. Ten Brook, Lieutenant R. Clench, Lieutenant Wm. Brant, Lieutenant Wm. Tweeny, Lieut. Jocal Swoos, Lieut. James Clements, Lieut. D. Swoos, all of Butler's Rangers; Captain James Brant, Indian Department; Captain H. Nelles, Captain James Young, Captain Robert Nelles, Captain Joseph Dockster, Captain C. Ryman, Lieut. J. Clement, Lieut. W. B. Shuhm, Lieut. A. Chrysler, Lieut. S. Secord, Lieut. F. Stevens, Surgeon R. Kerr, Commodore T. Merritt, father of the late Hon. W. H. Merritt, all of the Indian Department.

DIVISION II.

TRAVELING IN EARLY TIMES—ORIGINAL ROUTES.

CHAPTER XII.

Contents—Indian paths—Portages—Original French routes—Mer de Canada—Original names of St. Lawrence—Ontario—Huron—Route by Bay Quinté—Old French maps—Original English routes—Four ways from Atlantic to the Lakes—Mississippi—Potomac—Hudson—Indian name of Erie—From New York to Ontario—The Hudson River—Mohawk—Wood creek—Oneida Lake—Oswego River—The carrying places—West Canada Creek—Black River—Oswegotchie—The navigation—Military highway—Lower Canada—An historic route—The paths followed by the Loyalists—Indian paths north of Lake Ontario—Crossing the Lake—From Cape Vincent to the Bay Quinté—From Oswego by Duck Islands—East Lake—Picton Bay—Coasting Ontario—Two ways to Huron—By Bay Quinté and Trent; by Don River—Lake Simcoe—Point Traverse—Loyalists—Traveling by the St. Lawrence—First road—Long remembered event.

Although the European found the American continent a vast unbroken wilderness, yet the native Indians had well defined routes of travel. Mainly, the long journeys made by them in their hunting excursions, and when upon the war path, were by water up and down rivers, and along the shores of lakes. And at certain places around rapids, and from one body of water to another, their frequent journeyings created a well marked path. These portages or carrying places may even yet, in many places be traced, and are still known by such appellations. The arrival of the European in America was followed by his penetrating, step by step, to the further recesses of the north and west. The opening of the fur trade with the Indians led to increased travel along some of the original paths, and probably to the opening of new ones. While the French by the waters of the Lower St. Lawrence, found it convenient to ascend by the great streams, the English had to traverse the high lands which separate the sources of the rivers which empty into the Atlantic, from those which rise to flow to the lakes and rivers of fresh water to the north.

The original routes of travel taken by the French were up the St. Lawrence, at first called the "Grand River of Canada," while the gulf is marked Galpo di Canada O'S Larenzo. The water of the Atlantic, south of the Chesapeake River to Newfoundland and the gulf, was known as the *Mer de Canada*. From the seaboard the traveler sometimes, having ascended to the mouth of the Sorel River, turned west to lake Champlain, and thence into the western part of the present New York State, or continuing up the St. Lawrence to its confluence with the Ottawa, or as it was sometimes called Grand River, selected one or the other of these majestic streams, by which to continue the journey westward. Following the Ottawa, the way led to the north as far as Lake Nippissing, and thence westward to the Georgian Bay. Sometimes the voyager would continue to ascend the St. Lawrence to Lake Ontario, a portion of the St. Lawrence sometimes called Cataraqui River, or the Iroquois River, that is to say, the river which leads to Cataraqui, or the Iroquois country. Lake Ontario was called by Champlain, Lake St. Louis, and subsequently for a time it was known as Lake Frontenac. According to a map observed in the French Imperial Library the Indian name of Ontario was Skapiadono, 1688.

From Lake Ontario to Lake Huron, at first named Mer Douce, and, then after the Huron Indians, who were expelled from that region by the Iroquois in 1650, a very common route was up the Bay Quinté, the River Trent, Lake Simcoe, and to Georgian Bay. That this was a not unfrequent way is well exhibited by the old French maps, which, prepared to indicate the principle water ways to the traveler, had the waters of the Bay and Trent, even to its source, made broad, so that the observer might imagine that the bay and the river were one continuous bay of navigable waters.

As this route was adjacent to the territory of the Iroquois nation, it was only when the French were at peace with them that this course was taken, until the establishment of the fort at Cataraqui. Again, the French occasionally followed the south shore of Lake Ontario to the Niagara River and ascended it to Lake Erie, and thus approached the far west.

While the French with comparative ease, reached the vast inland seas, the English by more difficult channels sought the advantages, which intercourse with the lake Indians afforded. An early writer of American history, Isaac Weld, says: "There are four principal channels for trade between the ocean and the lakes. One by the Mississippi to Lake Erie, a second by the Potomac and French Creek to Lake Erie. (Lake Erie was at first called Okswego, and the territory to the south of Lake Erie was sometimes called Ontario Nous.) A third by the Hudson, and a fourth by the St. Lawrence." A later writer says: "It is worthy of notice, that a person may go from Quebec to New Orleans by water all the way except about a mile from the source of Illinois River." The last mentioned route we have seen belonged to the French, and was the best to follow, as well as the most direct to Europe. Of the other three, we have only to speak of that by the Hudson.

The distance from New York to Lake Ontario is laid down as being 500 miles. From New York Bay to Albany, the Hudson is navigable, 180 miles. Ten miles north of Albany the river divides into two branches. The western branch is the Mohawk and leads to Rome, formerly Fort Stanwix. A branch of the Mohawk, Wood Creek, leads toward Oneida Lake, which was reached by a portage. A branch of Wood Creek was called Canada Creek, and led toward Lake Champlain. From Oneida Lake, the larger lake, Ontario, is reached by the Oswego River. Weld probably refers to this route when he says that the distance over which boats had to be hauled by land, (perhaps, from New York to Ontario) was altogether thirty miles. This was no doubt the most speedy route by which to reach Upper Canada from the Hudson. Frequent reference is made to it, in the accounts of journeying, by the U. E. Loyalists, which have come under notice. It was by far the most commonly traveled way, taken by those who came into Canada after the close of the war. And, it is stated, 1796, that the chief part of the trade between New York and the lake is by this way. But sometimes, the traveler up the Mohawk, instead of turning into Vilcrik, or Wood Creek, would continue to ascend the Mohawk, which turned more toward the east; and then into a branch sometimes called, 1756, West Canada Creek, by which he was brought contiguous to the head waters of the Black River, which empties into the lake at Sacket's Harbor. But the Black River was sometimes reached by ascending the Hudson, above the mouth of the Mohawk, away eastward to the Mohegan mountains, where the Hudson rises. Crossing these mountains he would strike the Moose River, which is a tributary to the Black River. Occasionally, instead of Moose River, the Oswegotchie was reached, and followed to its mouth at La Présentation, the present town of Ogdensburgh. That this route was well known, is shown from the statement of Weld, that, "It is said that both the Hudson and Oswegotchie River are capable of being made navigable for light batteaux to where they approach within a short distance, about four miles." All of these branches of the Hudson are interrupted by falls.

Still another way was now and then taken, after having crossed the Mohegans, namely, by Long Lake which feeds Racket River, that empties into the St. Lawrence, at St. Regis, opposite Cornwall. Again, numerous accounts have been furnished the writer, in which the traveler followed the military highway to Lower Canada, by Whitehall, Lake Champlain, Fort Ticonderoga, Plattsburgh, and then turning northward proceeded to Cornwall. But this way was the common one to Lower Canada, and by the Sorel. This historic route was no doubt long used by the Indians, before the European trod it, and Champlain at an early period penetrated to the lake, to which his name is forever attached. Along this road passed many a military expedition; and during the wars between the colonies of France and England, here ebbed and flowed the tide of strife. The rebellion of 1776 witnessed Burgoyne with his army sweep by here westward to meet his disastrous fate; and thereafter set in the stream of refugees and loyalists, which ceased not to flow for many a year, along this path.

While the great majority of the loyalists who came to Canada, followed one or other of the routes above mentioned, there were some who came around by the Atlantic, and up the St. Lawrence. There were at least two companies, one under the leadership of Captain Grass, and one under Captain Van Alstine, who sailed from New York in ships under the protection of a war vessel, shortly before the evacuation by the British forces in 1783.

Directing our attention to the territory north of Lake Ontario, and the Upper St. Lawrence, we find some interesting facts relative to the original Indian paths; sometimes, followed on hunting and fishing expeditions, and sometimes in pursuit of an enemy. There is evidence that the Mohawks, upon the southern shore of Lake Ontario, were accustomed to pass across the waters, to the northern shores by different routes. Thus, one was from Cape Vincent to Wolfe Island, and thence along its shore to the west end, and then either to Cataraqui, or up the Bay Quinté, or perhaps across to Amherst Island, where, it seems, generally resided a Chief of considerable importance. A second route, followed by them, in their frail bark canoes, was from a point of land somewhat east of Oswego, called in later days Henderson's Point, taking in their way Stony Island, the Jallup Islands, and stretching across to Yorkshire Island, and Duck Island, then to the Drake Islands, and finally to Point Traverse. Following the shore around this point, Wappoose Island was also reached; or, on the contrary, proceeding along the shore westward they reached East Lake. From the northernmost point of this lake they directed their steps, with canoes on their heads, across the carrying place to the head of Picton Bay, a distance of a little over four miles. It is interesting to notice that upon the old maps, by the early French navigators, the above mentioned islands are specified a "*au des Couis;*" while at the same time the Bay of Quinté bears the name of *Couis*, showing unmistakably that the Mohawk Indians passed by this way to the head waters of the bay and to the Trent River. Herriot designates one of these islands, Isle de Quinté. Two maps in the Imperial library of Paris, give these islands, above mentioned, the name of Middle Islands, and the waters east of them are named Cataraqui Bay. It is not at all unlikely that Champlain, when he first saw Lake Ontario, emerged from the water of East lake. Again, instead of entering the Bay Quinté with a view of passing up the River Moira, or Trent, they would continue along the south shore of Prince Edward, past West Lake and Consecon Lake, and proceed westward, sometimes to the river at Port Hope, sometimes further west, even to the Don, and ascend some one of the rivers to the head waters of the Trent or Lake Simcoe. The early maps indicate Indian villages along at several points. Owing to the dangerous coast along the south shore of Prince Edward, sometimes they chose the longer and more tedious route through the Bay Quinté to its head. That here was a common carrying place is well attested by the statements of many. Indeed, at this point upon the shores of the lake was an Indian village of importance. An old graveyard here, upon being plowed, has yielded rich and important relics, showing that the Indians were Christianized, and that valuable French gifts had been bestowed.

It would seem from a letter of DeNonville, that there were two ways to reach Lake Huron from Lake Ontario: one by the Bay Quinté and the Trent; the other by the way of the Don River and Lake Simcoe, called by him "Lake Taranto." In the selection of routes they were guided by Indians.

The route by the Trent and the Bay Quinté was for many a day regarded as the most direct, and the best route to Lake Huron, even since the settlement by Europeans. Its supposed importance was sufficient to lead to the attempt to construct a canal with locks, to make it navigable. Gourlay says, sometime after the war of 1812, that "in course of time it may become an object of importance to connect Rice Lake by a canal with Lake Ontario direct, instead of following the present canoe route by its natural outlet into the Bay Quinté."

The Marquis DeNonville, in 1685, moved on the Five Nations with his little army in canoes, in two divisions. On the 23rd June, one-half proceeded on the south side from the fort Cataraqui, and the other on the north side of the lake, and met near Oswego. Now, there can be no doubt, that the latter party crossed the bay to Indian Point, passed along its southern shore, then across the bay by Wappoose Island, and then around, or crossing Point Traverse struck far into the lake, by the islands which constituted the guides of this early Indian route. It may be that this was so commonly traveled that the old name of Point Traverse was thus derived.

We have indicated the several routes followed by the Indians, the French, the English, and finally by the Refugees, so far as relate to the territory now comprising Upper Canada, that is by which it was originally reached and settled. Beside, there were some who found their way by land from the head waters of the Susquehana to Lake Erie and Niagara. But the vast majority of pioneers of Upper Canada entered by the channels aforesaid.

For many years, the only road from Lower Canada was by the St. Lawrence, ascending wearily up the dangerous rapids in canoes and batteaux; and it will be found that the lots in the first townships were surveyed narrow in order to secure a water frontage to as many as possible, because there was no other means of transit than by water. But those who settled in the second concessions, a year or two later, were obliged to tread the length of the long front lots, in order to reach the water. At the same time the communication with Lower Canada, up and down the rapids, was attended with many hazards and inconveniences. It consequently became a matter of no little importance to have a road through the settlements to Montreal, which might be traveled by horse, a King's highway from the eastern Provincial line. It was, however, some years after the first settlement before this was secured. The original survey for a road was made by one Ponair, assisted by one Kilborne. "The opening" Sherwood says, "of this road from Lower Canada to Brockville and thence to Cataraqui, a distance of 145 miles, was an event long remembered by the pioneers. At the end of each mile was planted a red cedar post with a mark upon it indicating the number of miles from the Provincial line."—(See First Years of Upper Canada—Construction of Roads).

CHAPTER XIII.

CONTENTS—Indians traveled by foot or by canoe—Seprating canoes—Primeval scenes—Hunting expeditions—War path—In 1812—Brock—A night at Myers' Creek—Important arrival—The North West Company—Their canoes—Route—Grand Portage—The Voyageurs—The Batteaux—Size—Ascending the rapids—Lachine—A dry dock—Loyalists by batteaux—Durham boats—Difficulties—In 1788, time from Lachine to Fredericksburgh—Waiting for batteaux—Extracts from a journal, travelling in 1811—From Kingston to Montreal—The expenses—The Schenectady boats—Trade between Albany and Cataraqui—The Durham boat—Duncan—Description of flat-bottomed boat by "Murray"—Statement of Finkle—Trading—Batteaux in 1812—Rate of traveling—The change in fifty years—Time from Albany to Bay Quinté—Instances—Loyalists travelling in winter—Route—Willsbury wilderness—Tarrying at Cornwall—The "French Train."—Traveling along north shore of Ontario—Indian path—Horseback—Individual owners of batteaux—Around Bay Quinté—The last regular batteaux—In 1819—"Lines" from magazine.

TRAVELING BY CANOE.

Having pointed out the several general routes by which the aborigines and the first Europeans in America, were wont to traverse the country from the seaboard to the far west; and indicated more particularly the smaller paths of the Indians around the Bay Quinté and Lake Ontario, we purpose glancing at the means by which they made their way through the wilderness.

The Native had but two modes of transporting himself from place to place; namely, by foot and by the canoe. He was trained to make long expeditions upon the war-path, or after prey. When his course lay along a water way, he employed his birch canoe. This being light, he could easily ascend rapids, and when necessary, lift it from the water, and placing it, bottom upward, upon his head, carry it around the falls, or over a portage with the greatest facility. When upon the chase, or about to attack a foe, the canoe was so carefully secreted, that the passing traveler would never detect its whereabouts. The French and English at the first followed this Indian mode of traveling. From the graphic descriptions which are given to us by the early writers, of this Indian mode of traveling in America, ere the sound of the axe had broken upon the clear northern air, and while nature presented an unbroken garment of green, it is not difficult to imagine that scenes of Indian canoe traveling were in the extreme picturesque. It is not necessary to go beyond the Bay Quinté, to find a place where all the natural beauty was combined with the rude usages of the aboriginal inhabitant, to create a picture of rare interest and attraction. In those primeval times there was no regular passage made between one part of the country and another. The Indian in his light canoe glided along here and there, as his fancy led him, or the probability of obtaining fish or game dictated. At certain seasons of the year there was a general movement, as they started off on their hunting expeditions; and at other times the warriors alone set out, when only intent upon surprising the hated foe. On these occasions one canoe would silently and swiftly follow in the wake of the other, until the place of debarkation was reached. For a long time the birch canoe was the only mode of traveling, and when the French came with their batteaux, the canoe continued for a long time the principal means of transit. Even so late as the war of 1812, canoes were employed, and many of the gallant ones who fought and conquered the conceited and unscrupulous Yankee invader, found their way to the front by the swift birch bark. Company after company of Red Coats were to be seen plying the trim paddle as the canoe sped on its way. We have it on good authority that Major General Brock, at the reception of the intelligence, that the United States had declared war against Great Britain, set out from Lower Canada in a birch canoe, and with a companion and their boatman, journeyed all the way to York, followed by a regiment of soldiers. Incidents of this passage are yet related by the living. He reached Belleville, or as it was then called

Myers' Creek, late one night, after having been traveling for some time without rest. With his companion, he went ashore and sought a place to sleep. They entered the public house of Captain Mc——, and after examining a room, decided to sleep there the night. But the host, hearing an unusual noise, rushed into the room demanding who was there. The General's companion, with the quickness, and in language somewhat characteristic of the army of that time, told him he would kick him to h–ll in a minute. Captain Mc—— somewhat disconcerted at the threat and tone of authority walked out, and meeting the boatman, ask him who the parties were. Upon being informed, he rushed away in a state of great alarm, not daring to shew himself again to the General. The house is still standing.

The following notice is from the Kingston *Gazette*.

"York, April 29, 1815."

"On Sunday evening last arrived in this town from Burlington, in a birch canoe, Lieutenant General Sir George Murray Knight," &c., &c.

BATTEAUX—SCHENECTADY BOATS—DURHAM BOATS.

Gourley, speaking of Lachine, says that "from Lachine the canoes employed by the North West Company in the fur trade take their departure. Of all the numerous contrivances for transporting heavy burthens by water, these vessels are perhaps the most extraordinary: scarcely anything can be conceived so inadequate from the slightness of their construction, to the purpose they are applied to, and to contend against the impetuous torrent of the many rapids that must be passed through in the course of a voyage. They seldom exceed thirty feet in length, and six in breadth, diminishing to a sharp point at each end, without distinction of head or stern; the frame is composed of small pieces of some very light wood; it is then covered with the bark of the birch tree, cut into convenient slips, that are rarely more than the eight of an inch in thickness; these are sewed together with threads made from the twisted fibres of the roots of a particular tree, and strengthened where necessary by narrow strips of the same materials applied on the inside; the joints in the fragile planking are made water-tight, by being covered with a species of gum that adheres very firmly, and becomes perfectly hard. No iron-work of any description, not even nails, are employed in building these slendor vessels, which, when complete, weigh only about five hundred weight each. On being prepared for the voyage, they receive their lading, that for the convenience of carrying across the portages is made up in packages of about three-quarters of a hundred weight each, and amounts altogether to five tons, or a little more, including provisions, and other necessaries for the men, of whom from eight to ten are employed to each canoe; they usually set out in brigades like the batteaux, and in the course of a summer, upwards of fifty of these vessels are thus dispatched. They proceed up the Grand, or Ottawa River, so far as the south-west branch, by which, and a chain of small lakes, they reach Lake Nippissing; through it, and down the French River into Lake Huron; along its northern coast, up the narrows of St. Mary, into Lake Superior, and then, by its northern side, to the Grand Portage, a distance of about 1,100 miles from the place of departure. The difficulties encountered in this voyage are not easily conceived; the great number of rapids in the rivers, the different portages from lake to lake, which vary from a few yards to three miles or more in length, where the canoes must be unladen, and with their contents carried to the next water, occasion a succession of labors and fatigues of which but a poor estimation can be formed by judging it from the ordinary occupations of other laboring classes. From the Grand Portage, that is nine miles across, a continuation of the same toils takes place in bark canoes of an inferior size, through the chain of lakes and streams that run from the height of land westward to the Lake of the Woods, Lake Winnipeg, and onwards to more distant establishments of the company in the remote regions of the north-west country. The men are robust, hardy, and resolute, capable of enduring great extremes of fatigues and privation for a long time, with a patience almost inexhaustible. In the large lakes they are frequently daring enough to cross the deep bays, often a distance of several leagues, in their canoes, to avoid lengthening the route by coasting them; yet, notwithstanding all the risks and hardships attending their employment, they prefer it to every other, and are very seldom induced to relinquish it in favor of any more settled occupation. The few dollars they receive as the compensation for so many privations and dangers, are in general, dissipated with a most careless indifference to future wants, and when at an end, they very contentedly renew the same series of toils to obtain a fresh supply."

"The batteaux," says Ex-Sheriff Sherwood, "by which the refugees emigrated, were principally built at Lachine, nine miles from Montreal. They were calculated to carry four or five families, with about two tons weight. Twelve boats constituted a brigade, and each brigade had a conductor, with five men in each boat, one of which steered. The duty of the conductor was to give directions for the safe management of the boats, to keep them together; and when they came to a rapid they left a portion of the boats with one man in charge. The boats ascending were doubly manned, and drawn by a rope fastened at the bow of the boat, leaving four men in the boat with setting poles, thus the men walked along the side of the river, sometimes in the water, or on the edge of the bank, as circumstances occurred. If the tops of trees or brush were in the way they would have to stop and cut them away. Having reached the head of the rapid the boats were left with a man, and the others went back for others," and so they continued until all the rapids were mounted. Lachine was the starting place, a place of some twenty dwelling houses. Here Mr. Grant had a dry dock for batteaux.

It was by these batteaux, that the refugees, and their families, as well as the soldiers and their families passed from the shores of Lake Champlain, from Sorel, and the St. Lawrence, where they had temporally lived, to the Upper Province. It was also by these, or the Skenectady, or the Durham boat, that the pioneers made their transit from Oswego.

Thus it will be seen that to gain the northern shore of the St. Lawrence and Lake Ontario, was a task of no easy nature, and the steps by which they came were taken literally inch by inch, and were attended with labor hard and venturesome. Records are not wanting of the severe hardships endured by families on their way to their wooded lands. Supplied with limited comforts, perhaps only the actual necessaries of life, they advanced slowly by day along dangerous rapids, and at night rested under the blue sky. But our fathers and mothers were made of stern stuff, and all was borne with a noble heroism.

This toilsome mode of traveling continued for many a year. John Ferguson, writing in 1788, from Fredericksburgh to a friend in Lower Canada, Lachine, says of his journey, "after a most tedious and fatiguing journey I arrived here—nineteen days on the way—horrid roads—sometimes for whole days up to the waist in water or mire." But the average time required to ascend the rapids with a brigade was from ten to twelve days, and three or four to descend.

One can hardly conceive of the toilsome hours formerly spent in passing from Kingston, or the seventh and eight townships of the bay to Montreal, and back. Before setting out, the traveler would make elaborate preparations for a journey of several weeks. There was no regular traffic, and only an occasional batteaux, laden with simple articles of merchandise, would start for the head waters of the bay. Individuals would often wait, sometimes a long time, for these opportunities, and then would work their passage, by taking a hand at the oars. Even up to the present century, it was the custom.

The following is a most interesting instance of batteaux traveling which has been placed in our hands by the Rev. Mr. Miles. It gives one an excellent idea of traveling at the beginning of the present century. "I left Kingston on the 6th of April, 1811, but as the traveling *then* was not as it is *now*, I did not arrive in Montreal till the 15th. I will just copy verbatim, the journal I kept on my passage. Durham boats were scarce on the Canada side at that time, but it was thought if I could get to the American shore, I would find one on its way to Montreal. Well, I found a man in Kingston, just from Grindstone Island, who had brought up some shingles and tar to sell, and he told me if I could get to Briton's Point, several miles down the river from Cape Vincent, and to which place he would take me, that he thought I would find a Durham boat there, and the following is my journal on that route.

"Grindstone Island, April 11th, 1811.—Left Kingston yesterday, April 6th, at 3 p.m., in an open skiff, with R. Watson, a clerk in Dr. Jonas Abbott's store,and two hands belonging to the skiff—head wind—rowed hard till about eight in the evening, when having blistered both hands, and being very much fatigued, we drew our skiff on shore, and camped on the shore of Long Island, about five miles above Grindstone Island—wind strong from the north—very cold and without victuals or fire—feet wet—slept some, walked some, and by daybreak was somewhat chilled. Strong head wind. Stuck close to our dear lodgings till about eight, when the wind abated, and we stuck to our oars till about eleven o'clock, when we made Grindstone Island, weary, and very hungry—eat a hearty dish of "sapon" and milk—rested about an hour—set off for Briton's tavern on the American shore, where we arrived about 4 p.m., the water being entirely calm. Had not been on shore ten minutes, as good luck would have it, before we engaged a passage for Cornwall in a Durham boat, and a breeze coming up directly from the south, our American boats immediately hoisted sail and proceeded about thirty miles, when the wind changed, and we put into a bay on Grenadier Island, about nine in the evening—eat some supper at a house owned by Mr. Baxter—spread a sail upon the floor, and seven boatmen and four passengers camped down before the fire. In the morning I felt my bones as though they had been lying on the soft side of a hard rough floor. April 8, head wind still. Wished myself either at Kingston or Montreal. April 9, still a head wind. Must take it as it comes. Reading and writing the order of the day. At 7 p.m., hoisted sail. At one a.m., arrived at a house on the Canada shore, and slept on the floor till daylight. April 10, left for Ogdensburg, where we arrived at 3 p.m. Found an old acquaintance and passed the afternoon quite agreeably. April 11, had a good night's rest. Still a head wind. Found the printing office and composed types the greater part of the day. April 12, still a head wind. April 13, left Ogdensburg and arrived at Cornwall. April 14, left Cornwall and arrived at M'Gee's, Lake St. Francis. April 15, left M'Gee's and arrived at Montreal about 8 p.m. Traveling expenses from Kingston to Montreal $9 75."

With the later coming refugees was introduced another kind of flat bottomed boat. It was generally small and rigged with an ungainly sail. It was generally built at the Town of Schenectady, and hence the name. Schenectady is a German word, and means *pine barren*. Families about to come to Canada would build one or more to meet their reqirements. There was never a large number of this particular kind of boat. Those that were to be seen, were upon the bay.

With the opening up of trade between Albany and Upper Canada, was introduced still another kind of vessel, which was adapted to the use of merchants, engaged in the carrying trade. One of the earliest traffickers from the Mohawk River to the lakes by the Durham boats was Duncan, of Augusta, who was, as will be seen, one of the first Legislative Councillors of Upper Canada. He finally removed to Schenectady. It is said that he introduced the trade between the Mohawk and Buffalo which led to the construction of the Erie Canal.

A writer, speaking of the boats used by the Canadians, says, the largest boats used by the Canadian boatmen is called the Durham boat, "used here and in the rapids of the Mohawk. It is long, shallow, and nearly flat bottomed. The chief instrument of steerage is a pole ten feet long, shod with iron, and crossed at short intervals with small bars of wood like the feet of a ladder; the men place themselves at the bow, two on each side, thrust their poles into the channel, and grasping successively the wooden bars, work their way toward the stern, thus pushing on the vessel in that direction." (Murray).

Mr. Finkle remarks that "the first mode of conveyance for travelers from Montreal to Kingston, after the settlement of Upper Canada, was by Canadian batteaux laden with merchandize (at this time there was no separate conveyance). The return cargo consisted of barrels of flour, peas, potash, north-west packs of furs, &c.; the men and conductors employed in this business were Lower Canadians. This mode of conveyance continued without interruption until 1809, when the Durham boats came from the Mohawk River and embarked in the carrying trade only between Montreal and Kingston. Being of commodious size, far above the batteaux, they materially interfered with them and lessened the trade by the batteaux. The men who managed the Durham boats came with them from the Mohawk River, these boats were entirely manned by men from that country.

The flat bottomed boat continued in use until some time after the war of 1812. Until the canal along the St. Lawrence was constructed it was the only way by which merchandize could be transported to the Upper Province through the rapids of the St. Lawrence. After the establishment of York as the capital of Upper Canada, there sprung up naturally, a trade between Kingston and the "muddy" capital, and regular batteaux communication was, after a little, established. Once a week the solitary boat left Kingston, and slowly made its way by oars, up the bay to the Carrying Place over which it was hauled by Asa Weller, a tavern keeper, upon low wheels or trucks drawn by oxen, and then continued its way along the shore of Ontario, to its destination. These boats carried not only merchandize but passengers. Beside the regular batteaux there were occasionally others, owned by small merchants and pedlars. It was by the flat bottomed boat and canoe that many of the troops ascended to the head of the lake in 1812, and by which many of the 1000 prisoners taken at Detroit were conveyed to Quebec. The rate of speed of the batteaux or Durham boat, as well as the Skenectady boat, can be approximated from the statement of "A traveller," writing in 1835. He says, "the line of boats which start from Albany to Skenectady, on their way to Upper Canada, go two-and-a-half miles an hour, taking in stoppages—charging one-and-a-half cents per mile, including board. This mode of traveling is preferred by large families and prudent settlers.

The conveniences of traveling then, as well as the time required, are so widely different from what we are accustomed to in this day, that we have to pause and wonder at the change which even fifty and sixty years have wrought. Even after Upper Canada had become somewhat settled, it was a momentous matter for a family to set out from the Hudson for Cataraqui, or the Bay Quinté, as they generally called the settlement in those days. For instance, Mr. Lambert, of Sophiasburgh, who came in 1802, was six weeks on the way between Albany and the bay, coming by the Mohawk and Oswego Rivers, and crossing from "Gravelly Point" to "Isle Tanti." We will give another instance:—Nicholas L., came from New Jersey with seven sons and two daughters. It took a month to come. Having reached Schenectady they waited to build a batteaux. This completed, they stored away provisions to last them until Cataraqui was reached. They also brought with them iron kettles, with which to make maple sugar, and "a churn full of honey." Mr. L., being a fanning mill maker, he brought also a quantity of wire guaze. At Oswego, the fort there being still held by the British, they were strictly questioned as to the use intended to be made of the kettles and gauze. Satisfaction being given on this point, the family continued their tedious journey along the shore toward Kingston. Barely escaping being wrecked off Stony Island, they at last reached the north shore. Three days more of weary rowing up the bay, and Hay Bay was reached, where they settled.

The loyalists not alone came in summer, by batteaux or the Schenectady boat; but likewise in winter. They generally followed, as near as possible, some one of the routes taken in summer. To undertake to traverse a wilderness with no road, and guided only by rivers and creeks, or blazed trees, was no common thing. Several families would sometimes join together to form a train of sleighs. They would carry with them their bedding, clothes, and the necessary provisions. We have received interesting accounts of winter journeyings from Albany along the Hudson, across to the Black River country, and to the St. Lawrence. Sometimes the train would follow the "military road" along by Champlain, St. George, and as far as Plattsburgh, and then turn north to the St. Lawrence, by what was then called the Willsbury wilderness, and "Chataguee" woods. At the beginning of the present century there was but one tavern through all that vast forest, and this of the poorest character. Indeed it is said that while provision might be procured for the horses, none could be had for man. Those who thus entered Canada in winter found it necessary to stay at Cornwall until spring. Two or more of the men would walk along the St. Lawrence to the bay

Quinté, and, at the opening of navigation, having borrowed a batteaux descend to Cornwall for the women, children, and articles brought with them. Often, indeed generally unacquainted with the use of the boat, the passage up and down the river was tedious and toilsome. While the families and sleighs were transported in the batteaux the horses were taken along the shore by the larger boys, if such there were among them. The "French train" was occasionally employed in their winter travels. It consisted of a long rude sleigh with several horses driven tandem style, this allowed the passage among the trees to be made more easily.

Many very interesting reminisences are known of traveling along the bay by the pioneers. A few are adduced.

TRAVELING TO YORK AND QUEENSTON.

Travelers from Montreal to the west would come by a batteaux, or Durham boat, to Kingston. Those who had business further west, says Finkle, "were conveyed to Henry Finkle's in Ernest town, where they commonly stopped a few days. Thence they made their journey on horse back. A white man conducted them to the River Trent, where resided Colonel Bleecker who was at the head, and had control of all the Mississauga Indians, and commanded the entire country from the Trent to Toronto. At this place the traveler was furnished with a fresh horse and an Indian guide to conduct him through an unsettled country, the road being little better than a common Indian path, with all its windings. The road continued in this state until about the year 1798. Sometimes the traveler continued his way around the head of the lake on horse back to Queenston, where resided Judge Hamilton.

During the time the surveyors were laying out the townships of the bay, batteaux occasionally passed up and down, supplying the staff with their requirements, or perhaps with some one looking for a good tract of land

In 1790 a batteaux was owned by Mr. Lambert, of the eighth township, and Mr. Ferguson, writing from Kingston to Mr. Bell, wished him to borrow it, to come to Kingston.

Among the first to use batteaux as a mode of traffic, was Captain Myers. He sailed one up and down the bay to carry, not only his own freight, but for the accommodation of others. He frequently went to Kingston, and now and then to Montreal, the mode pursued, was to charge for freight down, and then give the passenger a free passage back. This was followed for many years, with great profit. The Captain was accustomed to make the journey as pleasant as possible to the passengers. He always kept his grog in his "caboose," and would deal it out to all. There was no doubt much of jollity and pleasant yarn-spinning, during the long passages upon the tranquil waters of the bay. Captain Myers subsequently owned a schooner."

A letter written 11th November, 1790, by John Ferguson, to Wm. Bell, of Sidney, says, "As I suppose Mr. Lounsbury's boat is idle, I would be glad that you would endeavour to borrow or hire it and Sherrard's son and come down to the third township.

When persons had gone down the bay, and were expected to return upon a certain night, there would often be a fire kindled on the shore to guide them homeward. In dark nights this was really necessary. Many were the expedients resorted to make short cuts. The feat of swimming horses over the bay was now and then resorted to by the Wallbridges after they settled in Ameliasburgh. Wishing to go to Kingston, they would go down to the point where the bay is narrow, and swim the horses across to Ox Point, and then ride to Kingston by a bridle path. It would now and then happen at a late period, that a traveler passing to his place of settlement would have a lumber waggon. This would be ferried across the bay by placing it across two log canoes. Referring to swimming the bay by a horse, a colored man, yet living within the neighbourhood of Belleville, remembers when a boy, to have been put upon a horse, and then to have obeyed orders to swim him across the bay. This occurred near Belleville.

Long after steamboats were started on the bay, the batteaux continued to ply between Belleville and Montreal. The last to sail these was Fanning and John Covert. In 1830, Fanning arrived at Montreal from Belleville so early as to present his bills of laden upon the first of April. The following business notice cannot fail to be interesting:

"The subscribers having established a line of Durham Boats from this place, propose forwarding from the different ports of the lake to that of Montreal, on the following terms, viz.:

"From York, Niagara, Queenston, and the head of the lake, for each barrel of Flour delivered at the Port of Montreal, 5s. and 6d.

"From Kingston, to the Port of Montreal, for each barrel of Flour, 4s. and 6d.

"From York, Niagara, Queenston, and the head of the lake, for each barrel of Potash delivered at the Port of Montreal, 12s. and 6d.

10

"From Kingston to the Port of Montreal, for each barrel of Potash, 10s.

"From York, Niagara, Queenston, and the head of the lake, for each barrel of Pork delivered at the Port of Montreal, 8s. and 3d.

"From Kingston to the Port of Montreal, for each barrel of Pork, 6s. and 9d.

"Merchandize will be transported by the same means from Lachine to Kingston, at the rate of 5s. per cwt.

"An elegant Passage Boat will also leave Kingston every tenth day for Montreal, which will be fitted up in the most commodious manner and prevent any delay to passengers leaving the upper part of the lake in the Steam Boat *Frontenac*, it having been built for the purpose of leaving this place immediately after her arrival.

"These arrangements will take effect at the opening of the navigation, and be continued during the season.

"Thomas Markland.
"Peter Smith.
"Lawrence Herkimer.
"John Kerby.
"William Mitchell.

"Kingston, February, 1819."

Respecting the Canadian Batteaux, the following is from the Boston *Weekly Magazine* of an old date.

"Lines written while at anchor in Kingston Harbour, Lake Ontario, on hearing from several Canadian boats entering from the St. Lawrence—their usual songs.

Hark! o'er the lakes unruffled wave,
A distant solemn chant is sped;
Is it some requiem at the grave?
Some last kind honor to the dead?
'Tis silent all—again begin;
It is the wearied boatman's lay,
That hails alike the rising sun,
And his last soft departing ray.

Forth from yon island's dusky side,
The train of batteaux now appear,
And onward as they slowly glide,
More loud their chorus greets the ear.
But, ah! the charm that distance gave,
When first in solemn sounds their song
Crept slowly o'er the limpid wave,
Is lost in notes full loud and strong.

Row, brothers row, with songs of joy,
For now in view a port appears;
No rapids here our course annoy,
No hidden rocks excite our fears,
Be this sweet night to slumber given,
And when the morning lights the wave
We'll give our matin songs to heav'n,
Our course to bless, our lives to save.

CHAPTER XIV.

CONTENTS.—The first Vessel—The French—La Salle—The Griffon—Vessels in 1770—During the Rebellion—Building at Carleton Island—Captain Andrews The Ontario—Col. Burton—Loss of the Ontario—The Sheehans—Hills—Givins'—Murney's Point—Schooner 'Speedy'—Mohawk—Mississauga—Duke of Kent—Capt. Bouchette—Paxton—McKenzie—Richardson—Earle Steele—Fortiche—The Governor Simcoe—Sloop 'Elizabeth'—First vessel built at York—Collins' Report upon Navigating the Lakes—Navy in Upper Canada, 1795—Rochfoucault—Capt. Bouchette—Officers' Pay—York, the centre of the Naval Force—Gun Boats—The Loss of the "Speedy"—Reckoner—Dr. Strachan—Solicitor-Gen. Gray—Canada took the lead in building Vessels—First Canadian Merchant Vessel—The York—A Schooner on runners around the Falls—Sending Coals to Newcastle—Upon Bay Quinté—The Outskirts of Civilization—"The Prince Edward" built of Red Cedar—in 1812—Schooner "Mary Ann"—1817—Capt. Matthews.

THE FIRST SAILING VESSELS.

The first vessels, with sails, which navigated the waters of the lakes, were built by the French, to pursue their discoveries, and to carry on the fur trade. The first sailing vessel launched upon the Lakes, was built by LaSalle. He, with Father Hennepin and Chevalier de Tonti, set sail from Cataraqui, on the 18th November, 1678, for the mouth of the Niagara river, having on board his bark goods, and material for building a brigantine on Lake Erie. During the winter the vessel was commenced, six miles above the Falls, and was launched by the middle of summer, amid great display and ceremony. The vessel was named "Griffon," according to Garneau; but Father Hennepin says "Cataraqui." "She was a kind of brigantine, not unlike a Dutch galliot, with a broad elevated bow and stern, very flat in the bottom; she looked much larger than she really was. She was of sixty tons burden. With the aid of tow-lines and sails the Niagara river was, with difficulty, ascended; and on the 7th August, 1679, the first vessel that ever sat upon the lakes, entered Lake Erie." The end of this vessel was a sad one. (See Introduction).

We are indebted to the *Detroit Tribune* for the following interesting statements:

"In 1766 four vessels plied upon Lake Erie. These were the "Gladwin," "Lady Charlotte," "Victory," and "Boston."

"The two latter laid up in the fall near Navy Island, above Niagara Falls, and one of them was burned accidentally, November 30, of the same year. A vessel called the "Brunswick," owned and commanded by Captain Alexander Grant, made her appearance on the lakes during the year 1767, and was lost some time during the season following. Captain Grant was the Commodore of the lakes for two or three years. In 1769 Sterling and Porteous built a vessel at Detroit, called the "Enterprise," Richard Cornwall, of New York, being the carpenter. The boatmen, who went from Schenectady with the rigging and stores for this vessel to Detroit, were to have each £20, and ten gallons of rum. They were seventy days on Lake Erie, and two of the number perished from hunger, and their bodies were kept to decoy eagles and ravens. They returned to New York in February, 1760, by way of Pittsburg, then called Fort Pitt.

"In May, 1770, a vessel of seventy tons burthen was launched at Niagara, called the "Charity." The same year the Duke of Gloucester, Secretary Townsend, Samuel Tutchet, Henry Baxter, and four others, formed a company for mining copper on Lake Superior. In December they built at Point Aux Pins, a barge, and laid the keel for a sloop of forty tons burthen. Of the success of this enterprise we are not informed. Subsequent to the above period very little was accomplished in the construction of craft for lake navigation, and the few that came into commission were used solely as traders, as were in fact, all those previously named. A short time after, 1770, batteaux from Montreal and Quebec, employed by the Hudson's Bay Fur Company, made their annual tours westward, gathering large quantities of furs, and returning homeward in the fall. It has been stated that the first vessel built on Lake Ontario was in 1749, but this, we have reason to believe, is not correct."

During the Revolutionary War, the British Government built at Carleton Island, a few vessels to carry troops and provisions from place to place along the Lake, from Carleton Island to Niagara. The first Commissioner at the Dock Yard was Commodore James Andrews, Lieutenant in the Royal Navy. The "Ontario," a war vessel of considerable importance, carrying 22 guns, was built at Carleton Island. This vessel was commanded by Capt. Andrews. Some time between 1780 and 1783, as the "Ontario" was proceeding from Niagara to Oswego with a detachment of the King's Own regiment, commanded by Colonel Burton, with other officers, a storm arose at night, and the vessel was lost with all on board. Col. John Clark, in his memoirs, whose father belonged to the 8th regiment, says this event happened in 1780 or '81, in which belief he is supported by Mr. Sheehan, a descendant of Capt. Andrews: but other authority has it that the event took place in 1783. At all events, the occurrence produced a melancholy effect, which long remained in the minds of those acquainted with the circumstances. Captain Andrews left a widow, a son, and two daughters. The son returned to Scotland, the daughters married and settled in Canada. The Sheehan's, Hill's, and Givins' are descendants of Captain Andrews' daughters, whose husbands had been in the army.

After the settlement of Kingston, the Government built vessels at Murney's Point, and at Navy Point. Among the first built here was the Schooner "Speedy," and also the "Mohawk" and "Missisagua," and "Duke of Kent." Among the first commanders of vessels, most of whom were of the Royal Navy, were Capt. Bouchette, Capt. Paxton, Capt. McKenzie, Capt. Richardson, Capt. Earle, Capt. Steele and Capt. Fortiche.

"The first vessel built for trade upon Lake Ontario," that is after Upper Canada was settled, "may have been the 'Governor Simcoe,' for the North West Company; after she was worn out and laid up, Judge Cartwright, who was agent for the Company at Kingston, built another for that Company, and one for himself, both built at the same time, side by side, on Mississauga Point, at the mouth of Cataraqui Creek. Both were launched on the same day; the one for the Company named "Governor Simcoe," and the other "Sloop Elizabeth." These were built during my stay with Judge Cartwright, in 1808.

"The first, and only vessel for many years, built at York, was a small schooner about forty-five tons. Built by two brothers named Kendrick."—(*Finkle*).

The survey made by Deputy Surveyor-General Collins, at the request of Lord Dorchester, in 1788, included an examination of the lakes and harbors from Kingston to Michilmicinac. In reference to the lakes and vessels, the Surveyor says:—"Vessels sailing on these waters being seldom for any length of time out of sight of land, the navigation must be considered chiefly as pilotage, to which the use of good natural charts are essential and therefore much wanted. Gales of wind, or squalls, rise suddenly upon the lakes, and from the confined state of the waters, or want of sea-room, (as it is called), vessels may in some degree be considered as upon a lee shore, and this seems to point out the necessity for their being built on such a construction as will best enable them to work to windward. Schooners should, perhaps, have the preference, as being rather safer than sloops, they should be from 80 to 100 tons burthen on

Lake Ontario, and 50 tons burthen on Lakes Erie and Huron; but if not intended to communicate between these two lakes, they may then be the same size as on Lake Ontario; and if this system is approved there can be no necessity to deviate from it unless an enemy should build vessels of greater magnitude or force; but as the intent of bringing any such forward, at least the building of them can never remain a secret, there may be always time to counteract such a design by preparing to meet them at least on equal terms. It does not seem advisable, nor do I know any reason to continue the practice of building vessels flat bottomed, or to have very little draft of water, they are always unsafe, and many of the accidents which have happened on the lakes, have perhaps, in some degree been owing to that construction. On the contrary, if they are built on proper principles for burthen as well as sailing they will be safer, and will find sufficient depth of water proportioned to any tonnage which can be requisite for them upon these lakes."

Respecting the navy in Upper Canada, Rouchfoucault writes in 1795: "The Royal Navy is not very formidable in this place; six vessels compose the whole naval force, two of which are small gun-boats, which we saw at Niagara, and which are stationed at York. Two small schooners of twelve guns, viz., the "Onondago," in which we took our passage, and the "Mohawk," which is just finished; a small yacht of eighty tons, mounting six guns as the two schooners, which has lately been taken into dock to be repaired, form the rest of it. All these vessels are built of timber fresh cut down, and not seasoned, and for this reason last never longer than six or eight years. To preserve them, even to this time, requires a thorough repair; they must be heaved down and caulked, which costs at least from one thousand, to one thousand two hundred guineas. This is an enormous price, and yet it is not so high as on Lake Erie, whither all sorts of naval stores must be sent from Kingston, and where the price of labor is still higher. The timbers of the Mississauga, which was built three years ago, are almost all rotten. It is so easy to make provision for ship-timber for many years to come, as this would require merely the felling of it, and that too at no great distance from the place where it is to be used, that it is difficult to account for this precaution not having been adopted. Two gun-boats, which are destined by Governor Simcoe to serve only in time of war, are at present on the stocks; but the carpenters who work at them are but eight in number. The extent of the dilapidations and embezzlements, committed at so great a distance from the mother country, may be easily conceived. In the course of last winter a judicial enquiry into a charge of this nature was instituted at Kingston. The Commissioner of the navy and the principal ship-wright, it was asserted, had clearly colluded against the King's interest; but interest and protection are as powerful in the new world as in the old: for both the Commissioner and ship-wright continue in their places.

"Captain Bouchette commands the naval force on Lake Ontario, and is at the head of all the marine establishments, yet without the least power in money matters. This gentleman possesses the confidence both of Lord Dorchester and Governor Simcoe; he is a Canadian by birth, but entered the British service when Canada fell into the power of England.

"While Arnold and Montgomery were besieging Quebec, Lord Dorchester, disguised as a Canadian, stole on board his ship into that city, on which occasion he displayed much activity, intrepedity, and courage. It is not at all a matter of surprise that Lord Dorchester should bear in mind this eminent service. By all accounts he is altogether incorruptible, and an officer who treats his inferiors with great mildness and justice.

"In regard to the pay of the Royal Marine force on Lake Ontario, a captain has ten shillings a day, a lieutenant six, and a second lieutenant three shillings and sixpence. The seamen's wages are eight dollars per month. The masters of merchant-men have twenty-five dollars, and the sailors from nine to ten dollars a month.

"Commander Bouchette is among those, who most strenuously oppose the project of moving to York, the central point of the force on the lake; but his family reside at Kingston, and his lands are situated near that place. Such reasons are frequently of sufficient weight to determine political opinions.

Again, says the same writer, "Governor Simcoe intends to make York the centre of the naval force on Lake Ontario. Only four gun-boats are at present on this lake, two of which are constantly employed in transporting merchandise; the other two, which alone are fit to carry troops and guns, and have oars and sails, are lying under shelter until an occasion occurs to convert them to their intended purpose. It is the Governor's intention to build ten smaller gun-boats on Lake Ontario, and ten on Lake Erie. The ship carpenters, who construct them, reside in the United States, and return home every winter."

"On the 7th October, 1807, Mr. Justice Cochrane, Mr. Gray, the

Solicitor General, and Mr. Agnus McDonald, embarked at York, with several other passengers in the *Speedy*, a government schooner, commanded by Captain Paxton, for the purpose of going to Newcastle where the Assizes were to be held on the 10th. The vessel was seen a few miles from her destined port on the evening of the 8th. The wind commenced to blow, and the schooner was never heard of more. There were pieces picked up on the opposite shore. Mr. Cochrane was young in years, but not in piety." The above is extracted from the Kingston *Gazette*, written by "Reckoner," which was the name under which Dr. Strachan contributed to that paper. Colonel Clark, of Dalhousie, says "I recollect the loss of the *Speedy*," and he remarks of Solicitor General Gray, that he was "a noble character, noted for his sympathy on behalf of abolishing slavery." He says that there were upwards of twenty passengers, among them he mentions Jacob Herkimer, a merchant of York.

It will be seen that Canada took the lead in building the early vessels upon the lakes. The first American ship that navigated Lake Erie, was purchased from the British in 1796. She was called the *Detroit*. The first vessel built by the Americans, for the lakes, was constructed in 1797. The first Canadian merchant vessel built upon Lake Ontario, was by Francis Crooks, brother of the Hon. James Crooks. It was built to the east of the present United States fort, at the mouth of the Niagara river, in 1792, and was called the "York." She was wrecked at Genesee river. In 1800 a schooner of about 75 or 100 tons, was brought to Clifton, and during the winter of 1801 she crossed by the portage road on immense runners to Queenston, where she again found her native element in the Niagara river." She was, in 1804, lost in bringing a cargo to Niagara, with all on board.—(*Clark*).

It is a curious fact that in the American war of 1812, the British "Admiralty sent out the frame work, blocks, &c., of the Psyche frigate, which could have been procured on the spot in the tenth of the time and a twentieth part of the expense. At the same time there was furnished to each ship of war on Lake Ontario, a full supply of water casks, with an apparatus for distilling sea water," forgetting the fact that the waters of the lake were of the purest quality.

Directing our attention to the waters of the bay Quinté, it is found that until after 1812, but few sailing vessels entered the upper waters, although found east of Picton Bay. Strange as it may appear at the present day, there was a time when the head of Picton Bay, or Hay Bay, was regarded as the head of the bay, and the very outskirts of civilization, while going up the Long Reach, to the Mohawk tract was look upon like going to the Red River at the present day. The settlers above were too few, and their requirements too limited for a sailing vessel to ascend, unless occasionally to the Napanee mills. But as time passed, sloops and schooners, as well as batteaux found employment along the western townships.

In the first year of the present century, there was built in the township of Marysburgh, a short distance west of the Stone mills, a schooner of some celebrity. It was built by Captain Murney, father of the late Hon. Edward Murney, of Belleville. Captain Murney came to Kingston in 1797, at the solicitation of Mr. Joseph Forsyth. It was constructed for himself, and was made altogether of red cedar, a kind of wood formerly very plentiful along the bay, and which possesses a most agreeable odor, and is extremely durable. The vessel was named the *Prince Edward*. John Clark, of Dalhousie, says of this vessel, that he was on board the following year of her building, and that she was a "staunch good ship, with an able captain." Her size was sufficient to allow 700 barrels of flour to be stowed beneath her hatches. She ran upon Lake Ontario for many years, and made for her owner a small fortune. She was in good condition in 1812, and was employed by government as an armed vessel. A schooner called *Prince Edward*, probably the same, Captain Young, was the first vessel to land at the pier when erected at Wellington.

The Kingston *Gazette*, April 12, 1817, says: "On Thursday, 20th inst. at three o'clock p.m., arrived at Ernesttown, in the Bay of Quinté, the schooner *Mary Ann*, Captain J. Mosier, in twenty hours from York, and at this port yesterday afternoon with fourteen passengers, of whom eleven were members of the Provincial Parliament. This is the seventh voyage this vessel has made this season, to the great credit of her master. The *Mary Ann* sailed again in about half an hour for the Bay Quinté.

One of the early vessels upon the bay was commanded by Matthews, father of the rebel of 1836, who was executed.

DIVISION III.

THE LOYALISTS AS PIONEERS—THE ORIGINAL SURVEY.

CHAPTER XV.

CONTENTS—Major Gen. Holland—Surveying on Atlantic Coast—An adherent of the Crown—Removal to Montreal—Death—Major Holland—Information from "Maple Leaves"—Holland Farm—Taché—First Canadian Poem—Head Quarters of Gen. Montgomery—Hospitality—Duke of Kent—Spencer Grange—Holland Tree—Graves—Epitaphs—Surveyor Washington—County Surveyor—Surveyors after the War—First Survey in Upper Canada—Commenced in 1781—The Mode pursued—Information in Crown Lands Department—The Nine Townships upon the St. Lawrence—At the close of the War—Non-Professional Surveyors—Thomas Sherwood—Assisting to Settle—Surveying around the Bay Quinté—Bongard—Deputy-Surveyor Collins—First Survey at Frontenac—Town Reserve—Size of Township—Mistakes—Kottie—Tuffy—Capt. Grass—Capt. Murney—Surveying in Winter—Planting Posts—Result—Litigation—Losing Land—A Newspaper Letter—Magistrates—Landholders—Their Sons' Lawyers—Alleged Filching—Speculators at Seat of Government—Grave Charges—Width of Lots—Mode of Surveying—Number of Concessions—Cross Roads—Surveyors Orders—Numbering the Lots—Surveying around the Bay—The ten Townships—Their Lands—The Surveying Party—A Singer—Statement of Gourlay.

THE FIRST SURVEYS IN UPPER CANADA.

Among those who distinguished themselves at Louisburg and on the Plains of Abraham under General Wolfe, was Major Samuel Holland. Sabine says, he was "Surveyor-General of the Colonies north of Virginia." In 1773 he announced his intention to make Perth Amboy, near Jersey, his head-quarters, and wrote to a gentleman there to inquire for houses to accommodate himself and his assistants. He then completed the surveys as far west as Boston. Proposed in 1774 to get round Cape Cod, and to New London, and said it would be at best six years before he should be able to finish his labors. In 1775, he wrote Lord Dartmouth that he was ready to run the line between Massachusetts and New York. By a communication laid before the Provincial Congress of Massachusetts in July, 1775, it appears that he had loaned to Alex. Shepard, Jun., who was also a surveyor, a plan or survey of Maine, which Shepard disliked to return, fearing that it might be used in a manner prejudicial to the Whig cause, as Holland was an adherent of the Crown, and then in New Jersey. Congress recommended to

Shepard to retain Holland's plan. Major Holland went to Lower Canada, where he resumed his duties of Surveyor-General, in which capacity he served nearly fifty years. He died in 1801, and at the time of his decease he was a member of the Executive and Legislative Councils."

It was under Surveyor Holland that the first surveys were made upon the banks of the St. Lawrence and the Bay of Quinté. Major Holland was a gentleman of education, and known for his social and amiable qualities. We are indebted to the author of "Maple Leaves," J. M. LeMoine, Esq., for information respecting Surveyor Holland. Extending from the brow of St. Foy heights along St. Lewis Road at Quebec, was a piece of land of 200 acres which was known as the Holland Farm. This farm had belonged to a rich merchant of Quebec, Mon. Jean Taché, who wrote the first Canadian Poem, "Tableau de la Mer." He was the ancestor of the late Sir E. Taché. About the year 1740 he built upon an eminence a high peaked structure, which, during the seige of Quebec, was the head quarters of Gen. Montgomery. This place was bought by Gen. Holland in 1780, who lived there in affluence for many years, subsequent to the close of the war, 1783. The *élite* of Quebec were wont to resort here to enjoy his hospitality, and in 1791, he entertained Edward, afterward Duke of Kent, the father of our Queen. This place is now known as Spencer Grange; but the old building has long since been removed to be replaced by the present well-known mansion. From the St. Foy Road may be seen a fir tree known as the Holland Tree. Under that tree are several graves, which some years ago were inclosed with a substantial stone wall, with an iron gate. But now only the foundation remains. Two of the graves had neat marble slabs, with the names of Samuel Holland senior, and Samuel Holland, junior. "Here rest Major Surveyor Holland, and his son, who was killed in a duel at Montreal, by Major Ward of the 60th Regiment," by a shot from one of a brace of pistols presented to Major Holland by Gen. Wolfe. This farm is now in possession of the military authorities.

At the time of the rebellion the land of the thirteen Colonies was, in many cases, still unsurveyed, or so imperfectly laid out that frequent demands were made for the professional surveyor. In the very nature of things pertaining to the settlement of America, there was a general demand for surveyors. The country was constantly being opened up. Some of the most prominent men of the day had been surveyors. Gen. Washington commenced life as a country surveyor. In the war, both on the rebel and British sides, were to be found professional surveyors engaged in fighting. Consequently when the war terminated, there was no lack of surveyors to carry on the work of surveying the wilderness of Upper Canada. We have seen that Major Holland held the position of Surveyor-General, and there was duly appointed a certain number of deputies and assistants.

Even while the war was in progress, steps seem to have been taken to furnish the refugee Loyalists with new homes, upon the land still lying in a state of nature. The land in Lower Canada being in the main held by the French Canadians, it was deemed expedient to lay out along the shores of the upper waters a range of lots for their use. In pursuance of this, the first survey of land was made by order of Gen. Clarke, Acting Governor, or Military Commander, in 1781. Naturally the survey would commence at the extreme western point of French settlement. This was on the north bank of Lake St. Francis, at the cove west of Pointe au Bodet, in the limit between the Township of Lancaster, and the seigniory of New Longueil.

We have reason to believe that the surveyor at first laid out only a single range of lots fronting upon the river. In the first place a front line was established. This seems to have been done along the breadth of several proposed townships. In doing this it was desirable to have as little broken front as possible, while at the same time the frontage of each lot remained unbroken by coves of the river or bay. We are informed by the Crown Land Department that in some townships there could, in recent days, be found no posts to indicate the front line, while the side lines in the second concession were sufficiently marked.

The original surveyor along the St. Lawrence evidently did not extend his operations above Elizabethtown, which was called the ninth township, being the ninth laid out from New Longueil. This is apparent from the fact that while Elizabethtown was settled in 1784, the next township above, that of Yonge, was not settled until two years later. The quality of the land thence to Kingston was not such as would prove useful to the poor settler, and therefore was allowed for a time to remain unsurveyed. Hence it came that Cataraqui was the commencement of a second series of townships distinguished by numbers only. These two distinct ranges of townships, one upon the St. Lawrence numbering nine, and one upon the Bay numbering ten, were, when necessary, distinguished apart by the designation, the "first," "second," or "third" Township "upon the St. Lawrence," or "upon the Bay of Quinté," as the case might be.

It is impossible to say how far the work of surveying had progressed from Lake St. Francis westward, before the close of the war; it is very probable, however, that only a base line had been run, and some temporary mark placed to indicate the corners of each township. Such, indeed, is shown to be the case by the statement of Sheriff Sherwood, who says that his father Thomas Sherwood, who had been a subaltern in the 84th Reg., and who actually located on the first lot in the first concession of Elizabethtown, "was often called upon to run the side lines of the lots" for the settlers as they came one after another, and "to shew them their land." Mr. Sherwood was not a professional surveyor, but "he had the instruments and practically knew well how to use them, and he was ever ready to give his assistance and instructions to the new comers."

SURVEYING AROUND BAY QUINTÉ.

In the year 1783, Major Holland, Surveyor-General of Canada, received instructions from Sir Frederick Haldimand, Governor of the Province of Quebec, to proceed on duty to Western Canada. Prior to this, we have observed, there had been commenced a range of lots laid out at the easternmost limits of what now forms Canada West, to the extent of nine townships. Yet evidence is wanting that this range had been completed at the period stated. Holland set out with a sufficient staff of assistants and attachés, to simultaneously lay out several of the proposed townships along the St. Lawrence, and the Bay of Quinté. The party passed up the St. Lawrence, ascending the rapids in a brigade of batteaux manned by French boatmen. Surveyor Holland had, as his personal attendant, ——Bongard, who had been in the artillery under General Reidezel, of the Foreign Legion. From the son of this person, now living in Marysburgh, valuable information has been obtained, much of which has been substantiated by legal documents, published in connection with the law report of the trial respecting the Murney estate and the town of Kingston. Mr. Bongard says that Holland, as he passed up, detailed a deputy to each of the townships, stopping first at Oswegotchie, opposite Prescott, and that he passed up as far as the fourth township upon Bay Quinté, where he pitched his tent, and where he continued to hold his head-quarters, receiving the reports of the various Deputy-Surveyors as they were from time to time brought in. While it seems most probable that Holland came to the Upper Province in 1783, it is possible that he remained in Lower Canada until the spring of 1784, having deputed Surveyer Collins to commence a survey westward from the fort at Frontenac; or perhaps he visited that place with Collins whom he left to carry on the work during this first year.

Whether Surveyor-General Holland visited Fort Frontenac in the year 1783, or not, it was Deputy-Surveyor John Collins who made the first survey of the first township, and of the original town plot of Kingston. According to the sworn testimony of Gilbert Orser, who assisted Collins, in the year 1783, as well as others, the township was surveyed first, and the town plot afterward; although it appears that Holland's instructions were, first "to lay out proper reservations for the town and fort, and then to proceed and lay out the township, six miles square." The lots were to contain each 200 acres, to be 25 in number, each range. Mr. Collins placed a monument, it is averred, "at the south-east angle of lot 25, from which a line was run northerly the whole depth of the Township, six miles, where another stone monument was placed, making a line of blazed trees throughout." From this, it would seem, he continued to survey the township, leaving the land for the town, which he, no doubt, thought extensive enough, to be laid out into town lots, and leaving 40 feet of land, which was to form a road between the town and township. Respecting this line and lot 25, there has been a great deal of litigation. As nearly as the facts can be gathered, the following statement may be regarded as correct:

After Collins had completed the survey of the township, and had even made his returns, to the effect that it contained 25 lots, of 200 acres, he was importuned, or 'induced by the Commanding Officer at Fort Frontenac,' to make lot 25 contain only 100 acres, that more ground might thereby be had for the proposed town. More than this, it seems that there was some mistake in the said eastern side line, so as to subsequently limit lot 25 to even less than 100 acres. And, Capt. Michael Grass, when he took possession of this lot, in 1784, found that this line was inaccurately run. Deputy-Surveyor Kotte was requested to examine it; and finding there was an error, made representations to Government, who sent persons to correct it. One Deputy-Surveyor Tuffy was directed to re-survey the line, and he gave more land to lot 25. However, there was yet some error, which was a source of great trouble. Capt. Michael Grass sold this lot to Capt. Murney, who, subsequently finding it did not contain the amount of land which the patent assumed, applied legally for his rights.

The surveying party, among whom were some of those who subsequently settled in the township, and who must have belonged to Capt. Grass' company of refugees, returned to Sorel, where they spent the winter. At least this is the testimony of one of the grand-children of Capt. Grass. But if the surveying party did, this winter of 1783-4, retire from their work to Lower Canada, it appears unlikely they did the following winter. Indeed there are indications that surveying went on during the winter. In laying out the Townships, special attention was given to make the lots front squarely upon the Bay. In the winter the base line could be more closely run by the water edge upon the ice, than in summer, through the woods. We are informed, at the Crown Lands Department, that in some townships no posts or other marks had at first been found in the re-survey, although such were to be found in the 2nd concession. The inference was, that the posts planted in winter by the water, had, in the spring or summer been washed away, in the course of time. This, as may be supposed, led in time to great confusion, and no little litigation. For many years there was much trouble to establish the land marks all along the front; and cases are not wanting where it has been charged that fraudulent removals of posts were made. The straightforward settler, while engaged in his daily and yearly round of toil, thought not of the side lines of his farm, fully believing that a survey had been definitely fixed by marks that could not be altered, and too often when plenty and comfort had come, he was startled to find some one claiming some of his cleared or uncleared land. Although conscious that such and such were the boundaries of the land granted to him, it was not so easy to prove that such was the case. The annoyances of these direct and indirect attempts to disinherit, may easily be imagined. In this connection, the following letter may be given as exemplifying the feelings, if not the facts—perhaps both—which belonged to those days. It appeared in the Kingston *Gazette* in 1816, over the signature "A."

"SIR,—The situation of the old settlers in the Province of Upper Canada, is truly deplorable. These people settled in the wilds of Canada, then the Province of Quebec, under the surveys made by the acting Surveyor-General. Landmarks being established for the guidance of their improvements: no deeds were given them until the Parliament of Great Britain altered the Quebec bill, arranged a new constitution, similar to that they had lost during the rebellion, in the Province of New York, from whence they chiefly came to settle at Frontenac, now Kingston. After cultivating the country agreeably to those surveys for twenty years or more, deeds are issued to cover those lots, drawn and cultivated as above mentioned. The Surveyor-General, David William Smith, Speaker of the House of Assembly, knowing that these deeds were filled up by guess, the survey never having been made complete, wisely provided an Act of the Legislature to prevent the deeds from moving the old land-marks. This Act provides that when thirty freeholders apply to the Magistrates in session they shall make an assessment and collect the money to enable the Surveyor-General to erect monuments, in order to preserve their ancient land-marks and boundaries. What is the reason that this Act has not been complied with? Are the Magistrates all landholders and their sons Lawyers?

"An order from the Governor has lain in the Surveyor-General's office ever since the year 1801 for monuments to be erected in the Township of Kingston, agreeable to the intention of that Act. Why will not the Magistrates do their duty? The consequence is, that the licensed Surveyor, John Ryder, is running new lines every day, and moving the land-marks of the old settlers. People who have come into the country from the States, marry into a family, and obtain a lot of wild land, get John Ryder to move the land-marks, and instead of a wild lot, take by force a fine house and barn and orchard, and a well cultured farm, and turn the old Tory, (as he is called) out of his house, and all his labor for thirty years.

"These old settlers have suffered all that men could suffer; first in a seven years' rebellion in the revolutionized colonies; then came to a remote wilderness, some hundred miles from any inhabitant—not a road, not a cow, or an ox, or a horse to assist them; no bread during the winter, they wintered first at Cataraqui. A little pease and pork was all they could get until the ice gave way in the spring of 1785.

"The King, as an acknowledgment and mark of his approbation for the loyalty and sufferings of his faithful subjects, ordered lands to be granted them free from expense, and marked each man's name with the letters U. E., with a grant annexed to each child as it became of age, of two hundred acres of the waste lands of the crown.

"Now these children cannot get these lands agreeably to the intention of Government. They must sell their right to a set of speculators that hover round the seat of Government, or never get located. Or if they should have the fortune to get a location ticket, it is situated on rocks, and lakes, and barren lands, where they are worth nothing at all; the good lots being marked by the Surveyors, and located by those U. E. rights they have so purchased.

"Now, Sir, *was* I a scholar, I might draw you a much better description of this wickedness. But I have lived to see thirteen colonies, now States of America, severed from the British empire by the mal-administration of justice in the civil government of those colonies; the people's minds were soured to that degree that a few designing men overthrew the Government."

"After the conquest of Canada, the king ordered a thousand acres of land to be granted to each man. The land was granted; but the people to whom it was granted were deprived by a set of speculators, from ever getting a foot, unless they became tenants to those who, in a manner, had robbed them of their rights."

While the lots were generally made twenty chains in width, a few of the first townships were but nineteen, and consequently of greater depth to make the 200 acres, and the concessions were proportionally wider.

The base line being established, a second one, parallel thereto, was made at a distance generally of a mile and a quarter, allowance being made in addition, for a road. It is more than likely that in many townships the second line, or concession, was not immediately run out. The settlers could not easily traverse even a mile of woods, and for a time accommodation was made only at the front. But within a year, in most townships, the second row of lots had been surveyed and partially occupied. At the front line was always an allowance for a road of sixty feet, as well as at the second line for one of forty feet. The range of lots between the front and the second lines as well as between the second and third, and so on, was called a Concession, a term derived from the French, having reference to their mode of conferring land in the Lower Province, and peculiar to this counrty. Each concession was divided into lots of 200 acres each, the dividing lines being at right angles with the concession lines, and a quarter of a mile distant from each other. At intervals of two or three miles, a strip of forty feet between two lots was left, for a cross road. In Ameliasburgh it seems that this was neglected. The number of concessions depended on circumstances. Along the St. Lawrence, they numbered to even fifteen or sixteen. Along the bay they were seven and eight. Adolphustown has only four. The irregular course of the Bay Quinté, and the fronting of the townships upon its waters, gave rise to great irregularity in the interior lots, and produced a large number of Gores. This may be noticed moré especially in Sophiasburgh, and indeed throughout all of Prince Edward district.

Respecting the provision made for cross roads, Alex. Aitkins, who was Deputy Surveyor of Midland district for many years, says under date, 1797, in respect to the township of Sophiasburgh, "Mr. Kotte's orders 1785, were from Deputy Surveyor General, Mr. Collins, who was then at Kingston, to lay off cross roads between every six lots as he had done in the eastern part of the province, from township number one, now Charlotteburgh, to township number eight Elizabethtown, and, of no doubt, they would be found at the waters' edge on the Bay Quinté."

By looking at the township maps of the bay, it will be seen that the lots of the first three townships, are numbered from west to east, while as we have seen, the townships were numbered from east to west. It is inferred from this fact that the surveyor conducted his survey along the front, planting posts to mark the division of lots, and leaving allowance for roads, but did not complete the concessions until the breadth of the townships had been determined, when it was done from west to east, the lots being numbered accordingly.

The surveyor continued to chain the front, upon the north shore of the bay, until he reached the turn in the bay at the western point of Adolphustown. This portion of territory was divided into four townships.

The surveyor then crossed the bay and proceeded from the Upper Gap, to lay out lots in an irregular manner upon the water, along the bay and the lake to, and around Smith's Bay, and along Black Creek; also upon the east shore of Picton Bay. This constituted the fifth township. Following the bay shore of Prince Edward peninsula from Picton Bay, along the High Shore and around Green Point, another, the sixth township, was laid out; the lots always fronting on the bay. Still following the bay, the seventh township was created, the western boundary of which brought the surveyor to the head of the bay, or Carrying Place.

Turning eastward along the north shore of the bay, the eight township was laid out. Likewise, the ninth township, which brought the surveyor to a tract of land which had been reserved for, and given to the faithful Mohawk Indians. Passing by the present township of Tyendinaga, still another township was laid out fronting upon the Mohawk Bay, and Napanee River. This constituted the tenth town ship, Richmond. Thus the surveyors had made a complete circuit of the bay. These townships were, for many a day, designated by the numeral prefix; even yet may be found gray haired individuals who speak of them in no other way. Subsequently, however, these townships had given to them respectively, the royal names of Kingston, Ernesttown, Fredericksburgh, Adolphustown, Marysburgh, Ameliasburgh, Sophiasburgh; and the noble ones of Sidney, Thurlow, and Richmond.

There would at the present time, be nothing so interesting to the settlers of the bay, than to read a diary of the events connected with the original survey. Surveying the wilderness is weary work at any time; but when the persons who take part in striking the lines and fixing the boundaries, have constantly in mind that when their survey is completed, they cannot return to civilization and the comforts of a home, but that they have to remain to become citizens of the forest, they must experience many a heart pang. Yet there seems to have been a lightheartedness with most of them. The camp fire at night witnessed many pleasant hours of jovial passtime. Singing, storytelling, wiled away agreeably many an hour. Accompanying Collins' surveying party, was one Purdy, who gained no little renown as a capital singer.

We will close our remarks upon the original survey by giving the statement of Gourlay. He says that "such was the haste to get land surveyed and given away, that ignorant and careless men were employed to measure it out, and such a mess did they make of their land measuring, that one of the present surveyors informed me that in running new lines over a great extent of the province, he found spare room for a whole township in the midst of those laid out at an early period. It may readily be conceived, upon consideration of this fact, what blundering has been committed, and what mistakes stand for correction."

CHAPTER XVI.

CONTENTS—The term Concession—First Concession of Land in Canada—The Carignan Regiment—Seigniories—Disproportion of the sexes—Females sent from France—Their appearance—Settling them—Marriage allowance—The last seigniory—New Longeuil—Seigniory at Frontenac—Grants to Refugees—Officers and men—Scale of granting—Free of expense—Squatting—Disbanded soldiers—Remote regions—A wise and beneficent policy—Impostors—Very young officers—Wholesale granting of land—Republicans coming over—Covetous—False pretentions—Government had to discriminate—Rules and regulations—Family lands—Bounty—Certificates—Selling claims—Rear concessions—Transfer of location ticket—Land board—Tardiness in obtaining titles to real estate—Transfer by bond—Jobbing—Sir Wm. Pulleney—Washington—Giving lands to favorites—Reserves—Evil results—The Family Compact—Extract from Playter—Extract from Lord Durham—From Gourlay—Recompense to Loyalists—Rations—Mode of drawing land—Land Agent—Broken front—Traitor Arnold—Tyendinaga.

CONCESSION OF LANDS TO THE FRENCH.

It has been stated that the term concession, as well as the system of granting land to disbanded soldiers, was derived from the French. The first concession of lands to soldiers took place in 1665, to the Carignan Regiment, a name derived from a Prince of the house of Savoy, which came to New France with the first Viceroy. It was a distinguished corps in the French Infantry, having won renown on many a bloody field, and carried death to many an Iroquois Indian. The Indians having sought peace from the French, leave was granted to this regiment to permanently settle in the New World. Titles to land was conferred according to rank, and as well, sums of money to assist in the clearing of land. "The officers who were mostly noblesse obtained seigniories with their late soldiers for vassals." The settlement of this body of men increased the disproportion between the males and females in Canada. The home government considerately took steps to remedy this abnormal state of things and despatched "several hundred from old France." They "consisted of tall, short, fair, brown, fat and lean." These females were offered to such of the men as had means to support a wife. In a few days they were all disposed of. The Governor-General then distributed to the newly married ones "oxen, cows, hogs, fowls, salted beef," as well as money.—(*Smith.*)

The original grants of land by the French Government under the feudal system, was into seigniories. These were subdivided into parishes, "whose extents were exactly defined by De Vandreuil and Bigon, September 1721." For these grants of seigniorial tenure, certain acts of fealty were to be performed. pursuant to the custom of Paris.

After the British supremacy, grants of land were still made by government in Lower Canada. The last seigniory was conferred by the French in April, 1734, to Chevalier de Longeuil, and is known as New Longeuil. It constitutes the western boundary of the Lower Province.

CONCESSION OF LANDS TO THE LOYALISTS.

We have elsewhere seen that the first person, other than the natives, to possess land in Upper Canada, was De la Salle, the discoverer of the Mississippi River, to whom was granted a seigniory at Cataraqui, of four leagues, including the fort, and the islands in front of the four leagues of territory. Wolfe, Gage and Amherst Islands.

At the close of the war in 1783, it was determined by government to confer grants of land to the refugee loyalists in Canada, on the same scale to officers and men as had been done after the conquest of Canada, 1763, with the exception that all loyalists under the rank of subaltern were to receive 200 acres. The grants to the disbanded soldiers and loyalists, were to be made free of every expense.

In some of the townships, the settlers were squatting along the St. Lawrence and Bay Quinté, until late in the summer and fall of 1784, waiting to know the location of their lots. This might easily be, as although the forest had been surveyed, the lots had not been numbered. So, although the refugee soldier had his location ticket for a certain lot, it was often a long tedious time before he could know its precise situation.

The front part of the first, second, third, fourth and fifth townships upon the bay were definitely disposed of to disbanded soldiers and refugees, formed into companies. But the lands, then considered more remote, as along the north shore of Hay Bay, in the third and fourth towns; in some parts of the fifth; and more particularly along the shores of the western extremity of the bay, were at the service of any one who might venture to settle. It was considered quite in the remote part of the earth. Even the head of Picton Bay was considered a place which would hardly be settled. The result was, that many of the choice lots were taken up in the eight and ninth towns, before they were surveyed.

The policy pursued by the British Government, in recognizing the services of those who served in the British army against the rebels, and in recompensing the losses sustained by those who adhered to the British Crown in America, was most wise and beneficient. There were a few deserving ones in suffering circumstances, who failed to get the bounty so wisely granted. This sometimes was the result of the individual's own neglect, in not advancing his claims; sometimes the fault of an agent who, too intent in getting for himself, forget those entrusted to his care. While a small number thus remained without justice, there were on the other hand, a large number who succeeded unworthily in obtaining grants. It is no cause for wonder, that out of the large number who composed the U. E. Loyalists, there would be found a certain number who would not hesitate to so represent, or misrepresent their case, that an undue reward would be accorded. Finding the government on the giving hand, they scrupled not to take advantage of its parental kindness. In later days we have seen the United States, when in the throes of a great civil war, bleeding at every point of the body politic, by the unprincipled contractors and others, who the most loudly proclaimed their patriotism. In 1783, when a rebellion had proved successful, and so had become a revolution, and the nation, from which a branch had been struck off, was most anxious to repay those who had preferred loyalty to personal aggrandizement, we may not wonder that there were some willing to take all they could get.

It is also related that certain officers of the regiments were in the habit of putting each of their children, however young, upon the strength of the regiment, with the view of securing him land, and hence arose an expression the "Major won't take his pap," and "half pay officers never die," as the officer placed on half pay when a year old, would long enjoy it. But it will be often found that this mode was adopted by those in authority, as the most convenient to confer favors upon the chief officers, although a very ridiculous one.

For many a year no strict rules for discrimination, were observed in the granting of lands in Canada, and the petitions which literally crowded upon the government, were, in the main, promptly complied with. The time came, however, when more care had to be observed, for not a few of those who had actually rebelled, or had sympathized with the rebels, finding less advantages from republicanism than had been promised, and with chagrin, learning that those, whose homesteads and lands they had assisted to confiscate, had wrought out new homes upon land, conferred by a government more liberal, and of a nobler mind than the *parvenu* government, which had erected a new flag upon American soil, looked now with longing, covetous eyes toward the northern country, which those they had persecuted, had converted from a wilderness to comfortable homes. The trials of the first settlement had been overcome. The occasional visit of a Canadian pioneer to his old home in the States, where he told the pleasing tale of success, notwithstanding their cruelty, caused some to envy their hard earned comforts, and even led some who had been the worst of rebels, to set out for Canada with a view of asserting their loyalty and, thereby of procuring lands. Not a few of such unworthy ones succeeded for a time in procuring lands. It therefore became necessary, on the part of the government, to exact the most searching examination of parties petitioning for land. No reference is here made to those who came into the province in response to the invitation proclaimed by Governor Simcoe; but to those who entered under false colors, prior to the time of Upper Canada being set apart from Lower Canada.

Extracts from the Rules and Regulations for the conduct of the Land Office Department, dated Council Chamber, 17th February, 1789, for the guidance of the Land Boards.

"4th. The safety and propriety of admitting the petitioner to become an inhabitant of this Province being well ascertained to the satisfaction of the Board, they shall administer to every such person the oaths of fidelity and allegiance directed by law; after which the Board shall give every such petitioner a certificate to the Surveyor General or any person authorized to act as an Agent or Deputy Surveyor for the district within the trust of that Board, expressing the ground of the petitioner's admission, and such Agent or Deputy Surveyor shall, within two days after the presentment of the certificate, assign the petitioner a single lot of about two hundred acres, describing the same with due certainty and accuracy under his signature. But the said certificate shall, nevertheless, have no effect if the petitioner shall not enter upon the location, and begin the improvement and cultivation thereof within one year from the date of such assignment, or if the petitioner shall have had lands assigned to him before that time in any other part of the Province.

"7th. The respective Boards shall, on petition from the Loyalists already settled in the Upper Districts for the allotment of lands under the instructions to the Deputy Surveyor General of the 2nd of June, 1787, or under prior or other orders for assigning portions to their families, examine into the grounds of such requests and claims, and being well satisfied of the justice thereof, they shall grant certificates for such further qualities of lands as the said instructions and orders may warrant to the acting Surveyors of their Districts respectively, to be by them made effectual in the manner before mentioned, but to be void, nevertheless, if prior to the passing the grant in form, it shall appear to the Government that such additional locations have been obtained by fraud, and that of these the Boards transmit to the office of the Governor's Secretary, and to each others, like reports and lists as hereinbefore, as to the other locations directed.

"8th. And to prevent individuals from monopolizing such spots as contain mines, minerals, fossils, and conveniences for mills, and other similar advantages of a common and public nature, to the prejudice of the general interest of the settler, the Surveyor-General and his Agents or Deputy Surveyors in the different districts, shall confine themselves in the location to be made by them upon certificates of the respective Boards, to such lands only as are fit for the common purpose of husbandry; and they shall reserve all other spots aforementioned, together with all such as may be fit and useful for ports and harbours, or works of defence, or such as contain valuable timber for ships, building or other purposes, conveniently situated for water carriage, in the hands of the Crown. and they shall, without delay, give all particular information to the Governor or Commander-in-Chief for the time being, of all such spots as are hereinbefore directed to be reserved to the Crown, that order may be taken respecting the same. And the more effectually to prevent abuses and to put individuals on their guard in this respect, any certificate of location given contrary to the true intent and meaning of this regulation is hereby declared to be null and void, and a special order of the Governor and Council made necessary to pledge the faith of Government for granting of any such spots as are directed to be reserved.

FAMILY LANDS AND ADDITIONAL BOUNTY.

"Certificate of the Board appointed by His Excellency the Governor, for the District of———, in the Province of Quebec, under the rules and regulations for the conduct of the Land Office Department.

"Dated, Council Chamber, Quebec, 17th February, 1789.

"The bearer———, having on the———day of———, preferred to the Board a Petition addressed to His Excellency the Governor in Council, for a grant of———acres of land in the Township of———in the District of———. We have examined into his character and pretentions, and find that he has received——— acres of land in the Township of———, in the District of———, and that he settled on and has improved the same, and that he is entitled to a further assignment of———acres,———in conformity to the seventh articles of the rules and regulations aforementioned.

"Given at the Board at this———day of———, one thousand seven hundred and———.

"To———,

"Acting Surveyor for the District of———.

CERTIFICATE OF THE ACTING SURVEYOR.

"I assign to the bearer———the lot No.———in the Township of———, in the District of———, containing———acres,——— chains, which lands he is hereby authorized to occupy and improve, and having improved the same, he shall receive the same grant thereof, to him and his heirs or devisee in due form on such terms as it shall please His Majesty to ordain, and all persons are desired to take notice that this assignment and all others of a similar nature are not transferable, by purchase, donation or otherwise, on any pretence whatever, except by an act under the signature of the Board for the District in which the lands are situated, which is to be endorsed upon this Certificate.

"Given at———, this———day of———, one thousand seven hundred and———.

To———,

Acting Surveyor for the District of———.

But there were many a one who drew land, and never even saw it. It was quickly, thoughtlessly sometimes, sold for little or nothing. Sometimes for a quart of rum. The right jolly old soldier would take no thought of the morrow. A few did not retain their lands, because they were of little value for agricultural purposes; but the majority because they were situated in that remote region in the 4th or 5th concession of the third town, or away up in the 2nd concesssion of sixth town, or a long way up in the eighth town. Rear concessions of even the first and second townships were looked upon doubtingly, as to whether the land was worth having. Often the land would not be looked after. It not unfrequently was the case that settlers upon the front who had drawn land also in the rear townships, disposed of the latter, not from any indifference as to its future value, but to obtain the immediate necessaries of life, as articles of clothing, or stock, or perhaps foo d, or seed grain, and now and then in later days to pay taxes. The certificates of the children, entitling them to land when of age, were often disposed of. Even officers found it convenient, or necessary to sell rear land to new comers, for ready money.

Thus it came to pass that a good many never took possession of the land which a prudent Government had granted them. The statement has been made that persons holding prominent positions at the time, and possessed of prudent forethought, as to the value which would in the future attach to certain lots, stood ready not only to accept offers to sell, but to induce the ignorant and careless to dispose of their claims. Consequently when patents were issued, several persons became patentees of large tracts of land, which had been drawn by individual Loyalists, whose names never appeared in the Crown Land Office. The transfer of a certificate or "location ticket," consisted in the seller writing his name upon the back of the ticket. Occasionally a ticket would exchange hands several times, so that at last when it was presented to obtain the deed, it was difficult to determine who was the owner. The power to thus transfer the certificates, was allowed for several years. But in time Government discovered the abuses which had arisen out of it, and decided that all patents should, thenceforward, be in the name of the person who originally drew the land. Not unfrequently these certificates were lost. The losers, upon claiming land, could not establish their rights; but Government, to meet this misfortune, created a Land Board for each Township, whose duty it was to examine and determine the claims of all who presented them.

The following extract of a letter will explain itself:

"*For the Kingston Gazette, June 1st*, 1816."

"It has long been a subject of deep regret in the minds of judicious persons, that the inhabitants of this Province should be so neglectful as they are in securing their titles of real estate. When the country was first settled, the grants of land from the crown, on account of the existing state of the Province, could not be immediately issued. The settlers, however, drew their lots and went into possession of them, receiving only tickets, or certificates, as the evidence of their right to them. In the meantime, exchanges and sales were made by transfers of the possession with bonds for conveyances when the deeds should be obtained from the Crown Office.

"This practice of transferring land by way of bond, being thus introduced, was continued by force of usage, after the cause of its introduction was removed. In too many instances it is still continued, although, by the death of the parties, and the consequent descent of estates to heirs under age, and other intervening privations, many disappointments, failures, and defects of title, are already experienced; and the evil consequences are becoming still more serious, as lands rise in value, become more settled and divided among assignees, devisees, &c. In a few years this custom, more prevalent perhaps in this Province, than elsewhere, will prove a fruitful source of litigation, unless the practice should be discontinued."

In connection with free grants of land, and a certain degree of indifference as to the value, there must necessarily arise more or less speculation or land-jobbing.

Sir William Pullency has been called the first land-jobber in Canada. In 1791, he bought up 1,500,000, at one shilling per acre, and soon after sold 700,000 at an average of eight shillings per acre. But land-jobbing is not peculiar to Canada, nor has its practice militated against the public character of eminent men, either here or abroad. General Washington was not only a Surveyor, but an extensive land-jobber, and thereby increased immensely his private fortune.

We have seen elsewhere, that a few private individuals were wont to buy the location tickets of all who desired to part with them, or whom they could induce to sell. In this way a few individuals came to own large quantities of land, even from the first. Afterward, there was often conferred by the authorities, quantities of land upon those connected with influential persons, or upon favorites. Subsequently the mode of reserving Crown and Clergy lands increased the evil. And it was an evil, a serious drawback; not alone that, but favorites procured land without any particular claim or right. The land thus held in reserve, being distributed among the settled lots in the several townships, was waste land, and a barrier to advancement. Each settler had to clear a road across his lot; but the Government lots, and those held by non-residents, remained without any road across them, except such paths as the absolute requirements of the settlers had caused them to make. In this way, the interests of the inhabitants were much retarded, and the welfare of the Province seriously damaged. The existence of the Family Compact prevented the removal of this evil, for many a year, while favorites enjoyed choice advantages. In 1817, "The House of Assembly in Upper Canada took into consideration the state of the Province, and among other topics, the injury arising from the reserve lands of the Crown and the Clergy." In laying out the townships in later years, "The Government reserved in the first concession, the 5th, 15th, and 20th lots; and the Clergy the 3rd, 10th, 17th, and 22nd. In the second concession, the Crown reserved the 4th, 11th, 21st, and 23rd; and the Clergy, the 2nd, 9th, and 16th. And thus in every two concessions, the Crown would have three lots in one, and four in the other, or seven in all; and the Clergy the same; or 14 lots reserved in every 48, or nearly one-third of the land in each concession, and in each township. The object of the reservation was to increase the value of such land by the improvements of the settlers around it. The object was selfish, as the reserve lands injured all those who did them good. It was difficulty enough to clear up the forests; but to leave so many lots in this forest state, was a difficulty added by the Crown. To have one-third of a concession uncleared and uncultivated, was an injury to the two-thirds cleared and cultivated. Large patches of forest, interspersed with cultivated land, obstructs the water courses, the air, and the light; nurtured wild animals and vermin destructive to crops and domestic creatures around a farm house; and especially, are injurious to roads running through them, by preventing the wind and the sun from drying the moisture. Besides, no taxes were paid by these wild lots for any public improvements; only from cultivated lands. The Assembly, however, were cut short in their work of complaint, by being suddenly prorogued by the Governor, whose Council was entirely against such an investigation. Here was the beginning of the Clergy Reserve agitation in the Provincial Parliament, which continued for many years."—(*Playter*).

In this connection, the following extract from a report of Lord Durham, will be found interesting:

"By official returns which accompany this report, it appears that, out of about 17,000,000 acres comprised within the surveyed districts of Upper Canada, less than 1,600,000 acres are yet unappropriated, and this amount includes 450,000 acres the reserve for roads, leaving less than 1,200,000 acres open to grant, and of this remnant 500,000 acres are required to satisfy claims for grants founded on pledges by the Government. In the opinion of Mr. Radenhurst, the really acting Surveyor-General, the remaining 700,000 consist for the most part of land inferior in position or quality. It may almost be said, therefore, that the whole of the public lands in Upper Canada have been alienated by the Government. In Lower Canada, out of 6,169,963 acres in the surveyed townships, nearly 4,000,000 acres have been granted or sold; and there are unsatisfied but indisputable claims for grants to the amount of about 500,000. In Nova Scotia nearly 6,000,000 acres of land have been granted, and in the opinion of the Surveyor-General, only about one-eighth of the land which remains to the Crown, or 300,000 acres is available for the purposes of settlement. The whole of Prince Edward's Island, about 1,400,000 acres, was alienated in one day. In New Brunswick 4,400,000 acres have been granted or sold, leaving to the Crown about 11,000,000, of which 5,500,000 are considered fit for immediate settlement.

"Of the lands granted in Upper and Lower Canada, upwards of 3,000,000 acres consist of 'Clergy Reserves,' being for the most part lots of 200 acres each, scattered at regular intervals over the whole face of the townships, and remaining, with few exceptions, entirely wild to this day. The evils produced by the system of reserving land for the Clergy have become notorious, even in this country; and a common opinion I believe prevails here, not only that the system has been abandoned, but that measures of remedy have been adopted. This opinion is incorrect in both points. In respect of every new township in both Provinces reserves are still made for the Clergy, just as before; and the Act of the Imperial Parliament which permits the sale of the Clergy Reserves, applies to only one-fourth of the quantity. The select committee of the House of Commons on the civil government of Canada reported in 1828, that " these reserved lands, as they are at present distributed over the country, retard more than any other circumstance the growth of the colony, lying as they do in detached portions of each township, and intervening between the occupations of actual settlers, who have no means of cutting roads through the woods and morasses, which thus separate them from their neighbours. This description is perfectly applicable to the present state of things. In no perceptible degree has the evil been remedied.

"The system of Clergy Reserves was established by the act of 1791, commonly called the Constitutional Act, which directed that, in respect of all grants made by the Crown, a quantity equal to one-seventh of the land so granted should be reserved for the clergy. A quantity equal to one-seventh of all grants would be one-eighth of each township, or of all the public land. Instead of this proportion, the practice has been, ever since the act passed, and in the clearest violation of its provisions, to set apart for the clergy in Upper Canada a seventh of all the land, which is a quantity equal to a sixth of the land granted. There have been appropriated for this purpose 300,000 acres, which legally, it is manifest, belong to the public. And of the amount for which Clergy Reserves have been sold in that Province, namely, £317,000 (of which about £100,000 have been already received and invested in the English funds,) the sum of about £45,000 should belong to the public.

"In Lower Canada, the same violation of the law has taken place, with this difference—that upon every sale of Crown and Clergy Reserves, a fresh reserve for the Clergy has been made, equal to one-fifth of such reserves. The result has been the appropriation for the clergy of 673,567 acres, instead of 446,000, being an excess of 227,559 acres, or half as much again as they ought to have received. The Lower Canada fund already produced by sales amounts to £50,000, of which, therefore, a third, or about £16,000, belong to the public. If, without any reform of this abuse, the whole of the unsold Clergy Reserves in both Provinces should fetch the average price at which such lands have hitherto sold, the public would be wronged to the amount of about £280,000; and the reform of this abuse will produce a certain and almost immediate gain to the public of £60,000. In referring, for further explanation of this subject, to a paper in the appendix which has been drawn up by Mr. Hanson, a member of the commission of inquiry which I appointed for the colonies. I am desirous of stating my own conviction that the clergy have had no part in this great misappropriation of the public property, but that it has arisen entirely from heedless misconception, or some other error, of the civil government of both Provinces."

"The great objection to reserves for the clergy is, that those for whom the land is set apart never have attempted, and never could successfully attempt, to cultivate or settle the property, and that, by special appropriation, so much land is withheld from settlers, and kept in a state of waste, to the serious injury of all settlers in its neighborhood. But it would be a great mistake to suppose that this is the only practice by which such injury has been, and still is, inflicted on actual settlers. In the two Canadas, especially, the practice of rewarding, or attempting to reward, public services by grants of public land, has produced, and is still producing, a degree of injury to actual settlers which it is difficult to conceive without having witnessed it. The very principal of such grants is bad, inasmuch as, under any circumstances, they must lead to an amount of appropriation beyond the wants of the community, and greatly beyond the proprietor's means of cultivation and settlement. In both the Canadas, not only has this principle been pursued with reckless profusion, but the local executive governments have managed, by violating or evading the instructions which they received from the Secretary of State, to add incalculably to the mischiefs that would have arisen at all events.

"In Upper Canada, 3,200,000 acres have been granted to "U. E. Loyalists," being refugees from the United States, who settled in the province before 1787, and their children; 730,000 acres to Militia men; 450,000 acres to discharged Soldiers and Sailors; 225,000 acres to Magistrates and Barristers; 136,000 acres to Executive Councillors, and their families; 50,000 acres to five Legislative Councillors, and their families; 36,900 acres to Clergymen, as private property; 264,000 to persons contracting to make surveys; 92,526 acres to officers of the Army and Navy; 500,000 acres for the endowment of schools; 48,520 acres to Colonel Talbot; 12,000 acres to heirs of General Brock, and 12,000 acres to Dr. Mountain, a former Bishop of Quebec; making altogether, with the Clergy Reserves, nearly half of all the surveyed land in the province. In Lower Canada, exclusively of grants to refugee loyalists, as to the amount of which the Crown Lands' Department could furnish me with no information, 450,000 acres having been granted to Militiamen, to Executive Councillors 72,000 acres, to Governor Milne, about 48,000 acres, to Mr. Cushing and another, upwards of 100,000 acres (as a reward for giving information in a case of high treason), to officers and soldiers 200,000 acres, and to "leaders of townships" 1,457,209 acres, making altogether, with the Clergy Reserves, rather more than half of the surveyed lands originally at the disposal of the Crown.

"In Upper Canada, a very small proportion (perhaps less than a tenth) of all the land thus granted, has been even occupied by settlers, much less reclaimed and cultivated. In Lower Canada, with the exception of a few townships bordering on the American frontier, which have been comparatively well settled, in despite of the proprietors, by American squatters, it may be said that nineteen-twentieths of these grants are still unsettled, and in a perfectly wild state.

"No other result could have been expected in the case of those classes of grantees whose station would preclude them from settling in the wilderness, and whose means would enable them to avoid exertion for giving immediate value to their grants; and unfortunately, the land which was intended for persons of a poorer order, who might be expected to improve it by their labor, has, for the most part, fallen into the hands of land-jobbers of the class just mentioned, who have never thought of settling in person, and who retain the land in its present wild state, speculating upon its acquiring a value at some distant day, when the demand for land shall have increased through the increase of population.

"In Upper Canada, says Mr. Bolton, himself a great speculator and holder of wild land, "the plan of granting large tracts of land to gentlemen who have neither the muscular strength to go into the wilderness, nor perhaps, the pecuniary means to improve their grants, has been the means of a large part of the country remaining in a state of wilderness. The system of granting land to the children of U. E Loyalists has not been productive of the benefits expected from it. A very small proportion of the land granted to them has been occupied or improved. A great proportion of such grants were to unmarried females, who very readily disposed of them for a small consideration, frequently from £2 to £5 for a grant of 200 acres. The grants made to young men were also frequently sold for a very small consideration; they generally had parents with whom they lived, and were therefore not disposed to move to their grants of lands, but preferred remaining with their families. I do not think one-tenth of the lands granted to U. E. Loyalists has been occupied by the persons to whom they were granted, and in a great proportion of cases not occupied at all." Mr. Raudenhurst says, "the general price of these grants was from a gallon of rum up to perhaps £6, so that while millions of acres were granted in this way, the settlement of the Province was not advanced, nor the advantage of the grantee secured in the manner that we may suppose to have been contemplated by government." He also mentions amongst extensive purchasers of these grants, Mr. Hamilton, a member of the Legislative Council, who bought about 100,000 acres. Chief Justices Emslie and Powell, and Solicitor General Gray, who purchased from 20,800 to 50,000 acres; and states that several members of the Executive and Legislative Councils, as well as of the House of Assembly, were "very large purchasers."

"In Lower Canada, the grants to "Leaders and Associates" were made by an evasion of instructions which deserve a particular description.

"By instructions to the Local Executive immediately after the passing of the Constitutional Act, it was directed that "because great inconveniences had theretofore arisen in many of the colonies in America, from the granting excessive quantities of land to particular persons who have never cultivated or settled the same, and have thereby prevented others more industrious, from improving such lands; in order, therefore, to prevent the like inconveniences in future, no farm-lot should be granted to any person being master or mistress of a family in any township to be laid out which should contain more than 200 acres." The instructions then invest the governor with a discretionary power to grant additional quantities in certain cases, not exceeding 1,000 acres. According to these instructions 200 acres should have been the general amount. 1,200 the maximum, in special cases to be granted to any individual. The greater part, however, of the land (1,457,200 acres) was granted, in fact, to individuals at the rate of from 10,000 to 50,000 to each person. The evasion of the regulations was managed as follows: A petition, signed by from 10 to 40 or 50 persons, was presented to the Executive Council, praying for a grant of 1,200 acres to each person, and promising to settle the land so applied for. Such petitions were, I am informed, always granted, the Council being perfectly aware that, under a previous agreement between the applicants (of which the form was prepared by the then Attorney General, and sold publicly by the law stationers of Quebec), five-sixths of the land was to be conveyed to one of them, termed leader, by whose means the grant was obtained. In most cases the leader obtained the most of the land which had been nominally applied for by fifty persons."

Upon this subject we further give as worthy of attention, although we will not endorse all that is said, the remarks made by Mr. Robert Gourlay in his "Statistical Account." He says, "when we look back into the history of old countries, and observe how landed property was first established; how it was seized upon, pulled about, given away, and divided in all sorts of ways, shapes, and quantities; how it was bequeathed, burthened, entailed, and leased in a hundred forms; when we consider how dark were the days of antiquity,—how grossly ignorant and savage were our remote forefathers, we cannot be so much surprised at finding ourselves heirs to confusion; and, that, in these old countries, entanglement continues to be the order of the day. But when civilized men were quietly and peaceably to enter into the occupancy of a new region, where all could be adjusted by the square and compass; and when order, from the beginning, could have prevented for ever all possibility of doubt, and dispute, and disturbance; how deplorable is it to know, that in less than a life-time, even the simplest affairs should get into confusion! and so it is already in Upper Canada, to a lamentable degree. Boundaries of land are doubtful and disputed: deeds have been mislaid, lost, unfounded, forged: they have been passed again and again in review before commissioners: they have been blotted and blurred: they have got into the repositories of attornies and pettifogging lawyers; while courts of justice are every day adding doubt to doubt, delay to delay, and confusion to confusion; with costs, charges, cheating.

"Things are not yet beyond the reach of amendment, even in the old settlements. In the new, what a glorious task it is to devise plans for lasting peace and prosperity!—to arrange in such a way, as to bar out a world of turmoil in times to come!

"The present very unprofitable and comfortless condition of Upper Canada must be traced back to the first operations of Simcoe. With all his honesty, and energy, and zeal for settling the Province, he had really no sound views on the subject, and he was infinitely too lavish in disposing of the land—infinitely too much hurried in all his proceedings. In giving away land to individuals, no doubt, he thought he would give these individuals an interest in the improvement of the country,—an inducement to settle in it, and draw to it settlers; but he did not consider the character and condition of most of his favorites; many of them officers in the army, whose habits did not accord with business, and less still with solitude and the wilderness; whose hearts were in England, and whose wishes were intent on retirement thither. Most of them did retire from Upper Canada, and considering, as was really the case, their land grants of little value, forgot and neglected them. This was attended with many bad consequences. Their lands became bars to improvement; as owners they were not known; could not be heard of; could not be applied to, or consulted with, about any measure for public advantage. Their promises under the Governor's hand, their land board certificates, their deeds, were flung about and neglected. But mischief greater than all this, arose, is, and will be, from the badness of surveys. Such was the haste to get land given away, that ignorant and careless men were employed to measure it out, and such a mess did they make of their land-measuring, that one of the present surveyors informed me, that in running new lines over a great extent of the Province, he found spare room for a whole township in the midst of those laid out at an early period. It may readily be conceived, upon consideration of this fact, what blundering has been committed, and what mistakes stand for correction. Boundary lines in the wilderness are marked by blazing, as it is called, that is, chopping off with an axe, a little bark from such trees as stand nearest to the line. Careless surveyors can readily be supposed to depart wide of the truth with this blazing: their measuring chains cannot run very straight, and their compass needles, where these are called in aid, may be greatly diverted from the right direction by ferruginous substances in the neighbourhood, as spoken of. In short, numerous mistakes and errors of survey have been made and discovered: much dispute has arisen therefrom; and I have been told infinite mischief is still in store. It occurred to me, while in Canada, and it was one of the objects which, had a commission come home, I meant to have pressed on the notice of government, that a complete new survey and map of the Province should be executed; and at the same time a book, after the manner of Doomsday-book, written out and published, setting forth all the original grants, and describing briefly but surely all property both public and private. I would yet most seriously recommend such to be set about. It might be expensive now, but would assuredly save, in time to come, a pound for every penny of its cost."

We have seen elsewhere that, in the terms of peace made at Paris when hostilities ceased, justice was not done to the American Loyalists. But subsequently, when their claims became known to the British public, there was uttered no uncertain sound, upon the floor of Parliament, respecting the duty resting upon England towards the devoted but distressed loyalists who had laid all upon the altar of patriotism; and to the honor of England be said, every step was now taken to provide some recompense for the United Empire Loyalists. It is true, the old homes with their comforts and associations could not be restored; the wilderness was to be their home, a quiet conscience their comfort, and their associations those of the pioneer for many a day. But, what could be done, was done by the Crown to render their circumstances tolerable. Extensive grants of land were granted, not alone to the disbanded soldier according to rank, but to every one who had become a refugee. Three years supply of rations were allowed to all, as well as clothing; and certain implements were furnished with which to clear the land and prepare it for agriculture. The scale of granting lands was, to a field officer 5000 acres, captain 3000, subaltern 2000, private 200. The loyalists were ranked, with the disbanded soldiers, according to their losses, and services rendered, having taken the usual oath of allegiance; and all obtained their grants free of every expense. In 1798, complaints having been made to the Imperial Government respecting the profuse manner of granting lands, royal instructions were given to Gen. Hunter to limit the allowance to a quantity from 200 to 1,200. The grants of land when large, were not to be in blocks; but few secured more than 200 acres upon the front townships. The original mode of granting lands, at least to the soldiers, was by lot. The process was simple. The number of each lot, to be granted in each concession, was written on a separate piece of paper, and all were placed in a hat and well shaken, when each one to receive land, drew a piece of paper from the hat. The number upon the paper was the number of his lot. He then received a printed location ticket. In drawing lots, no one felt any particular anxiety. They were yet unacquainted with the country, they had not seen the land, and one number was as likely to prove as valuable as another.

It would seem that the Surveyor acted as Land Agent. Having surveyed the lots, he prepared the ballot, and arranged the time and place for the settlers to draw. It was no doubt this original mode of drawing by lottery, which gave the provincial term *drawing* land. We have the testimony of Ex-Sheriff Sherwood, that the Surveyor discharged this office. He recollects "Esquire Collins;" he was at his father's house, and his father assisted in the matter of drawing with those who had assembled for the purpose. The Surveyor had a plan by him, and as each drew his lot, his name was written immediately upon the map. Many of the plans, with names upon them, may be seen in the Crown Land Department. Some of the settlers upon the front acquired much more land than others by reason of the "broken front." It often happened that the base line, running from one cove of the Bay to another, left between it and the water a large strip of land. This "broken front" belonged to the adjacent 200 acres, so that often the fortunate party possessed even 50 or 100 acres extra.

One of the noted individuals to whom land was granted in Upper Canada, was Arnold the Traitor. 18,000 acres was given him, and £10,000.

The tract of land now constituting the Township of Tyendinaga, having been purchased from the Mississaugas, was deeded to the Mohawks. The deed bears the date of 1804. The land is granted to "the chiefs, warriors, people, women of the Six Nations." The chief, at the time they settled, was Capt. John Deserontyon.

CHAPTER XVII.

CONTENTS—Lines—Western Settlement, 1783—Population—Settlement upon St. Lawrence and Bay—Number, 1784—Proclamation to Loyalists—Society disturbed—Two kinds of Loyalists—St. Lawrence and Bay favorable for Settlement—Government Provisions—State of the Loyalists—Serving out Rations—Clothes—Utensils for clearing and farming—The Axe—Furniture—Attacking a last enemy—Tents—Waiting for their Lots—"Bees"—Size of dwellings—Mode of building—Exchanging work—Bedsteads—Clearing—Fireing trees—Ignorance of Pioneer Life—Disposing of the Wood—No beast of burden—Logging—Determination—All Settlers on a common ground—Additional Refugees—Advance—Simcoe's Proclamation, 1792—Conditions of Grants—The Response—Later Settlers—Questionable Loyalists—Yankees longing for Canada—Loyalty in 1812.

THE SETTLEMENT OF UPPER CANADA.

"CANADA."

BY ALEXANDER M'LACHLAN.

Land of mighty lake and forest!
Where the winter's locks are hoarest;
Where the summer's leaf is greenest;
And the winter's bite the keenest;
Where the autumn's leaf is searest,
And her parting smile the dearest;
Where the tempest rushes forth,
From his caverns of the north,
With the lightnings of his wrath,
Sweeping forests from his path;
Where the cataract stupendous
Lifteth up her voice tremendous;
Where uncultivated nature
Rears her pines of giant stature;
Sows her jagged hemlocks o'er,
Thick as bristles on the boar;
Plants the stately elm and oak
Firmly in the iron rock;
Where the crane her course is steering,
And the eagle is careering,
Where the gentle deer are bounding,
And the woodman's axe resounding;
Land of mighty lake and river,
To our hearts thou'rt dear forever!

Thou art not a land of story;
Thou art not a land of glory;
No tradition, tale, nor song,
To thine ancient woods belong;
No long line of bards and sages
Looking to us down the ages;
No old heroes sweeping by,
In their warlike panoply;
Yet heroic deeds are done,
Where no battle's lost or won—
In the cottage, in the woods,
In the lonely solitudes—
Pledges of affection given,
That will be redeemed in heaven.

In 1783, when a regular survey and settlement of Western Canada commenced, the inhabitants of the Lower Province extended westward, only a few miles above Coteau du lac, upon the St. Lawrence, at Lake St. Francis; but not a house was built within several miles of the division line of the two Provinces, which is above Montreal, about 40 miles, on the north shore. On the south side there was the Fort of Oswegotchie. Besides the squatters around the military posts at Carleton Island, Oswego, and Niagara, there were a few inhabitants at Detroit and Sandwich, of French origin, where a settlement had sprung up in 1750.

The entire population of all Canada at this time, has been estimated at 120,000, including both the French and English. Although refugees had squatted here and there upon the frontier, near to the several military posts, it was not until 1784 that the land, now surveyed into lots, was actually bestowed upon the Loyalists; yet it was mainly disbanded soldiers that received their "location tickets" in the year 1784. The grants were made to the corps under Jessup, upon the St. Lawrence, and under Rogers upon the Bay; and to Butler's Rangers at Niagara, at the same time, or very nearly. During the same season, a settlement was made upon the Niagara frontier and at Amherstburgh, by the Loyalists who had found refuge at the contiguous Forts. It is supposed that the number who became settlers this year, 1784, in Upper Canada was about 10,000. Thus the Province of Upper Canada was planted; thus the Refugees and disbanded soldiers found themselves pioneers in the wilds of Canada. Was it for this they had adhered to the Crown—had taken up arms—had sacrificed their all?

At the close of hostilities, a proclamation was issued to the Loyalists, to rendezvous at Sacket's Harbour, or Carleton Island, Oswego, Niagara, and Isle aux Mois, the principal military posts upon the frontier.

The tempest of war which had swept across the American Continent, severing thirteen Colonies from the parent trunk, had roughly disturbed the elements of society. It resulted that the cessation of hostilities left a turbulent ocean, which required time to compose itself. There were Loyalists who would not live under a flag alien to Britain. There were those whose circumstances would have induced them to abide the evil that had overtaken them in the dismemberment of the British Empire; but the fierce passions of the successful rebels rendered a peaceful or safe existence of the Loyalists among them impossible. Driven they were, away from their old homes. There were those who had been double minded, or without choice, ready to go with the successful party. Such wandered here and there looking for the best opportunity to secure self aggrandisement. It is of the first two classes we speak.

Forced by cruel circumstances, to become pioneers in a wilderness, there could not be found in America, a more favourable place whereupon to settle than along the banks of the St. Lawrence, and around the irregular shores of Bay Quinté, with its many indentations. They had to convert the wood-covered land into homes. The trees had to be felled, and the land prepared for grain, and the fruit of the soil to be obtained for sustenance within three years, when Government provisions would be discontinued. It can readily be understood that a water communication to and from the central points of settlement, as well as access to fishing waters, was most desirable. The smooth waters of the upper St. Lawrence and the Bay Quinté constituted a highway of the most valuable kind, for the only mode of travel was by the canoe, or flat-bottomed batteau, which was supplied by the Government in limited numbers; and in winter by rudely constructed hand-sleighs, along the icy shores.

THE FIRST SETTLERS.

The settlers of Upper Canada, up to 1790, may be divided into those who were forced away from the States by persecution, during and after the war; the disbanded troops; and a nobler class, who left the States, being unwilling to live under other than British rule.

To what extent were these pioneers fitted and prepared to enter upon the truly formidable work of creating homes, and to secure the necessaries of life for their families. But few of them possessed ought of worldly goods, nearly all were depending upon the bounty of Government. In the first place, they were supplied with rations; which consisted of flour, pork, and a limited quantity of beef, a very little butter, and as little salt. We find in Rev. Mr. Carroll's "Past and Present" that "their mode of serving out rations was rather peculiar." "Their plan was, to prevent the appearance of partiality, for the one who acted as Commissary, either to turn his back, take one of the articles, and say, 'who will have this?' or else the provisions were weighed, or assorted, and put into heaps, when the Commissary went around with a hat, and received into it something which he would again recognize, as a button, a knife, &c.; after which he took the articles out of the hat, as they came uppermost, and placed one on each of the piles in rotation. Every person then claimed the parcel on which he found the article which he had thrown into the hat."

They were also supplied with "clothes for three years, or until they were able to provide these articles for themselves. They consisted of coarse cloth for trowsers and Indian blankets for coats, and of shoes; beside, each received a quantity of seed grain to sow upon the newly cleared land, with certain implements of husbandry. To each was allotted an axe, a hoe, and a spade; a plough, and one cow, were allotted to two families; a whip and cross-cut saw to every fourth family; and, even boats were provided for their use, and placed at convenient points;" and "that nothing might seem to be wanting, on the part of the Government, even portable corn mills, consisting of steel plates, turned by hand like a coffee-mill, were distributed among the settlers." We have learned they were also supplied with nails, hand-saws and other materials for building. To every five families were given a "set of tools," such as chisels and augers, of various sizes, and drawing-knives; also pick-axes, and sickles for reaping. But, unfortunately, many of these implements were of inforior quality. The axe, with which the burden of the work was to be done, was unlike the light implement now in use, it was but a short-handled ship axe, intended for quite a different use than chopping trees and clearing land. Notwithstanding, these various implements, thoughtfully provided by Government, how greatly must they have come short in meeting the varied wants of the settler, in his isolated clearing, far separated from places whereat things necessary could be procured. However, the old soldier, with his camp experience, was enabled by the aid of his tools, to make homely and rude articles of domestic use. And, in farming, he constructed a rough, but servicable plow, and harrow, and made handles for his scythe.

Thus provisioned and clothed, and thus armed with implements of industry, the old soldiers advanced to the attack of a last enemy, the wild woods. Unlike any previous warfare, was this lifetime struggle. With location ticket in hand, they filed into the batteaux to ascend the rapids. A certain number of batteaux joined together, generally about twenty or twenty-five, formed a brigade, which was placed under the command of a suitable officer; if not one who had in previous days, led them against the foe. It is quite impossible to conceive of the emotions which found a place in the breasts of the old veterans as they journeyed along wearily from day to day, each one bringing them nearer to the spot on which the tent was to be pitched for the last time. Eagerly, no doubt, they scanned the thickly wooded shores as they passed along. Curiously they examined the small settlement, clustering around Cataraqui. And, it cannot be doubted, when they entered the waters of the lovely Bay Quinté, the beauty of the scene created a feeling of joy and reconciliation to their lot, in being thus cast upon a spot so rich in natural beauty. These disbanded soldiers, at least each family, had a canvass tent capable of accommodating, in a certain way, from eight to ten persons. These were pitched upon the shore, at first in groups, until each person had learned the situation of his lot, when he immediately removed thereto. But there were by no means enough tents to give cover to all, and many had only the friendly trees for protection. The first steps taken were to clear a small space of trees, and erect a place of habitation. We have seen what were the implements he had to work with—the materials he must use to subdue the forest tree standing before him.

Here, at the very threshold of Upper Canadian history, was initiated the "institution" of "bees." "Each with his axe on his shoulder, turned out to help the other," in erecting a log shanty. Small and unpretending indeed, were these humble tenements first built along the shores of the bay. The size of each depended upon the number to occupy it. None were larger than twenty by fifteen feet; and an old man tells me that his father, who was a carpenter, built one fifteen feet long and ten feet broad, with a slanting roof seven or eight feet in height. The back-woodsman's shanty, which may yet be seen in the outskirts of our country, is the counterpart of those which were first built; but perhaps many of our readers may never have seen one. "Round logs," (generally of basswood,) "roughly notched together at the corners, and piled one above another, to the height of seven or eight feet, constituted the walls.

Openings for a door, and one small window" (always beside the door) "designed for four lights of glass, 7 × 9, were cut out," (Government had supplied them with a little glass and putty); "the spaces between the logs were chinked with small splinters, and carefully plastered outside and inside, with clay for mortar. Smooth straight poles were laid lengthways of the building, on the walls, to serve as supports of the roof. This was composed of strips of elm bark, four feet in length, by two or three feet in width, in layers, overlapping each other, and fastened to the poles by withs." (The roof was some times of black oak, or swamp oak, bark,) "with a sufficient slope to the back, this formed a roof which was proof against wind and weather. An ample hearth, made of flat stones, was then laid out, and a fire back of field stone or small boulders, rudely built, was carried up as high as the walls. Above this the chimney was formed of round poles, notched together and plastered with mud. The floor was of the same materials as the walls, only that the logs were split in two, and flattened so as to make a tolerably even surface. As no boards were to be had to make a door, until they could be sawn out by the whip saw, a blanket suspended from the inside for some time took its place. By and by four little pains of glass, were stuck into a rough sash, and then the shanty was complete."—(*Croil.*)

Furniture for the house was made by the old soldier; this was generally of the roughest kind. They had the fashion of exchanging work, as well as of having bees. Some of them had been mechanics in other days. A carpenter was a valuable acquisition, and while others would assist him to do his heavy work, he would in return do those little nicer jobs by which the household comforts would be increased. No chests of drawers were required; benches were made of split basswood, upon which to sit, and tables were manufactured in the same style. The bedstead was constructed at the end of the cabin, by taking poles of suitable size and inserting the ends between the logs which formed the walls on either side. These would be placed, before the cracks were filled in and plastered.

CLEARING THE LAND.

A log hut constructed, wherein to live; and such plain rough articles of furniture as were really necessary provided, the next thing was to clear the land, thickly covered with large trees and tangled brush. Many a swing of the unhandy axe had to be made ere the trees could be felled, and disposed of; and the ground made ready for the grain or root.

A few years later, and the settler would, in the dry summer season, fire the woods, so as to kill the trees. By the next year they would have become dry, so that by setting fire again they would burn down. In this way much labor was saved. But sometimes the fire would prove unmanageable and threaten to destroy the little house and log barn, as well as crops. Another mode of destroying the large trees, was to girdle them—that is, to cut through the bark all around the tree, whereby it was killed, so that the following year it would likewise burn down.

A portion of the disbanded troops, as well as other loyalists, had been bred to agricultural pursuits; and some of them, at least those who had not been very long in arms, could the more readily adapt themselves to their new circumstances, and resume their early occupation. The axe of the woodsman was soon swung as vigorously along the shores of the well wooded river and bay, as it had been in the forests years before, in the backwoods of New England.

It is no ordinary undertaking for one to enter the primeval forest, to cut down the tough grained trees, whose boughs have long met the first beams of the rising sun, and swayed in the tempest wind; to clear away the thick underbrush, which impedes the step at every turn; to clear out a tangled cedar swamp, no matter how hardy may be the axe-man—how well accustomed to the use of the implement. With the best mode of proceeding, with an axe of excellent make, and keen edge; and, combined with which, let every other circumstance be favorable; yet, it requires a determined will, an iron frame and supple muscle, to undertake and carry out the successful clearing of a farm. But, the refugees and disbanded soldiers, who formed the pioneers of Upper Canada, enjoyed not even ordinary advantages. Many of the old soldiers had not the slightest knowledge of the duties of pioneer life, while others had but an imperfect idea. Some scarcely knew how to fell a tree. Hardy and determined they were; but they possessed not the implements requisite to clear off the solid trees. We have seen that the axe furnished by government was large and clumsy, and could be swung only with difficulty and great labor, being nothing more than the ship axe then in use. Slow and wearisome indeed, must have been the progress made by the unaccustomed woodsman in the work of clearing, and of preparing the logs for his hut, while he had, as on-lookers, too often a feeble wife and hungry children.

The ordinary course of clearing land is pretty well known. At the present day the autumn and winter is the usual time, when the wood is cut in sleigh lengths for home use, or made into cord wood for the market. The brush is piled up into huge heaps, and in the following season, when sufficiently dry, is burned up. Now, wood, except in the remote parts, is very valuable, and for those who can part with it, it brings a good income. But then, when the land was everywhere covered with wood, the only thought was how to get rid of it. The great green trees, after being cut down, had to lie until they had dried, or be cut into pieces and removed. Time was necessary for the first. To accomplish the second, involved labor with the unwieldly axe; and there were at first, no beast of burden to haul the heavy logs. The arm of the pioneer was the only motor power, and the trees had to be cut in short lengths, that they might be carried. To overcome the more heavy work connected with this, the settlers would have logging bees from place to place, and by united strength subdue the otherwise obstinate forces. Mainly, the trees were burned; the limbs and smaller portion first, and subsequently the large trunk. The fire would consume all that was flamable, leaving great black logs all over the ground. Then came "logging," that is, piling these black and half burned pieces into heaps, where, after a longer time of drying, they might be consumed. A second, perhaps a third time the pieces would have to be collected into "log heaps," until finally burned to ashes. It was by such means, that slowly the forest along the St. Lawrence, and surroundng the Bay Quinté, as well in the adjacent townships melted away before the daily work of the aggressive settler. Although deprived of all those comforts, which most of them had enjoyed in early life in the Hudson, and Mohawk valleys, and fruitful fields of Pennsylvania, they toiled on determined to conquer—to make new homes; and, for their children at least, to secure comforts. They rose early, and toiled on all day, whether long or short, until night cast its solemn pall over their rude quiet homes. The small clearing of a few acres gradually widened, the sound of the axe was heard ringing all the day, and the crash of the falling tree sent the startled wild beast to the deeper recesses of the wild wood. The toilers were not all from the same social rank, but now in the main, all found a common level; the land allotted to the half pay officers was as thickly covered with wood. A few possessed limited means, and were able to engage a help, to do some of the work, but in a short time it was the same with all; men of education, and who held high positions, rightly held the belief that it was an honor to be a refugee farmer.

At the close of the war a considerable number of the refugees found safety in New Brunswick and Nova Scotia. But a certain number, not finding such prospects as they had hoped, resolved to try Canada. Consequently, for five or six years after the peace, this class continued slowly to flow, to swell the number of inhabitants of Upper Canada. Some of them tarried, or remained in Lower Canada; but the majority ascended the Bay Quinté, and settled the new townships at the head of the bay; not a few would remain for a year or two in the townships already settled, working farms on shares, or 'living out,' until the future home was selected. A good many of the first settlers in the sixth, seventh, and eight townships, had previously lived for a while in the fourth township.

The advance of the settlements was along the bay, from Kingston township and Ernest town, westward along both sides. When the settlers in the first, second, third and fourth townships, had, to a certain extent overcome the pioneers first difficulties, those in the sixth, seventh, eight and ninth, were yet undergoing mostly all the same hardships and trials. Far removed from Kingston, they could, with difficulty, procure necessities, and consequently endured greater privation, and experienced severer hardships; but in time these settlers also overcome, and ended their days in comparative comfort.

Gen. Simcoe, after he became the first Governor of Upper Canada in 1792, held the opinion that there remained in the States a large number of Loyalists, and conceived the idea of affording them an inducement to again come under British rule, as they were British in heart. He, by proclamation, invited them to free grants of the rich land of Upper Canada, in the following words:

"A PROCLAMATION, to such as are desirous to settle on lands of the Crown, in the Province of UPPER CANADA, BY HIS EXCELLENCY JOHN GRAVES SIMCOE, ESQUIRE, Lieutenant-Governor and Commander-in-Chief of the said Province, and Colonel commanding His Majesty's Forces, &c., &c. Be it known to all concerned that His Majesty, both by his royal commission and instructions to the Governor, and in his absence, to the Lieutenant-Governor of the said Province of Upper Canada, gives authority or command to grant the lands of the Crown in the same by patent under the great seal thereof. I do accordingly make known the terms of grant and settlement to be:" &c.

Without introducing the somewhat lengthy terms given under the heads, it is sufficient to say that they were most liberal; in the meanwhile reserving what was necessary to maintain the rights previously granted to Loyalist settlers. No lot was to be granted of more than 200 acres, except such as the Governor might otherwise desire, but no one was to receive a quantity exceeding 1000 acres. Every one had to make it appear that he, or she was in a condition to cultivate and improve the land, and "beside taking the usual oaths, subscribe a declaration, vix: I, A. B. do promise and declare that I will maintain and defend to the utmost of my power, the authority of the king in his parliament as the supreme legislature of this province." These grants were free excepting the fees of office, "in passing the patent and recording the same." The proclamation was dated 7th February, 1792, Thomas Talbot, acting Secretary.

It was obligatory on settlers to clear five acres of land, to build a house, and to open a road across the front of his land, a quarter of a mile.

Whether Simcoe was right in his opinion, that many loyalists remained in the States, ready to avail themselves of a judicious opportunity of becoming citizens of British territory, may be questioned; that there were some, cannot be doubted. Not a few responded to his invitation, and entered the new province. The recall of Simcoe led to the abrogation of the terms specified in the aforementioned proclamation, and some of the new comers were doomed to disappointment. As may naturally be supposed, these later comers were not altogether regarded with favor by the first settlers, who now regarded themselves as lords of the soil. The old staunch loyalists were disposed to look upon them as Yankees, who came only to get the land. And it seems that such was often the case. We have the impartial statement of Rochefoucault, that there were some who "falsely profess an attachment to the British monarch, and curse the Government of the Union for the mere purpose of getting possession of lands." Even at this early day, they set about taking possession of Canada! Indeed, it was a cause of grievance in Walford township, Johnstown district, that persons from the States entered the country, petitioned for land, took the necessary oaths—perjured themselves, and having obtained possession of the land resold it, pocketed the money, and left to build up the glorious Union.

But, while so much has to be said of some Americans, who took land in Canada for mercenary motives, and committed fraud, it is pleasing to say likewise, that a large number of settlers from the States, who came in between 1794 and 1812, became worthy and loyal subjects of the Crown. How far all of them were at first Britons in heart, may be questioned. But the fact that the first settlers regarded them with doubtful eye, and often charged them with being Yankees, led many, for very peace-sake, to display their loyalty. But at last, when the war of 1812 broke out, they exhibited unmistakeable attachment to the British Crown. To their honor be it said, they were as active in defending their homes as any class. The number who deserted from Canada, was quite insignificant. As would be expected, the war of 1812 arrested the stream of emigration from the States. The Government of Canada thereafter discountenanced it, and instead, made some efforts to draw British European emigrants.

DIVISION IV.

THE FIRST YEARS OF UPPER CANADA.

CHAPTER XVIII.

CONTENTS—Father Picquet—Provision of Forts in Upper Canada just before Conquest—Frontenac—Milk—Brandy—Toronto—The Several Forts—Detroit—British Garrisons—Grasping Rebels—Efforts to Starve out Loyalists in Canada—Worse Treated than the Acadians—Efforts to Secure Fur Trade—The Frontier Forts—Americans Conduct to Indians—Result—Conduct of British Government—Rations for Three Years—Grinding by Hand—"Hominy Blocks"—"Plumping Mill"—The Women—Soldier Farmers—The Hessians—Suffering—The "Scarce Year"—Charge against the Commissariat Officers—Famine—Cry for Bread—Instances of Suffering—Starving Children—No Salt—Fish—Game—Eating Young Grain—Begging Bran—A Common Sorrow—Providential Escapes—Eating Buds and Leaves—Deaths—Primitive Fishing—Catching Salmon—Going 125 miles to mill—Disconsolate Families—1789—Partial Relief—First Beef Slaughtered in Upper Canada—First Log Barn—A Bee, what they Ate and Drank—Tea Introduced—Statements of Sheriff Sherwood—Roger Bates—John Parrott—Col. Clark—Squirrell Swimming Niagara—Maple Sugar—How it was made—Women assisting—Made Dishes of Food—Pumpkin Loaf—Extract from Rochefoucault—1795—Quality of Grain Raised—Quinté Bay—Cultivation—Corn Exported—The Grain Dealers—Price of Flour—Pork—Profits of the Merchants.

MODE OF PROCURING FOOD.

We have seen with what spirit and determination the loyalists engaged in the duties pertaining to pioneer life; how they became domiciled in the wilderness and adapted themselves to their new and trying situation. Thus, was laid the foundation of the Province of Upper Canada, now Ontario. Upon this foundation was to be erected the superstructure. Let us proceed to examine the circumstances of the first years of Upper Canadian life. And first with respect to *food.*

Father Picquet visited the Bay and Lake Ontario, from *La Présentation*—Ogdensburgh, the year of the Conquest. He speaks of his visit to Fort Frontenac, and remarks, "The bread and milk there, were bad; they had not even brandy there to staunch a wound." By which we learn that the French garrison had a cow, although she gave indifferent milk; and that even brandy for medicinal purposes could not be had. The missionary proceeded to Fort Toronto which was situated upon Lake Simcoe, no doubt ascending by the bay Quinté and Trent. Here he found "good bread and good wine" and "everything requisite for trade" with the Indians. The cession of Canada to the British by the French had been followed by a withdrawal of troops from many of the forts, around which had clustered a few hamlets, specks of civilization in a vast wilderness, and in most places things had lapsed into their primal state. And, when rebellion broke out in the Colonies of Britain, there were but a few posts whereat were stationed any soldiers, or where clustered the white settlers. There were a few French living at Detroit, and at Michilmicinac, and to the north-east of Lake Huron. We have seen that during the war, refugees found safety at the several military posts. The military rations were served out to these loyal men in the same proportion as to the soldiers, and when the war closed the garrisons continued to dispense the necessaries of life to the settlers upon the north shores of the lake, and St. Lawrence.

For ten years, after the terms of peace was signed between England and the Independent States, the forts of Oswego, Niagara, Detroit, and Michilmicinac, with the garrison on Carleton Island, remained in the possession of the British troops. To this the grasping Americans warmly took exceptions. Although it would have been next to impossible to supply these places with provisions for troops of their own, they nevertheless wished to dispossess the Royal troops; we learn that the object was to starve out the refugees who had found shelter upon the borders, and who would be depending for years to these forts, for the very necessaries of life. In this, their cruelty exceeded that practised towards the Acadians. Having driven away the loyalists and dispersed them at home, they would have followed them to their new wilderness home, there to cut off their supplies and leave them to perish. They wished to obtain possession of the forts not only to glut their vengeful feeling against the tories, but to secure the traffic carried on with the Indians. Dreams of aggrandizement floated through their avaricious minds. It was regarded an excellent stroke of policy to turn the current of the fur trade from the St. Lawrence, and starve out by degrees the refugees, and the French who would have none of *their* "Liberty." Hence their desire to get possession of the frontier forts. But it was destined that this valuable traffic should never come into the hands of the United States; or rather it should be said, the Americans had determined to pursue a course which would completely alienate the Indian tribes from them. Under such circumstances no possession of the forts could have turned the trade from its natural channel by the St. Lawrence, across the continent to New York.

The British Government never desired to stint the loyal refugees and the disbanded soldiers. At the close of hostilities it was determined that both alike, with their families, should receive while traveling, and for a period of three years, such rations as are allowed daily to the private soldier. And the Commissariat Department was instructed to make the necessary provision to have transported to each township by batteau, what should be requisite. Depôts were established, in addition to the different garrisons, in each township, to which some prominent and trusted refugee of their number, generally a half pay officer, was appointed as Commissary, and at which ample provisions of the specified kind, as well as certain implements, it was ordered should be stored, to be dealt out with regularity and fairness to each family, according to the number of children. In some of the townships two batteaux were provided to bring the provisions from Montreal. Besides the food thus obtained, they were often enabled to freely supply themselves with game of different kinds. The greatest trouble of all was to get the grain supplied to them, ground into flour. According to Carroll and Croil, the townships upon the St. Lawrence, were supplied with steel mills for grinding grain; but no word of such indifferent convenience for the settlers of the Bay, has by us been received; the settlers had to get the grain crushed as best they could. Various modes were adopted to do this; but in all cases the work was done by hand. Sometimes the grain was crushed with an axe upon a flat stone. Many prepared a wooden mortar, by cutting a block, of suitable length, about four feet, out of the trunk of a large tree, oak or maple. Sometimes it was the stump of a tree. In this a cavity was formed, generally by heating a piece of iron, and placing it upon the end. In some quarters, a cannon ball from the Garrison was used. By placing this, red hot, upon the wood, a hollow of sufficient depth could be made. These mortars, sometimes called "Hominy Blocks" and sometimes "Plumping Mill," varied in size; sometimes holding only a few quarts, sometimes a bushel, or even more. The pestle or pounder, was made of the hardest wood, six or eight feet long, and eight inches in diameter at the bottom end; the top sufficiently small to be spanned by the hand. The pestle was sometimes called the stamper; and the stump or block, with the pestle, was called the stump-mortar. Generally, it was by the unaided hand that the grinding was done; but after a time a sweep pole was arranged, similar to a well pole, and a hard weighty substance being attached to the pole, much less strength was required to crush the grain; at the same time a larger quantity could be at once done. The work was generally done by two men. The grain thus pounded was generally Indian Corn, and occasionally wild rice. To crush wheat required much more labor, and a small mortar. The bran was separated from the flour by a horse-hair sieve, one of which generally served a whole community, as they were possessed only by a few. This rude method continued for many years, especially in those townships remote from the flouring mills. Frequently, an individual would possess a large mortar, that would be used by a whole neighborhood. Mr. Diamond, of Belleville, a native of Fredericksburg, remembers when a boy, to have accompanied his father "to mill." The mill was one of these larger mortars which would contain a bushel of grain when being ground, but which would hold, even measure, two bushels. The grain was crushed by a sweep with a weight attached, of ten or twelve pounds.

But grinding grain in this rude manner, was very frequently done by the women; and was but one of the difficulties attending the production of meal. It was a hard task to prepare for use the corn supplied by Government; but when that supply was cut off, and the settler had but his own raising, it became much worse. Elsewhere we have seen the difficult process by which seed was planted, and the fruit of the soil reaped, and then thrashed. It had been thought by the Government that three years would suffice to give the settler ample time to reap sufficient grain for their sustenance. In most cases, industry and a right application of labor, enabled the farmer to accomplish what was expected of him. But the habits which some of the soldiers had acquired during the war, were highly detrimental to regular industry. When the three years' supplies were discontinued, many found themselves unprepared to meet the requirements of their new condition. It is said that some of them entertained the belief that "Old George," as they familiarly called the King, would continue to feed them, for an indefinite period of time, upon the bread of idleness. The Hessians, who had settled in the fifth township, who had no idea of pioneer life, were great sufferers, and it is stated that some actually died of starvation. Again, there was a considerable class who had not had time to prepare the land, and reap the fruit of the soil, prior to the supplies being stopped; or who could not procure seed grain. These were likewise placed in the most distressing circumstances. The fearful suffering experienced in consequence will be mentioned under the head of the "Scarce Year."

Notwithstanding, that Government supplied the settlers with provisions for three years, and also with spring wheat, peas, corn, and potatoes for seed, and took steps to furnish them, first with one mill at Kingston, and then a second one at Napanee, at the expiration of the three years, there were many unprepared. The mills were almost deserted, and the hearts of the people were faint because there was no grain to grind, and famine began to rest upon the struggling settlers, especially along the Bay Quinté. It has already been said that with some of the disbanded soldiers, there was some degree of negligence, or, a want of due exertion to obtain home-raised grain before the Government supplies were discontinued; also, that there was a certain number, who came with their families two or three years after the first settlement, who were not entitled to get Government rations, and who had not had time to clear the land. Many of these brought provisions with them, but the long distances traveled by them through a wilderness, allowed no large quantity of stores to be transported. And within a few months, or a year their store of food was exhausted. But the greatest evil of all it is averred, was the failure on the part of the Commissary Department to bring up from Lower Canada, the supplies which were required by those yet in the service, and who rightly looked to that source for the bread of life. And, it has been alleged that some who had charge of military stores forgot this public duty, in their anxiety to secure abundant supplies for their own families. And a spirit of cupidity has been laid to the charge of one or two for retaining for private use the bread for which so many were famishing. At this remote period it is impossible to arrive at positive conclusions relative to the matter. We can only examine the circumstances, and judge whether such a thing was likely. Of course the Commissary officers, whose duty it had been to distribute food in the several townships, would not be likely to disburse with a hand so liberal, that they should themselves become destitute; yet the fact that such had food, while others had none, would naturally create an erroneous impression. But the famine was not limited to the Bay region; although, being remote from Montreal, it was here the distress was most grievously felt. Throughout Lower Canada the pinch of famine was keenly experienced. Even there, in places, corn-meal was meted out by the spoonful, wheat flour was unknown, while millet seed was ground for a substitute. Still more, the opinion is given, that the accusation against certain parties is contrary to the spirit which pervaded the refugee settlers at that time. That they had laid up stores, and looked indifferently upon the general suffering, is contrary to the known character of the parties accused. In after days, as at the present time, there were aroused petty jealousies, as one individual exceeded another in prosperity. Family jars sometimes rise to feuds, and false surmises grow into untruthful legends.

The period of famine is even yet remembered by a few, whose memory reaches back to the immediately succeeding years, and the descendants of the sufferers, speak of that time with peculiar feelings, imbibed from their parents; and many are the touching stories even yet related of this sad first page in the history of Upper Canada, when from Lower Canada to the outskirts of the settlement was heard the cry for *bread! bread! bread!*

The year of the famine is spoken of sometimes as the "scarce year," sometimes as the "hungry year," or the "hard summer." The extreme distress seems to have commenced in the year 1787. With some, it lasted a part of a year, with others a year, and with others upwards of a year. The height of the distress was during the spring and early summer of 1788. But plenty to all, did not come till the summer of 1789. The writer has in his possession accounts of many instances of extreme suffering, during the famine, and for years after, through the ten townships. A few will here be given, as briefly as may be possible.

One, who settled in the Sixth Township, (who was subsequently a Member of Parliament for twenty years,) with wife and children, endured great suffering. Their flour being exhausted he sent money to Quebec for some more flour, but his money was sent back; there was none to be had. The wife tried as an experiment to make bread out of some wheat bran, which was bought at a dollar a bushel. She failed to make bread, but it was eaten as a stir-a-bout. Upon this, with Indian Cabbage, or "Cale," "a plant with a large leaf," also wild potatoes or ground-nuts, the family lived for many a week. In the spring they procured some potatoes to plant, but the potatoe eye alone was planted, the other portion being reserved for food. One of the daughters, in her extreme hunger digged up for days, some of the potatoe rind and ate it. One day, her father caught her at it, and seized hold of her arm to punish her, for forgetting the requirements of the future, but he found her arms so emaciated that his heart melted in pity for the starving child. Others used to eat a plant called butter-nut, and another pig-weed. Children would steal out at night with stolen potatoes, and roast them at the burning log heap, and consider them a great treat. One individual has left the record that she used to allay the pangs of hunger by eating a little salt. But the majority of the settlers had no salt, and game and fish, when it could be caught, was eaten without that condiment. Even at a later date, salt was a scarce and dear article as the following will show: "Sydney, 20th November, 1792—Received from Mr. John Ferguson, one barrel of salt, for which I am to pay nine dollars." (Signed), John German. Often when fish or game was caught, it was forthwith roasted, without waiting to go home to have it dressed. As spring advanced, and the buds of the trees began to swell, they were gathered and eaten. Roots were digged out of the ground; the bark of certain trees were stripped off and consumed as food. One family lived for a fortnight on beech leaves. Everything that was supposed to be capable of alleviating the pangs of hunger, whether it yielded nutriment or not, was unhesitatingly used; and in the fifth township some were killed by eating poisonous roots. Beef bones were, in one neighbourhood, not only boiled again and again, but actually carried from house to house, to give a little taste to boiled bran, until there remained no taste in the boiling water. In the fourth township, upon the sunny side of a hill, was an early field of grain, and to this they came, from far and near, to eat the milk-like heads of grain, so soon as they had sufficiently grown, which were boiled and eaten. The daughter of the man who owned the field, and gladly gave to all, still remains with us, then, she was in the freshness of girlhood; now, she is in the autumn of a green old age, nearly a hundred. She remembers to have seen them cutting the young succulent grain, to use her own words "as thick as stumps." This young grain was a common dish, all along the Bay, until it became ripe. One family lived several months solely on boiled oats. One day, a man came to the door of a house in Adolphustown, with a bag, and a piece of "calamink," to exchange for flour. But the flour was low, and the future doubtful, and none could be spared. The man turned away with tears of anguish rolling down his face. The kind woman gave him a few pounds of flour; he begged to be allowed to add some bran lying on the floor, which was permitted, and he went his way.

There were, scattered through the settlements, a few who never were entirely out of provisions, but who had procured some from Lower Canada, or Oswego. Many of these, even at the risk of future want, would give away, day after day, to those who came to their door, often a long distance, seeking for the very bread of life. A piece of bread was often the only thing to give; but thus, many a life was saved. These poor unfortunates, would offer various articles in exchange for flour or food. Even their lands—all they had, were offered for a few pounds of flour. But, with a few execrable exceptions, the last loaf was divided; and when flour was sold, it was at a fair valuation. A common sorrow knit them together in fraternal relationship. The names of some are handed down, who employed others to work all day for their board, and would give nothing for their famishing ones at home. One of them also, sold eight bushels of potatoes for a valuable cow. In some instances, families living remotely, forsook their houses and sought for food at Kingston. One family in Thurlow, set out for Kingston, following the bay shore on foot. Their only food was bran, which, being mixed with water, was cooked by the way, by heating flat stones and baking thereupon. As before stated, the settlers of the fifth township suffered fearfully, and it is stated, that some of them actually died. Mr. Parrott says, that he has heard it stated that persons starved to death. And the extraordinary statement is found in the M.S. of the late Mr. Merritt, that one old couple, too old to help themselves, and left alone, were preserved providentially from starvation, by pigeons, which would occasionally come and allow themselves to be caught. The fact is stated by others, that pigeons were at times, during the first years of settling, very plentiful, and were always exceedingly tame. Another person remarks, that although there was generally plenty of pigeons, wild fowl, fish and partridge, yet, they seemed to keep away when most wanted.

One family, four in number, subsisted on the small quantity of milk given by a young cow, with leeks, buds of trees, and often leaves were added to the milk. A barrel of bran served a good purpose for baking a kind of cake, which made a change on special occasions. At one time, Reed, of Thurlow, offererd a three year old horse for 50 lbs of flour. This family would, at one time actually have starved to death, had not a deer been miraculously shot. They often carried grain, a little, it is true, to the Napanee mills, following the river, and bay shores. And when they had no grain, articles of domestic use were taken to exchange for flour and meal. A woman used to carry a bushel and a half of wheat ten miles to the Napanee mills, and then carry the flour back.

Ex-Sheriff Ruttan says of his father's family, with whom his uncle lived, "We had the luxury of a cow which the family brought with them, and had it not been for this domestic boon, all would have perished in the year of scarcity. The crops had failed the year before, and the winter that followed, was most inclement and severe. The snow was unusually deep, so that the deer became an easy prey to their rapacious enemies, the wolves, who fattened on their destruction, whilst men were perishing for want. Five individuals, in different places, were found dead, and one poor woman also, with a live infant at her breast; which was cared for and protected." "Two negroes were sent to Albany for corn, who brought four bushels. This, with the milk of the cow dealt out day by day in limited quantity, kept them alive till harvest." "The soldiers' rations were reduced to one biscuit a day." Referring to other days after the famine he says: "Fish was plentiful"—the "fishing tackle was on a primitive plan; something similar to the Indians, who fixed the bait on part of the back bone of the pike, which would catch these finny tribe quite as expeditiously as the best Limerick hook; but our supply was from spearing by torchlight, which has been practiced by the Indian from time immemorial; from whom we obtained a vast deal of practical knowledge."

Roger Bates, near Cobourg, speaking of the first years of Upper Canada, says that his grandfather's family, living in Prince Edward for a while, "adopted many ingenious contrivances of the Indians for procuring food. Not the least simple and handy was a crotched pole, with which they secured salmon in any quantity, the creeks being full of them." He removed to the township of Clarke, where he was the first white settler, and for six months saw no white person. "For a long time he had to go to Kingston, 125 miles, with his wheat to be ground. They had no other conveyance than batteaux; the journey would sometimes occupy five or six weeks. Of an evening they put in at some creek, and obtained their salmon with ease, using a forked stick, which passed over the fish's back and held it fast. Sometimes they were so long gone for grist, in consequence of bad weather, that the women would collect together and have a good cry, thinking the batteaux had foundered. If their food ran short, they had a dog that would, when told, hunt a deer and drive it into the water, so that the young boys could shoot it."

The summer of 1789 brought relief to most of the settlers,—the heaviest of the weight of woe was removed. But, for nearly a decade, they enjoyed but few comforts, and were often without the necessaries of life. The days of the toiling pioneers were numbering up rapidly, yet the wants of all were not relieved. Those whose industry had enabled them to sow a quantity of grain reaped a goodly reward. The soil was very fruitful, and subsequently for two and three years, repeated crops were raised from a single sowing. But flour alone, although necessary to sustain life, could hardly satisfy the cravings of hunger with those who had been accustomed to a different mode of living. It was a long way to Montreal or Albany, from which to transport by hand, everything required, even when it could be had, and the settler had something to exchange for such articles; beside the journey of several weeks. Game, occasionally to be had, was not available at all seasons, nor at all times; although running wild, ammunition was scarce, and some had none. We have stated that Government gave to every five families a musket and forty-eight rounds of ammunition, with some powder and shot, also some twine to make fishing nets. Beef, mutton, &c., were unknown for many a day. Strangely enough, a circumstantial account of the first beef slaughtered along the Bay, probably in Upper Canada, is supplied by one who, now in her 90th year, bears a distinct recollection of the event. It was at Adolphustown. A few settlers had imported oxen, to use in clearing the land. One of a yoke, was killed by the falling of a tree. The remaining animal, now useless, was purchased by a farmer upon the Front, who converted it into beef. With the hospitality characteristic of the times, the neighbors were invited to a grand entertainment; and the neighborhood, be it remembered, extended for thirty or forty miles. A treat it was, this taste of an article of diet, long unknown.

The same person tells of the occasion when the first log barn was raised in Adolphustown, it was during the scarce period. The "bee" which was called, had to be entertained, in some way. But there were no provisions. The old lady, then a girl, saw her mother for weeks previous carefully putting away the eggs, which a few hens had contributed to their comfort; upon the morning of the barn raising, they were brought forth and found to amount to a pailful, well heaped. The most of the better-to-do settlers always had rum, which was a far different article from that sold now-a-days. With rum and eggs well beaten, and mixed with all the milk that could be kept sweet from the last few milkings, this, which was both food and drink was distributed to the members of the bee, during the time of raising the barn.

Tea, now considered an indispensable luxury by every family, was quite beyond the reach of all, for a long time; because of its scarcity and high price. Persons are yet living who remember when tea was first brought into family use. Various substitutes for tea were used, among these were hemlock and sassafras; there was also a plant gathered called by them the tea plant.

Sheriff Sherwood, in his most valuable memoirs, specially prepared for the writer, remarks, "Many incidents and occurrences took place during the early settlement which would, perhaps, at a future day be thought incredible. I recollect seeing pigeons flying in such numbers that they almost darkened the sky, and so low often as to be knocked down with poles; I saw, where a near neighbor killed thirty at one shot, I almost saw the shot, and saw the pigeons after they were shot." Ducks were so thick that when rising from a marsh "they made a noise like the roar of heavy thunder." "While many difficulties were encountered, yet we realized many advantages, we were always supplied with venison, partridge, and pigeon, and fish in abundance, no taxes to pay and plenty of wood at our doors. Although deprived of many kinds of fruit, we had the natural production of the country, strawberries, raspberries, gooseberries, blackberries, and lots of red plums, and cranberries in the various marshes all about the country, and I can assure you that pumpkin and cranberries make an excellent substitute for apple pie." Mr. Sherwood refers to their dog "Tipler," which was invaluable, in various ways, in assisting to procure the food. He also speaks of "Providential" assistance. "After the first year we raised wheat and Indian corn sufficient for the year's supply for the family; but then we had no grist mill to grind it; we made out to get on with the Indian corn very well by pounding it in the mortar, and made what we called samp, which made coarse bread, and what the Dutch called sup-pawn; but let me tell you how we made our mortar. We cut a log off a large tree, say two-and-a half feet through and about six feet long, which we planted firm in the ground, about four feet deep, then carefully burnt the centre of the top and scraped it out clean, which gave us a large mortar. We generally selected an iron-wood tree, from six to eight inches through, took the bark off clean, made the handle to it of suitable length, this was our pestle; and many a time have I pounded with it till the sweat ran down merrily. But this pounding would not do for the wheat, and the Government seeing the difficulty, built a mill back of Kingston, where the inhabitants, for fifteen miles below Brockville had to get their grinding done. In our neighborhood they got on very well in summer, by joining two wooden canoes together. Three persons would unite, to carry each a grist in their canoes, and would perform the journey in about a week. But in winter this could not be done. After a few years, however, when some had obtained horses, then a kind Providence furnished a road on the ice for some years until a road was made passable for sleighs by land. And it has not been practicable, indeed I may say possible, for horses with loaded sleighs to go on the ice from Brockville to Kingston, fifty years past."

Roger Bates says that "the woods were filled with deer, bears, wolves, martins, squirrels, and rabbits." No doubt, at first, before fire-arms were feared by them, they were plentiful and very tame. Even wild geese, it would seem, were often easily shot. But powder and shot were expensive, and unless good execution could be made, the charge was reserved. Mr. Sherwood gives a trustworthy account of the shooting of thirty pigeons at one shot; and another account is furnished, of Jacob Parliament, of Sophiasburgh, who killed and wounded at a single shot, four wild geese and five ducks. These wild fowl not only afforded luxurious and nutritious diet, but their feathers were saved, and in time pillows and even beds were thus made. Mr. John Parrott, of Ernest Town, descendant of Col. Jas. Parrott, says, "there were bears, wolves, and deer in great abundance, and there were lynx, wild cats, beavers and foxes in every directions; also martins, minks and weasels beyond calculation. In this connection, we may record a fact related by Col. Clark, respecting the migration of squirrels in the early part of the present century across the Niagara river, from the States. He says, "an immense immigration of squirrels took place, and so numerous were they that the people stood with sticks to destroy them, as they landed on the British shore, which by many was considered a breach of good faith on the part of John Bull, who is always ready to grant an asylum to fugitives of whatever nation they may belong to."

MAPLE SUGAR.

"Soon the blue-birds and the bees
O'er the stubble will be winging;
So 'tis time to tap the trees
And to set the axe a-ringing;

Time to set the hut to rights,
Where the girls and boys together
Tend the furnace fire o'nights
In the rough and rainy weather;

Time to hew and shape the trough,
And to punch the spile so hollow,
For the snow is thawing off
And the sugar-thaw must follow.

Oh, the gladdest time of year
Is the merry sugar-making,
When the swallows first appear
And the sleepy buds are waking!"

In the great wilderness were to be had, a few comforts and luxuries. Sugar is not only a luxury, but is really a necessary article of food. The properties of the sap of the maple was understood by the Indians, and the French soon availed themselves of the means of making sugar. To the present day, the French Canadians make it in considerable quantities. At first, the settlers of Upper Canada did not generally engage in making it; but, after a time a larger number did. The maple, the monarch of the Canadian forest, whose leaf is the emblem of our country, was a kind benefactor. In the spring, in the first days of genial sunshine, active operations for sugar making were commenced. Through the deep snow, the farmer and his sons would trudge, from tree to tree, to tap them upon their sunny side. The "spile" would be inserted to conduct the precious fluid into the trough of bass-wood, which had been fashioned during the long winter evenings. A boiling place would be arranged, with a long pole for a crane, upon which would be strung the largest kettles that could be procured. At night, the sap would be gathered from the troughs, a toilsome job, and put into barrels. In the morning a curling smoke would rise from amidst the thick woods, and the dry wood would crackle cheerily under the row of kettles, all the sunny spring day; and night would show a rich dark syrup, collected in one smaller kettle, for the more careful work of being converted into sugar. Frequently the fire would be attended by the women; and the men would come to gather the sap in the evening. In this way many a family would be provided with abundant sugar, at all events it had to serve them for the year, as they felt unable to purchase from the merchant. In another place, we have related how a few made a considerable quantity of sugar and sold it all, to pay for a farm, doing without themselves.

The absence of various articles of food, led the thoughtful housewife to invent new made dishes. The nature of these would depend in part upon the articles of food most abundant, and upon the habits peculiar to their ancestry, whether English, Dutch or some other. The great desire was, to make a common article as tasty as possible. And at harvest time, as well as at bees, the faithful wife would endeavour to prepare something extra to regale the tired ones. There was, for instance, the "pumpkin loaf," a common dish. It consisted of pumpkin and corn meal made into a small loaf, and eaten with butter. Another dish which seems to have been derived from the Dutch, was Pot Pie, which was always, and is even yet in many places, made to feed the hands at bees and raisings, and even was generally made to grace the board on a wedding occasion. We cannot give the space, if we felt prepared to speak, of the several made dishes commonly in use among the older Canadians of Upper Canada. Many of them are truly excellent in taste and nutritious in quality. They are often similar to, or very like the dishes in the New England and Midland States.

This subject will be concluded by giving a few extracts from Rochefoucault who wrote of what he saw and learned in Canada in 1795, and who may be regarded as quite correct.

He says, "It is asserted" (by Simcoe) "that all Canada, produces not the necessary corn for the consumption of its inhabitants, the troops are supplied with flour from London, and with salt meat from Ireland." But Simcoe then thought that Canada was capable not alone of feeding her inhabitants, but of becoming the granary, of England, and receiving commodities in Exchange. Speaking of Forty Mile Creek, he says: "Before it empties itself into the lake, it turns a grist mill and two saw mills, which belong to a Mr. Green, a loyalist of Jersey, who, six or seven years ago, settled in this part of Upper Canada." "Land newly cleared yields here, the first year, twenty bushels of corn. They plough the land after it has produced three or four crops, but not very deep. The price of flour is twenty-two shillings per hundred weight, that of wheat from seven to eight shillings per bushel. Laborers are scarce, and are paid at the rate of six shillings a day. Wheat is generally sown throughout all Upper Canada, but other sorts of grain are also cultivated." "Mr Green grinds the corn for all the military posts in Upper Canada."

Approaching Kingston by water he remarks that "on the left is Quinté Bay, the banks of which are said to be cultivated up to a considerable extent. The eye dwells with pleasure once more on cultivated ground. The country looks pleasant. The houses lie closer than in any of the new settled parts of Upper Canada, which we have hitherto traversed. The variegated verdure of the corn-fields embellishes and enriches the prospect, charms the eye, and enchants the mind."

"This district not only produces the corn requisite for its own consumption, but also exports yearly about 3 or 4000 bushels. This grain, which, in winter, is conveyed down the river on sledges, is bought by the merchant, who engage, on the arrival of the ships from Europe, to pay its amount in such merchandise as the sellers may require. The merchants buy this grain for government, which pays for it in ready money, according to the market price at Montreal. The agent of government causes part to be ground into flour, which he sends to the different ports in Upper Canada, where it is wanted; and the surplus he sends to England. The price of flour in Kingston is at present (12th July, 1795) six dollars per barrel. The district of Kingston supplied, last year, the other parts of Canada with large quantities of pease, the culture of which, introduced but two years ago, proves very productive and successful. In the course of last year, 1000 barrels of salt pork, of 208 pounds each, were sent from Kingston to Quebec; its price was eighteen dollars per barrel. The whole trade is carried on by merchants, whose profits are the more considerable, as they fix the price of the provisions which they receive from Europe, and sell without the least competition." Indeed, the profits of the dealers must have been immense. They sold to the military authorities at a rate which would remunerate them when the provisions came from England; and when the farmers of Canada began to raise grain to sell, they bought it, or exchanged merchandise for it, upon which they fixed the price, and continued to sell the flour at the same price to the military authorities.

CHAPTER XIX.

CONTENTS—Kingston Mills—Action of Government—The Millwright—Situation of the first Mill—Why Selected—The Machinery—Put up by Loyalists—No Toll—Only Mill for three years—Going to Mill, 1784—The Napanee Mill—Commenced 1785—Robert Clarke—An old Book—"Appenea" Falls—Price of certain articles—What Rum cost, and was used for—The Mill opened 1787—Sergt.-Major Clarke in charge—Indian Corn—Small Toll—Surveyor Collins in charge—Becomes the Property of R. Cartwright, 1792—Rebuilt—Origin of Napanee—Price of Butter, 1788—Mills at Four Mile Creek, Niagara Falls, Fort Erie, and Grand River—Mills on the St. Lawrence—The Stone Mills—Van Alstine—Lake of the Mountain—1796—Natural Beauty, *versus* Utility—The Mill—Van Alstine's Death—Wind Mill—Myer's Mill—Mill at Consecon.

THE FIRST FLOURING MILLS.

Government was not an indifferent spectator of the difficulty spoken of as to the grinding of grain—the procuring of flour, and at an early day, ordered means to meet the requirements of the pioneers. We have the certain statement of John C. Clark, of Ernest town, now dead, written ten years ago, that his father, Robert Clark, who was a millwright, "was employed by Government, in 1782-3, to erect the Kingston Mills preparatory to the settlement of the Loyalists in that section of Upper Canada." The place selected for erecting the mill, was upon the Cataraqui River, seven miles north of the Fort, now the entrance of the Rideau Canal, where are situated the first locks of that artificial water way. When in a state of nature, the place must have been strikingly beautiful; it is so at the present time, when the achievements of art give variety of attraction. This situation, selected for the first flouring mill, was central to the population strung along the banks of the St. Lawrence, and Bay Quinté. Every thing required for the construction of the mill, was furnished by Government, such as the mill stones, and the machinery. The rougher work, the walls of the building, was done by men detailed for the purpose, from the company of soldiers. The structure consisted of logs, or timber roughly squared, and was erected, as well as the mill house, by the combined efforts of the soldier settlers, collected for the purpose. All the settlers had their grists ground without paying toll. The original building was standing as late as 1836.

For nearly three years, the Cataraqui Mill was the only one in Central Canada. The settlers came from Cornwall in the east, and the most remote settlement up the Bay. At the present day, when railroads and swiftly running steamers assist so materially to annihilate space as it were, and bring distant places into close relationship, it would be regarded a matter of no little trouble and inconvenience, to carry grain from Cornwall on the one hand, and Sidney on the other, to Kingston, and wait to have it ground into flour; but how infinitely greater the difficulty, when a trackless woods covered the intervening spaces, when the only mode of carrying anything was upon the back, or in a canoe, or batteaux, or upon a raft, in summer; and upon a hand-sleigh in winter, drawn through deep snow, following the windings of the shore along many a dismal mile.

The increasing population around the Bay, caused the authorities to seek a proper site for a second mill. The Napanee River, with its natural falls, offered an advantageous place upon which to erect a second mill for the settlers, upon the Bay. We have been fortunate, through the kindness of Mr. P. Clark, of Collinsby, in being permitted to examine an account book kept by Robert Clark, the millwright, of both the Kingston and Napanee mills. By this, we learn that in the year 1785, Robert Clark, who had completed the Kingston Mill, removed to the second township, and, according to instructions received from Government, proceeded to construct a mill upon the Napanee River, at the site of the natural falls. In the absence of the full particulars relating to the building of the Napanee Mills, the following cannot fail to be of interest. In the account book aforementioned, the following references to the building of the mill, are found recorded:

"An accompt of articles bought for the use of the works, November 8." "To 4 Augers of different size, from Mr. Phillips, carpenters at Catariqui, 13s. 8d. To 3 quires of Writing Paper, 5s. December 6, To 20 lbs. of Nails, £1; December 22, To 6 Whip Saw Files, 3s. 9d." Omitting some items, and coming to March 23, 1786, we find "For Raising the Saw Mill," "2 gallons and 3 pints of Rum, 17s 6d." "April 20th, To 1 quart of Rum, 2s." On the "25th May, To 4 gallons and 1 quart of Rum, for Raising the Grist Mill, at 7s. 6d." The "26th, To 1 quart of Rum for the People at work in the water at the Dam." By this we learn the day upon which the Napanee mill was erected. On the 20th July, Government is again charged with "3 pints of Rum for raising the fenderpost," &c. On the 27th, a pint was again required, but for what special purpose is not mentioned. In December, 1786, we find "To making Bolt Cloth 15s." "To Clearing one acre and three-quarters of Land for a mill, at seven dollars per acre, £3." And we find that the iron or smith work for the mill was done by David Palmer and Conly. From the fact that the bolting cloth was not made until December, 1786, we may infer that the mill did not commence operations until the beginning of 1787. The mill was a great boon to the inhabitants around the Bay Quinté. not only because they had a shorter distance to travel, but the amount of work pressing upon the Kingston mill, made it very uncertain as to the time one would have to wait, to get his gristing done. Consequently many came from the Lower Bay, and the dwellers upon the South Bay in Marysburg, who followed the shores around Indian Point and up the Bay Quinté, To those living in Thurlow, Sidney, and at the Carrying Place, the mill was a great blessing.

The father of the late Col. John Clark, of Port Dalhousie, who had been Sergeant Major in the 8th Regiment, and who had, from 1777, been clerk and naval storekeeper at Carleton Island, removed to within three miles of Napanee, the same year the mill was built, to take charge of the works, in addition to his other duties. John Clark, who was then a small boy, says in his memoirs; the grain principally brought to be ground, was Indian corn; but as the clearances increased, wheat became more plentiful. He also speaks of the great industry which characterized the settlers. "A small toll was exacted to pay for the daily expenses of the mill, but this was a mere trifle, considering the advantages the settlers derived from loss of time in proceeding to Kingston." From this we infer that no toll was demanded at the Kingston mill. "When my father," continues Col. Clark, "was ordered to Niagara, the mill was delivered up to surveyor Collins, under whose directions it was continued in operation for many years, and then the mill site became the property of the Hon. R. Cartwright of Kingston." But, we find the statement elsewhere made that the land was originally granted to Captain McDonald of Marysburg, who sold it to Cartwright.

Robert Clark, in his account book, says, "Commenced work for Mr. Cartwright at the Napanee mills, the 28th August, 1792." This was probably the time when Cartwright became the owner. In the same year, reference is made to timber, for the "new mill," by which we learn that Mr. Cartwright found it desirable to re-build. The iron work for the new mill came to £14.

By the book, from which we have made extracts, we see that the name is spelled in different ways, the first being Appenea. For many years the name was spelled Apanee. It has been said that it was an Indian name, signifying flour, and was given by the Mississaugas, from the existence of the flouring mill. Napanee may signify flour, in the Indian language, but the inference drawn cannot be correct, as we find the name Appenea Falls given to the place in 1785, before the mill was commenced.

Cartwright having rebuilt the mill put in one run of stone at first, shortly after two, and then three. Robert Clark was the millwright, and one Profect was in charge of the works. The mill seems to have been constructed with some care, and Gourlay says, in 1817, that the Napanee mill is the best in the Province. The old account book from which we have gleaned, gives the price at which certain articles were vended. Thus, we learn that in June, 1787, and July 1788, butter sold at Napanee for 1s. per pound.

Some time after the erection of the Kingston and Napanee mills, others were erected in other parts of the Province; one at Four Mile Creek, one at the Niagara Falls, one at Fort Erie, another at the Mohawk Village, Grand River; and still later, one at Twelve Mile Creek. "In the year 1788, the first grist mill in Dundas was built by Messrs. Coons and Shaver in Matilda. It contained but one run of stone, and had a saw mill attached. It stood about a mile above the present village of Iroquois. It could grind 100 bushels of wheat per day, and turned out good flour. Soon after, another mill was built on a much larger scale, by John Munroe, also in Matilda, which had three run of stone." There was also a gang of saws. The machinery was driven by the St. Lawrence waters. At a still later period Van-Alstine's mill was erected, at the Lake on the Mountain.

The events connected with Captain, afterwards Major Van-Alstine, as a settler, are recorded in the settlement of Adolphustown. Directly opposite the rich and sloping land on the north shore, on which he settled, is a high prominent hill, which stands boldly up against the bay. This "mountain" is famous on account of the lake upon its summit, a particular account of which is given elsewhere. It is referred to here in a practical sense. While, upon the hill-top is the work of nature, presented in a striking manner; at its feet is the work of man, which, particularly in the past, was of no little consequence to the well-being of the settlers of the Bay. About the year 1796, the third flouring mill of the bay was erected at this place by VanAlstine, to whom had been granted a large tract of land. The surplus waters of the lake, in primeval days, made their escape over the cliff, falling into the bay, and forming, it must have been at times, a beautiful cascade. But, if Captain VanAlstine had a taste for the beautiful in nature, he also had a just appreciation of the wants of the people, and he proceeded to utilize the falling water. A canal was cut down the mountain side, to form a channel for the water to descend, and at the bottom was erected a mill, the machinery of which was to be propelled by the descending stream. From that day to this the work of grinding has been carried on. However beautiful the lake above, and delightful the prospect, they cannot exceed in interest the foundation of this mill. Imagination would almost give words to the sound of the mill, which so peacefully clicks the daily round of work. The down-rushing waters by the artificial channel would seem to utter reminiscences of the past—regrets that they may no longer tumble headlong over the hill-side to form a lovely cascade; but the water-witch has been driven away by the spirit of utilitarianism. This conspicuous hill has often been the point of hope, the goal to which the farmer turned his little bark, containing, it is true, but a few bushels of grain, yet so precious, and about which the hungry ones in the little log house, thought so frequently, with bodies long accustomed to suffer for the want of enough to eat. And, often this mountain stood up as a guide to the settler, as he trudged along wearily through the thick snow with a bag or two of grain upon a hand-sleigh. Although not the very first mill, it dates back to the last century.

The Kingston *Gazette* of the 16th April, 1811, contains an advertisement, signed by the executors of the deceased Major Van Alstine's will, namely, George W. Myers, Cornelius VanAlstine, and Thomas Dorland, in which it is stated that the mill contains two run of stone, one superfine and two common bolts.

A windmill was built at a somewhat early period, by Sergeant Howell, nearly opposite the Upper Gap, in Fredericksburgh. It was sold to one Russell, who was an Engineer in Kingston, in the war of 1812. The wind-mill was never much used, if at all.

About the beginning of the century, 1802, Capt. Myers built a flouring mill upon the Moira. (See Thurlow.) It seems to have been a good mill, for persons came a long distance to get grinding done. For instance: Isaiah Tubs, who lived at West Lake, would come, carrying a bag of grain upon his back.

In the year 1804, Mr. Wilkins says, a gristing mill was built at Consecon, to the south of the Carrying Place. Consecon is an Indian name, from Con-Cou, a pickerel.

CHAPTER XX.

CONTENTS—Clothing—Domestic and Farming Implements—Style of Dress eighty years ago—Clothing of the Refugees—Disbanded Soldiers—No Fresh Supply—Indian Garments of Skin—Deerskin Pants—Petticoats—Bed Coverings—Cultivating Flax—Sheep—Home-made Clothes—Rude Implements—Fulling—French Mode—Lindsay Woolsey—The Spinning-wheel—Industry—Young men Selecting Wives—Bees—Marriage Portion—Every Farmer his own Tanner and Shoemaker—Fashions—How odd hours were spent—Home-made Shoes—What Blankets were made of—Primitive Bedstead—Nakedness—Bridal Apparel—No Saddles—Kingston and Newark—Little Money—Bartering—Merchants from Albany—Unable to buy—Credit with Merchants—The Results—Itinerant Mechanics—Americans—Become Canadians—An old Stone-mason—Wooden Dishes—Making Spoons—Other Hardships—Indians Friendly—Effects of Alcohol upon the Mississaugas—Groundless Panic—Drunken Indians—Women, defending Themselves—An erroneous Statement about Indian Massacre in "Dominion Monthly Magazine"—Statement of an Old Settler, Sherwood—Wild Beasts—Few Fire-arms—Narrow Escapes—Depredations at Night—Destroying Stock—An Act of Parliament—"A Traveller's" Statement—The Day of Small Things—Settlers Contented—The Extent of their Ambition—Reward of Industry—Population in 1808—Importations—Money—The Youth.

CLOTHING—FURNITURE—DOMESTIC AND FARMING IMPLEMENTS.

The style of clothing worn by the refugees and disbanded soldiers was such as prevailed eighty years ago in England. A certain difference, no doubt, existed between the English and the Colonists, yet mainly the style was the same. Among the first settlers upon the bay were those who had fetched with them, and wore, at least occasionally, garments of fashionable cut and appointments. Tight knee-breeches and silver buckles would decorate the bodies of some, who had in other days mixed in the fashionable throng, perhaps luxuriated in the gay city of New York, where the presence of British soldiers always gave life and gaiety. Indeed some of the inhabitants had been commissioned officers in the regular army. Dr. Dougall, who had been in the navy, and who had settled in the sixth Township, is remembered as a wearer of "tights" and silver buckles. Also, Major VanAlstine wore this elegant attire, and the M'Leans, of Kingston. Those who left their homes hurriedly during the course of the war, and fled to Lower Canada and the several British Forts, brought only what was upon their backs. Those who came more leisurely might have a little more; but the distance to travel on foot would deter from undertaking to bring more than supplies of food. The disbanded soldiers had no more than what belongs to a soldier's kit, and no doubt the close of the war left many of them with well worn garments. A few year's of exposure to the wear and tear of pioneer life would quite destroy the best supplied wardrobe, however carefully husbanded, or ingeniously mended by the anxious wife. To replace the clothing was far from an easy matter to the settlers, many of whom had no money, certainly no time for a long journey to Montreal or Albany. After a few years, Kingston became a place of trade, but the supply of clothing was scant and dear, placing it beyond the reach of mostly all. The result was that the vast majority of the inhabitants had to look to the production of their lands wherewith to cover the nakedness of their families. Those living up the bay continued to want for clothing for a longer time, being unable to exchange with the merchants of Kingston, until peddlers began to visit the more remote settlers.

The faded garments, patched until the original material could no longer be distinguished, ultimately succumbed to the effects of time and labor.

The Indians, who as a general thing were friendly and kind, when they visited the settlement, gave to the settlers the idea of manufacturing garments out of deer skin. They, now and then exchanged skins for articles, the settlers could part with, and taught them how to prepare the fresh pelt so as to make it pliable. The process consisted in removing the hair and then working the hide by hand with the brains of some animal, until it was soft and white. Trowsers made of this material were not only comfortable for winter, but very durable. A gentleman who recently died in Sophiasburgh at an advanced age, remembered to have worn a pair for twelve years, being repaired occasionally, and at the end they were sold for two dollars and-a-half. Petticoats for women were often made of the same material. Roger Bates says "My grandmother made all sorts of useful dresses with these skins, which were most comfortable for a country life, and for going through the bush, could not be torn by the branches." Also, moccasins were procured from the buck-skin, and some had enough deer-skin to make covering for beds. But deer-skin was not sufficiently abundant to give covering to all, such as it was; and, certain clothing was required, for which it was unfit. Thus left to their own resources, the settlers commenced at an early period to cultivate flax, and as soon as possible to procure sheep. For many years almost every family made their various garments, for both sexes, of the coarse linen made from the flax, and cloth from wool raised at home and carded by hand. Preparing the flax for weaving, as well as spinning were done by hand, with inferior implements rudely made. But in later years, occasionally spinning wheels and looms were brought in by settlers. There were no fulling mills to complete the fabric. Even the mode adopted then, in Lower Canada, was not practised, which was as follows: A meeting of young folks, similar to a bee, was held from house to house, at which both sexes took part. The cloth to be fulled was placed in large tubs, and bare-legged youths would step in and with much amusement dance the fulling done. In Upper Canada, both high and low were glad to be able to don the home-made linen, and the linsey-woolsey petticoat.

"The growth of flax was much attended to as soon as lands were cleared and put in order." "Then spinning-wheels were all the go, and home-made linen, the pride of all families, manufactured substantial articles that would last a lifetime." The young men of industry would look for the spinning-wheel and loom before selecting a wife. "A young farmer would often be astonished to find on his marriage that his fair partner had got a good supply of linen for her marriage portion. I have known as much as sixty yards spun and manufactured at one bee or gathering."—*Clark*.

When the skins of sheep, and of calves and beef become available, every farmer became his own tanner, and dressed his leather; and then his own shoemaker. Fashions did not change, except as the continued practice of making for an increasing family, gave the maker ability to make something more like a boot than a moccasin. Rainy days, and the nights, were spent in doing such kind of work, not by candle light, but by the hearth fire. It was at the same time that an axe-helve, a wooden plow, a reaping cradle, a wooden fork, &c., were made. But many a child, whose grand children are now occupying positions of wealth and influence, stayed in the log cabin the winter through, because he had nothing with which to protect his feet from the snow. The writer's father was not a shoemaker by trade; but he remembers when a boy to have worn shoes made by him. They were not conspicuous for their beauty, but it was thought by the wearer they would last for ever; within his recollection there was not a shoemaker in Thurlow.

Much ingenuity was displayed in making clothes and blankets. What was called the "Kearsy" blanket was made at an early date; the writer has seen the first one said to have been manufactured in Upper Canada, certainly the first on the Bay Quinté. It is yet in use and belongs to one, nearly one hundred years of age, who is the daughter of the maker, whom we remember to have seen when a boy, who, although then in the sear and yellow leaf, was as tall and erect as if untold hardships had not crowned her life. Within fifteen miles of Belleville, across the Bay, was a log cabin, the occupants of which had for their first blanket, one made out of hair, picked out of the tanner's vat, and a hemp-like weed growing in the yard. The hair was first cleaned by whipping it; then it was carded and worked up with the hemp, and then spun. It was afterward doubled and twisted, and finally woven into a blanket. The individual whose wife did this, and whose descendants are among the most wealthy farmers, bought his farm for a horse. For many a day, they had no furniture, not even a chair, and the bedstead was made out of two poles, driven between the logs of the shanty; and basswood bark was twisted so as to bind them substantially together. Clean straw upon this, was really the only thing they had in the house. And so it was with very many, the exceptions being, some half pay officers, who had brought a table, or a chest of drawers. In 1790, the brother of an individual, holding an important post in Kingston, was near the head of the bay, staying at a house in a state of nakedness; in which condition his brother writes, "he must remain until I am able to go up." "I have agreed to put him to trial with a carpenter to learn the trade," he must therefore have been a large boy.

It was not until the close of the last century, that wearing articles, other than those made out of flax and wool, were to be obtained. A calico dress was a decided luxury. The petticoat, and short gown of linen, was more common. A long chintz dress to go to meeting, was the height of many a damsel's ambition, or a grogran dress and short petticoat. As years passed away, and a grown up daughter was about to be married, efforts would be made to array the bride in fitting costume. Often a dress, worn by the mother in other days, amid other scenes, which had been laid carefully away, was brought forth to light, and made by suitable alterations to do renewed service, although the white had assumed a yellow cast, and had lost its lustre.

As late as 1816, a farmer owning land in Sidney, and who died rich, made in winter a journey to Kingston with flour, wearing nothing on his feet, but a pair of shoes, and who had his trowsers strapped down to keep his ankles warm. Leg boots took too much leather. It was many years before a bridle and saddle were known, and then, but a few possessed such a convenience. Bare-back, or on a deer skin was the primitive mode.

After the erection of Upper Canada into a separate province; both Kingston and Newark, where there were always troops, and where articles of clothing were to be purchased from a few, who had gone into the mercantile business, exhibited a degree of comfort and even gaiety in dress.

At the first there was but little money in circulation. But few of the refugees, or disbanded soldiers had any when they entered the wilderness. The government were constantly paying a certain sum to the troops at Kingston and Newark, and likewise to the retired half pay officers. The few who could command money, were placed in a position of greater comfort, as soon as articles of provisions and merchandise, were brought to the new settlement. Mainly, however, trading was carried on by exchanging one commodity for another. Probably the first articles for trade, was the ticket for grants of land in the back concessions, often parted with so cheaply. The settlers required clothing, grain for sowing, and stock; these wants in time, led to trade, two kinds of which were introduced. One carried on by merchants established at Kingston, the other by pedlars, Yankee pedlars, who would come from Albany with their pack in a canoe or small batteau, and who plied their calling along the bay shore from clearing to clearing. Both the merchant at Kingston, who waited for his customers to come to him, and the pedlar who sought customers, asked for their wares, only grain or any other produce. But wheat was desired above all others. It was an event of no little interest to the back woodsman's family, when the pedlar's canoe or batteau came along, and halted before the log house, by the shore. And, even when their circumstances would not permit them to buy, it was a luxury to have a look at the things, which were so temptingly displayed. The toil-worn farmer, with well patched trowsers, would turn with an inward sigh from the piece of cloth, which although so much wanted, could not be got. The wife looked longingly at those little things, which would just suit baby. The grown up daughters gazed wistfully, but hopelessly at the bright calico prints, more valuable, in their eyes than the choicest silks are to their descendants to day. But a calico dress was a thing not enjoyed, but by few, until it was bought for the wedding dress. Frequently some articles of family use was exchanged for goods, which were deemed of more use. The trade of merchants at Kingston steadily increased ; but not a cash business. A credit system was initiated and carried on. Goods would be purchased with an engagement to pay in wheat or potatoes, or something else, at a certain time. Here and there along the bay were Indian fur traders. They, also, began to exchange with the settlers. While this was a great convenience, and gave immediate comfort to many a family, it, at the same time, led to serious results with many. Disappointed in the return of crops, or in some other way, the payment could not be made. Promissory notes were given at interest; and, after a few years, sueing and seizing of stock was the result. Sometimes even the farm went to satisfy the creditor. Unfortunately, there are too many such cases in the records of the settlers of the bay. Not alone did pedlars come from the States, to pick up the fruit of the industry, of those they had driven away; but there were itinerant Yankee mechanics who would occasionally come along, looking for a job. Carpenters, Masons, &c., after a few years, found much to do. We would not speak disparagingly of these Americans, because they served a good turn in erecting buildings, as houses, barns, &c. They also introduced many valuable articles of husbandry and domestic use. And finally, many of them forsook their republican government, and permanently settled under the King, and became the best of subjects. Even in the first decade of the present century, mechanics would go up and down the bay seeking work. For instance, there was one Travers, a stone mason, who found employment along the bay, and even up the lake. Of this we are informed by one of his apprentices who is now upwards of eighty years old. (We make place in our Review to state that John W. Maybee, referred to, aged 88, died 7th February, 1869.)

A hundred things enter into the list of what constitutes home comforts. But spare, indeed, were the articles to be found upon the kitchen shelves. Plain enough, was the spread table, at which the family gathered morning, noon, and night. Many had but one or two dishes, often of wood, rudely made out of basswood; and spoons of the same material. Knives and forks in many families were unknown. A few families had brought a very limited number of articles for eating, relics of other days, but these were exceedingly scarce. The wooden spoon was the most common table article with which to carry food to the mouth. By and by the pedlar brought pewter spoons, and once in a while the settler procured pewter and moulds and made spoons for himself.

VARIOUS HARDSHIPS.

Apart from the suffering arising from want of food, and clothing to wear, and furniture to make the house comfortable, there were others of more or less magnitude. It would naturally be expected that one of the first dangers in entering a wilderness, would be from the Indians, whose territory was being occupied. But in the main this evil was not added to their other distress. The considerate and just policy pursued by the British Government, left the Indians no cause of complaint, and they did not at any time assume an hostile attitude toward the infant colony. But that curse of the human race,—baneful curse to the Indians, alcohol, came with the white man; and, too often, the unscrupulous trader, and merchant would, not only sell the fire water to them, but rely upon its intoxicating qualities, to consummate more excellent bargains for furs. The evil thus inflicted upon the Indian, returned in some cases, upon innocent pioneers. The Indians under the influence of liquor are particularly savage and ungovernable; prone to exhibit their wild nature. Thirsting for the liquor, they would sometimes enter dwellings, when they new the men were absent, and endeavour to intimidate the women to give them rum. A few instances of alarm and actual danger, come to us, among the bay settlers. At one time particularly, there arose a wide spread alarm, (long remembered as the "Indian alarms,") that the Indians were, upon some fixed night, when the men were away to Kingston mills, going to massacre the settlers. This arose from some remarks, let fall by a half drunken Indian. A few of the settlers, did actually leave their homes, and sought protection in a more thickly settled locality, while active steps were taken to defend their homes against the Indians. Mrs. Dempsey, of seventh township, gathered up what she could, and with her children crossed in a canoe to the eight township. On another occasion, when her husband was absent, several half drunken Indians came to the house, and one stepping up to where she sat, trembling with fear, and with her little ones nestling close to her, drew his knife, and cutting a piece from the palm of his hand, held the bleeding wound before her face, crying out "look, look, Indian no fraid." Then he brandished his knife in the most menacing manner. She hearing the sound of a passing team, got up and slowly walked backwards to the door, looking the savage bravely in the eye all the time. Her husband had opportunely arrived, in time to save his family, which he did by a free use of the horse-whip. On another occasion, Mrs. D. savod her life and the childrens from drunken Indians, by rushing up a ladder with them, into the garret, which could only be reached by a small opening through the ceiling, and then hauling the ladder up. The Indians endeavoured to assist each other up, and through the entrance, but she having a knife succeeded by cutting their fingers, when they attempted to get up, in keeping them back. These hostile attempts were exceptions, and always the result of intoxication.

Since writing the above, an article has been published in the *Dominion Monthly Magazine*, in which it is stated that a family of settlers were massacred by the Indians upon the banks of the St. Lawrence in 1795. This statement is at variance with facts known to us, and with the testimony of one who cannot be mistaken. His statement is as follows:

BROCKVILLE, 13th April, 1868.

MY DEAR SIR,—

I am in receipt of your note of this date, adverting to the statement of the massacre of a family in Upper Canada, by the Indians in 1795. I noticed the same statement in some paper I have lately read, and at the time I thought it to be a mistake in the date, or an entire fabrication. I am not aware of the least hostility shewn by the Indians to any of the U. E. Loyalists since 1784, eleven years previous to date stated, and I do not believe a syllable of it.

Yours truly,

ADIEL SHERWOOD.

Although the native Indians did not, as a general thing, alarm the settler, there were wild beasts that did. For years the wolf, and the bear, and other ferocious animals were a source of terror and suffering. These animals, unaccustomed to the sight of man, were at first exceedingly tame. The settlers had but few fire-arms, and ammunition was very scarce; and the beasts knew no terror of them. They would even by day, come to the very door of the cabin, ready to seize the little child, or the scanty stock of poultry, pigs, or sheep, or calves, or salted provisions which had been left exposed, government stores, &c. And at night they made the most hideous and incessant howls, until morning. Many instances of their rapacity in robbing the scanty yard of the settlers, and of hair breadth escapes of individuals from wolves and bears, are mentioned. The destruction of stock by the wolf especially, caused the government of Canada, at an early date, (1793,) to legislate, with a view of gradually exterminating them; and an act was passed, granting a premium of four dollars to every one who should bring a wolf's head to the proper officer; and two dollars for a bears. It was withdrawn with regard to bears, in 1796. "A traveller," writing in 1835, remarks that in Kingston, resided a person who privately bred wolves to obtain the reward. But whether such an enterprising citizen did actually live in the good old town the writer saith not. Instances of narrow escapes from the wild beasts are still remembered, for instance, Lewis Daly, of Ernest town, was suddenly attacked by a bear within a mile of home. He sprung up a small tree, which bending over, he was in momentary danger of being reached. His cries brought help.

In those early days, the settler, looked not for great things; schooled by the hardships of civil war, and inured to want, and half starvation, they asked not for riches. Enough to eat, and to be warmly clad, and housed from the winter's cold, was the great point to which they stretched their longing hopes. Plenty in the future for the little ones, and for themselves, when they had grown old, was the single purpose of their toilsome life. A descendant of a first settler upon the front of Sidney, tells of his grandmother whom he had heard say, that her great ambition at first, was to raise vegetable, onions and other useful articles in her garden bed; to have poultry then, about her. After years she got the fowls; but a mink, in a single night killed them all. Then, again, they had got a breeding sow, and one morning a bear walked out of the woods, and with one hug destroyed all their hopes of future porkers.

Gradually, as years passed away, comforts began to reward the patient and industrious pioneers; acre after acre was brought under cultivation. The log house received an addition, a little stock was procured, and the future brightened up before them, and by the year 1808, the settlements in Upper Canada were increasing in number, and spreading in every direction. "The frontier of the country was fast filling up. Persons were taking up land several miles from the water's edge. Some had ventured to take up land in the second tier of townships, in the midst of the wilderness, and many miles from any habitation. The population was now increased to about 70,000 souls. The importations was chiefly liquors and groceries, which by the St. Lawrence and the United States, brought a revenue of nearly £7,000. The bulk of the inhabitants manufactured and wore their own clothing. The way of trade was mostly by barter, as gold and silver were scarce, and there were no banks to issue paper currency. Intemperance was very prevalent, and schools were scarce. The youth were too fond of foolish amusements."—(*Playter.*)

CHAPTER XXI.

CONTENTS—Sweat of the Brow—No Beast of Burden—No Stock—Except by a Few—Horses and Oxen—From Lower Canada—York State—Later comers, brought some—No Fodder—First Stock in Adolphustown—Incidents—Cock and Hen—"Tipler"—Cattle Driving—First Cow in Thurlow—First House in Marysburgh—The First Oxen—No Market for Butter and Cheese—Sheep—Rev. Mr. Stuart, as an Agriculturist—Horses at Napanee—An offer for a Yoke of Steers.

INTRODUCTION OF STOCK AND BEASTS OF BURDEN.

We have seen that the refugees and disbanded soldiers who entered Canada, brought but a limited number of implements, and those of an imperfect nature. The most of them had no means of lessening labor, no beasts of burden. All the work had to be done by the sturdy arm, and by the sweat of the brow. For years, mostly all alike thus labored, and for many years the increasing number continued to toil, being unable to procure beasts of burden, or any stock. The distance to go for them was too far, and the way too difficult to be undertaken easily. But, a greater difficulty, an insurmountable reason was that they had not the means to purchase, until years of struggling had extracted from the ground, covered with stumps, produce to exchange for the much required help, in the form of beasts of burden. Some of the half-pay officers, and other persons, favored by those holding some situations in the government, were enabled to get beasts of burden at first, or within a year or two. There were a few old soldiers who had a little money, received at being discharged; and again, some sold their location tickets of a portion of their land, and thereby were enabled to make purchase of cows or oxen.

For beasts of burden, they, as a general thing, preferred oxen in preference to horses, to work among the stumps with. Both oxen and horses were brought from Lower Canada and York State. The later comers, especially, fetched with them horses, oxen and cows from the latter place.

A few of the very first settlers, perhaps, brought one or more cows. We find it stated that the disbanded soldiers had a cow allotted to every two families; these must have been procured at Lower Canada, perhaps a few by way of Oswego, where were stationed some troops. Sheriff Ruttan, speaking of the famine, says: "We had the luxury of a cow which the family brought with them." Thomas Goldsmith came in 1786, and drove a lot of cattle to the Bay: but he could not get enough for them to eat and they starved to death, excepting one heifer and a yoke of oxen. The Petersons, who settled in the Fourth Town in 1785, and cleared a small lot of land, went "the following year to Montreal and brought up some horses and three cows, which comprised the principal stock then in the Township."

After a few years, when the settlers had become somewhat established, steps were taken more generally, to procure stock, so necessary to give ordinary comfort to their families; while those who now entered the country brought cows with them. Although the cows and oxen were procured occasionally from Lower Canada; the most of them were obtained from the States; but the horses were in the main at first, brought from Lower Canada. Many incidents attending the long and devious journey through the wilderness, are still told. Thomas Goldsmith, before mentioned, who settled in Prince Edward, came into Canada by way of the Mohawk, Wood Creek, Oneida Lake, and Oswego river, thence to Cataraqui. He undertook to drive some cattle through the woods to Cape Vincent, piloted by a friendly Indian, to swim them across the St. Lawrence. In this journey he suffered almost every privation—hunger, fatigue, exposure. Resting one night in the ordinary manner, with his head slightly raised, upon the root of a tree, with no other covering than the tree's branches, and sleeping very soundly, after a day's walking, he became benumbed from exposure, and knew not of the rapidly descending rain, which had actually covered his body when he awoke. Yet this man lived to be ninety years old. Driving cattle through the woods was no easy matter, and dogs were often employed for that purpose. Ex-Sheriff Sherwood, in his valuable memorandum, relates an incident which throws light upon those primitive days. After remarking how well he recollects the pleasure, he and an elder brother experienced from a present made them of a cock and hen, no common luxuries then, and with what care they watched over them, he says: "let me tell you the tragic story of our little 'Tipler,' she had become famed for driving cattle, and we thought much of her. Two persons, one named Urehart, from the Bay Quinté, and the other Booth, started to go through the woods to Fort Stanwix for cattle, and prevailed upon my father to let them take poor little 'Tipler.' We saw them safe across the river; but, sad to say, neither the men nor Tipler were ever heard of after."

John Ferguson, writing from Sidney, in July 1791, says that he cannot get horses for the farm until winter.

In the summer of 1787, Elisha Miller and Col. Richey brought from Saratoga County several cattle and horses. They were driven by way of Black River, and swam the St. Lawrence at Gananoque.

The Reeds, who settled in Thurlow, in 1789, had a cow, which afforded the principal means of sustenance. This, with basswood leaves and other greens, constituted their food for many a day.

Mr. Harrison, now living in Marysburgh, tells of the first horse " below the rock." It was brought, and owned by Colonel McDonald. This, and another were the only ones for many years. Afterward, oxen were brought in, as well as cows, by drovers from Lower Canada.

Rochfoucault says, 1795: "The cattle are not subject to contageous distempers; they are numerous, without being remarkably fine. The finest oxen are procured from Connecticut, at the price of seventy or eighty dollars a yoke. Cows are brought, either from the State of New York, and these are the finest; or from Lower Canada; the former costs twenty, and the latter fifteen dollars. These are small in size, but, in the opinion of the farmers, better milch cows, and are, for this reason, preferred. There are no fine bulls in the country; and the generality of farmers are not sensible of the advantages to be derived from cattle of a fine breed. In the summer, the cattle are turned into the woods; in winter, that is, six months together, they are fed on dry fodder. There is no ready market at which a farmer can sell that part of his cheese and butter which is not wanted for the use of the family. Of cheese and butter, therefore, no more is made than the family need for their own consumption." Sheep are more numerous here than in any part of the United States, which we have hitherto traversed. They are either procured from Lower Canada or the State of New York, and cost three dollars a head. They thrive in this country, but are high-legged, and of a very indifferent shape. Coarse wool, when cleaned, costs two shillings a pound."

The above information was derived, the writer says, from Mr. Stuart, the Curate of Kingston, "who cultivates, himself, seventy acres of land, a part of 2,000 acres which had been granted him as a Loyalist. Without being a very skilful farmer, he is perfectly acquainted with the details of agriculture." These statements refer no doubt, to the settlements of the Bay. There is reference to horses, by Col. Clarke, whose father, living at the Napanee Mills in 1788, had two favorite horses, Jolly and Bonny.

In an old account book, now before us, for which we are

indebted to Mr. P. C. Clarke, of Collinsby, and which belonged to his grandfather, Robert Clarke, who built the Napanee Mills, we find the following entry.

"Appenea Falls, 23rd November, 1785.

"Acct. of work for Adam Bower with his horses. Dec. 3, To "day's work, do., &c. He continued to work for sixty-two days with his horses."

The following supplies valuable information:

"Appanne Mills, 3rd Aug. 1788.

"Messrs. Collins and Frobisher, Dr." &c. (They must have been agents for the Government).

"Aug. 21st. To David Bradshaw, one day with his oxen, 6s. "June 11. To Samuel Browson, Jun'r., 2 days work with two "yoke of oxen, at 10s. March 28th. To 11½ days, Adam Arehart, "with a span of horses, at 6s.

"1789. Oct. 1. To Asa Riehard; 9 days work with a pair of "horses and a woman, at 9s.

There is a memorandum in Robert Clarke's book, as follows: "Mr. Joseph Crane got at Canada" (it will be remembered that the first settlers spoke of the Lower Province as Canada) "a bay horse six years old. A brown mare four years old. Second Township, 13th March, 1787."

The Dempsey's drove in, 100 miles, some cattle in 1789 to Ameliasburgh. He was offered 200 acres of land for a yoke of four-year-old steers, which offer he refused. At another time he was offered 100 acres for a cow.

CHAPTER XXII.

CONTENTS—Old Channels of Trade, and Travel—Art and Science—New Channels—The Wilderness—Loyalists Traveling on Foot, from Kingston to York—Formation of Roads—Act of Parliament—1793—Its Provisions—Crooked Roads—Foot-path—Bridle-path—King's Highway from Lower Canada—When Surveyed—Road from Kingston Westward—Its Course—Simcoe's Military Road—Dundas Street—Asa Danforth—Contract with Government—Road from Kingston to Ancaster—Danforth Road—1799—Misunderstandings—Danforth's Pamphlets—Slow Improvement—Cause—Extract from Gourlay—Thomas Markland's Report—Ferries—1796—Acts of Parliament—Statute Labor—Money Grants—Commissioners—Midland District—Distribution—The Cataraqui Bridge Company—The Petitioners—An Act—The Provisions—The Plan of Building—The Bridge—Toll—Completing the Bridge—Improvement of Roads—McAdam—Declines a Knighthood.

THE CONSTRUCTION OF ROADS THROUGH THE WILDERNESS.

The channels followed by the Europeans, as they penetrated the unknown wilderness of America, were those indicated by the Indians, who had themselves for centuries followed them, in their pursuit after the chase, or when upon the war path. The great routes mentioned elsewhere, are the natural ones, and no other could have been pursued. It was only when art and science followed emigration to the new world that new channels were opened up, and the canal and railroad superseded the old devious ways along the windings of rivers.

Prior to the visiting of Europeans, the Indian paths were more or less trodden as the requirements of food and the existence of prey led the hunter here or there, or the war cry led them to the deadly encounter. But when the Europeans initiated trade by giving for furs the attractive trinkets, and such articles as contributed to the Indian taste of comfort and grandeur, then there were more regular and frequent travelings from the sea-board to the far west.

The occupation of Western Canada found the country in its primeval state; a vast wilderness, and no roads. The only way of traveling from one clearing to another was by the canoe and batteau, or by foot through the trackless woods, guided by the banks of the bay, or a river, or the blazing of the trees. For a long time not even a bridle-path existed, had there been horses to ride upon. Even at a late date, journeys were made on foot from Kingston to York along the lake shore. The formation of roads was a very slow process. In the year 1793, an act was passed "to Regulate the Laying out, Amending, and Keeping in Repair, the Public Highways and Roads." The roads were to be not less than thirty feet, nor more than sixty wide. Each settler was under obligation to clear a road across his lot; but there was the reserve lands for the Clergy and Crown, which were not provided with roads. Any one traveling the older settled districts will be struck with the devious character of the highways. The configuration of the Bay Quinté, and the mode of laying out the lots to secure a frontage upon the water, tended to cause this irregularity. The settlements being apart, when a communication took place between them the shortest cut would be taken, so far as hill, and marsh, and creek would permit. The consequences were that many of the roads were angular with the lots, or running zigzag. In later years, some of these roads were closed up, but many remain to mark an original foot-path. The banks of the bay and of creeks and rivers were naturally followed, as sure guides, or perhaps as an Indian path. And thus sometimes the road was made not direct, but round-about. In the survey of the concessions, provision was made for roads between the concessions, and cross-roads were to be left between every fifth and sixth lots.

Many of the main roads were at first marked by the blazing of the trees, when made through the woods, after a while a foot-path could be seen, and then boughs were trimmed off, that one might ride on horseback; and in time the sleigh was driven, and finally a waggon road was made.

Government was slack in giving funds to open up the country, and the legislation, for many years, in reference to the subject, seemed as if it was intended to do as little as possible, forgetting the fact that "the first improvement of any country should be the making of good roads." But it soon became important to have a mail road between Montreal and Kingston, and between Kingston and York, and then by way of Dundas to the Thames, and to Niagara. Says Mr. A. Sheerwood, "I recollect when the King's highway was established from the Provincial line to Kingston, the line was run by a surveyor named Ponair, with a surveyor under his direction by the name of Joseph Kilborne. The distance from the Provincial line to my father's farm, three miles below Brockville, was ninety-five miles, and from Brockville to the fort, this side of Kingston, fifty miles, at the end of each mile was planted a red cedar post, marked on it the number of miles from the Provincial line, this line of road was made some years after the first settlement, but I have forgotten the year." The original mail road between Kingston and York did not altogether follow the present line. At first, from Kingston, the road followed the bay shore to Bath, and continued along the shore to Adolphustown to Dorland's Point, where was established a ferry to communicate with Marysburg at the Lake of the Mountain; thence the road followed the shore to the head of Picton Bay, and so on to Bloomfold, Wellington, Consecon, by the Carrying Place, and continued to closely follow the lake shore. Subsequently this great highway was called the York Road when going towards York, and the Kingston Road when going towards Kingston.

Gen. Simcoe intended to have a grand military road from one end of the Province to the other. This he lined out and gave it the name of Dundas Street. But he left the Province before his intentions were carried out, and but a small portion was then constructed; while settlers had located here and there along the proposed road, and had cleared land and built with the full expectation that the great thoroughfare would shortly be opened up. But years passed away, before this was done. Piece after piece was here and there made passable, until at last the road was made through the length of the Province.

The late Mr. Finkle of Ernest Town writes: "An American gentleman came into Canada, 1798, by the name of Asa Danforth, and made a contract with the Upper Canada Government, to open a road from Kingston through to Ancaster, at the head of Lake Ontario, which road he completed. Danforth's home was at my fathers (Henry Finkle), before and after the contract was taken. The work commenced in 1798, and was finished in three years time." This road passed through Prince Edward by Wellington. Danforth "became dissatisfied with the government when the settlement took place, and left Canada with a bitter feeling, so much so, that he, some time after, sent to my father a package of pamphlets, he had published to shew the injustice of the government transaction. He desired they should be circulated through the country along the road. However, the pamphlets were not distributed, and the fact never became generally known." For many years the main road was called the Danforth Road.

As time advanced, the road between York and Kingston was gradually improved. The great hindrance to road making is sufficiently indicated by the following, taken from Gourlay. It is the expression of a meeting of yeomen, held at the village of Waterloo, Kingston, February 2, 1818, Major John Everett in the chair. Among other things it is asserted that what retards the progress is that "great quantities of land in the fronts and public situations, that remain unimproved, by being given very injudiciously to persons who do not want to settle on them, and what is most shameful and injurious, no law is made to compel them to make or work any public road; but this is to be done by industrious people, who settle around. Such lands remain like a putrid carcass, an injury and a nuisance to all around: at the same time, to the owners, this land increases in value, without their being made to contribute towards it, at other men's expense. Our worthies, a few years ago, passed an act, that required a poor man to work three days upon the public roads, and these overgorged land-owners but twelve days, and others, with twenty times as much property, doing no more. It would excite surprise at Governor Gore's signing such a bill, if it was not known that the Parliament voted him £3,000. to buy a piece of plate."

Says Thomas Markland, in a General Report of Midland District:

"The same cause which has surrounded Little York with a desert, creates gloom and desolation about Kingston, otherwise most beautifully situated; I mean the seizure and monopoly of the land by people in office and favour. On the east side, particularly, you may travel miles together without passing a human dwelling; the roads are accordingly most abominable to the very gates of this, the largest town in the Province; and its market is often supplied with vegetables from the United States, where property is less hampered, and the exertions of cultivators more free, accordingly.'"

In 1797, Parliament passed an Act, which was the first "for the regulation of ferries."

In 1794, an Act was passed "to make further provisions respecting Highways and Roads." An Act was passed, 1798, respecting "Statute duties on Highways and Roads." In 1804 an Act was passed "granting £1,000 for repairing, laying out new roads, and building bridges in the several districts." Again, in 1808 £1,600 was granted for the same purpose; and again the same sum in the following year. In 1811, £3,450 was granted. In 1812, an Act was passed "to prevent damage to travelers on the highways of the Province. All persons meeting sleighs or waggons to turn out to the right, and give half the way. Two or more bells to be attached to every sleigh.

In 1812, it was found that "many roads were unnecessarily

laid out; to remedy this, every one had to be confirmed by Justices of the Peace, and if this were not done, the party who applied for the survey should pay for the same.

In 1814, £6,000 was granted for Highways and Bridges; and the year following, "£20,500 to be appropriated," and Commissioners were appointed on the road, to receive £25 each. Again, the year after, £21,000 was granted.

In 1819, Parliament passed an "Act repealing and amending certain portions of previous Acts," by which a more elaborate provision was made to secure statute labor. This was again amended in 1824. In 1826 was enacted to grant £1,200 for making and reparing roads and bridges—Item: "In aid of the Society for improving the Public Roads," in a part of Ernesttown and Kingston. In 1830, £13,650 was granted "for the improvement of Roads and Bridges," of which the Midland District received £1,900, to be expended as follows, by contract after public notice: "On the Montreal road, between the Town of Kingston, and the limits of the County of Frontenac, the sum of fifty pounds. Joseph Franklin, Elijah Beach, and James Atkinson to be Commissioners for expending the same: On the road leading from the Town of Kingston, to the Village of Waterloo, the sum of fifty pounds; and that Samuel Askroyd, Horace Yeomans, and Benjamin Olcott, be Commissioners for expending the same. On the leading road from Kingston to the Village of Bath, the sum of one hundred pounds, and that Henry Lasher, Joseph Amy, and Prentiss J. Fitch, be Commissioners for expending the same. On the road leading from the Village of Waterloo to the Napanee Mills, the sum of three hundred and fifty pounds; and that the Treasurer and Trustees of the Kingston and Earnesttown Road Society be Commissioners for expending the same. On the road leading from Loughborough to Waterloo, the sum of fifty pounds; and that Samuel Aykroyd, John Campbell, and Henry Wood be Commissioners for expending the same. On the road leading from the fifth Concession of Portland to the third concession of the Township of Kingston, fifty pounds; and that Jacob Shibly, Byron Spike, and Thomas Sigsworth, be Commissioners for expending the same. On the road leading from Bath to the Township of Camden, the sum of fifty pounds; and that Ebenezer Perry, Benjamin Clarke, and John Perry, be Commissioners for expending the same. On the road leading from Wessel's Ferry, in Sophiasburg, to Demorest's Mill, the sum of one hundred pounds; and that Abraham VanBlaricum, Daniel B. Way, and Guilliam

Demorest, be Commissioners for expending the same. On the road between the widow M'Cready's and the north-east of Chrysler's Creek Bridge, in the seventh concession of Thurlow, the sum of twenty-five pounds. On the road in the township of Huntington, leading to the township of Madoc, and surveyed by W. Ketcheson, in one-thousand eight hundred and twenty-eight, seventy-five pounds, and that Jacob Jowngs, of Thurlow, Garret Garritson, of Huntingdon, and James O'Hara, of Madoc, be Commissioners for expending the same. On the road leading from the Napanee Mills to Belleville, the sum of eight hundred pounds, and that Allan McPherson, John Turnbull, William Post, David B. Soles, and John Mabee, of Thurlow, be Commissioners for expending the same. On the road leading from VanAlstine's ferry to the Carrying Place, the sum of two hundred pounds, and that Simeon Washburn, Esquire, Charles Biggar, Esquire, and Jesse Henderson, be Commissioners for expending the same.".

During the same session, "there being reason to believe there would not be enough means on hand to meet the grant, "an Act was passed to raise by loan £8000. The year after another Act was passed to raise by debenture the sum of £40,000 more to be appropriated to the several districts. The Midland district to receive £2,200. Among the specifications, were "in the Indian woods" £200 for the bridge at the mouth of the little Cataraqui, £50 "to assist in erecting new bridge across Marsh Creek, near William Brickman's, in Ameliasburgh," £20. "To erect a bridge across East Creek, at the east end of East Lake, £50." "On the road leading from Belleville to the Marmora Iron Works, £250.

In March, 25, 1828, there was passed an Act respecting "a road between Ernesttown and the Gore of Fredericksburgh."

The Preamble says, "whereas, in consequence of a dispute having arisen between the Justices of the Peace of Ernesttown and Fredericksburgh, respecting the right of either party to take charge" of the road, and to which party the right of repairing it belongs, "in consequence of which dispute, the aforesaid road though much traveled from necessity, is dangerous and difficult to travel, on account of being left, in a great measure, for a long time past, without being mended," &c. It was enacted that the two townships should equally take charge and keep in repair the said road, certain portions being allotted to each.

In 1827 an act was passed to incorporate "The Cataraqui Bridge Company." Up to this time the communication between

Kingston and the opposite point of Frederick, was only by boat. The Act, or some portions of it cannot but be interesting: "Whereas John H. Glover, John Marks, John Macaulay, John Kerby, Christopher Alexander Hagerman, Michael Sproatt, John P. Hawkins, Robert Moore, Charles Jones, Stephen Yarwood, Augustus Barber, George Calls, Richard Williams, James B. Forsyth, George McBeath, Adam Kieu, John S. Cartwright, Robert D. Cartwright, Alexander Anderson, George O'Kill Stuart, Laughlin Currin, Donald McPherson, James Jackalls, the younger, Francis Archibald Harper, John Cumming, James Sampson, Elizabeth Herchmer, Catharine Markland, Anne Macaulay, John Jenkins, and Edward Forsyth, have petitioned to be incorporated," &c. (This furnishes us with the names of the more prominent persons at that time interested in Kingston). "And whereas, they have represented, by their agents, that they have made arrangements with His Majesty's Government, in case the object above recited be carried into effect, for the passage of Military and Naval stores, and of the officers and men belonging and attached to the various Military and Naval departments, for a certain consideration to be annually paid by the Government, and that for the purpose of this incorporation, they have subscribed stock to the amount of £6000."

The Act of Incorporation provided that "the said Company are authorized and empowered, at their own cost and charges, to erect and build a good and substantial bridge over the great river Cataraqui, near the town of Kingston, from the present scow landing on the military reserve, opposite to the north-east end of the continuation of Front Street to the opposite shore on Point Frederick, at the present scow landing on the Military Reserve, adjoining the western addition of the Township of Pittsburgh, with convenient access thereto at both ends of the bridge, to and from the adjacent highways, at present in use; that the said bridge shall be at least twenty-five feet wide, and of sufficient strength for artillery carriages," &c., &c.; they shall also be at liberty to build toll-houses, and toll-bars; Provided always, that there be a draw-bridge not less than eighteen feet, in some part, for the passage of all vessels, which bridge shall be opened at all hours required without exacting toll, and a space for rafts between the piers, forty feet."

The amount of toll to be demanded from man and beast, and vehicle, was fully specified in the Act.

The Company was to be managed by five Directors, Stockholders to hold office for one year from each last Monday in January. The bridge was to be completed within three years.

It was provided that no ferry should be allowed, nor other barge

The final clause enacted that after fifty years his Majesty might assume the possession of the bridge, upon paying to the Company the full value thereof, to be ascertained by three arbitrators.

March 20, 1829, an Act was passed extending the time for completing the bridge, two years from the passing of the Act.

We have seen how the roads throughout Canada, were gradually constructed. As time advanced steps were taken, sometimes however very tardily, to place public thoroughfares in a more passable condition. We believe the road from Kingston to Napanee, was the first to be macadamized, which for many long years was the exception in an execrable road, stretching between Kingston and York. The originator of macadamized roads was John Loudoun McAdam. He was born in Scotland in 1756; emigrated to New York when a lad, and remained in that City throughout the Revolution. Under the protection of the British troops, he accumulated a considerable fortune, as agent for the sale of prizes. At the close of the war he returned to his native land, with the loss of nearly all his property. His system of making roads is too well known to require description. The British Government gave him £10,000, and tendered the honor of knighthood, which he declined, but which was conferred on his son, James Nicholl McAdam. He died at Moffat, County of Dumfries, in 1836, aged eighty years.

CHAPTER XXIII.

CONTENTS.—Ode to Canada—Early events—First English child in America, 1587—In New England—First French child, 1621—First in Upper Canada, 1783—In Prince Edward—Adolphustown—Ameliasburgh—North of the Rideau—Indian marriage ceremony—Difficulty among first settlers to get clergymen—First marriage in America, 1608—First in New England, 1621—First in Canada, 1620—Marriageable folks—No one to tie the matrimonial knot—Only one clergyman—Officers marrying—Magistrates empowered—Legislation, 1793—Its provision—Making valid certain marriages—Further legislation, 1798—In 1818—1821—1831—Clergymen of all denominations permitted to marry—Methodist ministers—Marriage license, 1814—Five persons appointed to issue—A noticeable matter—Statements of Bates—Mode of courting in the woods—Newcastle wedding expeditions—Weapons of defence—Ladies' dresses—The lover's "rig"—A wedding ring—Paying the magistrate—A good corn basket—Going to weddings—"Bitters"—Old folks stay at home—The dance, several nights—Marriage outfit—Frontier life—Morals in Upper Canada—Absence of irregularities—Exceptional instances—Unable to get married, Peter and Polly—A singular witness—Rev. Mr. Stuart—Langhorn—McDowell—How to adorn the bride—What she wore—A wedding in 1808—On horseback—The guests—The wedding—The banquet—The game of forfeits—The night—Second day wedding—The young folks on horseback—Terpischorean—An elopement by Canoe—The Squire—The chase—The lovers successful—The Squires who married.

"ODE TO CANADA."

Canada faithful! Canada fair!
Canada, beautiful, blooming and rare!
Canada, happiest land of the earth!
Hail to thee, Canada! land of my birth!
Land of fair freedom, where bought not and sold,
Are sinews and sorrows, for silver and gold!
Land of broad lakes, sweet valleys and plains!
Land where justice for rich and poor reigns!
Land of tall forests, famed rivers and rills!
Land of fair meadows, bold mountains and hills!
Land where a man is a man, though he toil!
Land where the tiller is lord of the soil!
Land where a people are happy and free—
Where is the land that is like unto thee?
Thou hast for the stranger that seeketh thy shore
A smile, and a cheer, and a welcome in store;
The needy, relief; and the weary repose;
A home for thy friends; and a grave for thy foes.
Thy nobles are those whose riches in store
Is the wealth of the soul, and the heart's hidden lore;
They cringe to no master, they bow to no lord
Save Heaven's, each night and each morning adored.
Land of swift rivers, sweet-gliding along!
Land of my pride, and land of my song!
Canada, prosperous! Canada, true!
Canada loyal, and virtuous, too!
Canada, happiest land of the earth!
Hail thee, forever, sweet land of my birth!

THE FIRST NATIVES OF UPPER CANADA.

We turn from the sad pictures which have been truthfully, if imperfectly done, which represent the darker side of the pioneer life of the refugees, to others more pleasing. In those primitive times, events which now seem trivial to a general public, were of general interest, and the recollection cherished by a whole community. In the absence of those stirring events which characterize the present, incidents of comparative unimportance, became household words, and recollections. Hence, it comes that posterity may, in some instances, know who were first married in certain places in America, of the first birth, and who first died.

"The first child born of English parents in America, was a daughter of Mrs. Dore, of Virginia, October 18, 1587." "There is now standing in Marshalfield, Cape Cod, a portion of a house built by Perigrine White, the first male child born of English parents in New England.' According to the testimony of the registrar of Quebec, the first white child born in Canada, was upon the 24th October, 1621, which was christened the same day by the name of Eustache, being the son of Abraham and Margaret L'Anglois; Abraham was a Scotchman, named Martin Abraham. He was king's pilot, and married to Eustache. The plains of Abraham derive their name from him.

In the obituary notice of Rev. Mr. Pringle, a Methodist preacher, it is stated that he was born in Prince Edward, in 1780, but this must be a mistake. There is sufficient proof that the first settlement at Smith's Bay commenced in 1784, when the first part of Prince Edward became settled. Perhaps, indeed, very likely, the first children born of European parents, was the late Colonel John Clark, of Dalahousie, and an elder brother and sister. His father, an Englishman, came to Quebec, attached to the 8th regiment in 1768. From a sergeant-major, he was appointed in 1776, clerk and naval store keeper at Carleton Island. Here, Sarah and William Clark were born during the progress of the war. Col. Clark says, "I was born at Frontenac, now Kingston, in 1783, and was baptized by the Rev. Mr. Stuart.

The Rev. Mr. Pringle, before alluded to, was the first, or among the first-born in Prince Edward.

A son of Thomas Dorland, claimed to be the first white child born in the fourth township; but the honor was disputed by Daniel Peterson. Mrs. Wm. Ketcheson, now living in Sidney, daughter of

Elizabeth Roblin, of Adolphustown, was born there in 1784. She must have been one of the very first, as the first settlers came that same year. On the 16th January 1785, Henry VanDusen was born in Adolphustown, being one of the first natives.

Upon the 26th April, 1868, was buried Mrs. Bush, she was the first female born in Ameliasburgh. Mr. Bleeker, yet living at Trenton, was the first male child born in Ameliasburgh. Mrs. Covert, was also one of the first persons born in Ameliasburgh.

The first person said to have been born in Toronto, was Mr. J. Cameron, of Yonge Street, in 1798.

The first child born of white parents north of the Rideau, was Colonel E. Burritt, Burritt's Rapids, a relative of Elihu Burritt.

MARRYING IN EARLY TIMES.

The native Indians of America practiced no important ceremony in connection with marrying. Certain steps had to be taken by the one who might desire to have a certain female as his partner, and those proceedings were always strictly attended to. But the final ceremony consisted in little more than the affianced one, leaving the wigwam of her father and repairing to that of her future lord and master. In many cases the first settlers of America experienced some difficulty in obtaining the services of a Christian minister to solemnize matrimony. In French Canada there was not this difficulty, as from the first the zealous missionary was ever beside the discoverer as he pressed on his way.

The first Christian marriage solemnized in America, took place in Virginia in 1608, between John Loyden and Ann Burras. The first marriage in New England was celebrated the 12th May, 1621, at Plymouth, between Edward Waislow and Susannah White. The first marriage in the colony of French Canada, was between Guillaume Couillard and Guillmet Hebert, July 1620. This is found in the first parish register, which was commenced this year, 1620.

Among the pioneers of Upper Canada, were persons of every class as to age, from the tender infant at the breast, to the gray-headed man. There were young men and young women, as well as the aged, and as hopes and desires exist to-day in the breast of the young, so did they then. As the gentle influence of love animates at the present time, so it did then. But there was a serious drawback; the consummation of courtship could not easily be realized. Throughout the vast length of the settlements there were but few clergymen to celebrate matrimony, and many sighing swains had to wait months, and even years of wearisome time to have performed the matrimonial ceremony. At the first, when a chaplain was attached to a regiment, he was called upon, but when the settlers commenced to clear, there was no chaplain connected with the regiment. Indeed, Mr. Stuart, of Kingston, was the only clergyman in all Upper Canada for a few years. But the duties of the chaplain were frequently attended to by an officer, especially at Niagara, and many of the first marriages in the young colony were performed by a colonel, an adjutant, or a surgeon. Subsequently, magistrates were appointed, who were commissioned to tie the nuptial knot.

In the second session of the first Parliament, 1793, was passed "*An Act to confirm and make valid certain marriages heretofore contracted in the country now comprised within the Province of Canada, and to provide for the future solemnization of marriage within the same.*"

"Whereas many marriages have been contracted in this Province at a time when it was impossible to observe the forms prescribed by law for the solemnization thereof, by reason that there was no Protestant parson or minister duly ordained, residing in any part of the said Province, nor any consecrated Protestant church or chapel within the same, and whereas the parties having contracted such marriages, and their issue may therefore be subjected to various disabilities, in order to quiet the minds of such persons and to provide for the future solemnization of marriage within this Province, be it enacted and declared by the King's Most Excellent Majesty, by and with the advice and consent of the Legislative Council and Assembly of the Province of Upper Canada, that the marriage and marriages of all persons, not being under any canonical disqualification to contract matrimony, that have been publicly contracted before any magistrate or commanding officer of a post, or adjutant, or surgeon of a regiment, acting as chaplain, or any other person in any public office or employment, before the passing of this Act, shall be confirmed and considered to all intents and purposes as good and valid in law, and that the parties who have contracted such marriages, and the issue thereof, may become severally entitled to all the rights and benefits, and subject to all the obligations arising from marriage and consanguinity, in as full and ample a manner as if the said marriages had respectively been solemnized according to law.

"And be it further enacted, that in order to enable those persons who may be desirous of preserving the testimony of such marriage. and of the birth of their children, it shall and may be lawful at any time, within three years from the passing of this Act, for any magistrate of the district where any such parties as may have contracted matrimony as aforesaid, shall reside, at the request of either of said parties, to administer to each an oath that they were married on a certain day, and that there is now living issue of the marriage. This attestation to be subscribed to by the parties and certified by the magistrate. The Clerk of the Peace recorded these certificates in a register for the purpose, which thereafter was considered sufficient evidence of such matters.

It was further enacted, "That until there shall be five parsons or ministers of the Church of England, doing duty in their respective parishes in any one district," persons "desirous of intermarrying with each other, and neither of them living within the distance of eighteen miles of any minister of the Church of England, may apply to any neighbouring Justice of the Peace," who should affix in some public place, a notice, for which he should receive one shilling, and no more. The purport of the notice was that A. B. and C. D. were desirous of getting married, and there being no parson within eighteen miles, if any person knew any just reason why they should not be married, should give notice thereof to such magistrate. After which a form of the Church of England was to be followed, but should a minister reside within eighteen miles of either parties the marriage was null and void.

It is related that these notices of marriage were often attached to trees by the road side, and as it was considered desirable in those days to keep intending marriages secret, not unfrequently the intending parties would watch and remove the notice which had been put up.

In the year 1798, an Act was passed to extend the provisions of the first Act, which provided that "it shall be lawful for the minister of any congregation or religious community of persons, professing to be members of the Church of Scotland, or Lutherans, or Calvanists" to marry according to the rights of such church, and it was necessary that one of the persons to be married should have been a member of the particular church six months before the marriage. The clergyman must have been regularly ordained, and was to appear before six magistrates at quarter sessions, with at least seven members of his congregation, to prove his office, or take the oath of allegiance. And then, if the dignitaries thought it expedient, they might grant him a certificate that he was a settled minister, and therefore could marry, having published the intended marriage upon three Sundays previous.

In November, 1818, a brief act was passed to make valid the marriages of those who may have neglected to preserve the testimony of their marriage.

In the year 1821, an act was passed "for the more certain punishment of persons illegally solemnizing marriage, by which it was provided, that if persons, legally qualified to marry, should do so without the publication of banns, unless license be first had, should be guilty of a misdemeanor."

There was no further legislation until 1831, when provision was again made to confirm marriages contracted "before any justice of the peace, magistrate, or commanding officer of a post, or minister and clergyman, in a manner similar to the previous acts. It was at this time enacted that it should be lawful for ministers of the church of Scotland, Lutherans, Presbyterians, Congregationalists, Baptists, Independants, Methodists, Menonists, Tunkers, or Moravians, to solemnize matrimony, after having obtained certificates from the quarter sessions. According to the act of 1798, only the church of Scotland, Lutherans, and Calvinists, beside the English church, were permitted to marry persons. So it will be seen by this act of 1831, important concessions were made to different denominations. This act was by the Methodists, especially regarded as a deserved recognition of the constantly increasing number of that denomination. It certainly, at this time, seems remarkably strange, that so obvious a right, was for so long a time withheld, not alone from them, but other denominations. But the effort was strong, and long continued to build up the church of England to the exclusion of all others.

The restriction upon the Methodist ministers was to them greater from the fact, that for a long time they were members of a Conference existing, where all denominations were alike endowed with the power to perform the marriage ceremony. And it is recorded, that in a few instances, the ministers stationed in Canada, either forgot the illegality of marrying, or felt indisposed to submit to the unjust law, and did actually marry some persons. Elder Ryan was one, and was consequently banished; but was shortly pardoned by government, because of his known loyalty. His son-in-law, Rev. S. B. Smith, was another; but he defended himself at the trial and got free. Another was the Rev. Mr. Sawyer, who at once, on being accused, fled the country for a time.

It appears that on the 31st May, 1814, government appointed five persons to issue marriage licenses. One at Queenston, one at York, one at Kingston, one at Williamsburgh, and one at Cornwall. John Cumming was appointed for Kingston. Prior to this, licenses had been occasionally issued, probably, however, only by application to government. Marrying by license was so noticeable an event, that it was considered elegant to state in the marriage notice, "married by license."

According to a letter in our possession, sometimes the issuer of license would be without any, when he would give a certificate to the applicant, by which the party could get married, and subsequently he would furnish him with the license.

Having given the legal and legislative facts relative to marrying in early times, it may not be inappropriate to adduce some items of a social nature.

Roger Bates, of Newcastle, in his memoir at the parliament library, speaks thus pleasantly and graphically in referring to his father's courtship and marriage, which took place at the commencement of the present century. "The mode of courting in those days was a good deal of the Indian fashion. The buxom daughter would run through the trees and bushes, and pretend to get away from the lover; but somehow or other he managed to catch her, gave her a kiss, and they soon got married, I rather think by a magistrate. Time was too valuable to make a fuss about such matters." Whether this mode of courting was practiced elsewhere, than in Newcastle, it may be doubted. Speaking of the weddings, and the journey to get the knot tied, he says, "they generally furnished themselves with tomahawks and implements to defend themselves, and to camp out if required. The ladies had no white dresses to spoil, or fancy bonnets. With deer skin petticoats, home-spun gowns, and perhaps squirrel skin bonnet, they looked charming in the eyes of their lovers, who were rigged out in similar materials." Again, about the wedding ring, which could not then be procured, he says, "I have heard my mother say, that uncle Ferguson, a magistrate, rather than disappoint a happy couple, who had walked twenty miles, made search throughout the house, and luckily found a pair of old English skates, to which was attached a ring, with this he proceeded with the ceremony, and fixing the ring on the young woman's finger, reminded her, that though a homely substitute, she must continue to wear it, otherwise the ceremony would be dissolved. That curious token was greatly cherished, and is still among the family relics."

Mr. Sheriff Sherwood, speaking of his father, one of the first magistrates appointed by Simcoe, says "he probably joined more individuals together in the happy bonds of matrimony, than any other person ever has, in the county of Leeds. I have often heard him mention the circumstance of a young man asking him to marry him, but who said, I cannot get the money to pay you, but I will make you a good wheat fan, which he readily accepted, as it was an article much used at that time. At another time an old man came on the same errand, and said to him, I cannot get the money to pay you, but I will make you a good corn basket, with oak splints, and so tight that I will warrant it to hold water, and the old man punctually fulfilled his promise."

We have some interesting information from an old lady who settled in Ameliasburgh, and who still lives. Getting married at the beginning of the present century was a great event. The Carrying Place was the usual place of resort. "They placed in a lumber waggon, a number of chairs, and each gallant was supposed to support his partner upon his knee, and thus economise room. "Bitters" were indulged in, but no fighting allowed. If one began that, he was put out. Keeping good natured was a point of duty insisted upon. No old persons went to the wedding, but they joined in the dance, when the youngsters got back. A wedding without a dance was considered an insipid affair; and it was generally kept up two or three successive nights at different places. Francis Weese's was a half-way house between McMan's corners, (Rednerville), and the Carrying Place. Weese was a distinguished player upon the fiddle, and the wedding parties often stayed with him the first night.

"A yoke of steers, a cow, three or four sheep, with a bed, table, two dozen chairs, was regarded a very decent setting out for the bride. And if the groom was heir to 50 or 100 acres of land, with a little cleared, he was thought to have the worldly "goar," to constitute a first-rate match."

The history of frontier life; of the advance body of pioneers in the far west, frequently exhibits great irregularitiy in morals; a non-observance of God's commandments. But the record of the first settlers of Upper Canada is remarkably bright. When it is recollected that they were but scattered settlements in a wilderness; far away from civilized life; excluded from the world, and removed from the influence of the salutary power of public opinions, it is a matter of wonder, that great and frequent violation of God's law, with regard to marring did not take place. But such was not the case, as a general thing; the holy bonds of matrimony, were employed to bind man and woman together, whether through the officer, the magistrate or the clergyman. For years there was but few clergym'en to marry, and also but few magistrates, and there were secluded settlements where the clergyman or magistrate came not, and from which the inhabitants could not go, perhaps for many miles to get married. But a few, and they are very few instances, are recorded where parties deviated from the righteous way. Upon the shore of the bay, in a remote locality, about the year 1796, lived two individuals, whom we will call respectively Peter and Polly. They were living in the same family, she has a "help," and he has a hired man upon the farm. This couple had desired to enter the bonds of matrimony; but the ministers and squires lived some distance off, and they could not get away to be married, so they had to wait for the coming of one who would marry them; they had to wait, it would seem for several years, in the mean time they consoled themselves with genuine, and no doubt honest love. At last it came to pass that a Squire visited that neighbourhood, and stopped at the house where they lived.

The family bethought them of the wishes of Peter and Polly; and that now was the time to have the legal knot tied. So Polly was called from the kitchen just as she was, and Peter from the field besmeared with sweat, and clean dirt, and the two were made one. Among the witnesses of the interesting ceremony, was a bright eyed boy who trotted unceremonously from the bride to the groom, calling them respectively "mozzer" and "fadder." The time came when this same boy was the owner of the land whereon he had been born. This fact, from excellent authority, stands out as an exception to a general rule, although there is not about it that flagrant violation of moral principle which is too often seen at the present day, under other circumstances which afford no excuse.

The Rev. Mr. Stuart, living at Kingston, was not often called upon to marry, by persons outside of that village, and persons rarely found time to go all the way to him. When Mr. Langhorn came and opened a church at Adolphustown, and Bath, a more central place was supplied, and he consequently was often employed. But Mr. McDowell was the one who most frequently was required to marry. Being a minister of the church of Scotland, he enjoyed the privilege of marrying, and unlike Langhorn, he would marry them at their homes. So when making his rounds through the country, on his preaching excursions, he was frequently called upon to officiate in this capacity.

In the region of the Bay, were some who had in previous days, lived in comfort, had not wanted all that belonged to the well-to-do inhabitants along the Hudson, and at New York. In some cases, these families brought with them the fine clothes that had adorned their bodies in former times. Not only was it difficult for them, in many cases, to get some one to perform the marriage ceremony; but to the female, especially, it was a grave matter how to adorn the bride with that apparel which becomes the event. In those cases where rich clothes, which had been used by parents, were stored away, they were brought forth, and by a little alteration, made to do service; but by and by these relics of better days were beyond their power to renovate, and like others, they had, if married at all, to wear the garb mentioned by Roger Bates, or some other plain article; a calico print, bought of a pedlar, or a calamink, or linsey-woolsey petticoat, or a woolen drugget, were no common luxuries in the wilderness home. An old lady who is still living, tells us that she was married in 1807, and wore the last-mentioned; and was thought very extravagant indeed. A venerable lady, a native of the Bay, and now well-nigh eighty, remembers to have attended a wedding about the year 1708, up the river Moira. She was living with her uncle, Col. C. The wedding was one of some importance, as both parties were well-to-do. There was but a path along the banks of the river, and they went on horse back. At that time riding on horseback was a common practice, not a single person merely, but in couples. It was no unusual thing to see man and wife riding along together, also brother and sister, and as well lovers. The guests to this wedding all came on horse back, generally in pairs. They assembled early in the forenoon, and the happy pair were soon united. The bride's dress was unusually grand, being of lawn; the two bridesmaids graced the occasion by being dressed in muslin. She bears a distinct recollection of the entertainment. The banquet was crowned with a majestic chicken pie, in a pan capable of holding some twelve quarts; by roast goose, and with pies and cakes of all sorts, in abundance. The bride's father was the deacon of a church, and did not allow dancing, but the afternoon and evening were spent in joyous mirth and jovial "plays" in connection with which forfeits were lost and redeemed. But, however much these plays may have degenerated in recent days, they were then conducted with purity of thought, and innocence of soul. The party did not break up the first day. Half of the company repaired to the house of the groom's father, where beds were arranged for them. In the morning they went back to the scene of the wedding, upon the banks of the river, which at this point is particularly attractive. After breakfast, the young people, with the newly married pair, set out for the front, to the mouth of the river. They formed a joyous, and it must have been a picturesque cavalcade. Each gentleman selected his fair partner, and having mounted his horse, she was duly seated behind him. And thus they set out for their destination. Pleasant, indeed, must have been the ride; striking the scene, as they wended their way along the running water, and the bright autumn sun shone upon them through the variegated leaves which clothed the thickly standing trees. This night was spent at Myers' Creek, in following the notes of the fiddle with the nimble feet. This terminated the wedding party. This is adduced as an illustration of marrying in early times. Another will be briefly given, it was a case of elopement, and occurred many years before the wedding above mentioned. A certain Squire had been for many years in the enjoyment of wedded bliss. His wife was the daughter of Capt. ——, a half-pay officer, an honest but wayward Dutchman. The Squire's wife died, and, in due time, he sought the hand of another daughter of the Captains. But this the latter would not listen to; he was determined they should not marry; because she was his late wife's sister. The worthy Squire could not see the force of the objection, and the lady in question was likewise blinded by love. They resolved to run away, or rather to paddle away, in a convenient canoe. Clandestinely they set out upon the head waters of the bay, intending to go to Kingston to obtain the services of a clergyman. But the Captain learned the fact of their departure and started in pursuit with his batteau and oarsmen. According to one account, the flying would-be groomsman, who was paddling his own canoe, saw the angry parent coming, and made haste to quicken his speed, but finding that they would be overtaken, they landed upon an island in the bay, and hauled up the canoe; and concealed it, with themselves, in a cavity upon the island; and, after the Captain had passed, returned homeward and procured the services of a Squire to marry them. But, according to another statement, the lovers set out while the Captain was absent at Montreal, and arrived at Kingston, unfortunately, as he was returning home.

Seeing the Squire, he had his suspicions aroused, and began to look about for his daughter. She had, however, concealed herself by throwing an Indian blanket about her person, and over her head, and by sitting down among some squaws. The statement goes, that it was well the Captain did not find her, as he would, as soon as not, have shot the Squire. The end of it was, they were married, to live a long and happy domestic life. Although there may be a little doubt as to the details of this early elopement on the bay, there is no doubt that it took place in some such manner as described.

Among the Squires upon the Bay, the following were the most frequently called upon to marry: Young, of the Carrying Place; Bleeker, of the Trent; Lazier, of Sophiasburgh. The magistrates residing nearer Kingston and Adolphustown had less of this to do, as clergymen could there be more easily obtained.

CHAPTER XXIV.

CONTENTS—Burying Places—How Selected—Family Burying Places—For the Neighbourhood—The Dutch—Upon the Hudson—Bay Quinté—A Sacred Spot to the Loyalists—Ashes to Ashes—Primitive Mode of Burial—The Coffin—At the Grave—The Father's Remarks—Return to Labor—French Burying-place at Frontenac—Its Site—U. E. Loyalists Burying-place at Kingston—The "U. E. Burying Ground," Adolphustown—Worthy Sires of Canada's Sons—Decay—Neglect of Illustrious dead—Repair Wanted—Oldest Burying Ground in Prince Edward—Ross Place—At East Lake—Upon the Rose Farm—"The Dutch Burying Ground"—Second Growth Trees—In Sophiasburgh—Cronk Farm—In Sidney—Rude Tomb Stones—Burial-place of Capt. Myers—Reflections—Dust to Dust—In Thurlow—"Taylor Burying Ground"—The First Person Buried—Lieut. Ferguson—An Aged Female—Her Work Done—Wheels Stand Still.

THE EARLY BURYING PLACES UPON THE BAY QUINTE.

"Your fathers, where are they?"

Burying places in all the new settlements were, as a general thing, selected by the family to which death might first come. This was true of every part of America. Ere the forest had fallen before the hand of the axeman, or while the roots and stumps of the trees yet thickly encumbered the ground, before the scythe had been used to cut the first products of the soil, the great reaper death passed by, and one and another of the number were cut down. Some suitable place, under the circumstances, was selected for the grave, and quietly the body was laid away. In time, a neighbour would lose a member of the family, and the body would be brought and laid beside the first buried. And so on, until a certain circle would be found burying in a common place. But sometimes families would prefer to have a private burial ground, some conspicuous spot being selected upon the farm, where the ashes of the family might be gathered together, as one after another passed away. The Dutch are particularly attached to this custom. This may be seen even yet in those old sections of New York State, where the Dutch originally settled, especially at Hoboken, opposite New York City. Sacred spots were appropriated by each family upon the farm, in which the family was buried. The descendants of these Dutch who became such loyal subjects, and suffering refugees who settled around the bay, followed the same practice. These spots may be seen along the Hudson, and the Bay Quinté, which may be regarded as the Hudson of Canada, and are indicated by the drooping willow, or the locust or cypress. Some from whom reliable information has been received, state that the spot selected on the Bay Quinté was often that, where the family had first landed—where they had rested on the bare earth, beneath the trees, until a hut could be erected. This spot was chosen by the refugee himself as a suitable place to take his last rest. Indeed, the devotion of the settler to the land where he had wrought out his living, and secured a comfortable home, was sometimes of an exalted character. One instance by way of illustration:—There came to the shores of Hay Bay an heroic woman, a little rough perhaps, but one whose soul had been bitterly tried during the conflict between her king and the rebels. Her husband had been on many a battle-field, and she had assisted on many an occasion to give comfort to the British troops. The log hut was duly erected, and day after day they went forth together to subdue the wilderness. In the sear and yellow leaf, when competence had been secured and could be bequeathed to their children, when the first log tenement had fallen to decay, she caused her children to promise that her body should be laid upon the spot where that old hut had stood.

The mode of burial was often simple and touching, often there was no clergyman; of any denomination, no one to read a prayer over the dead for the benefit of the living. Frequently, in the hush of suspended work, through the quiet shades of the trees whose boughs sighed a requiem, like as if angels whispered peace to the sad and tearful mourners who silently, or with suppressed sobs, followed the coffin of the plainest kind, often of rough construction, which contained the remains of a loved one to the grave, in some spot selected. The rude coffin being placed in the grave, those present would uncover, and the father, in sad tones, would make a few remarks respecting the departed, offer a few thoughts which the occasion suggested, and then the coffin was hidden out of sight. The men would return to their labors, and the women to their duties.

We learn, on excellent authority, that the burial place for the French, at Fort Frontenac, was where the barracks now stand near the bridge. But not unlikely the French, when one died away from the fort at any distance, committed the dead to the earth in Indian burial places. The first burial place for the U. E. Loyalists in Kingston, was situated where St. Paul's Church now stands, on Queen Street, which was formerly called Grove Street.

No township is more rich in historic matters, pertaining to the U. E. Loyalists than Adolphustown. Here settled a worthy band of refugees whose lineage can be traced back to noble names in France, Germany and Holland. Here was the birth-place of many of Canada's more prominent and worthy sons, and here repose the ashes of a large number of the devoted pioneers.

As the steamboat enters to the wharf at Adolphustown, the observer may notice a short distance to the west, upon the summit of a ridge, a small enclosure in which are a number of second growth trees, maple and oak. He may even see indistinctly a few marble tombstones. If he walks to the spot he will find that the fence is rough, broken, and falling down. Casting his eye over the ground he sees the traces of numerous graves, with a few marble head-stones, and a long iron enclosure within which are buried the dead of the Casey family, with a marble slab to the head of each. The ground generally is covered with the *debris* of what once formed enclosures of individual graves or family plots. When visited by the writer, one grave, that of Hannah Vandusen, had growing out of its bosom a large poplar tree, while the wooden fence around was falling and resting against the tree. The writer gazed on these evidences, not alone of decay but neglect, with great regret, and with a sigh. For here, without any mark of their grave, lie many who were not only noble U. E. Loyalists, but who were men of distinction, and the fathers of men well known in Canadian History. Mr. Joseph B. Allison, accompanied us, and pointed out the several spots where he had seen buried these illustrious dead.

In the north-west corner of the ground, with no trace even of a grave to mark the spot, lies the old Major who commanded the company. Mr. Allison was present, although a little boy at his burial. The event is fixed upon his mind by the fact the militia turned out and buried him with military honors. We stood on the spot overgrown with thorn trees, and felt a pang that his name was thus forgotten, and his name almost unknown. Close by is a neat marble headstone to a grave, upon which is the following: "*Henry Hover, departed this life, August 23rd, 1842, aged 79 years, 5 months and 17 days.*" Noble man! Imprisonment with chains for nearly two years, with many hardships during, and after the war, did not make his life short, and we were thankful he had left descendants who forgot not to mark his resting-place. For account of this person see under "Royal Combatants."

The entrance gate to the ground is at the east side. To the right on entering, a short distance off, is an oak tree. Between the gate and tree was laid the body of Nicholas Hagerman. Sad to say, nothing indicates the resting-place of the earliest lawyer of the Province, and the father of Judge Hagorman. (See distinguished Loyalists). In the middle of the ground rests the dead of the Casey family. The two old couple whom we remember to have seen when a boy in their green old age, lie here. "Willet Casey died aged 86. Jane, his wife, aged 93." We would say to all here buried, *Requiescat in pace.* But the very crumblings of the enclosures which were put around the graves by sorrowing friends when they died cry out against the neglected state of the ground. The efforts which have repeatedly been made to put the place in repair ought to be repeated, and a stone wall at least made to effectually inclose the sacred dust.

The oldest burying place, we believe, in Prince Edward, is some distance from Indian Point, upon the Lake Shore, and east of the Rock, commonly known as Ross's Burying Ground. In this spot are buried some of the first and most distinguished of the first settlers of Marysburgh.

Another old burying place in Prince Edward is at East Lake, at the commencement of the Carrying Place. Here may be found the graves of some eighteen persons who made the first settlement of East Lake. The lot upon which it is situated belonged to Mr. Dyse. It is no longer used, but is partially in a ploughed field, and partially covered by a second growth of trees.

Upon the road along the south shore of Marysburg, a short distance west of the Rock, upon the Rose farm, are to be seen the lingering remains of the first church of this township. It was erected at an early date, and was twenty-four feet square. Here Weant was wont to preach to his flock of Lutherans, and here at times Langhorn from Bath also held forth. The situation is pleasant, upon the brow of a comparatively steep hill, overlooking a pleasant low-land, with the shining Ontario, and Long Point stretching away into its waters; while to the right is the well sheltered Wappoose Island. But another object attracts our attention. Almost immediately fronting us upon a sand-hill close by the water's edge is to be seen "the old Dutch burying ground." It is about half-a-mile from the road, and we will descend the hill and take the road through the fields along the fence, the way by which so many have passed to their long home. The old graveyard is overshadowed by good sized second growth pines, whose waving tops sigh not unharmoniously over the ashes of the old Hessian and Dutch settlers. The adjacent shore washed by the ever throbbing lake gives forth to day the gentlest sounds. These old burying places remind one that Canada is ever growing old. Here lie, not alone the early pioneers, but their grand-children; and over the spot cleared are now good sized second growth trees. The head boards are fallen in decay, the fence around the plots have crumbled in the dust.

The oldest burying place in Sophiasburgh is upon the Cronk farm east of Northport.

Nearly midway between Belleville and Trenton is situated the oldest burying ground of Sidney. It is pleasantly located upon an eminence by the bay shore, and affords a fine view of the bay, and opposite shore. The visitor will be struck with the irregularity of the graves in the place primarily used, as if the graves had been dug among the stumps. Some of them are almost north and south. At the ends of mostly all are placed stones, rough they are, but lasting, and have, in a large number of cases, more permanently indicated the position of the graves. Upon some of these rough stones are rudely cut the initials of the occupant of the grave. In a great number of cases tablets painted on wood have been placed to commemorate the individal deceased. But these are totally obliterated, and the wood is falling to decay. Probably the temporary mark of affectionate sorrowing was as lasting as the life of the bereaved. We lingered among the graves here, and they are numerous. We see the name Myers. And we know that old Capt. Myers was buried here, after an eventful life. Around him also repose his old acquaintances and friends—and enemies. They are gone with the primeval woods that covered the slopes by the Bay Quinté—gone with the hopes and aspirations, and prospects, and realizations that crowned their trying and eventful life—gone so that their ashes can no longer be gathered, like the old batteau which transported them thither—gone like their old log houses whose very foundations have been plowed up—gone like their rude implements of agriculture—gone by the slow and wearisome steps of time which marks the pioneer's life.

It is gratifying to see that while the ground has been extended, a new fence has been built, and elegant tomb-stones, 1868.

The first place set apart in which to bury the dead, in the township of Thurlow was the "Taylor Burying Ground." It is situated in Belleville, at the east of the mouth of the Moira, in view of the bay. The first person committed to the earth here was Lieut. Ferguson, who had been associated with Capt. Singleton. The second individual is supposed to have been the mother of John Taylor. She had been brought to the place by her son, her only son, two having been executed by the rebels during the war, when almost ninety years of age. But her stay on earth had almost ended; not long after, she was one day engaged in spinning flax, and suddenly ceased her work, and told them to put away the wheel, as she would spin no more. A few minutes after she ceased to live, and the weary wheels of life stood still. For many years this ground was the repository of the dead, about the mouth of Myers' Creek.

DIVISION V.

THE EARLY CLERGYMEN AND CHURCHES.

CHAPTER XXV.

CONTENTS.—French Missionaries—*First* in 1615—Recollets—With Champlain—Jesuits, in 1625—Valuable records—Bishopric of Quebec, 1674—First Bishop of Canada, Laval—Rivalry—Power of Jesuits—Number of Missionaries—Their "Relations"—*First mission field*; Bay Quinte region—"Antient mission"—How founded—First missionaries—Kleus, abbe D'Urfé—La Salle, to build a church—The ornaments and sacred vessels—The site of the "Chappel," uncertain—Bald Bluff, Carrying Place—Silver crosses—Mission at Georgian Bay—The "Christian Islands"—Chapel at Michilmicinac, 1679—The natives attracted—Subjects of the French King—Francois Picquet—La Presentation—*Soegasti*—The most important mission—The object—Six Nations—The Missionary's living—"Disagreeable expostulations—Putting stomach in order—Trout—Picquet's mode of teaching Indians—The same afterward adopted by Rev. W. Case—Picquet's success—Picquet on a voyage—At Fort Toronto—Mississauga's request—Picquet's reply—A slander—At Niagara, Oswego—At Frontenac—Grand reception—Return to La Presentation—Picquet in the last French war—Returns to France—By Mississippi—"Apostles of Peace"—Unseemly strife—Last of the Jesuits in Canada.

THE FIRST FRENCH MISSIONARIES.

In introducing this subject, we propose first to glance at the original French Missionaries, and then at the first Protestant Missionaries and clergymen, who labored in the Atlantic Provinces.

The first missionaries of christianity to America, came to Canada in the year 1615. They were four in number, and belonged to the order of Recollets, or Franciscans, of Spanish origin, a sect who attended to the spiritual wants of the people without accepting any remuneration. Four of these devoted men attended Champlain on his second visit to Canada in 1615. Three years later the Pope accorded the charge of missions in Canada to the Recollets of Paris. In 1625 members of the society of Jesus likewise entered the mission of America. Ignatius Loyola founded the Jesuit society in 1521. These two orders of Roman Catholics, especially the Jesuits, contributed much to the advancement of French interests in Canada, and by their learning assisted greatly to elevate the people. Side by side they traversed the vast wilderness of America, with the intrepid explorers, and by their close observations, committed to paper, they have left most valuable records of the country in its primeval state ; and the different tribes of savages that held possession of the country.

Canada was "constituted an apostolic vicariat," by the Pope, in 1657; and became an episcopal see, named the Bishopric of Quebec, about 1673. The first bishop of Canada was Francis de Laval, of the distinguished house of Montmorency. The rivalry which existed between the Jesuits and the Recollets, led to the withdrawl from the country of the latter. But they returned again about 1669. They were welcomed by the people, who preferred their self-supporting principles to the Jesuits, under Laval, who required sustentation from them, which was exacted by a system of tithes. The Jesuits became a very powerful ecclesiastical body, and commanded even sufficient political influence to secure the recall of the Governor, who was obnoxious to them, in 1665. Yet the people did not like them, in their usurpation of temporal power. The second bishop of Canada was M. de Saint Vallier, who was elevated to that position in 1688.

"Between the years 1635–1647, Canada was visited by eighteen Jesuits missionaries." It was due to these missionaries, who remained with, and adapted themselves to the Indian tribes, that Canada held such a position among the Aborigines. The relations of these missionaries are of thrilling interest, and deserve the attention of all who desire to become a student of history.

When there were no more than sixty inhabitants at Quebec, in 1620, the Recollets had begun to erect a convent and chapel upon the banks of the St. Charles River.

The Bay Quinté region may be regarded as the earliest mission field in America. Of the four Missionaries who came with Champlain from France, in 1615, one at least accompanied him in his journey up the Ottawa, across to Georgian Bay, and down the Trent to the Bay. This was in July, and Champlain was under the necessity of remaining in this region until the following spring, in the meantime visiting several of the tribes all along the north shore of Lake Ontario. During this period the zealous Recollet earnestly labored to lay the foundation of Christianity among the natives, and planted the "ancient mission" spoken of by father Picquet, 1751. We have positive statement to this effect. Probably when Champlain returned to Montreal, in the spring of 1616, he was not accompanied by the missionary; who stayed to establish the work he had commenced. We find it stated that the earliest missionaries to this region were M. Dolliere de Kleus, and Abbé D'Urfe, priests of the Saint Sulpice Seminary. Picquet remarks that the ancient mission at the Bay Quinté was established by Kleus and D'Urfé.

In June, 1671, DeCourcelles, as we have seen, visited Lake Ontario, coming directly up the St. Lawrence. On this occasion, it is recorded, he sent messages from Cataraqui "to a few missionaries residing among the Indians." Two years later, when Frontenac came, with a view of establishing a fort, we find it stated that as he approached Cataraqui, he was met by a canoe with the "Abbé D'Urfé, and the Captains of the Five Nations." The following year, 1674, LaSalle, in his petition for the grant of Fort Frontenac, and adjacent lands, proposed "to build a church when there will be 100 persons, meanwhile to entertain one or two of the Recollet Friars to perform divine service, and administer the sacraments there." In the reply to this petition by the King, it was stipulated that LaSalle should "cause a church to be erected within six years of his grant."

When Bradstreet, nearly a hundred years later, in 1751, captured Fort Frontenac, the Commandant, M. de Moyan, obtained the promise from Bradstreet, to "permit the ornaments and sacred vessels of the chapel to be removed in the luggage of the Chaplain."

By the foregoing, we learn the interesting fact, that for 150 years before the capture of Canada by the English, and nearly 170 before Upper Canada was first settled, there existed at the Bay Quinté an active mission of Roman Catholic Christianity. The exact location of the "chapel" cannot be fixed; but there is every reason to suppose that it was upon the shores of the Bay, at some distance westward from Cataraqui, inasmuch as reference is made to the chapel as quite apart from the Fort, at Cataraqui.

From the nature of the relics found in the Indian burying ground, near the Carrying Place, at Bald Bluff, by Weller's Bay, it might even have been situated there. Silver crosses, and other evidences of Roman Catholic Christianity, have been found in this place. Father Picquet remarks that the land was not good, but the quarter is beautiful.

There seems every probability that not many years after the establishment of the mission by the Bay Quinté, another was established in the neighborhood of Lake Huron, or Georgian Bay.

Upon the river Wye, some six miles north of Ponetanguishene, Pe-na-tang-que shine, so called by the Indians upon first seeing the sand banks, meaning "see the sand is falling," was established a French fort, at an early date, the foundation of which may yet be seen. It appears likely that at this point, at the Christian Islands, (a significant name,) situated between the Manitoulin Islands and the mainland; and also at Michilmicinac, were commenced missionary labors by the Recollets and others. We find it stated that in 1679 there was a chapel at Michilmickinac, which may refer to the Christian Islands. Here LaSalle, on his way westward, stopped and attended mass, with the celebrated Recollet, Pere Hennepin.

The natives were strongly attached to these French missionaries. Presents of porcelaine beads to make wampum, with a kind demeanor, soon won many of them to become Roman Catholics; and the cross was set up in their midst. And the time came when they were willing to acknowledge themselves under the protection of, and subject to the French King.

At the present site of Ogdensburgh, in the year 1748, "Francis Picquet, Doctor of the Sarbonne, King's Missionary, and Prefect Apostolic to Canada," began to found the mission of *La Presentation*. By the river Oswegotchie, then called by the Indians *Soegasti*, he succeeded in planting a mission, which became the most important in all Canada. The object was to convert the Six Nations to Roman Catholic Christianity, and thereby to win them from their connection with the English. M. Picquet was a devoted man. "He received at that time neither allowance nor presents. From the King he had but one half pound of pork a day, which made the savages say, when they brought him a buck and some partridges, "We doubt not, Father, but that there have been disagreeable expostulations in your stomach, because you had nothing but pork to eat. Here is something to put your affairs in order." They sometimes brought him trout weighing eighty pounds.

In 1749, when French interests were declining in the new world, and when every effort to secure the alliance of the Iroquois was devised, Governor de Veudreuil sent the Rev. Abbe Picquet of the missionary house at La Presentation, he being well and favorably know among the Five Nations. The object was to draw within the bounds of La Presentation many of the families, where they should not only be taught the Catholic religion, but also the elements of husbandry. It was somewhat the same idea as that which led the

Rev. William Case, in later days, to domesticate the Mississaugas on the Grape Island. L'Abbe Picquet was successful in his mission, and in 1751, he had 396 heads of families living at the place. Among these were the most distinguished and influential families of the Iroquois. The settlement was divided into three villages, and much taste and skill were displayed in the planning. Great attractiveness characterized the place up to the conquest of Canada.

In the month of June, 1751, Father Picquet set out upon a voyage up to Fort Frontenac, and thence up the Bay Quinté, and the River Trent to Fort Toronto, and so on around Lake Ontario. He embarked in a King's canoe, accompanied by one bark, in which were five trusty savages. The memoir of this trip is curious and edifying.

Proceeding to Fort Toronto, by way of the Trent, then an important trading post with the Indians, he found Mississaugas there who flocked around him; they spoke first of the happiness their young people, the women and children, would feel, if the King would be as good to them as to the Iroquois, for whom he procured missionaries. They complained that instead of building a church, they had constructed only a canteen for them. Abbe Picquet did not allow them to finish, and answered them, that they had been treated according to their fancy; that they had never evinced the least zeal for religion; that their conduct was much opposed to it;—that the Iroquois, on the contrary, had manifested their love for christianity, but as he had no order to attract them to his mission, he avoided a more lengthy explanation," (Paris Doc). This conduct on the part of Abbe Picquet must be regarded as heartless in the extreme. Such language ought not to come from the lips of a missionary. It shows that the Iroquois, because of his relationship with the English, had souls of far more importance than the Mississauga, whose character for peace rendered him of minor importance. The reflection upon the character was uncharitable; and, judging by the light supplied by later days, it was untrue—shamefully untrue. That the Mississauga Indians acquired a taste for the brandy vended to them by the French trader was certainly a fact; but that did not indicate an unwillingness on their part, to become christians. Missionaries, of the present century, have succeeded in raising the Mississauga, not alone from paganism, but from a degrading love of spirituous liquors acquired of the French, to a distinguished place among converted Indians.

Abbe Picquet went from Fort Toronto, probably by the River

Don, and thence across the lake, to Fort Niagara, to negotiate with the Senecas. Passing along the south shore, he visited the English fort at the mouth of the River Oswego, called *Choueguen*. He also visited the River Gascouchogou, (Genesee) and returned to Frontenac, where a grand reception awaited him. "The Nippissings and Algonquins who were going to war, drew up in a line of their own accord above Fort Frontenac, where three standards were hoisted. They fired several volleys of musketry, and cheered incessantly. They were answered in the same style from all the little crafts of bark. M. de Verchere, and M. de la Valtrie, caused the guns of the fort to be discharged at the same time, and the Indians, transported with joy at the honors paid them, also kept up a continual fire with shouts and exclamations which made every one rejoice. The commandants and officers received our missionary at the landing. No sooner had he landed than all the Algonquins and Nippissings of the lake came to embrace him. Finally, when he returned to *La Presentation*, he was received with that affection, that tenderness, which children would experience in recovering a father whom they had lost." Three years later war was, for the last time, in progress between the French and English in America. Father Picquet contributed much to stay the downfall of French domination. He distinguished himself in all the principal engagements, and by his presence animated the Indian converts to battle for the French King. At last, finding all was lost, he retired on the 8th May, 1760. He ascended the Bay Quinté and Trent by Fort Toronto, and passed on to Michilmicinac, and thence to the Mississippi; and then to New Orleans, where he stayed twenty-two months. Died 15th July, 1781, called the "Apostle of the Iroquois."

During the French domination in Canada, the dissentions between the Recollets and Jesuits were almost incessant. Now the one was sustained and patronized by the governor regnant, now the other, and many were the struggles between Church and State. The closing days of French rule witnessed scenes of unseemly strife between the clergy and the governors. The last of the Jesuits in Canada, Father Casat, died in 1800, and the whole of their valuable possessions came to the government.

CHAPTER XXVI.

CONTENTS.—First Church in New York, 1633—First Dominic, Rev. Everardus Bogardus—The Dutch, Huguenots, Pilgrims—Transporting ministers and churches—First Rector of New York, Wm. Vesey—Henry Barclay, 1746—First Catholic Bishop in America, 1789—Episcopalian Bishop, 1796—Moral state of Pioneers in Canada—Religion—No ministers—No striking immorality—Feared God and honored their King—The Fathers of Upper Canada—Religious views—A hundred years ago—"Carousing and Dancing"—Rev. Dr. John Ogilvie—First Protestant Clergyman in Canada—Chaplain 1759, at Niagara—A Missionary—Successor of Dr. Barclay, New York—Death, 1774 Rev. John Doughty—A Graduate Ordained—At Peekskill—Schenectady—A Loyalist—A Prisoner—To Canada—Chaplain—To England—Returns—Missionary—Resigns—Rev. Dr. John Stuart—First Clergyman to settle—His Memoir—The "Father of the U. C. Church"—Mission Work—The Five Nations—The Dutch—Rev. Mr. Freeman—Translator—Rev. Mr. Andrews—Rev. Mr. Spencer Woodbridge, Howley—New England Missionaries—Rev. Dr. Whelock—The Indian Converts—The London Society—Rev. Mr. Inglis—John Stuart selected missionary—A Native of Pennsylvania—Irish descent—A Graduate, Phil. Coll—Joins Church of England—To England—Ordination—Holy Orders 1770—Enters upon his work.

THE FIRST PROTESTANT CLERGYMAN IN AMERICA.

According to the Rev. J. B. Wakley, "The Reformed Dutch Church was the first organized in New Amsterdam, (New York). This year, 1633, the first church edifice was erected on this island, (Manhatten). It was built on what is called Broad Street. It was a small frail wooden building. The name of the first Dominie is preserved, the Rev. Everardus Bogardus. He came over from Holland with the celebrated Wanter Van Twiller. The Dutch and the Huguenots, as well as the Pilgrims, brought the church, the schoolmaster, and their bibles with them. They erected a dwelling for the Rev. Mr. Bogardus to reside in. This was the first parsonage built on the island, if not in America. This first minister in New Amsterdam met with a sad end. After spending some years in the new world, in returning to his native land, he, with eighty-one others, was lost off the coast of Wales. The Bogarts are probably descended from this pioneer minister, he having left children behind him in America, or some near connection. The first Rector of the Church of England in New York, was the Rev. William Vesey, pastor of Trinity Church. The Rev. Dr. Henry Barclay was the second Rector, who had previously been catechist for ten years to the Mohawk Indians. He became Rector October 22, 1746. "He was the father of the late Thomas Barclay, Consul-General of His British Majesty in the United States, and grandfather of Mr. Anthony Barclay, late British

Consul at New York, who was under the necessity of returning home during the Russian war, in consequence of the jealousy and partiality of the American Government.

We find it stated that Dr. Carroll, of Maryland, was the first Catholic Bishop in America, 1789.

Dr. Seabury, Bishop of Connecticut, was the first Episcopalian Bishop of that State, he died in 1796.

The circumstances of the settlers in Upper Canada were not such as would conduce to a growth of religion and morality. Apart from the effect upon them resulting from a civil war, and being driven away from home—isolated in a wilderness, far removed from civilization; there were circumstances inimical to the observance of religious duties. The earnest contest for life, the daily struggle for food, and more especially, the absence of ministers of the gospel, all combined to create a feeling of indifference, if not a looseness of morals. In a few instances, there was on the part of the settlers, a departure from that strict virtue, which obtains at the present time, and in which they had been trained. But on the whole, there was a close adherence, and a severe determination to serve the God of their father's. From many a log cabin ascended the faithful prayer of the followers of Luther; of the conscientious Episcopalian, and the zealous Methodist and Baptist. Yet, for years, to some the word of life was not preached; and then but rarely by the devoted missionary as he traveled his tedious round of the wilderness. After ten years, the average of inhabitants to the square miles, was only seven. This paucity of inhabitants, prevented regular religious sermons by clergymen, as it did the formation of well taught schools. This absence of educational and religious advantages, it might be expected, would naturally lead to a demoralized state of society, but such was not the case with the settlers of the ten townships. This sparseness of population, arose in part, it must be mentioned, from the system pursued by government, of reserving tracts of land, of granting to the clergy, and to non-resident owners, all of which remained to embarrass the separated settlers, and prevent advance of civilization, by begetting ignorance and indifference to religion.

When it is remembered how great had been the trials of the refugees during the continuation of the war; when we call to mind the school of training belonging to a camp life; and still more, when it is taken into consideration to how great an extent the settlers were removed from the salutary influences of civilized life, it at once strikes the thoughtful mind as surprising, that the early colonist did not relapse into a state of non-religion and gross immorality. But it is a remarkable fact that the loyalists who planted Upper Canada, not only honored their King, but feared God, and in a very eminent degree fulfilled the later commandment to love one another. Certainly there were exceptions. Even yet are remembered the names of a few who availed themselves of their neighbors' necessities to acquire property; and the story still floats down the stream of time, that there were those who had plenty and to spare of government stores, while the people were enduring the distress of the "Hungry Year." But even these reports lack confirmation, and even if true, are the more conspicuous by their singularity. There is no intention or desire to clothe the founders of Upper Canada with a character to which they are not entitled, to suppress in any respect facts that would tend to derogate the standing of the loyalists. This is unnecessary to place them upon an elevated ground, but were it not, it would be contrary to the writer's feelings, and unfair to the reader. There will be occasion to allude to a few instances, where gross evils manifested themselves, yet after all, they are but the dark corners which only serve to bring out the more gloomy colors of the picture presented. In arriving at a just estimate of their state of morals, it is necessary to take into consideration, that many of the views held by truly religious men a hundred years ago, differed widely from those held by many to day. Reference is made to certain kinds of amusements then unhesitatingly indulged in, which to-day are looked upon as inimical to sound christianity. One of these is the habit of using intoxicating liquors. It was also charged against them, that they were "wofully addicted to carousing and dancing."

REV. JOHN OGILVIE, D.D.

This divine was probably the first Protestant clergyman that ever officiated in Canada. He did so in the capacity of chaplain to a British Regiment in an expedition to Fort Niagara, in 1759, when that French stronghold was surrendered. Dr. Ogilvie, was a native of New York, and a graduate of Yale college. He was employed by the Society for the Propagation of the Gospel in Foreign parts, as a missionary with success. In 1765 he succeeded the Rev. Dr. Barclay, as Rector of Trinity Church, New York. He died in 1774. "A portrait of him is still preserved in the vestry office of Trinity Church." The next Protestant clergyman we believe, was the Rev. John Doughty.

"An Episcopal minister. He graduated at King's College, New

York, in 1770. He was ordained in England for the church at Peeks. kill, but was soon transferred to Schenectady. In 1775, political troubles put an end to divine service, and he suffered much at the hands of the popular party. In 1777, he obtained leave to depart to Canada, (after having been twice a prisoner,) where he became chaplain of the "Kings Royal Regiment," of New York. In 1781 he went to England; but returned to Canada in 1784, and officiated as missionary at Sorel. He resigned his connection with the society for the propagation of the gospel in foreign parts, in 1803."—(*Sabine.*)

The first clergyman to settle in Canada, and one of the refugee pioneers at the first settlement of Kingston, was the Rev. John Stuart. We are fortunate in having before us a transcript of the memoir of this distinguished person.

"*Memoirs of the Rev. John Stuart, D.D., father of the Upper Canada Church. He opened the first academy at Cataraqui—Kingston* 1786. *The last missionary to the Mohawks.*"

"The conversion and civilization of the American Indians, engaged the attention of Europeans at an early date." The Jesuits first gave attention to the Mohawks, 1642, a few years later, father Joynes laid down his life on the Mohawk River. The first colonizers, the Dutch did not give the subject much attention. "The government of New York, did not make any effort to christianize the five nations, further than to pay, for some time a small salary to the clergyman, at Albany, to attend to the wants of such Indians, as might apply to him." The Rev. Mr. Freeman, translated into the Mohawk language, the Church of England Prayer Book, with some passages of the Old and New Testament. "In 1712 Mr. Andrews was sent as a missionary to the Mohawk, by the society, for propagating the gospel, and a church was built at the mouth of the Schoharrie creek, but that missionary soon abandoned the place. As he was the first, so he was the last that resided among them for a great many years. After that the only ministration was at Albany. In 1748, the Rev. Mr. Spencer, Mr. Woodbridge and Howly, were sent successively by the people of New England," to this field of labor.

The French war soon interrupted this, and not until 1761, was anything more done, when the Rev. Dr. Wheelock, directed his attention to that quarter, with missionaries, and schoolmasters. The testimony mainly of all these mentioned, who labored among the Indians, is to the effect that, although they were quick to learn, and would for a time live a christian life, they mostly all lapsed into their former savage state. "The necessity of having missionaries of the Church of England, resident among the Mohawks, was again brought before the society for promoting of the gospel, a few years before the revolution, both by Sir William Johnson, and the Rev. Mr. Inglis, of New York, the last of whom also laid the subject before the government of England, in the form of a memorial. In 1770 the society again consented to ordain a missionary for the exclusive service of the Mohawks. John Stuart, who was selected for this purpose, was born at Harrisburgh, in Pennsylvania, in 1730. The family mansion in which he was born was still standing in 1836." His father, an Irishman, came to America in 1730. John Stuart had two brothers who sided with the Americans. When he "graduated at the college of Philadelphia, he made up his mind to join the communion of the Church of England." His father being a Presbyterian, this was extremely distasteful to him. But his father finally consenting, he proceeded to England for ordination, and received Holy Orders in 1770, and was appointed missionary to the Mohawks at Fort Hunter.

CHAPTER XXVII.

CONTENTS—At Fort Hunter—Mr. Stuart's first sermon, Christmas—Officiates in Indian tongue—Translates—The Rebellion—Prayers for the King—The Johnsons—Rebels attack his house—Plunder—Indignity—Church desecrated—Used as a stable—A barrel of rum—Arrested—Ordered to come before Rebel Commissioners—On Parole—Limits—Idle two years—To Albany—Phil—Determines to remove to Canada—Not secure—Exchanging—Security—Real estate forfeited—Route—Negroes—The journey, three weeks—At St. John's—Charge of Public School—Chaplain—At the close of the war—Three Protestant Parishes—Determines to settle at Cataraqui—Chaplain to Garrison—Missionary—Bishop of Virginia, Dr. Griffith—Visits Mr. Stuart—Invitation to Virginia Declined—"Rivetted prejudices," satisfied—"The only refugee clergyman"—Path of duty—Visits the settlement, 1784—Mohawks, Grand River—Reception of their old Pastor—First Church—Mohawks, Bay of Quinté—Remains in Montreal a year—Assistant—Removes to Cataraqui, 1785—His land—Number of houses in Kingston—A short cut to Lake Huron—Fortunate in land—5000 settlers—Poor and Happy—Industrious—Around his Parish, 1788—Two hundred miles long—By Batteau—Brant—New Oswego—Mohawk Village church, steeple, and bell—First in Upper Canada—Plate—Organ—Furniture—Returns—At Niagara—Old Parishioners—Tempted to move—Comfortable not rich—Declines a Judgeship—New Mecklenburgh—Appointed Chaplain to first House of Assembly—Mohawk Mission—At Marysburgh—Degree of D. D.—Prosperity—Happy—Decline of life—His duties—Illness, Death, 1811—His appearance—"The little gentleman"—His manners—Honorable title—His children—Rev. O'Kill Stuart.

MEMOIRS OF DR. STUART CONTINUED—"FATHER OF THE UPPER CANADA CHURCH."

Mr. Stuart immediately returned to America and proceeded to his mission, preaching his first sermon to the Mohawks on Christmas of the same year, 1770. He preached regularly every Sunday after the service had been read in Indian. In the afternoon he officiated in the Mohawk chapel to the whites, mostly Dutch. "In 1774 he was able to read the liturgy, baptize and marry in the Indian tongue, and converse tolerably well with them. He subsequently, assisted by Brant, translated parts of the Bible. After the commencement of the rebellion, until 1777, Mr. Stuart did not experience any inconvenience," although in other places the clergy had been shamefully abused; he remained at Fort Hunter even after the Declaration of Independence, and constantly performed divine service without omitting prayers for the king. Mr. Stuart's connection with the Johnson family, and his relations to the Indians rendered him particularly noxious to the Whigs. Although they had not proof of his being active in aiding the British, everything was done to make his home unbearable. "His house was attacked, his property plundered and every indignity offered his person. His church was also plundered and turned into a tavern, and in ridicule and contempt, a barrel of rum was placed in the reading desk. The church was afterwards used as a stable, July, 1778. He was ordered by the Board to detect conspiracies, to leave his home and repair forthwith with his family to Connecticut until his exchange could be procured." He was to leave within four days after receiving the orders, or be committed to close confinement. "Mr. Stuart appeared before the Commissioners two days after receiving the above order, and declared his readiness to convince them that he had not corresponded with the enemy, and that he was ready and willing to enter into any engagement for the faithful performance of such duties as may be enjoined him." The Board took his parole, by which he was obligated to abstain from doing anything against the Congress of the United States, or for the British, and not to leave the limits of Schenectady without permission of the Board. Soon after he writes there are only three families of my congregation, the rest having joined the King's forces, nor had he preached for two years. In the Spring of 1780, the Indians appeared in the county infuriated because of the conduct of General Sullivan the previous year. Mr. Stuart had to abandon his house and move to Albany. So imminent was the danger that the fleeing family could see the houses about in flames, and hear the report of arms. At Albany, Mr. Stuart received much civility from General Schuyler, and obtained permission to visit Philadelphia. Having returned, he made up his mind to emigrate to Canada, and communicated his resolution as follows: "I arrived here eight days from the time I parted with you (at Philadelphia) and found my family well, and after being sufficiently affrighted, the enemy having been within twenty miles of this place, and within one mile of my house in the country, considering the present state of affairs in this part of the Province, I am fully persuaded that I cannot possibly live here secure, either in regard to ourselves or property during the ensuing season; this place is likely to be a frontier, and will probably be burnt if the enemy can effect it. For these and other weighty reasons, materially weighed, I have resolved, with the approbation and consent of Mrs. Stuart, to emigrate to Canada, and having made an application for an exchange, which I have reason to believe will be granted.

Mr. Stuart applied by letter to Governor Clinton, to be exchanged, March 30, 1781. His application received prompt attention, and he was the same day allowed permission on certain conditions, which are stated by Mr. Stuart in a letter to Rev. Mr. White, of Philadelphia. The letter is dated Schenectady, April 17, 1781. "Being considered as a prisoner of war, and having forfeited my real estate, I have given £400 security to return in exchange for myself, one prisoner out of four nominated by the Governor, viz.: one Colonel, two Captains, and one Lieutenant, either of which will be accepted in my stead; or if neither of the prisoners aforesaid can be obtained, I am to return as a prisoner of war to Albany, when required. My personal property I am permitted to sell or carry with me, and I am to proceed under the protection of a public flag, as soon as it will be safe and convenient for women and children to travel that course. We are to proceed from here to Fort Arin in waggons, and from thence in Batteaux." The danger of the journey was adverted to, and the probability of obtaining a chaplaincy in Sir William Johnson's 2nd Battalion of Royal Yorkers, which is nearly complete on the establishment. "My negroes being personal property, I take with me, one of which being a young man, and capable of bearing arms. I have given £100 security to send back a white person in his stead."

"Mr. Stewart set out with his family, consisting of his wife and three small children, on his long and tedious journey, on the 19th of Sept., 1781, and arrived at St. Johns on the 9th of the following month, thus accomplishing the journey in three weeks, which is now done in twelve or fifteen hours. As there was no opening in Montreal, he took charge of a public school, which, with his commission as Chaplain, gave him support." In a letter to Dr. White, dated Montreal, October 14, 1783, he says: "I have no reason hitherto to dislike my change of climate; but, as reduction must take place soon, my emoluments will be much diminished, neither have I any flattering prospect of an eligible situation in the way of my profession, as there are only three protestant Parishes in this Province, the Pastors of which are Frenchmen, and as likely to live as I am. "Soon after, Mr. Stuart determined to settle at Cataraqui, where was a garrison, and to which a good many loyalists had already proceeded. He was promised the chaplaincy to the garrison, with a salary of one thousand dollars a year, and he writes, "I can preserve the Indian mission in its neighborhood, which, with other advantages, will afford a comfortable subsistence, although I wish it laid in Maryland. After the acknowledged independence of the United States, and the separation of the Episcopalian Church of America from the mother Church, Dr. Griffith, the Bishop elect of Virginia, invited Mr. Stuart to settle in his diocese; but Mr. Stuart declined. He writes, "The time has been when the chance of obtaining a settlement in that part of Virginia would have gratified my utmost desire; but, at my time of life, and with such rivetted principles in favor of a Government totally different, 'it is impossible.'" Though Mr. Stuart did visit Philadelphia in 1786, he never seems to have repented his removal to Canada. Yet the isolation in which he sometimes found himself, would sometimes naturally call up memories that could not fail to be painful. "I am," he writes, "the only Refugee Clergyman in this Province, &c." As a relief from such thoughts, he turned to the active duties of his calling. "I shall not regret," said he, "the disappointment and chagrin I have hitherto met with, if it pleases God to make me the instrument of spreading the knowledge of His Gospel amongst the heathen, and reclaiming only one lost sheep of the house of Israel." In this spirit he set out on the second of June, 1784, to visit the new settlements on the St. Lawrence, Bay Quinté, and Niagara Falls, where he arrived on the 18th of the same month. Already, 3,500 Loyalists had left Montreal that season for Upper Canada. His reception by the Mohawks, ninety miles from the Falls, was very affectionate, even the windows of the church in which he officiated were crowded with those who were anxious to behold again their old Pastor, from whom they had been so long separated." This church was the first built in Upper Canada, and it must have been commenced immediately after the Mohawks settled on the Grand River. He officiated also at Cataraqui, where he found a garrison of three companies, about thirty good houses, and some 1,500 souls who intended to settle higher up. He next proceeded to the Bay of Quinté, where some more Mohawks had settled, and were busy building houses and laying the foundation of their new village, named Tyendinaga. Though Mr. Stuart had now received from the Society, whose missionary he continued to be, discretionary powers to settle in any part of Canada, he remained in Montreal another year, as assistant to the Rev. Dr. DeLisle, Episcopal Clergyman of that town. He finally removed to Cataraqui, in August, 1785. His share of the public land was situated partly in Cataraqui, and partly at a place, which, in memory of the dear old place on the Mohawk River, was now called New Johnstown. Sometime in 1785, Mr. Stuart says, "I have two hundred acres within half a mile of the garrison, a beautiful situation. The town increases fast;

there are already about fifty houses built in it, and some of them very elegant. It is now the port of transport from Canada to Niagara. We have now, just at the door, a ship, a scow, and a sloop, beside a number of small crafts; and if the communication lately discovered from this place by water, to Lake Huron and Michilmackinac proves as safe, and short as we are made to believe, this will shortly be a place of considerable trade." Reference here must be made to the route up the Bay and River Trent. "I have been fortunate in my locations of land, having 1,490 acres at different places, in good situations, and of an excellent quality, three farms of which I am improving, and have sowed this fall with thirty bushels in them. The number of souls to westward of us is more than 5,000, and we gain, daily, new recruits from the States. We are a poor, happy people, industrious beyond example. Our gracious King gives us land gratis, and furnishes provisions, clothing, and farming utensils, &c., until next September, after which the generality of the people will be able to live without his bounty." The above must have been written in 1785, as in May, 1786, he opened an academy. In the summer of 1788, he went round his Parish, which was then above 200 miles long. He thus describes his voyage on this occasion. "I embarked in a batteau with six Indians, commanded by Capt. Brant, and coasted along the north shore of Lake Ontario, about 200 miles from the head of the lake; we went twenty-five miles by land, to New Oswego, the new Mohawk village on the Grand River; these people were my former charge, and the Society still styles me their Mohawk Vill. Missionary. I found them conveniently situated on a beautiful river, where the soil is equal in fertility to any I ever saw. Their village contains about 700 souls, and consists of a great number of good houses, with an elegant church in the centre; it has a handsome steeple and bell, and is well finished within." By this we learn, that not only was the first Protestant Church built at the Grand River, but as well here was the first steeple to contain a bell, which was the first to be heard in Upper Canada. Brant, when in England, collected money for all this. With the above, they had the service of plate, preserved from the rebels on the Mohawk; crimson furniture for the pulpit, and "the Psalmody was accompanied by an organ." "This place was uninhabited four years ago." "I returned by the route of Niagara, and visited that settlement. They had, as yet, no clergyman, and preached to a very large audience. The increase of population there was immense, and indeed I was so well pleased with that country, where I found many of my old Parishioners, that I was strongly tempted to remove my family to it. You may suppose it cost me a struggle to refuse the unanimous and pressing invitation of a large settlement, with the additional argument of a subscription, and other emoluments, amounting to near £300, York currency, per annum more than I have here. But, on mature reflection, I have determined to remain here. You will suppose me to be very rich, or very disinterested; but, I assure you, neither was the case. I have a comfortable house, a good farm here, and an excellent school for my children, in a very healthy climate, and all these I could not have expected had I removed to Niagara. But, that you may be convinced that I do not intend to die rich, I have also declined an honorable and lucrative appointment. Our new settlements have been divided into four districts, of which this place is the capital of one, called New Mecklenburgh, and Courts of Justice are to be immediately opened. I had a commission sent me, as first Judge of the Court of Common Pleas. But, for reasons which readily occur to you, I returned it to Lord Dorchester, who left this place a few days ago."

In 1789, Mr. Stuart was appointed Bishop's Commissionary for the settlements from Point au Boudette to the western limits of the Province, being the district now constituting Canada West. Though this appointment added nothing to his emoluments, it increased considerably his duties. At the meeting of the first Session of Parliament in 1792, he was named Chaplain to the Upper House of Assembly, an appointment which required for a time his presence at Niagara. "He occasionally visited and officiated for the Mohawk Village, at the Bay of Quinté. But, notwithstanding the laudable exertions of the society, and the partial indulgence of the British Government to this tribe, no flattering accounts can be given either of their religious improvements, or approach to civilization; on his return he usually stopped at Col. McDonnell's, Marysburgh, and preached in his house. In the year 1799, the degree of D.D. was conferred on Mr. Stuart, by the University of Pennsylvania, his Alma Mater, a complement he appreciated from his native state. About the same time he received the appointment of Chaplain to the Garrison of Kingston. "He had secured about 4000 acres of valuable land to which he occasionally made additions." In his prosperity and wealth he exclaimed: "How mysterious are the ways of Providence! How short-sighted we are! Some years ago I thought it a great hardship to be banished into the wilderness, and would have imagined myself completely happy, could I have exchanged it for a place in the City of Philadelphia,—now the best wish we can form for our dearest friends is to have them removed to us." It must be remarked that the above is taken from letters written to a friend in Philadelphia, and no doubt, being private and social in their nature, there is often a coloring favorable to the States which eminated from no love to that country. "The remainder of Dr. Stuart's life seems to have passed in the routine of his duties, interrupted however by attacks of illness, to which the increase of years, and the fatigue attendant on a mission in so new a country, could not fail to subject him." Dr. Stuart departed this life on the 15th of August, 1811, in the seventy-first year of his age, and was buried at Kingston, where he lives (says one of his cotemporaries) in the heart of his friends. "He was about six feet four inches in height, and from this circumstance, was known among his New York friends as "the little gentleman." His manners were quiet and conciliating, and his character, such as led him rather to win more by kindness and persuasion, than to awe and alarm them by the terrors of authority. His sermons were composed in plain and nervous language, were recommended by the affectionate manner of his delivery, and not unfrequently found a way to the conscience of those who had long been insensible to any real religious convictions. The honorable title of Father of the Upper Canada Church, has been fitly bestowed on him, and he deserves the name not more by his age and the length of his services, than by the kind and paternal advice and encouragement, which he was ever ready to give those younger than he on their first entrance on the mission." "By his wife, Jane O'Kill, of Philadelphia, who was born in 1752, he had five sons and three daughters." All of his sons subsequently occupied distinguished positions. His eldest son George O'Kill, graduated at Cambridge, England, in 1801, entered Holy Orders, and was appointed missionary at York, now Toronto, from whence he returned on his father's death to Kingston, where he became Archdeacon. He died in 1862, at the age of eighty-six.

CHAPTER XXVIII.

CONTENTS—A Missionary—Chaplain at Niagara—Pastor to the Settlers—Chaplain to Legislature—Visits Grand River—Officiates—A Land Speculator—Receives a pension, £50—1823—Rev. Mr. Pollard—At Amherstburgh—Mr. Langhorn—A Missionary—Little Education—Useful—Odd—On Bay Quinté In Ernesttown—Builds a Church—At Adolphustown—Preaches at Hagerman's—Another Church—A Diligent Pastor—Pioneer Preacher around the Bay—Christening—Marrying—Particular—His Appointments—Clerk's Fees—Generosity—Present to Bride—Faithful to Sick Calls—Frozen Feet—No Stockings—Shoe Buckles—Dress—Books—Peculiarities—Fond of the Water—Charitable—War of 1812—Determined to leave Canada—Thinks it doomed—Singular Notice—Returns to Europe—His Library—Present to Kingston—Twenty Years in Canada—Extract from Gazette—No One Immediately to take His Place—Rev. John Bethune—Died 1815—Native of Scotland—U. E. Loyalists—Lost Property—Chaplain to 84th Regiment—A Presbyterian—Second Legal Clergyman in Upper Canada—Settled at Cornwall—Children—The Baptists—Wyner—Turner—Holts Wiem—Baptists upon River Moira—First Chapel—How Built—Places of Preaching—Hayden's Corners—At East Lake—The Lutherans—Rev. Schwerdfeger—Lutheran Settlers—County Dundas—First Church East of Kingston—Rev. Mr. Myers Lived in Marysburgh—Marriage—His Log Church—Removes to St. Lawrence—Resigns—To Philadelphia—Mr. Weant—Lives in Ernesttown—Removes to Matilda—Not Supported—Secretly Joins the English Church—Re-ordained—His Society Ignorant—Suspicion—Preaching in Shirt Sleeves—Mr. Myers Returns, by Sleigh—Locking Church Door—The Thirty-nine Articles—Compromise—Mr. Myers continues Three Years a Lutheran—He Secedes—The End of both Seceders—Rev. I. L. Senderling—Rev. Herman Hayunga—Rev. Mr. Shorts—Last Lutheran Minister at Ernesttown, McCarty—Married.

THE FIRST EPISCOPALIANS, CONTINUED—PRESBYTERIANS, BAPTISTS, AND LUTHERANS.

The Rev. Robert Addison came as a missionary from the Society for Propagating the Gospel in Foreign Parts, in 1790. He probably discharged the duties of chaplain to the troops stationed at Niagara, and also was Clergyman, and officiated as such, to the settlers. When the government was formed at Niagara, in 1792, Mr. Addison, was appointed Chaplain. He occasionly visited the Grand River Indians, officiating through an interpreter, and baptizing and marrying. Col. Clark says, Mr. Addison was a land speculator. In 1823, an act was passed by Parliament, granting Mr. Addison a pension of £50 per annum during life, for service rendered as Chaplain to the House of Assembly for thirty years. Another Episcopalian Clergyman, who came to Canada about the same time, was the Rev. Mr. Pollard, whose station was at Amherstburgh.

A fourth Church of England Clergyman, and one with whom

we must become more familiar, was the Rev. Mr. Langhorn. According to the statement made to us by the late Bishop Strachan, Mr. Langhorn was sent to Canada as a missionary by a Society in London, called "The Bees," or some such name. He was a Welshman by birth, possessed of but little education or talent, yet a truthful, zealous, and useful man. Odd in his manner, he nevertheless worked faithfully among the settlers from Kingston to Hay Bay. Upon arriving he took up his abode in Ernesttown, living at Hoyts, the present site of Bath. Here he was instrumental in having, before long time, erected an English Church. Soon after coming he visited Adolphustown, and preached at Mr. Hagerman's, where Mr. Stuart had previously occasionally held service. Steps were at once taken to build a church also at Adolphustown, and Mr. Langhorn came to hold service regularly every second Sabbath. Mr. Langhorn was a diligent pastor in his rounds among his flock, over an extensive tract with great regularity, and once in a great while he went as far as the Carrying Place, where it is said he preached the first of all the pioneer ministers. He likewise occasionally visited Prince Edward, and preached at Smith's Bay, and at Congers, Picton Bay. He was very careful to have all the children christened before they were eight days old, and never failed to question the larger in the catechism. Marriage he he would never perform but in the church, and always before eleven in the morning. If the parties to be joined failed to reach the church by the appointed time, he would leave; and would refuse to marry them, no matter how far they had come, generally on foot, or by canoe. Sometimes they were from the remote townships, yet were sent away unmarried. After performing the marriage ceremony, he would insist on receiving, it is said, three coppers for his clerk. For himself he would take nothing, unless it was to present it to the bride immediately. Seemingly he did not care for money; and he would go in all kinds of weather when wanted to officiate, or administer to the wants of the sick. One person tells us that he remembers his coming to his father's in winter, and that his feet were frozen. No wonder, as Mr. Langhorn never wore stockings nor gloves in the coldest weather. But his shoe buckles were broad and bright; and a broad rimmed hat turned up at the sides covered his head. Upon his back he generally carried in a bag some books for reading. We have referred to his peculiarities; many extraordinary eccentricities are related of him, both as a man and clergyman. He was very fond of the water, both in summer and winter. "In summer," (Playter says,) "he would, at times swim from a cove on the main shore to a cove in the opposite island, three miles apart, and in winter, he would cut a hole in the ice, and another at some distance, and would dive down at one hole, and come up the other. He had some eccentricities, but he seemed to be a good and charitable man."

Mr. Langhorn, when the war of 1812 commenced, acquired the belief, it is said, that Canada would be conquered by the United States, and so determined to escape. The following somewhat singular "Notice" appeared in the Kingston *Gazette* :—"Notice—To all whom it may concern,—That the Rev. J. Langhorn, of Ernesttown, intends returning to Europe this summer, if he can find a convenient opportunity; and all who have any objections to make, are requested to acquaint him with them, and they will much oblige their humble servant,—J. Langhorn,—Earnesttown, March, 1813." The Rev. gentleman did go home, and some say that he was again coming to Canada, and was shipwrecked. Before leaving Canada, he made a valuable present to Kingston, as the following notice will show:

"The Rev. Mr. Langhorn, of Ernesttown, who is about returning to England, his native country, has presented a valuable collection of books to the Social Library, established in this village. The directors have expressed to him the thanks of the proprietors for his liberal donation. Many of the volumes are very elegant, and, it is to be hoped, will, for many years, remain a memorial of his liberality and disposition to promote the diffusion of useful knowledge among a people, with whom he has lived as an Episcopal Missionary more than twenty years. During that period his acts of charity have been frequent and numerous, and not confined to members of his own church; but extended to indigent and meritorious persons of all denominations. Many who have shared in his bounty, will have reason to recollect him with gratitude, and to regret his removal from the country."—(*Kingston Gazette*).

After his departure, the churches where he had preached were vacant for many a day; and, at last, the one in Adolphustown went to decay.

There died, at Williamstown, U. C., 23rd September, 1815, the Rev. John Bethune, in his 65th year. He was a native of Scotland. Came to America before the rebellion, and was possessed of property, all of which he lost, and was thereby reduced to great distress for the time being. The foundation was then laid for the disease of which he died. During the rebellion, he was appointed Chaplain to the 80th Regiment. At the close of the war he settled in Canada. He left a widow and numerous family.

Ex-Sheriff Sherwood, of Brockville, says that "the Rev. Mr. Bethune, a Presbyterian Clergyman, was the second legalized Clergyman in the country. He settled at an early period at Cornwall. He was father of the Rev. John Bethune, now Dean of Montreal, (1866)."

BAPTISTS—WYNER, TURNER, HOLTS, WIEM.

The first Ministers of this sect were Elders Wyner and Turner, a brother of Gideon Turner, one of the first settlers of Thurlow. One, Elder Holts, also preached around the Bay, but a love of brandy hindered him. Yet he was an attractive preacher. This was probably about 1794.

A considerable number of Baptists settled up the river Moira, in Thurlow. The first chapel built here was for that denomination, in the fifth concession. Its size was thirty feet square. But, prior to the building of this, a dozen or so would meet for worship at the house of Mr. Ross. The chapel was mainly built by each member going to the place and working at the building, from time to time, until it was completed.

Mr. Turner traveled through different sections, preaching wherever he found his fellow communionists. He occasionally preached at Capt. McIntosh's, at Myer's Creek, and now and then at the head of the Bay. The Baptists were, probably, the first to preach at Sidney, and Thurlow. Myer's Creek was not a central place at which to collect the scattered settlers until it became a village. Before that, the preaching place of the Baptists, and afterwards of the Presbyterians and Methodists, was up at Gilbert's house, in Sidney, or at Col. Bell's, in Thurlow. When the village grew, services were held at Capt. McIntosh's and Mr. Mitz's, at the mouth of the river, by different denominations, and still later, in a small school house. Preaching also was held up the river, at Reed's and Hayden's Corners.

The first Baptist Minister that preached at East Lake, Hallowell, was the Rev. Joseph Wiem. Not unlikely, he and Elder Wyner are the same.

THE LUTHERANS—SCHWERDERGER, MYERS, WEANT.

Among the early ministers of religion who attended to the spiritual interests of the pioneers, were several of the Lutheran

Church. Of this denomination, there was a considerable number in the County of Dundas, chiefly Dutch. There were also a community of them in Ernesttown, and another in Marysburgh. The first church built in Upper Canada, east of Kingston, perhaps the next after the one built at Tyendinaga, was erected by the Lutherans. It was put up in 1790, named Zion's Church, and a Mr. Schwerdfeger, who resided near Albany, was invited to be their Pastor. This invitation was gladly accepted, as he and his family had suffered severe persecution from the victorious rebels. He died in 1803.

At an ealy period, indeed it would seem probable before Mr. Schwerdfeger came to Canada, although the time cannot be positively fixed, the Rev. Mr. Myers, from Philadelphia, lived in Marysburgh and preached to the Lutheran Germans of that Township. He married a daughter of Mr. Henry Smith, one of the first settlers there, where stood his log church, about twenty-four feet square, upon the brow of a hill overlooking a lovely landscape. Mr. Myers removed to the St. Lawrence, and "in 1804 became Pastor of the Lutheran churches there." (History of Dundas). He resigned in 1807, not being supported, and removed to Pennsylvania.

The second Lutheran clergyman to preach upon the Bay, was the Rev. Mr. Weant. He lived a short distance below Bath, and went every four weeks to preach at Smith's Bay; and, in the meantime, preached to the Lutherans of Ernesttown, where he built a log church, the first there. In 1808, he received a call from the Lutherans of Matilda, "which he accepted, and for some time preached acceptably, residing in the parsonage. He, too, seems to have been inadequately supported by the people, and yielding to inducements, too tempting for most men to resist, he, in 1811, secretly joined the Church of England, and was re-ordained by Bishop Mountain, in Quebec. Upon his return, he pretended still to be a Lutheran minister, and preached, as usual, in German exclusively. Suspicions, however, soon arose that all was not right, for he began to use the English Book of Common Prayer, and occasionally to wear the surplice, practices which gave such offence to his former friends, that they declared they would no longer go to hear a man who proclaimed to them in his shirt sleeves. A few were persuaded by him to join the Church of England. The majority remained faithful. In 1814, the Lutherans again invited the Rev. Mr. Myers; upon his consenting to come, they sent two sleighs, in the winter, to Pennsylvania, and brought him and his family to

Dundas. But Mr. Weant would not give up the parsonage and glebe, and put a padlock on the church door, and forbade any one to enter, unless acknowledging the thirty-nine articles of the Church of England. A compromise resulted, and the Lutherans were permitted to use the building once in two weeks. For three years, Mr. Myers continued his ministrations as a Lutheran, in the meantime being in straitened circumstances. In 1817, strangely enough, Mr. Myers also forsook the Lutheran Church, and conformed to the Church of England. (Hist. of Dundas.) The end of Mr. Weant and Mr. Myers, according to accounts, was not, in either case satisfactory. The latter died suddenly from a fall, it is said, while he was intoxicated, and the former was addicted to the same habit of intemperance.

The successor of Mr. Myers was the Rev. I. L. SENDERLING. He came in 1825, and stayed only a short time.

In 1826, Rev. HERMAN HAYUNIGA became the Pastor; and succeeded, after many, years, in restoring to the church its former prosperity, notwithstanding much that opposed him. He had a new church erected. His successor was the Rev. Dendrick Shorts.

The *Kingston Gazette* contains a notice of perhaps the last Lutheran Minister at Ernest town. "Married. In Ernesttown, 29th Jan, 1816, the Rev. Wm. McCarty, Minister of the Lutheran congregation, to Miss Clarissa Fralick."

CHAPTER XXIX.

CONTENTS—Bishop Strachan—A teacher—A preacher—A student—Holy Orders—A Presbyterian—Becomes an Episcopalian—A supporter of the "Family compact"—Sincere—His opinion of the people—Ignorant—Unprepared for self-government—Strachan's religious chart—He was deceived—The Methodist—Anomalous connection—A fillibustering people—Republicanism egotistical—Loyalty of Methodists—American ministers—Dr. Strachan's position—His birth place—His education—A. M., 1793—Studying Theology—Comes to Canada—A student of Dr. Stuarts—Ordained Deacon—A missionary at Cornwall—Rector at York—Archdeacon—Bishop of Toronto—Coadjutor—Death—A public burial—Rev. Mr. McDowell—First Presbyterian at Bay Quinté—Invited by VanAlstine—On his way—At Brockville—Settles in second town—His circuit—A worthy minister—Fulfilling his mission—Traveling on foot—To York—Marrying the people—His death—His descendants—Places of Preaching—A Calvinist—Invites controversy—Mr. Coate accepts the challenge—The disputation—Excitement—The result—Rev. Mr. Smart—Called by Mr. McDowell—Pres. clergyman at Brockville—Fifty years—An earnest Christian—A desire to write—"Observer"—A pioneer—A cause of regret—Not extreme—Mr. Smart's views on politics—The masses uneducated—The "Family Compact"—Rise of responsible government—The Bidwells—Credit to Dr. Strachan—Brock's funeral sermon—Foundation of Kingston gaol—Maitland—Demonstration—Sherwood's statement.

BISHOP STRACHAN—REV. MR. MCDOWELL AND REV. MR. SMART.

Having elsewhere spoken of this distinguished man as the first teacher of Higher Education in Upper Canada, it is intended to give him a proper place among the first who preached the Gospel. Dr. Strachan, who had studied Divinity at Kingston, under the guidance of Mr. Stuart, took Holy Orders while engaged in teaching at Cornwall. Although he had been brought up in the Presbyterian faith, he deliberately connected himself with the Church of England, as the church of his choice.

From the first, Dr. Strachan took a decided stand in favor of the exclusive power claimed by the government and the "Family Compact." This step was no doubt, deemed by him the very best to secure the interest of the rising country, believing as he did, that the people generally were unfitted by want of education to perform the duties of legislation and self-government. His devotion to the government, led doubtless, in some instances, to errors of judgment, and on a few occasions placed him in a false position. Yet he was always seemingly conscientious. The course pursued by him, in preparing, and sending to the Imperial Government a religious chart, which subsequent investigation proved to be incorrect, had, at the time, an unfortunate effect. But it is submitted, that it has never been shewn, that Dr. Strachan was otherwise than deceived when preparing the document. He made statements of a derogatory nature with respect to the Methodist body; but can it be shewn that there was no reason whatever for his statements. The history of the Methodists of Canada, exhibits a loyalty above suspicion. But was there no ground on which to place doubts respecting the propriety of any body of Canadians receiving religious instruction from men who were subjects of another country—a country which was ever threatening the province, and who had basely invaded an inoffending people—a country that constantly encouraged her citizens to penetrate the territory of contiguous powers with the view of possessing it. While there is sufficient proof that the Methodist ministers who came into the country were actuated by the very highest motives, it cannot be denied that any one taught in the school of republicanism, will carry with him wherever he goes, whether among the courtly of Europe, the contented and happy Canadians, or the blood-thirsty Mexicans, his belief in the immaculate principles of republicanism. He cannot, even if he would, refrain from descanting upon the superiority of his government over all others. The proclamation of Gen. Hull, at Detroit, and of others, shews that the belief was entertained in the States, that many Canadians were favorable to the Americans. Whence could have arisen this belief? Not certainly from the old U. E. Loyalists, who had been driven away from their native country? Not surely by the English, Irish, or Scotch? Dr. Strachan, with the government, could not close their eyes to these facts, and was it unnatural to infer that American-sent Methodists had something to do with it?

Bishop Strachan was a man of education, and as such, he must be judged in reference to his opinion that Methodists were unqualified to teach religious truth, from their imperfect or deficient education. We say, not that much book learning is absolutely essential to a successful expounding of the plan of salvation, although it is always most desirable. But having taken our pen to do justice to all of whom we have to speak, we desire to place the reader so far as we can upon the stand of view occupied by the distinguished Divine and Scholar.

Dr. Strachan was born at Aberdeen, Scotland, 12th April, 1778. He was educated at the Grammar School, and at King's College, at that city, where he took the degree of M. A., in 1793. He then removed to the neighborhood of St. Andrews, and studied Theology, as a Presbyterian. As stated elsewhere, he came to America in 1799, reaching Canada the last day of the year. Disappointed in his expectations respecting an appointment to establish a college, he became a school teacher in Kingston, and at the same time a student of Divinity, under the guidance and friendship of Dr. Stuart. He prosecuted his Theological studies during the three years he was in Kingston, and in 1803, was ordained Deacon, by Dr. Mountain, the first Protestant Bishop of Quebec. The following year he was admitted to Holy Orders, and went as a missionary to Cornwall. Here he continued nine years, attending diligently to his duties as a minister, all over his widening parish; and also conducted a Grammar School. In 1812 he received the appointment of Rector at York, the capital, and in 1825 he was made Archdeacon. Enjoying political appointments with these ecclesiastical, he finally, in 1839, was elevated to be the first Bishop of Toronto. Dr. Strachan discharged the duties of his high office with acceptability. In 1866 Archdeacon Bethune was appointed as Coadjutor Bishop, the venerable prelate beginning to feel that his time was almost done. He died 1st November, 1867, having attained to his ninetieth year, and was accorded a public funeral. No higher marks of esteem and veneration could have been exhibited than were displayed by all classes at the death of this Canadian Divine.

The most of the settlers from the Hudson, not Lutherans, were Presbyterians, or of the Dutch Reformed Church. Mr. McDowell was the first Presbyterian minister to visit the Bay. He came about 1800, perhaps before; when yet there were but few clergymen in the province. We have seen it stated that he was sent for by Major VanAlstine, who was a Presbyterian. On his way he tarried a day in the neighborhood of Brockville. Adiel Sherwood was then teaching school, in connection with which he was holding a public exhibition. Mr. McDowell attended, and here first took a part as a minister, by offering his first public prayer in the country. He proceeded to Kingston, and settled in the second township. But his circuit of travel and places of preaching extended from Brockville to the head of Bay Quinté. The name of this worthy individual is too little known by the inhabitants of the bay. No man contributed more than he to fulfill the Divine mission "go preach;" and at a time when great spiritual want was felt he came to the hardy settlers. The spirit of christianity was by him aroused to no little extent, especially among those, who in their early days had been accustomed to sit under the teachings of Presbyterianism. He traveled far and near, in all kinds of weather, and at all seasons, sometimes in the canoe or batteau, and sometimes on foot. On one occasion he walked all the way from Bay

Quinté to York, following the lake shore, and swimming the rivers that could not be otherwise forded. He probably married more persons while in the ministerial work than all the rest in the ten townships around the bay. This arose from his being the only minister legally qualified to solemnize matrimony, beside the clergymen of the English Church, Mr. Stuart, of Kingston, and Langhorn, of Fredericksburgh. Persons wishing to be married repaired to him from all the region of the bay, or availed themselves of his stated ministerial tours. The writer's parents, then living in Adolphustown, were among those married by him, the cerificate of which now lies before him. Mr. A. Sherwood thus speaks of him, "He lived to labor many years in the service of his Master, and after an honorable and good old age he died highly esteemed by his friends and much respected by all who knew him." "Mr. McDowell had at least two sons and a daughter. The last is Mrs. Carpentor, now living at Demorestville. One of his sons removed to New York and there established a Magdalene Asylum. Mr. McDowell, used to pass around the bay twice or three times a year. He was one of the first, to preach at the extreme head of the bay, the Carrying Place, and for that purpose occupied a barn. Another of his preaching places was in Sophiasburgh. on the marsh front. He preached here four times a year. He was a rigid Calvinist, and preaching one Sabbath at the beginning of the present century in the Court House at Adolphustown, he offered to argue with any one publicly the question of Calvanism. The Methodist minister of the bay, the Rev. Samuel Coate, was urged by his society to accept the challange, and after a good deal of hesitation did so. So a day was appointed for the discussion. The meeting took place at a convenient place, three miles from Bath, in the Presbyterian church. The excitement was great; the inhabitants coming even from Sidney and Thurlow. Mr. McDowell spoke first, and occupied half a day. Then followed Mr. Coate. After he had spoken two hours Mr. McDowell and his friends left; why, it is not said. Mr. Coate continued speaking until night. We have the statement of the Methodists, that Mr. Coate had the best of it, but we never learned the belief of the other party. Mr. Coate's sermon was published by request, and thereafter, it is said Presbyterianism waned in the locality.

Rev. Mr. Smart,—This truly pious man, and evangelical minister, came to Canada in 1811. He never actually lived within the precincts of the Bay; but he was called to the wilderness of Upper Canada by the Rev. Mr. McDowell, at least he was chiefly instrumental in bringing him out, even before his student days were ended. For upwards of fifty years he discharged the duties of Presbyterian clergyman at Brockville, the first clergyman of any denomination within fifty miles. We shall ever remember the kind genial person with whom we spent a few pleasant hours in the evening of his eventful life, a life spent earnestly in the service of his Master, and for the welfare of his family, for, to use his own words, "In his day it was no easy matter to live and rear a family." This he said not complainingly, but because it hindered him from indulging a desire he once felt to do something with his pen—to record, as he was desired to do, the events connected with his early life in Upper Canada, and his cotemporaries. At first he did contribute to the *Kingston Gazette*, over the cognomen "Observer." But other things pressed upon him, and when repose came he fancied the fire of his early days, for scribbling, had too far sunk. This is much to be regretted, for as a close observer and upright man, and living in eventful times of Canadian history, he was pre-eminently qualified to treat the subject. Mr. Smart was always distinguished for moderate and well-considered views upon Religion, Political Government and Education. He lived when the battle commenced between the "Family Compact" and the people. While he firmly set his face against the extreme stand taken by the Rev. Mr. Strachan, he never identified himself with the party that opposed that worker for, and with the Government. On this point, Mr. Smart makes judicious remarks. In speaking of the rise and first days of the Province, he says, "it was necessary the Government in Council should create laws, and govern the people, inasmuch as the vast majority of the inhabitants were unlettered, and unfit to occupy places which required judgment and discrimination. There were but few of the U. E. Loyalists who possessed a complete education. He was personally acquainted with many, especially along the St. Lawrence, and Bay of Quinté, and by no means were all educated, or men of judgment; even the half-pay officers, many of them, had but a limited education. Many of them were placed on the list of officers, not because they had seen service, but as the most certain way of compensating them for losses sustained in the Rebellion. And there were few, if any, of them fitted by education for office, or to serve in Parliament Such being the case, the Governor and his advisers were at the first necessarily impelled to rule the country. Having once enjoyed the exclusive power, they became unwilling to share it with the representatives of the people. But the time came when the mass, having acquired some idea of Responsible Government, were no longer to be kept in obscurity, and thence arose the war between the Tory and the Radical. In all the contentions arising therefrom, Mr. Smart held an intermediate position with the Bidwell's and others. In speaking of all this, Mr. Smart is particularly anxious to give credit to Dr. Strachan for his honesty of purpose, saying that the Colony is much indebted to him in many ways.

Mr. Smart was called upon to preach the funeral sermon of Canada's great hero, General Brock.

He also delivered an address on the occasion of laying the foundation stone of the gaol in Kingston, in presence of the Governor, Peregrine Maitland, who was down from York, on which occasion there was great demonstration of Free Masons, and the farmers of the Bay.

Mr. Sherwood thus speaks of Mr. Smart: "On his arrival, he for some little time made his home at my house, he was then 23 years old, he has now (1866) entered his 78th year, has retired from a public charge, and is now residing quietly, and I trust comfortably, at Gananoque; and I feel quite sure, all that know him throughout the whole Province, will join with me, in wishing him long life and happiness, both here and hereafter."

CHAPTER XXX.

CONTENTS—The Quakers—Among the Settlers—From Penn.—Duchess County—First Meeting-house—David Sand—Elijah Hick—Visiting Canada—James Noxen—A first settler—Their mode of worship—In Sophiasburgh—The meeting-house—Joseph Leavens—Hicksites—Traveling—Death, aged 92—Extract, Picton Sun—The first preaching places—First English church—In private houses—At Sandwich—The Indian church at the bay—Ernesttown—First Methodist church—Preaching at Niagara—First church in Kingston—At Waterloo—At Niagara—Churches at Kingston, 1817—In Hollowell—Thurlow—Methodist meeting-houses, 1816—At Montreal—Building chapels in olden times—Occupying the frame—The old Methodist chapels—In Hollowell township—In the fifth town—St. Lawrence—First English Church, Belleville—Mr. Campbell—First time in the pulpit—How he got out—The old church superseded—Church, front of Sidney—Rev. John Cochrane—Rev. Mr. Grier—First Presbyterian Church in Belleville—Rev. Mr. Ketcham—First Methodist Church in Belleville—Healey, Puffer—The site of the church—A second one.

THE EARLY CLERGYMEN AND CHURCHES OF UPPER CANADA.—THE QUAKERS.—NOXEN, LEAVENS, HICKS, SAND.

Among the early settlers of the Bay were a goodly number of the Society of Friends Some of them were natives of Pennsylvania; but the majority were from the Nine Partners, Duchess County, New York, where had existed an extensive community of the followers of Fox. The first meeting-house built by the Quakers in Canada was in Adolphustown upon the south shore of Hay Bay, toward the close of last century.

About 1790, two Quaker preachers of some note visited Canada, they were David Sand and Elijah Hick. By appointment they held service in Adolphustown; it is uncertain whether this was before, or after the building of the meeting-house. The first and principal preacher among the Quakers was James Noxen, one of the first settlers of Adolphustown, under whom the Society was organized. He subsequently in 1814 removed to Sophiasburgh, where he died in 1842.

The worship of the Quakers consists in essentially spiritual meditation and earnest examination of the inmost soul, a quiet holding of the balance, to weigh the actions and motives of every-day life. To the proper discharge of these duties no place can be too quiet, too far removed from the busy haunts of men.

The sixth township, or Sophiasburg had among its settlers a good many of this sect, which at first had meetings at Jacob Cronks, until the year 1825, when they erected a meeting-house upon the northern front of the township.

Two miles below the village of Northport, is situated a Friends' meeting-house. Here twice a week, on Thursdays and Sundays, congregate few, or many of the adherents of this persuasion, to commune with their God. The meeting-house, reposing upon the very verge of the shore, and half shadowed by beautiful maples and evergreens, is a fit place in which to submit oneself to strict self-examination. There is nothing here to disturb the supreme quietude of the place, unless, the gentle ripples of the water, or the more restless murmuring of the wave.

JOSEPH LEAVENS "was an early settler of Canada, an emigrant from New York," he was for many years an esteemed preacher of the Hicksite branch of Quakers, and was accustomed to travel from place to place, to talk to his co-religionists. He had a place for preaching in a loft of his brother's store in Belleville. He was one of the first Quaker preachers in Canada and travelled through all the townships at the Bay, and to East Lake.

"Died in the township of Hallowell, about the 24th of May, 1844, the venerable Joseph Leavens, in the 92nd year of his age. He was amongst the early settlers of the Canadian forest, and emigrated from New York State, and probably was a native of Nine Partners District. He had long been a Preacher in the Religious Society of Friends, and though not possessed of more than one talent, yet it is believed that, as he occupied that to his Maker's glory, his reward will be as certain as though he had received ten talents. He was a diligént reader in the sacred volume. He was much beloved both by his neighbours and friends, and it is desired that his gospel labours may be profitably remembered by them and his relatives."—(*Picton Sun.*)

In speaking of the individual clergymen who first came to the Province we have referred to many of the first preaching places and churches: but there remains to be added some further remarks.

We have seen that the first church erected in Western Canada was at the Mohawk settlement, Grand River, which was built the first year of their habitation in that place—1785-6. Strange that the natives of the wood, should take the lead in erecting places of worship. It was several years later before even log meeting-houses were put up by the loyalists. For many years the pioneer clergymen or preachers officiated in private houses. Now the service would be at the house of one, to which a considerable number could come from a circuit of ten or fifteen miles, then it would be at the place of some settler whose larger log house afforded a more commodious place of worship.

A church was built at an early date at Sandwich, but the year, we know not. The first church erected upon the Bay, the Rev. Mr. Smart thinks, was at the Mohawk village, Tyendinaga. At an early period a log church was built in Ernesttown by the Lutherans and another on South Bay; one also for Mr. Langhorn to preach in, and then another in Adolphustown. The first Methodist church was built in Adolphustown in 1792, and a second one a month later in Ernesttown.

The Rev. Mr. Addison, went to Niagara in 1792. When Governor Simcoe lived in Navy Hall, the Council Chamber a building near the barracks it was said, was used alternately by the English Church, and Church of Rome.

The first English Church was erected in Kingston in 1793, and up to 1810 it was the only one. A Methodist church was built at a very early date at Waterloo, it was never finished, but used for many years. The first at Niagara, was in 1802.

In November 28, 1817, there were in Kingston, "four churches or meeting-houses, viz: 1 Episcopalian, 1 Roman Catholic and 2 Methodists; there were 4 professional preachers, viz: 1 Episcopalian, 1 Presbyterian and 2 Methodists. This enumeration does not include a chaplain to the army, and one to the royal navy." In Ernesttown there was one resident professional preacher, a Methodist.

In Sophiasburgh there were no churches; but the Quakers, Methodists and Presbyterians had meetings at private houses.

In Hollowell, says Eben. Washburne, "we have one Methodist, and one Quaker meeting-house; preparations are making also for a Presbyterian meeting-house. The former is attended by a circuit preacher every two weeks; the latter by a Quaker every Sabbath.

In Thurlow, "the Gospel is dispensed almost every Sabbath of the year, in different parts of the township, by itinerant preachers of the Methodist and Baptist sects.

In 1816, there were eleven Methodist meeting-houses in Canada. These were all of wood excepting one in Montreal, built in 1806, which was of stone. "The mode of building chapels in the olden times was by joint labor, and almost without the aid of money. The first step was for scores of willing hands on a given day, to resort to the woods, and then fell the trees, and square the timber; others, with oxen and horses, drawing the hewed pieces and rafters to the appointed place. A second step was to call all hands to frame the building, selecting the best genius of the carpenter's calling for superintendent. A third step was a "bee" to raise the building; and the work for the first year was done. The next year, the frame would be enclosed, with windows and doors, and a rough floor laid loose. As soon as the meeting house was thus advanced, it was immediately used for preaching, prayer meetings and quarterly meetings. Some of the early chapels would be finished inside; others, would be used for years in their rough, cold, and unfinished state. The people were poor, had little or no money, but loved the Gospel, and did what they could."

The oldest of the eleven chapels is the Adolphustown, on the south shore of the Hay Bay, and on the old Bay of Quinté circuit.

"The next for age is the chapel in the fourth concession of Ernesttown. It was not erected here at first, but on the front of the township, lot No. 27, and close to the Bay of Quinté. After some years, (some of the principal Methodists moving to the fourth concession), the frame was taken down, drawn to the present site, and put up again. It stands on the public road, leading from Napanee to Kingston, and near the village of Odessa. A rough-cast school-house, now stands on the old site, east of Bath. Some challenge the antiquity of the Ernesttown, with the Adolphustown chapel; but both were commenced at about the same time, by William Losee; the latter was first erected. As the traveler passes, he may look on this old and useful meeting-house, still used for public worship, and see a specimen of the architecture of the pious people settled in the woods of Ernesttown seventy years ago.

"About nine miles from Odessa toward Kingston is the village of Waterloo, and on the top of a sand-hill, formerly covered with lofty pines, is a well proportioned and good looking Wesleyan stone church. It is on the site of an ancient frame meeting-house, decayed, and gone, which bore an antiquity nearly as great as the other two chapels. The meeting-house in the Township of Kingston was an unfinished building, a mere outside, with rough planks for seats.

"Two miles from the Town of Picton, and in the first concession of the Township of Hollowell, is still to be seen one of the oldest Methodist chapels in Upper Canada. The ground and the lumber were the gift of Steven Conger. The first work was done in June, 1809. An account book, now existing, shows the receipts and payments for the building. Some paid subscriptions in money, some in wheat, some in teaming and work; and one person paid one pound "by way of a turn." The first trustees were named Conger, Valleau, Vanblaricum, Dougal, German, Benson, Wilson, and Vandusen. They are all dead, but children of some of them are still living in the vicinity. The building is square, with pavilion roof, of heavy frame timber, yet sound, having a school-house on one side, and a mill on the other. Here is a burying ground attached, in which lie many of the subscribers to, and first worshippers in, the chapel. It is still used as a place of worship, and for a Sabbath school. These four chapels were all in the old Bay of Quinté circuit.

"In the fifth township east of Kingston is another relic of the times of old, called the Elizabethtown chapel. It is now within the boundaries of the village of Lyn, about eight miles from Brockville, and near the river St. Lawrence. A chapel particularly remarkable for the assembling of the Genesse conference in 1817, and the great revival of religion which there commenced."

The first English Church erected west of Adolphustown, was at Belleville. It was commenced in 1819, and finished the next year. The Rev. Mr. Campbell was the first clergyman, and came to the place some little time before the building was completed. An anecdote has been related to us by one who saw the occurrence, which will serve to illustrate the character of those days. Mr. Campbell one day entered the church, when near its completion, and walked up a ladder and entered the pulpit; immediately one of the workmen, named Smith, removed the ladder, leaving the Rev. gentleman a prisoner; nor would they release him until he had sent a messenger to his home for a certain beverage. This church when erected was an ornament to the place, and is well remembered by many, having been taken down in 1858, the present handsome structure being completed. Mr. Campbell continued in charge until his death in 1835. During this time he caused to be erected a church at the front of Sidney, midway between Belleville and the Trent, and he held services there every second Sabbath, in the afternoon, for a time; but the congregation was never large. Methodism seemed to take more hold of the feelings of the people. Mr. Campbell's successor was the Rev. John Cochrane, who was pastor for three years, when the present incumbent, the Rev. John Grier, who had been at the Carrying Place for some years, took charge.

The first Presbyterian clergyman of Belleville, was Mr. Ketcham, under him the first church was built.

The first Methodist church to be built in the western part of the Bay country was at Belleville. It was probably about the beginning of this century that the itinerant Methodist began to visit the head of the Bay Quinté. They were accustomed to preach in private houses, and barns, here and there along the front, and up the Moira River, and at Napanee.

Healy and Puffer were accostomed to preach at Col. Bell's, Thurlow.

Belleville was laid out into lots in 1816; Mr. Ross applied to government for one, as the society was disqualified from holding landed property until 1828. The land was accordingly granted to him, and recorded, January 7, 1819. A frame building was immediately commenced 50 by 30 feet. Before it was inclosed, service was held within the frame. The building was never completed. The pulpit was of rough boards, and the seats were of similar material, placed upon blocks. In 1831, a second chapel was commenced, and the old one removed.

CHAPTER XXXI.

CONTENTS.—The first Methodist Preachers—The army—Capt. Webb—Tuffey—George Neal—Lyons—School-teacher—Exhorter—McCarty——Persecution—Bigotry—Vagabonds—McCarty arrested—Trial—At Kingston—Banished—"A martyr"—Doubtful—Losee, first Methodist missionary, 1790—A minister—A loyalist—Where he first preached—"A curiosity"—Earnest pioneer Methodist—Class-meetings—Suitable for all classes—Losee's class-meetings Determines to build a meeting-house—Built in Adolphustown—Its size—The subscribers—Members, amount—Embury—Those who subscribed for first church in New York—Same names—The centenary of Methodism—New York Methodists driven away—American Methodist forgetful—Embury and Heck refugees—Ashgrove—No credit given to British officers—Embury's brother—The rigging loft, N. Y.—Barbara Heck—Settling in Augusta—First Methodist Church in America—Subscribers—"Lost Chapters"—The Author's silence—What is acknowledged—"Severe threats"—Mr. Mann—To Nova Scotia—Mr. Whately "admires piety"—not "loyalty"—Second chapel, N. Y.—Adolphustown subscribers—Conrad VanDusen—Eliz. Roblin—Huff—Ruttan—The second Methodist chapel—The subscribers—Commenced May, 1792—Carpenters wages—Members, Cataraqui Circuit—Going to Conference—Returns—Darias Dunham—Physician—First quarterly meeting—Anecdotes—Bringing a "dish cloth"—"Clean up"—The new made squire—Asses—Unclean spirits—Losee discontinues preaching—Cause—Disappointment—Return to New York—Dunham useful—Settles—Preachers traveling—Saddle-bags—Methodism among the loyalists—Camp-meetings—Where first held, in Canada—Worshipping in the woods—Breaking up—Killing the Devil—First Canadian preacher—Journey from New York.

THE FIRST WESLEYAN METHODISTS IN CANADA.

The first Methodist Preachers both in Lower and Upper Canada were connected with the British Army; also, the second one in America, who was Capt. Webb. "In 1780, a Methodist Local Preacher, named Tuffey, a Commissary of the 44th, came with his regiment to Quebec. He commenced preaching soon after his arrival, and continued to do so at suitable times, while he remained," or until his regiment was disbanded in 1783. The second Methodist Preacher in Canada was George Neal, an Irishman. During the war he was Major of a cavalry regiment. He "crossed the Niagara river at Queenston on the 7th October, 1786, to take possession of an officer's portion of land, and soon began to preach to the new settlers on the Niagara river—his labours were not in vain." —(Playter).

"In 1788 a pious young man, called Lyons, an exhorter in the Methodist Episcopal Church, came to Canada, and engaged in teaching school in Adolphustown." He collected the people together on the Sabbath, and conducted religious services. "In the same year came James McCarty, an Irishman, to Ernesttown."

He was a follower of Whitfield, but acted with the Methodist, holding religious meetings. His preaching caused severe persecution against him on the part of certain loyalists, who held the doctrine that none could be true subjects who adhered not to the Church of England; but to oppose the Church was to oppose the King. Advantage was taken of this loyalty to try to prevent the introduction of any other religious denominations. A law had been enacted by the Governor in Council, that persons wandering about the country might be banished as vagabonds. McCarty was arrested on a charge of vagabondism in Adolphustown, and brought before a magistrate at VanDusen's tavern, at the front, who remanded him to Kingston. According to Playter, he was preaching at Robert Perry's when arrested; our informant is the Rev. C. VanDusen, at whose father's he was first arraigned. After being released on bail, he was finally tried before Judge C., and was sentenced to be banished, tradition says, upon an island in the St. Lawrence. At all events he was placed in a batteau and taken away by French boatmen. McCarty has obtained the name of *martyr*, but it is the belief of unbiassed persons that he was not left upon the island, but was conveyed to Montreal.

William Losee was the first regular preacher of the Methodist denomination in Canada. He first visited the country in 1790, preached a few sermons along the Bay of Quinté and St. Lawrence, and returned with a petition from the settlers to the Conference, to send him as a preacher. In February, 1791 he again came, as an appointed minister from the Methodist Episcopal Church of the United States. "Losee was a loyalist, and knew some of the settlers in Adolphustown, before they left the United States. He desired to see them and preach to them the glad tidings of salvation. Had he been on the revolutionary side, the warm loyalists would not have received him—rather would have driven him from the country."—(Playter). One of the first places at which he preached, was at the house of John Carscallian, in Fredericksburgh. The tavern of Conrad VanDusen, in Adolphustown, was another, and at Paul Huff's, on Hay Bay, another. "A Methodist Preacher was a curiosity in those days, and all were anxious to see the phenomenon; some would even ask how he looked, or what he was like! A peculiarity in Losee, too, was, that he had but one arm to use, the other being withered." A true pioneer Methodist, he set earnestly to work to form class-meetings and organize societies, and "during the summer his circuit embraced the settlements in the Township of Kingston, Ernesttown, Fredericksburgh, Marysburgh, and even Sophiasburgh. Class-meetings form the corner stone of Wesleyan Methodism. But little understood, often entirely misunderstood by others than Methodists, they are generally regarded as the abode of cant or of priestly control. No greater error could exist. Rightly conducted they are invaluable as a means of training the religious mind, and establishing it upon the Rock of Ages. It has been said that they are only suitable for the uneducated; not so, they are alike beneficial to the peasant and the noble, the clown and the *litératuér*. Losee, in accordance with the principles of Methodism, at once set to work to create classes, and on the Sabbath of February 20, 1792, in the 3rd concession of Adolphustown, at Paul Huff's house, he established the first regular class-meeting in Canada. The second class was formed on the following Sabbath, in Ernesttown, four miles from Bath.

A third class was formed in March, at Samuel Detlor's, three miles from Napanee. The following year the congregation had so increased, which met at Paul Huff's house, that a determination was formed to erect a meeting house. A paper was drawn up, in which was set forth the great blessing of God in sending a minister to their wilderness home, that a "Meeting-house or Church" is requisite. Then follows an agreement of the subscribers to build a Church, under the direction of Losee; to be thirty-six feet by thirty feet, two stories high, with a gallery. "Said house to be built on the north-west corner of Paul Huff's land, lot No. 18, third concession, Fourth Town;" and promising to pay the sums of money annexed to their respective names. This interesting document, with the names of subscribers, and the subscription of each, is to be found in Playter's History of Methodism, a work that ought to be in the hands of every Canadian, no matter what his creed, because of the fund of general knowledge upon Canada it contains. The total number of subscribers was twenty-two; the amount subscribed was £108. Among the names are those familiar to every inhabitant of the Bay, some known throughout Canada. To one, especially, reference must be made, Andrew Embury, a name of historic interest in connection with Methodism in America. It is a remarkable fact, that this and other names are to be found among those who planted Methodism in New York. The celebration of the centenary of Methodism in America, in 1866, was marked by frequent and glowing accounts of those who introduced Methodism into America. Too much credit, too much honor could not be given to the Emburys, the Hecks and others, which was was quite correct. But no reference was made in the United States, nor in Canada for that matter, to the dark days of the infant Society in New York, when the cruel rebellion interrupted the meetings in that place; and where persecution followed the retirement of the British forces, 1783. It is a page of history in connection with that body, which American writers of Methodism endeavor to wipe out, when the very founders of the Church in America were made to flee from their homes; and had all their property sacrificed. The names of Embury and Heck; of whom so much was said, were among the refugees from rebel oppression. No word has been said of the cause of the removal of these persons to the wilderness of Canada. Barbara Heck, who enjoys the everlasting honor of causing Philip Embury to begin Preaching, was driven away from his Methodist home. Philip Embury was not likewise treated, because death had sealed his eyes a year before the declaration of independence, ere the demon of rebellion was evoked by the spirit of radicalism, and unhallowed desire for neighbor's goods; otherwise his bones, the resting place of which they have given so glowing a picture, would likewise be sleeping in our midst, in the quiet shades of the Canadian forest, as do those of Paul Heck, who died in 1788; and of his wife, Barbara, who died in 1804. The remains of Philip Embury, instead of being urned, as they were, in 1822, in Ash Grove, Washington County, New York, after lying buried for fifty-seven years in the old burying ground of Abraham Beninger, should have found a burying place on Canadian soil, where rests his widow, the place to which his brother and the Hecks were driven. We have listened to some of the American orators, and read more of their speeches, and could not help noticing that they forgot to mention that their impetuous rebellion drove away from them the founders of Methodism; they forgot to give any credit to Capt. Webb, who was the second Methodist preacher in America; forsooth, because he was a British officer, and it would be unpleasant to associate such with centenary orations in this their day of Anglophobia.

Upon the north shore of Hay Bay, in Fredericksburgh, settled David Embury, brother of Philip, who officiated as a Methodist Minister in New York, in a Rigging Loft, on William St., about 1766. To do this he was urged by Barbara Heck, wife of Paul Heck, both of whom were among the first to settle on the St. Lawrence, in Augusta, in 1785. The first Methodist Church erected in America, was in 1768, on John Street, New York. Among the 250 subscribers, was the name of

David Embury, the same who settled on Hay Bay; he gave £2. Also, the name of Paul Heck, who contributed £3 5s. Twenty-four years later, and among the twenty-two subscribers to build the first Methodist meeting-house in Canada, again appears the name of Embury—Andrew, son of David Embury. The author of the "Lost Chapters of Methodism," gives interesting accounts of the formation of the Methodist Society in New York; but he is remarkably silent in this instance, as others are, about the treatment they received from the Americans; not a word to make it known that they were driven into the wilds of Nova Scotia and Canada by a relentless people. Yet, at the conclusion, he acknowledges this much: He says, "At the conclusion of the Revolutionary war, severe threats having been thrown out against the Loyalists who had taken refuge within the British lines, Mr. Mann thought it his duty to embark, with a considerable number of the Society, for the wilds of Nova Scotia." Mr. Mann was a class leader, and local preacher, and, during the war, at the request of the Trustees, kept the chapel in John Street open, after the regular preacher had left. "We see what became of a part of the Society, in John Street. Some of them had been so loyal to their sovereign, they were afraid they would suffer if they remained." Of course they were, and had they not sufficient reason from the "threats" which had been "thrown out." Mr. Wakely, the author, continues, "We can admire their piety without endorsing their loyalty." How kind. The second Methodist Church of New York was built on the land of DeLancy, who had his immense property confiscated.

Of the subscribers to the chapel in Adolphustown, Conrad Van Dusen gave the largest amount, £15. He had been a Tavern keeper on the front, and was one of the first fruits of Losee's missionary labors. "He lived a little east of the Court House. Of him many pleasing and amusing anecdotes are told; though a tavern-keeper, as well as a merchant, he opened his house for the Gospel, and when that Gospel entered his heart, he deliberately took his axe and cut down his sign posts."—(*Playter.*)

The second largest contributor, was Elizabeth Roblin, who gave £12. She was the widow of Philip Roblin, who died 1788. They had been among the first settlers of Adolphustown. (See U. E. Loyalists.) Mrs. Roblin afterwards became the wife of John Canniff, the founder of Canifton, and her remains now rest on the hill in the old family burying ground, in that village. She was the grand-parent of John P. Roblin, of Picton, "a man who has served

19

his country in several Parliaments of Upper Canada. Her daughter Nancy, born in 1781, is the mother of a large branch of the Ketcheson family in the County of Hastings."—(*Playter.*) She, with her husband, still live in the fifth concession of Sidney, yet hale and hearty, in the autumn of their genial, though toilsome, life. "The subscription of the widow was liberal; indeed, the Roblins of the Bay of Quinté have always been a hospitable and liberal minded people." Paul Huff and William Ruttan, each gave £10. The others gave smaller sums; but, considering the date, it is noteworthy that so much was contributed.

The same month, it is said, Losee undertook to build a second Church in Ernesttown, a short distance below Bath. "The principal persons who aided in building this meeting-house were James Parrot, John Lake, Robert Clarke, Jacob Miller, and others. There is evidence in the account book of Robert Clarke, who was a carpenter, that the chapel was commenced May, 1792. He credits himself with then working twelve and a-half days; and with working in October twelve and a-half days, at five shillings and six-pence per day, which shows carpenter's wages at that time. But like a good hearted man, seeing the building fund not too full, he reduced his wages to two shillings and nine-pence per day. His payment to the chapel was £10. James Parrot received the subscriptions. The two buildings were to be of the same size and form. As soon as these two chapels were inclosed, the congregations sat on boards to hear the preaching. They were the first Methodist Churches in Canada. At the end of the year Mr. Losee had 165 members enrolled in the "Cataraqui Circuit." He set out on his long journey to attend conference at Albany. Mr. Losee returned the following year, accompanied by Rev. Darius Dunham. The latter took charge of the Bay of Quinté district—the "Cataraqui Circuit," while Losee went to the St. Lawrence to organize a new society—this was called the "Oswegotchie" circuit.

On Saturday, September 15, the first "Quarterly" meeting was held, in Mr. Parrot's barn, 1st Con., Ernesttown, to which many of the settlers came from the six townships. Darius Dunham was a Physician by profession. "He was a man of strong mind, zealous, firm in his opinions." He labored well on the Cataraqui Circuit, and was in high repute by the people."—(*Playter*).

Many anecdotes are told of Dunham. On account of his quick and blunt way of speaking and rebuking evil doings, he acquired the name of "Scolding Dunham." Withal, he was witty, and he loved, it would seem, next to Godliness, cleanliness, so he would, if at a house, where it were not observed, according to his idea (and as there was only the one room, he could see the whole process of preparing for the table,) he would tell the housewife that the next time he came he would "bring a dish-cloth along," or perhaps, he would bluntly tell the woman to "clean up." Carroll relates the following story, yet often told and laughed at by the old settlers of the Bay. "His reply to the newly appointed magistrate's bantering remarks, is widely reported. A new-made 'Squire' rallied Dunham before some company, about riding so fine a horse, and told him he was very unlike his humble Master, who was content to ride an ass. The preacher responded with his usual imperturable gravity, and in his usual heavy and measured tones, that he agreed with him perfectly, and that he would most assuredly imitate his Master in that particular, but for the difficulty of finding the animal required—the Government having made up all the asses into magistrates." "A person of the author's acquaintance, informed him that he saw an infidel, who was a fallen Lutheran clergyman, endeavoring, one night while Dunham was preaching, to turn the whole into ridicule. The preacher affected not to notice him, but went on exalting the excellency of Christianity, and showing the formidable opposition it had confronted and overcome; when, all at once, he turned to where the scoffer sat, and fixing his eyes upon him,' the old gentleman continued: "Shall Christianity and her votaries, after having passed through fire and water," &c.—" after all this, I say, shall the servants of God, at this time of day, allow themselves to be frightened by the *braying of an ass.*" In those days it was believed, by some at least, that unclean spirits and devils might be cast out by the power of God through the faithful Christian, and Dunham had the credit of having, on several occasions, cast out devils.

Mr. Losee remained a preacher only two years, when he became mentally unfit, having encountered a disappointment of a crushing nature. The uncertainty of the cause of his discontinuing to preach, has been dispelled by Playter, in the most touching language, "He was the subject of that soft, yet powerful passion of our nature, which some account our weakness, and others our greatest happiness. Piety and beauty were seen connected in female form then as well as now, in this land of woods and water, snows and burning heat. In the family of one of his hearers, and in the vicinity of Napanee river, was a maid, of no little moral and personal attraction. Soon his (Losee's) attention was attracted; soon the seed of love was planted in his bosom, and soon it germinated and bore outward fruit. In the interim of suspense, as to whether he should gain the person, another preacher came on the circuit, visits the same dwelling, is attracted by the same fair object, and finds in his heart the same passion. The two seek the same person. One is absent on the St. Lawrence; the other frequents the blest habitation, never out of mind. One, too, is deformed, the other a person of desirable appearance. Jealousy crept in with love. But, at last, the preference was made, and disappointment, like a thunderbolt, overset the mental balance of the first itinerant minister in Canada." He subsequently removed to New York, where he continued to live for many years, and recovered his mental health. He had purchased lots in Kingston, which he returned to sell in 1816; at this time he was perfectly sound in mind, and was a good man. He visited Adolphustown, and other places, preaching here and there, and finally returned to New York.

Mr. Dunham proved a useful man, especially among the settlers of Marysburgh. He ultimately in the year 1800, retired from the ministry and settled near Napanee, having married into the Detlor family. But he continued to act as a local preacher.

The early preachers often traveled from place to place on horseback after a bridle-path had been made, with saddle-bags, containing oats in one part, and a few articles of wearing apparel in another, perhaps a religious book; thus the zealous preacher would travel mile after mile through interminable forests. Indeed there are plenty to-day who have done likewise.

There is one fact connected with the early Methodist preachers, which requires a passing notice.

The settlers were all intensely loyal; yet when the Yankee Methodist preacher came in their midst he was gladly received; it is true Losee the first who came was a loyalist; but many who followed were Americans and republicans. Although the Lutheran, Presbyterian, and English churchmen had preceded the Methodists into Canada, neither seemed to obtain that hold upon the hearts of the plain U. E. Loyalists, that the Methodists did. The people of every denomination as well as those belonging to none, flocked to hear them, and many stayed to become followers. These Americans were always regarded with suspicion by government, and serious doubts were entertained whether those who became

Methodists were loyal. But the war of 1812, exhibited in a thrilling manner the old fire of attachment to their sovereign the King. Their seemed to be an adaptability between the Methodist mode of worship and the plain old settlers, and for years there were many who left the church of their fathers, and joined the more demonstrative society of Wesleyanism. Not only was this mode of ordinary worship followed by the Methodist congenial, but especially the camp meeting engaged their hearty attention. This mode of worshipping in the woods was first known in Kentucky in 1801, and was initiated by two brothers named McGee, one of whom was a Methodist, the other a Presbyterian. There are many who regard the holding of camp-meetings as very questionable, even in the past. Whatever may be said about the necessity of such meetings at the present day, they were it is thought, highly appropriate in the infant days of the country. At the first, and for many long years, there were but few churches of any size. Then, the inhabitants had been buried as it were in the primeval forests, left to meditate in its deep recesses, far away from the busy haunts of men. No doubt the solemn repose, and silent grandeur awoke in their minds feelings of awe, and of veneration, just the same as one will feel when gazing along the naves of some old grand cathedral, with its representations of trees and flowers. It is not difficult to understand that the mind, trained by habit to meditation in the woods, with its waving boughs telling of other times, and of a mysterious future, would naturally find worshipping in the woods, congenial to the soul,—find it a fit place for the higher contemplation and worship of the great God. The first camp-meeting held in Canada was in 1805, on the south shore of Hay Bay, near the chapel. The meeting was attended by some from the distant townships, who went down in batteaux. This was a great event to the settlers. Its announcement, says Dr. Bangs, "beforehand excited great interest far and near. Whole families prepared for a pilgrimage to the ground, processions of waggons, and foot passengers wended along the highways." The ministers present were Case, Ryan, Pickett Keeler, Madden and Bangs. The meeting commenced on the 27th of September; the whole was characterized by deep religious feeling as well as decided demonstration, and the joy and comfort of believing, which ought always to be present with the Christian, was generally experienced, while there was an absence of that outside exhibition, too often seen in later years, around the camps. We quote from Carroll respecting the ending of this meeting.

The account is from Dr. Bangs, "The time was at hand at last for the conclusion of the meeting. The last night was the most awfully impressive and yet most delightful scene my eyes ever beheld. There was not a cloud in the sky. The stars studded the firmament, and the glory of God filled the camp. All the neighbouring forest seemed vocal with the echo of hymns. Turn our attention which way we would, we heard the voice of prayer and praise. I will not attempt to describe the parting scene, for it was indescribable. The preachers, about to disperse to their distant fields of labor, hung upon each other's necks, weeping and yet rejoicing. Christians from remote settlements, who had here formed holy friendships, which they expected would survive in heaven, parted probably to meet no more on earth. As the hosts marched off in different directions the songs of victory rolled along the highways."

Apropos of Methodist camp-meetings, Carroll tells an anecdote characteristic of the times, and as well of the honest Dutch. One of these old settlers was speaking of a recent camp-meeting from which he had just come said, "It was a poor, tet tull time, and no goot was tone, till tat pig Petty (the Rev. Elias Pattie) come; but mit his pig fist, he did kill te tuval so tet as a nit, and ten te work proke out. The Methodists of that day were fond of the demonstrative."

In the year 1806, a native of Prince Edward district entered the Methodist ministry. He was the first native Canadian preacher of any denomination, his name was Andrew Pringle.

The same year Thomas Whitehead was sent by the New York Conference. He was six weeks on the road through the woods with his wife and six children, "and during most ef the time they subsisted on boiled wheat."

CHAPTER XXXI.

SOME ACCOUNT OF HENRY RYAN.

A sketch of the early ministers who preached around the Bay Quinté, would be incomplete without a somewhat extended notice of Elder Ryan, after whom was called, a certain number of non-contented Methodists, *Ryanites*.

Henry Ryan, an Irishman, "of a bold energetic nature, with a powerful voice," commenced preaching in 1800. He was for five years stationed in the States. In the year 1805, he, with the Rev. Wm. Case, was appointed to the Bay Quinté circuit. It was they who arranged and conducted the first camp meeting. Carroll, writing of that period, says, "there was no society (of Methodists) then in the Town of Kingston, and its inhabitants were very irreligious. The market house was the only chapel of the Methodists, Case and his colleague (Ryan) made a bold push to arouse the people. Sometimes they went together, Ryan was a powerful singer too. They would ride into the town, put their horses at an inn, lock arms, and go singing down the streets a stirring ode, beginning with 'Come let us march to Zion's hill.' By the time they had reached the market-place, they usually had collected a large assembly. When together, Ryan usually preached, and Case exhorted. Ryan's stentorian voice resounded through the town, and was heard across the adjacent waters. They suffered no particular opposition excepting a little annoyance from some of the baser sort, who sometimes tried to trip them off the butcher's block, which constituted their rostrum; set fire to their hair, and then blew out their candle if it were in the night season." Proof was subsequently given that this preaching was not without effect.

Mr. Ryan continued ten years at the Bay Quintê, and then three years in the west at Long Point and Niagara. In 1810, he was presiding Elder. His duties, as such, was to visit every part of the Province, from Detroit to Cornwall. "Allowing for his returns home, he traveled about 1000 miles each quarter in the year, or 4000 miles a year. And what was the worldly gain? The presiding Elder was allowed $80 for himself, $60 for his wife, and what provisions he would need for his family. His entire allowance might have been £60 a year. Such was the remuneration, and such the labors, of the presiding Elder" of the Methodists fifty-three years ago—(Playter).

Henry Ryan continued a presiding Elder, for many years, in the whole of Upper Canada, a few years in lower Canada, and then when the Bay of Quinté district was set apart by division, he was appointed Elder to it. But in 1834, for some reason, Mr. Ryan was superseded in office. The reason of this can only be guessed. He was an Irishman by birth, and although sent to Canada by an American body, he seems to have been more a British subject, a Canadian, than American. During the war of 1812, he remained in Canada attending to his duties, with three other faithful men, Rhodes, Whitehead, and Pringle. More than that, as presiding Elder, he assumed the oversight of the preachers at the close of the first year. Others had been stationed in Canada who were British subjects, but they ceased before the war had closed, to discharge their duties. The Americans feared to come, or, having come, were warned off by proclamation. Those who continued in the ministerial field met under the presidency of Ryan. In the year of the commencement of the war, the conference was to have met at Niagara, in Upper Canada; but war was declared by the United States a month previous, and instead of venturing into the country where their fellow countrymen were about to carry the midnight torch, they turned aside to another place to hold their conference. "None of the brethren laboring on the Canada side went over. It is probable, although we are not certain, that they met at the place appointed, where some sort of deliberations would take place." The Rev. John Ryerson says Mr. Ryan "held a conference, and held three conferences during the war, the principal business of which was employing preachers, and appointing them to their different fields of labor." The Rev. Ezra Adams says, the second conference was held at Matilda," and "in 1814, it was held at the Bay of Quinté, at Second or Fourth Town"—Carroll. Mr. Ryan was impulsive and authoritative, at least the ministers thought so, and the rule of "Harry Ryan" was called "high-handed." The end of it all was that, although he was useful and liked by the people, his ministerial brethren in Canada did not like him, and the conference seemed glad to supersede one, who no doubt already manifested his desire that the Canadian Methodists should become independent of the Americans. In view of the political state of affairs, the objection felt by the government to have American preachers giving religious instruction to Canadians,—in view of the course pursued by Ryan during the war of 1812—in view of his whole career up to this time, the belief is forced upon the mind that it was not, only when Ryan had been superseded that he began to agitate for a separation. His labors during the war were severe and continuous, says a preacher of the times, "He used to travel from Montreal to Sandwich, to accomplish which he kept two horses in the Niagara district, and one for the upper part of the Province, and another for the lower. As his income was very small, he eked out the sum necessary to support his family by peddling a manufacture of his own in his extensive journeys, and by hauling with his double team in winter time, on his return from Lower Canada, loads of Government stores or general merchandise. Mr. Ryan, by his loyalty, gained the confidence and admiration of all friends of British supremacy, and by his abundant and heroic labors, the affections of the God-fearing part of the community." Much more might be said in the same vein, but probably enough has been said to establish his claim to the sympathy of every Bay of Quinté inhabitant, where he so long labored and where most of his subsequent followers lived. It may be added that he was brave and witty, and "had a ready answer for every bantering remark. Some wicked fellows are said to have asked him if he had heard the news? What news? Why, that the devil is dead. Then said he, looking around on the company, he has left a great many fatherless children. On another occasion, on entering a public house, a low fellow, knowing him to be, from his costume, a minister, remarked aloud, placing his hand in his pocket, "There comes a Methodist preacher; I must take care of my money." Ryan promptly said, "You are an impudent scoundrel." "Take care," said the man, "I cannot swallow that." "Then chew it till you can," was the fearless reply. —(Carroll). At camp meetings, when it came to pass that individuals came to create disturbance, and when there was no police to take care of rowdies, Mr. Ryan has been known to display his muscular power by actually throwing the guilty individuals over the enclosure to the camp ground.

Mr Ryan preached occasionally at Vandusens' tavern in Adolphustown. After one of his thundering sermons, a neighboring squire who was a daily visitor at the tavern, and who had recently attempted to cut his own throat, wrote upon the wall of the bar-room, "Elder Ryan, the Methodist bull, preaches hell and damnation till the pulpit is full;" whereupon some one wrote below it, "Bryan C——d, the magistrate goat, barely escaped hell and damnation by cutting his throat."

Mr. Ryan, upon his return from the General Conference in 1844, commenced an agitation for independence of the Canadian Methodists, and from Port Hope Creek to the Ottawa, he continued to urge the necessity of such an end.

"While not much liked by the preachers, Ryan was very popular among the people," especially along the Bay Quinté. Captain Breakenridge, a local preacher, living on the St. Lawrence, joined him, in holding conventions, and in procuring largely signed petitions, praying for separation. Ryan and Breakenridge, went to the General Conference, bearing these petitions, and were not received. But these petitions were the commencement of the separation, which it was quite time should take place for the well being of both parties. Concessions were made—a Canada conference was formed through the instrumentality of Elder Ryan; but under the superintendency of the United States conference. This did not satisfy Ryan, and his followers in the Bay Quinté circuit. Meetings were held at which it was resolved they would "*break off*" from the American Church without permission. For four months Ryan energetically appealed to the people. To allay this the Bishop had to come and say to the Canadians, that if they wished independence, the next general conference, which would meet in 1828, would no doubt grant it. The following year the first Canada conference was held at the village of Hollowell, (Picton). It was opened on the 25th August. There were thirty preachers present, and they continued in session five days. The agitation initiated by Ryan, had done its work, "a general desire existed, that the Canada body should become an independent body, not later than the general conference of 1828," and a memorial was prepared to be submitted to that body. After requesting to be set apart an independent body, the following reason, with others was given. "The state of society requires it. The first settlers having claimed the protection of His Britannic Majesty in the revolutionary war, were driven from their former possessions to endure great hardships in a remote wilderness. Time, however, and a friendly intercourse, had worn down their asperity and prejudice, when the late unhappy war revived their former feelings; affording what they considered, new and grievous occasion for disgust against their invading neighbors. The prejudices thus excited would probably subside if their ministry were to become residents in this country, as would be the case in the event of becoming a separate body." The fact that government regarded with dislike the connection was adverted to, also that they were not allowed to solemnize matrimony. Such was the fruit of Elder Ryan's proceedings, and to him belongs great credit, however much his motives may have been impugned. It has been acknowledged that he was disliked by the preachers, and this dislike was manifested this year by sending him as a missionary to the Indians. No wonder he was dissatisfied. Not because he was placed in a humble position, after acting nearly a quarter of a century as presiding Elder; but because of the animus of those who did it. And moreover, he entertained the belief that the general conference did not intend to give independence. The next year Ryan was placed among the superannuated ministers, and thus remained two years, the next year 1827, he withdrew, and resumed the agitation for independence. He had no faith in the United States conference, the cry was raised, Loyal Methodism against Republican Methodism. In this Ryan was countenanced by Government and the English Church, and Playter says, Dr. Strachan sent him £50 to carry on the work of separation.

The whole previous life of Ryan, lead us to believe that he was sincere and honest in his movements and statements, but it is said he was greatly mistaken. The people generally said, wait till we see what the general conference does. The preachers have said they will give us independence, pause till we see. The result of the conference was as had been promised; while already Ryan had separated, and, with a limited number of followers, mostly along the bay and St. Lawrence, had formed a new body with the name of *Canadian Wesleyan Methodist Church*. But it will always remain a question whether the general conference would have conceded the independence had it not been well known that Ryan would take almost all if they were not made free. It is not an unknown thing for a person who has worked for some public good to be robbed of the credit in a surreptitious manner. Ryan was deceived, and his kind, though impulsive nature resented the wrong done him. Though his name has been placed under a shadow by those who were indebted to him, yet his memory is even yet green and sweet in the hearts of some of the old settlers. Well might Elder Ryan, select as his text at the time, "I have raised up children and they have rebelled."

The general conference assembled at Pittsburgh, 1st May, 1828. The memorial from the Canada conference was duly considered, and whatever may have been the reasons, they granted in the most kindly spirit, the decided request of the Canadian Methodists. Ryan, it is said when he heard of it, "looked astonished, trembled and could scarcely utter a word."

The second Canada conference met at Ernesttown, the 2nd October, 1828, in Switzer's chapel. "Bishop Hedding came for the last time, and presided over the conference. No United States Bishop, no Bishop at all, has ever presided since." This year, Andrew Pringle, the first native Methodist preacher, was placed on the superannuated list. After due deliberation the conference resolved to organize into an independent body, and adopted the discipline of the Methodist Episcopal Church, as the basis of their own. The Rev. Wm. Case was appointed General Superintendent until the next conference.

It is not possible, nor would it be proper to give a connected history of Methodism, or any other religious denomination. But the aim of the writer is to supply facts relative to those who have lived and acted a part in connection with the early history of the bay, with such other facts as will throw light upon the matter. With this object in view, we will here introduce, in conclusion, a brief notice of the visit of Bishop Asbury to Canada in 1811. The account is from the pen of the Rev. Henry Bœhm, with remarks by Mr. Carroll. Reading this account, it called to our mind the account given to us by Father Bœhm, in 1854, while sojourning at Staten Island, New York, where we had the great pleasure of frequently meeting him and of enjoying the hospitality of his genial family. Mr. Bœhm was the traveling companion of Bishop Asbury when he visited Canada.

Bishop Asbury, the cotemporary of the Wesley's, being one whom Wesley ordained to preach, he came to America in 1771, as a missionary, being 25 years old. Of all the English preachers in the revolting colonies, he alone remained during the revolutionary war, and was under the necessity of concealing himself in Delaware. Created a Bishop by Dr. Coke, in 1785, he continued for many years in the oversight of the Methodist Church in America and in Canada. But although Methodism was planted in Canada in 1792, it was not until the year mentioned that a Bishop found his way to the remote settlements of Canada. Bishop Asbury, however, had for years a desire to see Canada. Two years before he came he wrote, "I shall see Canada before I die." Says Bœhm.

"We had a severe time on our journey. We crossed Lake Champlain, and Mr. Asbury preached in a bar-room in Plattsburgh. The roads through the woods, over rocks, down gulleys, over stumps, and through the mud, were indescribable. They were enough to jolt a hale bishop to death, let alone a poor, infirm old man, near the grave." "On entering the village (of St. Regis) as Mr. Asbury was leading his horse across a bridge made of poles, the animal got his foot between them, and sunk into the mud and water. Away went the saddle-bags; the books and clothes were wet, and the horse was fast. We got a pole under him to pry him out; at the same time the horse made a leap, and came out safe and sound. We crossed the St. Lawrence in romantic style. We hired four Indians to paddle us over. They lashed three canoes together, and put our horses in them, their fore feet in one canoe, their hind feet in another. It was a singular load; three canoes, three passengers, the bishop, Smith and myself, three horses and four Indians. They were to take us over for three dollars. "It was nearly three miles across to where we landed"—"did not reach the other side till late in the evening." The Indians claimed another dollar, because three could not be easily divided between four, this was "cheerfully paid." "We arrived in Canada on July 1st, 1811, landing at Cornwall, and about midnight reached the hospitable house of Evan Roise, who hailed the bishop's arrival with joy, and gave him and his companions a welcome worthy of patriarchal times." "We found it warm in Canada, and the Bishop suffered greatly. Here Henry Ryan, Presiding Elder of Upper Canada, met us. The next day Bishop Asbury preached," the day after the Bishop preached again and there was a love-feast, and the Lord's Supper." Proceeding up the River St. Lawrence, arrived at the eastern line of Matilda, "the Bishop rode in Brother Glassford's close carriage, which he called a 'calash,' and he inquired how they would get out if it upset. He had hardly asked the question before over went the carriage, and the venerable Bishop was upset, but fortunately no bones were broken; the saplings along side the road broke the fall. On Friday the Bishop preached in Matilda chapel, in what was called the German settlement. I followed, preaching in German. The Bishop was delighted with the people, he wrote, "here is a decent loving people. I called upon Father Dulmage, and Brother Heck." We tarried over night with David Breackenridge. He married and baptised a great many people, and attended many funerals. In 1804 he preached the funeral sermon of Mrs. Heck. who died suddenly, and it is said she claimed to be the person who stirred Philip Embury to preach the Gospel. On Saturday we rode twelve miles before breakfast to Father Boyce's, where we attended Quarterly Meeting. Bishop Asbury preached a thrilling sermon. "The Bishop greatly admired the country through which we rode. He says 'Our ride has brought us through one of the finest countries I have seen. The timber is of noble size; the cattle are well shaped, and well looking; the crops are abundant on a most fruitful soil. Surely this is a land that God, the Lord hath blessed.'" (Such was the testimony of one who had traveled all over the United States, concerning a country eighty years younger than the older States of the Union. Such the testimony respecting the pioneers of the country who twenty-five years previous came thereto into an unbroken wilderness—respecting the men the Americans had driven away and stigmatized by the application of the most degrading names). "On Monday we proceeded to Gananoque Falls, to Colonel Stone's. Father Asbury was very lame from inflammatory rheumatism. He suffered like a martyr. On Tuesday we visited Brother Elias Dulmage, a very kind family, and Bishop Asbury preached in the first Town Church" (Kingston Church). E. Dulmage, one of the Palatines, lived afterward a long time as jail-keeper."—(Carroll). The Bishop was so poorly he could not proceed on his journey, and was obliged to lie up and rest. He remained at Brother Dulmage's, where he found a very kind home, and I went with Henry Ryan to his Quarterly Meeting. in Fourth or Adolphustown, Bay of Quinté. On Friday we rode to Brother John Embury, Hay Bay. He was a nephew of Philip Embury, the Apostle of American Methodism. On the Lord's day we had a glorious love-feast, and at the Lord's Supper He was made known to us in the breaking of bread. In a beautiful grove, under the shade of trees planted by God's own hand, I preached to two thousand people, John Reynold's, afterward Bishop Reynolds, of Belleville, and Henry Ryan exhorted. (Exhorting after sermon was a common practice among the Methodists in those days). Mr. Bœhm had to return to Kingston the same night, in order that the Bishop might get to the Conference to be held in the States immediately. To do so they rode all night—35 miles. "To our great joy we found Father Asbury better"—"he had sent around and got a congregation to whom he preached in the chapel. He also met the Society and baptized two children. We were in Canada just a fortnight. The Bishop was treated everywhere as the angel of the churches. The Bishop preached six times in Canada, besides numerous lectures which he delivered to societies." The Bishop and Mr. Bœhm set out on the Monday for Sackett's Harbour, in a small sail boat. There was a heavy storm, and they were nearly wrecked. On the water all night without a cabin. Spent a fearful night, and reached Sackett's Harbour the next afternoon.

CHAPTER XXXII.

CONTENTS—McDonnell—First R. Catholic Bishop—A "Memorandum"—Birthplace—In Spain—A Priest—In Scotland—Glengary Fencibles—Ireland, 1798—To Canada—Bishop—Death in Scotland—Body removed to Canada—Funeral obsequies—Buried at Kingston—Had influence—Member of Canadian Legislative Council—Pastoral visitations, 1806—A loyal man—A Pioneer in his Church—The Bishop's Address, 1836—Refuting mal-charges—Number of the R. C. Clergy in 1804—From Lake Superior to Lower Canada—Traveling horseback—Sometimes on foot—Hardships—Not a Politician—Expending private means—Faithful services—Acknowledged—Roman Catholic U. E. Loyalists—First Church in Ernesttown—McDonnell at Belleville—Rev. M. Brennan—First Church in Belleville—What we have aimed at—The advantages to the English Church—The Reserves—In Lower Canada—Dr. Mountain—Number of English Clergymen, 1793—A Bishop—Monopoly initiated—Intolerance and Exclusion swept away—An early habit at Divine service.

THE ROMAN CATHOLICS—BISHOP MCDONNELL.

We are much indebted to J. P. McDonnell, Esq., of Belleville, for a "Memorandum of his grand-parent, the Rev. Alex McDonnell, first Bishop of Upper Canada."

"He was born in the year 1760, in Glengary, in Scotland, educated for the Priesthood at Valladolid College, in the Kingdom of Spain; for, at this time no person professing the Roman Catholic faith could be allowed to be educated in any part of the British empire. He was ordained Priest before the year 1790. Then came back to Scotland, his native country, and officiated as a Priest in Badenoch, a small district in North Scotland, also in the city of Glasgow; afterwards joined, in 1798, the Glengary Fencibles, then for duty in Ireland, under the command of Lord McDonnell, of Glengary, who was Colonel of said Fencible Regiment. He came to Canada in the year 1804; was consecrated first Bishop of Upper Canada in the year 1822, titled as the Bishop of Kingston." He died in Dumfriesshire, a County bordering on England and Scotland, in the year 1840. His body was laid in St. Mary's Church, Edinborough, until removed to Canada, in 1862. His remains was taken from the cars at the station at Lancaster, and carried to St. Raphael's Cathedral; in which Church he had spent some of his most useful days, administering the consolations of his religion to his numerous co-religionists throughout the Province of Upper Canada. His remains were escorted by thousands of people, of all denominations, from St. Raphael's Church to St. Andrew's Church, and thence to Cornwall depot, in order to convey his remains to Kingston, the head of his See; where his remains now lie in the vaults of the Cathedral of that ancient city, in which he, as Bishop, officiated for years, a favorite of both Protestants and Catholics. I may here remark, that no other man, either clergyman or lay, ever had more influence with the Government, either Imperial or Colonial than Bishop McDonnell. In fact he established the Catholic Church in Western Canada. All the lands that the church now possesses were procured by his exertions. The Bishop was a member of the Legislative Council for years in connection with the Venerable Bishop Strachan, of Toronto. About the year 1806, he passed on his way from Toronto, then York, to Kingston; celebrated mass at his relation's, Col. Archibald Chisholm, whose descendants are now living on Lot. Nos. 8 and 9, 1st Con., Thurlow, adjoining the Town of Belleville—carried his vestments on his back most of the way from Toronto to Kingston; and he took passage in a birch canoe from his friend's, Col. Chisholm, to another relation, Col. McDonnell, (McDonald's Cove,) on his way to Kingston.

"Although his religion was then proscribed by the British Government, and he was compelled to go to a foreign country to be educated, no more loyal man to the British Crown lived; no other man ever conduced more to the upholding of British supremacy in North America than he, and helped to consolidate the same.

We are also indebted to Mr. McDonnell for other valuable documents concerning the Bishop, who may be regarded the father of his Church in Upper Canada. At least, he was the pioneer of that denomination in the Bay region. To a great extent, his history is the early history of his Church. The worthy prelate will speak for himself, when at the advanced age of seventy-four, and he spoke under circumstances which precluded the possibility of any statement accidentally creeping in, which could not be fully substantiated.

Referring to an address of the House of Assembly, 1836, in which his character had been aspersed, and his motives assailed, he, in a letter to Sir Francis Bond Head, asks "the liberty of making some remarks on a few passages" thereof, and, among other things, says, "As to the charges brought against myself, I feel very little affected by them, having the consolation to think that fifty years spent in the faithful discharge of my duty to God and to my country, have established my character upon a foundation too solid to be shaken by the malicious calumnies of two notorious slanderers." To the charge that he had neglected his spiritual functions to devote his time and talents to politics, he, by plain declaration, refutes their "malicious charge," stating the following facts, which relate to the country from the year he entered it, 1804. He says, "There were then but two Catholic clergymen in the whole of Upper Canada. One of these clergymen soon deserted his post; and the other resided in the Township of Sandwich, in the Western District, and never went beyond the limits of his mission; so that upon entering upon my pastoral duties, I had the whole of the Province beside in charge, and without any assistance for the space of ten years. During that period, I had to travel over the country, from Lake Superior to the Province line of Lower Canada, to the discharge of my pastoral functions, carrying the sacred vestments sometimes on horseback, sometimes on my back, and sometimes in Indian birch canoes, living with savages—without any other shelter or comfort, but what their fires and their fares, and the branches of the trees afforded; crossing the great lakes and rivers, and even descending the rapids of the St. Lawrence in their dangerous and wretched crafts. Nor were the hardships and privations which I endured among the new settlers and emigrants less than what I had to encounter among the savages themselves, in their miserable shanties; exposed on all sides to the weather, and destitute of every comfort. In this way I have been spending my time and my health year after year, since I have been in Upper Canada, and not clinging to a seat in the Legislative Council and devoting my time to political strife, as my accusers are pleased to assert. The erection of five and thirty Churches and Chapels, great and small, although many of them are in an unfinished state, built by my exertion; and the zealous services of two and twenty clergymen, the major part of whom have been educated at my own expense, afford a substantial proof that I have not neglected my spiritual functions, or the care of the souls under my charge; and if that be not sufficient, I can produce satisfactory documents to prove that I have expended, since I have been in this Province, no less than thirteen thousand pounds, of my own private means, beside what I received from other quarters, in building Churches, Chapels, Presbyteries, and School-houses, in rearing young men for the Church, and in promoting general education. With a full knowledge of those facts, established beyond the possibility of a contradiction, my accusers can have but little regard for the truth, when they tax me with neglecting my spiritual functions and the care of souls. The framers of the address to His Excellency knew perfectly well that I never had, or enjoyed, a situation, or place of profit or emolument, except the salary which my sovereign was pleased to bestow upon me, in reward of forty-two years faithful services to my country, having been instrumental in getting two corps of my flock raised and embodied in defence of their country in critical times, viz., the first Glengary Fencible Regiment, was raised by my influence, as a Catholic corps, during the Irish rebellion, whose dangers and fatigues I shared in that distracted country, and contributed in no small degree to repress the rapacity of the soldiers, and bring back the deluded people to a sense of their duty to their sovereign and submission to the laws. Ample and honorable testimonials of their services and my conduct may be found in the Government office of Toronto. The second Glengary Fencible Regiment raised in the Province, when the Government of the United States of America invaded, and expected to make a conquest of Canada, was planned by me, and partly raised by my influence. My zeal in the service of my country, and my exertions in the defence of this Province, were acknowledged by his late Majesty, through Lord Bathurst, then Secretary of State for the Colonies. My salary was then increased, and a seat was assigned for me in the Legislative Council, as a distinguished mark of my sovereign's favor, an honor I should consider it a disgrace to resign, although I can hardly expect ever to sit in the Council, nor do I believe that Lord Glenelg, who knows something of me, would expect that I should show so much imbecility in my latter days, as to relinquish a mark of honor conferred upon me by my sovereign, to gratify the vindictive malice of a few unprincipled radicals. So far, however, from repining at the cruel and continued persecutions of my enemies, I pray God to give me patience to suffer, for justice sake, and to forgive them their unjust and unmerited conduct towards me. I have the honor to be Sir,—Your most obedient and very humble servant,—(Signed)—Alex. McDonnell. To T. Joseph, Esq., Sec'y to His Excellency, Sir Francis Bond Head, &c., &c., &c."

There were a number of Roman Catholics among the U. E. Loyalists. Among them were the Chisholm's on the front of Thurlow, to whose house Mr. McDonnell came to preach as he made his annual round. I am told by an old settler, that a very old Roman Catholic Church existed in Ernesttown west, a short distance from Bath. Probably Mr. McDonnell travelled all around the Bay, visiting members of his Church. There were several in Marysburgh. He was the first to preach in Belleville, when it had become a village. But the Rev Michael Brennan, who still lives, and is highly respected by all classes, was the first priest located in Belleville; he arrived in 1829. The frame of a building which had been erected for a Freemason's Lodge, was moved to the lot which had been received from Government, and was converted into a Church. The present Church was commenced in 1837, and completed in 1839.

We have now adverted to the several early clergymen of the different denominations in the young colony of Upper Canada, and have dwelt upon those facts, and related those events, which appertain to the work we have in hand. We have essayed to simply write the truth, without reference to the interests of any denomination, either by false, or high coloring, or suppression of facts.

From what we have recorded, it is plain that the Church of England stood the best chance of becoming the religion of Upper Canada. The seventh part of the lands were reserved for the clergy, and it was determined to erect an Ecclesiastical establishment in the Province. In Lower Canada the Roman Catholics had been secured by Act of Imperial Parliament. In Upper Canada it was resolved that the English Church should occupy a similar position. The Rev. Dr. Jehoshaphat Mountain was sent out from England in 1793, having been consecrated the first Bishop of Quebec, to take charge of the English establishment in all Canada. There were then in both Canadas five clergymen of the church. The monopoly thus instituted continued for many years, and other denominations could not even hold land upon which to build a place of worship. But time swept all intolerance and exclusiveness away. In the year 1828, was passed "An act for the Relief of Religious Societies" of the Province, by which it was authorized "That whenever any religious congregation or society of Presbyterians, Lutherans, Calvinists, Methodists, Congregationalists, Independents, Anabaptists, Quakers, Menonists, Tunkers, or Moravians, shall have an occasion to take a conveyance of land, it shall be lawful for them to appoint trustees," which body should hold perpetual succession, &c. But it was also enacted that no one Society should hold more than five acres.

This subject will be concluded by the following, the writer of which we fail to remember. It is within our own recollection when this habit still existed:

An early writer, a visitor to the Province of Canada, speaking about religious denominations says, "The worshipping assemblies appear grave and devout, except that in some of them it is customary for certain persons to go out and come in frequently in time of service, to the disturbance of others, and the interruption of that silence and solemnity, which are enjoyed by politeness, no less than a sense of religion. This indecorous practice prevails among several denominations."

CHAPTER XXXIII.

CONTENTS—First Sabbath teaching—Hannah Bell, 1769—School established, 1781—Raikes—Wesley—First in United States—First in Canada—Cattrick, Moon—Common in 1824—First in Belleville—Turnbull—Cooper—Marshall—Prizes, who won them—Mr. Turnbull's death—Intemperance—First Temperance Societies—Change of custom—Rum—Increasing intemperance—The tastes of the Pioneers—Temperance, not teetotalism—First Society in Canada—Drinks at Raising and Bees—Society at Hollowell.

SABBATH SCHOOLS.

The earliest attempt known to teach children upon the Sabbath was in 1769, made by a young lady, a Methodist, by the name of Hannah Bell, in England, who "was instrumental in training many children in the knowledge of the Holy Scriptures. In 1781, while another Methodist young woman (afterward the wife of the celebrated lay preacher, Samuel Bradburn) was conversing in Gloucester with Robert Raikes, a benevolent citizen of that town, and publisher of the *Gloucester Journal*, he pointed to groups of neglected children in the street, and asked: "What can we do for them?" She answered: "Let us teach them to read and take them to church!" "He immediately proceded to try the suggestion, and the philanthropist and his female friend attended the first company of Sunday-scholars to the church, exposed to the comments and laughter of the populace as they passed along the street with their ragged procession. Such was the origin of our present Sunday-school, an institution which has perhaps done more for the church and the social improvement of Protestant communities, than any other agency of modern times, the pulpit excepted. Raikes, and his humble assistant, conducted the experiment without ostentation. Not till November 3, 1783, did he refer to it in his public journal. In 1784, he published in that paper an account of his plan. This sketch immediately arrested the attention of Wesley, who inserted the entire article in the January number of the *American Magazine* for 1785, and exhorted his people to adopt the new institution."

In 1786, they were begun in the United States by the Methodist Bishop, Francis Asbury, in Virginia. In 1790, the Methodist conference "resolved on establishing Sunday-schools for poor children, white and black," since which time they have been in operation.

The first notice found of a Sabbath-school in Upper Canada, is in June, 1817, when a Rev. Mr. Cattrick proposed at Kingston to organize one. A communication from Wm. Moon, in the *Gazette*, expresses great pleasure thereat, and Mr. Moon offers for the purpose his school-room, and likewise his services. In 1824, "Sunday-schools were common in the old settlements, and were valued and encouraged by all classes of people. Not only did private benevolence contribute to the schools, but the Upper Canada Parliament granted £150, for the "use and encouragement of Sunday-schools," and of indigent and remote settlements, in the purchase of books and tracts—(Playter). A Sabbath-school was established in Belleville about 1826, by John Turnbull, Dr. Marshall, and Dr. Cooper who taught in the school. Some religious society granted books and tracts to schools. Four prizes were granted for good attendance and behaviour, consisting of two Bibles and two Testaments. They were awarded, the first to J. H. Meacham, who is now Postmaster of Belleville; the second to his sister, Anna

Meacham, the third to Matilda McNabb, the fourth to Albert Taylor. While these pages are going through the press, we receive the sad intelligence that John Turnbull, Esq., last living of the three mentioned, has passed away at the beginning of this new year, 1869, after a life of well-merited respect, and honor. The writer feels he has lost a friend.

INTEMPERANCE.—Total abstinence or teetotalism was unknown when Upper Canada was first settled. The first temperance society ever organized was at Moreau, Saratoga, County, New York, in 1808.

To taste and drink a glass of wine or grog, was not regarded as a sin by any one of that day. To the soldiers and sailors grog was dealt out as regularly every day as rations. Rum was the liquor more generally used, being imported from Jamacia, and infinitely purer than the rum sold to-day. It has to be recorded that at a comparatively early date, breweries and distilleries were erected, first in one township then in another, so that after a few years the native liquor was much cheaper than rum, and then followed the natural result—namely, increasing intemperance. It is not difficult to understand that the old soldier would like his regular glass of grog. In the long and tedious journeys made by boat, when food perhaps was very limited in quantity, the conveniently carried bottle would take its place, and extraordinary labor and severe exposure would be endured by the agency of unnatural stimulus. The absence of teetotal principles, the customs of the day; want of food; frequent and severe trials and exposures, would lead even the best of men to partake of spirituous liquors. As we see it to-day, so it was then, abuse arose from moderate use, and those who had no control over the appetite, or who loved to forget the bitterness of the day by inebriation, would avail themselves of the opportunity to indulge to excess. The mind naturally craves a stimulant. If this desire be not fed by legitimate food, it is too likely to appropriate the unnatural. The excitement of war had passed away; but had left in its wake the seeds of longing in the breast of the old soldier. The educated man shut out from the world, had but little to satisfy the usually active mind. With some, the remembrance of old scenes—of old homesteads, and their belongings, were forgotton in the stupifying cup. When all these facts are considered, is there not abundant reason to wonder that intemperance did not prevail more extensively. But it is a question after all, whether the loyalists became more addicted to the cup after they settled, than when at the old homes. Those who have charged the old settlers with the vice of drinking, have forgotten to look at them in comparison with other countries at that day, instead of the light set up at a later period.

But while the pioneers preserved themselves from unusual indulgence, it is to be regretted that their children too often forsook the path of soberness, and in losing their right minds, lost the old farm made valuable by their fathers' toil. It was often a repetition of what occasionally occurred when the soldiers were disbanded. They would often sell a location ticket, or two or three acres of land for a quart of rum; the sons would sell the fruit of a father's hard work of a life time.

One of the first temperance societies formed in Canada was in Adolphustown, on the 4th January, 1830. On this occasion the Rev. Job Deacon, of the Church of England, delivered an address, after which a respectable majority and three out of five magistrates present, adopted resolutions condemning the use of ardent spirits, and unitedly determining not to use or furnish drink for raisings, bees, and harvest work. At the same meeting a temperance society was formed and a constitution adopted under the title of "The Adolphustown Union Sabbath School Temperance Society." They pledged themselves not to use ardent spirits for one year.

According to the Hollowell *Free Press*, a temperence society was formed at Hollowell, in 1829; for it is announced that the "Second Anniversary" will be held 3rd June, 1831. It is announced April 12, 1831, that a temperance meeting will be held in the Methodist Chapel, when addresses will be delivered by Dr. A. Austin. The officers elected for the ensuing year are Asa Worden, Esq., M.P.P., President; Dr. Austin, Vice President; P. V. Elmore, Secretary and Treasurer.

CHAPTER XXXIV,

CONTENTS—The Six Nations—Faithful English Allies—Society for the Propagation of Gospel—First missionary to Iroquois—John Thomas, first convert—Visit of Chiefs to England—Their names—Their portraits—Attention to them—Asking for instructor—Queen Anne—Communion Service—During the Rebellion—Burying the Plate—Recovered—Division of the articles—Sacrilege of the Rebels—Re-printing Prayer Book—Mr. Stuart, missionary—The women and children—At Lachine—Attachment to Mr. Stuart—Touching instance—Mr. Stuart's Indian sister—Church at Tyendinaga—School teacher to the Mohawk—John Bininger—First teacher—The Bininger family—The Moravian Society—Count Zinzendorf—Moravian church at New York—First minister, Abraham Bininger—Friend of Embury—An old account book—John Bininger journeying to Canada—Living at Bay Quinté—Removes to Mohawk village—Missionary spirit—Abraham Bininger's letters—The directions—Children pleasing parents—"Gallowping thoughts"—Christianity—Canadian Moravian missionaries—Moravian loyalists—What was sent from New York—"Best Treasure"—The "Dear Flock"—David Zieshager at the Thames—J. Bininger acceptable to Mohawk—Abraham Bininger desires to visit Canada—Death of Mrs. Bininger—"Tender mother"—Bininger and Wesley—"Garitson"—"Losee"—"Dunon"—Reconciled to Methodists—Pitying Losee—Losee leaving Canada—Ceases to be teacher—Appointing a successor—William Bell—The salary—The Mohawks don't attend school—An improvement—The cattle may not go in school-house—The school discontinued.

THE SIX NATIONS—CONVERSION TO CHRISTIANITY.

From the first occupation of New York by the English, the Six Nations had almost always been their faithful allies. This devotion did not remain unnoticed. Returns were made not only of a temporal nature, but in respect to things spiritual. So early as 1702 the Society for the Propogation of the Gospel in Foreign Parts, the next year after its organization, sent a Missionary (Rev. Mr. Andrews) to the Mohawk Valley. Under his direction in 1714, the Church of England Common Prayers, was translated into their tongue. The first convert to Christianity was christened John Thomas, who died in 1727, aged 119.

It is said the English in their determination to secure the alliance of the Iroquois against the French prevailed upon certain chiefs to visit the Court of Queen Anne, in 1710, thinking that the greatness and splendour of England, would firmly fix their attachment.

There were four of them who crossed the water, and who were treated with distinction. Their names were "*Te Yee Neen Ho Ga Prow*, and *Sa Ga Yean Qua Proh Ton*, of the Maquas; *Elow Oh Roam*, and *Oh Nee Yeath Ton No Prow*, of the River Sachem. Portraits were taken of these four kings and placed in the British Museum. When presented to the Queen they made an elaborate speech, in which they spoke of their desire to see their "great Queen;" of the long tedious French war in which they had taken a part; they urged the necessity of reducing Canada, and closed by expressing a wish that their "great Queen will be pleased to send over some person to instruct" them in a knowledge of the Saviour. Consequently the Queen caused to be sent to the Mohawk church just erected among them, a valuable sacramental service of plate, and a communion cloth. This royal gift was ever held in the most fervent esteem by the tribe. The part taken by the noble Iroquois during the cruel rebellion of 1776-83 is elsewhere detailed; but in this connection is to be noticed an incident of a touching nature. The rebel commander of a blood-thirsty gang, stimulated by promises of the land which they were sent to despoil, came upon the tribe at an unexpected moment. The valuable—the costly—the revered gift from the Queen was in danger of being seized by the lawless horde which was approaching. Not forgetting them—not unmindful of things sacred, some of the chief members of the tribe decided to conceal them by burying them in the earth, which was accordingly done, the plate being wrapped in the communion cloth. These doubly valuable articles remained buried until the close of the war, when they were recovered. The plate had suffered no injury, but the cloth had been almost destroyed by the damp earth. These precious relics were divided between those who settled upon the Grand River, and the smaller branch that remained at the Bay. They are to this day used on sacramental occasions. Upon each of the articles, sacred to memory, and sacredly employed, is cut the following words:

"The Gift of Her Majesty Queen Anne by the Grace of God of Great Britain, France and Ireland, of Her Plantations in North America, Queen of Her Indian Chappel of the Mohawk."

When the lawless rebels came into their settlement, they destroyed the translated Prayer book. The Mohawks apprehensive that it would be lost, asked the Governor (Haldimand) to have an edition published. This was granted by printing a limited number in 1780 at Quebec. In 1787 a third edition was published in London, a copy of which before us, supplies these facts. In connection with it there is also a translation of the Gospel according to St. Mark by Brant. It is stated in the Preface that a translation of some other parts of the New Testament may soon be expected from Brant. But such never appeared.

The missionary employed at the commencement of the rebellion, by the Society for the Propogation of the Gospel in Foreign Parts, was the Rev. John Stuart. "In 1770, he was appointed to the Mission at Fort Hunter. He soon prepared a Mohawk translation of the Gospel by Mark, an exposition of the Church catechism, and a compendious History of the Bible. He was undisturbed in his labors, until after after the Declaration of Independence, though "he constantly performed divine service without omitting prayers for the King."

The women and children of the Indians when hurried away from their homes repaired to Lachine, where they mostly remained until the end of the war. The particulars of the history of their missionary is elsewhere given. There was a sincere attachment between him and the tribe, an instance of which is supplied by the conduct of a sister of Captain Johns. Mrs. Stuart had an infant child which was deprived of its natural food. The Indian woman weaned her own child that she might thereby be able to supply the missionary's child with food. This child was Charles O'Kill Stuart. When he became the Venerable Archdeacon, he did not forget the act of motherly kindness bestowed upon him. The faithful breast upon which he had nestled, had long since closed its heaving by death; but the daughter whom she had put away from the breast still lived. Dr. Stuart visited the Indian woods every year, and invariably went to see his sister, as he called her.

Early steps were taken to have built a church in which they might worship. The Rev. John Stuart had his home in Kingston, yet he often visited the Indians.

The first church was erected on Grand River by Brant in 1786, and as nearly as we can learn the plain wooden building at the settlement upon the Bay was, at the same time, or shortly after erected.

The Society for the Propagation of the Gospel in Foreign Parts, not only employed the Rev. Mr. Stuart, as a missionary, to labor with the Mohawks, but likewise set apart a sum of £30, as a salary to a teacher to instruct the children of the Indians upon Bay Quinté. Mr. Stuart lived at Kingston, however, and could but visit the Indian village occasionally. But a catechist was employed by him to supply spiritual instruction. Mr. Stuart also had the appointing of a school-teacher. The precise time when this school was opened, it is impossible to determine. The first reference we find to it is in a letter, (one of many kindly entrusted to us by Mrs.

Bininger of Belleville) written by John Bininger, then living in Adolphustown, to his father, the Rev. Abraham Bininger of Camden, New York, Moravian missionary. The letter is dated 18th September, 1792, and says, "being at Kingston, I heard as it were accidently, that the Rev. Mr. John Stuart wanted, on behalf of the society in England, to hire a teacher for the Mohawks up this bay, accordingly, I made an offer of my services." This may have been the commencement of the school. Mr. Stuart, not long after, accepted the offer, and John Bininger says he gave his employers notice that he should leave them. We learn that he was at that time, or had been a short time before, engaged as a book-keeper in Kingston. He was detained for two months before his employers would release him, immediately after which he removed to the Mohawk village.

Before proceeding with the record of the Mohawk school, we shall ask the reader to listen to a few of the facts in the history of the Bininger family.

The Moravian Society was founded by Count Zinzendorf. He visited New York in 1741, and seven years later, 1748, a Moravian Church was established in New York. The first or principal Moravian minister was Abraham Bininger, a native of Switzerland, from the same town where the immortal William Tell lived.—(Wakeley.) He was the intimate friend of Embury and the other early Methodists in America.

Of the sons of the Rev. A. Bininger, we have only to notice John. Before us is an old account book in which is found the following memorandum: "1791, May 30th, Moved from Camden in Salem, Washington County; June 2nd, Arrived at St. John's, Canada; June 8th, Arrived at Lachine for Kingston; 24th, arrived at Kingston, Upper Canada; July 2nd, Arrived at John Carscallians, Fredericksburgh, Bay Kanty; October 2nd, Moved from Fredricksburgh to Adolphustown, 1792; November 13th, Moved from Adolphustown to Mohawk Village." A letter written by John Bininger to his father, is in a fine distinct hand, and indicates both learning and piety, and that he was actuated, in taking the situation of teacher to the Mohawks, by a missionary spirit. His father wrote to him from time to time, the letters are dated at Camden, and usually refer to family affairs; but each has a large portion devoted to Christian advice, simply and touchingly, and sometimes quaintly given. They are signed Abraham and Martha. The first letter is addressed to "Caterockqua," and the request is made upon the corner of the letter to "please forward this with care and speed," "also to the care of Mr. John Carscallian, or Lieutenant Carscallian.' The rest of the letters are addressed to Adolphustown, and the Mohawk Village, "Bay Quinté."

In one letter he says "Remember children never please parents more than when they are willing to be guided by them; self-guiding is always the beginning of temptation, and next comes a fall that we must smart for it; we are to work out our own salvation (not with high gallowping thoughts) but with feare and trembling." In this way every letter beams with pure and simple Christianity. After his childrens' personal well-being, he is concerned about the Moravian missionaries in Canada, and also a considerable number of Moravian Loyalists who had settled upon the Bay Quinté, after whom he frequently inquires. In one letter he says "remember me to all my friends, in particular to old Mr. Carscallian and wife." One letter says, "We send you with Mr. McCabe a lag. cheese, weight five pounds and three-quarters, about half-a-pint of apple seed, from Urana's saving. I also send you part of my best treasure, the *Daily Word and Doctrinal Texts*, for the year 1792. The collection of choice hymns and sixteen discourses of my very dear friend, Count Zinzendorf." He says, "I would heartily beg to make Inquiry and friendship with the brethren among the Indians. They are settled in the British lines, I dont know the name of the place." Again he expresses a wish that he should inquire for the brethrens' settlement, and "make a correspondence with them," to think it his "duty to assist them in the furtherance of the Gospel, both on account of yourself and on account of your old father. If you can get any intelligence pray let me know, I am often concerned in my mind for the dear flock that believe in the Lord Jesus Christ. I think if any gentleman in your parts can give information, it is the Reverend Mr. Stuart, a minister of the Church of England, he is a gentleman that I have great esteem for, I know he will give you all the intelligence he possibly can." Subsequently, 1794, he wishes his son to correspond with the brethren at the river La Trenche (the Thames). As a result of this request, we see a letter received from David Zeisberger, dated at River Thames, 20th July, 1794, eighty miles from Detroit.

John Bininger was acceptable to the Mohawks of the Bay, as an instructor. His father writes 5th January, 1794, "It was a real satisfaction to me to see Mr. Hekenalder in New York, and more so when I heard the good character of the Indians of your place living among them." Writing February 23rd, he says, "was I able to undergo the hardships, I would certainly join with you and tell the poor Indians of God their Saviour, that would be the highest and happiest employ for me." In August, he says I would have ventured the hardships of the journey, but mother and Isaac wont approve of it, they think I am too old and feeble. I know that if I was with you I should have more contentment than I have here."

The last communication we have is dated February, 1804, in which the good old Moravian says to his children, John and Phœbe, that there "dear tender mother went happy to our dear Saviour;" at the funeral was so many, he wondered how so many could collect.

The Rev. Abraham Bininger was intimate with Wesley, whom he accompanied to Virginia. He also was familiar with Philip Embury, and Mr. "Garitson" who baptized his grand-child. The first two Methodist preachers in Canada were well known to him. Several letters, back and forth, are "per favor of Losee." In one letter he says, "Don forget to remember my love and regards to Mr. Dunon (Dunham) and Mr. Loese." The postscript of another letter says, "Isaac intends to send a young heifer, two pound of tea, a gammon, and a pise of smokt beef. Mother sends her love to Dunon and Mr. Loese." A letter dated April 12th, 1792, says John Switzers' son "was baptized by Mr. Garitson. Mr. Garitson is well approved of in these parts. I heartily wish, as much as I love him, that he were in your parts. I am of late more reconciled to the Methodists than I was before, I see they really are a blessing to many poor souls."

Writing 2nd August, 1794, he says "I heartily pity Mr. Losee for withdrawing his hand, he is now to be treated with patience and tenderness. I have sent last part of a discourse which I translated from the brethrens' writing. I did it chiefly on account of Mr. Losee, if you think proper send him a copy with a tender greet from me." John Bininger, writing January 12, 1795, remarks, Mr. Losee is just setting out for the States.

Mr. John Bininger ceased to be teacher to the Mohawks sometime in the latter part of 1795, or first part of 1796.

There are several letters before us, written by Mr. Stuart, in reference to the appointment of a successor to Mr. Bininger, the first one is directed to "Mr. William Bell, at the head of the Bay of Quinté, and dated at Kingston, September 26, 1796." He says "I received your letter respecting the Mohawk school; I can give you no positive answer at present: because I have agreed, conditionally with a school-master at Montreal, that is, if he comes up, he is to have the school; I expect daily to hear from him, although I do not think he will accept of the employment. Some time ago Mr. Ferguson* mentioned you as one who would probably undertake that charge. I told Captain John that if the person from Montreal disappointed me I would talk with you on the subject. The salary is £30 sterling, with a house to live in, and some other advantages which depend wholly on the pleasure of the Mohawks—but the teacher must be a man, and not a woman, however well qualified." The teacher from Montreal did not come, and Mr. Bell was appointed. The following seems to have been a copy of Mr. Bell's first call for payment, the half-yearly instalment.

"Mohawk Village, Bay of Quinté, July 5, 1797—Exchange for £15 sterling.

Sir,—At thirty days sight of this first of exchange, please to pay to Mr. Robert McCauley, or order, the sum of fifteen pounds sterling, being half-year's salary, from the 15th day of November, 1796, to the 15th day of May, 1797, due from the Society, without further advice, from, Sir, &c., (Signed), William Bell, school-master to the Mohawks. To Calvert Chapman, Esq., Treasurer to the Society for the Propagation of the Gospel in Foreign Parts—Duke Street, Westminster."

The Mohawks, it seems, did not appreciate the advantages which the establishment of a school among them was intended to afford, and Mr. Stuart is found writing as follows: "Kingston, August 18, 1799—Sir,—Unless the Mohawks will send such a number of their children to school as will justify me in continuing a school-master, in duty to myself, as acting for the Society, I shall be under the necessity of discontinuing the payment of your salary after the expiration of the present year. This information I think proper to give you, that you may govern yourself accordingly. I am, Sir," &c., (Signed), John Stuart.

But writing again, March 16, 1800, Mr. Stuart says, "I am happy to hear that the school is now furnished with a dozen or more scholars, and it is expected you will be very strict in your discipline, and see that prayers are read night and morning; that the children are taught the Lord's Prayer, and the Commandments—that children may not be sent home even if their parents do not send wood at the stated times; that the cattle may not be allowed to go into the school, but that it be kept clean, and the wood belonging to it may not be used unless in school hours."

Writing again, September 11, 1801, Mr. Stuart says, "I have waited with patience to see whether the Mohawks would send their children more regularly to school, but if the accounts I receive are true, the money is expended to no purpose. I am told that there has not been a scholar in school since last spring. And, as I never found that the fault was on your side, I cannot, in conscience, allow the salary of the Society to be paid for nothing. Therefore, unless Capt. John and the chief men of the village will promise that the school shall be furnished with at least six scholars, I must dismiss you from their service—as soon as you receive this notification. I hope you will see the reasonableness of this determination of mine, and you may show this letter to Capt. John and the Mohawks, by which they will see that the continuance or discontinuance of the school depends wholly on themselves."

The final letter upon the subject is dated "Kingston, 26th August, 1802," and says, "I have not yet received any letter from the Society; but, for the reasons I mentioned to you, I think it will be expedient to let the Mohawk school cease, at least for some time. I therefore notify you that after your present quarter is ended you will not expect a continuance of the salary." (Signed), "John Stuart." "To William Bell, school-master to the Mohawks, Bay of Quinté."

CHAPTER XXXV.

CONTENTS—The first Church at Tyendinaga grows old—A Council—Ask for Assistance—Gov. Bagot—Laying first stone of new Church—The Inscription—The Ceremony—The new Church—Their Singing—The surrounding Scenery—John Hall's Tomb—Pagan Indians—Red Jacket—His Speech—Reflection upon Christians—Indians had nothing to do with murdering the Saviour.

BUILDING A NEW CHURCH.

Their original edifice of wood, having served its purpose, and being in a state of decay; it was deemed necessary to have erected a new and more substantial building. They, consequently, held a Council, at which the Chief made the following speech, after hearing all the ways and means discussed—"If we attempt to build this church by ourselves, it will never be done. Let us, therefore, ask our father, the Governor, to build it for us, and it will be done at once." Reference here was made, not to the necessary funds, for they were to be derived from the sale of Indian lands; but to the experience requisite to carry out the project. Sir Charles, Bagot, the Governor, was accordingly petitioned. "The first stone was laid by S. P. Jarvis, Esq., Chief Superintendent of Indians in Canada; and the Archdeacon of Kingston, the truly venerable G. O. Stuart, conducted the usual service; which was preceded by a procession of the Indians, who, singing a hymn, led the way from the wharf." "The following inscription was placed in this stone:

TO

THE GLORY OF GOD OUR SAVIOUR

THE REMNANT OF THE TRIBE OF KAN-YE-AKE-HAKA,

IN TOKEN OF THEIR PRESERVATION BY THE DIVINE MERCY

THROUGH JESUS CHRIST,

In the sixth year of Our Mother Queen Victoria: Sir Charles Theopholus Metcalf, G.C.B., being Governor General of British North America;

THE RIGHT REV. J. STRACHAN, D.D., AND LL.D.,
Being Bishop of Toronto:

AND

THE REV. SALTERN GIVINS, BEING IN THE THIRTEENTH YEAR OF HIS INCUMBENCY.

The old wooden fabric having answered its end,

THIS CORNER STONE OF

CHRIST'S CHURCH TYENDINAGA,

WAS LAID

In the presence of the Venerable George O'Kill Stuart, LL.D., Archdeacon of Kingston;

By Samuel Peter Jarvis, Chief Superintendent of Indian Affairs in Canada, assisted by various Members of the Church,

ON TUESDAY MAY 30TH, A. D., 1843.

&c., &c., &c.

A hymn was sung by the Indians, and Indian children of the school. The Rev. Wm. Macauley, of Picton, delivered an address, which was followed by a prayer from the Rev. Mr. Deacon."—(*Sir Richard Henry Bonnycastle.*)

This edifice, with four lancet windows on each side, presents to the eye a very pleasing appearance upon approaching it. While the interior may not altogether appear so attractive, it is sufficiently interesting. There is the elevated desk, and the more elevated pulpit; and upon the wall, over the altar, are the ten commandments, in the Mohawk tongue. Here is grandly united the Mother Church, and the devoted piety of the once great Mohawk nation. Opposite the altar is a gallery, across the end of the building, in which is an organ. Therefrom proceeds, Sunday after Sunday, rich notes of tuneful melody, blending with the stout voices of the singers. From this church ascends, have we not reason to believe the adoration of hearts warmed into spiritual life by the pure principles of Christianity.

The view from the church upon the surrounding scenery is very pleasant, and, in the quietness of a summer day, one may linger gazing and meditating upon the past history of the race whose dead slumber hard by. The visitor's attention will be directed to a flat tomb, of blue stone, inclosed by a low stone wall, overgrown with shrubs. Upon the face of the tomb are the words:

"This tomb, erected to the memory of John Hall, Ochechusleah, by the Mohawks, in grateful remembrance of his Christian labors amongst them. During thirty years, he served as a Mohawk Catechist, in this settlement, under the Society for Propagating the Gospel, adorning the doctrine of God, his Saviour, and enjoying the respect of all who knew him. He died, generally regretted, June, 1848, aged 60 years." This stone also covers the remains of "Eloner, the exemplary wife of the Catechist, who died in the Lord, May 7, 1840, aged 50."

While the Mohawks always manifested a desire to learn the truth, as taught by Christians, there were some of the Six Nations who believed not, and steadfastly turned their backs upon the missionaries of the Cross. Among these stood prominent the Seneca chief Sagnoaha, or Red Jacket, one well known as an eloquent Sachem in all the Councils of his people. A Seneca council was held at Buffalo Creek, in May, 1811, when Red Jacket answered the desire of a missionary that they should become Christians, as follows:—

"Brother!—We listened to the talk you delivered to us from the council of black coats in New York. We have fully considered your talk, and the offers you have made us. We now return our answer, which we wish you also to understand. In making up our minds we have looked back to remember what has been done in our days, and what our fathers have told us was done in old times.

"Brother!—Great numbers of black coats have been among the Indians. With sweet voices and smiling faces, they offered to teach them the religion of the white people. Our brethren in the East listened to them. They turn from the religion of their fathers, and look up the religion of the white people. What good has it done? Are they more friendly, one to another, than we are? No, Brother! They are a divided people; we are united. They quarrel about religion; we live in love and friendship. Besides, they drink strong waters, and they have learned how to cheat and how to practice all the other vices of the white people, without imitating their virtues. Brother!—If you wish us well, keep away; don't disturb us. Brother!—We do not worship the Great Spirit as the white people do, but we believe that the forms of worship are indifferent to the Great Spirit. It is the homage of sincere hearts that pleases him, and we worship him in that manner." "Brother! For these reasons we cannot receive your offers. We have other things to do, and beg you will make your minds easy, without troubling us, lest our heads should be too much loaded, and by and by burst." At another time, he is reported to have said to one conversing with him upon the subject of Christianity, that the Indians were not responsible for the death of Christ. "Brother," said he "if you white people murdered the Saviour, make it up yourselves. We had nothing to do with it. If he had come among us, we should have treated him better."

CHAPTER XXXVI.

CONTENTS—Mississauga Indians—Father Picquet's opinion—Remnant of a large tribe—Their Land—Sold to Government—Rev. Wm. Case—John Sunday—A drunkard—Peter Jones—Baptising Indians—At a camp-meeting—Their department—Extract from Playter—William Beaver—Conversions—Jacob Peter—Severe upon white christians—Their worship—The Father of Canadian missions—Scheme to teach Indians—Grape Island—Leasing islands—The parties—"Dated at Belleville"—Constructing a village—The lumber—How obtained—Encamping on Grape Island—The method of instruction—The number—Agriculture—Their singing—School house—The teacher—Instructions of women—Miss Barnes—Property of Indians—Cost of improvements—A visit to Government—Asking for land—"Big Island"—Other favors—Peter Jacobs at New York—Extracts from Playter—Number of Indian converts, 1829—River Credit Indians—Indians removed to Alnwick.

THE MISSISSAUGA INDIANS—THEIR CONVERSION TO CHRISTIANITY.

We have learned that the French missionary, Father Picquet did not entertain a very high opinion, at least he professed not to, of the moral character of the Mississaugas, and their susceptibility to the influence of Christian religion. We will now see what was accomplished by the agency of the Rev. William Case. We refer to that branch at present called the Mississaugas of Alnwick, and formerly known as the Mississaugas of the Bay of Quinté. They were the remnant of the powerful tribe, which ceded a large tract in the Johnstown, Midland and Newcastle districts to the Government. This block contained 2,748,000 acres, and was surrendered in 1822, for an annuity of £642 10s.

In 1825 the Rev. William Case visited the Bay. Among the first to come under the influence of religion, from the preaching of the Methodists was John Sunday. The writer has conversed with many, who remember Sunday as a very filthy drunkard. Peter Jones and John Crane, Mohawks who had been converted to Methodism at the Grand River, visited Belleville. Peter Jones with simple eloquence, soon reached the hearts of the Mississaugas. The writer's father has heard Peter Jones preach to them in Indian near the banks of the Moira, just by No. 1 school-house in Belleville. In the spring of 1826 Case baptized 22 Indian converts, while 50 more seemed under the influence of religion. In June, a camp-meeting was held in Adolphustown, the Mississaugas attended. Special accommodation was afforded them. Their arrival is thus graphically given by Playter, and it supplies an excellent idea of Indian character in connection with religion.

"A message came that the Mississauga fleet was in sight. A few repaired to the shore to welcome and conduct the Indians to the ground. The bark canoes contained men, women and children, with cooking utensils, blankets, guns, spears, provisions, and bark for covering their wigwams. The men took each a canoe reversed on his head, or the guns and spears; each squaw a bundle of blankets or bark. The men marched first, the women in the rear and in file they moved to the encampment, headed by two preachers. The congregation seeing the Indians passing through the gate, and so equipped, was astonished. Reflecting on the former condition and the present state of these natives of the woods, gratitude and joy filled every bosom. God was praised for the salvation of the heathen. After the natives had laid down the burdens, they all silently prayed for the blessing of the Great Spirit, to the surprise and increased delight of the pious whites. The Indians next built their camp, in the oblong form, with poles, canoes, and bark. The adults numbered 41, of whom 28 had given evidence of a converted state, and the children were 17: in all 58. The natives had private meetings by themselves, and the whites by themselves; but in preaching time, the Indians sat on the right of the preaching stand. At the close of each sermon, William Beaver, an Indian exhorter, translated the main points for the Indians, the other Indian exhorters, Sunday, Moses, and Jacob Peter spoke to their people on different occasions. Beaver's first exhortation was on Friday, and produced a great effect on the natives.

On Sunday Beaver spoke to his people with great fluency. Upon being asked what he had been saying, "I tell 'em," said he, "they must all turn away from sin; that the Great Spirit will give 'em new eyes to see, new ears to hear good things; new heart to understand, and sing, and pray; all new! I tell 'em squaws, they must wash 'em blankets clean, must cook 'em victuals clean, like white women; they must live in peace, worship God, and love one another. Then," with a natural motion of the hand and arm, as if to level an uneven service, he added, "The Good Spirit make the ground all smooth before you."

"On Monday, the Lord's supper was given to the Indians and the whites, of the Indians 21 were also baptized, with ten of their children. The whole number of the baptized in this tribe was now 43, 21 children. As yet these Indians knew but one hymn, "O for a thousand tongues to sing, my great Redeemer's praise," and one tune. This hymn they sung, over and over, as if always new, and always good."

It has been the custom, of not alone the United States, but some in our midst, to regard the Indians as altogether degraded below the whites in intelligence, in natural honesty, and in appreciation of right and wrong. At the camp-meeting above referred to, there was a convert by name of Jacob Peter. He is described as "a sprightly youth of 18 years." At some subseqent date during the same year, the Indians held a prayer-meeting at the village of Demorestville. "Mr. Demorest being present with other white inhabitants, to witness the Indian's devotion, requested Jacob to speak a little to them in English; which he thus did:

"You white people have the Gospel a great many years. You have the Bible too: suppose you read sometimes—but you very wicked. Suppose some very good people: but great many wicked. You get drunk—you tell lies—you break the Sabbath." Then pointing to his brethren, he added, "But these Indians, they hear the word only a little while—they can't read the bible—but they become good right away. They no more get drunk—no more tell lies—they keep the Sabbath day. To us Indians, seems very strange that you have missionary so many years, and you so many rogues yet. The Indians have missionary only a little while, and we all turn christians."

"The whites little expected so bold a reproof from a youth belonging to a race which is generally despised."—(Playter).

Camp-meetings were peculiarly calculated to impress the Indians with solemn thoughts. These children of the forest deemed the shade of trees a fit and true place in which to worship the true God, just as seemed to the first settlers who had for so long a time had their homes within the quiet glades. And no more inconsiderate step could have been taken than that pursued by Governor Maitland, who, at the instigation of others, forbad the converted Indians at the River Credit to attend camp-meetings. The conversion of the Mississaugas at Belleville, and the Credit, soon became known to the other branches of the tribe scattered throughout Canada, and in time the whole nation was under the influence of Methodist teaching. Their change of life was as well marked as it has been lasting.

The Rev. William Case, "The father of Canadian Missions," determined to permanently settle the tribe, to teach them the quiet pursuits of agriculture, and their children the rudiments of education, as well as of christian knowledge. To this end the plan was adopted, of leasing two islands, situated in Big Bay, which belonged to the tribe, and establish thereupon the converted Indians. The parties to whom the tribe granted the lease for 999 years, for the nominal sum of five shillings, were "John Reynolds, Benjamin Ketcheson, Penuel G. Selden, James Bickford, and William Ross." The Chiefs, Warriors, and Indians conferring the lease, and who signed the indenture, were "John Sunday, William Beaver, John Simpson, Nelson Snake, Mitchell Snake, Jacob Musguashcum, Joseph Skunk, Paul Yawaseeng, Jacob Nawgnashcum, John Salt, Isaac Skunk, William Ross, Patto Skunk, Jacob Sheepegang, James Snake." It was "signed, sealed, and delivered in the presence of Tobias Bleaker, and Peter Jones." Dated Belleville, 16th October, 1826. The islands thus leased were Huff's Island, then known as "Logrim's," containing about fifty acres, and Grape Island with eleven acres.

Steps were promptly taken to carry out the object aimed at by the projectors, and arrangements were made to construct a village upon Grape Island. The lumber for the buildings was obtained by cutting hemlock saw logs upon the rear part of Tyendinaga, by the river Moira, under the direction of Surveyor Emerson, which were floated down to Jonas Canniff's saw mill, and there sawed into suitable pieces. These were again floated down in small rafts to the island. During the ensuing winter, the buildings not being as yet erected, a large number encamped upon Grape Island, while the rest went hunting, as usual. Instructions commenced immediately. Preachers visited them from time to time, and two interpreters. William Beaver and Jacob Peter taught them the Lord's Prayer and Ten Commandments. In January the hunting party returned, and "a meeting, lasting several days, was held in the chapel in Belleville, to instruct them also." "The tribe mustered about 130 souls, and the Society embraced every adult, about ninety persons."

A branch of the tribe living in the rear of Kingston, forty in number, came in May, the following Spring, and joined those at the island, and became converts. "In this month the buildings were commenced, and some land ploughed and planted. The condition of the people was every day improving. As many as 130 would assemble for worship. Their voices were melodious, and delightful was the singing. A school and meeting-house was built in July, 30 feet by 25 feet. William Smith was the first school-teacher, having thirty scholars in the day school, and fifty in the Sabbath school. The farming operations were under the superintendence of R. Phelps. The girls and women were instructed in knitting, sewing, making straw hats, and other work, by Miss E. Barnes.

"The public property of the Indians comprised a yoke of oxen, three cows, a set of farming tools, and material for houses, as lumber, nails and glass,—contributions of the benevolent. The improvements of the year were expected to cost £250, to be met by benevolence in the United States and Canada. In October, the meeting-house was seated, in connection with which was a room provided for a study and bed for the teacher. The bodies of eleven log houses were put up; eight had shingled roofs, and they were enclosed before winter."—(Playter).

Soon after, a deputation from Grape Island visited York, with a deputation from Rice Lake, and the Credit Indians, to seek an audience with the Government. A council was held with the Government officers on the 30th January, 1828. The speeches were interpreted by Peter Jones. John Sunday, after referring to their conversion, and having settled by the Bay Quinté, said, "that when they considered the future welfare of their children, they found that the island they claimed would not afford them sufficient wood and pasture for any length of time, and that they had now come to ask their great father, the governor, for a piece of land lying near them." "He then proceeded to ask the Government in what situation Big Island was considered; whether or not it belonged to the Indians? and, if it did, they asked their father to make those who had settled on it without their consent, pay them a proper rent, as they had hitherto turned them off with two bushels of potatoes for 200 acres of land. In the last place, he asked permission of their great father to cut some timber on the King's land for their buildings."—(Peter Jones).

In April of this year, Mr. Case, with John Sunday and Peter Jacobs, attended the anniversary of the Missionary Society in New York. The manifestation of Christianity displayed by these sons of the forest touched the hearts of the people present, and led to a considerable augmentation of the contributions previously supplied by private individuals. They visited other parts of the United States, and returned to the bay, May 12, "accompanied by two pious ladies, Miss Barnes, and Miss Hubbard." "The ladies came with the benevolent design of assisting the Indians in religion, industry, and education."

"In the tour Mr. Case received many presents of useful articles for the Indians; and among the rest ticking for straw beds. This was divided among twenty families, and made the first beds they ever slept upon." Among the conversions of this year, was an Indian woman, practising witchcraft, as the people believe, and a Roman Catholic."

The people were not only persevering in religious duties, but made progress in industry. Mr. Case collected the Indians together one evening, to show what they had manufactured in two weeks. They exhibited 172 axe handles, 6 scoop shovels, 57 ladles, 4 trays, 44 broom-handles, 415 brooms. The Indians were highly commended for their industry, and some rewards were bestowed to stimulate greater diligence."—(Playter).

According to the Annual Report of the Missionary Society of the Methodist Episcopal Church of the United States, there were "two hundred and twenty natives under the Christian instruction of one missionary, one hundred and twenty of whom are regular communicants, and fifty children are taught in the schools." Lorenzo Dow visited Grape Island, and writing July 29, 1829, says, "viewing the neatness and uniformity of the village—the conduct of the children even in the streets—and not a drunkard to be found in their borders. Surely what a lesson for the whites!"

The other communities of the Mississaugas that came under the religious teaching of the Methodists are the River Credit Indians, the Rice Lake Indians, and those at Schoogog, Simcoe, and the Thames River.

When the Indians from the Bay Quinté, and from Kingston, left Grape Island, they removed to Alnwick. A Report on Indian Affairs, of 1858, says, "they have now a block of land of 2000 acres divided into 25 acre farms."

DIVISION VI

EARLY EDUCATION IN UPPER CANADA.

CHAPTER XXXVII.

CONTENTS—Education among the Loyalists—Effect of the War—No opportunity for Education—A few Educated—At Bath—A common belief—What was requisite for farming—Learning at home—The School Teachers—Their qualifications—Rev. Mr. Stuart as a Teacher—Academy at Kingston—First Canadian D.D.—Mr. Clark, Teacher, 1786—Donevan—Garrison Schools—Cockerell—Myers—Blaney—Michael—Atkins—Kingston, 1795—Lyons—Mrs. Cranahan—In Adolphustown—Morden—Faulkiner—The School Books—Evening Schools—McDougall—O'Reiley—McCormick—Flogging—Salisbury—James—Potter—Wright—Watkins—Gibson—Smith—Whelan—Articles of Agreement—Recollections—Boarding round—American Teachers—School Books—The Letter Z.

THE FIRST SCHOOLS AND TEACHERS.

The majority of the refugees possessed but limited education. There were a very small number whose education was even excellent; but the greater portion of Loyalists from the revolting Colonies, had not enjoyed opportunities for even a common education. The state of society, for many years, precluded the teaching of youth. During the civil war, the chances for learning had been exceedingly slender. Apart from this, there did not exist, a hundred years ago, the same desire to acquire learning which now prevails. The disbanded soldiers and refugees, even some of the half-pay officers, were void of education, which, even in the back woods, is a source of pure enjoyment. There was, however, an English seminary at Quebec, and at Montreal, at which a few were educated during the war; for instance, Clark, who was a naval store-keeper at Carleton Island, had his children there at school. At the village of Kingston, there were a certain number of educated persons; but around the Bay there was not much to boast of. As their habitations were sparse, it was difficult for a sufficient number to unite to form good schools. Among the old, sturdy farmers, who themselves had no learning, and who had got along without much, if any learning, and had no books to read, there obtained a belief that it was not only unnecessary, but likely to have a bad effect upon the young, disqualifying them for the plain duties of husbandry. If one could read, sign his own name, and cast interest, it was looked upon as quite sufficient for a farmer. But gradually there sprung up an increased desire to acquire education, and a willingness to supply the means therefor. In most places, the children were gladly sent to school. And, moreover, in some cases, elder persons, without learning, married to one possessed of it, would spend their long winter evenings in learning from a willing partner, by the flickering fire light. Says Ex-Sheriff Ruttan, then living at Adolphustown, "As there were no schools at that period, what knowledge I acquired was from my mother, who would, of an evening, relate events of the American rebellion, and the happy lives people once led under British laws and protection previous to the outbreak." "In a few years, as the neighborhood improved, school teaching was introduced by a few individuals, whose individual infirmities prevented them from hard manual labor." We find it stated that the first school teachers were discharged soldiers, and generally Irish.

The Rev. John Stuart, subsequently D.D., (See first clergyman) was the first teacher in Upper Canada. So early as 1785, the year he settled at Cataraqui, as he called the place, he says, in a letter written to an old friend in the States, "The greatest inconvenience I feel here, is there being no school for our boys; but, we are now applying to the Legislature for assistance to erect an academy and have reason to expect success; If I succeed in this, I shall die here contented." "In May, 1786, he opened an academy at Kingston;" writing in 1788, he remarks, I have an excellent school for my children," that is the children of Kingston.—(Memoirs of Dr. Stuart). The degeee of D. D., which was conferred upon Mr. Stuart, in 1799, by his Alma Mater, at the University of Pennsylvania, was the first University degree of any kind conferred upon a Canadian, probably to any one of the present Dominion of Canada.

While the Rev. Mr. Stuart was engaged with the first school in Kingston, Mr. Clarke was likewise employed in teaching upon the shores of the Bay, probably in Ernesttown or Fredericksburgh. "We learn from Major Clark, now residing in Edwardsburgh, that his father taught the first regular school in Dundas. He arrived with his family in Montreal, in the year 1786, and proceeded to the Bay Quinté. He remained two years at the Bay, employed in teaching. In 1788, he came to Matilda, at the instance of Captain Frazer, who, at his own expense, purchased a farm for him, at the cost of one hundred dollars. A few of the neighbors assisted in the erection of a school house, in which Mr. Clark taught for several years. He was a native of Perthshire, Scotland."—(*History of Dundas*).

One of the first teachers at Kingston, was one Donevan.

As a general thing, all the British garrisons had, what was called, a garrison school, and many of the children at first derived the rudiments of education from these; that is, those living convenient to the forts. The teachers of these army schools, no doubt, were of questionable fitness, probably possessing but a minimum of knowledge, next to actual ignorance. However, there may have been exceptions. Possibly, where a chaplain was attached to a garrison, he taught, or superintended.

Col. Clark, of Dalhousie, says, "The first rudiments of my humble education I acquired at the garrison school, at Old Fort, Niagara. When we came to the British side of the river, I went to various schools. The best among them was a Richard Cockerell, an Englishman, from the United States, who left the country during the rebellion." He also speaks of D'Anovan of Kingston, as a teacher, and likewise Myers, Blaney, Mr. Michael, Irish, and another, a Scotchman. This was before 1800.

A memorandum by Robert Clark, of Napanee, says, "My boys commenced going to school to Mr. Daniel Allen Atkins, 18th January, 1791."

Rochefoucault says, in 1795, speaking of Kingston, "In this district are some schools, but they are few in number. The children are instructed in reading and writing, and pay each a dollar a month. One of of the masters, superior to the rest, in point of knowledge, taught Latin; but he has left the school, without being succeeded by another instructor of the same learning."

"In the year 1788, a pious young man, called Lyons, an exhorter in the Methodist Episcopal Church, came to Canada, and engaged in teaching a school in Adolphustown," "upon Hay Bay or fourth concession."—(*Playter*). Ex-Sheriff Ruttan tells us, that "At seven years of age, (1799), he was one of those who patronized Mrs. Cranahan, who opened a Sylvan Seminary for the young idea, (in Adolphustown); from thence, I went to Jonathan Clark's, and then tried Thomas Morden, lastly William Faulkiner, a relative of the Hagermans. You may suppose that these graduations to Parnassus, was carried into effect, because a large amount of knowledge could be obtained. Not so; for Dilworth's Spelling Book, and the

New Testament, were the only books possessed by these academies. About five miles distant, was another teacher, whose name I forget; after his day's work was done in the bush, but particularly in the winter, he was ready to receive his pupils. This evening school was for those in search of knowledge. My two elder brothers availed themselves of this opportunity, and always went on snow shoes, which they deposited at the door." It looks very much as if courting may have been intimately associated with these nightly researches for knowledge. Mr. Ruttan adds, "And exciting occasions sometimes happened by moonlight, when the girls joined the cavalcade." At this school as well, the only books were Dilworth, and the Testament; unless it were the girl's "looks." "Those primeval days I remember with great pleasure." "At fourteen, (1806), my education was finished." We learn that at an early period there was one McDougall, who taught school in a log house upon the south shore of Hay Bay. Says Mr. Henry Van-Dusen, one of the first natives of Upper Canada, "The first who exercised the prerogative of the school room in Adolphustown were the two sons of Edward O'Reily, and McCormick, both of whom are well remembered by all who were favored with their instruction—from the unmerciful floggings received."

About the year 1803, one Salisbury taught school on the High Shore, Sophiasburgh. The first teacher upon the Marsh Front, near Grassy Point, was John James. At the mouth of Myers' Creek, in 1807 or 8, James Potter taught school; but, prior to that, a man by the name of Leslie taught. About this time, there was also a Rev. Mr. Wright, a Presbyterian, who taught school near Mrs. Simpson's. He preached occasionally. In 1810, in a little frame school house, near the present market, (Belleville,) taught one John Watkins. One of the first school masters up the Moira, fifth concession of Thurlow, was one Gibson. Mrs. Perry, born in Ernesttown, rememembers her first, and her principal school teacher. His name was Smith, and he taught in the second concession of Ernesttown in 1806. He had a large school, the children coming from all the neighborhood, including the best families.

During the war of 1812, Mr. Whelan taught at Kingston, in the public school. The school house stood near the block house. It is stated, January, 1817, that he had been a teacher for ten years.

Before us, is a document, dated at Hollowell, Oct. 28, 1819. It is—"Articles of agreement between R—— L———, of the one one part, and we, the undersigned, of the other part: that is to say:

that R—— L——— doth engage to keep a regular school, for the term of seven months from the first day of November next, at the rate of two pounds ten shillings per month; and he further doth agree to teach reading, writing, and arithmetic; to keep regular hours, keep good order in school, as far as his abilities will allow, see that the children go orderly from school to their respective homes. And we, the undersigned, doth agree to pay R—— L—— the sum above named of ten dollars per month for the time above mentioned; and further, doth agree to find a comfortable house for the school, and supply the same with wood fitted for the fire. And further, to wash, mend, lodge, and victual him for the time of keeping said school. School to be under charge and inspection of the following trustees: William Clark, Peter Leavens, and Daniel Leavens."

To which is subjoined, quaintly, in Mr. L.'s hand writing:

"It is to be understood that the said R—— L—— has performed his business rightly till he is discharged,—(Signed) R——L——."

Below are the names of the subscribers, and the number of scholars each will send.

The practice already referred to, of setting apart for school teachers such members of the family as were physically incapable of doing hard manual labor, without any regard to their natural or acquired capabilities, was of Yankee origin, and continued in many places for many years. The writer had, among his early teachers, one who boarded round from family to family, whose sole qualification to teach consisted in his lameness. This prostitution of a noble calling, had the effect of preventing men of education for a long time, from engaging in the duties of this profession.

In different places, young men would engage for three or four months, in winter, to teach school; but, with the return of spring, they would return to the labor of the field and woods. After a while, young women could be found who would teach in the concession school house all the summer, to which the younger children would go.

Some of the first school teachers were from the old country, and some from the American States. The latter would naturally desire to have used American school books, and, as they were the most conveniently procured, they were introduced, and continued to be in use for many years. At least, by some schools, Dr. Noah Webster's spelling book was among the first to be used; and the writer commenced his rudimentary education in that book. It followed, from the presence of American teachers and school books, that peculiarities of American spelling and pronunciation were taught to the children of Canada. For instance, take the letter Z. This letter of the English alphabet is, according to original authority pronounced *zed*; but Webster taught that it had not a compound sound, and should be pronounced *ze*. This matter was brought before the public, by a letter over the signature of "Harris," which appeared in the *Kingston Herald*, in 1846. After adducing abundance of authority, he concludes that "the instructor of youth, who, when engaged in teaching the elements of the English language, direct them to call that letter *ze*, instead of *zed*, are teaching them error."

CHAPTER XXXVIII.

CONTENTS—Mr. Stuart's school—Simcoe—State Church and College—Grammar Schools—Hon. R. Hamilton—Chalmers—Strachan—Comes to Canada—Educational history—Arrival at Kingston—The pupils—Fees—Removes to Cornwall—Pupils follow—Strachan, a Canadian—Marries—Interview with Bishop Strachan—His disappointment—A stranger—What he forsook—300 pupils—Their success—Stay at Cornwall—Appointments at York—A lecturer—At Kingston—Member of Legislative Council—Politician—Clergy Reserves—Founds King's College—The thirty-nine articles—Monopoly swept away—Voluntaryism—Founds Trinity College—Bishop Strachan in 1866—What he had accomplished—Those he tutored—Setting up a high standard—"Reckoner"—Sincerity—Legislation, 1797—Address to the King—Grammar Schools—Grant, 1798—Board of Education—Endowment of King's College—Its constitution—Changes—Upper Canada College—Endowment—"A spirit of improvement"—Gourlay—The second academy—At Ernesttown—The trustees—Bidwell—Charges—Contradicted—Rival-school—Bidwell's son—Conspicuous character—Bidwell's death—Son removes to Toronto—Acadamy building, a barrack—Literary spirit of Bath—Never revived—York.

HIGHER EDUCATION—FOUNDATION OF UNIVERSITIES—STRACHAN—BIDWELL.

Up to the time that Upper Canada was set apart from the Province of Quebec, as a distinct Province, and even until 1799, when Dr. Strachan came to Kingston, the Rev. Mr. Stuart continued to be the only teacher who imparted anything like a solid education. But his scholars consisted mainly of boys not far advanced. No doubt many of them, however, received from him the elements of a sound, and even classical education.

Governor Simcoe, soon after assuming office, impressed with the importance of higher education, even for an infant colony, took early steps to procure from the mother-country a competent person to place at the head of a College he had determined to establish in connection with a State Church. His scheme of education to further that object, was to establish a system of grammar schools, and a University as the head.

The Hon. Robert Hamilton, of Queenston, had at this time a brother living in Scotland, and it was through him that an offer was made first to the celebrated Dr. Chalmers. But not desiring to come, although he had not yet attained to his greatness, he mentioned the name of his friend Strachan, to whom the offer was then made. Mr. Strachan decided to come. Thus it was the veteran school-teacher, the divine, the founder of Universities, who but recently passed away, was led to Canada to become the occupant of one of the most conspicuous places in the Province of Upper Canada. So intimately is the name of Dr. Strachan associated with the history of education, as well as with the Episcopalian Church, that it becomes necessary to supply here a somewhat lengthened account of his educational history. He arrived at Kingston the last day of the year, 1799, having sailed from Greenock the latter part of August, and having been over four months on the way. But when Strachan arrived, Simcoe had been recalled, and his scheme was at least, in abeyance.

Col. Clark says that "a school was established at Kingston, 1800, by the Hon. R. Cartwright for his sons, having Mr. Strachan for teacher, who had the privilege of taking ten additional scholars at £10 each per annum. Among these ten were the late Chief Justice Robinson, Chief Justice Macaulay, the Hon George Markland, Bishop Bethune, the successor of Dr. Strachan; the Rev. W. Macaulay, Picton; Captain England, Royal Engineers; Justice McLean, Col. John Clark, and the two sons of Hamilton, James and Samuel. These, with four sons of Richard Cartwright, formed Mr. Strachan's first school for the higher branches of education.

Mr. Strachan continued to teach in Kingston for three years, when he removed his school to Cornwall.

All of his pupils at Kingston, except John Clark, of Niagara, followed him to that place, and continued for years under his instruction.

The high standard of education now set up by Mr. Strachan had a beneficial effect. He trained here for usefulness and distinction, some of the first men of the Province. In addition to those mentioned as distinguished pupils, was Christopher Hagarman. Here Mr. Strachan, it may be said, became a thorough Canadian, and began to identify himself with the higher interests of the country. He shortly after married a lady of Cornwall, Miss Woods, who lived to within a few years of the Bishop's death.

Dr. Strachan, in conversation with the writer, referred to the time of his coming to Canada with no little feeling. He evidently felt the disappointment arising from the departure of Governor Simcoe very keenly, which left him quite to his own resources in the new country, far from his home which he had forsaken, in view of certain promises of advancement, congenial to his taste. He was, to use his own words, "a lonely stranger in a foreign land, without resources or a single acquaintance." But in coming to speak of his pupils, of which there had been about 300, and whose course in life he had been permitted to see; whose success he had been proud to note, he spoke of them with all the kindness and regard of a parent. He dwelt upon the character and high position to which so many had attained, especially the late Chief Justice Robinson. Speaking of himself, he said his "early life was of too busy a nature to allow him to keep a journal." And we find it stated that he had to support a mother and two sisters.

Mr. Strachan continued at Cornwall nine years, teaching, when he removed to York. The Government recognised his ability, and to increase the sphere of his usefulness, and to establish a Provincial College, he was requested to remove to the capital of Upper Canada, and had offered to him every advantage, pecuniary and otherwise. In these early efforts to establish higher education, says the Rev. Mr. Smart, whose testimony is important, too much praise cannot be given to Dr. Strachan.

Although Mr. Strachan had removed to Cornwall, Kingston was occasionally favored by his presence as a public lecturer, as the following notice which appeared in the *Gazette*, December, 1810, will show:

"Mr. Strachan's annual course of popular lectures on Natural Philosophy, will commence on the second Monday in January, the course consisting of thirty-six lectures, to be completed in two months. Tickets of admission, four guineas; students taught at any of the District Schools of Upper Canada, entitled to tickets for one guinea. This money to be appropriated to the purchase of scientific books, for the use of those who attend the lectures."

In 1818 Dr. Strachan was appointed a member of the Legislative Council, and also of the Executive Council. In these positions he was a consistent worker to secure the establishment of a State Church; and for the twenty-two years he took part in the politics of Upper Canada he ceased not to work for the cause, and the preservation of the Clergy Reserves. Dr. Strachan never forgot the original purpose which brought him to Canada, the foundation of Grammar Schools and a University. In 1827, after using the influence which his political position allowed him to secure this object, he procured a royal charter for a University which he named King's College after his *Alma Mater*. This institution was intended for the exclusive benefit of those who would subscribe to the Thirty-nine Articles. For nearly twenty years this University continued under the control of the Church of England. But the spirit which obtained in the public mind of Canada was hostile to this monopoly, and the time came when the University he had founded became more truly a national one. Although at this time an old man, when it might have been supposed he would yield to the adverse influence which had overcome his college, he never thought of resting satisfied, but, in direct opposition to the principle against voluntaryism, for which his life had been so far spent, he set about laying the foundation of another University, and the Trinity College of Toronto is a second monument to his untiring energy and success; a monument which renders another unnecessary to commemorate him.

We penned the following remarks in 1866: This widely known worthy still animates the church he has been mainly instrumental in erecting to a high and ever influential position in Canada, and whose untiring energies, guided by a brilliant intellect and a noble purpose, has made him the parent of higher education in the Province. The result of his doings—the traces of his vigorous mind, the repletion of his noble life may be seen, not alone upon the page of Episcopalian Church History; but in all the departments of Provincial life—in the halls of learning, in the recorded charges from the Bench, by the mouth of those he educated; in the speeches of many of Canada's earliest and foremost statesmen. For it was he tutored the mind of a McLean, a Hagerman, a Robinson, of the Sherwoods, Jones, besides a large number of others who have acted a conspicuous part in the history of the country. While the trees of the forest yet overshadowed the muddy soil where Toronto now proudly rears her graceful spires and domes, and while the wild duck found a safe resting place in the bay, now thickly dotted with crafts of every

22

size, Dr. Strachan by pen, and by word of mouth, was setting up a high standard of learning; and by worthy means, was stimulating the minds of the future men of Canada to attain that high mark. Read the easy flowing words that appeared in the Kingston *Gazette*, over "Reckoner," and it will strike one that if he took the *Spectator* as a model, he abundantly succeeded in imitating the immortal Addison. His school at Cornwall was pre-eminently good, "he had the welfare of those committed to him at heart, (says the Rev. Mr. Smart,) as well as the youth of the country generally."

Five years after the erection of Upper Canada into a distinct Province, 1797, steps were taken by the two Houses of Parliament to establish schools for the higher branches of learning. A joint address was presented to His Majesty, Geo. III., asking that he "would be graciously pleased to direct his Government in this Province, to appropriate a certain portion of the waste lands of the Crown, as a fund for the establishment and support of a respectable Grammar School in each District thereof; and also a College, or University, for the instruction of youth in the different branches of liberal knowledge." The Imperial Government replied, enquiring in what manner, and to what extent, a portion of the Crown lands might be appropriated and rendered productive towards the formation of a fund for the above purposes." The Executive Council of Canada recommended "that an appropriation of 500,000 acres, or ten townships, after deducting the Crown and Clergy sevenths, would be a sufficient fund for the establishment and maintenance of the royal foundation of four Grammar Schools and one University." It was also suggested, that the Grammer Schools be established at Cornwall, Kingston, Newark (Niagara), and Sandwich, and the University at York." It is not known what action was taken on this recommendation.—(Lillie). But, in 1798, "a grant was made of 549,000 acres of land in different parts of the Province, to carry out the design of the Grammer Schools and University." "Of the above land endowment, 190,573 acres were, up to the year 1826, assigned to (or disposed of by) a public body, known as the Board of Education, the proceeds having been applied to the support of Common and Grammar Schools." The residue of the grant, amounting to 358,427 acres, appears to have been regarded as properly constituting that portion of the royal gift which had been intended for the support of the contemplated University."

Through the influence and exertion of Dr. Strachan, the University of King's College was established by Royal Charter of

Incorporation, 15th March, 1827, with an endowment of "225,000 acres of crown land, and £1,000 for sixteen years. The Council or Governors were to consist of the Chancellor, President, and seven Professors or Graduates of the institution. All were to be members of the Church of England. This exclusive feature of the College continued to exist until 1843, when the charter was modified whereby parties were eligible to hold office by a declaration of their "belief in the authenticity and Divine incorporation of the Old and New Testaments, and in the doctrine of the Trinity. Various changes were made by Legislative enactment until the present institution became established, in 1853, when the faculties of Law and Medicine were abolished, the name changed from King's College to University College, and the University and College made two distinct institutions.

The Royal Grammar School was merged into Upper Canada College in 1829, and this institution was opened the following year. "In the years 1832, 1834, and 1835, it received endowments of land, amounting, in all, to 63,268 acres, irrespective of two valuable blocks in York—on one of which the present College buildings stand." "The College further received an allowance from Government of £200 sterling, in 1830; £500 in 1831; and £1,000 sterling per annum since."

ACADEMY AT ERNESTTOWN—BIDWELL.

While to Dr. Strachan belongs the honor of establishing the first school whereat a liberal education might be obtained the efforts and labors of others must not be forgotten. Shortly after the commencement of the present century, there arose, perhaps as a result of the teaching of Strachan, a greater desire for advanced learning. Says a writer in 1811, "A spirit of improvement is evidently spreading, the value of education, as well as the want of it, is felt. Gentlemen of competent means appear to be sensible of the importance of giving their children academical learning, and ambitious to do it without sending them abroad for the purpose. Among other indications of progress in literary ambition, I cannot forbear referring to the academy lately erected in Ernesttown, by the subscription of public-spirited inhabitants of that, and the neighbouring townships, who appear to be convinced that the cultivation of liberal arts and sciences is naturally connected with an improvement of manners and morals, and a general melioration of the state of society."

The academy above referred to was the second school of importance established in Upper Canada. It was also situated upon the shores of the Bay of Quinté. The following is from the *Kingston Gazette*:

"ERNESTTOWN ACADEMY.—The subscribers hereby inform the friends of learning that an Academical School, under the superintendence of an experienced preceptor, is opened in Ernesttown, near the church, for the instruction of youth in English reading, speaking, grammar and composition, the learned languages, penmanship, arithmetic, geograhy, and other branches of Liberal Education. Scholars attending from a distance may be boarded in good families on reasonable terms, and for fifteen shillings a year can have the use of a valuable library. School Trustees: Robert McDowel, Benjamin Fairfield, William Fairfield, Solomon Johns, William Wilcox, Samuel Neilson, George Baker.—Ernesttown, 11th March, 1811."

The person selected for teacher was Mr. Barnabas Bidwell, who had a few years previously come to Canada from the State of Massachusetts, where he had been, according to a writer in the *Kingston Gazette*, Attorney-General of that State. The same writer made charges of a serious nature against Mr. Bidwell, as to the cause of his leaving his country; but one of the above committee vindicated Mr. Bidwell's character; by asserting that although Mr. B. had been "unfortunate in business, and became embarrassed, he was honest, and had left property to pay his debts when he left—that he had been a tutor at the first college in America—that he avoided politics and devoted himself to literary pursuits." It was about the commencement of the present century, when Mr. Bidwell came to Bath to live.

Probably the academy at Bath was regarded somewhat as a rival to the school existing at Cornwall.

Barnabas Bidwell remained at Bath about eight years when he removed to Kingston, with his son, Marshal Bidwell, who became a lawyer, and a very conspicuous character in Canada. B. Bidwell died at Kingston, July 26, 1833, aged 70. His son removed to York in 1830, where he practised his profession until the eventful year of 1837.

The academy, at the commencement of the war of 1812, was in a prosperous state, but very soon all was changed,—the school was broken up, and the building converted into a barrack. The close of the war unfortunately saw no return of the old state of things, the teacher was gone, and the students scattered, "having resorted to other places of education, many of them out of the province. The building is now, (1822), occupied as a house of public worship, and a common school. It is to be hoped, however, that the taste for literary improvement may be revived, and this seminary be re-established." But these hopes were never realized. The literary glory of Bath had departed. The capital of York was now to become a centre to which would gravitate the more learned, and where would be established the seats of learning. The limited, though earnest rivalry which had existed between Kingston and Bath, was to be on a more important scale, between the ancient capital, Kingston, and the more promising one of York.

CHAPTER XXXIX.

CONTENTS—Extract from Cooper—Educational institutions—Kingston—Queen's College—Own's Real Estate—Regiopolis College—Roman Catholic—Grammar School—Attendance—School houses—Library—Separate Schools—Private Schools—The Quaker School—William Penn—Upon the Hudson—Near Bloomfield—Origin of school—Gurnay—His offer—Management of school—The teaching—Mrs. Crombie's schools—Picton Ladies' Academy—McMullen, proprietor—Teachers—Gentlemen's department—Popular—The art of printing—In America—Book publishing—First in America—Books among the loyalists—Few—Passed around—Ferguson's books—The Bible—Libraries at Kingston and Bath—Legislation—In Lower Canada—Reading room at Hallowell—Reserves for Education—Upper Canada in respect to education—Praiseworthy—Common School System Bill introduced 1841—Amended, 1846—Dr. Ryerson's system—Unsurpassed.

HIGHER EDUCATION, CONTINUED.

The subjoined statement we extract from Cooper, which was written in 1856. We have no doubt the last twelve years has been attended with a steady increase in the importance of the Educational institutions of Kingston.

"EDUCATIONAL INSTITUTIONS.—There are in Kingston two colleges, Queen's College and Regiopolis; the County Grammar School, 11 Common Schools, 2 separate R. C. Schools, one School connected with the Nunnery, or Sisters of Charity, with numerous good private schools for boys, private schools for girls, infant schools and other minor educational establishments, such as evening schools, classes for teaching continental languages, &c., in all between 20 and 30.

"Queen's College.—Queen's College is an educational institution of very considerable importance, and from it have issued graduates in arts, divinity and medicine, of no despicable attainments. It was incorporated by Royal Charter in 1842, and is under the management of a Board of Trustees and Senate. It has a Principal and four Professors in Arts and Divinity, besides six Medical Professors. It confers Scholarships of the aggregate value of £200, the highest being worth £12 10s. It numbers during the present year, 47 medical students, 30 in Arts, 10 in Divinity, connected with it is a Preparatory School, where great pains are taken to prepare pupils for matriculation at the college. A good library, containing some 3,000 volumes belongs to the College. A series of meteorological observations are taken by the graduates, with the able supervision of the Rev. Professor James Williamson, under whose assiduous attention this branch of knowledge, so much neglected in Canada has been carefully fostered.

"This institution owns valuable real estate, and is aided by an annual grant from the Legislature of £750, and £250 to the medical branch.

"Regiopolis College is a Roman Catholic Seminary of learning; it has three Professorships, the duties of which are discharged by Roman Catholic clergymen. Beyond its own walls, and its own community, it is little known as an educational institution.

"The County Grammar School is supported as those in other counties, that is, by a grant from Government of £100 per annum, and the tuition fees of pupils. It possessed formerly a small endowment; this for the present has been consumed in creating a fund for the liquidation of some debt on the school-house, a plain substantial building in a healthy and elevated part of the town; it is under the control of a Board of Trustees, appointed by the County Council, and is managed by a head-master and under-master. It is one of the three Grammar Schools first established in the Province, and created by Royal Charter—the other two being at Cornwall and Niagara.

"The Common Schools are, as in other places, under the management of the department of education, and the local control of a Board of Trustees, and local Superintendent. There is a great want of proper and sufficient school-houses, a want which it is anticipated will soon be supplied, the Board having in contemplation, the immediate erection of proper buildings. The free school system has been adopted here; the difficulties usually attendant on its establishment have not been altogether escaped—the public seeming loth to tax themselves to any extent, for the purpose of general education. A marked increase in the attendance at the city schools has taken place during the last two years, and there are now taught as large a number of children in the common schools of Kingston as in any other Canadian city, in proportion to its population: the standard of education may or may not be as high as in Toronto, Hamilton or Brockville, but if it is more elementary, it is not less sound. In free public schools, such as now established, it is perhaps as well not to aim at a higher standard than is here attained to. When good school-houses are erected, it will doubtlessly be found necessary to adopt the Central School system, on the model of that so successfully carried out in Hamilton, Perth and St. Catharines, and perhaps elsewhere. When such is the case the present schools will rank high as primary schools, whilst the central schools will have to compete with other similar institutions in the province, and will not likely be behind them in character and value; these changes are in contemplation, and will before long be carried into effect. The people of Kingston do not fail to appreciate the benefits of sound education of its inhabitants in elevating the position of a city. A public library, containing some 2,000 volumes, has been established in connection with the city schools.

"The Roman Catholic Separate Schools are under the management of a separate Board of Trustees; they are supported as are the Common Schools, by a Legislative grant, proportionate to the average attendance of pupils, and by a rate settled by the Board, collected from all rate-payers; in the case of the Separate Schools, from the parents of pupils and supporters of the schools, who are exempt from all other taxation for school purposes. The rate in their case is usually very low. The wealthier supporters of the schools, with a praiseworthy zeal, voluntarily contribute largely to the required fund. Among the private schools are many excellent academies for both boys and girls, which afford both ornamental acquirements and substantial, classical and commercial education."

Quaker Schools—The noted and good William Penn founded a school for the children of the Friends at an early date. Subsequently a Quaker Boarding School was established upon the banks of the Hudson, near Poughkeepsie.

Toward the latter part of 1841, a school for the children of the Quaker denomination, was opened near the pleasant village of Bloomfield, about 4 miles from Picton. The origin of the school we believe, was pretty much as follows: An English gentleman, John Joseph Gurney, brother to Elizabeth Fry, a member of the Quaker Society, and we believe a minister, was travelling in Canada, and discovering the wants of that denomination, with respect to education, offered to bestow a certain sum, (£500), on condition that another specified sum were raised, a suitable place bought, and buildings prepared. His offer being accepted, and at this juncture, Mr. Armstrong being desirous of selling his farm of 100 acres, with a good brick house just completed, the present site of the school was procured. In addition to the means thus obtained there was also a limited sum held by the society, it is said a bequest, for educational purposes. Additional buildings were erected, and the school duly opened. The first teachers were Americans. The school was managed by a committee chosen annually by the Society, until the latter part of 1865, when it was leased to Mr. W. Valentine, to whom we are partially indebted for the foregoing facts. The school continues under the supervision of a managing committee, appointed by the Society. Its capacity does not extend further than to receive 30 pupils of each sex, who are taught the usual branches of a good English education, and sometimes the rudiments of the classics and the modern languages.

In 1836, Mrs. Crombie and her sister Miss Bradshaw opened a "Female Academy" in Picton, which promised to give "substantial and ornamental accomplishments."

The Picton Ladies' Acadamy was opened in December, 1847, by the Rev. D. McMullen, as sole proprietor. It was continued by him until May, 1851, when Miss Creighton rented the premises and took charge of the school. It continued under her management nine months, when it finally was closed. The first teachers were the late Mrs. N. F. English, and Miss Eliza Austin. Afterwards Miss M. E. Adams was preceptress, and Miss Ployle was teacher.

A male department was established by Mr. McMullen, with the hope of having it connected with the Grammar School. But this was not done. The principal of the school was C. M. C. Cameron, now Dr. Cameron of Port Hope, and a graduate of Victoria College. He was assisted by Mr. Samuel W. Harding; the school existed but one year. Both of these schools were well attended, and were deservedly popular. When closed it was generally regarded as a public loss, by those most capable of judging.

UPPER CANADA ACADEMY—VICTORIA COLLEGE.

We have accorded to Dr. Strachan a prominent and foremost position in connection with the subject of higher education. We considered it a duty as well as a pleasure, to thus honor one whose praise was in all the land when he ceased to live. But the fountain of education opened by him did not flow, shall we say, was not intended to flow to the masses. Dr. Strachan's educational establishment was rather created for a select circle, for an expected Canadian aristocracy. It remained for others to originate a stream of learning that should water the whole land, and come within the reach of every Canadian family—that should give intellectual life to the whole of the country, irrespective of creed or origin. To the Wesleyan Methodists belongs the greater honor of establishing an institution of higher learning, whose doors were opened to all, and within which any one might obtain learning without hindrance, no matter what his belief. While religious oversight was to be extended, no peculiar dogma was to be enforced, no sectarian principle was to be inculcated.

In the month of August, 1830, when the Wesleyan Conference met upon the Bay Quinté, the Rev. Wm. Case, being General Superintendent, and Rev. James (now Dr.) Richardson, Secretary, and while Cobourg was yet embraced within the Bay Quinté District, the following Resolution was adopted by that body:

"That a Committee of nine be chosen by ballot, consisting of three from each District, to fix the location of the Seminary, according to some general instructions to be given them by the Conference." The committee consisted of "J. Ryerson, T. Whitehead, S. Belton, David Wright, J. Beatty, Wm. Ryerson, Thos. Madden, Wm. Brown, James Richardson."

"The following Constitution for the Upper Canada Academy, was adopted:

"1. That nine Trustees be appointed, three of whom shall go into office annually.

"2. That a Board of Visitors, consisting of five, be chosen annually by the Conference." That these two bodies should jointly form a Board to appoint the Principal and Teachers, and govern, and generally superintend the institution.

The Conference, in the Pastoral Address, asked for the liberal support of the members, in the establishment of the proposed Academy. A general agent was appointed, and active steps taken to carry out the object. It is noteworthy, that the call thus made to the farmers, many of whom were yet struggling for the necessaries of life, was promptly and nobly responded to. Agents continued to be appointed from year to year, and in the Conference address of 1835, it is said, "We are happy to be able to say that the buildings for the Upper Canada Academy are nearly completed. We trust the Institution will soon be open for the reception of pupils." There had been delay "for want of funds." Arrangements were making to accommodate one hundred and seventy pupils, with board and lodging. In 1836, it is found stated, that "the Conference and the friends of general education, and of Wesleyan Methodists in Canada, have at length, by their unremitting efforts, succeeded in preparing the Upper Canada Academy for the reception of pupils, and we expect, in a few days to see it in operation." In 1837, we find that Matthew Ritchey, A. M., was the Principal of the U. C. Academy. If we mistake not, the Rev. Egerton Ryerson had, previously been named to fill the office. At all events, we have every reason to believe that this distinguished Canadian educationist was chiefly instrumental in securing the foundation of an abiding institution, probably, indeed, was the originator of the scheme. He not only stimulated others to work; but obtained from Government a grant, so often begrudged. He also, as a representative to the British Conference, was the means of procuring a donation of one hundred pounds' worth of books, beside other contributions. In 1840, the Rev. Mr. Ritchey ceased to be Principal. During his time of service, it is stated, the Academy increasingly progressed in efficiency and in increase of pupils. Mr. Ritchey's successor, in 1841, was the Rev. Jesse Hurlburt, A. B. Daniel C. VanNorman was Professor of Mathematics, a post to which he had been appointed a year previous.

The year 1842 saw the Upper Canada Academy changed into the Victoria College, by Provincial Legislative enactment, possessing the usual powers and privileges of a University. The Rev. Egerton Ryerson was made Principal; Jesse Hurlburt, A. M., and D. C. VanNorman, Professors; and James Spencer, English Teacher. Dr. Ryerson continued Principal until 1845. In 1845, Alexander MacNab, A. M., was appointed Acting Principal, and in 1847 he became Principal, and held the position until 1850.

In 1851, the Rev. S. S. Nelles, A. M., was elected to the office which he now continues to hold with so much credit and dignity, having been instrumental in materially advancing the reputation of the previously well known College.

BOOKS, LIBRARIES—PRINTING.

The art of printing was not old when the colonies of France and Great Britain were planted in America. The discovery of this art, with the avenue which the discovery of America, opened for the pent up millions of Europe, wrought out the most striking changes which ever marked the history of the human race. It struck the final blow to the spirit of feudalism, while America supplied an asylum for those who found not full freedom of conscience and an opportunity to rise in the scale of human existence.

Book publishing being once introduced into England, rapidly became of vast magnitude, and thus everywhere scattered the food essential for the human mind. It was in the year 1639 that printing was introduced into America; but it was sixty-two years before it became of any account, during which time the business was mostly in Philadelphia. Altogether there were but four presses in the country. The first book printed in America was made in 1640. It was a reprint of the Psalm Book, and afterwards passed through many editions, while it was reprinted in England in eighteen editions, and twenty-two in Scotland, being seventy in all.

Whatever may have been the state of education in the British Colonies, and the general desire to read books at the time of the rebellion, it is quite certain that the hasty manner in which many left their homes, the long distance to travel, and necessity of carrying quantities of provision which took all the strength of the refugees, precluded the possibility of carrying many, or any books to the wilderness of Canada. Even after the peace the long distance to come, and the frequent impoverished condition of the settler, allowed not the desire, if such existed, to fetch books for instruction and mental enjoyment. However, there were some brought by them, but mostly by the officers recently out from the old country. During the first ten years the books among the settlers were very few; but these few were circulated from one township to another—from one person to another, who had the desire to, and could, read. We have in our possession, a letter from John Ferguson to Mr. Bell, who was then, 1789, at Kingston, in which the latter is requested to tell Mr. Markland, that he, Mr. Ferguson, had sent h'm from the Eighth Township, by the bearer, the History of France. The same person writing from Fredericksburgh in 1791, desires to have sent from Sidney to him, "some books, viz.: five volumes of the History of England, by Horn, and the two volumes of Andrew's History of France."

But while few, or no books of a secular nature, were brought by the settler, a large number, true to their conscience, carried a copy of the Bible, even many of the disbanded soldiers had one, especially the Lutherans. These were often in the German, or Dutch language. Some of these venerable and sacred relics we have seen; one in German, which belonged to Bongard of Marysburgh.

For many years Kingston took the lead in everything that pertains to education. The history of the *Kingston Gazette* shews that, not only did the leading men of the place give the patronage necessary to establish and maintain a newspaper, independent of Government support, and give interest to the columns of the paper by contributions; but there is evidence of early and successful efforts to form a public library. Reference is made to the "Social library established in this village (Kingston) in 1813, when the Rev. Mr. Langhorn presented to it a valuable collection of books, (see the first clergyman). This library had probably been in existance for some years. Another library was established at Bath prior to this time. Gourlay says, in 1811, "books are procured in considerable numbers, social libraries are introduced in various places." And, no doubt, the High School at Cornwall, under Mr. Strachan, had attached to it a select library.

The *Kingston Gazette* announces, August 1, 1815, that "A small circulating library" has been opened at the *Gazette* office, "on the most reasonable terms."

In 1816, an act was passed "to appropriate a sum of money for providing a library for the use of the Legislative Council and House of Assembly of this Province." The sum granted was £800 to purchase books and maps.

While the growth of Upper Canada was attended by a corresponding increase of private and public libraries, Lower Canada, there is reason to believe, was maintaining the character it had acquired under its original rulers, for educational privileges and individual efforts to create centres of learning.

We find the statement "that the library of F. Fleming, Esq., Montreal, comprising 12,000 volumes, sold by auction, September 8, 1833, was the largest ever offered for sale on the American continent."

In the *Hallowell Free Press*, 15th February, 1831, is the following: "Library notice."—"A meeting of the inhabitants of the village of Hallowell is requested to-morrow evening, at Strikers' Inn, at seven o'clock, to take into consideration the propriety of establishing a Reading-room in the village." The next issue of the Journal says, "we are glad to see our friends have established a reading-room."

"At an early period of British dominion in America, blocks of wild land were set apart, to make provision, by a future day, for public institutions. Since the revolution, the United States have followed out, in part, this practice, by allotting lands for schools, and in Canada, whole townships have been appropriated for the same purpose." While this forethought respecting schools indicated a proper desire to secure educational interests, it must be observed that the reserves, like those of the Crown and Clergy, very materially prevented the opening up of the country by settlers, and kept apart the settlers, over a wide field, and thus preventing advancement in civilization.

Looking back at the history of legislation, relative to education, one is struck with the fact that much, very much, was done by the young colony of Upper Canada. The establishment of the Common Schools especially, which first took place 1816, has been regarded as most wise, and the grants of money most praiseworthy.

The present Common School system of Upper Canada was introduced in 1841. The Bill was brought forward by the Hon. S. B. Harrison. The fundamental principle, being the allotment of money to each county, on condition of its raising an equal amount by local assessment. This act was amended and improved in 1843, by the Hon. Francis Hincks, and in 1846, by the Hon. W. H. Draper. In 1849, the Hon. J. H. Cameron introduced an act, establishing schools in cities and towns. In the year following, these two acts were in corporated into one, with further improvements.

The Common School system, as we find it to day, is, in a great measure, the production of Dr. Ryerson's long continued and intelligent labor. Borrowing the machinery from the State of New York, and the mode of support from Massachusetts, taking the Irish national school-books for instruction, and making use of the Normal School system of Germany, he has, by the addition of what was necessary, built up a system of Common School education in the Province of Ontario, that cannot be surpassed, if equalled, in the whole world.

CHAPTER XL.

THE FIRST NEWSPAPERS IN THE WORLD.

The first newspaper published in the world, says Galignani, bears the name of Neuremberg, 1457. But according to Tacitus, newspapers, under the name of *diurna,* circulated among the Romans so early as the year 66. The first English newspaper was issued in 1622, and the first French in 1631. The first in America was the *Newsletter*, published at Boston, 1704. It was discontinued in 1776. The first published in New York, was by Wm. Bradford, in 1773. In 1775, there were but thirty-seven in the British colonies. By 1801, there were in the United States 203, and in 1810, 358. The first newspaper in Canada was the Quebec *Gazette,* first issued in 1776. Although now upwards of a hundred years old, it continues to live an active and useful life. The founder of it, Mr. Brown, brought his press from Philadelphia in 1763. By his heirs it was sold to Mr. Nelson, who left the establishment by his will to his brother, the late Hon. John Wilson, long the experienced and able editor of the paper. There were, in 1763, not more than twenty newspapers in the breadth and length of the then American colonies; and the Quebec *Gazette* is the oldest in the British North American Provinces. For nearly thirty years it remained without a competitor; but about 1788 the Quebec *Herald* was started, which had but a brief existence. About the same time, the old Montreal

Gazette was established by one Mesplet, and was published in French; but was soon discontinued until 1794. About the same date *Le Temps* newspaper was published at Quebec, in French and English, and was of short life. The Quebec *Mercury*, published in English, by Thomas Cary, commenced its career in 1804, and the *Canadien* followed it in 1806; but was stopped by the seizure of the press by the Government, in 1810. The *Canadien Courant* was founded at Montreal about 1808. The *Royal Gazette* and *Newfoundland Advertiser*, the first newspaper in Newfoundland, appeared in 1707. The *Upper Canada Gazette* or *American Oracle*, the first paper in Upper Canada, was established by Governor Simcoe, in 1793. It was first published on the 18th April, by Gideon Tiffany. Naturally its circulation was limited, as the population was sparse, and communication difficult. It was supported mainly by Government. Rochefoucault says, in 1795 it was "not taken by a single person in Kingston. But the Quebec *Gazette* was by two."

The second journal published in Upper Canada, was the *Upper Canada Guardian*, in opposition to Government, at York, by Mr. Joseph Wilcox, an Irishman, in 1807, whose history is not of the most satisfactory nature. He had been a Sheriff in the Home District; but was displaced for voting at an election for one Thorpe. Mr. Thorpe had been sent out from England as one of the Justices of the King's Bench. Notwithstanding this position, he became a candidate for member of Parliament; but, being opposed by the Government, he was defeated. Subsequently he was recalled by the Secretary of State, at the request of Governor Gore. Wilcox, having lost his office, commenced publishing the *Guardian*, and was very bitter in his opposition to the Government. He was prosecuted for libel, but was acquitted, and becoming popular, was elected to Parliament. Having used language considered unbecoming or seditious, he was arrested, and confined in York jail, a miserable log building, "in a filthy cell fit for a pig." Subsequently, he became the leader of the opposition, and had a majority in the House; for a time becoming more and more an object of Ministerial dislike. At the commencement of the war of 1812, he gave up his paper, and shouldered his musket. He fought at Queenston against the Americans; but afterward deserted, taking with him a body of Canadian militia, and became a Colonel in the American army. He was killed, finally, at Fort Erie, by a musket ball, when planting a guard during the seige.

Mr. Miles remarks that "When he came to Kingston, in 1810,

there was but one paper published in York, by the Government, called the *York Gazette*, printed by Cameron and Bennet; and one at Newark, by Joseph Wilcox. These were the only papers then printed in Upper Canada; but the one at Newark was discontinued in 1812, and the other was destroyed when York was taken by the Americans, in April, 1813. The Kingston *Gazette* was the only paper then printed in Upper Canada, till 1816, when the Government *Gazette* was again commenced. The Rev. Mr. Carroll says of the *York Gazette*, the number "for November 13, 1801, now lies before the writer, a coarse, flimsy, two-leaved paper, of octavo size; department of news is pretty large, but "news much older than their ale." On this, November 13, they have, wonderful to say! New York dates so late as October the 23rd; Charleston, of October the 1st; Philadelphia and Boston, of October the 19th; and a greater exploit still, Halifax dates of Oct. 19, &c."

We are indebted to the Rev. Stephen Miles, of Camden East, for the facts relating to the establishment of the first newspaper in the Midland District, indeed the first between Montreal and York, at Kingston. Mr. Miles is not only the sole pioneer of journalism in Upper Canada, now living, but he is the faithful *parent of the fourth estate in the province*, and probably the oldest journalist now living in America or Europe. The history of such an one cannot but be interesting, while it is especially appropriate to the work upon our hands. Mr. Miles, although a native of Vermont, is of English and Welsh extraction. Born October 19, 1789, he was brought up on the farm until 1805, when he was placed as an apprentice to the printing business, at Windsor, Ver., in the office of Nahum Mower. In the spring of 1807, Mr. Mower moved his printing materials to Montreal, Lower Canada, to which place Mr. Miles accompanied him. "At that time there was only one printing establishment in Montreal, under the management of Mr. Edward Edwards, who was also the Postmaster there; the paper printed was the *Montreal Gazette*, of small demy-size, two columns on a page, one in French the other in English. Mr. Mower, commenced printing the *Canadian Courant*, in Montreal, about the middle of May, 1807. Mr. Mower, says Mr. Miles, giving me three months of my time, my apprenticeship expired on the 19th July, 1810." Not long after "I made arrangements in connection with an excellent young man Charles Kendall, who had worked as a journeyman, to go to Kingston, Upper Canada, and commence publishing a paper." Accordingly having purchased our material from Mr. Mower, we left Montreal 1st September, 1810, in the old fashioned Canadian batteau (17 in number) and arrived at a wharf in Kingston just the west side of where the barracks now are, on the morning of the 13th. We took an excellent breakfast at a tavern opposite, and at once set about to procure a suitable room for a printing office." Upon the 25th September, the first number of the *Kingston Gazette*, was published under the names of "Mower and Kendall," Mr. Miles not being of age. At this time there were five papers in Lower Canada. The following March, Mr. Miles sold out his share to Mr. Kendall, who finished the first volume. At the close of the year, Mr. Kendall wishing to retire, disposed of the office and contents "to the late Hon. Richard Cartwright, the Hon. Allen McLean, Thomas Markland, Esq., Lawrence Herchimer, Esq., Peter Smith, Esq., and John Kerby, Esq." These gentlemen saw the necessity of having a public journal in Kingston, and became the proprietors. They immediately wrote to secure the services of Mr. Miles, to conduct the office, and even desired him to take it off their hands. Mr. Miles promptly came "expecting that the proprietors would wish to be publishers as well, and that I should attend only to the mechanical part, but it was their unanimous wish that I should take the whole concern off their hands, continue to print the paper, and do the best I could with it." Mr. Miles speaks feelingly of the kindness of these gentlemen who would accept no other terms than that he should take possession and pay them when convenient, "and by God's blessing all were promptly paid." These kind friends, says Mr. Miles, "have all passed into the spirit world, and the prayer of my heart is, that God may greatly bless their posterity." "After some unadvoidable delay, the second volume of the Gazette was commenced by me, and printed and published in my name, till December 31, 1818." Before proceeding with Mr. Miles' history, as a journalist, we will copy from the volumes which he has kindly placed at our service, such items as are appropriate.

"KINGSTON, Tuesday, November 19, 1811.—The establishment of the Kingston Gazette, being now in the possession of the subscriber, he takes the earliest opportunity of re-commencing its publication, as he intends that it shall be conducted in the same impartial manner as heretofore practiced by his predecessors, he confidently expects and solicits the patronage and support of its former patrons, and of the public in general. He will not intrude upon the patience of his readers by making a multiplicity of promises, but will merely observe that he asks the patronage of the public no longer than he shall be deserving of it. Former correspondents of the Gazette, and gentlemen of science generally, are respectfully invited to favor us with their communications.—(Signed)—S. Miles.

"Printed and published by Stephen Miles, a few doors east of Walker's hotel. Price fifteen shillings per annum, five shillings in advance, five shillings in six months, and five shillings at the end of year. Exclusive of postage."

In the beginning of 1819, John Alexander Pringle, and John Macaulay, Esquires, to whom Mr. Miles had sold his printing establishment, commenced publishing the *Kingston Chronicle*, Mr. Miles having charge of the mechanical part for nearly three years.

In Feburary or March, 1819, the *Upper Canada Herald*, owned and edited by Hugh C. Thompson, Esq., was first issued. In 1822 Mr. Miles took charge of the work of printing of this Journal, and continued in charge until the spring of 1828.

On the 15th of May, the same year, Mr. Miles commenced printing on his own account the "*Kingston Gazette* and *Religious Advocate*," in quarto form, which he continued till August 6, 1830. Again, Mr. M. took charge of printing for Ezra S. Ely, who commenced August 13, the *Canadian Watchman*, and continued it for one year. In December 1831, Mr. Miles moved to Prescott; and on the 3rd June, 1832, commenced printing the first paper in that place, and continued till April 1833. In July he disposed of his establishment and returned to Kingston, and engaged as printer of the *Kingston Chronicle*, which was now published by McFarlane & Co., with whom he remained till December, 1835. This ended Mr. Miles' career as a printer and publisher; and he then entered upon the calling of a Wesleyan minister.

Mr. Miles although a native of the States was a truly loyal subject, and proved himself such during the war of 1812. The Gazette of May 5, 1813, says "our attendance at *military* duty prevented the publishing of the Gazette yesterday." This was the time when Kingston was threatened by the Americans, and every man turned out as a volunteer. Mr. Miles tells of the occasion that he saw, among those shouldering the musket in the market place, the late Arch Deacon Stuart. Mr. Miles belonged to Captain Markland's company. "Col. Cartwright seeing him, called him and desired him to go to his office and he would be sent for when wanted." The principal contributors to the Gazette were Col.

Cartwright, who wrote a good deal, sometimes over Falkiner, Barnabus Bidwell, Christopher Hagerman, generally Poetry, while a student with McLean, Solomon John, who kept a book store ; and particularly Rev. Mr. Strachan, over *Reckoner*.

We cannot leave Mr. Miles without expressing here our sincere thanks and regard for the interest, trouble, and encouragement he has favored us with, nor can we forgo recording the following. Says he, "the only watch I ever owned I purchased in Montreal, on the 1st January 1810, price $20. It has travelled with me in all my journeyings from that day to the present time, and still keeps good time. It was made at Liverpool." A faithful man and a faithful watch; both for time, one for eternity.

About the year 1816 the *Gazette* had the following, under the caption of "*A good chance:*"

"A sober, honest, persevering man, would find it to his advantage to undertake the circulation of the *Kingston Gazette*, weekly, on the following route: say, to start from Kinston every Wednesday morning, go through the village of Ernesttown, from thence to Adolphustown, and cross either at Vanalstines or Baker's Ferry, and so on through Hallowell, &c., to the Carrying place; cross the River Trent, and return to Kingston by the York post road. The advantages to be derived from an undertaking of this kind, exclusive of the papers, we are persuaded would be many; and any honest, persevering man, who could produce good recommendations as to his sobriety, &c., and will give security for punctual payment once a quartér, will make a good bargain by applying to the publisher of the *Kingston Gazette*. There is not a doubt but that four or five hundred papers might be distributed on this route to great advantage." We learn from another source, that at an early period there was one Shubal Huff, who went around the Bay every fortnight, carrying the *Kingston Gazette* with other papers, pamphlets, &c., and also tea and sugar.

The following indicates the character of the times when the *Gazette* was established. It is a notice from the *Gazette*:

"Subscribers to the *Kingston Gazette*, in the neighbourhood of York, will please apply at the store of Q. St. George, where their papers will be delivered once a fortnight. Payments made to him in grain, &c., will be acceptable. He will also receive subscriptions." (Signed), Mower & Kendall.

In addition to the papers already mentioned, there was the *Kingston Spectator*, issued about 1830, and lasting three or four years.

The *Patriot* was commenced in 1829, by T. Dalton. Subsequently there was the *Argus*, *Commercial Advertiser*, and *Churchman*. The *British Whig* was started in 1832, by Dr. Barker, and is still published. *The Chronicle and News* began in 1830, is also still published. *The British Whig* was the first Daily published in Upper Canada.

For many years the subscribers to the *Gazette* and other papers were indebted to footmen who traveled through the more thickly settled parts of the settlement, which were generally along the front. But after a time there were scattered along in the second or more remote concessions, subscribers to whom the footman could not go. These individuals would often place boxes upon the path followed by the carrier, into which could be dropped the paper, and letters as well. These boxes were attached to a tree and made water-tight, and the owner would go for his paper at his convenience.

One of the first newspapers in Upper Canada, east of Kingston, was the *Recorder*. Says Adiel Sherwood, Esq., in a letter to the writer, it was "the first and only paper of note, of early date in this district. It was first got up in 1820 by one Beach, who continued but a short time when he sold out to William Buel, Esq., and about 1848 Mr. Buel sold out to the present proprietor and editor, D. Wylie, Esq. It was got up as Reform paper, and has ever continued as such."

The following is extracted from an American paper:

"In 1818, D. McLeod, a retired soldier, who had fought at Badajoz, and other places in the campaign under Wellington, and at Queenston, Upper Canada, Chrysler's Farm, Lundy's Lane, and then under General Picton, at Waterloo, "purchased a farm in Augusta, a few miles back of Prescott, moved on it, and commenced the business of farming; not succeeding well in his new avocation, he removed to Prescott and opened a classical school, at which the late Preston King received his rudimentary Greek lessons, and subsequently accepted the appointment of Clerk of the new court of Commissioners, for the collection of debts. He purchased a printing establishment and commenced the publication of a paper at Prescott, called the *Grenville Gazette*, taking a decided stand against the "Tory Compact" administration, and continued a zealous advocate of reform until the insurrection broke out in December, 1837, when he was forced to leave the country, when his press, type, and the various paraphernalia of the printing office were seized by the Tories. A mob of Tories visited his house, after he left the place, at midnight, to the terror of his unprotected family, seized, and carried off his books, letters, and other papers, and his elegant sword, as the trophies of their midnight raid. He was chosen by the insurgents as their major-general, and acted in that capacity during the continuance of the insurrection, At this time large rewards were offered for his arrest on each side of the line, on the Canadian side, for his rebellion against that government;" on the United States side for an alleged violation of the Neutrality Laws,," in being supposed the leader of the party of men who captured and burned the Canadian Steamer, "Sir Robert Peel," Well's Island.

McLeod settled in Cleveland, Ohio, and is yet alive, being upwards of eighty-four years of age. The Cleveland *Herald*, from which we learn the above, records the celebration of "General D. McLeod's fiftieth anniversary of his marriage."

The *Prescott Telegraph*, "The first number" said an exchange "published by Messrs. Merrell & Miles, (1831) is now lying before us. From the appearance of the first number, and the known ability of the proprietors, we anticipate that the *Telegraph* will be a valuable acquisition to the best of newspapers in this Province, and also to the principles of reform."

The *Christian Guardian* was established in the year 1829. Rev. E. Ryerson being the Editor.

The following were so-called "Reform" papers: The *Colonial Advocate*, by McKenzie, The *Canadian Watchman*, The *Brockville Recorder*, and The *Hamilton Free Press*, &c.

CHAPTER XLI.

NEWSPAPERS—CONTINUED.

The first newspaper published between Kingston and York, was the *Hallowell Free Press*, of demy size, the first number of which was issued 28th December, 1830, by Joseph Wilson, Esq., now of Belleville; W. A. Welles, Esq., editor, a gentleman from Utica, New York. Attempts had been made at Cobourg, Port Hope, as well as at Hallowell, prior to this, to establish papers, prospectus having been acknowledged by the *Kingston Gazette*. A letter in the first number of the *Free Press*, signed "Recluse," says, "a number of attempts have been made to publish a journal in this county, proposals circulated, subscriptions obtained to a considerable amount, and the expectations of the public wrought up to the highest degree, yet every attempt hitherto made, has proved abortive, except the present; repeated imposition has, no doubt, had a tendency to create in the public mind, a spirit of indifference and apathy respecting newspapers."

Mr. Wilson had his press of wood, made by one Scripture, of Colborne. Although a very indifferent affair, it was used for a year, when Mr. Wilson procured an iron press from New York. Probably one of the first iron printing presses in the Province. The *Free Press* was continued for five years. Mr. Welles was editor for a short time only. This journal was evidently intended for the public weal. No one can read the first issues of the paper without being convinced that the proprietor was intent upon rendering service to the public. He allied himself to no party: the contending political aspirants of the day, had equal access to the columns of the *Press*, and could thereby challenge unbiased attention. "*The Traveller, or Prince Edward Gazette*," published every Friday, by Cecil Mortimer, Editor and Proprietor, "John Silver, Printer," 12s. 6d., per annum, in advance. Commenced April, 1836, and continued about four years, when the printing press was removed to Cobourg. In 1840, the *Prince Edward Gazette* appeared, J. Dornan, Publisher. It was continued under this name by Rev. Mr. Playter. In 1847, and in 1849, Mr. Thomas Donnelly became Editor and Proprietor, changing the name to the *Picton Gazette*, which name it still bears. Mr. Donnelly was succeeded as editor in 1853, by Maurice Moore, and he again by S. M. Conger, in 1856, who still continues to publish this old and popular journal. The *Picton Sun*, established in 1841, by Mr. J. Douglas, who was succeeded in 1845, by J. McDonald, and he again in 1849, by Mr. Striker, who removed it to Cobourg in 1853. The following year Dr. Gillespie and R. Boyle commenced the *Picton Times*, which still continues to be published by Mr. Boyle. The *North American* removed from Newburgh in 1861, published by McMullen Brothers. The *New Nation* succeeded it in 1865.

The *Anglo Canadian* was established in Belleville in February, 1831. It was "printed and published by Alexander T. W. Williamson, Editor, and W. A. Welles. Printed at four dollars per annum, payable in advance." A copy of this paper is before us, and is very respectable as to size and quality, and is readable. This was the first journal published in Belleville. The *Phœnix* arose from the ashes of the *Anglo-Canadian*. It was first issued in the early part of July, 1831, "published every Tuesday by T. Slicer, Editor and Proprietor, at his office, Water Street, Belleville, U. C., 20s. per annum—if sent by mail, 22s. 6d., payable half-yearly." A few copies before us resemble, in appearance, its predecessor, the *Anglo-Canadian*. In one of the early copies is a prospectus of the *Canadian Wesleyan*, the subscribers to the announcement are "H. Ryan," and "J. Jackson," dated Hamilton, August, 1831.—(See first clergyman, H. Ryan).

The last number of the *Phœnix* issued July 3, 1832, and which was "published by William A. Welles, for the Proprietors," says, "As the present number completes the year, it is intended to give the paper a new name; which, though less classical, may be considered more appropriate" The name selected was the "*Hastings Times*," No. 17, of the *Times* now before us, was published by Rollin C. Benedict, every Saturday.

"The *Reformer*" of Cobourg, published every Friday, J. Radcliff, Editor, was first issued, June, 1832.

"The *Intelligencer*, of Belleville," was founded by George Benjamin, in September, 1834, who continued its editor until 1848, when McKenzie Bowell, Esq., now M. P., succeeded him, who remains the proprietor. Mr. Benjamin was an Englishman, born 1799, and died 1864. He was a gentleman of more than ordinary ability, a consistent politician, and a true friend. He held the highest municipal offices, and was Member of Parliament from 1856 to 1863. He had talent to adorn any position.

The *Victoria Chronicle* was founded in 1841, by S. M. Washburn and Sutton, who had removed from Brockville. Sutton remained partner for two years. In 1849 the establishment was purchased from Washburn by E. Miles, Esq., who, with T. R. Mason, Esq., continues proprietor. The name was changed many years ago from *Victoria to Hastings Chronicle.*

A Magazine of *cheap miscellany* was issued monthly, by Seth Washburn, &c., Belleville, 1847 & 8.

Playter, writing of the year 1824, says, "books, periodicals, and newspapers were scantily supplied to, and not much desired by the people as yet, the country was not old enough to give much encouragement and support to literature. Still, in the Methodist connection. the *Magazine*, (Methodist) was tolerably well circulated, no less than seventy subscribers were among the friends on the Bay of Quinté circuit at once. Newspapers were on the increase; nineteen were now published in Canada, and six of them twice a week. Quebec printed four, (of which one was French; Stanstead one, Brockville one, Kingston two, York two, Niagara one, Queenston one."

The *Colonial Advocate* was issued in the latter part of 1824, by William Lyon McKenzie.

We have a copy of the *Upper Canada Herald* before us, dated June 27, 1832, vol. xiv. which gives us the period at which it was started.

Barker's Canadian Magazine, published at Kingston, by Edward John Barker, M. D., commenced May, 1846.

The *Victoria Magazine*, a monthly periodical, was issued first in September, 1841, by Joseph Wilson, of Belleville, formerly of the Hallowell *Free Press*. Like many a one subsequently commenced. the *Magazine* had but a brief existence. It continued just one year.

The editors were Sheriff Moodie, and his accomplished wife, whose writings have gained for her a European reputation of no ordinary standing. Mrs. Moodie may be regarded as the pioneer of Canadian literature, and, as a long standing inhabitant of the Bay, she claims a brief notice in these pages, to give which affords the writer but a meagre opportunity to express his own high estimation of, and gratitude to a personal friend, whose kind words of encouragement has so frequently been a stimulus to action, when his energies flagged in this undertaking.

Morgan, in his *Bibliotheca Canadensis*, a most useful compilation, says: Mrs. Moodie is "well known in Canada and Great Britain for her works, and as an extensive contributor to the periodical literature of both countries. Born at Bungay, County of Suffolk, England, sixth December, 1803. She is a member of the talented Strickland family, of Beydon Hall, in the above County; four of her sisters, Elizabeth, Agnes, (the best known), Jane, and Mrs. Trail, have each contributed to the literature of the day. Both Mrs. Moodie and her sisters were educated by their father, who is represented to have been a gentleman of education, refined taste, and some wealth. Mrs. M. was only in her thirteenth year, when her father died. As early as her fifteenth year, she began to write for the press generally, for annuals and for periodicals, contributing short poems and tales for children. About 1820, she produced her first work of any pretension—a juvenile tale, which was well received by the public and the press. In the following year she married Mr. Moodie, a half-pay officer from the 21st Fusileers, and, in 1832, emigrated with her husband, to Canada. They bought a farm near Port Hope, which, however, they only held for a short time, removing to the back woods, ten miles north of Peterborough, where they settled. There they remained for a period of eight years, experiencing all the trials, mishaps and troubles incident to early settlers, and which are so graphically narrated and depicted by Mrs. M. in her "*Roughing it in the Bush.*" In 1839, Mr. Moodie was appointed Sheriff of Hastings, (an office from which he retired a few years since,) and, with his wife, took up his residence at Belleville, where they have since lived. During the existence of the *Literary Garland*, (Montreal), Mrs. M. was the principal contributor of fiction to its pages. For some years she edited the *Victoria Magazine*, (Belleville). Her contributions to these and other annuals, magazines, and newspapers, would fill many volumes."

The work for which Mrs. Moodie became more especially famous, was "*Roughing it in the Bush*;" but other volumes are exceedingly interesting, as "*Flora Lindsay*," "*Mark Hurdlestone*," "*Geoffry Moreton*," or the "*Faithless Guardian*," and "*Life in the Clearings*."

"John Wedderburn Dunbar Moodie, formerly Lieutenant in

the 21st Reg. of Fusileers," saw action in Holland, where he was wounded; he was a writer for the *United Service Journal*, *Literary Garland*, (Montreal), and author of "*Ten Years in Africa*," and "*Scenes and Adventures as a Soldier and Settler, during half a Century*."

The *Victoria Magazine* was succeeded by the *Eclectic Magazine*, Joseph Wilson being Editor and Proprietor. This monthly was also continued only one year. Mr. Wilson now commenced a "family paper called *Wilson's Experiment*, and soon after, in connection with it, *Wilson's Canada Casket*. These were issued alternately every two weeks, and were continued for two years. They had a large circulation, as Mr. Wilson avers, at the last about 6,000. The subscribers were not only in Canada, but in the Lower Provinces. The journals were discontinued, not because they did not pay; but in consequence of embarassment from other causes.

The *Bee* was the first newspaper published in Napanee, in 1851, by the Rev. G. D. Greenleaf, Editor and Proprietor. It was a small sheet, and semi-political, at one dollar per year. It was printed on a press of the owner's own construction, and continued two years, when it was succeeded by the *Emporium*, published by the same person, at the same office. It was somewhat larger than the *Bee*, and was two dollars a year. Its existence extended but little over a year.

The *Standard* was the third journal established at Napanee, 1853, by a joint-stock company. It was in the interest of the Conservatives. Its first editor was Dr. McLean, formerly of Kingston. Subsequently, the paper came under the management of Alexander Campbell, Esq., and continued for a few years. It then passed into the hands of Mr. A. Henry. It is still published by Henry and Brother.

The next paper, after the *Standard*, to be issued was the *Reformer*, by Carman and Dunham. There have subsequently been published the *North American*, *The Ledger*, and the *Weekly Express*. Besides the above, there was published, in 1854, continuing for two years, *The Christian Casket*, by E. A Dunham.

Trenton first possessed a newspaper in 1854. It was published and edited by Alexander Begg, and its name was the *Trenton Advocate*. The first number was issued March 4, 1854. About a year, afterward, the paper changed owners, and took the name of of *British Ensign*. It was continued about two years longer.

We have before us several copies of *The Canadian Gem and Family Visitor*, published at Cobourg; and edited by Joseph H.

Leonard, 1848. It is very readable. and exhibits no little enterprise. Also, we have *The Maple Leaf*; published at Montreal by R. W. Loy, 1853. Mr. Loy died not long after its issue. This also contains many interesting articles of a local and general nature.

In 1853, 158 papers are mentioned in the *Canada Directory*, of which, 114 are issued in Upper Canada. At the present time the number has much increased. Respecting the newspapers of Canada, Mr. Buckingham, who visited Canada in 1840, says that they are generally superior to those of the Provincial towns of the United States.

The following cannot fail to be of interest:

A Boston paper says, "Died—In the early part of the year 1813, Wm. Berczy, Esq., aged 68; a distinguished inhabitant of the Province of Upper Canada, and highly respected for his literary acquirements. In the decease of this gentleman, society must sustain an irreparable loss, and the republic of letters will have cause to mourn the death of a man, eminent for genius and talent."

CANADIAN IDIOMS.—The loyalist settlers of Upper Canada were mainly of American birth, and those speaking English, differed in no respect in their mode of speech from those who remained in the States. Even to this day there is some resemblance between native Upper Canadians and the Americans of the Midland States; though there is not, to any extent, a likeness to the Yankee of, the New England States. While the Yankee, and to some extent, the whole of the American people have steadily diverged from the pure English, both with respect to accent and idiom, as well as in the meaning attached to certain words; in Canada this tendency has been arrested by the presence of English gentlemen, often half-pay officers, and their families, by the officers of the Army and Navy, and as well by the school teachers, high and low, which were often from the old country. The accent of Canadians, and their idioms to-day, are to a certain extent peculiar, *sui generis*, which peculiarity is constantly increasing, even as the British American is assuming in appearance a distinct characteristic. Taking all classes of Canadians, it may be said that for a people far removed from the source of pure English, that is the Court, they have a very correct mode of speaking, the criticisms of English travelers to the contrary, notwithstanding. As education becomes more diffused among the masses there will ensue a very decided improvement in the mode of speaking among Canadians. Listening to the children at any school, composed of the children of Englishmen, Scotchmen, Irishmen, Americans, and even of Germans, it is impossible to detect any marked difference in their accent, or way of expressing themselves.

SUPERSTITION.—Although a few of the settlers had books to read, many had none. And as there were no school teachers very many children grew up without being able to read, or at most very little, and entirely unable to write, unless it might be their name. The writer has been struck with the difference between the composition and penmanship of many of the settlers and that of their immediate children, the former being good, the latter bad; while the parent could write a bold signature, and express himself in writing a letter, intelligibly, the offspring either could do nothing of the kind, or else made a very poor attempt. The result of this was, that the mind, starved for want of mental food of a wholesome nature, did not become inactive, but sought other kinds of pabulum. They derived a certain amount of information from the legendery tales told and retold of former days of happiness and plenty. Excluded from the world of literature, and secluded in a forest of eternal silence, except the tones uttered by the voice of nature, sometimes whispering in the gentle murmurs of the sighing wind, and sometimes thundering forth in the loudest voice,—shut up with nature they listened to her words, and not educated to understand her meaning, they undertook to interpret her speech, and oftentimes superstition of the deepest kind took possession of their minds. This prevailed perhaps more especially among the Dutch. Belief in ghosts, or "spooks" was a common thing, and before the bright and flickering light of many a hearth fire, during the winter nights, were told "stories" which lost nothing in their relating. And along the Bay were many old houses, once the homes of the settler which it was declared, was occasionally visited by the spirit of the builder, who returned to discharge some duty which rested heavily upon him in the spirit world, or who desired to reveal the place of concealment of some hoarded gold which had been so safely buried in some cranny nook.

A company of neighbours spending the evening would take their turn in telling of what they had seen or dreamed, or heard told; and at last when the bright sparkling fire had sunk into subdued embers, the consciousness of having to go home through the woods, or past a grave yard, would arouse the talkers. Shuddering at the thought, with imagination heightened by the conversation, they would set out on their path. It was at such times that the spirit of some recently departed one would be seen hovering over the grave, or floating away at the approach of footsteps. Strange voices came from the midst of the darkness, and unnatural lights flashed in the eyes of the midnight traveler. Should no sound or sight present themselves on the way, there was still a chance to experience much in dreams, when revelations of the gravest import would be made, which only had to be repeated three nights in succession to obtain the status of absolute certainty.

The traditions and recitals made known to the children were sometimes, not alone exaggerated, but untrue. The old soldier, or loyalist in his great hatred to the rebels, would sometimes unduly blacken the character of the fathers of the American Republic, for instance, the writer has heard it several times, told as a fact, that Washington was the illegitimate son of King George.

By some means a belief obtained, that at a place called Devil's Hill, at the Indian Woods, was concealed in the earth, a quantity of money, and parties used to actually go and dig for it. There was a huge rock here which was supposed to cover the precious metal, and a "bee" was formed, on one occasion to overturn it, but they found nothing to reward them for their pains.

DIVISION VII.

THE TERRITORY OF UPPER CANADA—THE BAY QUINTE.

CHAPTER XLI.

CONTENTS— The Indians—Their origin—Pre-historic Canada—Indian relics—Original inhabitants—Les Iroquois du nord—Original names—Peninsula of Upper Canada—Champlain exploring—Ascends the Ottawa—His route to Lake Nippissing—To Lake Huron—French River—The country—Georgian Bay—Lake Simcoe—Down the Trent—A grand trip—Bay Quinté, and Lake Ontario discovered—War demonstration—Wintering at the Bay—A contrast—Roundabout way—Erronous impressions.

CHAMPLAIN'S DISCOVERY OF THE BAY QUINTE, AND LAKE ONTARIO.

In this work but brief reference can be made to the general history of the Indians. Perhaps it is hardly necessary to explain that the term Indian, applied to the aborigines of America, took its origin from the fact, that when the New World was discovered it was supposed to be a part of the Indias (East Indias), the riches of which had led the intrepid navigator to seek a more direct route thereto. And consequently the natives were called Indians.

It does not lie within the scope of this work to speak of the several theories which have been given with respect to the origin of the natives, nor to advance any particular view. It is sufficient to remark that the character of the various tribes, their features, their traditions, and customs, all indicate most unmistakably that Asia was the original birthplace of the aborigines of America. Of course, reference is made only to those Indians whose representatives occupied the continent when discovered by Columbus, and not to those who had in some long past day held possession, who have left here and there indications of their rude character, and primitive mode of life, and who were swept away by the more powerful and warlike invaders—the predecessors of the aborigines of whom we now write.

In our researches we have collected a good many Indian relics, of the origin of which we have no record, and can only guess, while science strives to explain. We offer no views of our own, but give the following upon

PRE-HISTORIC CANADA.

From the Manchester *Guardian*. "At a meeting of the Manchester Anthropological society, on Monday, Mr. Plant made a communication upon some curious relics which he exhibited, of a race of pre-historic men, for which he was indebted to Mr. J. S. Wilson, of Perrytown, Canada West. These objects were obtained from the soil of the lands which have been cleared of the forests and brought into cultivation. It is only in the spring, when the snow has disappeared, that these objects are found, the winter snow acting like a riddle to the soil, and bringing to the surface the pebbles and broken pieces of pottery, flint, weapons, &c. The most interesting features connected with these relics is, that the localities where they are so frequently found are situated on the high level ground of ancient terraces, or beach lines, which may be traced at about 600ft. above the sea level, all around the great Canadian lakes, or, in fact, all around the high lands of the River St. Lawrence basin. There are three terraces at descending levels to the present shores of the great lakes. The highest terrace is the most ancient, and the evidences connected with this terrace all seem to point to the conclusion that it belongs to an age very remote, when the area now occupied by the great fresh-water lakes was filled by an inland bay, connected by a wide strait with the Atlantic, and was subject to the action of glacier ice from the land, as well as flows of icebergs from the current flowing from the north-east. The high terraces are, therefore, of marine origin, and the pre-historic objects found in them are indicative of a race of men whose habits were consistent with the physical features of the land and sea; a race of hardy fishers, living upon the whale, the walrus, the shark, and marine sources of food, together with the reindeer and Arctic animals. Since this remote time, the whole of the land about the lakes has risen from 600 to 1,000 feet above the sea, slowly and evenly through a great length of time, pausing twice sufficiently long to form two lower terraces; and at present is forming a fourth on the shore lines of the lakes. The pre-historic objects consist of great quantities of earthenware of rude make, quartz arrow heads, black stone adzes and hatches, sharp splinters of bone worked to a point, teeth drilled and bone needles, and bowls and stems of smoking pipes about six inches long. These last are singular and most interesting objects, and are solely confined to the North American continent, proving that the habit of smoking some narcotic plant has been indulged in by mankind from the most remote ages to which the geologist assigns the relics of pre-historic man, the age which immediately succeeded the glacial period."

All around the bay, as well as in other parts of Canada, may be found here and there indications of an extinct people whose sepulchral remains can be traced. Along the western portion particularly, are faint traces of mounds or tumuli which have been found to contain not only human remains; but objects of curiosity. For a more particular account of these the reader is referred to an interesting paper in the *Canadian Journal* for September 1860, by T. C. Wallbridge, Esq., of Belleville.

THE ABORIGINES OF UPPER CANADA.

"Dark as the frost-nipped leaves that strew the ground,
The Indian hunter here his shelter found;
Here cut his bow, and shaped his arrows true,
Here built his wigwam and his bark canoe,
Speared the quick salmon leaping up the fall,
And slew the deer without the rifle ball;
Here his young squaw her cradling tree would choose,
Singing her chant to hush her swart pappoose;
Here stain her quills, and string her trinkets rude,
And weave her warrior's wampum in the wood.

BRAINARD."

For many long years, perhaps centuries, before the white man saw the pleasant shores of the Bay, the Indian war-whoop was often heard, and the war dance performed along its borders. We know but little of those primal days. We cannot estimate the cruelties of barbaric warfare, natural to the aborigines, which have been enacted. We cannot count up the number of Indian braves who have moved upon its wood-begirted waters, as conquerors, or as captives, nor the woman and children carried away from their kindred—nor yet the total of the bleeding scalps which have hung at the girdle of the returning warriors, as they pursued the devious trail.

Early French travelers, generally Jesuits, have marked roughly the territory, which embraces in its area, the land extending from the Ottawa westward to Lake Huron, and from the St. Lawrence and Lake Ontario, northward to the French River, and Lake Nippissing. This was named the country of *Les Iroquois du Nord*, and, according to a map in the Imperial French Library, the land north of Bay Quinté, was called in 1656, *Tout-hatar*, and the land west to Lake Huron, was named *Conchradum*. There were, at the same time indicated at the eastern borders, the "antient

Hurons" and the "Outtawas" at the west, occupying the peninsula of Upper Canada, the *Neutre Nation de truite*, and at the mouth of the French river, *Mississagues*. It would seem at first, that the inhabitants were a branch of the Iroquois, or Six Nation Indians. But it may be that they had given to them the name Iroquois from their peculiar mode of expression, like the Indian to the south of the lake;—although not immediately connected. According to a map, examined by the writer, in the Imperial library at Paris, all the land between the Ottawa and Lake Huron was the Algonquins. A map by Champlain calls the land north of the Bay Quinté, *Lien force cerfs*. The northern Iroquois was divided into several tribes, each of which had a distinct name, and lived in considerable communities, here and there. The old maps are marked with sites of Indian villages, where, no doubt, they lived a greater portion of their time; probably the families remained most of the time, and also the males, except when away up the rivers to the north, upon hunting expeditions. Among these tribes and villages was the *Kentes*. Their village was situated at the east of Hay Bay, according to some maps; according to others, it was placed upon the south shore of Prince Edward, west of West Lake. Another tribe mentioned is *Gaungouts*. And along the north shore of the Mohawk Bay near Napanee, is marked an Indian village called *Gaunaroute*. Upon another map the village here is called *Gameydoes*. Just above the Carrying Place, near the harbour of Presq' Isle, is another village called *Ganaraske*, and a second one designated *Gonetoust*. Some of the maps here alluded to, bear date as late as 1703, while others are much earlier.

The waters of the bay and the lake adjacent, were looked upon as valuable for fishing, and the land as abundant in game. McMullen, in his History of Canada, speaks thus of the bay region. Referring to the year 1692, he states, "the Aborigines and French ravaged the frontiers of Massachussets, and revenged upon its helpless borderers the injuries suffered by the Canadians; detachments of troops swept the favorite hunting grounds of the Iroquois along the beautiful Bay of Quinté; and an expedition from Montreal did considerable injury to the Mohawks in their own country."

The peninsula of Upper Canada was called, in 1686, *Saquinan*—(Paris documents). The "Neutre Nation" was exterminated by the the Iroquois prior to 1650.

It is an interesting fact that Champlain arrived at Lake Ontario, or "fresh water sea," as he called it, being the first European to gaze upon its broad blue waters, by the way of the Bay of Quintè. This was in 1615. Prior to that he had penetrated by way of Sorel river, and the lake which has been named after him, and explored some part of the territory to the south of Ontario lake; but probably was not north of the Mohigan mountains, at least he did not then discover Lake Ontario. His principal object at this time was to create terror of the French arms, on behalf of the Six Nation Indians.

It was after a return from France, with a commission granting him extensive powers in the peltry traffic, that Champlain, with the view of protecting that trade, erected a fort on the site of Montreal. This done he directed his attention to the country lying unexplored to the north. Aware of Hudson's discovery in the north, of the bay now bearing his name, he was led to hope that by following the river Ottawa, of which the Hurons gave him some information, to its upper waters, he would be brought into close proximity if not actually to the bay, explored by Hudson. He accordingly set out accompanied by one or more of the four Recollet missionaries he had brought with him from France, and a considerable force of Hurons, with the view of ascending the Ottawa to its source. How far he penetrated into that rugged region, or how long a time he expended, does not appear. But it would seem that failing in his attempted discovery, he retraced his steps down the Upper Ottawa, until he reached the mouth of the Mattawan river, which empties into the Ottawa, and rises in the high lands to the west, approaching Lake Nippissing. As nearly as can be learned, Champlain was here joined by more warriors, who persuaded him to follow them and assist in a proposed attack upon the Iroquois nation to the south of Lake Ontario. His course was up the Mattawan river, through *la petite rivière* to *lac du Toulon.* Thence across to Trout Lake, Upper Trout Lake, and traversing the high lands, from which the waters flow in opposite directions; some into the valley of the Ottawa, and others towards the west. he descended the river *La Vase* into Lake Nippissing. Crossing this lake, he descended the French river into the Georgian Bay. In passing it may be observed that all the names, some of which are in French, and some in English, have a special meaning, and were applied, at least some of them, by the Indians. The Ottawa is so called not from the fact that the territory through which it runs was the home of the Ottawa tribe, but, because it was by its waters that they came to visit the French. The Ottawa river, that is, the river by which the Ottawas came. On the other hand the French river, which discharges into the Georgian Bay, was so called by the Indians, because it was the river by which the French came to their western domain. The length of French river is about 61 miles, and is a chain of lakes, connected by short rapids. Lake Nippissing is 69 feet above Lake Huron.

It is now 253 years since this voyage of discovery was made by Champlain, guided by the Indians. The appearance then presented to the intrepid navigator must have been exceedingly wild and beautiful, as he passed along the unknown way. Now swiftly gliding in the birch canoe upon the glassy waters of a lake, now dancing down the rapids, among rugged rocks, and green-clad islands; and anon, threading the devious path of a *portage*, beneath the lofty arches of the wilderness, making the first European footprints upon the virgin soil.

Deputy Surveyor-General Collins, writing to Lord Dorchester, by his command, in 1788, speaking of the French river says; "The entrance is composed of a considerable number of small islands and channels," the westernmost is the best navigable—about 250 feet wide, and has from two to three fathoms depth of water. It is narrower a little way up, and at about half a league from the entrance becomes exceedingly intricate, on account of the small islands and channels, which are here so numerous in every direction, and so much resembling each other in appearance, as to make it extremely difficult without a guide to find the true navigable channel, which, although deep in some places, is so narrow there is scarce room for two canoes to pass each other. The bank in these situations, is a steep rock, almost perpendicular, and there are very strong currents or rapids. The term Souters, sometimes given to the Mississauga Indians by the French, means to jump up and down, in reference to their living upon this river, and being expert in navigating its channels. "The country adjoining to; and near this, (river) is a rocky desert, nothing growing but small scrubby bushes and pine trees not thirty feet high—the same dreary prospect continues, I am informed, all the way up to Lake Nippissing, which is recorded twenty-five leagues." He states that the coast from the mouth of the river eastward is dangerous, for even canoes, although they may find shelter among the islands which lie along most of the coast. It is equally rocky and barren. Such was the nature of the way by which Champlain was led.

He now directed his course southward along the wild and irregular shore of the Georgian Bay, through the myriad islands that give beauty to that coast. Arrived at the mouth of the Severn river, he ascended that devious stream, and entered Sparrow Lake. Thence he crossed to Lake *Cowchouching*, which, at its southern extremity approaches to Lake Simcoe. Crossing the portage to this Lake, he ascended the River Talbot, in a north-east direction, and by frequent portages reached Balsam Lake. Then, through Cameron Lake, past Fenelon Falls, and into Sturgeon Lake. So on, by Pigeon Lake, Buck Hare Lake, Deer Lake, into Salmon Trout Lake. Turning south, by Clear Lake, he descended the Otanabee, or *Pamoduscoteong*, past the present site of Peterborough, and entered Rice Lake. Again turning east, he entered the head waters of the River Trent. Around by Heely's Falls, down by Cambellford, then, by Chisholm's Rapids, he arrived at the head of the Bay of Quinté, sometime in July, 1815.

Champlain took this route from the Ottawa, which had long before been traveled by the Indians, at the request of the Indian warriors who accompanied him, to make an attack upon their bitter enemy the Iroquois.

At the present day it would be a grand trip to make, by the way pursued by Champlain, when he visited the Bay region. But how wonderfully magnificent must it all have been to the bold, but educated French explorer of the primeval forest.

Champlain crossed the Lake to a point not far from Oswego. Whether he passed through the upper, or lower gap to the opposite side of the Lake, and coasted the south shore; or whether he ascended Picton Bay and crossed the Indian Carrying-place to East Lake, and thence into Ontario, may be questioned. But in order to make an unexpected attack upon the enemy, he had need to conceal his advance; hence it is reasonable to suppose he would take the nearer route by Picton Bay, although it would involve the crossing of the portage. This could scarcely be regarded as a serious difficulty, as he had already passed many in the devious route by the Ottawa.

Strange enough, that a European should discover Lake Ontario by entering the head waters of the Trent River, and sailing through the Bay of Quinté. Strange enough that a warlike demonstration should be made by this route, against a foe living upon the south shore of the Lake.

Champlain, notwithstanding his caution, found his Indian foes prepared to receive him, having well entrenched themselves, and he suffered a serious defeat, being glad to secure a safe retreat in the Bay of Quinté region, probably Prince Edward, after having himself received two wounds.

Failing in his efforts to obtain a guide to conduct him down the St. Lawrence, to his fort at Montreal, Champlain was compelled to spend the winter months, which were by this time approaching, in the vicinity of the Bay of Quinté. Probably six or nine months were passed by him upon the northern shores. He did not remain all the time at the Bay, as it is stated he visited the neighbouring Indian nations, especially the neutral nation which occupied the peninsula between Lakes Erie and Huron, and the head of Ontario. We can readily imagine the wide difference between a long winter thus spent in 1615–16, mid the wild scenes of aboriginal life by the ice-locked waters, and one spent in this latter part of the 19th century, with the highly cultivated land, and advanced civilization. Then, the trees of the forest, in one unbroken denseness, was the sole home of the savage, and wild beast, and waved in solemn mournfulness over the wintry landscape; while few other than nature's sounds disturbed the stillness of the wilderness. Now, the dark forest has disappeared and human habitations of comfort and luxury thickly stud the land. The wild beasts, as well as the original owners of the territory, have almost disappeared. The snow of the ice-covered bays and streams no longer remain unbroken by human foot. Sleigh roads thickly intersect the surface, and joyous shouts of the skater break upon the light pure air, while the gingle of sleigh bells indicate the everflowing stream of travelers. The strings of telegraphs sigh in the wind, instead of the tall trees' bough. The iron horse snorts along through the snow hills, instead of the beast from his lair. Towns and cities rest in peaceful security, where there were thick jungles of cedar and furs.

It was by this roundabout way that the Bay of Quinté was discovered; and it was fifty years later when DeCourcelles, pursuing the Iroquois from the Lower St. Lawrence ascended for the first time the river, direct from Montreal to Lake Ontario. But during this time missionaries had been at work among the Indians, upon the northern shores of the Lake—(See early Missionaries).

The impressions made upon the minds of these first explorers, respecting the Bay, seem to have been very erroneous; at least they have left maps not only rude, but incorrect. Thus, we find upon an old map intended to represent Lake Ontario and the Bay, with the country north of the Lake, the Bay is made to extend northward, at right angles with the Lake, for some distance, and then, turning westward somewhat, its extremity is brought very near to another bay, which empties into Georgian Bay.

CHAPTER XLIII.

CONTENTS—Name—Letter, Daily News—"Omega" Lines—The writer—Conjectures—Five Bays—Indian origin—Kentes—Villages—*Les Couis*—Modes of spelling—Canty—The occupants, 1783—Mississaugas—Origin—With the Iroquois—The *Souter*—Mississaugas, dark—At Kingston—Bay Quinté—Land bought—Reserves—Claim upon the islands—Wappoose Island—Indian agent—Indians hunting—Up the Sagonaska—Making sugar—Peaceable—To Kingston for presents.

THE NAME OF BAY QUINTE—THE ABORIGINAL INHABITANTS OF UPPER CANADA IN 1783.

There appeared in the "Daily News" of Kingston, October 20, 1856, the following letter and verses:

"SIR,—I send you a few lines in connection with what I believe to be an historical fact, though not generally known, even in the vicinity of the bay. When the French first took possession of Canada, or shortly after, they established posts at Frontenac, Niagara and Detroit.

In the fall following their establishment, the men under Col. Quinté, who commanded at Niagara, were driven out by the Indians, and pursued and harrassed several days, when following the lake shore to the west of the bay, they took the south shore of the bay and got to the reach. The snow was falling and ice making on the bay, without sufficient strength to carry them; when, nearly starved and exhausted, they started back two or three miles to what is known as Stickney's Hill, where (an extremely cold night coming on) they nearly all perished, including Quinté himself. Only two of the party (the ice having become strong) reached Frontenac. Hence the name of the bay."—(Signed,)—"Omega."

This note was accompanied with the following lines:

QUINTE.

On the Bay of Quinté gliding,
O'er its smooth and tranquil breast,
Whilst the sun is fast declining
To its waters in the west;
"And the gorgeous leaves of autumn,
In their varied gold and green,
Adds fresh glory to such beauty
As the eye hath seldom seen.

Yet this Bay had once its terrors,
Ere the red men were subdued,
And the scene that's now so lovely,
Was terrific, wild and rude,
When the gallant Quinté flying
From the savage of the west,
On the cheerless hills lay dying,
With fierce cold and hunger pressed;
And his bones were left unburied,
But his name won't pass away,
While there's beauty on thy hill-side,
Or thy waters gently play."

"STEAMER BAY OF QUINTE."

Mr. T. C. Wallbridge, to whom we are indebted for the foregoing, informs us that upon the day this was written, a learned judge (Robinson) now dead, was a passenger from Belleville to Kingston, and the inference was that *he* penned the lines, which must have been based upon what he considered facts. The same tradition has been received also, from other sources, and many living upon the bay, regard it as true. But it becomes our duty to question the matter. In the first place unfortunately, for the plausibility of the statement, the name of no such French officer can be found.

The nearest approach to the name of Quinté, held by any Frenchman known, was that of Prince de Conti. This person was a particular friend of Cavalier de la Salle, to whom was ceded the Seignory of Cataraqui. "Chevalier de Tonti, went with him, proposing to share his fortunes," in western explorations. Now La Salle, named one of the islands near Cataraqui, (Amherst,) after this officer, and even yet may be found living, persons who call that island, "Isle Tanta." Well, it might reasonably be supposed that La Salle would wish to do honor to his friend the Prince de Conti, and therefore named the bay after him. From Conti, it might gradually change to Canta, or Quinté. Now, however probable this may seem, it cannot be regarded as the origin of the name.

Again, it has been supposed to be derived from the Latin Quintanus, or Quinta,—the *fifth* place,—having reference to five bays, namely, the Lower Bay, Picton Bay, Hay Bay, the Reach, and Upper Bay; or, as some aver, it refers to five Indian stations, formerly existing in the vicinity of the bay. But, however much may be advanced in support of the plausibility of these theories, we think a more certain origin is perfectly intelligible.

The word Quinté, as at present spelled and pronounced, when

rightly done, is undoubtedly a French one, being one of the few remaining memorials of French possession; but its origin can be distinctly traced to an Indian source.

We have seen elsewhere that the country lying north of Lake Ontario was called the "Country of the Northern Iroquois." To the south of the lake was the Iroquois country proper. Among the several nations which composed the Iroquois Confederation, was the Seneques, or commonly called Seneca. Wentworth Greenhalgh in the "London Documents," writing of a journey in May, 1677, from Albany to the Indians, westward, says "the Seneques have four towns, viz: Canagora, Tiotohalton, Canoenada," (how like Canada), "and Keint-ho—which contained about 24 houses, and was well furnished with corn." In connection with this we find a statement made in the documentary History of New York, that some of the tribes belonging to the Iroquois proper, separated from them, and removed to the north of the lake. Now the Indian term, "Keint-he," be it remembered, was written by an English explorer, and of course was spelled in accordance with the pronunciations of the Indians. Every one knows that the letters of the alphabet have a different sound in the French language. If therefore, a French writer were to write the English term Keint-he, it is not unlikely he would spell it Kanta or Kente. Examining the old French maps, made by some of the early travelers through Canada, but bearing date subsequent to 1677, we find marked with distinctness, an Indian village, sometimes in one place, sometimes another, by the name of Kente. This may be seen on quite a number of different maps, which we have examined in various libraries in Canada, and in the Imperial Library in Paris. It is not always spelled Kente, sometimes it is Kante, and upon one it is Kenti, and upon a map in the Imperial Library, Paris, it is Kento. This Indian village has its location upon most of the maps, at the eastern extremity of Hay Bay; but upon a few it is placed at the south shore of the peninsula of Prince Edward; upon one map it is put at South Bay; while in another Wappoose island, is called Isle de Quinté. Hence it is inferred, that a branch of the Seneca tribe separated from the main body, and removed to the north of the lake, and settled probably first at South Bay, and afterward, or at certain seasons visited at Hay Bay, to which, in time they gave their name—that of Kente, according to the pronunciation of the French. It was an easy matter to convert Kente into Quinté. In other words, we find that *K* and *Qu* are used indifferently among early writers of New France; for instance, Quebec is spelled by early writers, Kebec. The origin of the word Quinté seems to be in this way perfectly clear.

The Indian village of Kente was situated at the eastern extremity of Hay Bay, and it seems plain that this was regarded as the head of the bay by the French, and the waters leading to the village, was designated the Bay Kente, or the Bay to the Kentes. The waters above the entrance to Hay Bay were looked upon rather as the mouth of the River Trent; and as quite another bay, to which was given a different name. This was a water way from Lake Ontario to Lake Huron. Travelers passing along would at times receive imperfect ideas respecting the names of the several bays and lakes. Again, the early French explorers, and the Jesuits, in their maps would frequently give the names, derived from the Indians, in Latin, while later French travelers gave the names in French. The consequence was that several different names were at times bestowed upon the waters stretching between Lakes Huron and Ontario.

One of the old French maps, and perhaps, it may have been prepared before the Kentes had settled upon its shores, gives to the bay the name "Bayedes Couis," while several islands between the south shore of Lake Ontario, and the north, are called "*au des Couis*, as if indicating a line of travel. There is one larger island, called *Les Couis*.

The waters west of the Long Reach are, in several maps which have been examined, named *Lac St. Lion*, and *Lionel*. But whether this name was limited to the uppers waters of the bay, or applied to the Trent, with Rice Lake, is doubtful, inasmuch as the maps represent the River Trent as being very wide and seemingly navigable up to almost the river's source. Again, the name of *Quinto* and *Quintio* are found upon a few maps, and are applied to Rice Lake. A map in the Imperial library, dated 1777, gives to Rice Lake, Quinto, and close by is the village of *Tonnaonto;* and the Bay Quinté proper, is called Lake *Tento*. Another map names it *Kentsio*. There is also a map which gives to Simcoe Lake, the name of *Œntarion* Lake, instead of Lake Taronto. From these varieties of names, we discover an indistinct connection between the words Kente and Toronto. Their origin and meaning it is impossible to trace. Perhaps they were names used only for a short time. It is worthy of remark, that upon an ancient map examined in the Imperial library, we find Lake Erie called *Lac. Conty*.

The word Quinté is in one or two places spelled Quintee, and also Quintie. The most common mode of pronunciation was that used by the loyalists. They spelled it generally Canty, or Kenty. Such they heard it called by the French and Indians when they came here; and, unacquainted with the French mode of spelling, they naturally rendered it according to the English idea; and we have found it in letters written, by the first settlers, mostly always spelled "Canty," or "Cante," and occasionally "Canta." The last of these approaches the nearest to the correct way of pronouncing the name; and it is a cause for regret that some years ago there arose the belief that it ought to be called "Quinty." We would request the inhabitants of the bay, to return to the old fashioned, and correct pronunciation.

The settlement upon the bay was sometimes identified with Cataraqui; being known by the refugees, as well as by those who stayed in the States, only by that name. Indeed, it may be said that all of Upper Canada was, for a few years, designated by that name; the settlements at Detroit and upon the Niagara, contiguous to the fort, being regarded as merely military stations. For many years the name Canada, was limited to the lower Provinces. After a few years the settlement along the bay came to be generally called, both by the settlers, and those who knew them abroad as that of the Bay "Canty." The writer has in his possession a letter dated from one of the townships upon the bay, in which reference is made to Canada as a place quite distant and distinct from the British settlements.

Mr. Ferguson, in a letter dated at Sidney, 23rd July, 1791, to a person at Kingston, says, "I'll send you a memorandum of what you'll want from Canada, and he further speaks about taking an Indian to Canada. By this we learn that the new townships were regarded as quite apart from Canada.

Before proceeding to speak of the appearance of the bay, a space must be given to speak more particularly of those Aborigines who occupied the territory of the bay, and Upper Canada generally, at the time of the revolutionary war, and from whom the British Government purchased the land to bestow upon the U. E. Loyalists, namely, the Mississaugas.

The meaning of the word Mississauga has reference to "many outlets," or a place of settlement by the "fork of a stream." The first noticewe have found of this name is upon a map in the Imperial library, dated 1620. It is applied to a lake,—*L'Missauga*, or

Buade. The location is not far from the source of the Mississippi River, and there is a small stream represented as running from this lake to empty into the Mississippi, the lake is doubtless the Itasca Lake in Minesota. The Indians, then inhabiting that region, was the "Eastern Sioux." There is no doubt some identity as to origin and meaning, between Mississippi and Mississauga. It will be remembered, we have in the north of Upper Canada a River Mississippi as well as River Mississauga. The Mississauga Indians first came into notice about the middle of last century, some time before the rebellion. They were then living east of the Georgian Bay upon the lake and the river, both of which have derived names from this tribe. Capt. Anderson thinks they took the name from living by this river, which has *many outlets.* It may be regarded as a question whether the river gave a name to the tribe, or the tribe a name to the river.

The Mississaugas have been more generally regarded as a branch of the Otchipewas. Father Charlevoix says, they are a branch of the Algonquins.

Towards the end of the seventeenth century, the Iroquois had quite overrun the territory formerly designated by the French "the country of the Northern Iroquois," and now constituting Upper Canada. As the Six Nations retired to their territory upon the south of Lake Ontario, the Chippewas, or Otchwas and the Mississaugas descended to the north shore of Ontario, the St. Lawrence, and around Bay Quinté. The exact time at which these tribes obtained possession of the land around the Bay, and its Islands, and other parts of Canada, is uncertain. But, long before the settlement of Upper Canada, they were the acknowledged owners of the soil, and Great Britain purchased from them the right of ownership. The first record we have of surrender of land, was by the Chippewas, in 1781, to Gov. St. Clair. The Mississaugas seem to have been a neutral nation, at least, they never appear to have taken any part in the wars between the French and English. But we find that "at a great assembly of chiefs and warriors, at Albany, in August 17, 1746, the chief speaker of the Six Nations, informed the English Commissioners that they had taken the Mississaugas as a seventh nation. There certainly seems to have been a very friendly relationship between the Iroquois and Mississaugas.

The Mississaugas were divided into several tribes, or rather, were divided into several villages. which were scattered all along the St. Lawrence, from the river Gananoque to the Bay Quinté, and

Lake Ontario. Thus, we find it recorded that "They were dispersed along Lake Ontario, South of Frontenac." This means Prince Edward particularly; but they were as well settled in little villages at different points. Charlevoix speaks of the Mississaugas as having a village at Niagara and upon Lake St. Clair; most likely at the mouth of the Thames. They likewise had villages along the upper waters of the Trent, and at the Don. Their armorial bearing, or "totem" was the crane, crow, muskrat, and beaver. The Kentés and Ganneyouses, two tribes of the Mississaugas, although taking no part in the wars against the French, had practised upon them a base act of treachery. In 1687, M. de Nonville, who was then Governor of Canada, being at Frontenac, invited these two tribes to the fort to hold a conference, and while there, seized forty or fifty men, with eighty women and children, who were sent prisoners to France.

The French called the Mississauga, while living in the west, the *Souter*, or Jumpers, because of the numerous rapids in the river Mississauga down which their canoes were wont to *jump*.

The Mississaugas are of a darker hue than any other tribe in the northern part of America.

The uncertainty that attaches to the Mississaugas as to origin, and the fact that they were not given to warfare; but seemed to be at peace with all native tribes, causes us to think that possibly they may have sprung from the dispersed "Neutral Nation."

At the time of the settlement of Upper Canada, the Mississaugas seem to have been the principal, if not the sole aboriginal occupants of the land. There are a great many "Mississauga Points" along the Bay, even at the present day, and there was a greater number at the first, all of which indicated the site of an Indian Village. At Cataraqui, just by the old fort, and Tete du Pont, was a Mississauga point, so called from its being the site of an Indian village. For years after the refugees entered, the Indians continued to dwell here, at least during certain periods of the year. The ground whereon a portion of the railway is laid, used to be the scene of many an Indian dance, to the tune of other music than the screaming of the iron horse, although no less inharmonious. Peter Grass was wont to tell of these scenes, whereat fearful orgies were witnessed by the lurid glare of their rude torches. "At the time of the peace, in 1783, the Mississaugas ceded to the Crown large tracts of land in the Johnstown, Midland and Newcastle Districts."—(Report).

The whole of the land contiguous to the Bay was purchased from the "Mississaugas of the Bay Quinté." The Indians, in relinquishing their claims to the land, had guaranteed to them certain stipulated payments yearly, in presents. We find it stated that "every man received two blankets, cloth for one coat and one pair of trowsers, two shirts, several small articles, besides a gun, ammunition, kettles, and other things."—(Playter).

"They claim, however, to have retained the following reserves." *Mississauga Point*, six miles below Belleville, about 1,200 acres; *Grassy Point*—in Sophiasburgh—about 600 acres; *Cape Vesey*, in Marysburgh, six miles east of Wappoose Island, 450 acres; *Bald Head*, at Weller's Bay, Ameliasburgh, 100 acres. "They also claim the islands eastward from Presqu Isle to Gananoque, Nicholsons' Island, in Lake Ontario, 250 acres, near West Lake, Wellington; Weir's or Tubb's Island, McDonald's Island, and Sugar Island, in all about 1,000 acres. The islands from Trenton to Kingston, and thence to Gananoque. Also, Green's Island, Timber Island, False Ducks, with others in Lake Ontario."

The Commissioners considered that the Indians had claims to compensation for their lands. As for the islands, the following extract from a letter from Sir John Johnson to the Military Secretary, dated Lachine, 9th October, 1797, will show their right to the Islands. "No islands were ceded to the Crown but Grenadier Island and the Islands between it and Kingston; two of which were granted to me, with the lands at Gananoque, by the Governor and Council, together with the Island of Tontine above Kingston, at the entrance of Lake Ontario." This was Amherst Island.

The portion of the Mississaugas to which the land belonged, were those subsequently known as the Bay Quinté, and the Kingston Indians. The same that lived for a time at Grape Island, and who now reside at Alnwick.

"The acceptance of the surrender of the Indians in 1856, by the Government, is an acknowledgment that these islands had never been ceded by them."

We thus learn that the Indian claims made to the islands and reserves in Prince Edward, were allowed by the Government. But the Indians claimed also that the treaty of cession, as they understood it when made, did "not include, a portion of land bounded on the north by a line which marks where the waters flow into the Ottawa River, and thence to the south, some thirty miles, to the head waters of some streams which flow towards the Lake, with a length of some sixty miles." But this claim was not considered as tenable.

According to the testimony of the first settlers, Wappoose Island, at the opening of Smith's Bay, was the abode of the Indian Chief; at least, he came here yearly to receive the rates from the settlers who had squatted upon it. The Indians went from this to Kingston, to get their presents, which they obtained from one Lyons, who it is said, was the first Indian agent there. He lived a quarter of a mile from the Market Place.

From the several villages, placed by the water board, the Mississaugas were accustomed to ascend up the rivers to the interior of the country for game. Of the different rivers, the *Saganaska*, (Moira), was, perhaps, more generally selected. Stoco Lake was a favorite hunting and fishing region, so named after a famous Mississauga Chief, Stougoong. They had a lot reserved at the mouth of the river, and also lot number four, in the second concession of Thurlow,—altogether 428 acres, which was sold in 1816, for £107. They generally ascended about the last of March, and returned the latter part of December. The writer can remember to have seen their birch canoes, well laden, passing up and down the river. Before the settlement of Belleville, they had their encampment on the plains by the river's mouth, but in later years they selected grounds some way up the stream. At first the trading post, kept by Chisholm, east of the river on the bay, was a point of attraction to them.

The Indians would make sugar in the spring, and bring it to the settlers in small basswood bags, which they would exchange for different articles.

The Mississaugas being a race of naturally peaceful disposition, the settlers never had any reason to fear them, even had the Canadian Government, like the American, forgot to recognize the rights of the natives, and owners of the soil. When under the influence of liquor they might assume a mock heroic character to intimidate women and children, in order to get something; but no attempt was ever made to disturb the settlers along the Bay.

Every year the Indians would go to Kingston to receive their presents, annually given by Government; sometimes there would be a hundred canoes.

CHAPTER XLIV.

CONTENTS—Appearance—Mouth of Bay—Length—The Peninsula of Prince Edward—Width of Bay—Long Reach—Course of Bay—The High Shore—Division of bay—Eastern, central, western—Taking a trip—Through the Reach—A picture—A quiet spot—Lake on the mountain—A description—Montreal Gazette—Beautiful view—Rhine, Hudson—Contrast—Classic ground—A sketch—Birth place of celebrated Canadians—Hagerman—A leading spirit—Sir J. A. McDonald—Reflections—A log house—Relics of the past—Lesson of life—In the lower bay—Reminiscences—The front—Cradle of the province—Shore of Marysburgh—In the Western Bay—Cuthbertson—Up the bay—A battle ground—Devil's Hill—Stickney's Hill—In the depths—Prosperity—Geological supposition—Head of bay—The past.

BAY QUINTE CONTINUED—ITS APPEARANCE.

Perhaps there is no sheet of water in Upper Canada possessed of greater natural beauty than this arm of Lake Ontario. At the eastern extremity of Ontario, where it merges into the St. Lawrence, with its 1692 islands, on the northern shore, is found the entrance to the Bay Quinté. In the early days of the settlement the name was limited to the waters west of Indian Point, at the extremity of Prince Edward Peninsula. At the present time the Bay Quinté is understood to include the sound between Amherst Island, and Wolfe Island, upon the south, and the mainland to the north. Our history is intended specially to embrace the events connected with the settlement of this region.

The bay, commencing where the St. Lawrence begins its mighty flow, extends in an irregular manner inland to a distance of some 70 miles, its western extremity approaching to within a short distance of the lake; and thus creating a lengthy peninsula, varying in breadth, the greatest being about 25 miles; but with a neck so narrow, that the peninsula is almost an island. The width of the bay varies, averaging about a mile; but in some places it is two miles. Not only is the bay irregular in its direction; but there are many indentations, some several miles in length, which increase the irregularity, and add beauty and variety to the scenery.

The course of the bay from the lower gap, is at first, for some 35 miles almost due west. It then makes a turn toward the north, tending a little to the east; while to the south is an indentation forming the Picton Bay. This portion of the bay is called the Long Reach, and in its length, presents some of the most striking beauties of the whole bay. Extending to the south of the Reach is a lengthy indentation five or six miles long, forming Hay Bay. At the northern extremity of the Long Reach, is another small bay into which the Napanee River empties, called the Mohawk Bay. Here the main body of water makes another turn, and again, stretches almost directly westward, to the head of the bay. At a distance of eight miles from Mohawk Bay there is a material widening of the water. This portion is called Big Bay. The width does not appear so great in consequence of the existence of islands, one of which, the Big Island, stretches along the south shore even the whole length of Big Bay. At the western limits of the wide part, the bay is very narrow by reason of two opposite points, Mississauga and Ox Points, approaching to within a half mile of each other. It is the opinion of geologists, that the channel between these two points is of comparatively recent formation, caused by a sinking of the land, and that the old channel was through the marsh which divides Mississauga point from the peninsula.

The High Shore, which forms so prominent a feature in the scenery of the bay, and the highest summit of which is at the Lake on the Mountain, is a remarkable formation. Commencing in Marysburgh, near the East Lake by the shore of Lake Ontario, it follows the course of Smith's Bay eastward, down the shore to what is called "the Rock," thence across the peninsula to the bay and so follows the course of the bay upward, around Picton Bay, and thence along the eastern front of Sophiasburgh to a point opposite Hay Bay. Here the hill leaves the bay shore and takes a westerly course, and stretches away toward the lake, to the south of the Carrying Place.

The Bay of Quinté may be divided into three portions—an eastern, a western, and a central portion. The eastern and western portions, we have seen, run east and west. The middle portion, connecting these two together, is a reach of some twelve miles and mostly north and south, from Picton Bay to Mohawk Bay. Undoubtedly the "Long Reach" possesses the most attractive scenery, from the waters themselves, along the whole sheet, from Kingston to the Carrying Place. To obtain some idea of the scenery here presented, the reader is invited to accompany the writer, in imagination, upon the steamer from Mill point, Tyendinaga, or the Indian Woods, to Kingston. It is upon a bright morning in September. Leaving the wharf at Mill Point, our boat makes a graceful sweep and turns here prow down the bay toward the Reach. The power of the sun is beginning to be felt, and the mist which has rested upon the waters is gradually rising. After leaving the wharf a few minutes, an angle is reached from which we can look up through the Big Bay almost to Belleville, and, at the same time down the Reach, into Picton Bay. This morning, on glancing upwards, a lovely view presents itself. The water is like glass, from which the mist, here and there, is rising like a sheet of the purest snow. Resting in the glassy bed are several schooners, whose white sails and rigging are perfectly mirrored by the unrippled surface of the water. Turning our gaze down through the Reach, even a more beautiful sight is before us. From this stand point we seem to be looking through, as it were, a telescope, at the distant shores of Picton Bay. The sun's rays have not yet reached the deep and narrow channel, so that a thick covering of white mist hides the water, excepting here and there, where its lovely blue may be seen, as it reflects the azure sky. A vessel with snowy sails, seems to be resting against the high shore, while its hull is half enshrouded in the fog. To the right, over a point of low land, may be seen the top mast of another vessel, which, in an indentation of the bay, is as if left upon the dry land by a retiring flood. It has always seemed to the writer that this is the most delightful and picturesque spot upon the bay, and he has endeavored, in but an imperfect way, to draw to it the attention of tourists, who may desire to see the more enchanting scenes connected with the bay. Proceeding on our way down the Reach, the steamer stops at Roblin's wharf upon the right. Here, in a little dell, leading into a peaceful valley pleasantly wooded, which leads up to the high shore, is situated Mr. Roblin's buildings. For a quiet place in which to live during the summer, where one may forget the cold artificial world, it is unequalled. To the right is the bold high shore, which protects from the northern wind. Spread out before, is a beautiful landscape. There, is another view of Adolphustown, with its many points, and corresponding indentations, the home of peace and plenty. There, is the entrance to Hay Bay, and more directly opposite, the elevated shore, well crowned with trees, still clothed in green.

We now continue our voyage close to the precipitous rocks which form the shore, and presently we approach the mouth of Picton Bay. Here again is obtained a varied and delightful prospect, ere we leave this "Grand Bay," as it was at first called.

Issuing again from Picton Bay, our steamer glides along in the shadow of the eastern shore, and approaches the Stone Mills, at the foot of the lake on the mountain. The captain will wait until we have ascended, and viewed the lake, and the magnificent prospect spread out around. But the brief time allowed to accomplish the ascent affords no adequate chance to take in the exceeding loveliness, and call to mind the historic events connected with the country within view. So we shall detain the tourist for a days' inspection of the scene.

The Lake of the Mountain is a curiosity of no mean order. The following, taken from the Montreal *Gazette*, published in the summer of 1834, is worthy the place we give it:

"The Lake of the Mountain is one of the most remarkable objects in the District of Prince Edward. This singular body of water is about five miles distant from Hallowell, (Picton). It is situated on the top of a lofty eminence, about one hundred and sixty feet above the level of the Bay of Quinté. The manner in which it is bounded is rather singular. In one direction it is only separated from the waters of the Bay below by a ledge of limestone rock, about eighty feet high, and by a precipitous embankment, which extends half way around it. In every other direction it is skirted by a ridge which rises to the height of 40 feet above the level of its surface. This Lake is about five miles in circumference. Its waters are at present applied to propel only a grist mill and a fulling machine. An artificial canal has been cut, along which the water is conveyed to the edge of the embankment, from whence it is conducted by a wooden raceway to the mills, which are situated near the margin of the bay below. The original outlet of the lake is at a few paces distance from the raceway. At this place the surplus waters formerly escaped through an orifice in the precipice I formerly mentioned, and after dashing over the rocks below, ultimately found their passage into the Bay.

"When I first heard of this lake, the most incredible stories were related to me concerning it. The gentleman who first directed my attention to it, absolutely told me that it was supplied by a subterraneous passage from Lake Erie, that there was no inlet in the neighborhood, capable of affording it a supply, and lastly, that it was unfathomable, or that its bottom was lower than that of the adjoining part of the Bay of Quinté. Such information as this, communicated by a well-informed Barrister, did not fail to excite my curiosity, and I accordingly set out to examine it with feelings of considerable anxiety.

"What led to the absurd idea that this lake was supplied from Lake Erie, I am at a loss to understand. It contains no springs, and the banks of that part especially from which it is viewed by strangers, being all so low that no inlet is visiblo, it might, perhaps, have been thought impossible to account for its source by any other means. The absurdity of the notion is, however, so glaring, that I would not spend a single moment in exposing it, had it not taken strong hold of the imagination of a great proportion of intelligent people residing in this part of the country.

"If the Lake of the Mountain were supplied from Lake Erie, its waters should experience a corresponding rise and fall with those of Lake Erie. This, however, they do not, for last year the waters of Lake Erie were higher than usual, while those of the Lake of the Mountain were very low. Again, this year, the waters of Lake Erie were lower than usual, while those of the Lake of the Mountain are very high.

"Further, if the Lake of the Mountain were supplied from Lake Erie, it should be altogether uninfluenced by any state of the weather in its neighborhood. This, however, is not the case, for in wet weather it becomes high, and in dry weather it becomes low. When I first visited this lake, its waters were nearly upon a level with its banks, and when I saw it some months afterwards, they were seven or eight feet above them. This was after a continuance of dry weather.

"From all this it is evident that Lake Erie does not furnish the supply of the Lake of the Mountain, and that it must be looked for in some other quarter. Being determined to discover from whence this supply was derived, I proceeded along the east side of the lake for about a mile, upon the top of the eminence which separates it from the Bay of Quinté. I then entered the woods and began imperceptibly to ascend, until I found, by again coming in site of the lake, that I had reached an elevation of about forty feet above it. Continuing to proceed for two or three miles, I descended, in the same imperceptible manner, to the place from which I first set out. In the course of this journey, I crossed no less than five different water-courses, four of which were dry at the period of my first visit, but all of which I have since seen pouring out very considerable quantities of water. The fifth is a beautiful stream flowing into the lake over successive ledges of limestone rock, underneath the rich foliage of the trees by which it is overarched. This stream affords the chief supply to the lake, and judging from the appearance of its channel, it must be sometimes upwards of a foot deep. In the spring and fall, when the greatest quantities of water are discharged by it, I have distinctly heard the noise which it makes at a distance of two miles, and on the opposite side of the lake, as it dashes over the rocks. The whole of these rivulets proceed from two extensive swamps. That from which the largest arises is situated to the south west of the lake, and is about three or four miles in circumference.

"The depth of the lake next claimed my attention. Having procured a sufficient length of line, I pushed out upon its waters in a small scow. For a considerable distance we distinctly perceive the bottom, which consists of dissolved, or rather corroded lime, so loose and light that with little or no exertion one may push the whole length of his oar into it. Continuing to look downwards upon the beautiful white bottom as we sail along, we start instinctively upon finding that we all at once loose sight of it, and that we gaze into a deep, dark, frightful abyss, which is formed by the sudden appearance of a precipitous ridge, running right across the lake. Nothing can exceed the amazement—terror, I had almost called it—which some people express on finding themselves surrounded by lofty, dark woods, and floating upon the surface of water as black as ink, over an abyss which they have been told is quite unfathomable.

"After having sailed over the lake in every different direction, and taken an immense number of soundings, I found its greatest depth to be only ninety-one feet. The bay below I found to be eighty-two feet. Now as the lake is about one hundred and sixty feet above the level of the bay, it follows that the bottom of the lake is one hundred and fifty-one feet higher than that of the bay.

"Thus, then, it appears that the Lake of the Mountain does not derive its supply from Lake Erie, that its source is to be found in its immediate neighbourhood, that it is not unfathomable, and that its bottom is not lower than that of the Bay of Quinté.

"The Lake of the Mountain is however, an object of sufficient interest, without adding to its wonders those of a subterraneous communication with Lake Erie, and an unfathomable depth. There is, for instance, the very singular manner in which it is separated from the Bay of Quinté, by a wall of solid rock, and the extraordinary form of its basin. The fine views, too, with which the mountain abounds, ought to be sufficient to attract the attention of all those whose minds are capable of enjoying the various forms in which beauty may be contemplated.

"Nothing can surpass the savage grandeur of the scene we look upon from the summit of the limestone rock I have so often mentioned, nor can a lovelier prospect be anywhere found than that which breaks upon the view, on first reaching the top of the mountain. To the north and west, we behold the Bay of Quinté, stretching far away into the land, and dividing itself into many beautiful inlets. There are too, the promising settlements and clearances all along the coast, which can never fail to raise and exhilarate the spirits of every one who wishes well to the destinies of his species. There is, however, one view at this lake, which, above all others, I have most delighted to enjoy. It is from the woods, upon the most elevated part of the eminence which bounds the lake to the south. From this we behold the deep dark waters of the lake beneath our feet, the bay of an hundred arms, with its smiling coast, and far away we gaze upon forest rising behind forest, until we are lost in the interminable—the dreamy distance.

"I have visited this place when the surrounding woods shone in all the gorgeousness of summer sunshine. I have viewed it again by the pale moonlight, when the splendour and magnificence of the scene surpassed even what it exhibited when viewed by the broad light of day. The lake below, and the distant bay, appeared like sheets of molten silver, and every object was softened down by the mellow light under which they were viewed. At first the sky was perfectly cloudless, but, in the course of the evening, the scene gradually underwent a change. On the one hand, the moon shone out with a degree of splendour which no one can have any idea of, save they who have beheld her chaste countenance peering above a Canadian forest. On the other hand the thin, fleecy-looking clouds rapidly chased each other up towards the zeinth. As the evening advanced, gleams of purple lightning at intervals streamed forth. At length one large cloud which seemed to be the nucleus of the whole, shot from around its margin successive flashes of pure white lightning, unaccompanied by the slightest noise of thunder. As I gazed on the brilliant spectacle before me, it seemed instantly to assume the shape and form of the bust of some gigantic being. The longer I looked at it, the brighter did the lightning blaze around it, and the more forcibly was I impressed with the resemblance. It might have seemed to a superstitious or highly imaginative mind, as if the great Spirit of nature had deigned to reveal himself, amid the grandeur and sublimity of a scene so congenial to his character."

We would supplement this just tribute of praise, and interesting statement; and we venture to say, after having viewed many lovely spots in the old and new worlds, that we know of no lovelier panoramic view than that to be obtained from the Lake of the Mountain, not even excepting the far-famed Hudson, and the classic Rhine. Of course we except the rich relics of the old feudal days, which so picturesquely adorn the mountain tops along the swift running Rhine. But even here we are not destitute of historic reminiscences. True, we have no embattled towers, resting on rugged summits; no castle keeps, with mysterious dungeons, upon whose walls may be traced the letters laboriously cut by long retained captives; no crumbling walls and half-filled moats; no magnificent ruins of graceful architecture. We possess no Tintern Abbey by the quiet waters, to tell of the olden time; no gloomy cloisters where comfortable monks did dwell; nor romantic cathedral whose antique windows admitted but dim religious light. Still, there is something to be said of the past, in connection with our country. From our position here we may examine the classic ground of Upper Canada, and trace the course of settlement followed by our fathers, the pioneers.

At our feet is the bay, and seemingly so near, that one could toss a stone into the clear blue water; and across, at the distance of a mile, though apparently much nearer, lies the low rich land of Adolphustown. To the right stretches, in almost a straight line, the waters of the bay, along which may be seen the well settled shores even to Ernesttown, and over which we get a view of the Upper Gap, where the waters of the bay co-mingle with the more boisterous flood of Ontario. Upon this bright autumn day the view is almost enchanting. The surface of the waters of the several indentions, especially Hay Bay, as well as the main channel, have imparted to them the bright blue of the sky, while the fields of rich green and gold give variety to the scene. This rich landscape spread out before us is really the classic ground of Upper Canada. Within the compass of our view was for several years the western limit of the settlement. We can see, where landed the refugee loyalists to take possession of the land. Along that green and golden sloping shore has slowly passed the batteaux laden with the settlers and their limited household effects; there also has gone the Skenectady boat with its ungainly soil, and toiling rowers. There, upon the rich land of Fredericksburgh and Adolphustown, lived and died many of the fathers of Canada. In the old homesteads, which there gradually arose, were born, and spent their boyhood days, a host of sons, who, moving further west up the bay and lake, planted the townships. From that spot sprang many of Canadas earliest public men, who passed their younger days among these natural beauties which belong to the bay. Under our eye is the birth-place of Judge Hagerman, Sheriff Ruttan, and others, who have left a name upon the pages of Canadian history. There, upon the front of Adolphustown stands the old Court House, where were held the first Courts of Law of Upper Canada; there flourished the earliest lawyer of the Province, Judge Hagerman's father, and there pleaded McLean of Kingston, in his robes and powdered wig. And, there yet stands the house where lived the little boy, who, now a man, is the leading spirit in our enlarged Canada. Upon this hill, and up and down its slopes, often played this, the foremost man in British America, Sir John A. McDonald. Those four townships, Kingston, Ernesttown, Fredericksburgh, and Adolphustown, were the early homes of those who faithfully served their country. How many thoughts are suggested as the student of history looks abroad on this the first inhabited land of Western Canada. Many of the present inhabitants here never heard of the noble ones, who have struggled, and whose bones now decay in yon "U. E. burying ground," just across the water.

Descending the mountain, we will continue our voyage toward Kingston. The next stopping place is Adolphustown, the history of which is given elsewhere. We have to cross the water, and as we approach the landing, we may see the splendid farm where lived the leader of the original settlers, Major VanAlstine. The village of Adolphustown, once one of the most important places in Upper Canada, is now a quiet but pleasant spot, especially during the summer days.

Proceeding on our way, we may observe, just west of Coles' Point, where settled the very first person in Adolphustown, a small log house. It is much larger than those which sparsely dotted the bay shore seventy years ago. But it reminds one, of the first domiciles here erected. Divided into two, one part having been first built, and the other, when a growing family made it desirable, and means possible. This old log house close by the shore is a lingering specimen of an almost extinct feature of the bay. See here and there those tall poplar trees, brought in by the early settlers from the Hudson valley, and planted in front of the dwelling; many of them are yielding to the tooth of time. These trees generally mark the spot where the settler erected his second home after years of labor had prospered him. In many places they stand erect, but with age stricken limbs, as faithful sentinels over the ashes of the old homestead. Ashes indeed! For the crumbling chimney alone indicates where was once the abode of the pioneer—of life's cares and hopes, of doubt and expectation—of all the ins and outs belonging to the home of the pioneer. We have read to us the lesson of life; there, are the graves of the brave old veterans and pioneers, and there, the dust of their earthly dwellings. Ashes to ashes! Dust to dust!

In the lower bay particularly have come to pass many events of varied import, and fraught with thrilling interest. Here, in times anterior to the French rule in Canada, did the native tribes come to hold their councils, to make treaties, form alliances, or declare war. Here, at the mouth of the Cataraqui; or along the shores toward the little Cataraqui, the French first fixed their place of meeting, and trade with the Indians who lived afar off in the west. Over these waters have Champlain, the French Recollets, the first discoverers, La Salle, Father Hennepin, Chevalier de Tonti, La Barre, Denonville, Conte de Frontenac and others, passed time after time. Over the waters here floated the English under Bradstreet, upon the 25th August, 1750, who, at the break of day were to besiege Fort Frontenac, and to capture it.

The close of the war in 1783, brought the disbanded soldiers and many a refugee. Along the shores passed the whole of the

Mohawk Indians on their way to their lands. Here the Nation separated, a small party under Captain John, passing up the Bay of Quinté, while the majority passed up the south shore of the lake to the Grand River For years after might have been seen day after day, batteaux, singly, or in brigades, and at a later date Skenectady boats, freighted with families old and young, and with a few precious household effects, slowly and laborously pulling their way to their place of destined settlement. In the war of 1812, the American fleet ventured in at the upper gap and passed along at a safe distance from the field artillery that occupied the shore at Herchimer's Point. They were essaying to capture the Royal George; but this attempt was as vain as that to over-run our province. Into these waters entered the vessel of war, bearing the officers of Hull's army from Detroit, which they boastingly had declared would conquer Canada. From these waters issued some of the first sailing vessels of Lake Ontario. Here was likewise built the first steamboats upon the lake and bay, the *Frontenac* and *Charlotte*.

Upon the shores of these pleasant waters was commenced the survey of the ten townships around the bay. Here was the starting point of settlement. Here, for many a year, was the central point of Upper Canada. Along from Cataraqui up to Collin's Bay was the great front of the infant settlement. Going up the bay, even to Adolphustown, was regarded for several years as going far into the backwoods.

Along the north shore of the bay to Adolphustown, were enacted those scenes which constituted the very first events of Upper Canadian history. The front of Kingston township may, indeed be called the birth place, and the front of Adolphustown the cradle, of the province. Every farm along this shore has its history, which if written in the noble spirit that animated the British American Loyalists, would command the attention of the world. These quiet old homesteads now reposing upon the gentle slopes in peace and plenty, tell not of the hardships of the old soldiers and refugees, who, with ticket in hand entered to commence the earnest work of clearing. Mainly, in the third and fourth townships, the officers settled by the bay, while the rank and file took up lots in the second and rear concessions. The first four townships are indeed, the classic ground of Canada.

Nor is the south shore of the bay, Marysburgh, devoid of interest in an historic sense. Reserving for another place a full account of the first settlement by the Hessians, we can but glance at the fact that a band of men without any knowledge of the English language, and unacquainted with the first principles of pioneer life, constituted the first settlers. There, in McDonald's Cove landed he, after whom the name is given; and there, amid the woods and upon the bright waters, he passed his days.

We commenced our trip and observations at Mill Point, and proceeded down the bay. Let us return, and starting from the same place proceed to the head of the bay, the Carrying Place. This part of the bay possesses less of that picturesque beauty than is found in the part over which we have passed; yet there is much to engage the attention of the tourist.

Mill Point, although a name suggestive of enterprise and of the existence of mills; cannot be regarded with approbation, and it is to be hoped that some appropriate name, commemorating some past event or person, connected with the place, will be bestowed upon it. It was for many years known as "Culbertson's wharf." The proper name, however, was Cuthbertson. It was from the son of a Scotch fur trader who became connected with the Mohawks. He lived at Kingston for many years, leaving when he died a natural son and daughter, by a daughter of Captain John. After his death, she and the two children removed to the Mohawk village. It was this son who first built the wharf here, and hence the original name.

Continuing our way up the bay, leaving to the east the pleasant inlet stretching up to Napanee, the first thing to attract our attention is the Parsonage and Indian Church, embowered in the beautiful forest trees. The Parsonage first strikes our view, where resides the amiable and worthy clergyman Mr. Anderson. In front of it is a solitary poplar with the branches partially decayed. It marks the spot upon which the tribe first landed, when they came to the place in 1784. Here they first spread their tents. Somewhat to the east of this stood the first English Church, the foundation of which can yet be traced. Near by sleeps the remains of Captain John, the leader of the tribe, and likewise many other warriors.

A half mile to the west of the Church, is an eminence, which tradition points to as the battle ground between the ancient Missisaugas and the Hurons. Further westward is Devil's Hill, so called because a drunken Indian declared he there had seen, one night, his Satanic Majesty, and chased him all night. Then comes Eagle Hill, once the abode of this Imperial bird. To the south, first lies the low island, known as Captain John's, bought by Cuthbertson who built the wharf, from the Mississaugas. Then comes the north front of Sophiasburg, rich in agricultural beauty. The first eminence by the shore is Stickney's Hill, once the burying place of Indians, but erroneously supposed to be the spot where a Col. Quinté, with his army, perished from hunger and cold. In the depths of the waters over which our boat now glides, it has been recorded, have been seen cannon and ammunition, and other warlike material, which Col. Quinté vainly endeavored to take across on his way to Fort Frontenac. But the truth is, if such material have been seen, they were the contents of a military sleigh which, while passing up through here in the winter of 1812-13, heavily laden, broke through the thin ice. We now enter Northport, at the eastern side of Big Bay; and the land, on every hand, tells of comfort and thrift, and quiet peace. Next, the wider portion of the Bay, which has received the name of Big Bay, is passed over. To the left is Big Island, and Grape Island, where the Rev. Mr. Case endeavoured to civilize and Christianize a community of Mississaugas. We now pass through the Narrows, and the spires of Belleville Churches may be seen in the distance. From Big Bay to the Carrying Place, there is great uniformity in the appearance of the land on either side, excepting upon the south shore at about seven miles from the head of the Bay. Here, where is the Village of Rednersville, is a somewhat remarkable hill, which, commencing at this point, extends up along the Bay toward the end. It is separated from the western extremity of the High Shore by a valley, through which, at one time, the waters of Ontario flowed; and, when this hill was an island. The rock of this hill consists of shaly limestone, similar to that which forms the bed of the Moira. We now approach the end of our voyage, and, as the steamer enters the port at Trenton, we can see the basin which forms the end of the bay, in which rests one Island known as Indian Island. Taking the Bay Quinté in its whole extent, the events of the past belonging to this quiet sheet of water, are of no ordinary interest. The tourist of to-day, while he admires the beauty as he passes along, sees no trace of the past. The placid water, no more reflects the trim and light canoe of birch, no longer the clumsy, but staunch batteau, or Durham boat, nor the Skenectady boat. No more is heard the oar of the Canadian voyaguer. keeping time by tuneful voices.

CHAPTER XLV.

THE SEVERAL BAYS.

In looking at the main channel, we have mentioned several indentations, which have, from their size, received distinct names. We will now examine these more particularly.

About twenty miles from the Carrying Place, and eight miles east of Belleville, is *Big Bay*, meaning, originally the big part of the Bay. As before stated, its size does not appear so well marked as it otherwise would, from the existence of a large island which lies in the south part of the Bay, and which is, seemingly a part of the main land. To the north is a small bay, where the Salmon River empties. Between Mississauga point, which forms the western boundary of Big Bay, and Huff's Island, is another inlet from Big Bay, which is called by the inhabitants *Musketoe Bay*, or sometimes, erroneously, "Miscouter" Bay. It is, mainly, but a marsh, in which the Muskrat finds a home, the wild duck a safe retreat, and where myriads of musketo may, in their season, be found. This last mentioned fact explains the origin of the name. It is stated that, before the adjacent land was cleared, the swarms of insects was so thick as to actually cloud the air.

At the junction of the western and middle portions of the Bay is the *Mohawk Bay*. This name is derived from the residence here of the Mohawk Indians, who came in 1784, and consequently is of no older date than the settlement of Upper Canada. The original name was *Ganeious*. The Bay is about five miles in length, and a mile wide at its mouth; it gradually lessens until it forms the mouth of the Napanee river. In summer the scenery along this Bay is very agreeable, and in some places really beautiful. The second flouring mill having been built in 1785, Mohawk Bay and the Napanee River were well known by early settlers, and along these shores, now well cultivated fields, there have passed many a time the batteau laden with grain, or the canoe with a bag of gristing; or along the shore trudged the pioneer with a bushel of corn on his back, or in winter hauled it upon a hand sleigh.

Hay Bay.—From the entrance of Mohawk Bay southward, along the reach about seven miles, is another inlet. This is *Hay Bay*, and, by far, the largest of the several Bays. By looking at the map, it will be seen that this indentation is somewhat divided into two almost equal portions by a narrow channel; and that the eastern part is considerably broader than the western. This narrow channel was originally called, according to an old map of Fredericksburg, dated 1784, the "Long Reach," and the east end, the "Eastern Bay." This was then regarded as the real end of the Bay Quinté. The "North Channel," leading to the Mohawk settlement, was but little known, and not taken into consideration. It must be remembered that the names originally given to the several portions of the Bay were such as the circumstances of the settlers would be likely to suggest. The soldiers who settled on the front of the third township soon learned that in the rear was a Bay, by which they could reach the back concessions. Some crossed the peninsula, while others reached their lots by making a circuit of the Fourth Town shore. The distance to them as they toiled in the batteaux, seemed a long stretch, and hence it was called the "Long Reach," while the wider portion, at the end of the Bay was named Eastern Bay, or the most eastern bay. Here, as we have seen, dwelt the ancient Kentes. The name of Hay Bay must have been given to this sheet of water about 1786. In the absence of any certain knowledge of the origin of the name, we have concluded that it was so called, out of respect to his memory, after Lieut-Governor Hay, who died at Detroit, 29th August, 1785, "after twenty-nine years service." This was the year previous to the time of the first settlers locating here. The name was, most likely, given by the Surveyor, who, in accordance with the custom, named everything after some influential or prominent person, or friend. While advancing this theory of the origin of the name, we must not omit to mention, that when the country was opened up there was, growing in some places upon the bay shore, wild hay. This may possibly have given rise to the name; or the name may have been taken from Chief Justice Hay. Hay Bay, although possessing no particular features of beauty, has a charm peculiarly its own, as being the original Kente Bay. It is not wanting in historic interest. Along its shores, now so fertile, for long years existed abundant game; a fact well known to all the neighboring tribes. Although no settler took up land here until 1786, there were among them individuals who took no unimportant part in the war against rebellion. Upon the south shore lived and died some families who acted more than ordinarily venturesome parts during the contest, as the Huycks, Miss Loyst, who married a Diamond, and whose two brothers were with Sir John Johnson at Hungry Bay. Here settled three Embury's, David on the north shore, who was brother of Philip Embury, the first Methodist Preacher in America. On the south side lived Andrew, and John Embury, and the first family of the Bogarts of Canada, descendents of the first Moravian minister, to America. Also, here lived Judge Fisher, Squire Beegle, James Knox, the first Quaker Preacher in Canada. Upon the north bank, while the colony was yet in its infant days, was committed, probably, the first act of suicide in the country. An event even yet remembered by some. And, more than all, it was upon these waters where occurred an accident, which filled the whole Bay country with horror; and awakened emotions of the keenest sympathy, which produced an impression throughout the whole Province, exceeded only by the loss of the schooner "Speedy," with all on board.

The accident on Hay Bay took place on a Sunday morning, 20th August, 1819. On the south shore of the bay, in the Methodist meeting-house, was this day a Quarterly Meeting. Quarterly meetings, in the early days of the country, were always largely attended, persons coming from a considerable distance. On this occasion there were present many from the adjacent townships. Not a few came from the banks of the Napanee. Those living to the north of the bay had to cross to the place of meeting by boat. It was a bright sunny Sabbath morning, and already had many crossed and were joining in the religious services, when there put off from the north shore, a short distance from Casey's Point, a boat load, consisting of eighteen young men and women, most of whom lived along the bay. "They were all dressed in good and modest apparel as befitted the day, and the house and worship of God. Buoyant with the cheerfulness of youth, and the emotions of piety, they sang as they stepped into the boat, and as they made progress to the other shore. The boat being rather leaky, and so many, pressing it too near the water's edge, the water came in and increased fast, and they had no vessel to bail with. Unhappily, the young men did not think of bailing with their clean hats, or did not like to do so, until it was too late. The boat filled and sank, when near the other shore, and these eighteen young men and women, crying and shrieking, went down into the deep water.

At the time of crossing, there was a prayer meeting proceeding in the chapel. One those present was now engaged in prayer, and had just uttered the petition that "it might be a day long to be remembered," when a shriek was heard, another, and another. The prayer was stopped, and some ran up to the pulpit to look out, and saw the youths struggling in the water. All ran to the shore, and some plunged in to render assistance. Eight were taken to the shore. Ten bodies were yet in the water. A seine was prepared, and so the bodies of these unhappy youths, a few hours ago so blythe and cheerful were brought dripping to the land. One was not recovered till the next morning. Two young men were drowned, and eight young women. Two were of the German family, two Detlors, one Bogart, one Roblin, one McCoy, one Clark, one Madden, and one Cole. The grief of the families, so suddenly bereaved, gathered together on the shore, gazing at the loved bodies, may be better imagined than described. The grief, too, was shared by the large congregation assembled, and by the minister. No public worship was attended to, but preparations for the solemn funeral.

"Monday was a day of mourning. News of the disaster soon spread far, and a great congregation was assembled. Nine coffins were laid in order outside the chapel. One of the corpses was buried in another grave-yard. Mr. Puffer took for the text, Job xix. 25–27, "I know that my Redeemer liveth," &c. He stood at the door and tried to preach to those within and without, but was so affected by the catastrophe, the weeping congregation, and the coffined dead before him, that he confessed he could not do justice to the subject, or the occasion. But he offered consolation from the gospel to the stricken families mourning. Next, the coffins of the youthful dead were opened, that friends and neighbours, and young acquaintances, might take a last look and farewell. Six of the graves were in rotation, and the coffins were placed in the same manner. The others were near departed friends in other parts of the ground. After the reading of the burial service, the graves, one after another, received the dead, and then were closed up again, until the day when "the trumpet shall sound, and the dead shall be raised incorruptible."—(Playter).

The writer has often heard his father relate the touching circumstances here told. He was then at home, his father being a resident of the south shore, and was an eye witness of the scene. His father's steelyards were used, the hooks being attached to a pole, to grapple for the bodies.

PICTON BAY.—Where the eastern portion of the Bay Quinté and the Long Reach unite, the waters are comparatively wide. This was at the first called the *Grand Bay*. The south side of the Grand Bay forms the mouth of Picton Bay, which stretches southward some five miles, and which has at its head the town of Picton, after which the bay has been named.

The view presented upon passing up this indentation of the Bay, and as well in returning, and looking up the long reach, is one of the most attractive perhaps in all Canada. As the tourist approaches the head of the Bay he will be struck with the extraordinary beauty. To the left are two pictoresque buildings, one the Ontario College. Rising up majestically at the very head of the Bay, is an almost precipitous mountain, whose gray sides, and wood-crowned summit, gives a grand, though sombre appearance. Nothing seems to be wanting but the crumbling walls of an old castle to make the picture complete.

When the refugees first came to the Bay, the inlet, now called Picton Bay, was regarded with some degree of aversion. The high barren-looking shores, covered with dwarf firs and cedars, offered no inducements to the settler. During the first two or three years a party of three or four ascended to the head of the Bay, but observing the thick cedars and firs on either hand, and withal suffering much from the musketoes, they returned and reported that no man could ever inhabit it, that it was fit only for the musketoe. But before many years the Congers, the Johnsons, Washburns and Steeles, had taken up their abode here.

We have seen that this Bay constituted a part of an Indian route from the west to the south shores of Ontario.

To the east of "Grand Bay," the peninsula of Adolphustown is indented by two bays.

Between the extremity of Prince Edward peninsula and Amherst island, where Lake Ontario joins the Bay, at a point which formerly was regarded as the mouth of the Bay of Quinté, is a space nearly a mile. This is called the *Upper Gap*. Between the eastern end of Amherst and Grape Island is the *Lower Gap* which is something more than a mile wide. Directly to the north of the east end of Amherst Island, upon the coast of Ernesttown is an indentation where empties a small stream, this is called *Collins' Bay*, after Deputy Surveyor Collins.

The only remaining bay of which we shall specially speak, is the Kingston Bay.

Perhaps no piece of water can be found in Western Canada possessed of more natural beauty than the Bay of Kingston, during the season of navigation by water. Whether one enters it from the Great Lake with its rough swell, or the quiet waters of Quinte, or the bright St. Lawrence, whose waters are beautiful with a thousand isles; or whether he gazes from the curving shore at the City's front; or from the Cataraqui Bridge; or instead, takes his stand at the point of Frederick or Fort Henry, there is spread out the same pleasing view; one upon which the eye can long gaze with admiration. Encircled by a border of green clad islands, with the massive city upon one side, the waters of the harbour are peaceful and secure. The former beauties such as Champlain and Frontenac looked upon, have passed away. There is less of the natural beauty entering now into the view, but art has taken the place. The barracks at the *Tête du Pont*, the buildings at Navy Yard, the strong fort, the warlike martello towers, and the city of solid stone, give a different, but yet a pleasing picture. Kingston Bay affords a safe place for boating in summer, and in winter, its coating of ice is the theatre of attraction for the joyous skater.

Respecting the events which have come to pass by the Bay of Kingston in the early history of the country, the reader is referred to the history of Kingston. We will only add that the "ship-yards and marine railways at Kingston, Garden Island, and Portsmouth, have launched on the inland seas the greatest in number and largest of tonnage of Canadian vessels in Canada West; Kingston being second only to Quebec in the extent of its ship-building."

Here in 1814 was built the three decked ship of war "*Saint Lawrence*," at a cost of £500,000. The chief cause of this enormous cost was the expense of transportation of stores and equipments from Montreal. In 1853, the aggregate tonnage of the vessels built at the ship-yard in Kingston alone, apart from those built at Portsmouth and Garden Island, amounted to 2,500 tons; the cost of these vessels was £26,000, of which £14,000 was paid for labor.

We will here introduce an interesting notice of the several lakes lying north of the Bay in the adjacent townships, from Cooper. "Through the whole tract of country lying north of the Township of Kingston, and in these and the neighbouring counties, are a multitude of lakes of various sizes, from that of a mere pond up to that of a lake twenty miles in extent. The water of these lakes is extremely pure and clear, and they are furnished with abundance of fish; they are mostly connected by streams of water, and are navigable, and the streams are capable of floating canoes or small boats. Through these lakes and streams are annually floated immense quantities of lumber and timber, and in the absence of the roads now in course of construction, they have been the highway to the city from many a fine farm on their banks. Around them, in some places, the land is much broken, rocky and waste, but between such broken and rough tracts are lands of great richness and fertility, and of the first quality. The scenery throughout this tract of country, and in the neighbourhood of these lakes and rivers is extremely picturesque, and in many places even grand, varied with rock, valley, streamlets and wood. When as the country gets older, localities are sought not only with regard to their flat unvaried richness of soil, but with some consideration of their beauty of location and scenic charms; there is little doubt that many a romantic glen here will have its accompanying cottage, hamlet or mansion, and that many a pretty homestead will be embowered among these woods and water-falls; even now, many a good farm is being brought under cultivation in these parts. If any surpass the rest in picturesque beauty, we should incline to give the palm to Buck Lake and its vicinity. The neighbourhood of these lakes abound in deer.

CHAPTER XLV.

CONTENTS—Islands—Possessed by Indians—The "Thousand Islands"—Carleton Island—History of Island—During the rebellion—Wolfe Island—The name—Howe Island—Old name—County of Ontario—Garden Island—Horseshoe Island—Sir Jeffry Amherst—The size—Indian name—"Tontine"—Johnson's Island—The Island won—Present owner—First settler—The three brothers—Small Islands—Hare Island—Nut Island—Wappoose Island—Indian rendezvous—Captain John's Island—Bartering—Hunger Island—Big Island—First settlers—Huff's Island—Paul Huff—Grape Island—Hog Island—Smaller Islands—Mississauga Island—A tradition—The Carrying Place—Its course—Original survey—History—American prisoners—Col. Wilkins.

THE ISLANDS OF BAY QUINTE.

The reader who has kindly followed us thus far in examining the bay, and its several coves, or indentations, is invited to accompany us once more along its course, and note the several islands which stud its bosom. They are not numerous; but the numerous points all along, as well as the turns in the bay recompense any lack arising from the absence of islands.

When the Mississauga Indians ceded the land along the bay to the British Government, they reserved certain points of land, and mostly all the islands between the head of the bay and Gananoque. Those excepted were Grenadier Island, and the small islands between it and Kingston, and Amherst Island.

The islands of the St. Lawrence are famed almost the world over, they are called the "Thousand Islands." But Howison says, that the commissioners appointed to fix the limits between Canada and the United States, counted the islands of the St. Lawrence and found there were 1692. The islands below Gananoque belonged to the Iroquois.

CARLETON ISLAND—The first island is Carleton Island, called by the French the island of Chevreux, Goat's Island; situated between the American shore of the St. Lawrence, and Wolf Island. It was a military and naval station during the American rebellion, at which government vessels were built for navigating the lake, and possessed fortifications. Its name is derived from Guy Carleton, Esq., "his Majesty's Captain-General and Governor-in-chief, and over his Majesty's province of Quebec, afterward Lord Dorchester." This military post, as we have seen, afforded a retreat for the refugees, who fled from the Mohawk valley. Says the Rev. William Mcaulay, "Jay's treaty of peace, as it was called, in 1783, found Carleton Island occupied by the 84th Regiment, a body of Highlanders levied in the Carolinas, and subsequently adopted into the line." Upon the erection of the northern line of the United States, Carleton Island came within the boundary of the State of New York. But it continued in common with other military posts, in possession of the British, until 1796. Indeed, according to the gentleman whose words we have quoted above, it remained in possession of the British until 1812, when the Americans crossed and seized a sergeant's guard stationed there. It would seem that parties entering Canada were required to procure a passport here. A copy of one, extracted from the history of Dundas, is as follows, directed "To whom concerned."

"Permit the boat going from this to pass to Kingston with their provisions, family, clothing, beding, household furniture, and farming utensils, they having cleared out at this post, as appears by their names in the margin. (John Loucks, two men, two women, three children)."—Signed "C. McDonell, P. O."

Among the refugees here during the war was Mr. Mcaulay. In 1776, Sergeant Major Clark, of the 8th, or King's Own Regiment, was appointed clerk and naval store keeper at Carleton Island, where he remained till 1790. This was father of the late Colonel Clark, of Dalhousie. For further particulars of Carleton Island the reader is referred to the history of Kingston.

WOLFE ISLAND—This is a considerable island, 25 miles long, stretching along near the American shore, directly opposite Kingston. It contains 28,129 acres of good land. The name is found often spelled wolf, leading us to infer that it is derived from the presence of that animal upon the island at some time. But it is no doubt after General Wolfe, who fell at Quebec. The original Indian name, as given in the document conferring a seigniory at Cataraqui upon La Salle, including this and Amherst Island, was *Ganounkouesnot*. The French called it the *Grande Island*, and Simcoe in his proclamation 1792, directed it to be called Wolfe Island. Mr. Detlor says that "it would seem the greater part of Wolfe Island was granted to the heirs of Sir William Johnson, the clergy and Crown reserves excepted.

We observe a notice in the *Kingston Gazette*, that Wolfe Island, with Pittsburgh, was conjoined to Kingston for municipal purposes in 1812.

HOWE ISLAND—Is situated in the St. Lawrence, somewhat below Kingston, it is a large, long island in front of the township of Pittsburgh, and one part of it is almost conjoined to the mainland.

It is a township by itself, and contains about 8000 acres. It was called by the French, Isle Cauchois; but was named by Simcoe, or his advisers, Howe Island.

When Upper Canada was erected into a province, it was divided into nineteen counties; the seventh of these consisted of Howe Island, Wolfe Island, Amherst Island, Gage Island, with all the other islands between the mouth of the Gananoque and the point of Marysburgh. They constituted the county of Ontario.

GARDEN ISLAND.—Upon the north of Wolfe Island, in Kingston Bay, is *Garden Island*, containing some sixty-three acres. Near the western extremity of Wolfe Island, is another small island, which received the name of *Horseshoe Island*, and separated from the large island by a narrow channel, which was named Batteau Channel, is *Gage Island*, after Brig. General Gage, which was also sometimes called *Simcoe Island*. The name given to it by the French was *Isle aux Foret*. It contains some 2164 acres of rich land.

AMHERST ISLAND.—So called after "Sir Jeffrey Amherst, of the honourable and military order of Bath, Colonel of of the Third and Sixteenth Regiments of Infantry, Lieutenant-General in the Army, and Commander-in-Chief of all His Majesty's Troops and Forces in North America." This beautiful island, stretching along opposite, and about a mile and a half from Ernest-town; being some twelve miles in length, causes an extension of the Bay Quinté to a corresponding distance. It contains about 14,015 acres of very rich land. The channel separating it from Gage and Wolfe Islands, forms the Lower Gap, and that which flows above, between it and Marysburg, is the Upper Gap.

In the time of LaSalle, the Indian name of this island was *Kaouenesgo*. It formed a part of his Seigniory, and he, some time after his arrival to build Fort Frontenac, 1678, named the island *Isle de Tonti*, after a brave French officer, with one arm, who accompanied him. This name, modified to "Isle Tanta," clung to the island until recent years. Sir John Johnson, to whom it was granted, with other land, at the close of the war, 1783, in a letter to the Military Secretary, calls it the "Island of Tontine." This may have been a fancy name of the owner, as we find no other reference to it. The present name was bestowed in 1792, after Gen. Amherst, who acted so conspicuous a part in the wars. Upon some old maps the Island is designated "Sir John Johnson's Island." We find an indefinite statement that the island was claimed by the

Mohawks, and that they ceded their rights to Col. Crawford, who accompanied Sir John, and who, in turn, transferred it to Johnson. But, as he and Brant were on the most intimate terms, they could, no doubt, arrange any difference between themselves.

We do not see that there can be any objection to record a statement which has been told for many long years by the inhabitants of the Bay, that the Island was subsequently won by an aristocratic gambler, Lady B——, in England, at a game of cards, who afterwards disposed of it to the present owner, Lord Mountcashel.

Some of the farm lots have been, we believe, disposed of, but the island is mostly held by tenants, under lease from the Earl. The oldest settler upon the island was Lieutenant McGinnis, of Johnston's Regiment. He lived here in some comfort, having several slaves to do the work.

Off the east end of Amherst Island, in the Bay, are three small islands, called the *Three Brothers*, "famous for black bass fishing, and for deep rolling sea."

Leaving the waters of the Lower Bay, and directing our course westward, we find the Bay comparatively free of Islands. Here and there, all along its course, may be seen small islands, close to the shore. These received names, as a general thing, after the person who owned the adjacent land. There are, however, a few more islands which need special notice.

Upon an old plan of Fredericksburgh, dated 1784, is to be seen in Hay Bay, three islands; one near the north shore, at its eastern extremity, is called *Hare Island*. To the south, at the eastern shore, are the other two; the north one is called *Nut Island*; the more southern one is *Wappoose Island*. This island, from its name, must have been the place of residence of the principal chief of some Indian tribe, probably the Kente Indians. Here, must have been a place of considerable importance to the Indian—a rendezvous, whereat they met, and whereat the chief held his simple, but dignified court.

Opposite the Mohawk Church, in the Indian Village, just off Grassy Point, of Sophiasburg, is a low island, containing fourteen acres. This island originally belonged to the Mississaugas, as did most of the islands in the Bay, until a comparatively recent date. John Cuthbertson, a grandson of Capt. John, purchased the island from John Sunday, and other Mississauga chiefs. The price paid was a cow and a yoke of steers. A quit claim deed was received by Mr. Cuthbertson, which is yet to be seen. This bargain led to some trouble with the Government, who held that the Mississaugas had no right to sell their land except to Government. However, finally, the receipt held by Cuthbertson was allowed to be a legal document. This Island is known as Capt. John's Island.

There are three small islands in Mohawk Bay, the largest of which is called Hunger Island. It is situated a short distance from the mouth, near the north shore, and contains about seven acres of land.

Along the north shore of Sophiasburg is *Big Island*. As its name implies, it is an island of considerable size, containing over 3,000 acres of excellent land. The channel separating this long narrow island from the mainland, especially at its east end is very narrow, and is spanned by a short bridge, and may even be forded. Long grass abundantly grows all though the channel, which, in summer, covers the water, and seems to form the island and mainland into one. Here, is the constant abode of the muskrat, and at certain seasons the resort of the wild fowl.

It is said that Samuel Peck and Samuel Shaw were the first settlers on this island. The older inhabitants along the bay remembers when this island was thickly covered with wood of the most heavy description. It was for many years, at the beginning of the present century, the scene of lumbering operations. Winter after winter, large quantities were cut down, and in the spring, rafted and conveyed to Montreal.

The writer has heard it stated, this island was originally, when no longer owned by the Indians, bestowed on one Hall, and that early maps designate it Hall's Island.

Huff's island is situated to the west of Big Island, and forms a part of Ameliasburgh, from which it is separated by a marsh, and to which, at one point it is connected by a low neck of land. To the north is Mississauga Point. The island obtains its name from the first settler, Solomon Huff, who settled there in 1825. Solomon Huff was the son of Paul Huff, one of the original settlers of Adolphustown, who came from Long Island, New York, with Van. Alstine. The writer has conversed with the wife of Solomon Huff when in her 91st year, who retained a vivid récollection of the time of their settling, from the fact, that when crossing the ice to the island they broke through with their furniture. At the time of their settlement their nearest neighbours were on one hand at Demorestville and on the other at Walbridge's, on the north shore of Mississagua Point.

Immediately to the east of Huff's Island, is Grape Island. It received the name it bears from the great quantities of wild grapes that at one time grew spontaneously upon it. This Island, now barren and treeless, was, at one time, the home of domesticated Indians. Even yet, may be seen, the traces of the wooden cabins, where the Mississaugas lived under the paternal care of the Rev. Mr. Case.

Continuing westward from Big Bay, there are to be seen several small islands close to the shore, the names accorded them are not beautiful, but probably have in their origin something significant. Thus, there is one called Hog Island, and opposite Belleville is another known as Cow Island. An island west of the mouth of the Moira, is yet called Zwick's Island, after the person who once owned the adjoining land. This island was, at one time, an Indian burying ground.

We next come to the island upon which are extensive sawing mills, commonly called Baker's Island. It was formerly called Myers' Island, after Captain Myers, who lived adjacent thereto. He, for several years, paid rent to the Indians for it. Telegraph Island is about four miles above Belleville; and "Nigger" Island nine miles.

The last island we have to notice, belonging to the bay, is Indian Island, situated at the extremity of Bay Quinté, west of the mouth of the Trent River. Upon a map, to be seen in the Crown Land's Department, this is designated Mississauga Island. It has also been called Fighting Island. There is a tradition respecting this island, to which the existence of human bones found there, seems to give some degree of plausibility. It is even now related, that at an early date, a company of Mohawks, who had crossed from the south side of the lake, were encamped upon this island. A band of Mississaugas, learning the fact, approached the island cautiously at night, took away their boats so they could not escape, and then suddenly, with superior numbers, fell upon the Mohawks, and killed and scalped them all. But the bones found there may have been placed there for burial.

THE CARRYING PLACE.

The distance between the head of bay Quinté, and the waters of Lake Ontario, at the narrow part of the isthmus is about a mile and three-quarters. By this narrow neck of land the peninsula of Prince Edward is saved from being an island. This was called in the first proclamation of Simcoe, "the isthmus of the Presqù isle de

Quinté." It is from this source that the harbour on the lake west of the isthmus has received the name Presqû isle.

We have elsewhere spoken of the fact that a Carrying Place had existed here from time immemorial. From the Indian villages, which at times were located, now along the lake shores of the peninsula, and now upon the bay, the Indians started forth, perhaps to ascend the Trent, or the Moira, or to pass down the waters of the bay, or perhaps to coast along the shore of the lake, westward to the mouth of some river. And, when the French had possession of the country they found this a well marked Indian path. The French had not occasion to cross it, as they either ascended the Ottawa, the Trent, or if desirous of going to the head of Lake Ontario, they passed along its south shore. But in the early years of Upper Canada, this portage was frequently crossed by those passing back and forth from the lower parts of Canada to the west. This was the case particularly after the forts of Oswego and Niagara were handed over to the United States in 1796.

The original Indian Carrying Place can yet be traced. Its course is indicated by a road which leads from water to water. The street is consequently somewhat crooked, and is in some places wider than in others. When the land was originally surveyed, this path was made the base line of a row of lots on either side. The surveyor being ill and entrusting the matter to an assistant; the Indian path was faithfully followed. While this irregular dividing line between Ameliasburgh and Murray may appear unseemly, it cannot be regretted that the old path is thus indubitably known. Upon the Murray side of the road the fence is comparatively straight, but upon the opposite side it is very devious. This pretty nearly marks the old Indian path. While used as a Carrying Place for batteaux, which were transported upon low wheels, the road was no doubt, to a certain extent, straightened; yet mainly the old route remained.

The old days, when Weller used to haul the batteaux from water to water, have left no memorial; and even more recent days when the first steamboats invariably came to this place, have left but little to mark their history. Here is the remains of the wharf and frame store house where once was life and enterprise; but now all is in decay, and rural solitude prevails. But there is beauty here, as well as interest. All along the street between the head of the bay and Weller's Bay of the lake are buildings, consisting of private residences, and churches. The tourist will find abundant food for thought at the Carrying Place ; whether he contemplates the far remote past ere the Indian was disturbed in his native abode ; or the days when the French Recollet Missionaries followed the footsteps of those whom they sought to convert; or the time when the pioneer surveyor and settler first trod the path ; or whether he reflects upon the many human beings who have come and gone on their way of life, now going one way now another; or thought of the trader intent on pressing his business into the very outskirts of the settlements ; of the soldiers—regulars, and militia, who pressed onward for the conflict, to drive off the invading foe; or of the thousand prisoners carried captive through the province, which they had boastingly came to conquer. If the writer were there again, he would ponder, in addition to all this, upon the sad, yet natural occurence, that, of all those who had come and gone, the one who imparted much information to him, who came to the Carrying Place long years ago, is now gone the way of all the earth. The history of the place is inseparably associated with the life of the Hon. Col. Wilkins, whose loss was expressed by the presence of many" as he was carried to his grave.

DIVISION VIII.

THE FIRST TEN TOWNSHIPS IN THE MIDLAND DISTRICT.

CHAPTER XLVI.

CONTENTS—The French—Their policy—Trading posts—Cahiaque—Variations—Name of river—Foundation of Fort Frontenac—A change—Site of old fort—La Salle's petition—A Seigniory—Governors visiting—War Expedition—Fort destroyed—Rebuilt—Colonial wars—Taking of Fort Oswego—Frontenac taken—End of French domination.

HISTORY OF THE FRENCH OCCUPATION.

It was the policy of the French, to penetrate, as far as possible, into the interior of the country, and, by all possible means, secure the peltry traffic with the Indians. The Recollets and the Jesuits, while seeking to convert the Pagan Indian, endeavoured as well, to win him to the interest of their country. As soon as practicable, trading posts were established at convenient points, at which to buy furs of the Indians. Not sure, even at the first, of the continued friendliness of the natives, and subsequently exposed to tribes, who assumed a hostile attitude, they proceeded to fortify their trading depots against sudden attacks; not alone to secure this, but to maintain a constant menace to those who might venture to assume such attitude. It was in carrying out these designs, that M. de Courcelles, in 1670, ascended the St. Lawrence, direct to Lake Ontario, from the mouth of the Ottawa, being the first European to do so. Two years later, he convened a meeting at the head of the St. Lawrence, of Indian chiefs of the region round about, when, concealing his ulterior object, he gained permission to erect a fort; but being immediately thereafter recalled to France, it was left for his successor, Conte de Frontenac, to establish the fort.

The first name which is found applied to the place, where the fort was founded, is *Cahiaque*, or *Cadaroque*. It is an Indian name, and most probably signifies "the strongest fort in the country." This is inferred from the following fact:—When certain of the chiefs of the Mohawks, were in London, in 1710, desirous of doing honor to their host, where they stayed, at King Street, Covent Garden, they called him *Cadaroque*, meaning "the most powerful man in London." Or, possibly, in using the word, in connection with Frontenac, they may have referred to the strong expedition which accompanied him. For many years the fort was known by this name, or one derived from it. It must be remembered that this word, with many others spoken by the Indians, was written by the French according to the particular idea of the person hearing the pronunciation. Hence it is that we find this word changed frequently as into the following. Beside the two already mentioned are found Catarcoui, Catarouy, or Cataraccouy, Catarakvy, Catarakouy, Catarasky, Cataracto, Catara-couy, Cadaraque, Cadarachqui, Kadaraghke, Kadaraghkie, Kodakag-kie, Cadarochque, Cadaacarochqua, Catarocoui, Cuadaraghque, Cre-deroqua, Cataraqui.

While the fort, or place of the fort, was thus known mostly by the Indians, it was, according to Charlevoix, called by the French, the fort of Lake St. Louis, the name then applied to Lake Ontario. Subsequently, the fort was spoken of as the one built by Frontenac; and ultimately, it came to be permanently designated *Fort Frontenac.* After the conquest, and at the time of the revolution, the place was known in the rebel colonies, as Cataraqui; and, in speaking of going to Upper Canada, they would say to Cataraqui. The river between Ontario and Montreal, was sometimes called Cariqui, or Iroquois.

The following account of the foundation of the fort, is extracted from Draper's Brochure. He says "the expedition was a vast one for those days, 120 canoes, 2 batteaux, and 400 men." He then quotes from a journal of Frontenac's voyage, describing the entrance into the river Cataraqui;—"12th, broke up camp very early in the morning, and having proceeded till ten o'clock, halted three hours to rest and eat. On approaching the first opening of the lake, the Count wished to proceed with more order than had been already done, and in line of battle. He accordingly arranged the whole fleet in this wise:—

"Four squadrons, composing the vanguard, went in front and in one line. The two batteaux followed next. After these came Count de Frontenac at the head of all the canoes, of his guards, of his staff, and of the volunteers attached to his person; having on his right, the squadron from Three Rivers, and on his left, those of the Hurons and Algonquins.

"Two other squadrons formed a third line, and composed the rear guard.

"This order of sailing had not been adhered to for more than half a league, when an Iroquois canoe was perceived coming with the Abbe D'Ursé, who, having met the Indians above the River Katarakoui, (Cataraqui) and having notified them of the Count's arrival, they were now advancing with the captains of the Five Nations.

"They saluted the admiral, and paid their respects to him with evidence of much joy and confidence, testifying to him the obligation they were under to him for sparing them the trouble of going further, and for receiving their submissions at the River Katarakoui, which is a very suitable place to camp, as they were about signifying to him.

"After Count Frontenac had replied to their civilities, they preceeded him as guides, and conducted him as guides, and conducted him into a bay, about a cannon shot from the entrance, which forms one of the most beautiful and agreeable harbors in the world, capable of holding a hundred of the largest ships, with sufficient water at the mouth, and in the harbor, with mud bottom, and so sheltered from every wind, that a cable is scarcely necessary for mooring." "On the 13th of July, 1673, the fort was commenced, and on the 19th, it was finished, and De Frontenac left on the 27th for Montreal, having laid the foundation of the future City of Kingston."

How different was the appearance then from that presented to-day. No clearing, as yet, broke the woody shores. At this conference between Frontenac and the Iroquois chiefs, the charms of nature only were displayed. Where now stands the city of Kingston, was then a dense forest. The gently curving shore, which now forms the front of the city, with its line of piers, was undisturbed, except by the birch canoe. The quiet Bay, within the Point, then more prominent than now, stretching up with its low sand banks, and begirt with marshes, was then the safe abode of the wild fowl and muskrat. Across the inlet of the bay, and where now is the Navy Yard, the land was thickly covered with the greenest foliage; as well as was the higher and more beautifully wooded peninsula of Point Henry. And still beyond, to the south, the third point, stretching out almost to the rugged little island, called Cedar Island, increased the variety of the picture; and the two indentations where now is Navy Bay, and the "Dead Man's" Bay, at one time called Hamilton's Cove, added thereto. Then, turning toward the south, there reposed the magnificently green, long island, now

Wolfe Island, with Gage Island in its front; and still extending the view around the Bay, was to be seen the islands, now called Simcoe and Amherst, all richly clothed with the garments of nature. One would wish to look upon a faithful picture of this primeval appearance of Kingston Bay, before even the French had planted a post or cleft a tree. However beautiful Kingston of to-day may be regarded, with its graceful architecture, as displayed in its public and privte edifices; however grand the strong fortifications, which silently utter words of warning to the passing stranger whose nation covets our territory, while pretending to depreciate it; however striking the combination which composes the picture of Kingston and its harbor of to-day, they cannot exceed, as a whole, in attractiveness, the prospect seen by Frontenac, of wood and water so remarkably associated, and charmingly blended, ere the hand of man had marred it.

It was immediately after this conference, between Frontenac and the chiefs, when he concealed the true designs he entertained, that the erection of the first fort was proceeded with. Its site was upon the point of land by the entrance of the bay, near the *Tete du Pont*, and commanded the entrance to Cataraqui Creek. It seems, from the testimony of early settlers of Kingston, that the fort was separated from Kingston by a deep trench, so that the point was converted into an island, upon which was built the original village of Cataraqui. In later years, this ditch has been obliterated by the filling in of material, and, in like manner, a portion of the bay, immediately north of the point has disappeared.

In the following year, LaSalle, who has been particularly referred to in the introductory chapter, presented the following petition to King Louis XIV.

"The proposer, aware of the importance to the Colony of Canada, of the establishment of Fort Frontenac, of which he was some time in command, and desiring to employ his means and his life in the King's service, and for the augmentation of the country, offers to support it, at his expense, and reimburse its cost, on the following conditions, to wit:—That His Majesty be pleased to grant in Seigniory, to the proposer, the said fort, four leagues of country along the border of Lake Frontenac, the two islands in front, named Ganounkouesnot and Kaouenesgo, and the interjacent islets, with the same rights and privileges obtained hitherto by those who hold lands in the country in Seigniory, with the right of fishing in Lake Frontenac and the adjoining rivers, to facilitate the support of the people of said Fort, together with the command of said place and of said lake, under the orders and authority of His Majesty's Governor, Lieutenant-General in the country; on which condition, the proposer will be bound:—1st. To maintain the said Fort; to place it in a better state of defence; to keep a garrison there, at least as numerous as that of Montreal, and as many as fifteen to twenty laborers, during the two first years, to clear and till the land; to provide it with necessary arms, artillery and ammunition, and that so long as the proposer will command there, in His Majesty's name, and until some other persons be authorized to settle above the Long Sault of the River St. Lawrence, through which people pass to the said Fort, without being charged with similar expense, or to contribute to that which the proposer will be obliged to incur for the preservation of the said Fort.

"2nd. To repay Count de Frontenac, His Majesty's Governor and Lieutenant-General in Canada, the expense he incurred for the establishment of said Fort, amounting to the sum of 12,000 to 13,000 livres, as proved by the statements thereof prepared.

"3rd. To make grants of land to all those willing to settle there, in the manner usual in said country; to allow them the trade (*la traite*) when their settlements will be in the condition required by the Edicts and Regulations of the Sovereign Council of said country. 4th. To grant them land for villages and tillage; to teach them trades, and induce them to lead lives more conformable to ours, as the proposer had begun to do with success, when he commanded there. 5th. To build a Church, when there will be 100 persons; meanwhile, to entertain one or two Recollet Friars, to perform Divine service, and administer the sacraments there. 6th. His Majesty, accepting these proposals, is very humbly supplicated to grant to the proposer letters of noblesse, in consideration of the voyages and discoveries which he made in the country at his expense, during the seven years he continually lived there, the services he rendered in the country, and those he will continue to render; and all the other letters necessary to serve him as titles possessory to said Seigniory."

In the succeeding year this petition was granted, and a decree to that effect was issued by the King on the 13th May, 1675, and a Patent of Nobility issued to La Salle; and Fort Frontenac, with four leagues of the adjacent country, was created a Seigniory of Canada, and LaSalle its first Seignior.

In the decree making the grant, it is specified that LaSalle shall "induce the Indians to repair thither, give them settlements, and form villages there in society with the French, to whom he shall give part of said land to be cleared, all which shall be cleared and improved within the time and space of twenty years. * * His Majesty wills that appeals from the Judges (to be appointed by La Salle), be to the Lieutenant-General of Quebec." But, the subsequent checquered career and early death of La Salle, probably prevented the carrying out of these intentions.

When La Salle set out on his western exploring expedition, he "left Sieur de la Forest in charge of the fort." As before stated, La Salle had many enemies, and among them the Governor, M. de la Barre, "who actually sequestered Fort Frontenac and took possession of it, pretending that La Salle had abandoned it. This was in 1682."

The history of the French occupation of Cataraqui is marked by occasional visits of the French Governor, and the presence of large and small bodies of armed forces. In 1684 M. de la Barre, the successor of Frontenac, tarried at Cataraqui two weeks with his convoy, which was composed of 130 regular soldiers, 700 armed Canadians, 200 savages, and a mixed body of several hundred from the west. It must have been a picturesque sight, the encampment of this army. The veterans from France in their uniform attire, the Canadians in their various hued garments, and the Algonquins and Ottawas in their wild garb of paint and feathers formed the components of a picture truly striking. A year or two later and De Nonville, another Governor, was likewise found encamped here with an army of 2000. At this time the original fort of wood was at its greatest pitch of renown and glory. Here was kept stored within the palisaded walls, arms, amunition, and provision, beside furs. It was while enjoying this considerable power that De Nouville committed the act of treachery toward the Ganneyouses and Kentes Indians. But this act was followed by an attack by the Indians, and the fort was in a state of siege for the space of a month; "but was not taken." Two years later, however, finding it difficult to maintain this out-post so far from Montreal, De Nonville ordered De Valrenne, the commander, to blow up the fort, which was accordingly done, and "three barks on the lake were scattered," and "property to the extent of 20,000 crowns," was sacrificed.

The fort thus destroyed was rebuilt by the orders of Frontenac, and in 1695 he sent 700 workmen for the purpose. (For the circumstances and the opposition respecting this, see Introductory.) The fort being completed it was garrisoned with 48 soldiers. "The expense of re-victualling and re-establishing the fort, cost 12,000 livres, or between £600 and £700."—(Draper).

Respecting the situation of the fort, a manuscript published in 1838, under the direction of the Literary and Historical Society of Quebec, says, "it was situated *at the bottom of a bay*, which a little river flowing into Lake Ontario forms, close to the junction of Lake Ontario and the River St. Lawrence. It consisted of four stone curtains, 120 feet each, defended by four square bastions. The walls were defended by neither ditches nor palisades. There was no terrace to sustain it on the inside. A wooden gallery was built all round for communicating from one bastion to another. The platforms of these bastions were mounted on wooden piles, and the curtains were pierced for loop-holes."

Father Charlevoix, writing in 1720, says of Fort Frontenac, "that it is a square with four bastions built of stone, and the ground it occupies is a quarter of a league in compass; its situation has something very pleasant; the sides of the river present every way a landscape well varied, and it is the same at the entrance of Lake Ontario."

Fort Frontenac now fully re-established on a stronger basis, continued for many years to be an important post, with respect to trading, and likewise offensive and defensive operations against the Indians, and also the English. Here was deposited vast stores of provision, and materials of a war-like nature for the use of other forts.

In the first years of the 18th century, rivalry and jealousy between the French and English Colonists, assumed a more determined form. Already was gathering the fierce elements of Colonial war, which were to culminate in the siege of Quebec, and spend its fury upon the Plains of Abraham. We have seen that the two powers tried zealously, and often by unscrupulous means to secure the alliance and aid of the savages, whose love of war and desire to engage in the bloody attack, with the allurements of promised presents, led them too often to scenes of blood and rapine. The regions about Cataraqui were often the place of sudden attack and cruel torture. The fort was an object of dread to the Iroquois, of jealousy to the English, and with the view of breaking the chain of forts, of which this was so important a one, the English set about erecting one at Oswego.

In 1754 the eventful seven years war began, and one of the first events was the sending of a force of 4000 men and 12 guns by the French Governor, to attack Fort Oswego. But when the force reached Cataraqui, it was found necessary to recall a portion of them to Lower Canada, and defer the attack. One battalion was ordered to Niagara, while one or two battalions were encamped under the walls of Frontenac. The total force of Canadians and savages in arms west of Cataraqui at this time was 1000. The following year, it is found stated that, on "June 26, 1756, English vessels were seen across the Bay of Quinté, coming toward Frontenac. The French gave chase, and captured a sloop."

July 29, 1757, witnessed the arrival at the fort of a considerable body, and for days armed men continued to rendezvous here. The woods around the fort were alive with soldiers. The attack upon Fort Oswego, contemplated three years previous, was now about to be made. On the evening of the 4th August, the party, of no small dimensions set out for the attack. It consisted of 80 batteaux laden with artillery luggage and provision, and canoes to carry the force of 3100 men. They started at night, when the shades of darkness were gathering, and stealthily directed their way, one boat after another, for the opposite shore. At the approach of morning they came to a stop, where the thick woods met the southern shore of the lake. The bushes were parted, and without noise, the batteaux were, one by one, withdrawn from the water and carefully covered with leaves, so that unless one passed directly by the way, no indications could be observed of their existence. By the dawn of day there was not a ripple upon the waters from the party, and the woods were hushed, except by the denizens of the forest. All the day long the party lay concealed. After night had fallen, re-embarkation took place, slowly and calmly beneath the mild summer's sky. For five days and nights the same course was pursued, by which time they had reached the neighbourhood of Fort Oswego, where reposed the English garrison, unconscious of danger. The attack was so unexpected, and carried on with so much spirit, that the garrison had to succumb before reinforcements could be obtained, and the French returned to Fort Frontenac laden with spoils.

But the time was approaching when the glory of Fort Frontenac should depart. At this time the building itself was beginning to decay. Sixty years had told upon the walls, and a writer of 1758 says they "were not good." However, had the fortifications been never so strong, the course of events would have all the same witnessed the final fall of this strong-hold. "In this year, the commandant at Fort Frontenac was a Monsieur de Noyan, King's Lieutenant for Three Rivers. He was an old man, but brave as a lion." We have seen that de Levis having withdrawn, the fort was left with but a few men, Garneau says seventy; but Warburton, one hundred and twenty Frenchmen and forty Indians. Even with this number it was but an easy success for Bradstreet, with his three thousand men and eleven guns, to possess himself of a fort weakened by age. Having descended the Oswego River, Colonel Bradstreet crossed to the Upper Gap and approached Cataraqui along the shore, observing great caution, and landed about a mile to the west of the fort, August 25, in the evening. During the following night he cautiously approached the place of attack, and upon the ground where now stands the market buildings, he erected a battery. So silently was this done, and with such despatch, that before the morning of 27th August, 1758, he had it all completed. The morning light revealed to the French how imminent was their danger. Dismayed, but not discouraged, the intrepid commander ordered every man to his post; but a few shots from the English guns showed to him how futile was resistance. Having signified his intention to surrender, which was about seven o'clock in the morning, he became, with his garrison, prisoner of war. The conquerors found in "the fort sixty pieces of cannon, sixteen mortars, an immense supply of provisions, stores and ammunitions, with all the shipping on the lake," also, "several vessels richly laden with furs, to the value, it is said of 70,000 louis d'ors. There was also a large quantity of merchandise intended for the western forts, beside some of the booty which had been brought thither after the capture of Oswego. Colonel Bradstreet had no intention of holding the fort; but to destroy, which he accordingly did, with the vessels.

There was a feeble attempt to restore the fort in the fall, and "a small detachment of troops and Canadians, under the command of the Chevalier Benoit, was sent to Frontenac partly to protect merchandize and ammunition passing up and down, and partly to rebuild the fort; and subsequently the *Sieur de Cresse*, an assistant engineer, with Captain Laforce, a sailor, were sent there to construct two new schooners, to endeavor to maintain the supremacy on the lakes." But the following year the presence of Wolfe before Quebec, and Amherst at Carillon, rendered the restoration of Frontenac an impossibility. The glory of Fort Frontenac had forever departed. But the spirit of bravery again appeared, in later days, in a people of another language, though, nevertheless Canadians. In 1812-13 the Americans approached Kingston, but the hostile and determined attitude assumed by the militia and troops deterred them from attempting to touch the soil here, and when they did attempt, both above and below, great indeed was the repulse and discomfiture.

CHAPTER XLVII.

CONTENTS—Cooper's Essay—Loyalists naming places—King's Town—Queen's Town—Niagara—Spanish names—Cataraqui from 1759 to 1783—Desolation—The rebellion—Station, Carleton Island—Settling—Refugees at New York—Michael Grass—Prisoner at Cataraqui—From New York to Canada—Captain Grass takes possession of first township—First landholders—A letter by Captain Grass—Changes—Surveying forts and harbors—Report to Lord Dorchester—Kingston, *versus* Carleton Island—The defenses—Troops—King's township—First settlers—"Plan of township No. 1"—First owners of town lots—Names—Settlers upon the front—First inhabitants of Kingston—A naval and military station—The Commodore—Living of old—Kingston in *last century*—New fortifications.

SETTLEMENT AT CATARAQUI BY THE LOYALISTS.

It would be impossible to write of Kingston without traveling the ground already taken by writers, especially in an admirable essay written by C. W. Cooper, Barrister-at-law, being a prize essay published in 1856. We shall accept very many of the statements therein contained except we find trustworthy grounds for controverting them. Much, however, of the subject matter we had laboriously collected before this pamphlet was placed in our hands by our friend M. Sweetnam, Esq., P. O. Inspector.

The practice of naming places, rivers, &c., after royal personages and those occupying prominent places in the public service, naturally arose from the intense loyalty which reigned in the bosoms of all who had forsaken their old homes to settle under the old flag in the wilderness. The pre-eminence of Kingston is indicated by the name, which seems to have been given it at a very early date, as surveyor Collins uses that name in 1788. This, the first township surveyed and settled, was named *King's* township. Afterwards the town and township came to be called Kingston In this connection reference may be made to *Queenstown* at the head of navigation upon the Niagara River. Trade with the west along Lake Erie was carried on, and boats were accustomed to pass up and down on their way to and from Montreal. These boats had to be carried around the Falls of Niagara. Already many of Butler's Rangers and persons connected with the Indian department, began to settle upon the Canadian side of the Niagara. There was very shortly a collection of houses at the point of landing, and the commencement of the portage, and nothing was more natural than this, the second village formed by the United Empire Loyalists, should receive the name of Queenstown, not unlikely the name was bestowed by the Hon. R. Hamilton.

As we proceed, it will be observed how general was the habit to give names derived from Great Britain and Englishmen. The most notable exception to this is to be found in connection with those places that received names during the time of Sir Peregrine Maitland, who had a fancy for bestowing Spanish names.

During the time which elapsed between the evacuation of Frontenac, the year after the destruction of the fort, in the autumn of 1759, until the commencement of the American rebellion, and until its close, ruin and desolation prevailed at Cataraqui. It is found intimated, but not on the best authority, that there continued to live at this place a certain number of French families and half-breed Indians. That such was the case is quite possible, though, as yet, no positive proof is to be found. But, at the most there was a few log huts around the ruins of the fort, and upon the cleared ground adjacent thereto, or perhaps upon the site of the ancient chapel of the Recollets. No doubt the Indians frequently encamped in this vicinity, perhaps had a permanent village. The words of Captain Grass, penned twenty-seven years later, may probably be accepted as correct, that "scarse the vestige of a human habitation could be found in the whole extent of the Bay of Quinté."

The rebellion led to the establishment of a military post at the Island of Chevereux, or Goat Island, subsequently named Carleton Island. This position was found more convenient than the site of old Fort of Frontenac. After the defeat of General Burgoyne, at Saratoga, in 1778, there were many refugees who sought protection at the several military posts along the northern frontier of New York, that of Carleton Island among the rest. Indeed, it is probable that to this place a large number escaped, as being more safe than Oswego or Niagara. A communication was with some regularity kept up between this place and Montreal, and also the Fort of Niagara. By the army boats, refugees may have passed to Montreal; but it would seem that a considerable number remained domiciled at Carleton Island, eating the food supplied by government. Of course, able bodied men would be at once enrolled into the companies, to do military service; yet there would remain a certain number of males, besides the women, who were incapaciated for military life. During the continuation of the war, there is every reason to believe that individuals, perhaps families, would cross to the old fort at Cataraquí, to stay for a while, or even take up their abode.

It may have been, that there were here some advantages in cultivating the cleared land, which did not exist at Carleton Island. In the absence of active duty, not unlikely the soldiers and officers would pass over to fish or hunt, or perhaps to examine the land as to quality, and facilities for settlement. Bongard says his father, who was with Holland, said that a small village existed at Cataraqui. But it was not until the close of the war 1783, that a systematic settlement commenced. That settlers existed, during this year, at Cataraqui, there is no doubt. It was sometimes referred to in Lower Canada as Seignory, No. 1. Col. John Clark, whose father was in the Commissariat Department during the war, says, that he was born at Cataraqui, in 1783, and was baptized by the Rev. Mr. Stuart. The family must then have been living on the mainland, as he speaks of another brother as being born on Carleton Island. The probability is that at this date, there were a few families living in the vicinity of the fort.

At the close of the war, it was a question of considerable importance, what can be done to ameliorate the condition of the loyalists? While the commissioners, who completed the terms of peace at Paris, chose to sink the interests and welfare of the loyalists in their unseemly haste to complete the treaty, the officers commanding in America, everywhere felt the deepest sympathy, and keenest compassion for the refugees. Among these was the officer commanding at New York. At this juncture of affairs, when they were undecided, whether to embark for Nova Scotia, or Lower Canada, it came to the ears of the General, that one Michael Grass, of New York, had been a prisoner of the French, before the conquest at Cataraqui. He caused that person to appear before him, and to report as to the character of the country, and the probabilities of its being a suitable place for refugees to seek homes. Mr. Grass having rendered a favorable report, the result was that he was commissioned Captain, and placed at the head of a band of loyalists, staying at New York. They were dispatched in King's ships, under the care of a man-of-war.

Mr. Robert Everett Grass, of Sidney, the grandson of Captain Grass, says, that the party of refugees set sail from New York in a fleet of seven vessels, and after a long voyage of nine weeks, during which they encountered a severe gale, lasting eight days, and nearly wrecking them, they reached Sorel. This was probably in the early part of 1783. The men of the party ascended the St. Lawrence in batteaux, and landed at the mouth of Little Cataraqui Creek, thence proceeding westward, prospecting as far as Collin's Bay. Crossing to the west side of this little bay, Captain Grass attempted to drive a stake in the ground, with the intention of fixing a tent, or commencing a survey, whereupon he found it rocky. Remarking that he had come too far to settle upon a rock, he returned to the east of the cove, and took possession of the first township of the Bay Quinté. There seems some reason to believe that, when Grass arrived in Canada, and explained to the Government his mission, that Surveyor General Holland, directed Deputy Surveyor Collins to proceed with Captain Grass to Cataraqui, so that he might be guided by him. If such was the case, the base line along the front of the first township, must have been run before Captain Grass crossed to the west of Collins Bay, and rejected the land lying to the west thereof. Captain Grass, as well as the surveying party, returned to Sorel for the winter, and, in the spring, they returned, accompanied by all of the families, under Captain Grass. It was the summer of 1784 that the first township was occupied. There was some dissatisfaction at the preference accorded to Captain Grass by those who had been in Canada. His superior claim was however acknowledged. At the same time, there appears to have been some compromise, from the fact, that while Captain Grass himself obtained the first lot adjoining to the reserve for the town, the second one, which was by number, lot 24 was granted to the Rev. Mr. Stuart, and the next to Mr. Herkimer, neither of whom had any connection with Captain Grass' company.

The following extract of a letter written by Captain Grass, at a subsequent period, reveals to us the appearance the place presented to him, at the time of his settling. The old gentleman had some grievance to make known to the public, respecting a road, and he commences his communication thus:—

"Seven and twenty years, Mr. Printer, have rolled away since my eyes, for the second time, beheld the shores of Cataraqui. In that space of time, how many changes have taken place in the little circle in which fate had destined me to move! How many of the seats of my old associates are now vacant! How few of these alas! to mourn with me the loss of the companions of our sufferings, or to rejoice with me at the prosperous condition of this our land of refuge! Yet will I not repine; they are gone, I trust, to a better land, where He who causeth the wilderness to smile and blossom as the rose, hath assigned to them a distinguished place, as a reward for their humble imitation of his labors. Yes! seven and twenty years ago, scarce the vestige of a human habitation could be found in the whole extent of the Bay of Quinté. Not a settler had dared to penetrate the vast forests that skirted its shores. Even on this spot, now covered with stately edifices, were to be seen only the bark-thatched wigwam of the savage, or the newly erected tent of the hardy loyalists. Then, when the ear heard me, it blessed me for being strong in my attachment to my sovereign, and high in the confidence of my fellow-subjects, I led the loyal band, I pointed out to them the site of their future metropolis, and gained for persecuted principles, a sanctuary—for myself and followers a home." "Kingston, 7 Dec. 1811." (Signed) "G."

On the 29th May, 1788, Lord Dorchester, the Governor of Canada, issued instructions to John Collins, Surveyor, to make a survey of "forts, harbours, &c., from Carleton Island to Michilmacinac." His report was found among the "Simcoe papers." The report, dated Quebec, 6th Dec., 1788, says:—

My Lord—"In obedience to your Lordship's instructions, wherein is specified, that doubts being entertained whether Carleton Island or Kingston" (and this shows how early the royal name had been given to the first township) "is the most eligible station for the King's ships of war to protect the navigation of Lake Ontario, and the upper part of the river St. Lawrence, I am to make this particularly an object of my attention, and report how far it may be necessary to occupy either, or both, and what works I judge advisable for that purpose." "With respect to Kingston, and what is there called the harbour, and where the town is laid out, is not the best, situation on this side for vessels, as it lies rather open to the lake, and has not very good anchorage near the entrance, so that they are obliged to run a good way up for shelter; the most eligible situation is to the east." After referring to the more frequent directions of the wind, he concludes, that to get into the lake, it is as easy from Kingston as from Charleton Island, but that the latter affords the best shelter. "Having brought forward all the material information and observations I have been able to make and procure, and having duly weighed the several properties, both of Kingston and Carleton Island, relative to naval purposes only," he concludes, "that the preference rather leans on the side of Carleton Island. If the object was that of trade only, or regarded merely by the transport of goods to Niagara, I do not see that Carleton Island has any material advantage over Kingston; but, as a station for the King's ships of war, I am induced to think that Carleton Island is the best," as it possessed many natural advantages. Respecting Kingston, a fort and out-works could be constructed to protect the harbour; but an enemy might advance in the rear, and bombard the fort and the navy. "In regard to the present condition of the works at this post, the whole is so far in ruins as to be altogether defenceless, and incapable of being repaired, the ditch which is in the rock, has never been sufficiently excavated, the other works have been completed, but it strikes me they were never capable of any serious defence, as well as from the bastions, as well as the oblique manner in which their faces are seen from the other works, but the whole could only be considered as a temporary matter. The green logs with which the fort was built, could not be expected to last long; the ground is favorable for a fort of greater capacity and strength, but it is probable that such a system may have been originally adopted for the works, at the place it might have been thought adequate to its importance, to the number of troops designed for its defence, and the strength it was likely an enemy would be able to bring against it; and there ideas would again be brought into consideration, if this post should be established, or any new system adopted. Without, therefore, going, in this place, into a detail of particular works, I will remark, that as the ground in front widens and extends somewhat over the extremities of the work, particularly on the right, precaution should be taken to strengthen those points towards the field, to contract, in some degree, the advantage an enemy attacking might have in the extent of his flanks. The barracks, although partly dismantled, and in a very bad condition, may be still repaired."

From the foregoing, it may be inferred that the troops had all been withdrawn from the head of the St. Lawrence, and that only a Commissariat Department remained at Carlton Island. Probably, it was only when Canada was erected into a distinct Province, that regular troops again were stationed here, and then, it having been ascertained that Carleton Island would belong to the United States, Kinston superseded it.

Although the "King's Township" was mainly settled by the band of Loyalists who came by way of the St. Lawrence, from New York, there were several others who received grants of land here, a few of whom, no doubt, reached Kingston at as early a date as 1783, and, as we have seen, they may have visited the place, previous to that date. Among these, was Col. Hanjost, or John Joost, or Joseph Herkimer, who had been compelled to forsake his home at the German Flats, where his father lived. Looking at "A Plan of Township No. 1," (now Kingston), "in the District of Mecklenburgh, surveyed in 1783, with the proprietor's names on the lots," in the Crown Lands Department, the following may be observed. Just by the grounds of the Fort, the water is called Cataraqui Harbor. Across the mouth of the Bay, and between Points Frederick and Henry, is Haldimand Cove. Beyond Point Henry, is Hamilton Cove. Passing up the river, the first lot has upon it the name of Joseph and Mary Brant. This lot was not numbered, however. (Capt. Brant came to the place in 1785, and remained living there for a time). Still proceeding along the west shore of the river, lot No. 1, has the name of Neil McLean; No. 2, Henry Wales; No. 3, James Clark; No. 4, Capt. Crawford; No. 5, Lieut. Brown; No. 6, Sovereign; No. 7, at first was granted to Lawrence; this name is superseded by the name of Braton. To the west of the road, is a block of land, of 700 acres, for "Capt. James McDonnell;" but this name is erased, and Robert Macaulay written instead. Probably Macaulay became the purchaser. To the east of the road, is another block of land, for John Macaulay. The island in the mouth of the river, called "Isle Aux Père," was granted to Neil McLean, "by order of General Haldimand." Turning to the south of the Fort, the first lot has the name of Capt. Grass; the second from the Fort, Rev. Mr. Stuart; the third has the names upon it of Lawrence Herkimer, Sam. Hilton, Capt. Jost Hartman; the fourth, Francis Lozion, Rockland, James Brown, John Moshier; fifth, Lieut. Ellerbeck; sixth, John Stuart, Lieut. Gallary, Lieut. Mower, Charles Paudor; seventh, Capt. McGarrow; eighth, Lieutenant Atkinson; ninth, Robert Vanalstine; tenth,

Richard Moorman ; eleventh, R. Gider : this lot lies on the "Petite Cataraqui ;" twelfth, Lieut. Kotte, Surveyor, and afterward John Stuart; thirteenth, Capt. Grass, also Capt. Everett; fourteenth, Grass; fifteenth, Capt. Harkman; sixteenth Nicholas Herkimer. This brings us to Collins' Bay, or, as the orginal name appears "Ponegeg." Continuing westward, among others, are to be seen the names of Purdy, Capt. Wm. Johnson, Wm. Fairfield, Senr., Daniel Rose, Matthias Rose, Robert Clark, James Clark, Sen., Sergt. John Taylor, Capt. J. W. Myers, who has two lots; (these two last became the first settlers in Sidney and Thurlow); Lieut. James Robins, Sergt. Williams, Lieut. Best, Lieut. John Durenbury, and then there was a lot (No. 18) for the "King's saw mill," subsequently Booth's Mills. Of the foregoing, it is uncertain how many became settlers. But the most of them seem to have obtained these front lots, irrespective of Captain Grass.

Of the other early settlers, the following are, doubtless, the principal ones. For their names, I am partially indebted to Mr. G. H. Detlor, himself the descendant of an Irish Palatine. "Wm. MacAulay, Thomas Markland, John Kirby, John Cummings, Peter Smith, England, John Ferguson, Lyons, Pousett, McDonnell, Boyman, Cook, Taylor, Smyth, DeNyke, Murney, Cuthbertson, Alcott. The Rev. John Stuart, Hon. Richard Cartwright, Allen McLean." These did not probably come the first year, but within the first two or three years.

It is said that John Fralick or Freeligh, who had held a commission in the army, was one of the first settlers in Kingston, and built the fourth house erected. Other names given, as among the first inhabitants of the village of Kingston, are John Forsyth, Joseph Forsyth, Anderson, Punbee, Merrill, Stoughton, Gray, Hix, Cassady, Ashley, Burley, Stower, Donald McDonald, James Richardson, Patrick Smith, John Steel, Ebenezer Washburn. Early settlers on the front of the Township, beside those before given, were Holmes, Day, Ferris, several Wartmans, and Graham.

Before proceeding with the history of Kingston, it is desirable to notice more particularly some events connected with the occupancy of Kingston, as a Naval and Military station. We have seen that Surveyor Collins gave the preference for Carleton Island. But Lord Dorchester decided that Kingston was the most desirable place for purposes of defense, and it is a striking fact that the views held by him have been, to a certain extent, reiterated by Gen. Michel, in 1867. Both seemed to hold the opinion that Canada, west of

Kingston, was untenable against an invading foe. When Simcoe assumed the Government of the newly formed Upper Province, it was the declared desire of Lord Dorchester, that he should select Kingston as the capital, and make it a well fortified town. Already steps had been taken to establish a naval as well as a military station. Haldimand's Cove, between Point Frederick and Point Henry, had been selected for the Naval depot, and here was a Dock Yard and Stores, which were continued for many years. These were commenced about 1789, and the same year barracks were built by soldiers, upon the ruins of the old fort, which was the commencement of the Military Station, and the head-quarters of the troops in Upper Canada, and the residence of the Commander-in-Chief; also a staff of the Ordinance and Engineer Departments was kept up. Cooper, writing 1856, says: "Of late years, a general reduction has been made,—a small garrison only is now kept, and the Artillery is wholly withdrawn." (This was at the time of the Crimean war). The establishment was, some dozen years ago, greatly reduced, and is now wholly abandoned. In years past, however, the officers and crew of Her Majesty's ship Niagara, were regularly piped to quarters in a handsome stone building in the Dock Yard, which was manned, and the crew disciplined in complete man-o'-war fashion. In these bygone days, Kingston was the residence of the Commodore in charge of the Naval Department, who lived in a style which would have quite outshone that of some of our economical Governors. Those connected with this and other departments, followed the worthy Commodore's example, and as the population was not then great, the influence of that example rendered the town, if not a very prosperous, certainly a very gay, and seemingly happy one. Times have certainly changed since then, as far as the expenditure of Imperial money is concerned."

After Kingston had been selected as a military station, it naturally grew more rapidly. The presence of the soldiers and of seamen, and their expenditure of money, had the effect of starting into quicker life, the infant town; but when Simcoe, in 1792, passed it by, and sought his gubernatorial residence at Newark, it received a material check in its growth. Being the largest collection of houses in Upper Canada, Kingston had claims, irrespective of the existence of the two arms of the service. During the first decade in the history of Upper Canada, Kingston did not rise above a small village, although it was honoured, sometimes, with the appellation of "city." Rochefoucault says, 1795, that Kingston "consists of about 120 or 30 houses. The ground in the immediate vicinity of the city, rises with a gentle swell, and forms, from the lake onwards, as it were, an amphitheatre of lands, cleared, but not yet cultivated. None of the buildings are distinguished by a more handsome appearance from the rest. The only structure, more conspicuous than the others, and in front of which the English flag is hoisted, is the barracks, a stone building surrounded with palisades. All the houses stand on the northern bank of the bay, which stretches a mile further into the country. On the southern bank are the buildings belonging to the naval force, the wharfs, and the habitations of all the persons, who belong to that department. The King's ships lie at anchor near those buildings, and consequently have a harbour and road separate from the port for merchantmen."

"Kingston, considered as a town, is much inferior to Newark; the number of houses is nearly equal in both. Kingston may contain a few more buildings, but they are neither so large nor so good as at Newark. Many of them are log houses, and those which consist of joiners' work, are badly constructed and painted. But few new houses are built. No town-hall, no court-house, and no prison have hitherto been constructed. The houses of two or three merchants are conveniently situated for loading and unloading ships; but, in point of constructure, these are not better than the rest.

"Kingston seems better fitted for a trading town than Newark, were it only for this reason, that the ships, which arive at the latter place, and are freighted for Lake Erie, pass by the former, to sail again up the river as far as Queen's Town, where the portage begins."

Cooper remarks that "Fort Frontenac existed for several years after the conquest, the remains of the tower in the interior being removed in 1827. The present barracks were built, the officers' quarters in 1821, the men's stone barracks in 1827, and the frame barracks in 1837. At the commencement of the war in 1812, Point Henry, the site of the present extensive military works, was covered with trees; in the following year a rude fort of logs and embankment was thrown up. A year or two after its erection two large and substantial stone towers were added to the defences, they were lofty, square towers, rounded at the corners. These remained until 1826 or '28. Stone magazines, ordnance offices, and armoury were built outside the fort during the years 1816, '17 and '18.

Extensive stone barracks, roofed with tin, were built between 1818 and 1820; one of these within the fort was 230 feet in length; another building which stood where the advanced battery has since been built, was 80 feet in length, and formed the officers' quarters.

"These barracks stood until 1841, when they were pulled down and the material sold. Two large houses in Brock Street, and one in Barrack Street, were built from the stone, which, it may be remarked in passing, is not the ordinary blue limestone in general use, but a much whiter material, apparently not so durable. The erection of the present fort was commenced in 1832, several previous years having been spent in the quarrying and preparing material. It was first occupied in 1836. On Point Frederick the first works were a breastwork of logs and earth, with traversing platforms for guns; within the breastwork was a block house. These works were built during or just after the war; this block house was burnt in the year 1820. There were also built, about the same time, a block house surounded with a strong stockade on the hill on Princess Street, on the lot formerly owned by the late Mr. Jacob Ritter; a small redan on Ordnance Street; a battery at Mississauga Point; a block house near the present Marine Railway; one on Stuart's or Murney's Point; another at Snake Island; one which stood until recently, near the present new court house, with those now standing, one of them on the hill to the east of the city, and the other at the west end of Wellington Street. These block houses, excepting, of course, that on Snake Island, were all connected by a strong stake fence, or stockade; portions of which still exist, and formed a chain of defences surrounding, what was then, the whole city."

From the first, it will be seen that the village of Kingston was to a great extent indebted to the public service for its prosperity. Isaac Wild, writing in 1796, says that from 60 to 100 men are quartered in the barracks.

CHAPTER XLVIII.

CONTENTS—The situation of Kingston—Under military influence—Monopolist—Early history of legislation—In 1810—Gourlay's statement—Police—Modern Kingston—Lord Sydenham—Seat of government—Perambulating—Surrounding country—Provisions—An appeal for Kingston as capital—Barriefield—Pittsburgh—Building of small crafts—Famous—Roads—Waterloo—Cemetry—Portsmouth—Kingston Mill—Little Cataraqui—Collinsby—Quantity of land—Early and influential inhabitants—Post masters—"Honorable men"—Deacon, Macaulay, Cartwright, Markland, Cummings, Smiths, Kerby—Allen McLean, first lawyer—A gardener—Sheriff McLean—"Chrys" Hagerman—Customs—Sampson, shooting a smuggler—Hagerman, M.P.P.—Removes to Toronto.

THE FIRST TOWNSHIP——EVENTS IN ITS EARLY HISTORY.

It must be admitted, the place did not possess from its geographical situation the requisites for becoming a great city, although its situation at the head of the St. Lawrence, would always secure for it a certain degree of importance. There are evils incident to places, depending upon the military and naval bodies, and these can be seen in connection with the history of Kingston. Anything which drew away for a time, to any extent, either arm of the service, had a damaging effect upon the prosperity, and stagnation resulted in business.

Early Kingston must be regarded as a town growing up in the back woods, with a population governed and influenced more or less by the society of officers and soldiers, and while the former gave dignity and tone to the higher classes, the lower portion of society was correspondingly and for evil, affected by the presence of the soldiers, with the numerous grogeries, and low houses of entertainments, which particularly in former days, were found to exist in connection with military establishments.

In the first years of Canada, speculation was common with a certain class. Land claims could be purchased for a mere song. The holder of a "location ticket," would often part with his title for a few quarts of rum, while many other holders were glad to sell for a few pounds of ready money, or certain articles of stock. It came that in time, a certain number of monopolists, living at Kingston, held land in the rear concessions and neighboring townships. The Imperial money in Kingston was often spent without contributing to the improvement of the adjacent country. But the time came when the encircling settlers compelled a more generous course of conduct.

But, much obscurity rests upon the history of the first seven or ten years of the village of Kingston. The effort has been made to gather up the fragments partaining thereto, and arrange them so as to form a connected whole.

Cooper says that "the town was laid out in 1793, being then confined to what is now the eastern portion in the vicinity of the *Tete du Pont* barracks, and what was then known as the Cataraqui Common, lots 25, 24, 23, on which is situated the chief part of the city, were then farm lots of 200 acres each, and uncleared."

According to the census roll in the office of the clerk of the peace 1794, the population of Cataraqui village was 345. It would seem that the appearance of the village was not very pleasing. But the surroundings had a certain wild beauty. The first buildings were of the most inferior kind. Kingston now so beautiful in its fine buildings and well appointed streets, had in its first days but the humblest of log tenements, with the rude Indian wigwam for a neighbor. Instead of fair broad streets, and a well ordered park, there was the Indian foot path, and the thick tangled wood, with the stately pine.

In 1793 an act was passed "to fix the times and places of holding the courts of quarter sessions, within the several districts," according to which it was provided that the courts of the midland district should be held in Kingston, in April and October of each year. This added somewhat to the dignity of the place. Then in 1801, there was created an act to empower commissioners of the peace, to establish a market at Kingston, where might be exposed for sale "butchers' meat, butter, eggs, poultry, fish, and vegetables." It was further enacted that all "rules and regulations shall be published by causing a copy of them to be affixed in the most public place in every township in the district, and at the doors of the church and court house of the said town of Kingston, &c.

In 1810, Kingston was yet a small place. Mr. Miles who moved there at the time says there was not a sidewalk or pavement, and he for a time boarded in one of several log houses close by the market place, "where was no lack of mud in the spring and fall, and it was no uncommon thing for waggons to be pried out by fence rails just north of the market place. Pine trees of the forest yet waved almost over the market place. A thick wood covered Point Henry, and the ground, where now is erected St. Andrew's Church and parsonage. The limit of the town on the north was at Store Street, now Princess, the last house being on the north east side, Alcott's old store, and on the west side where Mr. Meadows now resides. The road, for it was then such only after passing, Alcott's turned to the right, and went a zig-zag course northwards, till it reached the second concession, now Waterloo road. This was a distance of five miles from the foot of Store Street."

A resident writing to the *Kingston Gazette*, December 26, 1815, among other things, says that the town of Kingston, "possessing so many advantages, it is time that its inhabitants should adopt some plan of improving and embellishing of it. The streets require very great repairs, as in the rainy seasons it scarcely possible to move about without being in mud to the ankles; from the breadth, they will admit of very wide foot-paths on both sides, which ought to be paved, at least in every part of the town where the buildings are connected. Lamps are required to light the streets in the dark of the moon. Trees should be planted on each side. The streets should be kept free of lumber of every kind, and piles of wood. A fire engine, with a certain number of buckets, with a company of firemen should exist. But first the legislature must form a code of laws, forming a complete police. To meet expense, government might lay a rate upon every inhabitant householder in proportion to value of property in house."

Another correspondent under the signature of Citizen, says, "January 27, 1816, that he approves of "A Residents" remarks, and in addition, he suggests that the lower classes follow the example of the liberal spirit manifested among heads of society in the previous summer in contributing to the turnpiking of the streets, and paving the footpaths before their own doors. They ought to imitate, though faintly, that noble and generous example." Besides this, among other things, Citizen speaks against persons who work at their trades on Sunday, instead of going to church. "Luther," another correspondent says, there is the noise of hammers and axes from sunrise to sunset, on Sundays.

According to the *Kingston Gazette*, August 14, 1829, the census taken that year shewed the population of the town to be 3528, but this did not include the military. The number of inhabitants in 1836 was 6000.

At the present time, 1867, Kingston is said to cover an area of 2930 acres, while Toronto boasts of 5885 acres.

R. Gourlay says, in 1816, that Kingston "is now progressing rapidly in population and buildings, as well as in business. From 1811 to 1816 the number of dwellings increased from 130 to 300;

but it is estimated that 100 more will have been erected at the close of this year." Much of this prosperity was doubtless due to the war, causing so many troops to be stationed there; at the same time business and general growth of the City received an impetus which the close of the war failed entirely to arrest. This year a bill passed Parliament "to regulate the police, within the town of Kingston." More ample provision was made in 1824.

In 1821, a writer says, Kingston was the largest town in Upper Canada, containing about 5000 inhabitants including the military. "The people live in good style, but are not very hospitable; they are mostly in the mercantile business." The number of inhabitants is probably over estimated, as in 1824 it is stated on good authority, that the population amounts to 2336. "The buildings are of such an inferior description as scarcely to be worthy of notice."

MODERN KINGSTON.

The events chronicled in this work are mainly those which came to pass prior to 1830, and the history of the first township here recorded must mainly be limited to those early days. It will not, however, be inappropriate to glance, and it will be a mere glance at the Kingston of modern days. The greatest event in connection with Kingston, was the selection by Lord Sydenham, when the Upper and Lower Provinces were united in 1840, into one, for the capital of United Canada. Its claim to that honor as the most central city cannot be questioned. It may fairly be questioned on the other hand whether it was a wise and judicious policy, which caused Kingston to be forsaken, and the perambulatory system to be substituted. Had the Seat of Government permanently rested at Kingston, much expense to the country would have been saved, and at the same time a great deal of heart bitterness stirred up by political agitators, likewise prevented. But the hopes of Kingston as the capital were shortlived, and with the death of Lord Sydenham, in 1842, resulting from an accident, who had been mainly the cause of Kingston becoming the capital, the brightest prospects of the oldest town in Upper Canada, were buried.

In 1845 Government was removed to Montreal. The motives according to Cooper, which had much to do in determining the removal were not such as are supposed to actuate statesmen. After rebutting the charge which it seems had been made, that there was "no surrounding country calculated to furnish marketable produce to a large non-producing population," and referring to the undoubted facts that the townships along the Bay of Quinte were far more than adequate to meet all the gastronomists wants, he concludes. "It may seem a small consideration when treating of so important a branch of the subject, to take into account these circumstances, but there is no ignoring the fact that the absence of some of these minor luxuries had a serious effect on the minds, and perhaps digestion of some of the officials of Her Majesty's Provincial Government, and some people at a distance are persuaded that Kingston is a city built on a rock, surrounded with barren and stoney wilds, out of which a bare existence is wrung by the occupants, and but a scanty supply afforded to the City, and in deference to those thus unenlightened, facts are dwelt on which may seem trivial to those in the least acquainted with the neighborhood. Since 1845, when the Government was removed to Montreal, this City has greatly increased in the number of well built and commodious houses, which, with a well regulated and well supplied market, tempting the most fastidious, would prevent even the temporary inconveniences which in that year were felt. If any families had to adopt double-bedded rooms, and to import their own celery in those days, we can now assure them '*nous avons changes tout cela.*' In short we claim for a City central, indeed almost in the very centre of the Province to be governed, proverbially healthy, substantially built, strongly fortified, well lighted, thoroughly drained, pleasantly situated, abundantly supplied, easy of access, the focus of a net-work of good roads, the outlet of the produce of several rich countries, provided with a good harbour, and enjoying many other advantages, a pre-eminence among all Canadian Cities, as the permanent Seat of the Government of the Province."

The existence of the Seat of Government at Kingston, although of short duration, had a beneficial effect; many handsome buildings were erected besides those used for the several Public Departments. "The Municipal Legislature of the City was encouraged to make improvements in streets, drainage, side-walks, and otherwise, and to erect the present handsome and expensive edifice, the City Hall and Market House, though not so useful as it would have been had the Government remained here. The whole building is occupied, and produces a revenue exceeding in amount the interest on its cost. On the whole it may fairly be considered that the

City was improved by the temporary location of the Government here."

BARRIEFIELD.—The Cataraqui Bridge, which spans the great Cataraqui River connects Kingston with the Township of Pittsburgh, the origin of which name is sufficiently well indicated. Close by, is the village of Barriefield, "named after Commodore Barrie, who was head of the Naval Department for many years." "It forms a sort of suburb to the city, and though not a place of much increase, has been long settled. It has an elevated ground, and from it the visitor obtains a very favorable and pleasing view of Kingston, with its harbors, forts and towers. At Barriefield, are built the best small crafts, skiffs, and pleasure boats in use throughout the Province. They are sent hence to all parts, and their character and build are well known to the aquatic sportsman, and amateur mariner. Not only in the Province, but abroad, these boats are sought after, and in use, some of them being now afloat on the Lake of Geneva. The Kingston, Pittsburgh, and Gananoque, and the Kingston and Phillipsville Macadamized Roads run through this township, opening up the township beyond, and affording to the settler a ready access to a never-failing market. Within this township, are upwards of thirty-eight miles of thoroughly macadamized roads, besides good country roads to and between the concessions. That part of Pittsburgh where Barriefield stands, and for about two miles eastward, was formerly part of the township of Kingston. When the site of the Town of Kingston was first selected, the spot where this village is situated was suggested, but was overruled in favor of the present locality of Kingston, which certainly offered greater advantages for the site of a city."

Kingston Township contains, not only the city of that name, but various villages; "one of the nearest to that city is that of *Waterloo*, a very pretty and neat little hamlet, about three miles from town. It contains about 300 inhabitants, and has its Town Hall, Church, Stores, Inns, &c."

"In the neighborhood of this village, is the *Cataraqui Cemetery*, laid out on a rising ground crowned by a grove of small pine trees. Much care and skill in landscape gardening has been displayed in rendering the ground picturesque and pleasing; a fine and extended view of the surrounding country, and a pretty glimpse of the Bay is obtained from the Cemetery grounds. This spot is not excelled in beauty and appropriateness, by anything in the Province, and is compared by travelers, who view it, to Greenwood Cemetery, in

Brooklin, N. Y. It covers some sixty-five acres of land, and when ornamented by such numerous and elegant monuments, as the living have erected to mark their respect to the beloved dead in older places of sepulture, will be unsurpassed by the oldest and most beautiful cemeteries known."

"*Portsmouth* is another village, about equi-distant from Kingston with Waterloo, lying westward on the Lake shore; it was at one time, a very bustling spot, and much enterprise was evinced in ship-building. It suffered, for a time, from the withdrawal of the Seat of Government, and the construction of the St. Lawrence canals, but has now recovered its former prosperity, which promises to continue. The ship-building business has revived, and is carried on with energy and success. In its neighborhood are several handsome houses and villa-residences: the surrounding country offering very inviting spots for building. It contains about 350 inhabitants, and a large amount of rateable property, and has an exceedingly neat unique little Church, in old English style, with a belfry." Portsmouth is now united to Kingston, by the erection of buildings between them.

Within the Township of Kingston, about five miles from the city; is the old "Kingston Mill." It is situated upon the Rideau Canal. The traveler, as he passes along by train, over a tubular bridge, will be struck by the beauty and grandeur of the scene. (For particulars, see "Early Years of Upper Canada.")

Little Cataraqui is a stream of small dimensions, confined to the township. In addition to the Little Cataraqui stream, there is running across the township, the Collins Creek, so named after Surveyor Collins. Not far from its source, in the north east part of the township, is a small, pleasant lake, of the same name, while, at its mouth, is Collins' Bay. This is a beautiful inlet of the Bay Quinté, and forms a good harbour. The place is known as Collinsby, and is situated about five miles west of Kingston.

The quantity of land in the township, is about 47,906. The soil is principally clay upon a limestone foundation; but still there is much of it capable of bearing good crops, to the careful and scientific farmer.

Thomas Deacon, father of the present Post Master, was Post Master from 1800 to 1836, when his duties in the Commissariat Department obliged him to resign that office. The Hon. John Macauley occupied the post from 1813 to 1836, when he resigned, and was succeeded by the present incumbent, Robert Deacon.

We will supplement the reference we have made to the leading men of Kingston, by giving extracts from a communication we have, at the last moment received, written by one who, now well advanced in life, spent his earlier years of manhood in Kingston, when the first inhabitants were in the afternoon of their life.

The Hon. R. Cartwright, the pioneer merchant, and Judge of Mecklenburgh, seems to have stood next in importance and influence to the Rev. Mr. Stuart. "Among the prominent merchants was Thomas Markland, John Cummings, Peter Smith, John Kirby, and John Macaulay." They were "all honorable men," and "members of the English Church," and of undeviating loyalty. Mr. Markland left a son. John Cummings left no issue. He was a man of "great energy; a magistrate, and filled other offices under the Government." Peter Smith was "highly respected, upright in all his dealings, and free from any moral or political reproach." "A fine specimen of an English gentleman." He "carried with him evidence that he was no stranger to good dinners, and understood the qualities of good wine." He died at an advanced age, 1825, leaving a son and two daughters.

"John Kirby was another fine specimen of an Englishman. He loved good wine and good dinners. Extremely affable, always in good humor, universally respected. His highest ambition, in the evening of his days, seemed to be the enjoyment of domestic tranquility, and a quiet home, made happy to him by a wife of rare sense, intelligent, and possessed of many amiable accomplishments." The Hon. John Macaulay had a well disciplined mind, possessed great energy of character, and was decided in his political opinions no doubt, from conscientious motives. In his business transactions "he was scrupulously exact." "Extremely temperate in his habits. Was one of those who passed through life without exposing themselves to the obloquy of their political opponents. Allen McLean, Esq., the first Lawyer of Kingston; created such by an order in Council. His "abilities were moderate," and "his original education defective." "A man of considerable taste, modest, dignified in his deportment. For many years, was the only legal adviser in the place. He was a faithful representative in Parliament for many years. Was liberal in his political opinions." "As proof of his good taste, he was proprietor of one of the best gardens in the Province. It covered one acre of ground, and contained many choice fruit trees, such as apples, plums, pears, peach, &c.,—all tastefully arranged, kept in prime order, and defended from the wind by a high wall. He took an honest pride in showing his garden to his friends who called npon him, and was not stinted in distributing its lucious products." Mr. McLean left one daughter, who became the wife of John McLean, Esq., Sheriff of the Midland District. Christopher Hagerman resided for many years in Kingston. "Was, for many years, Custom House Officer, and while so, one of his students (Mr. Samson, afterwards of Belleville) detected a man, by the name of Lyons, in the act of carrying smuggled goods, and ordered him to stop. On his refusing to do so, Mr. S. discharged his pistol, which took effect, the ball passing through the chest. Lyons rushed to his house, a few doors off, and fell exhausted from loss of blood. Mr. Samson, frightened at what he had done, hastened to summon two doctors, Drs. Armstrong and Sampson. This occurred before daylight, on the morning of the 26th June, 1824. The life of Lyons was despaired of for many days; but, eventually, he grew better, and gained a moderate degree of health. It is creditable to Mr. Hagerman, that he cheerfully paid the medical attendants. Mr. Hagerman represented Kingston in Parliament several years. He removed to Toronto, a few years previous to the rebellion of 1836.

CHAPTER XLIX.

CONTENTS—The second town—Ernest's town—King George—His children—Settlers of Ernesttown—Disbanded soldiers—Johnson's regiment—Major Rogers' corps—The "Roll"—Number—By whom enlisted—An old book—Township surveyed—Settling—Traveling—Living in tents—A change—Officers—Names—Occupants of lots—Mill Creek—The descendants—Quantity of land—Village—The settlers in 1811—The main road—Incorporation of Bath—Trading—Fairfield—The library—Bath by Gourlay—Bath of the present—Bath *versus* Napanee—In 1812—American Fleet—Wonderful achievement—Safe distance from shore—Third township—Fredericksburgh—After Duke of Sussex—Surveyed by Kotte—A promise to the disbanded soldiers—Johnson—Fredericksburgh additional—A dispute—Quantity of land—Extract from Mrs. Moodie—Reserve for village—Second surveys.

THE SECOND TOWNSHIP—ERNESTTOWN—BATH.

The first township was named after His Majesty, the King's Town, and all of the other townships, both upon the St. Lawrence and Bay Quinté, received names after distinguished loyality, or some distinguished nobleman, or general of Great Britain, then occupying a prominent position. King George the Third, who died in 1820, aged eighty-two, having reigned sixty years, had a family of fifteen children, whose names were George, Frederick, William Henry, Charlotte Augusta Matilda, Edward, Sophia Augusta, Elizabeth, Ernest Augustus, Augustus Frederick, Adolphus Frederick, Mary, Sophia, Octavius, Alfred, Amelia. These royal names were appropriated to the townships, towns, districts, &c.

Ernesttown was so named after Earnest Augustus, the eighth child of the King.

The first township, we have seen, was chiefly granted to Captain Grass and the band of loyalists who came from New York under his guidance, notwithstanding some objection from Sir John Johnson, and the officers of his regiment. The second township, however, and also the third, were alloted to the 2nd battalion of the 84th regiment, commonly called Sir John Johnson's regiment, also the King's New York Royal Rangers. The regiment was generally designated, by the rebels, as the Royal Greens. This body of men took a conspicuous part in the war—took a noble part, although those who feared them, and were unequal to meet them in successful combat, endeavoured to malign them. The history of this regiment is referred to elsewhere, and as well that of the distinguished founder. The writer has in his possession the "roll of the 2nd battalion of the King's Royal Rangers, New

York," containing the names of the parties by whom each of the soldiers was enlisted, which will be found in the appendix.

By this it is learned that the whole number of the company was 477. That Sir John Johnson enlisted 88, Major Ross 47, Captain Leahe 17, Guminall 38, Munrow 29, Anderson 1, Lieutenant Halbert 1, Captain McKay 95, Morrison 30, Singleton 1, Major Gray 2, Captain Crawford 2, John McDonell 2, Lieutenant Langan 30, Langhn 2, Lieutenant Wair 1, French 1, C. McAlpine 1, Ensign Thompson 1, Lieutenant McKay 2, Sergeant Howell 2, Tipple 1, Ensign Smith 3, and 69 by whom, it is not stated, they were enlisted. This roll was afterwards a precious document, when it became necessary to prove that one was truly a U. E. Loyalist. The book in which this roll is found, seems to have been an account book kept by the Adjutant, Fraser, and is dated at Oswego, 28th November, 1782. Subsequently, it was used as an account book by "Captain Crawford's company." We believe it was after his death that the book came into the possession of Mr. Sills. It is an interesting relic of the past, and ought to find a lodgement in some museum.

Many of these disbanded soldiers were from the Mohawk valley and Upper Hudson. The majority were from the old Johnston district, and not a few of Dutch origin. These honest and industrious settlers are represented to-day by wealthy and valuable citizens, whose names unmistakably indicate the stock from which they have descended.

This township was surveyed probably in 1784. It may be that a base line was run in the fall of 1783. By looking at the map of this township, it will be seen that the lots are marked, like those of Kingston, from west to east, showing that the base line was run along the whole length, and then subsequently the survey completed from the west.

In the early spring of 1784, came the soldier settlers; the 1st battalion, commonly called Jessup's Corps, settled on the St. Lawrence, in Edwardsburgh and Augusta, while the second, or Rogers' Corps, passed up to the Bay of Quinté. Respecting this regiment, the following will prove appropriate, from the pen of the historian of the County of Dundas. "At the close of the war, this regiment was stationed at the Isle aux Noix, a fortified frontier post at the northern extremity of Lake Champlain, which has been mentioned as an important fortress during the old French war. Here they passed a whole year, and were employed in adding to the already extensive fortifications of that island. While they remained there thus employed, two Government surveyors, named Steichmann and Tewit, were actively engaged surveying the County of Dundas, for their future occupation. Late in the autumn of 1783, the soldiers were joined by their wives and little ones, who had wandered the weary way afoot, to Whitehall, through swamps and forest, beset with difficulties, dangers, and privations, innumerable. The soldiers from Isle aux Noix met them there, with boats, and conveyed them the rest of their journey by water, through Lake Champlain. Imagination fails us when we attempt to form an idea of the emotions that filled their hearts, as families, that had formerly lived happily together, surrounded with peace and plenty, and had been separated by the rude hand of war, now met in each others embrace, in circumstances of abject poverty. A boisterous passage was before them in open boats, exposed to the rigors of the season—a dreary prospect of a coming winter, to be spent in pent up barracks, and a certainty, should they be spared, of undergoing a life-time of such hardship, toil, and privation, as are inseparable from the settlement of a new country. As soon as the journey was accomplished, the soldiers and their families, were embarked in boats, sent down the Richelieu to Sorel, thence to Montreal, and on to Cornwall, by the laborious and tedious route of the St. Lawrence. The difficulty of dragging their boats up the rapids of this river was very great; to us it is really quite inconceivable. Arrived at Cornwall, they found there the Government Land Agent, and forthwith proceeded to draw by lottery the lands that had been granted to them. On the 20th of June, 1784, the first settlers landed in the County of Dundas."

Not unlikely some of the 2nd battalion were stationed at Carleton Island and Oswego, up to the time that settlement took place. We learn that Captain Crawford's company at least was at the latter place in 1782. However, it seems clear that most of the battalion was in Lower Canada, and came up with the first battalion. The survey was not yet completed, and they pitched their tents along the shore, waiting until the work of drawing lots was accomplished. In the meantime, they passed their days as best they could; not knowing where their lot would be cast, they could not proceed with the clearing of land. The writer has been told by one who, passing up during this summer, saw the tents spread along the shore, upon whose brink the primeval forest yet stood in all its native beauty. Now, had they been stationed at Carleton Island or Oswego, it is not likely they would have thus come before they could enter upon their work of settling.

The camp tents in use by these disbanded veterans were the same they had occupied in their campaigning. How great the change to them. The alarm of the coming foe, the thought of approaching battle, the cannon's roar, the rattle of small arms, no longer disturbed their dreams, nor sounded upon their ears. The battle cloud had passed away, leaving but a wreck of their worldly goods, and there was a great calm—the calm of the desert wilderness, unbroken even by the sound of the pioneer's axe—the calm of a conscience quieted by the thought that all had been sacrificed in a righteous cause. They had met and conquered many a foe; but the fate of war had driven them to the desert wild, to encounter new fears, to fight the battle of the pioneer. How they succeeded; how glorious the victory, is written, not merely by our own feeble hand elsewhere—it is indellibly inscribed upon the pages of the townships, by the tillers of the soil.

In this township as well as elsewhere, the officers seem to have had the choice of lots upon the front, while the rank and file took possession of the rear lots. Among the officers who settled on the front of Ernesttown and Fredericksburgh, may be found the names of Lieut. Church, Lieut. Spencer, Capts. Crawford and Thompson, Ensign Fraser, Capt. Howard. According to John Collins Clark, son of Robert Clark, the first lots were taken up in the following order, commencing at the easternmost lot, No. 42:

Lot 42 was first occupied by David Purdy; Joshua Booth, Esq., married to a daughter of David Fraser, lived on Lot 40 or 41; Mr. Nicholas Lake, Lot 39, but soon left it; Lot 38 was settled by Capt. Wm. Johnson; William Fairfield, sen., Lot 37. He had twelve children, all of whom lived to marry. Daniel Rose commenced a settlement on Lot 30, but in a few years left, and removed to the third concession. Matthias Rose, sen., settled on Lot 35, he died in his 90th year. Lot 34 and east half of 33, were settled by Robert Clark, Esq. His wife was a Ketcham, they had five sons and a daughter; he died at the age of 80 years. His eldest son, Matthias, had twelve sons. West half of Lot 33 was occupied by John Longwell. The east half of Lot 32 was first owned by John Sayer; the west half by Simon Swarts. Lot 31 was school land, first occupied by Michael Phipps and William Sole. East half of Lot 29, owned by a German named Gedd, west half occupied by Daniel Fraser, Esq., though not the first settler on that lot. Sebastian Hogle, John Lake and John Caldwell settled Lots 27 and 28, but soon removed back into the concessions. James Parrot, Esq., a half-pay officer, settled Lot 26; he afterward sold this lot to Adam Stanring, from the Mohawk River. The next settlers, continuing westward, were Jacob Miller, Frederick Baker, Wigant (Lutheran clergyman), John Mabee, Joseph Huff, a waggon maker, Adam Peat, a tailor, Nicholas Amey, Simon Snider, David Williams, generally called Sergeant Williams, a blacksmith, Joseph Losee, Lieut. John Dusenbury. Lieut. Best soon left, and Dusenbury died. Lot 19, has latterly been partially laid out into village lots, and a number of buildings erected. Lot 18 was a Government mill lot. It was leased for some years by Joshua Booth. From the number of mills subsequently erected on the stream, that empties here, it obtained the name of "Mill Creek." Lot 17, settled by William Cottier which was afterward owned by A. D. Foward. There were several occupants of the next lot; and the next was settled by Brisco, and the next by Richard Robins. Then came one by John George. Lot 11, now a part of Bath, was owned by George McGinnis, a half-pay officer, who sold to Fairfield. No. 10, on which is situated most of the village of Bath, was occupied by John Davy. No. 9 was owned by James Johnson, father of the celebrated "Bill" Johnson, the traitor of 1812. The next was settled by Jeptha Hamley, Esq. Westward lived Matthias Rose, William Rose, Wilcox, Shibley, then Finkle, Brisco, Huffman, Pruyn, Williams, Church, &c. As a general thing, the sons of the first settlers, settled in the rear concessions. At the present time, says Clark, there are not more than 10 or 12 of the farms on the front owned by the descendants of the original settlers.

The township of Ernesttown contains 68,644 acres, all of which is excellent land with the least exception, so that the pioneers were not the losers in having this township allotted to them instead of Kingston. However, at that time the distance from Carleton Island and Cataraqui seemed considerable. The land being good, and the settlers industrious, as a general thing, the time was not long, when the township became the best cultivated, and most wealthy, not alone around the Bay of Quinté but in the whole of Western Canada. The richness of the soil, and lying more immediately at the mouth of the Bay, contributed to its prosperity, and a village before many years sprung up, which for a time rivalled even Kingston itself, in respect to rapid increase of inhabitants, the establishment of trade, building of ships, and from the presence of gentlemen of refinement and education, and in the foundation of a library and a seminary of higher education.

Gourlay says, in 1811, that "the settlers are most of them practical husbandmen. Their farms are well fenced, well tilled. and accommodated with barns. There are now above 2,300 inhabitants, a a greater number than are found in any other township in the Province. They have three houses of public worship, one Episcopalian one Presbyterian, and one Methodist. In 1817, Ernesttown had "one parochial academy in the village, and thirteen common schools over the township."

In some of the townships first surveyed, a plot was reserved at the front, and subsequently laid out into town lots. Such was the case in Ernesttown, seemingly. At all events a village sprung up at an early period, on the front of the tenth lot. It was for a long time known as the Village of Ernesttown; but in time, after the war of 1812, it acquired the name of Bath, probably after the beautiful English town of that name. The distance of Bath from Kingston is about eighteen miles, and the road leading thereto was one of the first constructed in Upper Canada, and the country there was regarded as the very centre of civilization in the Province. For a long time the main road between Kingston and York passed by Bath, even after it was no longer solely by the way of Prince Edward and the Carrying Place. A branch of the main road passed from this place to Napanee, and thence to Thurlow and Sidney. Bath was regarded as a city in embryo. Its progress was onward, until the war of 1812. Gourlay says of it in 1811, that "it promises to be a place of considerable business." But the war dealt a serious blow to the place, from which it never recovered fully. The *Kingston Gazette*, of 1816, remarks, to the effect, that the village is emerging from its depression, and that it ought to be made a post town, and a port of entry. In the summer of this year Samuel Purdy started a public conveyance between Kingston and Bath. The following year the Steamer *Frontenac* and *Charlotte* were commenced here. In 1818 a bill was introduced into Parliament "to constitute the town of Bath—to provide for laying out and surveying town lots and streets, and a market-place therein, and regulating the police thereof."

The first person to engage in the trading business at Bath was Benjamin Fairfield.

Thus wrote Gourlay, of Bath, in 1811: "From the lake shore the ground ascends about seventy rods, and thence slopes off in a gentle northern descent. The ascent is divided into regular squares by five streets, laid parallel with the shore; one of them being the lower branch of the main road, and all of them crossed at right angles by streets running northerly. One of these cross streets is continued through the concession, and forms that branch of the main road which passes round the Bay of Quinté. On the east side of this street, at the most elevated point, stands the church, and on the opposite side is the academy, overlooking the village, and commanding a variegated prospect of the harbour, the sound, the adjacent island, the outlets into the open lake, and the shores stretching eastward and westward, with a fine landscape view of the country all around. The situation is healthy and delightful, not surpassed perhaps in natural advantages by any in America. The village is increasing in buildings, accommodations, inhabitants, and business, and seems calculated to be the central point of a populous and productive tract of country around it."

A stranger visiting Bath to-day, having read of its early and enterprising days, will not unlikely feel a pang of disappointment. We are sorry to say that the place presents a tumbling-down appearance. A large brick building, built in 1809, to accommodate what was then the largest Free Mason lodge in the province, has a large rent in it, as if an enemy's cannon ball had penetrated and shattered it. Prominently situated it attracts great attention. The quietness of the place reminds one of Goldsmith's deserted village. Within our own recollection, ship building was carried on here; but now nothing indicates the place of busy enterprise; there is nothing but the plain unbroken beach, where was constructed the first steamboats built in Upper Canada. The literary spirit that led to the establishment of a library here at an early date, we fear has departed—gone with the spirit of those who nobly conceived the project — gone as lawyers Macaulay, Fairfield, and Bidwell, who here entered upon promising careers of professional usefulness. The glory of Bath has not ceased to depart; year after year it has lost some element of importance to its existence. The rich country around for many years poured into this charming village its ever increasing supplies. The merchants of Bath exchanged goods for the produce, and became rich; but now, Napanee, affording a greater variety of the necessaries and luxuries for family use, draws a large majority of the well-to-do yeomen, who there spend their money. Occasionally, a grain buyer may be able to offer a little higher price here, yet the farmer takes his money to spend in Napanee. Times, indeed, have changed since the denizens of Bath regarded their village as a rival of Kingston; when enterprise sought here a larger field in which to drive business, and men of education adorned society, and gave refinement and superior advantages to its people. Then Napanee was in the backwoods—a place regarded as we do now the settlements upon the Hasting's Road; and those who lived there were removed from the centre of civilization. But now the iron horse speeds along by the old York Road; and Bath of Canada, like its great namesake at home, although still beautiful, is interesting, mainly from its past associations.

It was the citizens of Bath who first saw the American fleet in 1813 approaching the shore. The early morning sun saw the inhabitants very shortly aroused to action. The old veterans, who for so many years had used the plow and the axe, anxiously enquired for their old weapons of warfare. Mrs. Perry tells us that she distinctly remembers that the word came to her father's while they were at breakfast, that the enemy was entering Bath. Her father, then fifty-eight, forsook his breakfast and sought his gun. But before he and his sons reached the village, the fleet had passed on toward Kingston. Three of his sons, hurried on to Kingston. In like manner, all along the front, arose the men of seventy-six, with their sons; and their arms flashed in the morning sunlight. The enemy had won at Bath a great victory. They had stolen in at the early dawn, when no foe was there, and actually had succeeded in taking and burning the schooner *Benjamin Davy*.

THE THIRD TOWNSHIP—FREDERICKSBURGH.

The early settlers sometimes called it the "Township of Frederick." It was called after Augustus Frederick, the Duke of Sussex, ninth child of the king.

According to the original plan of this township, preserved in the Crown Lands' Department, it was "surveyed in 1784 by James Pearly Lewis Kotte, Henry Holland, and Samuel Tuffe."

The limits of the second township having been defined, the third was also planned. Having fixed the base line, which formed a slight angle with that of the second town, over the width of twenty-five lots, it was at first, the intention to limit the township to this extent of frontage; and the lots were consequently completed and numbered from west to east, as had been done with the first two townships. But it turned out that this would not meet the requirements of Sir John Johnson's disbanded soldiers, to whom the promise had been made that they should be located in a township by themselves. The result was, that the wishes of this corps' were gratified, and the township was enlarged to the extent of thirteen additional lots, which the map will show are numbered from east to west, and which indicate that the lots were completely surveyed before they were numbered. That portion of the third town included in the portion first numbered, received the name of "Fredericksburgh Original," and that subsequently added, was called "Fredericksburgh Additional." The original intention of the surveyor, was to have the latter portion form a part of the fourth township, which would have effected a more equal division of the land; but the disbanded soldiers did not wish to pass under the control of other officers, such as held command of the settlers of the fourth township. Indeed, as will be more particularly pointed out in connection with that township, Adolphustown had well nigh been entirely consumed by the renewed arrivals of Rogers' men. There need be no wonder that the old soldiers should thus desire to remain side by side under a common commander, in the wilderness field, to fight the stern battle of pioneer life, and to convert the wilderness into homesteads. The fact that numbers of each battalion were unwilling to settle, except under their own officers, reveals the spirit of the times: it tells us how much the settlement partook of a military character, and the feeling of attachment which existed between the officers and men, as well as among the rank and file. It would not do that the same lots should be occupied as a part of the fourth town under Captain VanAlstine; they must be severed from that township, and united to Fredericksburgh, under the jurisdiction of their old major.

Fredericksburgh contains 40,215 acres of the very best quality of land. The following is taken from Cooper's Essay, by the pen of the talented Mrs. Moodie. "We approach Fredericksburgh: this too is a pretty place, on the north side of the bay; beautiful orchards and meadows skirt the water, and fine bass-wood and willow-trees grow beside, or bend over the waves. The green smooth meadows, out of which the black stumps rotted long ago, show noble groups of hickory and butternut, and sleek fat cows are reposing beneath them, or standing midleg in the small creek, that wanders through them, to pour its fairy tribute into the broad bay." In 1811, the township had "a large population, and many excellent farms, an Episcopal Church (subsequently burnt), and a Lutheran Meeting-house."—(Gourlay).

There was also a "reserve" for a village in this township at the front, which, however, never grew into a village.

In 1798, an act was passed, the object of which was to ascertain, and establish the boundary lines between the townships by which irregularities might be removed. In 1826, a special act was obtained "to make provision for a survey of the first, second, and third, concessions of Fredericksburgh, original, and the whole of Fredericksburgh, additional." It was enacted that the eastern boundary line of the said township, otherwise known as the line between lots number twenty-five, and the Gore, in the said second and third concessions, shall be, and the same is hereby declared to be, the course or courses of the respective division or side lines of lots or parcels lying in the aforesaid tract of land; and all surveyors shall be, and are hereby, required to run all such division or side lines of any of such lots or parcels of land, which they may be called upon to survey, to correspond with, and be parallel to, the aforesaid eastern boundary line."

CHAPTER L.

CONTENTS—The Fourth Township—Adolphustown—After Duke of Cambridge—Quantity of Land—Survey—Major VanAlstine—Refugees—From New York—Time—Voyage—Their Fare—Names—Arrived—Hagerman's Point—In Tents—First Settler—Town Plot—Death—The Burial—A Relic—Commissary—Dispute of Surveyors—The Settlers—All things in common—An Aged Man—Golden Rule—Old Map—Names—Islands—The Township—Price of Land—First "Town Meeting"—Minutes—The Officers Record—Inhabitants, 1794—Up to 1824—First Magistrates—Centre of Canada—Court Held in Barn—In Methodist Chapel—"A Den of Thieves"—Court House erected—Adolphustown Canadians—Members of Parliament—The Courts—Where first held—Hagerman—Travelers tarrying at Adolphustown.

SETTLEMENT OF ADOLPHUSTOWN.

The Fourth Township westward from Fort Frontenac, was, some time after its survey and settlement, named Adolphustown, after Adolphus, Duke of Cambridge, the tenth son of King George III. The Township contains about 11,459 acres, and was surveyed in 1784, by Surveyor-General Holland.

In the year 1783, a party of Loyalists sailed from the port of New York. They were under the command of Capt. VanAlstine, with a fleet of seven sail, and protected by the Brig "Hope," of forty guns. Some of this band had served in the army, in an irregular way, more had been in New York as refugees. VanAlstine although commissioned to lead this company, it would seem, had not been in the service—was not a military man, but a prominent Loyalist of the Knickerbockers. But these refugees, in setting out for the unknown wilderness, were provided with camp tents and provision, to be continued for three years, and with such implements as were given to the disbanded soldiers, as well as a batteau to every four families, after arriving at their place of destination. The company were mostly from the Counties of Rockland, Orange, and Ulster, on the east side of the Hudson, and Westchester, Duchess, and Columbia, on the west.

They sailed from New York on the 8th Sept. 1783, and arrived at Quebec, 8th Oct. Many were undecided whether to remain in the Lower Provinces, or go on to Canada. The events of this voyage; this departure from old homes, to penetrate the unknown north, are even yet held in remembrance by their descendants. Thus, it is told, that after leaving New York a few days, a shark was observed following the vessel, which created no little consternation. It continued to follow for many days, until a child had died and been consigned to the deep, after which it was no longer seen. The Government rations with which they were supplied, consisted, as the story has been told the writer, of "pork and peas for breakfast; peas and pork for dinner; and for supper, one or the other." The party proceeded from Quebec thence to Sorel, where they spent the winter. They inhabited their linen tents, which afforded but little protection from the intense cold. While staying there, it was determined to grant them a township on the Bay Quinté. The first Township had been granted to Capt. Grass, the second and third were to be possessed by Johnson's Second Battalion; so VanAlstine's corps were to have the next township. Surveyor Holland was engaged in completing the survey, and even then, had his tent pitched on the shore of the fourth township. The party left Sorel 21st May, 1784, in a brigade of batteaux, and reached the fourth township on the 16th June. The names of some of those who composed this party, were: VanAlstine, Ruttan, Huycks, Velleau, Maybee, Coles, Sherman, Ballis, three families of Petersons, Loyce, VanSkiver, Philip and Thomas Dorland, Cornelius VanHorn, VanDusen, Hagerman, father of the late Judge Hagerman, Angel Huff, Richard Beagle, John and Stephen Roblin, Fitzgerald, Michael Stout, Capt. Joseph Allan, Hover, Owen Ferguson, John Baker, Wm. Baker, German, Geo. Rutter, James Noxen, John Casey, Benj. Clapp, Geo. Rutledge, David Barker, Owen Roblin.

It is a curious fact, fully attested by the Allison's, the Hover's and others, that as the batteaux slowly wended their way along the shore, having passed the mark which indicated the boundary of the Third Township, several of the passengers, gazing upon the woods, expressed a wish to possess certain places, according to the fancy of each; and, strangely enough, the Cole's, the Hover's, the Allison's, the Ruttan's, and others, did actually come respectively into possession, by lot, in accordance with their previously expressed wish.

The company had reached the land whereon they were to work out their future existence. The writer has driven upon the ice along the Bay, following, it must have been, almost the way taken by this party, as they landed. They passed along the present Adolphustown wharf, westward nearly half a mile, and rounded a point known as Hagerman's Point. Here a small, but deep stream empties itself, having coursed along a small valley, with sloping sides, in a westerly direction. They ascended this creek for nearly a quarter of a mile; and proceeded to land upon its south side. Between the creek and the bay is a pleasant eminence; it was upon its slopes the settlers, under VanAlstine, pitched their tents. The boats were hauled up; and among the trees, the white tents were duly ranged. Thus housed, and thus far removed from the busy haunts of men, this community continued to live for many days. Steps were taken at an early day to draw lots for land. As so much of the township was washed by the waters of the bay, there was not the same anxiety among the settlers with respect to the decision of the ballot. Every one drew his number, with one exception, and this was a notable one, as indicating the noble feeling of brotherhood which lived in the breasts of the noble band of refugees. The exception was not in favor of the person in command, or a particular friend. Mr. Cole had expressed a liking for the first lot, now known as Cole's Point, and he, having a large family and consequently more anxious to get on his land, and get settled for the winter, and the land ready for the next summer, was immediately, by universal consent, put in possession of the lot; and he even that year raised some potatoes.

In addition to the 200 acres granted to each of the company, there was a town plot, consisting of 300 acres, regularly laid out into town lots of one acre each, and one of these was granted to each of the settlers. This plot thus surveyed, it was believed in time would become the site of a town.

While they were yet living in their tents one of their number died, a child it is said by some. The dead was buried close by, under a tree. When others came to die, they also were buried here, and thus was formed the "U. E. Loyalist burying ground."

The second person buried in this place, while it was yet a woods, was Casper Hover. Shortlived was his career as a pioneer. But a few months had passed, and he had barely taken possession of his land when, one day engaged in clearing off the land, he was struck by a falling limb and killed. A blow so sudden was felt not alone by his own family, but by all the settlers. Imagination cannot call up the heart-stirring scene of this burial in the woods by his comrades. As there was yet no roads nor path, not unlikely the body was conveyed by batteau from Hover's farm to the burying ground. The coffin must have been made of rough green boards, split out of logs, or perhaps made with a whip saw. There was no minister to discharge any rights belonging to the dead, or improve the events for the spiritual welfare of the living.

Casper Hover had for his wife Barbara Monk, a relative of Barbara Heck, well known for her connection with early Methodism in the new world. There remains now in possession of Joseph Allison, of Adolphustown, whose wife was a Hover, a pewter platter which belonged to Barbara Monk. It is a relic of no ordinary interest. Barbara Monk was a descendant of the Palatines, and this platter was carried by her ancestors when they were forced to leave the Palatinate. They took it with them to Ireland, thence to New York, and finally it was brought by Barbara to Adolphustown, with VanAlstine's company. The writer has had the satisfaction of examining this relic of former days. It is a round dish, of solid metal, 16 inches broad, and weighing over five pounds. It bears no signs of wearing out. This article of household usefulness is, or was in the past, regarded as a township one, and was famous for its associations with innumerable pot pies. For many a year when there was a bee, or a raising, or a wedding, the pewter platter was engaged to do service.

The stores of provisions for the settlers in this township, were placed under the care of VanAlstine himself; but it would appear, from the statements of some, that Philip Dorland gave his assistance, and to some extent, was responsible, acting under the instructions of a committee, for the distribution to the families. Also, one Emery, was connected with the department.

It would seem that Surveyor General Holland, who surveyed the fourth town, and Deputy Surveyor Collins, who surveyed third town, had same trouble with respect to "Fredericksburgh additional." The number of lots composing the third township at first, was not enough to supply the whole of the battalion; having been promised lots in the same township. When it was seen that all could not be accommodated in the lots of third township, it was determined to take a certain number from the fourth township. To this Surveyor Holland consented, probably with the concurrence of Major VanAlstine. But more of Rogers' company continued to come; and Collins wished to absorb the whole of the fourth town, to accomodate them. In this he was, no doubt, supported by officers of the battalion; Sir John Johnson among the rest. But Holland, in the interest of the company, which had already settled in the fourth town, under VanAlstine, objected. The statement come to us that Holland and Collins had well nigh fought a duel in connection with the matter. As Collins was a deputy under Holland, there must have been some strong influence supporting the former, which was probably through Sir John Johnson. But Holland, having completed the survey of the side lines as he desired, started precipitately to Quebec with his report. Collins hearing of this, started after. Whatever may have been the contest at head quarters, Holland's report of the fourth township was received, and the third township was limited to its present size.

Mr. Joseph Allison, says, respecting the settlement, that "what was one's business was everybody's business, they were all dependent on each other. Each concession was considered a neighbourhood, each being about four miles in length. After the trees were felled and the brush burnt, then came on the logging bees, and every man had to give an account of himself, if he should be missing when notified. There were no aristocrats, from Major VanAlstine down to the humblest individual. Each had to do what he could. They were perfectly organized in this branch of business, being divided into companies or squads of six; and each squad had to take a regular "through" of about six or seven rods wide, piling all the timber in their respective "throughs." These logging bees were always attended with much strife, all striving to be ahead; and as they were always used to their rations of rum, they must, on these occasions, have all they wanted. Then, in the evening, they must have their dance. It was considered the privilege and duty of all the women in the neighbourhood to attend and assist in cooking, as many of the settlers were bachelors. Indeed, if there was a wedding, in one of the concessions, all had a right to attend, belonging to the neighbourhood.

These pioneers of Adolphustown were a wonderfully hardy set of men, possessed of great physical powers, although inured to hardships of a very pressing kind. They lived to a great age; very few of them died under eighty, and two of them lived to be over a hundred. John Fitzgerald was the oldest man that came with VanAlstine, he died in 1806, aged 101; Daniel Cole was 106, when he died. The leading men of the settlement were VanAlstine, Captain Peter Ruttan, Michael Stout, the Dorlands, and Nicholas Hagerman. If any dispute or grievance arose, it would be left to some one to settle, but they all, with very few exceptions, tried to do as they would wish to be done by.

"Joseph Allison was a whip-sawyer by trade, and assisted to saw the first boards that were used in the buildings. He drew lot 17."

Examining an old map in the Crown Lands Department, certain names are found written upon the Islands and Points of Adolphustown. The southern extremity has upon it the name of Lieutenant Michael Vandervoort. The adjacent island has Lieutenant Samuel Tuffee, and P. V. Dorland. Proceeding around the point to the north, the first indentation of the bay is named Bass Cove. The next point is for John Speers, and Humphrey Waters—called on the map "Speers and Waters lot, 150 acres." The next cove is called Perch Cove, and the next point is for Lieutenant Samuel Deane, 100 acres. Then comes Little Cove. The bay off these points is called "Grand Bay," northward to where Hay Bay commences, it is called "The Forks," while Hay Bay is designated "East Bay," and up toward the Mohawk Bay it has the name of "the North Channel;" Casey's Point on the north shore of Hay Bay is called Green Point, and the land there is allotted to Philip and Owen Roblin.

Beside those mentioned, as forming a part of VanAlstine's company, there were, among the first settlers of Adolphustown, and probably of VanAlstine's party: Angel, William and John Huff, Thomas Casey; and at a later period came "Billy" Monroe, John Roblin, John and James Canniff, Philip Flagler, Carnahan, Robert Short, Fisher, and Captain Allan."

In some respects Major VanAlstine's company were better off than the soldier pioneers. Although they had to come a long distance by ship, and ascend the St. Lawrence in small boats, which precluded the possibility of bringing to the country many articles for family use; yet they could fetch with them some things to contribute to family comfort, beside clothing.

The township being almost surrounded by water, and having

many indentations of the bay, there was thereby afforded the most advantageous place for the settlers, whose only mode of traveling was by boat. Every concession has communication with the bay. The township is the smallest in the Province, containing but 11,459 acres. The land at first, it is said, could be had for "one shilling an acre," and half of lot 15, of 100 acres, was sold for a "half joe"—$8.00. In contrast to this, in 1817, there was "no land in the township which could be procured for less than £4 an acre," and few would sell at that price. Although so well provided with a water way for travel, good roads were early constructed.

The following are the minutes of the first "Town meeting" held in Adolphustown, on the 6th of March, 1793, for which we are indebted to Mr. J. B. Allison.

"The following persons were chosen to officiate in their respective offices, the ensuing year, and also the regulations of the same."

"Ruben Bedell, Township Clerk; Paul Huff, and Philip Dorland, Overseers of the Poor; Joseph Allison, and Garit Benson, Constables; Willet Casey, Paul Huff, and John Huyck, Pound Keepers; Abraham Maybee, and Peter Rutland, Fence Viewers."

"The height of fence to be 4 feet 8 inches. Water fence voted to be no fence. Hogs running at large to have yokes on 18 by 24 inches. No piggs to run until three months old. No stalion to run. Any person putting fire to any bush or stuble, that does not his endeavour to hinder it from doing damage, shall forfeit the sum of forty shillings."

(Signed) PHILIP DORLAND, T. C.

It is most likely that Philip Dorland was merely secretary for the meeting.

Ruben Bedell was successively, elected town clerk for three years, when, in 1795, Archibald Campbell was appointed, who served for four years. In 1800, Daniel Haight was appointed. In 1801. William Robins filled the office, and continued to fill it for three years, when in 1804, Ruben Bedell was again elected. The following year Bryan Crawford was appointed; the next Daniel Haight, who continued four years; John Stickney then filled the office three years, and Daniel Haight was again appointed, 1813.

There is in the Township Records, a Return of the inhabitants for 1794, March, with the names of each family, and the number of members in each. They are as follows: Ruben Bedell, 5; Paul Huff, 6; Solomon Huff, 10; William Griffis, 5; Caspar VanDusen,

6; Nicholas Peterson, 8; Nicholas Peterson, Sen. 3; Isaac Bern, 1; Thomas Jones, 4; Alexander Fisher, 10; James McMasters, 8; James Stephenson, 1; Russel Pitman, 7; Joseph Clapp, 4; George Brooks, 6; John Halcom, 3; Martin Sherman, 3; Joseph Cornell, 5; Peter Valleau, 5; William Clark, 6; Joseph Clark, 1; Albert Cornell, 8; Peter Delrya, 4; John Huyck, 6; Alexander Campbell, 5; Buryer Huyck, 2; Albert Benson, 4; Gilbert Bogart, 2; Abraham Bogart, 3; Christopher German, 5; William Casey, 6; Edward Barker, 3; David Kelly, 4; Battin Harris, 8; John Canniff, 13; Nathaniel Solmes, 10; Peter Wanamaker, 4; Garret Benson, 1; William Mara, 4; John Roblin, 3; John Elms, 3; John Wood, 2; Peter Ruttan, Jun'r., 3; Owen Roblin, Jun'r., 2; Owen Roblin, Sen'r., 8; Benjamin Clapp, 8; George Rutter, 7; Jacob Bullern, 6; Cornelius VanHorn, 6; Robert Jones, 5; Paul Trumper, 8; William Hanah, 4; Michael Slate, 4; Peter Ruttan, Sen., 5; Denis Oscilage, 1; Joseph Carahan, 8; Thomas Dorland, 6; Philip Dorland, 9; Willet Casey, 8; Peter VanAlstine, 3; John VanCott, 7; David Brown, 3; Peter Sword, 2; William Brock, 5; Nicholas Hagerman, 8; Cornelius Stouter, 3; Abraham Maybee, 7; Henry Tice, 3; Thomas Wanamakers, 1; William Button, 5; Joseph Allison, 2; John Fitzgerald, 2; Matthew Steel, 5; Conrad Vandusen, 5; Henry Hover, 3; Arion Ferguson, 2; Henry Redner, 4; Andrew Huffman, 4; Daniel Cole, 11; Henry Davis, 5; James Noxen, 1.—Total 402.

The total number of inhabitants in 1800, was 524, and in 1812, 575. The returns are given, yearly, up to 1822, when the nnmber was only 571. It is observable that the number fluctuates from year to year. This was due to the fact that families would come to the township, from the States, remain a few years working a farm on shares, and then would move up the Bay, to another township.

Major VanAlstine, as the military commander, was the chief officer. But there lives no account of dissensions and litigations, for many a year. When the Government appointed Magistrates, probably not until after Upper Canada was erected into a separate Province, VanAlstine was the first to receive the commission. There were, likewise, appointed at the same time, or soon after, several others, viz., Thomas Dorland, Nicholas Hagerman, Ruttan, Sloat, and Fisher, afterwards Judge. It is said the Magistrates did not always agree. Ruttan and VanAlstine had dissentions; and VanAlstine claimed certain power, by virtue of his command over the corps who peopled the township. Whereupon Ruttan, at the next meeting, donned his suit of clothes, which he had worn as an officer of the Regular Army, and declared no one was his superior, and, it is said, gained his point.

The time came, when Adolphustown was almost the Centre of Canada. It is true, Kingston was the great point to which the military and naval forces centred, and the circumstances of such gave that place a status which it could not otherwise have obtained. But Adolphustown was really the centre of the settlements in the central part of Canada—the Midland District. So it came that the court was alternately held at the Fourth Town and Kingston, being twice a year in each place. The first court in this township, was held in the barn of Paul Huff, which served the purpose very well in summer. The next occasion was in winter, and some building had to be procured. Application was made for the Methodist Chapel. Some objection was made, on the ground that a "house of prayer" should not be made a "den of thieves," referring to the criminals, not to the lawyers. But the Chapel was readily granted for the second court held in Adolphustown. It is said that a proposition was made, in due form, that if the inhabitants of the Fourth Town would build a Court House, the court should be held there twice a year. The offer was accepted, and a subscription set on foot, which resulted in the erection of a Court House. When the court ceased to be held, in accordance with the agreement, the Court House reverted to the Township.

The building of the Court House was followed by the growth of a village, and among its population were those whose names became household words in every Canadian home. It continued a place of importance for many a year; and, even when the court ceased to be held, the village, by virtue of its situation, and the standing of the township, continued for a long time of no little repute.

Adolphustown contributed, during the first years of Upper Canada, a good many worthy individuals to the welfare of the country, indeed Adolphustown took the lead for many years in political, as well as more general matters relating to the country. The general elections, at one time, resulted in the election of four natives of this township to Parliament, viz: two Hagermans, Sam'l Casey, and Paul Peterson. Says Joseph B. Allison, of Adolphustown, "Our township, though, perhaps, the smallest in the Province, (if it were consolidated, it would not be more than three miles and a half square,) has furnished as many statesmen and judicial officers as any of the larger townships. From the humble abodes of Adolphustown, have gone to the Legislative Halls of Canada, Thomas Dorland, John Roblin, Christopher A. Hagerman, Paul Peterson, Dr. W. Dorland, Willet Casey, Henry Ruttan, Samuel Casey, Dan'l Hagerman, David Roblin, John P. Roblin, who represented the County of Prince for many years. The Hon. John A. M cDonald although not born here, spent his juvenile years, and attended the common schools in Adolphustown. Now, we challenge any township in the Province, that has not a city or town connected with it, to turn out eleven members of Parliament, all of them U. E. Loyalists."

Roblin, who settled in the third concession, was elected three times to Parliament, in 1808, 1811, and 1812. At first, he sat for two years; but, when sent the second time, he was expelled, because he was a *local* Methodist Preacher. His constituents re-elected him, and again he was expelled, to be a third time elected; but he died before the Parliament again met, on the last day of February, 1813, aged 44.

It was in the year 1793, in the second Session of Parliament, that an Act was passed "to fix the time and place for holding the Courts of General Quarter Sessions of the Peace." The Act provided "that the Courts of General Quarter Sessions of the Peace for the Midland district of this Province, shall commence and be holden in Adolphustown, on the second Tuesday in the month of July, and on the second Tuesday in the month of January; and in Kingston, on the second Tuesday in the month of April, and on the second Tuesday in the month of October." The other places were Michilmackinac, Newark, New Johnstown, and Cornwall. In this second year of Upper Canada, no mention is made of Toronto, nor yet of York. Where now stands the splendid Osgoode Hall, with its chaste and beautiful decorations; and, indeed, now exists the whole of Toronto, with its unrivalled University building, its Colleges, its handsome Churches and elegant mansions was then a tangled forest, and, except an Indian path along the Don, marking a portage to Lake Simcoe and Fort Toronto, there was no indication of human existence. Moreover, about this time, upon the shores of Adolphustown was born Christopher Hagerman, who was destined to adorn the bar and grace the bench; who saw arise the Courts of Law, the organization of the Law Society, and assisted to establish them at Toronto, where he spent his latter days, and where now his ashes repose.

Among those who first came to Adolphustown are some who had seen service in an irregular way, as well as the refugees. The names of some of them will be found among the loyal combatants and loyalists.

For several years, the families that came from the States would stop at the Fourth Township, where they would "work out," or take a farm on shares, or perhaps rent a farm, until they could find a suitable place on which to permanently settle, in the back townships, such as Sophiasburgh, Ameliasburgh, Sidney and Thurlow. The ordinary terms for working a farm on shares was for the owner to furnish team, seed, &c., and take one-half of the produce when gathered.

Conrad VanDusen kept the first tavern west of Kingston, and at his house travelers up and down the Bay would stop. Also, new comers to the Bay would here first tarry, until decided where to settle.

CHAPTER LI.

CONTENTS—Marysburgh—Origin—Once part of a Seigniory—Survey—Hessians—Old map—The lots—Officers of 84th Regt.—Original landowners—Indian Point—McDonnell's Cove—Grog Bay—"Accommodating Bay"—"Gammon Point"—Black River—"Long Point"—Reserves—Course pursued by the Surveyor—Number of Hessians—Their sufferings—Dark tales—Discontented—Returning to Hesse—A suitable location—Not U. E. Loyalists—Received land gratis—Family land—Their habits—Capt McDonnell—Squire Wright Sergt. Harrison—The Smith's—Grant to Major VanAlstine—Beautiful Scenery—Smith's bay—"The Rock"—Over a precipice.

THE FIFTH TOWNSHIP—MARYSBURGH.

This township is so called after Mary, Duchess of Gloucester, eleventh child of the King.

It is more than likely that the extremity of Prince Edward Peninsula was frequently visited during the French occupancy of Frontenac. Indeed, it is quite probable that the Seigniory granted to La Salle included a portion of the present township of Marysburgh. And no doubt, the beautiful bay, long time called South Bay, that is the body of water lying between Indian Point and Long Point, with Wappoose Island, was often visited during the American rebellion.

The original surveyor, Mr. Collins, having been instructed to lay out a fifth township on the shores of the Bay, recognized the south shore as a desirable place upon which to settle disbanded troops. The forked peninsula, with the coves, and the Black River, supplied valuable facilities for the intending pioneer. The surveying was commenced in 1784, and finished in '85 or '86. Referring to the loyal combatants, it will be seen that the Foreign Legion composed of Hessians, and a few Irish and Scotch, had offered, to such of them as desired to remain in Canada, grants of land. It was the Fifth Township in which the Government determined they should be located. Having been staying in Lower Canada for a time, they ascended in batteaux in 1785, and, we believe, under the care of Archibald McDonnell, proceeded to occupy the township; while the surveying was still going on along the bay. Great pains had been taken to secure a frontage upon the water either of the Bay Quinté, the South Bay, or Black River. By referring to the oldest map of the township in the Crown Lands Department, it is found that while most of the land was allotted to the Hessians, a considerable portion was taken up by commissioned and non-commissioned officers of the 84th Regt.

By looking at the map of Marysburgh, it will be seen that great irregularity exists in the formation of the lots, and it will be observed that great care has been taken to secure a frontage upon the water to as many lots as possible. This was, as elsewhere shown, to procure a water communication to the central points of the settlement; and as well facilities for fishing, to the settlers. By maps preserved in the Crown Land Department, it may be seen to whom was originally granted certain parts of the township, from the names written thereupon. The names of places are, as well, very suggestive. It would seem that Collins, as well as others, engaged in laying out the townships, did not forget to make claim to eligible lots, here and there, for himself. To these he was doubtless entitled, and acted no unjust part.

At the extremity of what is now called Indian Point, but formerly designated Point Pleasant, was a considerable tract of land which was not laid out into lots, but which has marked upon it, as the original owner, Surveyor John Collins. Subsequently, Collins conveyed it to Alexander Aitkins, a lawyer. Proceeding up the Bay of Quinté, we come to a small cove, known now as McDonnell's Cove; but maps exist upon which this is called Grog Bay. In the absence of fact, it may not be well to relate the traditionary origin of this name. It is sufficient to say that it most likely arose from the habit, then far more common than now, of visiting this place to fish, and drink grog. Adjacent to this bay was a large block of land granted to Archibald McDonnell. Upon the south shore of Point Pleasant the water, now Smith's Bay, is marked "Accommodating Bay." When we remember the great necessity for each settler to have access to the water, and the constant course pursued by the surveyor to secure it; we have no difficulty in arriving at the conclusion that this name arose from the increased facilities this indentation of the lake supplied, in this respect. The point of land stretching out between "Accommodating Bay" and Prince Edward Bay, and Black River, a name due to the dark color of its water, which is north of the furthermost point of the peninsula, is called "Gammon Point." This name was given, most likely from the fancied resemblance it bore to a ham; the term gammon being the word commonly used by the old settlers for ham. Looking at the hill from the south-west, it does bear such a resemblance.

The lots were surveyed with their front upon the north shore of the Black River, and, then returning to the water, and continuing towards the extremity of Prince Edward's Bay, the lots were made to front upon the water, making them angular with the others. At the very end of the Bay, they are changed again, so as to have a front at right angles with the others. There are four of these lots. The surveyor had now reached the rock of "Long Point," as it is called, at the present day. Here we find, again, that the lots front to the north, upon Prince Edward's Bay. The surveyor next proceeded to survey the base line as far as Bluff Point, and then returning, formed fifteen lots, which brought him to the rear of those laid out at the head of the Bay. He then crossed over to the Lake Shore, and commenced to survey westward. The point was then named "Point Traverse," from the fact, we fancy, that the surveyor crossed here to continue his survey without laying out the extremity of Long Point, which offered no inducements for the settlers. Upon Point Traverse, was set apart a block of land, containing 2,500 acres, which is marked "Military Lands." Probably, with some idea of erecting here some military post. These were afterwards conveyed to "Capt. Joseph Allen." Upon the same map, in the Crown Lands Department, we learn that a block of land near Black River, was originally granted to James Brock, Esq. To the west of the fifteen lots laid out at the neck of Point Traverse, and fronting upon the Lake, was a reserve for the Clergy. This seems to have been the extent of the first survey in this section.

Returning to the Bay of Quinté, we find that at this time lots were laid out along the shore westward, to within about two miles of the Lake on the Mountain. The land thence not being attractive, it was not then surveyed. Subsequently when laid out, the lots were placed at a slight angle with those to the east, in order to front upon the Bay. Sixteen lots brings us to the entrance of Picton Bay. Again a change is found to take place, so that the lots may front upon the east shore of this bay. Six lots reach to the head of the bay, which appears to have been the termination for a time But subsequently, the survey was continued, being slightly altered, that the base line might follow the old Indian Carrying Place. There were nine lots in this row. Turning to East Lake and West Lake, it will be seen that the lots were arranged to front on either side, as well as at the ends. The time at which these lots mentioned were surveyed, is somewhat uncertain, but probably before 1786.

It is impossible to state the exact number of Hessians who settled in Marysburgh; but judging from accounts, and the names taken from the Grantee's list, it is surmised there were about forty. Unacquainted with the English languish, and unaccustomed to the profound solitude of the forest, and the flittings of the dark-skined Indian, often in a state of semi-nudity, it is no reason for wonder, if the Hessians felt otherwise than contented in their wilderness home. Although upon the borders of a lovely bay, rich in valuable fish, they were ignorant of the mode of catching them; and, when the Government supplies, which were continued to them, as to the other settlers for three years, was withdrawn; although this valuable article of diet was at their very door, they were exposed to the terrors of actual starvation. Even during the time that rations were to be given them, it is related they were often in want. A dark tale of cupidity, and heartless carelessness on the part of officials, to whom were entrusted the duty of furnishing the necessary stores, has been told. How much of truth there may be in this report, it is now impossible to say. When we remember the circumstances of the times; the settlers scattered along hundreds of miles of uncleared land, that the stores had to be transported from Montreal, and Lachine by batteaux, and that, necessarily, many persons became responsible for the transit, as well as the distribution, we need not be surprised if there was now and then carelessness and neglect; and now and then reprehensible appropriation of stores, which were intended by a paternal Government for the mouths of the hungry. Many of the Hessian settlers would gladly have escaped from all the terrors which encompassed them; but it was now too late. As a general thing, they had not the means of removing. But there were a few who managed to extricate themselves, and who returned to the old country. One John Crogle went to Kingston, mortgaged his farm for £6 to Rev. Mr. Stuart, and took his departure for the fatherland; another mortgaged his lot to Captain Allan and left, leaving his wife; and never returned.

Probably no place in the country afforded a better location for these foreigners who were entirely ignorant of the rugged duties of pioneer life, and had but an imperfect conception of agricultural pursuits, and moreover, were quite unable to speak the English language. It has been said, indeed, that the Government exercised a thoughtful regard in placing them, where a means of existence was at their very door, by the catching of fish, beside what the soil might bring forth. But the fact that they were of a different nationality—essentially a different people from the loyalist settlers, militated against them. Many of the latter were Dutch, and could speak little or no English; but the former could understand Dutch no more than they could English, German was their native tongue. The Hessians were not U. E. Loyalists, and they were often made to feel this by not receiving for themselves and family the same allowance of land, and by the behaviour manifested toward them by the loyalists. The writer recollects the tone of disparagement toward the "fifth towners," by an old inhabitant of the fourth town. These things combined to delay prosperity to the township, as a general thing.

They received land gratis; but subsequently when the title deed was given, a sum of £5 was demanded, being the amount of expense incurred at the time of their enrolment into the service. This was protested against upon the floor of the Parliament, but without avail. The quantity of land each should receive was to depend upon the number of children. Beside the allotment to each, at the time of settling, he was to receive an additional fifty acres at the time each child attained the age of twenty-one. This took the name of "Family Lands."

Although prosperity did not come to the township of Marysburgh as quickly as to the first four townships, yet the time eventually arrived when it partook of the general spirit of advancement. From several sources we have the statement that the old soldiers were for many years given to somewhat irregular habits; and that an important instrument in effecting a reformation among them, was the Rev. Darius Dunham, the first Methodist preacher to visit them.

Beside those of the foreign legion who settled in this township, were several officers, and non-commissioned officers of the 84th regiment, and a few who had been in the regular army. The most important of these was Captain Archibald McDonnell, who arrived at the township in 1784, and landed in the cove, which now bears his name, and there on the shore pitched his tent, until he had erected a log cabin.

Then, there was "Squire" Wright, who was supreme in authority in the township for many a day, even before he was appointed magistrate. He was the Commissary Officer, and the old soldiers were; wont to come to him, to settle any differences that might arise among them.

Sergeant Harrison was an early settler, he has a son still living now in his 88th year; yet hale as a man of sixty-eight. He was born in St. John's, Lower Canada, and was five years old when he came with the family to the place, an elder brother having preceded and erected a hut. He tells us that the Hessians were to have three years' provisions, but for some reason only received two years. He remembers when blazed trees alone marked the way, from one house to another; and then the bridle path, which in time was widened into a road. The first horse brought to the township is well remembered, it was owned by Colonel McDonnell. This one, with another, were the only ones, for many a year, in the place.

Among the first settlers were William Carson, Daniel McIntosh, and Henry Smith, a German, who had several sons: John, William, Benjamin, Charles, Barnit, and Ernest. Smith's Bay is so called after Charles.

Major VanAlstine had granted to him a large block of land in this township. The original grant is now before us, and gives the information that the quantity was 437 acres, consisting of lots number five and six in the first concession. The document is dated "4th June, 1796," signed "J. G., S." (John Greaves, Simcoe). "Peter Russell, Auditor General. Registered, 17th June, William Jarvis, Registrar."

This lot of land included the high hill, with the lake at its summit, so well known to excursionists. The Major at once proceeded to erect a mill here, which proved a great convenience to the inhabitants of the township .The lake was for a time called VanAlstine's Lake. In 1811, Major VanAlstine having died, the land, with 30 acres cleared, and a dwelling-house, and another for the miller, and out-houses are found offered for sale by the executors.

We cannot leave the township of Marysburgh without commending the beautiful scenery to those who may not have visited it, especially the interior, and the shores of South Bay. A trip by carriage from Picton across the rugged hill, which seems to encircle in an irregular manner, the whole township, to the Black Creek. whose dark and narrow waters, inclosed by muddy banks, contrast so markedly with the bright blue of the bay into which it empties, hard by Gammon Point, is one that will well repay any one making it. The irregularity of the roads makes the drive none the less interesting. Approaching the bay, there is spread out a view whose beauty we have never seen surpassed, and rarely equalled either in the new world or the old. Having obtained a close view of Prince Edward Bay, and observed the far-stretching Point Traverse with the three prominent Bluffs; and still further away to the south, the Ducks, and Timber Islands, the tourist should follow us closely as may be the changing shore, that forms the head of Smith's Bay, to the north side, where another delightful prospect will lay before him.

About six miles east of Wappoose Island, is a bold point standing out into the Lake. It presents a bold and precipitous front of about 100 feet in height. It is now commonly designated the "Rock." Formerly, it was called "Cape Vesey Rock." Here was a reserve for the Mississauga Indians, of about 450 acres. This was not surrendered by the Indians until 1835, although some time prior, a settler by the name of Stevenson, had been in occupation. Some years ago, there was overhanging the brow a mass of rock, which one day fell, with a thundering crash. And the old inhabitants tell of a deer and an Indian huntaman, whose bodies were found lying at the foot of the rock both having approached the brink with such speed that, to turn aside was impossible, and both bounded over the perpendicular rock to meet a common doom.

CHAPTER LII.

CONTENTS—Sixth township—Name—Survey—Convenient for settlement—First settlers—A remote township—What was paid for lots—"Late Loyalists"—Going to Mill—Geological formation—Along the fronts—High shore—Grassy Point—Its history—Marsh front—Central place—Stickney's Hill—Foster's Hill—Northport—Trade—James Cotter—Gores—Demerestville—The name—"Sodom"—First records—Township meetings—The Laws of the township—Divided into parishes—Town clerk—Officers—The poor—The committee—Inhabitants, 1824—Fish Lake—Seventh township—The name—Survey by Kotte—At the Carrying Place—Surveyor's assistant—No early records—First settlers.

SIXTH TOWNSHIP—SOPHIASBURGH, NORTHPORT, DEMERESTVILLE.

This township is named after Sophia, the twelfth child of King George III. In the year 1785, Deputy Surveyor General Collins, who was then at Kingston, instructed his assistant Louis Kotte, to lay out a sixth township, commencing at the southern extremity of South (Picton) Bay, and proceeding northward along the west coast of the Bay Quinté, the lots to front upon the bay. Those were measured along the high shore to Green Point, forty-four lots. Following the bay, which at Green Point turns westward, a row of lots were laid out to the head of the bay, sixty-four lots of which were to form the northern front of the sixth township. By referring to the map it will be observed that this township was also a convenient place for a new settlement, having two sides of a triangle upon the bay. The comparatively straight high shore; and the equally even coast upon the north, enabled the surveyor to obtain a uniformity which had been impossible in the fifth township, although securing an extensive frontage for the settlers. About 1788, probably, the first settlers of this township took up their land at the head of Picton Bay, sometimes called Hallowell Bay. They were two Congers, Peterson, Spencer, Henry Johnson ; and at a later date came Barker and Vandusen.

Respecting this township generally, Mr. Price, who has kindly exerted himself to procure facts, observes, "I find there is some difficulty in getting information. "The first settlers are all dead, with one or two exceptions, and many of the farms on the north shore were bought from the U. E. Loyalists who never lived on them." The occupation of the township generally, may be regarded as a later settlement. This rich, and now, long settled place, was once considered as a remote settlement, as Rawdon, Huntington, and Hungerford, were thirty years later. All, or nearly all, who took up land here and became the pioneers, had at first lived in one of the townships upon the lower part of the bay, most of them in Adolphustown. Guilliam Demerest, John Parcels, and Roblin, were among these. Some of the settlers drew land here; but many purchased, and lots, now worth the highest price, were procured for a very small sum, or for a horse, or cow, or a certain quantity of grain. Some of the settlers had formerly lived in the Lower Province, or in New Brunswick and Nova Scotia. Also, there was continually coming in, those who felt no longer at home under the new form of government in the States, or who were glad to escape persecution. These were not in time to secure land, and were often called the "Late Loyalists." Then, again, a few years later, when the bitterness of spirit, which had led the rebels to commit such serious acts of cruelty to the loyalists, had subsided, and a degree of intercourse had commenced between the two, it came to pass that many, who had not taken an active part on either side in the contest, and who had friends in Canada, emigrated to the shores of the bay, or, as they called Canada then, Cataraqui. For instance, the Cronks and Ways, who were among the first settlers upon the Marsh front, as the north shore was called, were but the precursors of several others of the same name, who entered about the beginning of the present century. Some of these were, no doubt, influenced by the proclamation issued by Simcoe. Nathaniel Solmes was one of the older settlers. He came from Duchess County in 1792, lived in Adolphustown two years, then settled on lot No. 10, 1st concession.

One of the first settlers upon the north front was John Parcels. He was of Captain VanAlstine's company, and settled in that township, where he continued to live until 1809, when he removed to lot No. 24, where Northport now stands. His wife having died in 1787, he married Mrs. Parliament. Their first-born, named Richard, was the first, or one of the first white children born in Sophiasburgh. Mrs. Parcel's son, George Parliament, says, in a memorandum, "I recollect having to go to Napanee Mills, in company with my brother Jacob, a distance of nearly twenty miles, to get our grinding done, we had our wheat on a hand-sleigh, as the roads were not passable by any other mode of conveyance."

The land was often purchased at a very low price; for instance, lot No. 16, in the 1st concession, was purchased for a horse, harness, and gig. A farm belonging to Matthew Cronk, was bought for a half barrel of salmon. The Foster-place, where Benjamin Way, used to live, was sold for an old horse. This is one of the best farms in Prince Edward, now, perhaps valued at seven or eight thousand dollars. In 1793, Nicholas Lazier paid $25 to Tobias Ryckman, for 200 acres.

The geological formation of Sophiasburgh and Ameliasburgh, is not without interest. That the mountain about Picton, and the high shore at one time formed the shore of the bay, or perhaps, what is more likely, stood up as an island in a lake, with much broader boundaries than Lake Ontario now has, there is but little doubt. It will not be possible to discuss such points to a great extent, at the same time, it will be well to make a few observations as we proceed. It has been seen that this township has two long fronts upon the bay.

These join at what is known as Grassy Point. Commencing at the head of Picton Bay, the reader is invited to follow the course of the bay, and to observe the points of interest which may be found. No one can travel by the road on the summit of the high shore, without been deeply impressed with the beauty of the scenery. From this height, is an extended view of the bay, stretching down toward Kingston, with the rugged shore of Marysburgh on the right, and the lower and more attractive lands of Adolphustown, and Fredericksburgh on the immediate left, while beyond the Reach, lies the placid waters of Hay Bay. About fifteen miles from Picton, the high shore recedes from the bay, and turns to the west, stretching away almost to the waters of Ontario. From this part of the coast, to Grassy Point, a distance of over nine miles, the land is low; but the road is a pleasant one, until it turns to cross to the north shore. Continuing along the south shore, although walking in silence, and quite removed from human habitation, we are treading upon ground, which, in the past, was a place of note. The following notice respecting Grassy Point supplies information.

"On Wednesday, the 27th of June, at the Court House, will be sold by auction to the highest bidder, that beautiful property, consisting of 843 acres of excellent land, of which a large portion is cleared, situated in one of the finest parts of the Bay of Quinté, being the residue of a reserve for military purposes, and afterwards granted to Sir John Harvey. on which there is a Ferry crossing to the Six Nation Tract. In the neighborhood, there is an extensive settlement of respectable farmers. The premises and the vicinity abound with game, and the bay with fish of every description peculiar to Lake Ontario. It is particularly suitable for grazing, and is within 40 miles of Kingston, which is a never failing ready money market."

Sir John Harvey was afterward, for his services in the war of 1812, appointed Governor of Nova Scotia. The land was sold to Samuel Cluse, Civil Engineer, the person who surveyed the Welland and Rideau Canals. He died at Ottawa some years ago, and left this property to his daughter, Anna, now Mrs. Paul Peterson, who resides upon the place. The agent who advertised the land for Sir John, as 'excellent land,' was scarcely correct. Much of the land is rocky, with but few inches of soil. Clumps of scraggy trees exist with patches of plain. But along the shores are pleasant nooks, in which agreeable fishing may be found. The Point is divided into two, by a small bay. The more eastern of the two points is known as Grassy Point, and the other Green Point. The intervening cove has been known as Louis Cove, from a Frenchman of that name who long lived here. The land to the East of the cross roads, between lots two and three, is useless, almost, for agricultural purposes.

Grassy Point, from its geographical position, naturally became a place at which the early settlers, in passing up and down the Bay, made a rest. At that time, but few trees were growing, the Point being a green plain. Most likely, it had been the site of an Indian village. The first settler here, who came at an early date, was Haunce Trumpour. His house was well known to the pioneers; and the navigator, wearily toiling in the batteau, gladly welcomed the appearance of his hospitable roof. Passing around the extreme northerly point, off which is Capt. John's Island, we are upon the north shore, or marsh front, of Sophiasburgh.

Grassy Point was not only a convenient place for resting, to those passing along; but it likewise was regarded as the most central point at which to hold township meetings. And here, the whole militia, which comprised mostly all the male population of Prince Edward, even from the extreme point of Marysburgh, were wont to meet, to have their annual trainings. At these times, John Trumpour's house became one of no little importance. The training took place here so late as 1802.

Proceeding on our way westward, the land becomes very much better. At the northern termination of the cross-road before mentioned, is a ferry, which has long existed. The first settler here, who established the ferry, was Richard Davenport. It originated from the necessity of the settlers of the Sixth Township, having to go to Napanee to mill. Many a bushel of grain has been backed from this township to Napanee mills, and the flour carried back. Mr. Paul Peterson now lives here.

Proceeding on our course. As the land improves, it is no longer level, but becomes uneven, and, on lot eight, is found a considerable eminence, known as Stickney's Hill, which stands closely against the Bay. This hill has attracted no little attention, on account of the large number of human bones which the plow has, year after year, turned to the surface. Various stories have gained currency relative to the origin of the bones; the most notable of which is, that here perished Col. Quinté, with a number of men. (Respecting this, see History of Bay). The most likely explanation is, that here, for years, the Indians living on Grassy Point buried their dead. Upon this hill, in the burying ground of the Solmes family, reposes the remains of Dr. Stickney, after whom the place is named, and who was the first physician to practice in this township. Since we visited this spot, but a few short months ago, another pioneer has found here a resting place. A faithful Canadian, an exemplary citizen, Richard Solmes, having lived to see the wilderness truly blossom as the rose, full of years, has passed to the grave, followed by a whole community of people, and mourned by a highly esteemed family.

West of Stickney's Hill, the land gradually rises; and a few miles gradually brings us to a higher eminence, called now, Foster's Hill, which is noticeable for many miles up and down the Bay. It was once, no doubt, an island in the midst of a great lake. Being covered with wood, adds, in summer, very much to the beauty and interest of the scenery. At the summit of this prominent hill is a table land of rock covered with but little soil. But very soon the soil increases in depth, and away, on every hand, stretches a fertile land. Near the foot of the hill, and upon the shore, where the land is pressed out into the bay, almost to form a point, is situated the Friends' Meeting House. No one acquainted with the mode of worship practiced by this exceedingly conscientious denomination, can help being impressed with the truly suitable locality for deep spiritual communing. Two miles further westward, at the commencement of the channel, between the mainland and the Big Island, brings us to the pleasant village of *Northport*, so called from its situation, upon the north shore of the township. The situation is charming, and here may be seen the very essence of rural happiness. The village, consisting of some 200 inhabitants, has two stores, but no place where intoxicating liquors are sold. The trade is confined to the inhabitants of the township, with an occasional customer from the Mohawks, across the Bay. The view, looking westward, through Big Bay and the Narrows, along the shore of Thurlow, to Belleville, is, upon a lovely summer night, very pleasant to the gaze.

The village of Northport was built partly on the property originally owned by James Morden and Isaac Demill; James Morden having built first here in 1791. The first merchant to commence business here was Orton Hancock, in 1819. The first wharf built here was in 1829; but prior to that Jacob Cronk had constructed one on his farm, lot twenty-one, probably in the second year the Charlotte run.

In addition to the names already given, of the first settlers of Sophiasburgh, we may mention the following: three families of Ostrom's, the Short's, Brown, the Cole's, Barse, Abbott, Cronks, La Zier, Spencer, Basker, Peck, De Mill, Fox, Spragg, Goslin, Trippen, Mowers.

James Cotter was an early settler, became the first Justice of the Peace, and, in 1813, was elected to Parliament, and served four years.

The township having been surveyed so that the lots might front upon both sides, there resulted a certain number of Gores, designated respectively by the letters B C D and G. The first of these Gores settled was by Philip Roblin, who was one of the first settlers of the township.

DEMERESTVILLE.—This village, which is situated upon lots 38 and 39, of the marsh front, is named after the original settler, Guillame Demerest. The old settlers called him "Demeray." He was a native of Duchess County, N. Y., and was a boy during the rebellion. He was often engaged in carrying provision to the British army. He continued to live in Duchess County, until 1790, when he came to Canada. He failed to prove his right as a U. E. Loyalist, and consequently "lost a fine grant of land." He died at Consecon, 1848, aged seventy-nine. The village sprung up from the mills, which were here erected. It was, for many a day, called Sodom. This name, it is stated, arose from the fact that when Mr. Demerest's first wife was on her death-bed, a ball was given in the place, at which the inhabitants generally attended, and created some little noise, whereupon she said they were "as bad as the inhabitants of Sodom." The village of Demerestville was incorporated in 1828.

We copy the following from the first record of the township of Sophiasburg, by which it will be seen that their mode of procedure was unlike that observed by other townships. All of the townships were acting by virtue of a common law, but seem to have given the law a widely varying interpretation.

"Passed, at Sophiasburg, at a regular town meeting, held on the 3 day of March, 1800.

"For the better ascertaining astrays, and knowing and describing horses and neat cattle, sheep or swine. Be it understood by this town meeting, that every inhabitant and householder shall, within six weeks from the passing of this Act, have their mark and brands recorded, according to law by the Town Clark.

"And be it further enacted by the authority aforesaid, that any astrays, horses, neat cattle, sheep or swine, that shall be found on any open or improved lands from the twentieth of November to the first of April yearly, and every year the owner or owners of such improvement or cleared lands shall give in their natural mark, or artificial marks, and describe their age, as near as possible, to the Town Clark, who is hereby ordered to record the same in a book, to be kept for that purpose; for which such informer shall receive one shilling for each horse or neat cattle; and sixpence for each sheep or swine. Provided always, and be it so understood, that such astrays above mentioned, is not one of his near neighbors, which shall be left to the Town Clark to decide; and the Clark shall send word to the owner or owners, if he knows them, by the mark or brands; and, if unknown to the Town Clark, he is hereby ordered to advertise them in three different places in this township; for which he shall be entitled to receive from the owner, or owners, as followeth, viz: For sending word, or writing, or recording, or informing any way, one shilling and three-pence; if advertised, one shilling and six-pence, for each horse or neat cattle; and for each sheep or swine, six-pence per head. And be it further enacted by the authority aforesaid, that if any inhabitant or householder who shall leave any astrays, as above mentioned, on his or her cleared lands for eight days, from the 20th day of November to the first of April, and neglect to give notice thereof, as by the above Act mentioned, shall loose the reward for finding, or feeding such astrays, and pay the owner one shilling for each horse or neat cattle; and six-pence for each sheep or swine. And be it further enacted. by the authority, that if no owner or owners shall appear by the first Monday in April, to prove their property, then, and in that case, the Town Clark shall advertise for sale, all such astrays, in three townships, viz., Ameliasburg, Sophiasburg, and Hallowell, for the space of twenty days, describing the marks and brands, color and age, as near as possible; and if no owner or owners shall appear and prove their property, then the Town Clark shall proceed to the sale of such astrays, by appointing the day of sale, to the highest bidder; and, after deducting the expenses, to be adjudged by persons hereafter appointed by each parish, in this town, and the overplus shall be delivered into the hands of a Treasurer, hereafter to be appointed.

"And be it observed—That all well regulated townships is divided into parishes. Be it enacted, by the majority of votes, that this town shall be divided into parishes, and desbribed as followeth, that is to say: That from lot No. 45, west of Green Point to lot No, 19, shall be a parish by the name of St. John's, and by the authority aforesaid, that including No. 19, to No. 6, in the Crown Lands, west of Green Point, shall be a parish by the name of St. Matthew. And be it further enacted, by the authority aforesaid, That including the tenants on the Crown Lands, and including lot No. 28, shall be a parish by the name of St. Giles; and from Nicholas Wessel's, to Hallowell, shall be a parish by the name of Mount Pleasant.

"Whereas, all the fines and forfeitures that may incur within our limits, shall be appropriated to charitable uses; we, the inhabitants of Sophiasburg, in our town meetings, on the 3d day of March, 1800, do think it necessary to appoint our Treasurer, in this town, out of the most respectable of its inhabitants, to be Treasurer to this town, to receive all forfeitures and other sums of money that is, or shall be, ordered to be appropriated to charitable uses; which Treasurer is hereby ordered to serve in that connection during good behaviour, or till he shall wish a successor. And be it enacted by the authority aforesaid, that we do appoint and nominate Peter Valleu, who is appointed Treasurer, who is to keep a book and receive all the moneys coming into his hands, and enter by who received, and for what fined; and when a successor is appointed, he shall give up all the monies he has belonging to said town, with the book and receipts, to the successor, and deliver the same on oath, if required; and that each parish shall nominate one good and respectable inhabitant, who together with the Overseer of the Poor, shall be inspectors to inquire and see that all the fines and forfeitures of this town is regularly received and delivered to said Treasurer. And if any person who comes and proves of any astrays that had been within one year and a day, then the Treasurer and those Parish Inspectors, and the Overseers of the Poor, shall refund such moneys as was delivered to the Treasurer, deducting two shillings on the pound for its fees of said Treasurer. And be it enacted by the authority aforesaid, that when there is any money in the hands of the Treasurer, and a necessity to lay it out on the same charitable use—this body corporate shall have the sole management and disposing of, who is to receipt to the Treasurer for the same end, have recorded in his book, and the use they had applied the same and the Treasurer, Overseers of the Poor, and the Parish Inspector may hold meetings and adjourn the same when and as often as they or the major part of them shall choose so to do and shall be a body corporate to sue and be sued on anything that may appertain to their several offices."

We find no further record until the year 1820, which is as follows: "An Act passed at a town meeting, held at Sophiasburg, 3rd January, 1820, for the relief of the poor in the township of Sophiasburg.

"Report of the Committee on the subject.

"We, the Committee appointed, who have the care of the poor of the said township, have agreed to report that one half-penny on the pound, of each man's rateable property, be paid for the present year, and it is seen of the Committee that when any person is agreed with to keep any of the poor, that they endeavour to get them to take produce in payment for defraying said poor. Signed on behalf of the Committee,

JAMES NOXEN, *Chairman.*

Sophiasburg, 3rd January, 1820.

"Passed at a regular town meeting, held at Sophiasburg, 1st January, 1821.

"The report of the Committee to the care of the poor for the present year is, that one farthing on the pound, of each man's rateable property, will be sufficient for the present year.

"By order of the Committee.

(Signed) JAMES NOXEN, *Chairman.*"

The following year, a somewhat similar report is found, signed by Tobias Ryckman, Chairman.

It is not until the year 1822 that any record is found of the appointment of officers, that is, the Township Constables, Assessors, Collectors, &c.

"At a regular town meeting, held at Sophiasburg, at the house of John Goslins, on the first January, 1822, the following officers were chosen and elected": "Town Clark, John Shorts; Lewis Ketchum, David Birdett, Sylvenus Doxy, Constables; Thomas D. Apleby, John Shorts, Assessors; Sylvenus Day, Collector," &c.

John Shorts was successively elected until 1826, when Thomas D. Appleby was appointed. We find a note appended to the report of this year as follows: "Our laws at present be as they will. We have them long, and keep them still."

The next year, 1827, the town meeting was held at the inn of John Goslin, and John Smith was elected Town Clerk. A note says "Farmers Town Laws, as heretofore—Hogs not to run at large in Demerest Vill." John Smith was Town Clerk until 1832. This year S. W. Randell was elected.

It is found stated that in 1824 there were 1796 inhabitants, and in 1825, there were 1793.

In some respects, it would be found interesting to notice the township to a later period; but we have already devoted as much space to this town as we had intended.

Within this township is Fish Lake, situated a short distance east of Demerestville, it was so named from the countless numbers of fish which inhabited its waters when discovered, which was in the year of the famine, or "scarce year." The food thus supplied saved, it is said, many from suffering and death.

AMELIASBURGH.

This township took its name from the fifteenth child, and seventh daughter of the King. She died in November, 1811, aged 27 years. Upon the oldest chart of this township, to be found in the Crown Lands Department, is the following note: "The front of this township is a continuation of Lieut. Kotte's survey from Green Point to the head of the Bay of Quinté, whose orders were in 1785, to have cross roads between every six lots." This note was most probably, made in consequence of there being an absence of three cross roads, when the settlement of the county made them necessary.

Coming to the Carrying Place, or portage, from the head of Bay Quinté to Weller's Bay, it will be seen that a row of lots somewhat smaller in size, is formed on either side of the road. But while the road seems to have a straight course upon the map, by visiting the place, one will observe that the course is not altogether direct. We have it from one, who, no doubt knew, that the surveyor's assistant, a mulatto by the name of Smith, was told to lay out a double row of lots; both to front upon the Indian path, which instructions were literally carried out, whereas it was intended they should be straight. The lots upon the west side of the road extended to the small marshy creek. This row of lots, numbering twelve, originally forming a part of Ameliasburgh, now belong to Murray, the Carrying Place being the dividing line between the two townships.

We have been unable to find any early record of Ameliasburgh.

According to information furnished us by Mr. Ashley and others, the first family that settled in this township was George Angel Weese, with three sons, John, Henry and Francis, natives of Duchess County; they came here in 1787. The second settler was Thomas Dempsey, who came in 1789. (See U. E. Loyalists). Among the other settlers were Bontors, Sagers, Bleekers and Coverts.

The names of other early settlers of Ameliasburgh are mentioned elsewhere, and are among the first patentees. Among them was Elijah Wallbridge, a native of Duchess County. He came to Canada in 1804, and purchased on Mississauga Point, of one Smith, 1200 acres of land, all of which, we believe, is still retained in the family. Two years laters his family came by French train in winter.

William Anderson, sen., who is still living, aged 88 years, a native of Ireland, emigrated to America with his parents in 1793. He came to Canada in 1803. In 1806 he settled on Mississauga Point, having married Miss Polly Way, a descendant of the U. E. Loyalists.

CHAPTER LIII.

PENINSULA OF PRINCE EDWARD.

The name of this district is derived from Prince Edward, Duke of Kent, the father of our Queen, who visited Canada at an early date (see under Early Government).

The peninsula is a rich and beautiful tract of land stretching away from the main land, to be washed on the one hand by the quiet waters of the bay, and on the other by the more turbulent waves of Ontario. It is some seventy miles in length, and varying in breadth from two to twenty miles. The neck of land, or isthmus which separates the head waters of the bay from Lake Ontario, is something less than a mile-and-a-half across. It is known as the Carrying place.

Prince Edward district is irregular in outline, on both the lake and bay sides. Along the lake coast there are numerous bays extending inward, two or three being of considerable size. The larger ones are Weller's bay, Consecon Lake, West Lake, and East Lake. In places, the shore is rendered exceedingly picturesque, by the presence of irregular and beautifully white sand-hills. They have been gradually formed by well washed sand which the waves have carried shoreward, so that the wind might, in the lapse of time, deposit it heap upon heap. The mariners regard this coast with justifiable concern, at the extreme southerly portion, off Long Point, in the vicinity of the Ducks, where many a vessel has come to grief.

The geological formation of the peninsula is of considerable interest; and the observant student of this interesting science; may trace many steps which indicates the geological history.

In a valley, upon the second concession road of Ameliasburgh, may be seen a huge mass of rock, known as Gibson's rock, whose history carries us back, far into the remote past, when the continent of America was covered by a vast ocean, and when massive icebergs, cast loose from their native place in the frozen north, carried with their icy scales huge rocks from the north land coast. Then, carried southward by wind or tide, and reaching water of a milder temperature, the ice became melted, and the rocks were deposited in the depths of the ocean. When the continent of America was upheaved, and the waters departed to their present limits, this huge body of stone, unlike the stone forming the geological bed of this region, was found fast fixed to the soil, ever to form a part of it.

In the whole of Upper Canada, there is not, perhaps, any section so full of historic interest, excepting Frontenac, as Prince Edward. We have seen that the forked peninsula was well known by the Aborigines, and that they were accustomed to cross from the south side of the lake to Point Traverse. It was always a favorite hunting and fishing ground, where abundant supplies were obtained. And, not unlikely, some portion of Indian Point belonged to the Siegniory, granted to La Salle. Moreover, the two points stretching far into the lake, became early locations for the refugees and disbanded soldiers.

In the history of Marysburgh, reference has been made to the early settlement of the point east of Picton Bay, which commenced in 1784. But it appears by the statement of John C. Young, that his grandfather, Colonel Henry Young, made the first settlement in the summer, or fall of 1783. For an account of this half-pay officer, the reader is referred to the Royal combatants of the rebellion of 1776.

With a brother officer, Young left Cataraqui, or, Carleton Island, in a canoe, and ascended what was then called (perhaps first by these parties), the South Bay, now Picton Bay. They landed at the commencement of the Indian Carrying Place, subsequently, for some time known as Hovington's Landing, after the individual who here built a convenient house. They left their canoe here, and set out southward. We have been told that they intended to seek the bay now known as Smith's Bay; but, according to his descendant it would seem they had no particular point in view, desiring only to examine the land. Following, no doubt, the old Indian path, they came out at the north corner of East Lake, a point afterward called the Indian Landing, which name it still retains. Following the east shore of this lake to the south corner, they were surprised to hear the roaring of Lake Ontario, having thought they were following the shore of an inland lake. They crossed the strip of land covered with cedar, spruce, and balsam, and taking off their shoes, waded from the beautiful sand-beach across the outlet of the lake to the opposite point, and proceeded along the west side to the north corner of the lake, to where David McDonald now lives, having entirely walked around East Lake. They here constructed a hut, of cedar bushes, in which to stay the night. The following morning they set out in a north-west direction, and came to West Lake, following the east side, they reached the sand-beach. Traversing this, they arrived at the point where Wellington now stands. Here they stayed the night. The next day they continued on around the north side of West Lake through the woods, and the same evening regained their canoe. They observed plenty of deer and other game, and fish, the former of which Ensign Young's wife, subsequently assisted him to hunt. The succeeding day they returned to Carleton Island. Mr. Young, from this rich land over which he walked, selected the west side of East Lake for his future abode. His eldest son Daniel, who had belonged to the Engineers, was at Carleton Island, having been with his father during his stay at Fort Oswego. His second son, Henry, was at St. John's with the rest of the family. He sent a message for him to come up. This must have been in July or August. In September, the father and two sons, having procured a large canoe, loaded it with provisions, and other necessaries, and ascended to the Indian Carrying Place, Hovington's Landing. They carried their provisions across, and constructed another boat with which they conveyed their things to the point selected for settling, about three miles. Here they proceeded to build a log shanty. Sometime after, the father left, leaving behind his two sons, to winter alone in this out-of-the-way place. They were the first settlers in Prince Edward County. Mr. Young descended to St. John's, where his family still remained, and stayed the winter.

In the spring he came up the St. Lawrence with his family as far as Fredericksburgh, where he left his daughters while he went to see how his sons fared, and had passed the winter. He found them all well; and remained the summer with them, during which they built a more commodious log house. In October, he returned to Fredericksburgh for his daughters, who accompanied him to the wilderness home. These four daughters, Elisabeth, Mary, Catherine and Sarah, subsequently married Henry Zuveldt, Jonathan Ferguson, William Dyre, and John Miller. They all lived to be upwards of eighty years.

"On the first day of January 1800, the settlement at East Lake, in the township of Hallowell, consisted of the following families, in the following order, commencing at Silas Hills, at the head of East Lake, near the place now known as the Cherry Valley, and proceeding around the north side of lake, viz:—

"Colonel John Peters and family, half-pay officer; Major Rogers and family, do; David Friar, Mr. Friar, U. E. L.; Roswell Ferguson, do; Elisha Miller, do; Blasdall Tailor; Caleb Elsworth, Lieut. Heny Young, half-pay officer; Henry Young, Jun., U.E.L.; Augustus Spencer, half-pay officer; George Wait, U. E. L.; Benjamin Wait, do; William Dyre, do; George Elsworth."

"*List of settlers on the south side of the lake.*—Henry Zuveldt, (Zufelt) U. E. L.; Johnathan Ferguson, Sen., U. E. L.; Johnathan Ferguson, Jun., do; Anthony Badgley, do; John Miller, do; Farnton Ferguson, do; William Blakely, do; Sampson Striker, do; Barret Dyer, do; Daniel Baldwin, John Ogden, U. E. L.; Richard Ogden, do; Solomon Spafford, Joseph McCartney, Joseph Lane, William Ensley, Col. Owen Richards, U. E. L.; James Clapp, do; Charles Ferguson."

"At this time there were no settlers in the second concessions neither side of the lake."—(Rev. G. Miller.)

East Lake is about five miles long and one and a half wide. It was for a time called Little Lake. West Lake is about fifteen miles in circumference.

Prince Edward was one of the original nineteen counties of Upper Canada, established by the proclamation of Simcoe in 1792. By this proclamation, we learn that the Peninsula was called by the French "Presque isle de Quinté." Originally it was divided into the three townships of Marysburgh, Sophiasburgh, and Ameliasburgh. Subsequently the townships of Hallowell and Hillier, were formed, and in later days the township of Athol.

In 1831, and act was passed to erect the county into a district, "so soon as the Governor shall be satisfied that a good and sufficient gaol and court house has been erected therein, when a proclamation should announce the formation of the new district." The act specified that the "gaol and court house should be erected in the village of Picton, upon a certain block of land, containing two and a half acres, granted, or intended to be granted and conveyed to Asa Worden, Simeon Washburn, and James Dougal, Esquires, agreeably to a resolution adopted at a public meeting in May, 1826," unless a majority of Justices of the Peace of the Midland District should declare the site ineligible.

We find the following respecting the division of Prince Edward. "Pro. Parliament," "Prince Edward division bill." Mr. Roblin moved the adoption of the Preamble in a few remarks, stating its (the Peninsula) geographical position, the population being 10,000, the remoteness of the inhabitants from the location of the District Court House and Gaol, at Kingston, the earnest desire of the people for separation. Mr. Samson moved, as an amendment, that the village should have a member when it contained 1,000 souls. The debate upon the bill, resulted in one of those fierce encounters that was then not unfrequent between William Lyon McKenzie, and the Solicitor General, afterwards Chief Justice Robinson.

If we may credit the *Free Press*, there were plenty of applicants for office in the newly erected district, there being no less than sixteen seeking the office of Sheriff.

HALLOWELL.

We find in Sabine, that "Benjamin Hallowell, of Boston, Commissioner of the Customs in 1774, while passing through Cambridge in his chaise, was pursued toward Boston by about one hundred and sixty men on horseback, at full gallop. In July, 1776, he sailed for England. While at Halifax, he said, in a letter, "If I can be of the least service to either army or navy, I will stay in America until this rebellion is subdued." It appears from another letter that he frequently tendered himself to the Commander-in-Chief without success. In the autumn of 1796, Mr. Hallowell came to Boston. He was accompanied by his daughter, Mrs. Elmsley, and by her husband, who had just been appointed Chief Justice of Upper Canada. He died at York, Upper Canada, in 1799, aged seventy-five, and was the last survivor of the Board of Commissioners. The British Government granted him lands in Manchester, and two other towns in Nova Scotia, *and a township in Upper Canada, which bears his name.* He was a large proprietor of lands on the Kennebec, Maine, prior to the revolution; but proscribed and banished in 1778, and included in the Conspiracy Act a year later, his entire estate was confiscated. His country residence at Jamacia Plain, was used as a hospital by the Whig Army during the seige of Boston; and his pleasure grounds were converted into a place of burial for the soldiers who died."

We are unable to learn whether any part of the township of Hallowell was granted to Benjamin Hallowell, or not, but, it is not at all unlikely, that at first he did hold some portion of the land.

At all events, there seems every reason to believe that the name was derived from him. On July 3, 1797, an act was passed, whereby it was provided "that a township shall be struck off from the southern-most parts of the townships of Marysburgh and Sophiasburgh." The reason set forth was, that "the inhabitants of the townships experience many difficulties from the uncommon length of the said townships." The Governor was by proclamation, "to declare the name of such township before the first day of August next. Mr. Hallowell's brother-in-law, Mr. Elmsley, had recently been appointed Chief Justice, and doubtless the distinguished position Mr. Hallowell had held, led to the naming of the new township to commemorate his loyalty.

Surveyor Gen. William Smith, was the person employed to lay out the new township.

The first record of this township is at follows: "The annual meeting of the inhabitants of the township of Hallowell, held on Monday, the fifth day of March, 1798, held by virtue of an act of the legislature of the Province of Upper Canada, before Augustus Spencer, and John Stinson, Jun., two of his Majesty's Justices of the Peace, the following persons were chosen town officers for the ensuing year:" Bazel Ferguson, Town Clerk; Caleb Elsworth, and Peter D. Conger, Assessors; James Blakely, and Thomas Goldsmith, Town or Church Wardens; Benjamin Wail, John Miller, Owen Richards, Henry Zufelt, Ichabod Boweman, Aaron White, Carey Spencer and George Baker, Overseers of Highways and Fence Viewers; Daniel Young, and Isaac Bedal, Pound Keepers; Samson Striker, Henry Johnson, Samuel Williams, and Isaac Garret, Constables.

At the first township meeting, "it was enacted that no fence is to be lawful in the township under the height of four feet eight inches high, sufficiently made." Horses, horned cattle, hogs, sheep, were to be permitted to run at large with certain exceptions. "It is enacted that if any freeholder shall suffer any Canadian thistle to go to seed on his farm, he shall forfeit and pay the sum of twenty shillings." A law was also passed, that if any one set fire to any rubbish or brush, whereby his neighbors property was endangered, without previously making two of his neighbors acquainted, he should pay a fine of forty shillings, to be expended for the benefit of the highways. Bazel Ferguson, who seems to have discharged his duty as Town Clerk, recording the proceedings in a neat legible hand, was successfully elected to that office for ten years. In 1810,

31

James R. Armstrong was appointed, and again the following year. The next following, Arra Ferguson was elected, who continued in office three years, when Simeon Washburn received the appointment, and remained in office two years, when Arra Ferguson was again selected, and continued for three years. Robert Scott was Town Clerk two years, and then again followed Arra Ferguson for eight years. William Barker then was appointed.

The three Justices of the Peace, before whom the annual meeting continued for many years to be held, were John Peters, Augustus Spencer, and John Stinson, doubtless the first magistrates in the township. In the year 1815, we notice as "present" at the annual meeting, Stephen Conger, Barret Dyer, Ebenezer Washburn, Justices of the Peace.

The town meeting was held in the year 1801, "at the house of Richardson and Elsworth," "near Hallowell Bridge;" likewise the following year. In 1803 the meeting was held "at the house of Thomas Richardson." The following year 1805, it is "the house of the late Thomas Richardson." In 1806, the meeting was "at the dwelling house of Thomas Eyre." In 1807 it is "the Inn of Thomas Eyre." Here the annual meeting was successively held for many years.

HILLIER.

In the year 1823 there was an act passed for the division of the township of Ameliasburgh, in consequence of the inconvenience of the inhabitants to meet on public occasions. The dividing line was established between the fourth and fifth concessions. The act went into force on the first of January, 1824. The Lieutenant-Governor at that time was Sir Peregrine Maitland, who had for his secretary, Major Hillier. There is no doubt the new township was called after Major Hillier.

PICTON.

At the beginning of the present century the ground on which the town of Picton now stands, was covered with a dense forest of pine and hemlock, while in the low land existed a thick and tangled cedar swamp. A bridge of very inferior construction was erected across the creek about the time of the war of 1812, it was on the road between Kingston and York, and was called for a long time Hallowell Bridge. Thus we find in an advertisement, in the *Kingston Gazette*, 1815, that "Richard G. Clute sold goods and groceries at Hallowell Bridge."

The first settlers of Picton are said to have been Ebenezer Washburn, Henry Johnson, Abraham Barker, Harry Ferguson, James Dougal, Cary Spencer, Congers, Peterson, Richard Hare, Captain Richardson.

Among the early settlers of Picton were Dr. Armstrong, elsewhere spoken of, and Dr. Andrew Austin. The latter was a native of Vermont, and a doctor of medicine of the University of New York. He came to Picton in 1822, having obtained his license to practice in Canada. Remained practicing his profession, very much respected, until his death in 1849.

Some time after the war of 1812, the Rev. William Macaulay, bestowed the name of Picton upon a small collection of houses situated at the south side of the stream which empties into the head of Picton Bay, in the township of Marysburgh. The name was given in memory of the celebrated British General who had recently fallen upon the field of Waterloo. At a late visit to St. Paul's Cathedral, we felt no little pleasure with a touch of sadness in gazing upon the memorial which has been erected to commemorate a nation's appreciation of military worth. We transcribe the following :—

"Erected by the public expense, to Lieutenant-General Sir Thomas Picton, K.C.B., who, after distinguishing himself in the victories of Buzaco, Fuentes de Onor, Cindaet Rodrigo, Badajoz, Vittoria, the Pyrenees, Orthes, and Toulouse, terminated his long and glorious military service in the ever memorable battle of Waterloo; to the splendid success of which his genius and valour eminently contributed," &c.

Prior to the naming of this collection of buildings, the village upon the west of the stream, upon the first lots in Sophiasburgh, was known as Hallowell. The Rev. Mr. Macaulay with the enthusiastic loyalty, characteristic of his family, desired that both places should be known as one village, under the distinguished name of Picton. The citizens of Hallowell Village, however, were opposed to any other name than Hallowell, and we find in a map published in 1836, the names of Picton and Hallowell respectively applied to the two places. But when the whole was incorporated by Act of Parliament, Mr. Macaulay had sufficient influence, we are informed, to secure the name of Picton for the corporation; yet we have the town of Hallowell spoken of in 1837. The growth of Picton was not particularly rapid. "At a meeting held at Eyre's Inn, Feb. 14, 1818, over which Ebenezer Washburn, Esq., presided, it was stated that there was in the township of Hallowell, which included Picton, but two brick houses, one carding and fulling-mill, one Methodist chapel, now known as the old chapel at Congers, one Quaker meeting house; and that preparations were being made to build a church, that is for the Episcopalians. Orchards, it was stated were beginning to be planted.

There seems to have been no little antagonism between the villages of Picton and Hallowell. While an effort was earnestly made to make the east side, the heart of the community, the inhabitants of Hallowell strove to fix the central point upon the west side. When Prince Edward was erected into a district, in 1831, and it became necessary to erect a jail and court house, it became a warm question as to the site of the building. The Hallowell *Free Press* became the channel of a sharp discussion.

In the Press of June 21,1831, is a letter signed, "A farmer of Sophiasburgh," one paragraph of which says, "Among all these advantages pointed out in the most striking colours, I have discerned none so great as the $200 so liberally offered by Mr. Macaulay, which $200 must otherwise be paid by the rateable inhabitants of the county."

The year 1831 seems to have been an important one to the inhabitants, not only of Picton, but the peninsula. Enterprise was the order of the day, and improvements of a public character were in various ways proposed. The *Free Press* of 5th July, says, under the heading "Another Steamboat," "We understand that a number of the enterprising inhabitants of this village, have it in contemplation to build a steamboat to ply between this place and Prescott, to perform their trips in a week. A number of merchants and capitalists have offered to take stock. We are of opinion that a boat built and owned by the inhabitants of this county, would be not only useful to the inhabitants of the Peninsula, but profitable to the stockholders. We would suggest to them the propriety of having the channel in the bay at the lower end of the village cleared, so as to allow steamboats to pass up as far as the bridge."

The present English Church, standing on Church Street, was the first built in Picton. It was erected by the Rev. Wm. Macaulay, aided by a partial loan in 1825. Mr. Macaulay was the first minister; he came to the parish after seven years of officiating at Cobourg, and has remained as Rector ever since. The Roman Catholic chapel, now standing on Church Street, was the first erected, in 1828 or 9, the land having been given for that purpose by Mr.

Macaulay. The new stone church was built in 1839. Rev. Mr. Frazer was first minister, in 1828; Rev. Mr. Brennan, occasionally from 1832 to 1836; the Rev. Mr. Lalor from 1836 to the present time.

CHAPTER LIV.

CONTENTS—Eighth Township—Sidney—Name—Survey—Settlement, 1787—Letter from Ferguson—Trading—Barter—Potatoes—Building—Cows—No salt to spare—First settlers—Myers—Re-surveying—James Farley—Town Clerk at first meeting—William Ketcheson—Gilbert's Cove—Coming to the front River Trent—Old names—Ferry—Bridge—Trenton—Its settlement—Squire Bleeker.

THE EIGHTH TOWNSHIP—SIDNEY—ITS SETTLEMENT.

No Royal name being available for this township, the noble one of SIDNEY was conferred. The name is derived from Lord Sidney, who, at the time of the Revolutionary War, was His Majesty's Secretary for the Colonial Department.

A map in the Crown Lands Department, has written upon it "Sidney, in the District of Mecklenburgh, was surveyed in 1787, by Louis Kotte." This was probably written by Kotte himself. It is most probable that the first lots only were then laid out. While Kotte was the chief surveyor to whom was entrusted the duty, it is gathered from different sources that he was not present to superintend the work. Mr. William Ketcheson, of the fifth concession, who came with his father to the place, in 1800, says that one McDonald was the surveyor, and laid out the land as far back as the 5th concession, when he died.

While the townships fronting upon the two shores of the Bay were being surveyed in the western portion, not a few were on the look out for a good location. These parties consisted of all classes, but it appears most likely that the majority of those who had the first choice were individuals connected with the surveyors, and who had influence with them. The officers, naturally, enjoyed greater privileges, and some of them sought suitable spots with the view of trading with the Indians, or streams of water to supply power for sawing and flouring-mills.

As illustrative of those times we will make use of a letter lying before us, written at that time.

In the year 1789, John Ferguson and Wm. Bell opened a store in the Eighth Township. It appears with the view of trading with the Indians, and such of the settlers as could pay for the goods they might buy. A letter written by Ferguson, in 1790, from Kingston, to his partner, says: "As to again taking up goods for trade, had I money I would not think it worth while—notwithstanding all I said and begged of you, you nevertheless have let the white people have almost everything we had. When do you think they will pay for it?" By the foregoing we may learn the difficulties attending mercantile pursuits, as well as the procuring of the common necessaries of life. It was no doubt a matter of first importance to Ferguson to see that the goods brought a return. It was no hard-heartedness that caused him to find fault; for in the same letter he says, "Forsyth is arrived, and I know not how I'll pay him." On the other hand, Mr. Bell, with his little stock of goods upon the Bay Shore, in the distant Eighth Township, is applied to by the needy settlers for necessaries. They have no money; it is an article almost unknown among them, but they want this and that, and who could refuse? Ferguson afterward says, "You must oblige every one to pay you in wheat, or otherwise I will want bread before winter is over—if they will not take 3s. 9d. for wheat, make them pay in money immediately, or else send me down their accounts, and I'll summon every one of them. Let your half bushel be examined before Squire Gilbert. Do not spare a potatoe to any one soul. I hope to get a barrel of pork here, but do not trust to that."

In the same letter Mr. Ferguson says, "If convenient, I could wish you'ld get cut and brought home, as many logs as would build a house the width of the one we have, and 14 feet long. Let them be small and handy—we have plenty of small pine handy—and it soon can be put up when I get home. If Johnson will saw ten logs about 14 feet long, for us, into inch boards, and find himself. He shall have the loan of the saw from the time he finishes them until the 15th day of April next." "The cows must be sent up. I do not know how the calf will be kept. I have bought two pairs of ducks which I'll take up, and also some fowls if I can get them." "Spare no salt to any one, as none is to be had here, but at a very dear rate." "The Indian prints goes up, which will spoil the trade this season, as after this the Indians cannot want clothing until the spring." "Rum I must endeavour to take up, as without that nothing can be had."

The late Mr. Bleeker, of Belleville, tells us that among the very first settlers upon the front of Sidney, were Chrysler, Ostrom and Gilbert.

The interesting history we give elsewhere, of Capt. Myers, as a loyalist and pioneer, shows that he was one of the first inhabitants of Sidney. A pioneer in the construction of mills upon the River Moira, he had previously built in 1794 or '5, a sawing mill upon a small uncertain stream which empties into the Bay a few miles east of Trenton.

We have seen that the survey took place in 1787. It is questionable, however, whether more than the first concession was at this time laid out. There is some reason to believe that Louis Kotte did not attend very closely to his duties, but left the surveying to an incompetent assistant. Probably he thought it did not matter whether the side lines were correct or not, in a remote township so far removed from civilization, as Sidney. At all events, in later days, it was found necessary to re-survey the township, which was done by Atkins.

The first settlers, most likely, came in 1787, yet it may be that one or two had previously squatted by the Bay Shore. We do not find in the Crown Lands Department any map with the names of grantees upon the different lots, such as exist in connection with other townships.

No doubt that in Sidney, as in other places, many lots were drawn, and subsequently disposed of before the patents were issued, so that the original owner cannot be traced. By the close of last century the township was pretty well settled. An early settler who has recently passed away, and who leaves highly respectable descendants, was James Farley. He came in 1799.

The first township meeting was held the following year at Gilbert's Cove, and James Farley was chosen Town Clerk; but Surveyor Smith was present and did the writing on that occasion. Another early settler, the first one in the back concessions was Wm. Ketcheson. Reference is made to him elsewhere. His son, now almost 90 years of age, remembers full well the days of their coming, and settling. The 400 acres of land was bought of Martin Hambly, who lived by the Napanee River, at one dollar per acre, in 1800. Gilbert's Cove was the place of landing, which was for many years a central spot. Here the batteaux unloaded their contents, and the provision was stored. William Ketcheson, my informer, says, "he used to come every Saturday during the season, through the trackless woods, some seven-and-a-half miles, and carry upon his back provisions of pork, peas and flour, sufficient to serve three of them for a week. After a while they would come to the Front by the way of the River Moira. To do this they constructed a scow which was kept near the present village of Smithville, in which they crossed the river.

In the western part of the township is the River Trent, which empties into the Bay, somewhat to the west of the boundary line between Sidney and Murray. This river possesses no little interest as one of the original routes of Indian and French travelers; and as the way by which Champlain entered the Bay, and discovered Lake Ontario. The Indian name we find upon an old map was *Ganaraske*. Upon many ancient maps the bay and river are very imperfectly distinguished. It is named Quintio occasionally.

The Trent being a stream of considerable size, it formed a barrier to journeying up and down, from Kingston to York. A ferry was established here about the beginning of the present century, by the Bleekers, after which the main road between Kingston and York gradually became fixed to the north of the Bay, instead of by Prince Edward.

The construction of a bridge across the Trent, which took place in 1834, was a great benefit. It was 750 feet long and 32 broad. It was for many years "the best bridge in Upper Canada." The *Hastings Times*, of Belleville, has an advertisement for tenders by the Commissioners, &c., C. Wilkins, Reuben White, and James G. Bethune, dated River Trent, 9th March, 1833.

At the mouth of the Trent there naturally sprung up a village. Up to 1808 the site of the village was a dense cedar swamp. Two years before A. H. Myers had removed from Belleville and erected a mill about a mile from the mouth of the river, first a saw mill, afterward a flouring mill. Excepting the mills, and a very narrow road, the place was a perfect wilderness. The land upon the west side, where the village stands, originally belonged to "old Squire" Bleeker. The portion of land between the river and Sidney was held by Dr. Strachan. The first lot in Sidney was owned by Judge Smith.

Old Squire Bleeker was probably the very first settler between the Trent and the Carrying Place. He was a trader with the Indians, and was probably Indian Agent. At all events he was a man of considerable authority among them.

CHAPTER LV.

CONTENTS—Ninth town—Thurlow—Name—When surveyed—Front—Indian burying ground—Owner of first lots—Chisholm—Singleton—Myers—Ferguson—Indian traders—To Kingston in batteau—Singleton's death—Ferguson's death—Distress of the families—Settled, 1789—Ascending the Moira—Taking possession of land—Fifth concession—John Taylor—Founder of Belleville—Myers buying land—Settlers upon the front—Municipal record—Town officers—1798—Succeeding years—Canifton, its founder—Settling—The diet—Building mill—Road—River Moira—Origin of name—Earl Moira—Indian name—Indian offering—"Cabojunk"—Myers' saw-mill—Place not attractive—First bridge—The flouring-mill—Belleville—Indian village—Myers' Creek—Formation of village—First inn—Permanent bridge Bridge Street—In 1800—Growth—A second mill—McNabb's—Sad death—Captain McIntosh—Petrie—Inhabitants, 1809—Dr. Sparcham—Naming of Belleville—Bella Gore—By Gore in council—Petition—Extract from Kingston Gazette—Surveying reserve—Wilmot—Mistakes—Granting of lots—Conditions—Board of Police—Extent of Belleville—Muddy streets—Inhabitants in 1824—Court-house—First Court, Quarter Sessions—Belleville in 1836.

THE NINTH TOWN—THURLOW.

The oldest map in the Crown Lands Department, states that this township was surveyed in 1787, by Louis Kotte; perhaps only the front concession. By this map, we learn that at the mouth of the river had been, probably on Zwick's Island, an Indian burying ground; and a lot is reserved for the Indians, for a burying ground. The map informs us that lot No. 1, in both the first and second concessions, was at first given to John Chisholm. Lot No. 2, in first and second concession, to David Vanderheyden; No. 3, to Alexander Chisholm; No. 4, the reserve for the "Indian burying ground;" Nos. 5 and 6, to Captain John Singleton. These are the only names which appear upon the map; but it is likely that lot No. 7, was granted at first to Captain Myers. The late George Bleeker, Esq., told the writer that Captain Myers having stayed in Lower Canada three years, came and settled upon lot 7, where he built a hut and lived for a year, before going to Sidney. This was probably in 1787, when the surveying was proceeding. Thus it was that Captain Myers, who afterward gave a name to the river and place, was the first squatter. About this time, Captain Singleton, who had been a first settler in Ernesttown, came to Thurlow with a brother officer, Lieutenant Ferguson, both having recently married and settled upon lot No. 6. Their object in coming was to carry on a fur trade with the Indians, who regularly descended the River Sagonoska to barter, and subsequently to get their presents. The single log house which was first built, was shortly added to, by a second compartment, into which was stored furs and goods for barter. The life of these first settlers of Thurlow was a brief one, and the termination a sad one. Both had just married, and with their faithful servant, Johnson, and his wife, they hoped for a future as bright as the wood and water which so beautifully surrounded them. It mattered not to them that no human habitation existed nearer than the Mohawk settlement, and the Napanee River. Many trips with the batteau were necessary to obtain a complete outfit for Indian trading, and ample provisions had to be laid up, with stores of rum. These articles were procured at Kingston. Singleton had rented his farm in the second town; but reserved a room, where he might stop on his way up and down. In September, 1789, Captain Singleton, his wife, child, some eight months old, with Lieutenant Ferguson, his wife, and the servants, Johnson and wife, set out for Kingston and Ernesttown in a batteau. The women were to visit in Ernesttown, while the men proceeded to Kingston to purchase flour and other articles. Not long after starting, Singleton was taken ill. They stopped at Captain John's, at the Mohawk settlement, and Indian medicines were given him; but he continued to grow worse, and when he reached his home, in Ernesttown, he was dangerously ill. A doctor from Kingston was procured; but Captain Singleton died nine days after, from what seems to have been a malignant fever. His faithful servant, Johnson, contracted the disease and also died. Thus, Lieutenant Ferguson was left with three women and a child, away from home, which could only be reached after much toil. Captain Singleton was spoken of as a "pleasing gentleman, and beloved by all who knew him." His infant son grew to man's estate, and became one of the first settlers of Brighton, where his widow, now far advanced in years, and descendants reside.

Lieutenant Ferguson went to Kingston, exchanged his load of furs for a barrel of flour, then very dear, and other articles, and returned with his charge to Thurlow. But Ferguson's days were also numbered; and, in three months' time, he died, and there were left in the depth of winter, alone, upon the front of Thurlow, three widowed women, and an infant; with but little to eat, beside the barrel of flour; which, before long, was to be the only article of food, and used by cup-fulls to make spare cakes.

Lieutenant Ferguson, the associate of the first settler in the township, was at first a refugee from the Mohawk valley in New

York, and latterly served, probably in Johnson's regiment. He had lived a short time at Sorel before coming to Thurlow. His body was buried upon a pleasant elevation, between their house and the plains to the east of the river. The first one of the loyalists to die in Thurlow, his body was the first to be interred in the "Taylor burying ground."

In the spring of 1789, a party of about fifty, reached the bay. They were all refugee loyalists, and most of them had been since the close of the war in the States, looking up their families, and arranging to take them "to Cataraqui." This party settled in Sidney and Thurlow. Those who settled in Thurlow, finding no land available at the front, prepared to ascend the river. Among them were John Taylor, William Reed, with four sons, John, William, Samuel, and Solomon; Richard Smith, Cavelry, Robert Wright, John Longwell, Sherard, Zedic Thrasher, Asa Turner, Stephen and Laurence Badgley, Solomon Hazleton, Archibald McKenzie, McMichael, William Cook, and Russell Pitman. The party reached the mouth of the river late in the day, and pitched their tent among some cedar shrubs upon the east bank of the river, just by the site of the upper bridge. The following day, they followed the bank of the river, searching for indications of good land The surveyor had not yet laid out any but the front lots; but the pioneers had been assured that any land they should choose to occupy, would be granted them. When they reached the point where now is the fifth concession, they felt that they had reached their destination, and proceeded to take possession of such land as struck their fancy. William Reed, and his four sons, possessed themselves of 600 acres in a block, through which the river wound its way. The land here was unmistakeably good; and four generations have now reaped the fruit of the soil, while two generations lie buried there. But the first years of pioneer life with those first settlers of the fifth concession, were years of great hardship and want (see First years of Upper Canada). They all went to Napanee at first to mill. Sometimes took articles to exchange for flour.

John Taylor settled in the fifth concession, where he remained a year, when he came down to the mouth of the river. A sketch of this old soldier is elsewhere given. Among the settlers who came in, a few years later, were Richard Canniff, and Robert Thompson.

In some respects, the settlers of these townships, at the western extremity of the bay, suffered in a peculiar manner. They were far removed from Kingston, and from the necessaries of life to be procured there. And they were settling after the period when Government allowed provisions.

The name of Captain Myers must ever stand identified with the early history of Thurlow. He cannot be regarded as the founder of Belleville; yet he was the first to give a name to the village at the mouth of the river. Captain Myers saw service during the revolutionary war (see Royal Combatants). At the close of hostilities, having tarried for a time at Lower Canada, he came to the bay, and squatted at first upon the front of Thurlow. He first became a settler upon the front of Sidney, a few miles east of the Trent River. Being a man of enterprise, and with forethought, he did not content himself with clearing a farm and cultivating its soil. He saw the wants of the settlers, that they required sawed lumber, and greater conveniences for grinding grain. Hence he is found, even before 1790, erecting a sawing mill upon a small stream on his land in Sidney. The water-power was very inefficient, and he looked about for a more suitable place. The waters of the Moira presented the inducements he sought. A bargain was effected with John Taylor for the rear half of lot No. 5, which embraced a portion of the stream, affording the desired mill-site. It was, most probably, in the year 1790, that Captain Myers came to Thurlow, and built his log hut upon the banks of the river, a few rods above the present mill-dam. Within a year, the first dam erected upon the river was finished, and a log saw mill built upon the east bank.

The late Colonel Wilkins, of the Carrying Place, says, that when he came to the bay, in 1792, Myers had his mill built, the one farthest west, until they came to where is now Port Hope.

The following are the names of those who settled upon the front, as supplied by the late G. Bleeker, Esq. Commencing at lot No. 1, the first settler was John Chisholm; No. 2, Coon Frederick; No. 3, Crawford, the lot having been drawn by A. Chisholm. Coming to No. 7, it was settled upon by A. Thompson, who sold the right to Schofield; No. 8, by Arch. Chisholm; No. 9, by Samuel Sherwood, who was an Indian trader. Then Fairman, William Johnson, Edward Carscallion, J. Carscallion, Fairman, Biddell.

There is no record of the first municipal transaction. Most likely, no record was kept. The following, however, takes us back a long way:—

"At the annual town meeting, for the township of Thurlow, held the fifth day of March, 1798, whereat the following persons were chosen town officers, viz., John McIntosh, Town Clerk, John

Chisholm and William Reid, Assessors; Joseph Walker, Collector; Samuel B. Gilbert, John Reed, William Johnson, Pathmasters; John Cook and Daniel Lawrence, Town Wardens; John Taylor, Pound-keeper; John Fairman, Constable."

John McIntosh, remembered as Capt. McIntosh, was Town Clerk for three years, and was succeeded by Jabez Davis. The following year, the occupant was Caleb Benedict. The year succeeding, Roswell Leavens was appointed, and continued to hold the office for three years, when John Frederick was chosen, who held the place two years, when John McIntosh was again selected; he held it two years. Then John Thompson was appointed, who held it one year. The next year it was Roswell Leavens; the next, John Frederick; the next, R. Leavens, who continued uninterruptedly in office for twelve years, up to the year 1826. During that time very many changes are observed in the names of those holding the other municipal offices in the Township. The Town Clerk, in the year 1826, was Daniel Canniff, who held it two years; the next was James McDonnell, who filled the post seven years. In 1835, D. B. Sole was appointed, who held it two years. The year ensuing, Dr. Hayden was appointed. It would seem that during the year following, Dr. H. escaped as a rebel, while his wife refused to hand over the township records.

CANIFTON.—Up to the year 1806, the way from Myers' mill up the river to where stands Corby's mill, a distance of four miles, was unbroken by a single clearing. There was but a poor waggon road, which had been cut by the two individuals who alone could afford the comfort of a waggon. But in that year another settler was added to Thurlow, and a third waggon to the community. John Canniff, having bought some 800 acres of land from one McDougall, and one Carle, in the third concession, commenced the work of clearing upon the present site of the village of Canifton. John Canniff was a U. E. Loyalist, and was born at Bedford, in the County of Westchester, in the present State of New York, in the year 1757. There is no reliable statement handed nown as to the part he took in the war against the rebellion. That he took an active part is believed by those most capable of judging. The name of Lieut. Candiff appears among the officers of a New Jersey regiment, which is thought to have been one of the family. John Canniff was a refugee at the close of the war in New Brunswick, where he remained a few years. He then came to Canada, in 1788, and first settled in Adolphustown, where he lived until his removal to Thurlow. He had witnessed and experienced the suffering of the year of the famine. And it is known that he actually saved one family from death by starvation. Before bringing his family to Thurlow, in 1807, he had cleared a considerable piece of land, on the east side of the river, around the present site of the bridge; built a mill-dam, a saw-mill, and a frame house, which stood a short distance above the site of the Methodist Church. Although this took place near the end of the first decade of the present century, yet the settlement was attended by no little hardship. The necessaries of life were not always to be had, and it is authentically related, that for a time pea bread constituted the principle article of diet, while a fish, now and then caught, was a great luxury.

About the year 1812, Canniff erected a flouring-mill, having for mill-stones those made on the spot, out of hard granite; the man who made them yet lives. These relics of the past may yet be seen. But in two years he procured a pair of Burr stones from the Trent.

In the year 18—, Mr. Canniff removed to the front of Thurlow, and lived upon lot number eight, where he continued to dwell until his death, 21st Feb., 1843. He was in his 87th year when he died. His remains are buried near the front of the Episcopal Church, in Belleville. He was a great uncle to the writer.

Up to the year 1715, there was but one small house in Canifton, beside that occupied by Mr. Canniff, this was occupied by a cooper, named Ockerman.

For four years after John Canniff settled upon the river, there was an unbroken wood between his place and Myers' mill, while but a rough road existed, which followed the river's bank. In the spring of 1811, James Canniff, the writer's father, commenced to clear land, midway between Myers' mill and John Canniff's. At this time, the road remained almost impassable, for the half-dozen waggons, owned in the township. Some years later, the road was somewhat straightened and improved; but although now, and for a long time, so great a thoroughfare, the road continued to be, for many years, the most execrable.

THE RIVER MOIRA.—This river is named after the Right Hon. the Earl of *Moira*, afterward Marquis of *Hastings*, and previously, when a soldier, serving in the American war, known as Lord *Rawdon*. At his death the title became extinct. His body was buried in his native town in Ireland. While in America, he formed a strong attachment to Brant.

The Moira takes its rise in the township of Tudor, and in its windings to the Bay Quinté, passes through the townships of Madoc, Marmora, Rawdon, Huntingdon, Hungerford, Tyendinaga, and Thurlow. It was well known, and yearly ascended by the Indians for the excellent hunting which it afforded. They called it *Sagonasko*, which name may be found on the first maps issued by the surveyor. It was sometimes spelled *Saganashcocon*.

The Indians, when about to pass up on their hunting expeditions, leaving many of the women and children in wigwams upon the plains near its mouth, would make an offering to their pagan god, of tobacco, which was dropped upon the east shore, near its mouth, just below the site of the first bridge. A thank offering was repeated upon their return.—(B. Flint).

When the first mill dam was erected by Capt. Myers, the obstruction was called by them *Cabojunk*.

When the land was surveyed, the Government reserved at the mouth of the river 200 acres, ostensibly, for an Indian burying ground. But the place of burying was upon Zwick's Island, in the Bay, near the river's mouth.

Upon the old maps, this river is called Singleton's River, after Capt. Singleton.

About the year 1790, Capt. Myers settled upon the river, and erected a dam and log saw mill. It consequently took the name of Myers' Creek, which it retained, until after the war of 1812, and by some, to within the writer's recollection, thirty years ago. The writer remembers to have seen the Indians, in their birch canoes, ascending and descending the river. The fact that the word Moira has some resembling sound to that of Myers, has led some to suppose that the latter name became gradually changed into the former. But the fact is as stated above.

The appearance of the place, presented to the first adventurers in pursuit of land on which to settle, was not attractive. It was a barren plain with a cedar swamp covering the shores on either side. There were, however, on the east side, at the mouth, some tall and good sized oaks, indicating deep soil, while the land around was rock; this land, like the two islands upon which mills are built, was rich, and had been made from the washings of the river's sides for centuries, and carried down from the back country.

The first bridge upon the Moira, was a floating structure, and was placed quite at the mouth of the river, with the view of escaping the current; but it was soon carried off. The bridge was built about 1800; prior to which time there had been a ferry for foot passengers, when the stream was not fordable. At certain seasons, crossings could take place almost anywhere. The first spring freshet carried away the bridge. In the winter of 1802, according to Mrs. Harris, who then lived in the place, a more substantial structure was commenced; but again it was carried off by ice breaking over Myers' dam. Possibly, this may be the first one. The first permanent bridge must have been completed in 1806 or 7.

The excellent water power was first employed by Capt. Myers, and the second person to use it was the Reeds, at the place where is now situated Corby's mill. The benefit of a flouring mill to the Reeds will be understood when it is known that they had previously, to carry on their back the grist to the Napanee mills, a distance of some forty miles, and thus occupying four days.

BELLEVILLE.

The early *voyageurs*, passing along in their birch canoes, bound for the far west, by the way of the River Trent to Lake Simcoe, were never attracted to the low, thick woods, which bordered the river called by the Indians *Sagonoska*. It is true, there was generally an Indian village upon the plains situated to the east of the river's mouth. But the collection of rude tents offered no special invitation. While the French, it would seem, never ascended the river; the Indians of the Missisauga tribe inhabited the region, and mostly always had a village upon the bay shore. As we have seen, the Government, at the time of surveying, reserved lot number four, which included the river and the plains, for the Indians. About 1789 or 90, Captain Myers, having purchased a part of lot number five, of John Taylor, for $100, endeavored to obtain a lease of the Indian lot for a long period of years; and he subsequently claimed the lot, averring that it had been leased him for ninety-nine years. This claim of Capt. Myers, it has been stated, led to the name which so long obtained, Myers' Creek. But the claim was never recognised by Government, although there is some reason to think that the Indians did actually bargain it away. The settlement upon the river, by Captain Myers, very soon came to be known as Captain Myers', and the inhabitants up and down the bay, spoke of the settlement, as well as of the river, as Myers' Creek. But, at the same time, Myers' mill and house were quite remote from the first collection of houses at the mouth of the river. Apart from the water privileges, there was nothing to attract to the place, and, until the beginning of the present century, there was not even a hut at the mouth of the river. If public meetings were held, they were up the front, or back near the fifth concession, afterward known as Hayden's Corners.

The village began to form upon the east bank of the river, a little distance below Dundas street, and, for many years, it did not extend further north than that street. The first place of habitation so far as can be learned, was a log house, built and occupied by Asa Wallbridge, a trader, who was well known by the early settlers. Then came John Simpson, in the year 1798, and constructed a log hut, 20 x 12. This house, the first public house in Thurlow, was for many years known from Kingston to York, as a place of public entertainment. Within its rough walls rested many an important traveler, and here, in later days, convened the men of dignity and office, to discuss matters of great import concerning the village. Here met, in jovial companionship, the inhabitants of the village at night. Around this rude public house centered the crowd upon training days, or when the race course was a point of attraction. For many years, the heart of the village was at the corner of Dundas street. At this place was the ferry, and afterwards the first bridge.

John Simpson, who was Sergt.-Major of the Militia when first organized, died shortly after coming to Myers' Creek; but his widow, Margaret, continued the hostess for many years. She endeavored to keep pace with the wants of the growing village, and made one improvement after another, and finally had built the frame structure now converted into the agreeable residence of the Hon. Lewis Wallbridge. About the year 1800, a second inn was opened in the village, the descendant of this is the present Railroad House.

When it became necessary to build a bridge across the river, about 1806-7, the question of site was one of no little consideration. It seemed the most natural that it should be erected on Dundas Street, which was the great mail road between Kingston and York; and those living in the heart of the village could see no reason in having it placed elsewhere. But a majority of those having a voice in the matter, looked at the question in a more practical light; and rightly thought a bridge would cost less where the river was the narrowest, while it should not be too far for convenience. The result was that it was built on the site of the present lower bridge, and so gave to the street the name of Bridge Street.

Retracing our steps to the beginning of the present century, we present the statement of Mr. William Ketcheson, who settled in Sidney, and also of James Farley, both of whom say that there was not then even a village at the mouth of the river, there being but two or three shanties, among them Simpson's tavern, at the rude bar of which the sole drink was a home brewed beer, which, however, possessed intoxicating properties. Another building was an ash house, owned by Asa Wallbridge.

During the first years of the present century, the place grew to the importance of a village, whose inhabitants, with those of the adjacent farmers, made up nearly a hundred persons. Important additions had been made, and enterprise was at work. Two noble and loyal Scotchmen had come to the place several years before, and purchased lot number three, and had built a second mill dam, and mills. These were Simon and James McNabb. They subsequently took an active part in everything relating to the village. James McNabb became Collector of Customs, and the first Post-Master and Registrar, and both were officers in the militia. The melancholy death of James McNabb, is hardly yet forgotten. During the rebellion of 1836, there was an alarm in Belleville, and Capt. McNabb, while running through an unlighted hall, was fatally wounded by a careless militiaman, who was trailing his musket with bayonet fixed.

Capt. McIntosh was an early settler in Belleville, as well as a pioneer with sailing vessels. He built the first frame store house at Belleville, which was taken down in 1867. The house he built is still standing, a quaint edifice, at the lower extremity of front street. Within its walls rested General Brock, when on his way westward, at the commencement of the war of 1812; also General Gore, after the close of the war. Capt. McIntosh met an untimely death by drowning while attempting to swim from his schooner, which was wind-bound off Ox Point, to the shore, 23rd Sept, 1815.

In the year 1809, Alexander Oliphant Petrie, came to live at Myers' Creek. He found the following persons living in Belleville at that time. Commencing at the lowest part; there first lived Capt. John McIntosh, who kept a store; John Johnson, a saddler; Dr. Sparehan; John Thompson, who had been a soldier in the King's Rangers; Peter Holmes, a carpenter, who had also been in the Rangers; Mrs. Margaret Simpson, inn-keeper; Roswell Leavens, a blacksmith; John Simons; one Ames, a cooper; Hugh Cunningham, store-keeper, at Mrs. Simpson's; Simon McNabb, who lived across the river; Ockerman, a cooper; Benj. Stone, a sawyer; Wm. Maybee, and Abraham Stimers. In the neighborhood of the village lived John Taylor; James Harris, a hatter, and Capt. Myers. The only road was along the river, while foot paths led to the different dwellings. Respecting Dr. Spareham, there is the following notice in the Kingston *Gazette*: "Died, Friday 20th, 1813, Dr. Thomas Spareham, at Kingston; aged about 88. He was one of the first settlers in the country."

The McNabbs had a flouring-mill, and there was a small cloth factory on the west side of the river, at Myers' dam. Harris had a small shop on the bank of the river; and just below the present market, back from the river, stood a little frame school house, where taught one John Watkins. About the year 1810, Mr. Everitt, from Kingston, erected a fine building for a hotel, outside of the village, near Coleman's, formerly McNabb's mills. This was near the Victoria buildings.

The naming of Belleville took place in 1816. The circumstances attending it were as follows: There met one evening at Mrs. Simpson's tavern, Captain McMichael, the two McNabbs, Wallbridge, R. Leavens, and S. Nicholson. These gentlemen, at the suggestion, it is said, of Captain McMichael, determined to invite Lieutenant-Governor Gore, to name the newly surveyed town. The request was complied with, by calling it after his wife *Bella*. In reference to this, we find in the *Kingston Gazette*, Aug. 24, 1816, the following: "The Lieutenant-Governor, in council, has been pleased to give the new town (formerly known by the name of "Myers' Creek" at the River Moira, the name of "BELLEVILLE," by the request and petition of a great number of the inhabitants of that town and the township of Thurlow." In the issue of 7th September, the *Gazette* remarks, "We mentioned in our paper of the 24th ult., that the new town at the River Moira, was now called Belleville," &c. We were under the impression, from the very pleasant situation of that town that its name was derived from the French; but we have since been informed that it has been given the name of Bellville, in honor of lady Gore at the request of the inhabitants." We have it also, on the authority of Mr. Petrie, who could not be ignorant of the facts, that the name is after Lady Bella Gore. It will be observed that the name was originally spelled Bellville, instead of Belleville, as at the present time. In all letters and public documents where the town was mentioned, we find it spelled Bellville for many years. The writer will now, quote himself from another work. "The same year (1816) the Government instructed surveyor Wilmot to lay out the 200 acres of Indian reserve, lot number four, into town lots of half an acre each. It cannot be recorded that Mr. Wilmot discharged his duty to his credit or the advantage of the town. In the first place he made the serious mistake (it has been questioned whether it was a mistake) of placing the line between Sidney and Thurlow, upwards of sixty feet to the east of that marked by the original survey. The consequence was, that the line between lots numbers three and four (at the front) instead of being mainly in the river, where it ought to have been, was established where now is Front Street, and thereby, a valuable strip of land belonging to the Reserve, was added to private property on the western side of the river; while the owner of lot number five, Mr. Taylor, was a loser to a corresponding extent. Another mistake was the very few cross streets laid out, the inconvenience of which is felt daily by many; although some new ones have been opened latterly. A third error was the respect he made to a hotel which stood a little to the east of where now stands the Victoria buildings. This hotel had been erected on the ground, where the street, in surveying, happened to come. The result is the unseemly turn in its course at Pinnacle Street. While the hotel gave a name to the street, the name commemorates the cause of its uglinesss. The town lots were disposed of by Government to petitioners, true subjects of His Majesty, on a payment of a fee of thirty dollars. No one could obtain more than a single lot. Seven plots were reserved: one for a hospital, one where stands the Catholic Church, the Grammar School, the English Church, also, the Parsonage house, the old Market Square, and the Jail."

The lots were granted to applicants upon presenting a petition signed by two citizens, to Government. The grantee was obligated to build, in a given time, a house, one story and a half high, and 18 x 30 feet.

Belleville is the oldest town in Upper Canada. At the time it was named, where now stands Cobourg, were but three houses. In 1816 the *Kingston Gazette* says, "A Post Office is now established in the new and flourishing town of Bellville, S. McNabb. Esq., Post Master."

In the year 1834, a petition was submitted by the inhabitants of Belleville to Parliament, the result of which was "An act to establish a Board of Police in the town of Belleville, passed 6th March, 1834."

It would seem that the act passed did not come into operation, for in 1836, an act was passed respealing the former one. This latter act was in many respects the same, but making further provisions. The same year the town record begins. The boundaries were, "commencing at the limits between lots number five and six, in the first concession, so as a line at right angles will run on the northerly side of Wonnacott's bridge, thence south seventy-four degrees, west to the limits between lots numbers two and three, thence sixteen degrees east to the Bay of Quinté, thence easterly following the winding of the bay to the limits between lots numbers five and six aforesaid; thence north sixteen degrees, west to the place of beginning, together with the island and the harbour." There were two wards, each of which elected two members of the Board of Police, and the fourth selected a fifth. The body then selected one of themselves for President. Those elected the first year were, Wm. McCarty and Asa Yeomans, for first ward; Zenas Dafoe, and Wm. Connor for second ward; Billa Flint was elected the fifth member, and was also chosen President; Geo. Benjamin to be clerk to the Board.

Up to this time there had been no sidewalks, and at the same time there was no drainage. The consequence was, that in the rainy season the streets were almost impassible, quite as bad as those of Muddy York are said to have been. The first pavement was laid in 1836, the stones of which were taken from the river.

It is impossible to say definitely what was the number of inhabitants at any one period. These were, however, in 1818, according to Talbot, about 150; about 500 in 1824; 700 in 1829, and in 1836 more than 1,000. But McMullen, writing in 1824, says that between Kingston and York, there are two or three very small villages, the largest of which is Belleville, containing about one hundred and fifty inhabitants.

After this the town increased more rapidly in size and importance. Steps were taken to have built a Court House and Jail, as the nearest place of confinement of prisoners was at Kingston; and, in 1838, just at the close of the rebellion, the present building was finished.

The first court of Quarter Sessions held at the Court House in Belleville, was November, 1839, Benjamin Dougall presided; Edmund Murney, Clerk of the Peace; J. W. D. Moodie, Sheriff. The principal business of the court was to organize, and take the oaths of office. The second court was held in March, 1840, in the Court House; there were the same officers, except that W. H. Ponton was Clerk of the Peace.

A writer in the *Intelligencer*, in 1836, says, Belleville is said to contain about 1,800 inhabitants. There is an English and Scotch Church, a Roman Catholic and Methodist Chapel, also a congregation of Episcopal Methodists, and one of American Presbyterians; 25 merchants' shops, 2 Apothecaries and Druggists', 12 huxters' and grocery shops, 9 taverns, 3 breweries, 3 butchers', 2 flouring mills, 4 saw, and 2 fulling and carding mills, 1 pail factory, 7 blacksmiths' shops, 3 tanneries, and mechanics of almost every description. In Front Street there are a number of spacious brick, stone, and frame buildings; being the most central part of the town for business. The town has recently being called East and West Belleville; separated by the river Moira. The later has been laid out in town lots by the present owners; and the streets and lines defined. On Coleman Street there are already erected a handsome brick and other stone and frame buildings; a Trip-Hammer Forge and Axe manufactory carried on by Mr. Proctor, celebrated for making the best axes in the province. A saw mill in operation and a flouring mill for four run of stone now erecting, and another for six run in contemplation of being built next summer by our enterprising townsman, Mr. Flint. A cabinet-maker, blacksmith's shop, and a tavern, together with a variety of lots unsold, some of which are calculated for hydraulic purposes; and for which there are abundance of materials for stone buildings. The same street leads to the extensive wharfs and store houses belonging to Mr. Billa Flint.

CHAPTER LVI.

CONTENTS—Tenth township—Richmond—Origin—Quantity of land—Shores of Mohawk Bay—Village on south shore—Original land holders—Names—Napanee—The falls—The mill—Salmon River—Indian name—Source of Napanee River—Its course—Colebrook—Simcoe Falls—Name—Clarke's Mills—Newburgh—Academy—The settlers—"Clarkville"—No records.

THE TENTH TOWNSHIP—RICHMOND.

This township is called after the Duke of Richmond, and contains about 50,000 acres.

At an early period, the shores of the Mohawk Bay were occupied by settlers. At first, upon the Fredericksburgh side, and shortly after upon the north shore. The facilities for erecting a flouring-mill at the falls, upon the river which empties into the Mohawk Bay, attracted the attention of Government so early as 1785, in which year the first mill was erected. The existence of this mill caused something of a village to spring up on the south shore. About the same time, the land upon the north shore of the bay and river, was taken up by the loyalists. We can find nothing to indicate the year in which this township was originally surveyed; but it was most probably done in the latter part of 1785, or in the spring of 1786, after the front of Thurlow had been surveyed. Upon the old chart of this township in the Crown Lands Department, may be seen the names of certain officers, as claimants of land near the mouth of the river. The names are in the main, now unknown, and it seems that the land passed into other hands. The second and third concessions seem to have been settled at a comparatively early date. We believe that some of the first settlers on Mohawk Bay, were, Alexander Nicholson, Woodcock, Peterson, Campbell, Richardson, Detlors.

Napanee, a name given to the river, and to the town upon its banks, is of Indian origin. Originally it was Appanee, which signifies, in the Mississauga language, flour, or the river where they make flour. This designation, it has been supposed, arose from the existence of the flouring-mill, built here at an early date (see first days of Upper Canada). The place was first visited by loyalists, in 1784. The beauty of the scenery, the waters of the river, tumbling over the rocks, down a distance of thirty feet, and sweeping down through a muddy bed, and widening into Mohawk Bay, and the surrounding hills clothed in natures rugged habiliments, would naturally attract the settler. Then, when Government placed a mill, at which the settlers could get their grain ground, a consideration of great importance, the land in the vicinity would be eagerly sought, upon which to settle. And, it can readily be inferred, that the more valuable lots in the township of Richmond were, at an early date, appropriated and settled upon.

Running across the back part of this township, from east to west, and continuing across the township of Tyendinagua, is the Salmon River. It takes its rise in Crow Lake, in the Township of Kenebec. It empties into the Bay Quinté, at the border line between this township and Thurlow. Near its mouth is the Village of Shannonville. The Indian name of the Salmon River was *Gosippa.*

The Napanee River, of which we have spoken, takes its rise in the townships of Hinchinbroke, Bedford, Loughborough, Portland, which are thickly strewn with beautiful lakes and streams, all connected so as to form a sort of net work, The Napanee then crosses the front part of Camden, and pursues its way along, forming the southern boundary of Richmond, to empty into the Mohawk Bay. Along the course of the stream are several villages, all possessed of more or less beauty. There is the village of Colebrook, having upward of 300 inhabitants; Simcoe Falls comes next, beautiful and picturesque, with some 250 of population. The village is named after the Falls, which are some forty feet high. The name is derived from Governor Simcoe, who at one time owned here 1000 acres of land. Four miles further down the stream is the pleasant village of Clark's Mills, after a family name of which we have elsewhere spoken, as a distinguished U. E. Loyalist. Continuing down the river we come to Newburgh, a village picturesquely situated, and of considerable importance. Beside its grist-mills, saw-mills, factories, machine shop, foundry, and other machinery worked by the water; Newburgh has a very respectable academy. Perhaps there is no stream in Canada which possesses the same number of mill privileges as the Napanee. There are numerous rapids and several falls along its course, and the banks on either side are often strikingly beautiful. The original settlers along the stream were mostly the children of loyalists.

NAPANEE.—The settlement of Napanee is pretty fully given in the chapter upon the first flouring-mills. We there have stated that Sergeant Major Clark of the 84th regiment, was ordered to Napanee to act as superintendent of the works in connection with the building of the mill; second flouring-mill in Upper Canada. The mill was situated upon the Fredericksburgh side of the river. Upon an early map of the township, by P. V. Elmore, a village is marked here by the name of Clark ville.

Napanee was incorporated in the year 1854.

We regret our inability to procure the township record of Richmond.

DIVISION IX.

THE EARLY GOVERNMENT OF UPPER CANADA.

CHAPTER LVII.

CONTENTS—Military rule—Imperial Act, 1774—French Canada—Refugees—Military Government in Upper Canada—New Districts—Lunenburgh—Mecklenburgh—Nassau—Hesse—The Judges—Duncan—Cartwright—Hamilton—Robertson—Court in Mecklenburgh—Civil Law—Judge Duncan—Judge Cartwright—Punishment inflicted—First execution—New Constitution of Quebec—1791, Quebec Bill passed—Inhabitants of Upper Canada.

UPPER CANADA FROM 1783 TO 1792—THE GOVERNMENT, MILITARY AND CIVIL.

For three years after the conquest the Province of Quebec was governed by military laws, but in 1774, the British Government introduced a Bill, conferring civil rights upon the Canadian French, with a governing council of not more than 23, nor less than 17. The laws, religion and language were secured to the Province, as before the conquest, so that in most respects, excepting the presence of an English Governor, Canada remained a French Colony. The timely concessions of the British Government, and the natural antipathy felt by the Canadians to the New Englanders, prevented in a most positive way, any desire or intention, on the part of the Canadians, to take sides with the revolting British Provinces. When the loyalist refugees began to pick their way into Canada they found themselves as it were in a foreign country. A colony it is true, under the government of an English Governor, but nevertheless consisting of a people entirely dissimilar to themselves. While the war continued the presence of a large number of British troops made the country seem less foreign in its character; but the close of the war, and the disbanding of many of the companies, and withdrawal of others, left the unhappy refugees in a society to them altogether unnatural. It was under such circumstances that steps were taken to survey land upon the upper waters, to which the loyalists might go. The plan pursued by Government was, not to extend the operation of the laws belonging to Lower Canada, and therefore French and unnatural, to the settlements in Upper Canada; but to marshal the pioneer in bands under officers, with the necessary appointments, to secure order, protect interests, and administer justice. The first settlers of Upper Canada, then came in military order, by word of command, and were directed to the point where each should find the land allotted him, and meet his wilderness foe.

All alike were governed by military law, until 1788. Says the historian of Dundas, "It was decided by Government that the first settlers should live under MARTIAL LAW, till such times as it should be rescinded, and replaced by competent courts of justice. But by martial law was meant only, that the English laws, having by the settlement of this part of Canada, been introduced, should be its laws for the present, and that these laws, which very few knew, should be martially executed by the Captain in command, having the superintendence of the particular locality."

Upon the 24th July, 1788, Lord Dorchester issued a proclamation, dated at the Castle of St. Louis, Quebec, forming a certain number of new districts in the Province of Quebec. Upper Canada was formed into four districts, viz.: *Lunenburgh*, which extended from the borders of Lower Canada "to the River Gananoque, now called Thames," *Mecklenburgh*, which included the settlement from Gananoque to the Trent River; *Nassau*, extending from the Trent to Long Point on Lake Erie; *Hesse*, which embraced the remaining parts of Western Canada, including Detroit. The division was based upon the number of settlers rather than the extent of territory.

To each of these districts was appointed a Judge, a Sheriff, &c. The Judge seems to have been clothed with almost absolute power. He dispensed justice according to his own understanding or interpretation of the law, and a Sheriff or Constable stood ready to carry out the decision, which in his wisdom, he might arrive at. These four courts of Common Pleas constituted it seems the whole machinery of the law in Upper Canada, after the people ceased to be under military jurisdiction. It may have been, however, probably was, that appeal could be made against the Judge's decision, to the Governor and Council. There were no other magistrates, and no lawyers in those primitive happy days.

Of the four Judges appointed to the districts, positive knowledge can be obtained but of three; these are Richard Duncan, Judge of Lunenburgh, Richard Cartwright, Judge of Mecklenburgh, and Robert Hamilton, Judge of Nassau. Not unlikely, William Robertson, of Detroit, was Judge of Hesse. This opinion is ventured from the fact that this gentleman was the most successful and prominent man in that locality; the same as Duncan, Cartwright, and Hamilton were in theirs.

Respecting the Judgeship of *Mecklenburgh*, the Rev. Mr. Stuart writes, 1788, that "our new settlements have been lately divided into four districts, of which this place (Kingston,) is the Capital of one called *New* Mecklenburgh. I had a commission sent me as first Judge of the Court of Common Pleas, which I returned to Lord Dorchester, who left a few days ago." The office thus refused was subsequently filled by Mr. Richard Cartwright. In a letter before us, written by John Ferguson, dated 29th December, 1788, it is stated that "our Courts are opened, but they have done nothing particular, but I suppose will in a few days." This was the commencement of other than martial law at the Bay of Quinté. 1788 then, is the year in which civil law began to be administered. This was considered a boon by the British Americans, who objected quite as much to military law, when the individual might not by education, be qualified to dispense judgment and justice, as they did to the French laws of Lower Canada. Indeed the loyalists of Lower Canada complained very much that they had lost the protection of British laws. And probably many were induced to ascend to Upper Canada where the British law was in operation. At the same time Upper Canada remained a part of the Province of Quebec.

Reference is made in the History of Dundas, to Judge Duncan, of Lunenburgh as follows: "As a soldier he was generous and humane." The Court sat at Mariatown, of which he was the founder." He "seemed to have monopolized every office. A store-keeper, and holding a Captain's rank, he dealt out law, dry goods and groceries alternately." The court room was at the place of Richard Loucks, who kept a store and tavern, about a mile below the present eastern limits of the County of Dundas. The name of the Sheriff was Munro, probably John Munro, who was subsequently called to the Legislative Council.

With respect to Judge Cartwright, the reader is referred to individual U. E. Loyalists for a notice of his history. The fact that he was selected as the Judge after the office was refused by Mr. Stuart, shows that he was a man of influence, education and wealth.

and persons are now living who remember him as a "big man," along the Bay. From all that we can learn, it is most probable that Judge Cartwright held his court at Finkle's tavern, Ernesttown, It is stated that he convicted the first man that was hanged in Canada. The crime charged against him for which he was executed was watch stealing. The article was found upon him, and although he declared he had bought it of a pedlar, yet, as he could not prove it, he was adjudged guilty of the crime, and sentenced to be hanged. Dr. Connor, of Ernesttown, stood up in court and appealed against the decision of the Judge, but he was hissed down, and the law took its course. The man was hanged, and subsequently the pedlar from whom the watch had been purchased came along and corroborated the dying words of the unfortunate man.

The most common punishment inflicted upon those convicted of high offences, was that of banishment for a certain number of years, or for life, to the United States, "a sentence next to that of death, felt to be the most severe that could be inflicted." "Minor offences were atoned for in the pillory. For a long time there stood one such primitive instrument of punishment, at Richard Louck's Inn, the centre of law and justice for the Lunenburg District." (History of Dundas).

The first person executed at Niagara was in 1801, a woman by name of Loudon, who was convicted of poisoning her husband, at Grimsby.

The difference between the French and British in Canada, as to religion, language and laws, was so great that, although efforts were earnestly made to unite the two races, the divergence of views continued to increase. And the result was, that a Bill was introduced into the Imperial Parliament, by the Government, which duly became law.

On Friday, 4th March, 1791 "Mr. Chancellor Pitt moved, "that His Majesty's message concerning the New Constitution for Quebec might be read. It was read accordingly."

"George R.—His Majesty thinks it proper to acquaint the Commons, that it appears to His Majesty, that it would be for the benefit of His Majesty's subjects in the Province of Quebec, that the same should be divided into separate provinces, to be called the Province of Upper Canada and the Province of Lower Canada; and that it is accordingly his Majesty's intention so to divide the same, whenever His Majesty shall be enabled by Act of Parliament to establish the necessary regulations for the government of the said Provinces. His

Majesty therefore recommends this object to the consideration of this House," &c., &c. The discussion which arose in connection with the passage of this Bill was of unusual interest, and produced that historic scene between Burke and Fox, during which "tears trickled down the cheeks" of the latter, as "he strove in vain to give utterance to feelings that dignified and exalted his nature." The Bill passed its third reading on the 18th May.

At this time there were distributed along the St. Lawrence, the Bay of Quinté, Niagara frontier, Amherstburgh, with the French settlement on the Thames, and the Indians at Grand River, about 20,000 souls, or double the number, who came at the first as refugees, and disbanded soldiers.

For a list of the Governors of Upper Canada see Appendix.

CHAPTER LVIII.

CONTENTS—Simcoe—His arrival in Canada—Up the St. Lawrence—An old house—"Old Breeches' River"—Simcoe's attendants—The old veterans—"Good old cause"—"Content"—Toasting—Old officers—Executive Council of Upper Canada—First entry—Simcoe inducted to office—Religious ceremony—"The proceedings"—Those present—Oath of office—Organization of Legislative Council—Assembly—Issuing writs for elections—Members of Council—Simcoe's difficulty—At Kingston—Division of Province—The Governor's officers—Rochfoucault upon Simcoe—Simcoe's surroundings—His wife—Opening Parliament in 1795—Those present—Retinue—Dress—The nineteen counties—Simcoe's designs—Visit of the Queen's father—At Kingston—Niagara—A war dance.

ORGANIZATION OF THE UPPER CANADA GOVERNMENT BY SIMCOE, 1792.

Colonel John Graves Simcoe, the pioneer Governor of Upper Canada, and the Lieutenant-Governor under Lord Dorchester, entered upon the duties of his office. July 8, 1792.

His arrival in Canada was signalled by much rejoicing, as he passed along in a fleet of bark canoes from Lower Canada, by the St. Lawrence. A writer, in 1846, relates some interesting facts respecting this passage. He speaks of one house then remaining in Johnstown, which remained in all its original proportions. "It is built in the Dutch style, with sharp-pointed roof, and curious gables. This house was framed of oak of the finest growth; and, considering that it has been drawn from lot to lot, until it has traveled almost the entire extent of the bay, (at Johnston) within the last half century, it certainly is a remarkable edifice. It is now a hostelrié, as it has always been, and no sign of repentance can be yet seen in its huge sign-board, exhibited at the top of a taper pine, on which some cunning disciple of Michael Angelo, hath depicted a tolerably sized square, and a pair of exquisitely expansive compass, striding classically, in imitation of the Collosus of Rhodes, with the staring capitals of "*Live and let live*—St. John's Hall—*Peace and plenty to all mankind*"—thrown in as a sort of relief to the compass, and as a sweet inducement to the weary and dust-begrimmed traveler to walk in, and make himself as comfortable as the little peculiarities of the lazy-eyed landlord, and the singular temperament of the land-lady, will allow.

"This house is Governor Simcoe's house. In it John Graves Simcoe, the first Governor of the U. E. Loyalists, himself a hearty, brave old colonel, who fought in the cause of these men, held his levee, on his first arrival in Upper Canada. Time hallows all. Young Canada has her antiquities—although she may be more prone to look forward to the future with hope, than back on the past with regret. Yet the house in which John Graves Simcoe reposed himself, and cast his martial eye over the gracefully curving bay, the sparkling river, and the dilapidated fortifications of the old French fort, built during the French ascendancy; on the point and islands below, may still be an object of interest to more than those who reside in the vicinity, in a Province, which owes so much of its present prosperity to the good commencement made by one possessed of his historic heroism, humanity, and noble self-denial in the cause of an exiled race. The house stood on a point of land formed by the bay, and a small stream which passes from the north westward, called formerly by the French, "Riviere de la Vielle Culotte," which being translated, probably means "Old Breeches' River." Governor Simcoe had, but a short half-hour previously, taken his departure for Niagara, in one of the large bark canoes with which the passage on the St. Lawrence, and along the shore of the lakes, was then generally made. A brigade of smaller canoes and boats followed him, conveying his suite, and a few soldiers; and never since the year 1756, when Montcalm led his army upward to the attack of Oswego, had the swelling bosom of the wild forest river borne so glad a sight as on that sparkling morning.

"The old piece of ordnance, obtained from the island fort below, had ceased to belch forth its thunders from the clay bank; whereon, fort want of trunnions it had been deposited. The gentry of the surrounding country, collected together for the occasion, and looking spruce, though weather-beaten, in their low-tasselled boots, their queer old broad-skirted military coats, and looped chapeaux, with faded feathers fluttering in the wind, had retired to the inn, and were toasting in parting goblets, the "good old cause for ever," previously to betaking themselves to their woodland path homeward, or embarking in their canoes to reach their destinations by water, above or below.

"Now I am content—content, I say, and can go home to reflect on this proud day. Our Governor—the man of all others—has come at last—mine eye hath seen it—drink to him gentlemen—he will do the rest for us,"—cried Colonel Tom Fraser, his face flushed and fiery, and his stout frame drawn up to its full height at the head of the table.

"We do—we do!" vociferated young Kingsmill, emptying his glass, and stamping to express joy. "Bonhomme" Tom Fraser then got on his legs, and shouted a brawny young soldier's echo to the toast of his relative.

The mild, placid countenance of Dr. Solomon Jones, was lighted up by the occasion, and he arose also, and responded to the toast, recounting some of the services performed by the newly appointed Lieutenant-Governor in the late war.

Captain Elijah Bottum, a large portly person, having at his side a formidable basket-hilted claymore, then addressed them in brief military phrase, and gave one of the old war slogans. Major Jessup followed in the same strain, and proposed a sentiment which was received with vociferous cheers by the younger portion of the company. Captain Dulmage, Captain Campbell, Pay-master Jones, Commissary Jones, Captain Gid. Adams, Lieutenant Samuel Adams, Ephraim Webster, Captain Markle, Captain Grant, and numerous other captains and officers, managed to make themselves heard on the joyful occasion, until finally the meeting broke up, and the company separated not to meet again until the next fourth day of June, in the following year."

The first entry in the journals of the Executive Council of Upper Canada, gives an account of the induction of Colonel Simcoe into the gubernatorial office at Kingston. The event was made one of solemnity and religious observance, the proceedings taking place on a Sunday, in the old church of wood, which stood opposite the market-place. We quote an extract from the proceedings of the Executive Council.

Kingston, July 8, 1792.

"His Excellency John Graves Simcoe, Esq., Lieutenant-Governor of the Province of Upper Canada, colonel, commanding the forces in the said Province, &c., &c., having appointed the Protestant church, as a suitable place for the reading and publishing of his Majesty's commissions, he accordingly repaired thither, attended by the Hon. William Osgoode, Chief Justice; the Hon. James Baby, the Hon. Peter Russell, together with the Magistrates and principal inhabitants, when the said commission appointing his Excellency (Grey) Lord Dorchester, Captain-General and Governor-in-chief, &c., &c., of Upper and Lower Canada, and also the commission appointing the said John Graves Simcoe, Governor of the Province of Upper Canada, were solemnly read and published."

The oaths of office were then administered to his Excellency. According to the Royal instructions to Governor Simcoe, he was to have five individuals to form the first Executive Council. The five named were William Osgoode, William Robertson, James Baby, Alexander Grant, and Peter Russell, Esqs. The next day, Monday, Osgoode, Baby, and Russell were sworn into office, as Executive Councillors. Robertson was not then in the Province; Grant was sworn in a few days after.

Upon the 17th of July, a meeting of the council was held at the Government House, at Kingston, when the first steps were taken to organize a Legislative Council, and assembly writs were issued, summoning the gentlemen who were to form the first Legislative Council. These were, in addition to those forming the Executive Council, Richard Duncan, Robert Hamilton, Richard Cartwright, Junr., John Munro, and we believe, Thomas Fraser. These constituted the Legislative Council.

Two of the nine, it would seem, never took upon themselves the duties of the high place thus alloted them. One was Richard Duncan, who lived at Mariatown, County of Dundas. He was a captain, and had, in 1788, been appointed Judge of the Lunenburgh district. When Upper Canada became a separate province, Judge Duncan, as well as Cartwright, Judge of Mecklenburgh, were appointed Legislative Councillors. Duncan was a man of extensive business, and highly respected; but "some transactions in connection with banking business, were so imprudent," that "he left the country somewhat abruptly for the United States," and "never dared to return," (Croil). This unfortunate affair, whatever its nature may have been, probably occurred about the time of the above mentioned appointment, as he shortly after removed to Schenectady, New York, where he continued to live until his death. The other was Mr. Robertson, a resident of Sandwich, where he had become a successful merchant. He never took his seat in the council, the reason of which does not appear.

It is stated that, according to the despatches of Simcoe to the Imperial Government, he found no little difficulty in obtaining suitable persons to fill the offices of the Executive and Legislative Council, who would absent themselves from home for the purpose.

The Executive Council continued to hold meetings at Kingston up to the 21st July, when Simcoe proceeded westward, and determined to make the village at the mouth of Niagara River, his capital.

Upon the same day that the Governor and Council issued summonses to the gentlemen of the Legislative Council, the 16th July, a proclamation was likewise issued, forming the Province into Counties, and specifying the number of representatives to be elected by the people to constitute the Legislative Assembly. And these proclamations were speedily conveyed and posted in every settlement.

The following were the officers connected with the Governor while at Newark. "Military Sec. Major Littlehales; Provincial Aide-de-Camp, Thomas Talbot; Solicitor General, Mr. Gray; Clerk of Executive Council, Mr. Small; Civil Secretary, William Jarvis; Receiver General, Peter Rusell; Surveyor General, D. W. Smith; Assistant Surveyor General, Thomas Ridout and William Chewitt." The Council Chamber was a building near to Butler's barracks on the hill, where the Episcopal and Catholic Churches assembled occasionally, and alternately. The first meeting of the Executive at Newark, was held on the 29th September. Ten days after this was the opening of Parliament. Peter Clark was appointed Clerk of the Legislative Council; John G. Law, Usher of the Black Rod. The superintendent of the Indian department, was Colonel John Butler, of Butler's Rangers of the Revolutionary war.

John White, the first Attorney-General of Upper Canada, came to the country, accompanied by Thomas Ward, in 1792.

The Duke de la Rochefoucault, Linancourt, a French nobleman, traveling in America, in 1795, visited Governor Simcoe, and remarks in his writings that "Upper Canada is a new country, or rather a country yet to be formed. It was probably for this reason General Simcoe accepted the government of it. He was fully aware of the advantages which his native land might derive from such a colony, if it attained perfection; and imagined that means might

33

be found adequate to this purpose. This hope was the only incitement which could impel a man of independent fortune, to leave the large and beautiful estates he possesses in England, and to bury himself in a wilderness, among bears and savages. Ambition, at least, appears not to have been his motive; as a man, in Gen. Simcoe's situation, is furnished with abundant means of distinguishing himsel by useful activity, without removing to a great distance from his native country. But, whatever have been his motives, his design has been attended with consequences highly beneficial. The plan conceived by General Simcoe for peopling and improving Upper Canada, seems, as far as he has communicated to us, extremely wise and well arranged." The same writer says, that Simcoe had a hearty hatred against the United States, that he had been a zealous promoter of the war, in which he took a very active part. "In his private life Governor Simcoe is simple, plain, and obliging. He inhabits a small miserable wooden house, which formerly was occupied by the Commissaries. His guard consists of four soldiers, who every morning come from the fort, and return thither in the evening. He lives in a noble and hospitable manner, without pride. Mrs. Simcoe is a lady of thirty-six years of age. She is bashful, and speaks little, but she is a woman of sense, handsome and amiable, and fulfils all the duties of a mother and wife with the most scrupulous exactness. The performance of the latter she carries so far as to act the part of Secretary to her husband. Her talents for drawing, the practice of which she confines to maps and plans, to enable her to be extremely useful to the Governor." The "The Governor is colonel of a regiment of Queen's Rangers, stationed in the Province. His servants are privates of this regiment which is stationed elsewhere."

During our residence at Navy Hall, the Session of the Legislature of Upper Canada was opened. (This was 1795). The Governor had deferred it till that time, on account of the expected arrival of a Chief Justice from England, and from a hope that he should be able to acquaint the members with the particulars of the treaty with the United States. But the harvest has now begun, which in a higher degree than elsewhere engages, in Canada, the public attention. Two members of the Legislative Council were present instead of seven; no Chief Justice appeared who was to act as Speaker; instead of sixteen members of the Assembly only five attended. The law requires a greater number of members for each House, to discuss and determine upon any business, but within two days a year will have expired since the last Session. The Governor has therefore thought it right to open the Session. The whole retinue of the Governor consisted in a guard of fifty men of the garrison of the fort. Dressed in silk, he entered the Hall with his hat on his head, attended by the Adjutant and two Secretaries. The two members of the Legislative Council gave, by their Speaker, notice of it to the Assembly. Five members of the latter having appeared at the bar, the Governor delivered a speech," &c.

When Simcoe undertook the administration of the newly established Province, a proclamation was issued which divided the Province into nineteen counties. In the creation of this division, Simcoe had a view to military organization. Rochefaucault says, "The maxims of government professed by Gen. Simcoe are very liberal and fair; he detests all arbitrary and military government, without the walls of the fort; and desires liberty in its utmost latitude, so far as is consistent with the constitution and law of the land. He is, therefore, by no means ambitious of investing all power and authority in his own hands; but consents to the Lieutenants, whom he nominates for each county, the right of appointing the Justices of the Peace, and Officers of the Militia."

"A Justice of the Peace could assign, in the King's name, 200 acres of land to every settler, whom he knew to be worthy, and the surveyor of the district was to point out to the settler the land allotted him."—(Rogers). Simcoe desired to populate the Province as speedily as possible, no doubt he felt anxious the United States should not get too far ahead. The schemes conceived by him for the settlement, government, and defence of the Province, have received the approval of most men capable of judging. But he remained not to carry out the plan intended. In 1796, shortly after the close of the first session of the second Parliament, he was instructed by the Imperial authorities to repair to St. Domingo, to assume the same duties; and the Hon. Peter Russell, President of the Council, was delegated to discharge the duties belonging to the office of Governor, and he enjoyed all the emoluments and perquisites arising therefrom.

During the occupancy of Simcoe, an event came to pass which may be here appropriately referred to. It was a visit to Upper Canada of the Duke of Kent, father of our much loved Queen. Prince Edward was stationed at Quebec with his regiment, having arrived a short time before the division of the Province of Quebec, and consequently before Simcoe came. Desiring to see the Upper

Province, he set out in a *calashe*, drawn by a French pony, accompanied by his suite. At Montreal he took a batteau, manned with Frenchmen, for Kingston. At Oswegotchie, "the royal party was met by a pleasure barge from Kingston, manned by seamen and military, accompanied by Peter Clark, of the Naval Department at Kingston." From thence they were speedily rowed to Kingston, where the King's schooner, the 'Mohawk,' Commodore Bouchette, commander, was in waiting to receive him. The Prince went on board, and after a tedious passage, safely reached Newark, where he was received by the firing of guns. "As soon as horses and saddles could be mustered, the royal party wended their way by a narrow river road on the high banks of the Niagara river to the Falls. The only tavern, or place of accommodation, was a log hut for travelers to refresh themselves. There, the party alighted, and, after partaking of such refreshments as the house afforded, followed an Indian path through the woods to the Table Rock. There was a rude Indian ladder by which to descend to the rocks below, 160 feet. This consisted of a long pine tree with the branches cut off, leaving length enough at the trunk to place the foot upon, and hold on by the hands, in ascending or descending. (This Indian ladder continued in use several years later, when it was superseded by a ladder furnished from money, given by a lady from Boston to the guide). Our illustrious traveler availed himself of this rude mode of descent. The Prince and party lunched at the Hon. Mr. Hamilton's on their way back. In the evening, the Prince was amused by a war dance by the Mohawks, headed by Brant himself. The next day, the Prince re-embarked, and proceeded to Quebec. There is a tradition in Marysburgh that he stopped on his way down in Smith's Bay, to admire the beauty of that place.

CHAPTER LIX.

CONTENTS—General Hunter—Peter Russell—Francis Gore, 1806—Alex. Grant—Brock—1812—United States declare war—Prompt action—Parliament—Proclamation—The issue—Second proclamation—General Hull—His proclamation—Bombast and impertinence—The Indians—Proclamation answered—Hull a prisoner—Michigan conquered—To Niagara—At Queenston heights—"Push on York Volunteers"—Death of Brock—McDonnell—War of 1812, the Americans—Extract from Merritt—What Canadians did—Brock's monument—General Sheaffe—General Drummond—Invading the States—What Canada will do—Lord Sydenham—A tribute by Dr. Ryerson—Union of the Provinces.

THE GOVERNORS OF UPPER CANADA, FROM SIMCOE TO LORD SYDENHAM.

Lieutenant General Peter Hunter, who had been Colonel of the 24th Regiment stationed at Newark, was the second Governor for Upper Canada; his accession to office was on the 17th August, 1799. During the two previous years, Hon. Peter Russell had been President. He continued to hold the position until his death, which took place at Quebec, 21st August, 1805. His age was sixty-nine.

The third Governor of Upper Canada was His Excellency Francis Gore, who assumed the gubernatorial functions on the 25th August, 1806. In the interim between this period and the death of Hunter, the Hon. Alexander Grant having been President. The reign of Gore was one of ease. No conflicting parties as yet disturbed the political arena of the Province. Year after year he convened Parliament, which enacted laws for the growing requirements of the colony, with a degree of harmony not subsequently present. In 1811, he resigned, when *Sir Isaac Brock* became *President*, upon the 30th September. Although but the President, and not a Lieutenant-Governor, he requires some notice.

GENERAL BROCK.—In the year 1812, in June, the United States declared war against Great Britain, ostensibly, on the question of the right of England to take her seamen from American vessels to which they had deserted; but, in reality, the object of the war was to acquire Canada, and as England was engaged with an European war, it was deemed a favorable opportunity by President Madison, to subjugate the people whom they had once dispossessed of their inheritance. The declaration of war was quickly made known to General Brock, even sooner than the enemy thought possible, who promptly took necessary steps to secure the defence of the Province, against the dastardly intentions of the invader. On the 20th

June, he issued orders to Captain Roberts, at St. Joseph, which issued in the capture of Fort Michilmacinac, with seventy men, beside valuable cargoes of furs. On the 28th July, he met the Parliament at York, which continued in session eight days, and sent forth a proclamation to the people, with these concluding remarks: "We are engaged in an awful and eventful contest. By unanimity in our councils, and by vigor in our operations, we may teach the enemy this lesson, that a country defended by freeman, enthusiastically devoted to the cause of their King and constitution, can never be conquered." Remarkable words! How true the sentiments. And so, animated by this belief, strong in the consciousness of right, indignant at an unprincipled foe, he went on his way showing to all an example of "vigor," and displaying the bravery which freemen alone know how to practice, until in the hour of victory, death overtook him on Queenston Heights. The address of General Brock was supplemented by one from the Legislative Assembly, and no excuse need be offered for introducing it here *in extenso*. It ought to be read by every Canadian, and the truths it contains made known to the rising generation, that they may know the history of the fathers of those who support Fenianism. Know how unscrupulous the neighbours we have upon our southern borders, have ever been.

"Already have we the joy to remark, that the spirit of loyalty has burst forth in all its ancient splendour. The militia in all parts of the Province have volunteered their services with acclamation, and displayed a degree of energy worthy the British name.

"They do not forget the blessings and privileges which they enjoy under the protection and fostering care of the British Empire, whose government is only felt in this country by acts of the purest justice and most pleasing and efficacious benevolence. When men are called upon to defend everything they call precious, their wives and children, their friends and professions, they ought to be inspired with the noblest resolutions, and they will not be easily frightened by menaces, or conquered by force. And, beholding as we do, the flame of patriotism, burning from the one end of the Canadas to the other, we cannot but entertain the most pleasing anticipations. Our enemies have indeed said that they can subdue this country by proclamation; but it is our part to prove to them, that they are sadly mistaken; that the population is determinedly hostile, and that the few who might be otherwise inclined, will find it their safety to be faithful. Innumerable attempts will be made, by falsehood, to detach you from your allegiance, for our enemies, in imitation of their European master, trust more to treachery than to force, and they will, no doubt, make use of many of those lies, which unfortunately, for the virtuous part of those States, and the peace and happiness of the world, had too much success during the American rebellion; they will tell you that they are come to give you freedom, yes, the base slaves of the most contemptible faction that ever distracted the affairs of any nation,—the minions of the very sycophants who lick the dust from the feet of Bounaparte, will tell you that they are come to communicate the blessing of liberty to this Province; but you have only to look at your situation to put such hypocrites to confusion. Trusting more to treachery than open hostility, our enemies have already spread their emmissaries through the country to seduce our fellow-subjects from their allegiance, by promises as false as the principles on which they are founded. A law has therefore been enacted for the speedy detection of such emmissaries, and for their condign punishment on conviction. Remember when you go forth to the combat, that you fight, not for yourselves alone, but for the whole world. You are defeating the most formidable conspiracy against the civilization of man that ever was contrived. Persevere as you have begun, in your strict obedience to the laws, and your attention to military discipline; deem no sacrifice too costly, which secures the enjoyment of our happy constitution; follow, with your countrymen in Britain, the paths of virtue, and like them, you shall triumph over all your unprincipled foes."

This address was followed by a second one from General Brock, on the 22nd July, 1812, in which he reviewed an address which had been issued by the American General, who had invited the Canadians to seek voluntarily, the protection of his government; also the threat to show no quarter if the Indians appeared in the ranks; Brock eloquently defended their right to defend their homes against an invading foe.

General Brock having prorogued Parliament, pushed on to the scene of Hull's invasion, where he had issued a proclamation to the Canadians characterised by absurdity, falsehood, and Yankee brag. Indeed, it seems quite impossible for any American General to indite an address or proclamation, without exposing himself to ridicule. Having already collected an army at Detroit, General Hull, the commanding officer, crossed over to Sandwich on the Canadian side, and issued the following modest! address to the

"INHABITANTS OF CANADA."—"After thirty years of peace and prosperity, the United States have been driven to arms. The injuries and agressions, the insults and indignities of Great Britain, have once more left them no alternative but namely, resistance or unconditional submission. The army under my command has invaded your country, and the standard of Union now waves over the territory of Canada. To the peaceable and unoffending inhabitants it brings neither danger nor difficulty. I come to find enemies, not to make them. I come to protect, not to injure you. Separated by an immense ocean, and an extensive wilderness, from Great Britain, you have no participation in her councils, nor interest in her conduct. You have felt the tyranny, you have seen her injustice, but I do not ask you to avenge the one or redress the other. The United States are sufficiently powerful to afford you every security consistent with their rights, and your expectations. I tender you the invaluable blessings of civil, political, and religious liberty, and their necessary result, individual and general prosperity; that liberty which gave decision to our councils, and energy to our conduct, in our struggle for independence, and which conducted us safely and triumphantly through the stormy period of the Revolution. That liberty which has raised us to an elevated rank among nations of the world, and which has afforded us a greater measure of peace and security, of wealth and improvement, than ever fell to the lot of any people. In the name of my country, and by the authority of my country, and by the authority of my government, I promise protection to your persons, property, and rights. Remain at your homes, pursue your peaceful and customary avocations; raise not your hands against your brethren, many of your fathers fought for the freedom and independence we now enjoy. Being children, therefore, of the same family with us, and heirs of the same heritage, the arrival of my army of friends must be hailed by you with a cordial welcome. You will be emancipated from tyrany and oppression, and restored to the dignified station of free men. Had I any doubt of eventual success, I might ask your assistance, but I do not. I come prepared for every contingency, I have a force which will look down all opposition—and that force is but the vanguard of a much greater. If contrary to your own interests, and the just expectation of my country, you will be considered and treated as enemies, the horrors and calamities of war will stalk before you. If the barbarous and savage policy of Great Britain be pursued, and the savages are let loose to murder our citizens, and butcher our women and children, this war will be a war of extermination. The first stroke of the tomahawk, the first attempt with the scalping knife, will be the signal of one indiscriminate scene of desolation. No white man found fighting by the side of an Indian, will be taken prisoner; instant destruction will be his lot. If the dictates of reason, duty, justice, and humanity, cannot prevent the employment of a force which respects no right, and knows no wrongs, it will be prevented by a severe and relentless system of retaliation. I doubt not your courage and firmness; I will not doubt your attachment to liberty. If you tender your services voluntarily, they will be accepted readily. The United States offer you peace, liberty, and security. Your choice lies between these and war, slavery, and destruction. Choose then, but choose wisely; and may he who knows the justice of our cause, and who hold in his hands the fate of nations, guide you to a result the most compatible with your rights and interests, you peace and prosperity."

But it was not long till the same Gen. Hull was a prisoner among them, and in his journey from Detroit to Quebec he had abundant opportunity of seeing not only the loyalty of the Canadians, but that they knew how to treat a conquered foe with consideration—that without crying it out they could grant every "protection" to their ancient foe, notwithstanding the cruel treatment they had sustained when made exiles.

On the 18th July, with the intrepidity characteristic of the British officer, Brock crossed the Detroit, advanced upon the town with his brave militia and handful of regular troops, and demanded of Gen. Hull the surrender of the place, following up the demand with preparations to assault; but soon the white flag appeared, and Gen. Hull, so brave in writing proclamations, with the whole American army, became prisoners of war. They were conveyed to Quebec in parties, some going by vessels of war from York to Kingston, some in small boats along the shore and across the Carrying Place, by the Bay of Quinté. Most of them were confined in hulks in the St. Lawrence, at Quebec, where they remained until exchanged. Gen. Brock after this brilliant conquest of Detroit, which included the whole of Michigan, lost no time in hastening to the Niagara frontier, where another army was threatening to invade.

Upon the 12th October the Americans were preparing to cross from Lewiston to Queenston. Gen. Brock was at Fort George,

Niagara, and hearing the cannon's sound, hurried to the field of battle. He placed himself at the head of the troops, and triumphantly led them up the heights of Queenston, against the enemy, who had obtained a footing there; but with the deep river between them and safety, the enemy rallied for a time in a struggle for life, and Brock's men, inferior in number, retired, until his reinforcements had come, for which he would not previously wait. Then again he essayed to lead them on, but his hour had come, and while his cheering voice was ringing out "Push on York Volunteers," a musket ball struck him down. But the spirit of the brave General was infused into every Canadian. As soon as Gen. Sheaffe had arrived they advanced to conquer the polluters of Canadian soil. Again the whole American army became prisoners of war, and had the privilege of marching the length of the Province to Quebec, and Gen. Scott among the rest, who was favored with a passage down the Bay of Quinté.

Gen. Brock's Aide-de-Camp, McDonnell also fell, mortally wounded. Brock was buried in a bastion of Fort George, but subsequently his remains found a resting place upon the heights where he fell, and where now rises the monument to his memory. This illustrious Chief was much beloved by the Canadians, and he was held in great veneration. To him—to the energetic and heroic Brock is due to a great extent the subsequent success by which the enemy, ever boasting, was kept at bay, so that when peace was sought by the United States, after three years of war, because England, no longer at war at home, was about to deal heavy blows, there was not a foot of Canadian territory in the enemy's possession.

Of Gen. Brock the Hon. William H. Merrit, in 1853, speaks as follows:

"It will be in the recollection of many now present, that in the commencement of the war of 1812, only one regiment of British troops, the 48th, was left to defend Upper Canada, from Kingston to Michilimackinac, a distance of one thousand miles, and during the whole campaign, only two companies of the 48th could be spared on this frontier. Although this fact is one of the most striking events connected with that war, it has never yet been brought prominently before the public; yet it clearly proves that the defence of Canada, then rested with its inhabitants. We find that though they consisted principally of the old U. E. Loyalists and their descendants, the native Indians who had been dispossessed of their possessions in the United States, and their descendants, together with residents from the United States—emigration from the Mother Country not having been commenced to any extent,—a population thus composed, not exceeding in Upper Canada, at most 90,000, without troops, without munitions of war, without resources, and without the least expectation of any timely aid from the mother country, with a few troops, unable to contend against a powerful nation, numbering about 8,000,000, with munitions of war, and resources without limit, within a comparative short distance from maritime cities, also numerous forces at command, of which they were not slow of apprising us, in the proclamations circulated from time to time,—it was under those circumstances that the character and ability of Sir Isaac Brock were brought to light. Well knowing on whom he had to depend for the defence of the country, he directed his personal attention to the clothing, arms, equipment, mess, and personal comfort of the militia, and took every opportunity of gaining the good will of the Indians."

The estimation in which General Brock was held by the people of the Province, was duly evinced by Parliament in passing an act, 14th March, 1815, "to provide for the erection of a monument to the memory of the late president, Major General Sir Isaac Brock." The value of his wisdom, his councils, his energy, his wise plans, as well as his bravery, and the effects thereof, are fully set forth in the preamble. It was resolved to grant £1,000 for the purpose referred to, and erect the monument at Queenston Heights. Thomas Dickson, Thomas Clark, and Robert Nichol, Esquires, were appointed commissioners to carry out the act. In January, 1826, an act was passed granting £600 more "to complete the monument on a scale which appears to the commissioners worthy of the object."

Major General Sheaffe, became President, 20th October, 1812, and continued in office until January 19, 1813, when Major General de Rottenburgh assumed the office, and remained until December 12, of the same year. At this date

Lieutenant General Sir Gordon Drummond was inducted as President. It was immediately after this that the infamous American General McClure, set fire to Newark when unprotected, burning 150 houses, and leaving 400 women and children homeless in the middle of December. This act of villany was fully avenged by General Drummond. Having occupied Fort George, a night attack was made upon Fort Niagara, with brilliant success. Then, the burning of Newark was remembered, and from Lewiston to Buffalo the frontier was laid waste, including those two towns. In this connection, we would remark, that in the event of another war with the United States, it would be no doubt the policy of Canada to make frequent disastrous raids into the States, wherever the opportunity presented. The Americans may as well understand that destruction of property will not be all on one side.

These brief sketches of the first Lieutenant-Governors of Upper Canada, will be finished by alluding to one who devised the scheme of uniting the two Canadas, who successfully accomplished that noble design, and became the first Governor of United Canada. He fixed the capital at Kingston, as the most central place suitable for both Provinces, indeed, it is generally understood, that it was a part of the plan when the union was made, that Kingston should become the permanent seat of government. "It virtually formed part of the contract between the respective provinces." But with the death of Lord Sydenham, also died the opportunity of Kingston remaining the capital of Canada.

Lord Sydenham died at Kingston, in September, 1841, and was buried beneath St. George's Church. Says Dr. Ryerson, in an affecting letter communicated to the public at that time: "Unlike the close of the session of legislature, which was ever held in either Province of Canada, the termination of the late session will produce throughout Canada the opposite feelings of grateful joy, and melancholy grief. The same post which conveys to the people of Canada, the tidings of the harmonious and happy conclusion of a session unprecedented in the productiveness of comprehensive and valuable measures for the general improvement and social and intellectual elevation of the province, conveys to them the appalling announcement that death has terminated the earthly career of the noble mind which conceived those improvements and originated those institutions which will form a golden era in the annals of Canadian history, by laying the foundation of Canadian prosperity and greatness. While blessings are multiplied us, the agent of those blessings is removed from us, and our country is, at the same moment, thrilled with joy and consternation—and on the same day vocal with thanksgiving and clothed in sackcloth; luminous with hope and involved in mourning. Thus do the strokes of Providential chastisement accompany the outbeamings of Providential munificence; and the brightest picture of human life is shaded with disappointment, suffering, and bereavement. It is in heaven only that death is unknown, that pain is never felt, and tears are never shed.

"Lord Sydenham belongs essentially to Canada. His nobility was fairly earned in her service; the ripest fruits of his experience and acquirements are embodied in her institutions; his warmest and latest sympathies are blended with her interests; his mortal remains repose, by choice, among her dead; and his name is indelibly inscribed in the affectionate esteem and grateful recollections of her inhabitants.

"It is not easy to determine which is most worthy of admiration, the comprehensiveness and grandeur of Lord Sydenham's plans, the skill with which he overcame the obstacles that opposed their accomplishment, or the quenchless ardor and ceaseless industry with which he pursued them. To lay the foundations of public liberty, and at the same time to strengthen the prerogative; to promote vast public improvements, and not increase the public burdens; to promote a comprehensive system of education upon Christian principles, without interfering with religious scruples; to promote the influence and security of the government by teaching the people to govern themselves; to destroy party faction by promoting the general good; to invest a bankrupt country with both credit and resources, are conceptions and achievements which render Lord Sydenham the first benefactor of Canada, and place him in the first rank of statesmen. His Lordship found a country divided, he left it united; he found it prostrate and paralytic, he left it erect and vigorous; he found it mantled with despair, he left it blooming with hope. Lord Sydenham has done more in two years to strengthen and consolidate British power in Canada by his matchless industry, and truly liberal conservative policy, than have been done during the ten previous years by the increase of a standing army, and the erection of military fortifications. His Lordship has solved the difficult problem, that a people may be colonists and yet be free; and, in the solution of that problem, he has gained a triumph less imposing, but not less sublime and scarcely less important, than the victory of Waterloo; he has saved millions to England, and secured the affections of Canada.

"In the way of accomplishing these splended results, the most formidable obstacles oppose themselves. At the foundation of these lay the hitherto defective theory, and worse than defective system of Colonial Government; a system destitute of the safety-valve of responsibility, of the attributes of freedom, and of the essential materials of executive power; a system which was despotic from its weakness, and arbitrary from its pretences to representation; a system inefficient in the hands of good men, and withering in the hands of mistaken or bad men."

CHAPTER LX.

CONTENTS—Kingston—First capital—First act of government—Niagara—Selecting the capital—Niagara in 1788—Carrying Place—Landing Place—Newark—In 1795—Mr. Hamilton—The inhabitants—Little York—The Don—The Harbor—Survey—De la Trenche—London—Inhabitants of the Don—Yonge Street, a military road—Governor at York—Castle Frank—York in 1798—The Baldwins—In 1806—Buffalo—York, 1813—Taken by the Americans—The Combatants—Toronto—"Muddy York"—A monument required.

THE CAPITALS OF UPPER CANADA.

The site of the old Fort Frontenac, the first township to be surveyed, and the place whereon to form the first village in Western Canada, was in reality the first capital of Upper Canada. Here the first Governor was inducted solemnly upon a Sabbath to his office; here he formed his first cabinet, the Executive Council; here he selected the gentlemen to form his first Legislative Council; here he issued his proclamations forming the province into counties and arranging the representation. Although the first Parliament did not meet here, the first acts of government were here performed, and public documents were dated at "the Government House, Kingston, 1792."

We have elsewhere spoken of Niagara River and the early French Fort here erected, and its capture by the English. We have learned that the place was garrisoned by troops during the rebellion, and that many refugees here found a safe retreat.

Lord Dorchester desired Simcoe to make Kingston the capital of the new province. But he was unwilling to do so until he had informed himself of the advantages which other places might offer. It seems that he became impressed with the belief that the seat of government should be placed in the peninsula of Upper Canada, and finally determined to fix it at the mouth of the River Niagara, notwithstanding the recommendation of Dorchester, the wishes of Bouchette, the Commodore of the Navy, and the urgent requests of the Kingston merchants.

Collins in his report 1788, speaks of Navy Hall, near Niagara; that the buildings of Navy Hall, are for the most part in exceeding bad repair, and the wharf is in ruins. Of the Ranger's Barracks one pile has been so far dismantled as to be past re-establishing, one end indeed, might perhaps, with some fitting up, be made to serve for some time as a blacksmith's shop to the Indian Department, which they say is much wanted; the other pile is capable of being repaired, and might also answer for a temporary accommodation, (at least in part) this same department, their storehouses, &c., on the Niagara side as already observed being in absolute ruin and not repairable; the fitting up of this pile of buildings would cost about £35. The storehouse at the landing place, which is of round log work, is mostly rotten, and altogether in exceeding bad repair, and should be rebuilt; the dwelling house is much out of repair. The ways, wharf, cradle, and capstan, want some repair, which may be done for about £20, all the picketing and small platforms in the angles of Fort Schlosser, are rotten and in a tottering state, part of the wharf has been washed away, and the remainder cannot last long. The barracks and store houses are not in much better condition, they have been kept standing by the temporary repairs which have been annually performed, merely to keep the weather out.

"From Niagara to the landing place, below the Falls, is about seven miles and a quarter, there is a tolerable good road, but the merchandise, store, &c., are carried up the river in batteaux or vessels, there being sufficient depth of water all the way up, and also alongside the wharf to unload, beyond this place the current becomes too strong to proceed any further by water without great difficulty, boats, indeed, but not vessels, go about half a mile higher, but no advantage can be obtained from it as the shore then becomes impracticable, being a precipice of loose rock about three times as high as where the present landing is. From the wharf at the landing, goods are drawn up the side of the bank about fifty feet high upon ways, on easy slope by a capstan fixed at the top; from this place there is a waggon road of seven miles to Fort Schlosser, a mile and a half above the Falls, where the goods are again put into boats and carried up eighteen miles to Fort Erie, from whence they are conveyed in vessels across Lake Erie to Detroit.

"I think a better situation for a landing place might be chosen below the present one, about half a mile distant by land, and three-quarters by water. The bank of the river here is not half the height of the other; the water is sufficiently deep at a short distance from the shore for vessels to unload; and by raising a wharf and lowering some of the bank for a road, the labor and delay of hauling goods up by ways, as is the present practice, and would be avoided; it would also be much more convenient and expeditious for vessels to come up to, as the worst part of the navigation would be avoided, which in passing round a point between this place and the landing. The length of road to be made from this proposed landing place, will be about half a mile, but it is mostly good ground and will not require mnch expense. The real length of land carriage, however, to Fort Schlosser, will not be increased, or at most more than 100 or 150 yards."

The original British fort at Niagara was upon the east side of the mouth of the Niagara River, upon the present site of the American Fort. By a treaty entered into in 1794, Great Britain was to vacate this fort, with others situated to the south of the lakes, namely, Oswego, Detroit, Miami, and Michilmacinac, which was done in 1796. Upon the west side of the river, upon a point known as Mississauga Point, had sprung up a small village. This, it is said, was the largest collection of houses after Kingston when Governor Simcoe arrived, and here he decided to make his residence, and the permanent capital of the new province. He lived "in a small frame house, half a mile from the village." To this place he gave the name of *Newark*. There was up the river, at the end of navigation, and at the commencement of the portage around the falls to Lake Erie, a small village which had arisen from the course of travel upwards to the western lakes. The boats which left Kingston, on their way westward, were here unloaded. And this place had taken the name of Queen's Town, a name which it retains to the present day. Rochefoucault says, in 1795, "The different buildings, constructed three years ago, consist of a tolerable inn, two or three good storehouses, some small horses, a blockhouse of stone, covered with iron, and barracks. Mr. Hamilton, an opulent merchant, who is concerned in the whole inland trade in this part of America, possesses in Queen's Town, a very fine house, built in the English style; he has also a farm, a distillery, and a tan-yard. The portage was formerly on the other side of the river; but as this, by virtue of the treaty, falls under American Dominion, government has removed it hither." The same writer, speaking of Newark says, "About a hundred houses, mostly very fine structures, have already been erected, but the progress of building will probably be arrested by the intended removal of the seat of government. The majority of the inhabitants, especially the richest of them, share in the administration; and consequently will remove to whatever place the government may be transferred. In point of size and elegance, the house of Colonel Smith, of the 5th Regiment, is much distinguished from the rest, being constructed, embellished, and painted in the best style."

YORK—Governor Simcoe was thoroughly English; unlike Governor Maitland, who gave foreign names in his time, he was intent upon erecting another England in America One new England had alienated itself, and he determined another should arise in its place, and hence he gave to his new capital the name of York. The present New York had been named York, after James Duke of York, brother to Charles the II. The term new being prefixed to distinguish it from old York of England. To distinguish the new capital of Canada from both of the others he designated it *Little York*.

As soon as Simcoe learned that the Niagara fort was to be delivered to the United States, he saw the necessity of removing the capital, as it would never do to have it under the guns of a foreign government. The extreme dislike with which he saw the fort pass into the Republic's hands no doubt led to the haste with which he set about the removal of the Seat of Government. After examining several points upon the upper lakes, and Lake Ontario, he selected the present site of the City of Toronto, back of which was a fort of the same name, or rather Taranto. Upon this spot, which then had for inhabitants but two families of Mississauga Indians, Governor Simcoe immediately quartered one division of his old regiment, the Queen's Rangers, which came the 1st July, 1793. The same summer Bouchette, of the Royal Navy, surveyed the harbour or bay.

The harbour of Toronto was first examined, by Deputy Surveyor Collins, in 1788, when he made a survey of all of the waters of the Upper Lakes, and the several forts, by instructions from Lord Dorchester. In his report he says, "The breadth at the entrance is about half a mile, but the navigable channel for vessels is only about 500 yards, having from three to four fathoms water, the north of the main shore the whole length of the harbour, is a clay bank from 12 to 20 feet high, and rising gradually behind, apparently good land and fit for settlements. The water is rather shallow near the shore. The shoalness of the north shore as before remarked, is also disadvantageous as to creating wharfs, quays, &c. In regard to this place as a military post, I do not see any striking features to recommend it in that view, but the best situation to occupy for the purpose of protecting the settlement and harbour would, I conceive, be on the point A, near the entrance thereof."

Subsequently however, Simcoe relinquished the intention of making York the Capital, and determined to erect one at a central point in the peninsula lying between Lakes Ontario, Erie and Huron. He selected a site upon the river De la Trenche, which he named the Thames, and, to the intended Capital he gave the name of London. He also gave the name to the town of Chatham, a place intended by him, in carrying out his plan of forming a navy, for a navy yard, which he intended to have communicate with a route between Lake Huron and Lake Ontario. In the mean time he kept troops to work, to cut a military road to the Thames, which he called Dundas Street after the Home Minister. At the same time he "intended York the centre of the naval force on Lake Ontario." In 1795 there had not been more than twelve houses built in York, which stood on the bay near the Don. This year the land was was surveyed into lots. "The inhabitants" says Rochefoucault do not possess the fairest character, to which Gourlay adds, in spite, "Nor have they yet mended it." The River Don was an old Indian route to the waters of Simcoe Lake and the Huron. The portage to a Lake, subsequently named after the Governor, was thirty miles. The barracks, where Simcoe's regiment was stationed, was two miles from the Don, the present site of the old barracks. At that time, in a circumference of 150 miles, the Mississauga Indians were the only neighbours of York.

The desire of Simcoe to fix the capital at London was overruled by Lord Dorchester, who, although a true friend of Canada, seemed to oppose Simcoe. Having decided upon Toronto as the capital, Simcoe proceeded to have constructed a military road from the waters of Lake Ontario to Lake Simcoe. This road is now Yonge Street. From 1794 the Governor resided at York, part of which time was in his camp tent, until his departure.

Governor Simcoe caused to be built at York, upon the Don River, about three miles up, on a beautiful eminence, a somewhat large frame building, which he named after his son, Castle Frank. This building was standing in 1829.

By the kind favor of Mrs. Murney, relict of the late Hon. E. Murney, of Belleville, and her most estimable parent, Mrs. Breckenridge, sister of the late Hon. Robert Baldwin, we are able to give some particular notice of the appearance of York at a later date. Mrs. Breckenridge's father, with his family of three sons and four daughters, arrived from Ireland after innumerable delays and losses, dangers, and escapes by sea and land, at York in 1798. They found it composed of about a dozen houses, "a dreary dismal place, not even possessing the characteristics of a village. There was no church, school-house, nor in fact any of the ordinary signs of civilisation, being in fact a mere settlement. There was not even a Methodist chapel, nor does she remember more than one shop. There was no inn; and those travelers who had no friends to go to, pitched a tent and lived in that so long as they remained. My grandfather and his family had done so during their journey. The Government House and the garrison lay about a mile from York, with a thick wood between. After remaining a few days at York, the family proceeded to take possession of a farm in the township of Clarke. They traveled in an open batteau, when night came pitching their tent on the shore of the lake." The following year Mrs. Breckenridge, then a young girl, accompanied her father and sister to New York, whither the latter was going to be married to Mr. Morgan, grandfather of Gen. Dix, the United States Minister to France. She returned in 1806, and found many changes and improvements—"where cities now stand, there was then only woods, for instance, at Buffalo, where she passed a night, was a solitary inn with a swinging sign. But York was mostly changed, there was a church, a jail, a light-house building, and many nice houses, and the woods between the garrison and town were fast disappearing. Governor Gore was then there.

On the 27th April, 1813, 2,700 Americans landed a little west of Toronto. Two companies of the 8th, or King's Own, with some Indians, one company being the grenadiers, the other being the 3rd company, under Capt. J. H. Eustace, both being led by Capt. McNeale, were sent to oppose the landing. The portable magazine of the advance battery was accidentally blown up killing some twenty of the grenadiers, Capt. McNeale, was also killed. This accident led to Sir R. H. Sheaffe's retreat, and the destruction of the magazines. The total loss was 97, including two officers and four non-commissioned officers. "The force engaged, including the two companies of the 8th, consisted of one company of Newfoundland Fencibles, one company of Glengarry Light Infantry, a detachment of Royal Artillery, Militia, Volunteers and Indians—in all about 600 men. Among the volunteers was the present highly esteemed Chief Justice of Upper Canada, Sir J. B. Robinson, and Sir Allan McNab." The gallantry of these two gentlemen was most conspicuous. The unequal contest continued for 4 hours. The month following the remnant of the 8th was nearly annihilated at the attack upon Sackett's Harbour. The above facts and eulogium upon two distinguished Canadians are derived from

Edward Hincks, who was Lieut., and who was present in charge of a two gun battery, and "Another of the surviving officers of the 8th regiment," published in London in 1860, upon the discovery of human remains near the old fort at Toronto, which proved to be some of the grenadiers who were killed by the explosion of their magazine.

The name of York continued to belong to the capital till 1834, when it received the more appropriate name of Toronto, an Indian word we are told, which signifies "trees growing out of the water," referring to the low level shore, with the trees at the waters edge. For many years before the name was changed; from the vast quantity of mud which made the streets almost unpassable, the place obtained the designation of "Muddy York."

In 1820 a Parliament House was built near the site of the present County Jail, at the front of the present Parliament Street; this building was burned down in 1824.

In 1830 an address was carried by the House, to be presented to the Governor, "to remove the Seat of Government from York to a place of security," but no action was taken in the matter.

The wisdom in the choice of selecting this situation upon which to found a capital for Upper Canada cannot be questioned. The proof is found in the handsome and richly circumstanced City of Toronto. Should not Toronto, now again the Capital of Ontario, the seat of learning, of magnificent Universities, the home of refinement, the abode of wealth, erect a monument to the memory of its founder, the illlustrious first Governor of the Colony?

CHAPTER LXI.

CONTENTS—Parliament—Simcoe's Proclamation—Nineteen counties formed—Names, and boundaries—First elections—Names of members—Officers of the House—A Quaker member—Chaplain—Meeting of Parliament—The Throne, a camp stool—Address—To both houses—Closing address—Acts passed—Simcoe s confidential letters—A contrast—A blending—2nd Session The Acts—Quarter Sessions—3rd, 4th, 5th Sessions—New division of Province—1798—Modes of punishment—Burning the hand—Whipping—Salaries of officers—Revenue first year—The members of Parliament—Education—Offering for Parliament—A "Junius"—Early administration of justice—"Heaven-born lawyers"—First magistrates.

THE LEGISLATIVE ASSEMBLY.

Upon the 16th July, 1792, Lieutenant-Governor Simcoe issued a proclamation in the name of the King, having for its object the organization of a Legislative Assembly composed of persons, to be elected by the people, of which there should be sixteen, and dividing the province into counties. It was as follows:

"Know ye, that our trusty and well-beloved John Graves Simcoe, Esquire, our Lieutenant-Governor of our Province of Upper Canada, hath, and by this our proclamation doth, divide the said Province of Upper Canada into counties, and hath and doth appoint and declare the number of representatives of them, and each of them, to be as hereinafter limited, named, declared, and appointed," &c.

Nineteen counties were formed, namely: "Glengary, Stormont, Dundas, Grenville, Leeds, Frontenac, Ontario, Addington, Lenox, Prince Edward, Hastings, Northumberland, Durham, York, Lincoln, Norfolk, Suffolk, Essex, Kent."

For the purpose of representation in Parliament, the following arrangements were made: Glengary was divided into two ridings, each riding to send a representative to the Legislative Assembly; Stormont, to send one member; likewise Dundas and Grenville each to have a representative; Leeds and Frontenac together, to send one representative; Ontario and Addington to send one representative; Prince Edward, together with the late township of Adolphus, in the County of Lenox, to send one member; Lenox (except Adolphustown) with the Counties of Hastings and Northumberland, to elect one member; Durham and York, and the first riding of Lincoln, to be represented by one member; the second riding of Lincoln to have one member; the third riding of Lincoln to have one member; the fourth riding of Lincoln, and the County of Norfolk, to have one member; Suffolk and Essex to have one member; the County of Kent, which included all the west not Indian territories, to the Hudsons Bay, to have two members. The proclamation was dated Government House, Kingston, 16th July, 1792, William Jarvis, Secretary.

The elections must have followed hard after the issuing of the proclamation, as Parliament met on the 17th of September following. They probably took place in August. Simcoe writing in November, to the Secretary of State for the Colonies, speaks of the elections in these words:—"On my passage from Montreal to Kingston, I understood that the general spirit of the country was against the election of half-pay officers into the Assembly, and that the prejudice ran in favour of men of a low order, who kept but one table, that is, who dined in common with their servants."

The names of those first elected to Parliament were John McDonnell, who was elected Speaker; Joshua Booth; Mr. Baby; Alexander Campbell; Philip Dorland, (but being a Quaker, he would not be sworn and did not take his seat, and Peter VanAlstine was elected in his place); Jeremiah French; Ephraim Jones; William Mocomb; Hugh McDonnell; Benjamin Pawling; Nathaniel Pettit; David William Smith; Hazleton Spencer; Isaac Swazy; —Young; John White—16. Simcoe, in a despatch, spoke of the last mentioned:—"It was by good fortune that the temporary residence I made at Kingston created sufficient influence to enable us to bring the Attorney General White, into the House.

The oaths to the members were administered by the Governor's Civil Secretary, William Jarvis, Esq., who was also the first registrar of the Province. McDonnell, the member for Glengary, was unanimously elected to the speakers chair. Angus McDonnell was clerk to the Assembly; George Law, Sergeant-at-arms. In the matter of Philip Dorland, of Adolphustown, a Quaker, who refused to take the oaths. A resolution was unanimously passed by the House, that he was incompetent to sit and vote in Parliament unless he took the necessary oath, and consequently a writ was issued for a new election.

A chaplain, the Rev. Mr. Addison, was elected to the House of Assembly, and he, on the day of prorogation, preached a sermon to them before they were summoned to meet the Governor in the Legislative Council Chambers. Mr. Addison continued a chaplain for thirty years, and was then granted a yearly pension of £50.

This first Upper Canadian Parliament assembled at Newark, now Niagara, on the 18th September, and was prorogued 15th October following. The circumstances of this infant legislation were well fitting the new-born colony. The Governor himself was a soldier by profession. Most of the members elect had been inured to the life of the camp, though subsequently to the settling of the wilderness, and they could, with no ordinary interest, and with appropriate intelligence, direct themselves to the work of legislation. The first Parliament of Upper Canada met in no stately hall; the proceedings must have borne some resemblance to a court-martial. The collective wisdom of Upper Canada assembled in a camp-tent on the plains of Niagara On the 18th September, the Governor, with his Secretary, and probably adjutant, took his seat, not upon the throne, but a camp-stool, and delivered the following address:

Honorable Gentlemen, &c.—I have summoned you together under the authority of an Act of the Parliament of Great Britain, passed last year, which has established the British constitution, and all the forms which secure and maintain it in this distant country.

"The wisdom and beneficence of our most Gracious Sovereign and the British Parliament, have been eminently proved, not only in importing to us the same for government, but also in securing the benefit, by the many provisions that guard this memorable act. So that the blessing of your invaluable constitution, thus protected and amplified, we may hope will be extended to the remotest posterity. The great and momentous trusts and duties which have been committed to the representatives of this Province, in a degree infinitely beyond whatever, till this period, distinguished any other colony, have originated from the British nation, upon a just consideration of the energy and hazard with which its inhabitants have so conspicuously supported and defended the British constitution.

"It is from the same patriotism, now called upon to exercise with due deliberation and foresight, the offices of civil administration that your fellow-subjects, of the British Empire, expect the foundation of that mien of industry, and wealth of commerce and power, which may last through all succeeding ages.

"The natural advantages of the Province of Upper Canada are inferior to none on this side of the Atlantic; there can be no separate interest through its whole extent. The British form of government has prepared the way for its speedy colonization; and, I trust, that your fostering care will improve the favourable situation; and that a numerous and agricultural people will speedily take possession of the soil and climate, which, under the British laws, and the munificence with which His Majesty has granted the lands of the Crown, offer such manifest and peculiar encouragement."

The session was closed the 15th October. The Governor delivered the closing speech.

"HONORABLE GENTLEMAN, &c.—It is with very great satisfaction that I have considered the acts which you have found it expedient to frame, and to which, in consequence of the power delegated to me, I have this day given my assent, that they shall become laws of the Province of Upper Canada.

"As the division which His Majesty, in his wisdom, thought proper to make of the late Province of Quebec, obviated all inconveniences, and laid the foundation for an establishment of the English laws in the Province, it is natural to presume, that you would seize the first opportunity to impart that benefit to your fellow-subjects; and by the act to establish trials by jury, and by that which makes the English law the rule of decision, in all matters of controversy, relative to property and civil rights, you have fully justified the public expectation. Your other acts seem calculated to promote the general welfare and commerce of the Province, &c.

"HONORABLE GENTLEMEN, AND GENTLEMEN.—I cannot dismiss you without earnestly desiring you to promote, by precept and example, among your respective counties, the regular habits of piety and morality, the rarest foundations of all private and public felicity; and, at this juncture, I particularly recommend to you to explain, that this Province is singularly blest, not with a *mutilated constitution*, but with a constitution which has stood the test of experience, and is the very image and transcript of that of Great Britain, by which she has long established and secured to her subjects, as much freedom and happiness as is possible to be enjoyed, under the subordination necessary to civilized society."

The modest and matter-of-fact Parliament passed eight Acts at this the first session. Chapter I., An Act to Repeal certain parts of an Act, passed in the fourteenth year of His Majesty's Reign, entitled, "An Act for making more sufficient provisions for the Government for the Province of Quebec, in North America, and to introduce the English Law as the rule of decision in all matters of controversy relative to Property and Civil Rights." Chapter II., "An Act to establish Trials by Jury." Chapter III., "An Act to establish the Winchester Measure, and a Standard for other Weights and Measures." Chapter IV., "An Act to Abolish the Summary Proceedings of the Court of Common Pleas in actions under Ten Pounds Sterling." Chapter V., "An Act to prevent Accidents by Fire." Chapter VI., "An Act for the more easy and speedy Recovery of Small Debts." Chapter VII., "An Act to Regulate the Toll to be taken in Mills, not more than one-twelfth for Grinding and Bolting." "Chapter VIII., "An Act for Building a Gaol and Court-house in every District within the Province, and for altering the names of the said Districts.) The District of Lunenburgh to be henceforth called the Eastern District; Mecklenburgh, the Midland District; Nassau, the Home District; Hesse, the Western District."

Thus was the new-born colony, whose germ had been planted in the wilderness eight years previous, ushered into life, and thus the functions thereof were commenced.

Simcoe, it would seem, wrote frequent despatches to the Colonial Secretary; and in one he gives his opinion of this first meeting of the representative body of Upper Canada: "At this first meeting they were active and zealous for particular measures, according to the promises they had made, or the instructions they had received. Many bills were accordingly framed, which required only a little time to evince their impropriety or futility. Having offices to create and salaries to bestow, they were rather too liberal of their patronage, and pledged their credit to £174 annually to different officers. The Legislative Council made no engagements, but, of course, their expenses must be equal. The sum of £348 was, therefore, the first item." "Upon the whole, I have no reason to be dissatisfied with the disposition and conduct of the Assembly, considering that it is composed of persons of not any restrictive method, and unacquainted with power. I hope that by treating them with temper and moderation, they may become a beneficial establishment to the Province." McMullen says, by way of contrast, that "the Upper Canadian Parliament, with its "homespun" members, took five weeks to do what had taken the Lower Canadian Seigniors seven months to accomplish.

How great the change wrought by seventy-five years! As the log hut in the wilderness has been superseded by the elegant mansion, handsome villa, with thriving towns and cities, so has the tented capital of Newark been forgotten in surveying the magnificent proportions of the buildings at Ottawa; and the camp stool, and nature's carpet of green, in the elegant halls. And as the Legislature, whose infant days were passed within the sound of the majestic Niagara, where its waters are precipitated over a stupendous fall, and sweep on to fill a mighty lake, has, after numerous mutations, and many uncertainties, found a safe home upon the rugged cliffs overlooking the Ottawa, where still may be heard the swelling sound of falling waters, as they rush down the Chaudiere; so may the confederated Provinces forming the New Dominion, after many changes, and frequent political uncertainties—hope alternating with fear, not alone meet in formal union,—not as incompatible elements of an unwise and unequal connection, but as one people; even as the waters of the great Ottawa, mighty in itself, meet and unite with the farther coming St. Lawrence,and, commingling, form the grand stream of the Lower Lawrence, upon whose bosom the proudest ships rest, and which is a highway of trade, unsurpassed in the world.

The *second session* of the parliament of Upper Canada, was opened at Newark, 31st May, 1793; prorogued 9th July, following. At this sessions were passed thirteen bills, most of which were important and useful measures. The first was "for the better regulation of the Militia;" the second, respecting the appointment of town officers; the third, having respect to assessments and rates, and payment of assembly-men; the fourth, about highways; the fifth, concerning marriage; sixth, of courts of Quarter Sessions within the several districts; the seventh, a most important one—an everlasting one of honor, "to prevent the further introduction of slaves," and to limit the time of servitude of those in slavery; the eighth, respecting courts of Probate; ninth, to establish regulations about duties between Upper and Lower Canada; tenth, for paying salaries of officers of Legislative Council and Assembly; eleventh, to encourage the destruction of wolves and bears; twelfth, returning officers of the several counties; thirteenth, also about officers, and taxing wine and spirituous liquors.

The places fixed for the holding of Quarter Sessions were Cornwall, New Johnson, Kingston, Adolphustown, Newark, and Michilmacinac. For the Midland District, it was enacted that they should "commence and be holden in Adolphustown, on the second Tuesday in the month of July, and on the second Tuesday in the month of January; and in Kingston on the second Tuesday in the month of April, and on the second Tuesday in the month of October."

The *third session* of the 1st parliament met at Newark, on the

2nd June. 1794, and prorogued 9th July following. At this session there was a continuation of that wholesome legislation which had characterized the two previous sessions. Twelve acts were passed.

The *fourth session* was at Newark, commencing 6th July, 1895, when four acts were added. It was prorogued 10th August, following.

A *fifth session* of first parliament met at Newark, 16th May, 1796, and was prorogued 3rd June following. Seven acts were passed. This was the last meeting of parliament under the governor ship of Simcoe.

The second parliament opened at York, 16th May, 1797, under the presidency of the Hon. Peter Russell. It was prorogued 3rd July, following. Eighteen measures passed.

Second session under Hon. P. Russell, met at York, 5th June, 1798, prorogued 5th July. Passed eight bills. Among these bills was one "to ascertain and establish the boundary lines of the different townships of the province." Stone or other durable monuments to be set up, to mark the corners of lots; and any person wilfully defacing or removing such, to "be adjudged guilty of felony, and to suffer death without the benefit of the clergy." Another important act, which the growing province demanded, was "for the better division of the province," into townships, counties and districts. According to this, there were formed eight districts, with twenty-three counties, and one hundred and fifty-eight townships. The districts were the Eastern, Johnson, Midland, Newcastle, Home, Niagara, London, and Western. The Midland district, with which we have more particularly to do, "was composed of four counties, with land in their rear to the northern limits of the province." The first county was Frontenac. In this we have Kingston, as well as the townships Pittsburgh, Lougborough, Portland, Hinchinbroke, Bedford, and Wolfe Island. The second county, the incorporated counties of Lenox and Addington; consisted of the townships of Ernesttown, Fredericksburgh, Adolphustown, Richmond, Camden, Amherst Island, Sheffield. The third county, Hastings; contained Sydney, Thurlow, Mohawk land, Tyendinaga, Hungerford, Huntingdon, and Rawdon. The fourth, Prince Edward, had Marysburgh, Hallowell, Sophiasburgh, and Ameliasburgh.

The third session met at Newark, 12th June, 1799, and was prorogued 29th of the same month; five acts having been passed.

The fourth session met at York, 2nd June, 1800, prorogued 4th July, under Lieutenant-General Hunter. Six acts were passed, the first of which was "for the further introduction of the criminal law of England, and for the more effectual punishment of certain offenders." The third clause is as follows: "That whereas the punishment of burning in the hand, when any person is convicted of felony within the benefit of clergy, is often disregarded and ineffectual, and sometimes may fix a lasting mark of disgrace and infamy on offenders, who might otherwise become good subjects and profitable members of the community; be it therefore enacted by the authority aforesaid, that from, and after the passing of this act, when any person shall be lawfully convicted of any felony, within the benefit of clergy, for which he or she is liable by law to be burned or marked in the hand, it shall, and may be lawful for the court before which any person so convicted, or any court holden for the same place with the like authority, if such court shall think fit, instead of such burning or marking, to impose upon such offender such a moderate pecuniary fine as to the court in its discretion shall seem meet; or otherwise it shall be lawful, instead of such burning or marking, in any of the cases aforesaid, except in the case of manslaughter, to order and judge, that such offender shall be once or oftener, but not more than three times, either publicly or privately whipped; such private whipping to be inflicted in the presence of not less than two persons, besides the offender and the officer who inflicts the same, and in case of female offenders, in the presence of females only; and such fine or whipping so imposed or inflicted, instead of such burning or marking, shall have the like effects and consequences to the party on whom the same, or either shall be imposed or inflicted, with respect to the discharge from the same or other felonies, or any restitution to his or her estates, capacities, and credits, as if he or she had been burned or marked as aforesaid."

In 1801 the salaries of the officers of the parliament stood thus; per annum.

Clerk of Legislative Council, £145. Usher of the Black Rod, £50. Master in Chancery, attending the Legislative Council, £50, Chaplain of the Legislative Council, £50. Door-keeper of ditto £20. Speaker of the House of Assembly, £200. Clerk of ditto, £125. Sergeant-at-Arms, £50. Chaplain of the House of Assembly, £50. Door-keeper of ditto, £20. Copying Clerks, £50. Total, £805.

The first tax raised by statue in the province, was to pay the members, who received $2 per day.

The revenue of the whole province the first year was £900.

Elsewhere the fact has been stated that many of the settlers were devoid of a liberal education; while the stern duties of pioneer life precluded the possibility of any mental culture whatever. At the same time competent school teachers for the young were not to be had. With a population made up of such material, the question might be asked with becoming seriousness, " Where are we to get our representative men to carry out responsible government as accorded to the young province of Upper Canada? Many of the first Assembly men were not possessed of book learning, and all along the list of those who have been M.P.P.'s, up to the present, may be found very many who were limited in their education. Yet, the first members convened in the tent, on the green slopes of Niagara, discharged their duty with much decorum and despatch.

It would be an interesting chapter to introduce some account of the first members of Parliament, and the political contests in the early days of Upper Canada. In the absence of complete information, we give such items relating thereto as have come under notice. We have already given the names of those elected to the first Parliament.

Among the early members was James Wilson, of Prince Edward, he was first elected in 1808, or 9, and remained a member for some twenty-four years. Simeon Washburn, was also a member for a time. Allen McLean, in a notice dated Kingston, 18th May, 1812, says " To the independent electors of the County of Frontenac. Having had the honor of representing you at three successive Parliaments, I again make you a tender of my services, and beg leave to solicit your votes and interest at the ensuing election."

Amos Ansley, Esq., says, in an address, dated at Kingston, May 20, 1812: "To the Electors of the County of Frontenac. Having had the honor to represent this County in the first foundation of its happy constitution, I again make you a tender of my services, and beg leave to solicit your votes and interest, &c." James Cotter, of Sophiasburg, was elected to Parliament in 1813, and served four years.

A man of sterling integrity, and good common sense may make a useful Member, if he be not egotistical. In recording the early events of the Bay, we must not hesitate to mention an incident which, at the time, created no little comment with the public, but brought chagrin to an M. P. P. A member, who shall be nameless, whose early advantages for education had been extremely limited, but with any amount of self-confidence, was, on one occasion, sarcastically, but humorously, brought to task in the Kingston *Herald*, by an anonymous writer. The member replied, and in so doing, "copied verbatim, nearly the whole of the first part of Sir William Draper's letter to Junius, dated Jan. 26, 1769, in defence of his friend Lord Granby, over his own signature. Macaulay, a young lawyer of Bath, noticed the plagiarism, and exposed the M. P. P.," which we believe, resulted in the political demise of that individual.

THE EARLY ADMINISTRATION OF JUSTICE.

For two years, Upper Canada, after becoming a distinct Province, was without any lawyers. But, in 1794, such a number of Acts were found upon the statute books, that it was necessary to create some to interpret, not mystify the law. It was provided that his "Majesty should appoint not more than sixteen, whom he should deem, from their probity, education, and condition of life, best qualified to receive the license to practice law." This appointment of lawyers by the Executive, gave rise to an expression of derision in after days, of "heaven-born lawyers."

The first lawyer appointed in Johnson District, was Samuel Sherwood, who had studied law two or three years with lawyer Walker, of Montreal. Jacob Farand, was the first lawyer in the Eastern District. Allen McLean, the first lawyer for Kingston, and Mr. Hagerman, the first for the Bay Quinté.—(See U. E. Loyalists). James Clarke was appointed for Niagara District; also, William Dickson, of Niagara, and Angus McDonald for Cornwall.

After the formation of Upper Canada into a Province, a number of magistrates were appointed to each District, to form a Court of Quarter Sessions. The four gentlemen who had been the judges of Lunenburgh, Mecklenburgh, Nassau, and Hesse, respectively, no longer had so extensive a jurisdiction. We have no farther information of Robertson, in this respect, and Duncan left the Province. But Cartwright and Hamilton continued to fill the same positions, as chairmen of the Quarter Sessions, in their respective Districts. After the death of Cartwright, in the Midland District, Colonel Thompson was appointed to the office, and his successor was Alex. Fisher, of Adolphustown. John Ferguson was also Judge of the District Court.

Among the first appointments for magistrates, was Thomas Sherwood, of Leeds. Also, Dr. Solomon Jones, who was afterward Judge of the District Court.

Charles Stuart, Esq., was, for many years, Sheriff of the Midland District; he died while yet young, in 1816. The first Sheriff of Niagara District, was Alex. McDonnell; the next was Barrack-master Clark, and afterwards Thomas Merritt was appointed.

Among the first, probably the first, magistrates appointed in Thurlow, were Col. Wm. Bell, Col. Hazelton, and James McNabb. Most likely Bell had the commission before the others. Bell generally held his Court of Requests at Mrs. Simpson's Inn. On 19th April, 1822, it was held at the house of John Taylor.

DIVISION X.

THE EARLY MILITIA OF UPPER CANADA.

CHAPTER LXII.

CONTENTS.—Militia Act, 1792—Simcoe—No faith in the Americans—His views—Military Roads—Division of Districts—Military purposes—The officers—Legislation—The expenses—Repeated Legislation—Aggressive spirit—The Enrolment—Hastings Battalion—"Something brewing"—List of Officers—Col. Ferguson—Col. Bell—Leeds Militia—Officers' Clothing—The Midland District—Prince Edward—Training Places.

THE MILITIA.

Any magisterial power that the military commanders of the first settlers may have possessed was lost by the proclamation of Lord Dorchester, in 1788, forming Upper Canada into districts, and appointing to each a staff of civil officers. From this period until 1792, after the meeting of the second session of the First Parliament, the military organization was a dead matter, although there must have been in force some law relating to such, inasmuch as the first Act passed at this Session was "for the *better* regulation of the Militia in this Province."

Governor Simcoe was a man of a military turn of mind. He had taken an active part against the American rebels, and he continued to entertain strong feelings of hostility to the American cause, believing not in the integrity of their professed principles. In many respects he was a well chosen person to take charge of a people who had been under a military rule, and who shared his antipathy to the republican people. Not only did Simcoe conceive schemes of settling the forests, and improving it, but also for securing the country against attack, likewise of drawing into the country many who he believed remained in the States because they could not help themselves, and to whom the Republican form of government was exceedingly distasteful. Simcoe never felt any doubt about his ability to defend the Province against the Americans, and he even had vague ideas that he might concentrate a force of sufficient strength upon Upper Canada soil, to enable him to invade the States, with a good prospect of success. Imbued with these views, and animated by such feelings and desires, he lost no time in taking the necessary steps to organize and train the Militia, and to establish a Naval force for the Lakes. The regular soldiers under his immediate command were put at work to cut roads, one from Lake Ontario to the Thames, which was called the Dundas road, the other from Lake Ontario to the Lake Simcoe, which has received the name of Yonge Street.

The four districts of Upper Canada were subdivided into counties. This division was, according to Rochfoucault, who visited Simcoe, and procured his information from him, "into counties is purely military, and relates merely to the enlisting, completing and assembling of the Militia. The counties are about twelve in number. The Militia of each county are assembled and commanded by a Lieutenant; they must be divided into regiments and companies. They assemble once a year in each county, and are inspected by the Captains of the different companies, at least twice a year. Every male inhabitant is considered a militia man from the age of sixteen to fifty. He is fined four dollars if he does not enlist at the proper time; and officers, both commissioned and non-commissioned, who do not join their regiments at the time the militia is assembled, pay a fine, the former of eight dollars, and the latter of two. An officer who, in case of insurrection, or an attack, who should not repair to his assigned post, would be punished with a pecuniary penalty of £50, and a petty officer with a fine of £20. A militia man who sells either the whole, or a part of his arms, amunition or accoutrements, is fined £5, and in default of payment, imprisoned for two months. The Quakers, Baptists, and Tunkers, pay, in time of peace, twenty shillings a year; and during a war of insurrection, five pounds sterling for their exemption from military service. Out of these fines and ransoms the Adjutant-General of the Militia receives his pay, and the remainder is at the Governor's disposal. This is nearly the substance of the first act of the legislative body of Upper Canada, passed in 1793."

The following year an additional Act passed, relative to the Militia, the chief regulations of which tended to improve and define more accurately the internal form of the regiments, battalions and companies, and to render the assembling of detachments more easy and expeditious. This Act determines, that, in time of war, the obligation to carry arms in defence of the country shall not cease before the age of sixty, and that, of consequence, Quakers and others who enjoy exemption from military service, shall pay for their immunity up to that age. It also obliges the militia to serve on board of ships and vessels, to act as cavalry, and to extend their service beyond the Province, on condition, however, that the same men be not bound to serve more than six months successively. The exemptions from military service are confined to the officers of justice, and other public functionaries, whose number is very small. The whole militia is estimated at nine thousand men. All the expenses of the civil and military administration of Upper and Lower Canada are defrayed by England." The expense, including money and presents to the Indians, "amounts for Upper Canada to one hundred thousand pounds."

In all the measures introduced by Simcoe and passed into law by Parliament, can be discovered a military mind actively at work. The arrangements by which he endeavored to settle the country—to secure it against invasion—to keep alive a spirit of military order—to keep aglow the flame of patriotism, a love for the mother country, were eminently judicious and commendable. There is no doubt that the military spirit of Simcoe was pleasing to the old soldier-farmers, and in them he found willing and zealous abettors of his military schemes. Had it not been for the short-sighted policy of Lord Dorchester, who, it is averred, became envious of his Lieutenant-Governor, and tried to thwart the designs, and had he not succeeded in having him re-called before time allowed for carrying out those designs, there can be no doubt that Upper Canada would have advanced more rapidly than she subsequently did advance, and would have far surpassed any State in the Union.

In 1797, an act for still further regulation of the militia was passed; but the nature of it does not appear in the statutes.

There was also passed an "Act for the better securing the province against the King's enemies."

In 1801, there was still further legislation, and again in 1808 when there was "an act to explain, amend, and reduce to one act of Parliament the several laws now in being for the raising and training of the militia." And a suitable salary was to be allowed to the Adjutant-General. Legislation at this time was deemed necessary, because of the aggressive spirit manifested by the United States. The game of conquest was already begun by the selfish statesmen of America, and even foul means were being adopted to subvert British power on the continent. The year prior, Lower Canada had taken steps under Mr. Dunn, to protect themselves against a wily enemy. General Brock was earnestly engaged in perfecting the defences of Quebec. In 1809 an act was passed respecting billeting Her Majesty's troops, and the Provincial Militia, and furnishing them on the march, and impressing horses, carriages, oxen, boats, &c.

Respecting the enrolment of the militia in accordance with the acts first and subsequently passed, comparatively little can be said by the writer. The earliest, and indeed the only account of an official nature to be obtained, refers to the organization of the Hasting's Militia. Through the kindness of Mr. Sager, of the front of Thurlow, grandson of the late Colonel William Bell, we have had placed in our possession, a portion of the papers left by Colonel Bell, of an official and semi-official character. In a communication dated at Kingston, 29th November, 1798, John Ferguson, of that place, writes to "Mr. William Bell, of the Mohawk village as follows: "Having been appointed Lieutenant of the County of Hastings, and being ordered to enrol the militia without delay, I must request you will immediately proceed with the enclosed notices, and cause them to be put up as directed. This is the beginning of your duty, as I have recommended you to be Adjutant, as well as captain of a company, and I have the satisfaction of telling you that the President has assured me he will approve of my appointments." In a separate communication, Lieutenant Ferguson authorizes Captain Bell "to give notice to the inhabitants of the county to attend a meeting of Lieutenancy on Saturday, the 8th December next, at ten o'clock, at the house occupied by David Harris, on lot 34, in the first concession of Sidney, for the purpose of enrolment."

It would seem that the second in command of the Hastings battalion, was Major A. Chisholm.

Ferguson, writing 22nd February, 1799, says, "It appears from the President's letter, that there is something brewing to the westward."

On the 25th February, 1799, Ferguson writes to Adjutant Bell, to require the officers commanding companies "to cause the volunteers and drafts in their respective companies to assemble, with such arms as they may have, at the house of Ferguson, on the point of Sidney, lot 23, to be made acquainted with the purport of a letter received from the Hon. Peter Russell, President."

Colonel Ferguson writing again on February 26, to Captain

Bell, informs him that the President has been pleased to approve of the appointments made, and that he must meet him at Sidney, 5th of March, to receive his commission. On the 1st March, he further writes thus, "there is some appearance of the militia being embodied next spring, and that Captain Bell is appointed to take command of the detachment should such an event take place.

In a communication dated, 10th March, 1799, Colonel Ferguson refers Captain Bell to an inclosure from President Russell, giving directions as to .teaching the volunteers and drafts, "who are to assemble at Wallbridge's every other Saturday," for platoon exercise, &c.

"List of officers of the Hastings Militia, as approved of by His Honor, the President, with the dates of their commission."

"John Ferguson, Lieutenant of County; date of commission, 1798. The following officers were commissioned in December following:—Major Alexander Chisholm, Captain Wm. Bell, Captain Samuel Sherwood, Captain George W. Myers, Captain Lieutenant Matthias Marsh, Lieutenant Gilbert Harris, Lieutenant John Stuart, Lieutenant John Chisholm, Lieutenant John Fairman, sen., Lieutenant L. W. Myers, Ensigns David Simmons, Jacob W. Myers, Alexander Chisholm, Robert Fairman, Samuel B. Gilbert, Adjutant William Bell, Quarter-Master, John McIntosh.

At the commencement of the war of 1812, John Ferguson, of Kingston, was Colonel; William Bell, of Thurlow, Lieutenant-Colonel, and Alexander Chisholm, Simon McNabb, S. B. Gilbert, Jacob W. Myers, L. W. Myers, David Simmon, Gilbert Harris, John McIntosh, were Captains of 1st Regiment Hastings Militia. John Thompson who had been a soldier in the King's Rangers, was Major.

In May, 1810, a notice was posted in Hastings to "all persons of the battalion having in their possession arms and accoutrements belonging to Her Majesty, to bring them in good order on the 4th of June, and they will be furnished with powder and ball to shoot at a mark."

We are informed by Mr. Adiel Sherwood, that James Breakenridge, who had been an officer in Rogers' corps, was appointed the first Lieutenant of the County of Leeds under Simcoe, with authority to organize the body and appoint the officers. Mr. Sherwood received his first commission as Ensign, from him, to the first regiment of Leeds Militia ,in 1796. He was shortly after commissioned a Lieutenant, which he remained until 1808, when he was made Captain.

OFFICERS' CLOTHING.—No sooner had the officers received their commissions than the matter of military clothing came into consideration, and steps were promptly taken to obtain suitable outfits, in the way of scarlet coats, swords, and so forth. Reading the letters which have come under notice, one is struck with the fact of men putting themselves to trouble to procure costly uniform, when very many of them could scarcely collect money enough to meet their wants. At that time money was scarce and bartering was the ordinary mode of proceedings between the farmer and dealer. The merchants of Kingston did not find it necessary to keep material for officers' dress, and consequently it had to be procured at Montreal. The officers without money and unknown, in Montreal, could scarcely expect to get credit there. It was under such circumstances that Colonel Ferguson, the Lieutenant of the County of Hastings, undertook to assist the officers under him. Concerted action on their part was necessary, that all the coats might be alike, and moreover, they might expect to have them supplied at a cheaper rate. The following will now become intelligible:

"We, the following officers of Militia of the County of Hastings, having agreed to have uniform clothing, do empower John Ferguson, Samuel Sherwood, Matthias Marsh, and John McIntosh, to agree with any person to furnish the materials, and we will pay for it as agreed upon by the above persons—the uniform to be red coats with blue facings; long yellow buttons and white lining with shoulder-straps—the Light Infantry to have short coats with wings. Thurlow, 7th October, 1800." (Signed)—John Ferguson, William Bell, John Chisholm, Daniel Rose, "John McIntosh, David Simmons, John Fairman, junr., Samuel Sherwood, Matthias Marsh."

A few days later Colonel Ferguson supplies a memorandum to Major Bell, recommending James Dawson, Kingston, as the person to be employed to make the coats, the material, or at least the cloth, to be bought at Mr. Cumming's. Ferguson also suggests that each person give his note of hand for the sum until paid, from which it seems evident that he wished to be free from personal responsibility. Three months later, and no steps had been taken except by Ferguson, who, it appears, applied at Montreal for his coat. He writes, "I have received my coat pattern from Montreal," and the cost of cloth and trimmings amounted to £4 7s. 7d., and "the common price of making a regimental coat" was £1 3s. 4d., the epauletts ready-made were £3 each. In another place, Colonel

Ferguson says, "if any of those gentlemen wish to have a coat from Montreal, and will put into my hands sixteen bushels of wheat, as a part payment, I will send for them, and they will surely find their profit in it.

The following were among the first Militia officers connected with the force in the Midland District.

Thomas Dorland, one of the first settlers of Adolphustown, was the first captain commissioned in the township. He commanded a company in 1812, at Kingston. His company partook of the loyal spirit which actuated the captain, who indignantly said of the Americans, "they drove us from our homes once and now come after us." Captain Dorland was much liked, as an officer, by his men.

Captain Trumpour, who commanded a company of horse, was generally estimated as a commander.

Christopher Hagerman, a native of Adolphustown, arose by promotion from an Ensign, to be Aide-de-Camp. The following is from the *Kingston Gazette*:—"Head Quarters, Upper Canada, York, 15th December, 1813. District General order. The Lieutenant-General commanding and President, has been pleased to appoint Christopher Hagerman, Esq., to be Provincial Aid-de-Camp to his Honor, and to enter the Provincial Rank of Lieutenant Colonel on Mr. Hagerman."

Major Spencer, who had been Colonel in Major Rogers' regiment during the Revolutionary war, died at the breaking out of the war of 1812, and was buried in Fredericksburgh on his own place with military honors, he was succeeded by Captain Thompson. Crawford was Colonel of a regiment of Militia.

The following were officers in Ernesttown: Lieutenant Colonel James Parrot, Captain Joshua Booth, C. Fralick, Noris Briscoe, Peter Daly, Robert Clark, Shelden Hawley. Lieutenants: Davis Hamby, Henry Day, John Richards, Daniel Fraser, Robert Worlet. Ensigns: Isaac Fraser, David Lockwood, Daniel Simmons, Abraham Amey, Solomon Johns, John Thorp, senr."

Major Young, formerly ensign in Sir John Johnson's regiment, was an officer in the Prince Edward Militia for some time. He was at Kingston in 1812, and died while on duty. Captain McDonnell of Marysburgh, was also on duty at Kingston at that time. Captain Young, of the Carrying Place, was likewise there, as well as his Ensign, W. H. Wallbridge, who became Captain in 1831, Owen Richards being the Colonel. Lieutenant Richard Howard, of Sophiasburgh, died March 1, 1814. Dengin Conger "held a commission in the first battalion of the Prince Edward Militia during twenty-four years, fourteen of which he was Captain. William Ketcheson, of Sidney, was commissioned Ensign in 1804; Lieutenant in 1812: Captain toward the close of the war, served nine months at Kingston. Coleman, of Belleville, was Captain of Provincial Light Dragoons.

The Militia of Adolphustown, Fredericksburgh, Ernesttown, and probably of Kingston, were accustomed to meet on Finkle's Place, below the wind mill, before the war, 1812. Strange as it may now seem, the place for training of the Prince Edward Militia was, for many years, at Grassy Point, in the Sixth Town. All the way, not only from the extreme point of Marysburgh, but from Amherst Island, and from the western part of Ameliasburgh, the sparsely settled inhabitants were wont to come, by anything but even roads, to this point for their stated training. They met at this place until the year 1800, after which they all met at Hallowell, Picton. Those from Ameliasburgh required two days to reach the training place. Some years later a second place was allowed.

CHAPTER LXIII.

CONTENTS.—In 1812, around Bay Quinté—The declaration of war—The news at Kingston—The call to arms—Hastings—Events of Kingston—In 1813—Attack upon Sacket's Harbour—Oswego—American Fleet before Kingston—Royal George—Kingston prepared—Chrysler's farm—A "Postscript"—Along the St. Lawrence—Ribaldry—The Commissary—Capt. Wilkins—Quakers—Rate of pay—American prisoners—The wounded—Surgeons, Dougal, Meacham—Jonathan Philips—Militiamen's reward—Militia orders—Parliamentary grants.

THE WAR OF 1812.

The call to arms was promptly and loyally responded to by the inhabitants of the Midland District, including the militia of Northumberland. The old veterans of former days, who had for so many years been engaged in the peaceful occupation of farming, were aroused to a high degree of indignation that their old enemies, who had driven them away from old homes, should now threaten them in their hard earned new ones. No wonder that these old sturdy loyalists and their sons quickly obeyed the call to come in defense of their homes. To a certain extent the Bay region was free from immediate danger. Excepting at Kingston the inhabitants were not alarmed by the trumpet blast. There was not here enacted such stirring events as transpired at Detroit, upon the Niagara frontier, and below upon the St. Lawrence. Nevertheless there was diligent preparation made for any contingency that might come with the tide of war. The several regiments of militia called out, were taken to Kingston and prepared for service whether it might be offensive or defensive. Kingston being a naval station and having a dock-yard as well as a military depot; and at the same time situated within a short distance of the enemies' territory, it was necessary that it should be well garrisoned, and the surrounding country constantly watched. And here the raw militia man was drilled for service, while they were ready to defend the place.

The news of the declaration of war reached Kingston by a private letter to Mr. Forsyth, from the States, and an hour and a half afterwards, says one who was there, a letter having been conveyed to Col. Benson, the drum beat to arms, and couriers were on their way with all haste to warn out the militia along the Bay and in Northumberland. The belief was entertained that Kingston would be a place of attack at once, and the flank companies were ordered there immediately.

Upon the 27th June, 1812, John Ferguson, Colonel commanding 1st regiment Hastings Militia, wrote from Kingston, to Lieut.-Colonel William Bell, of Thurlow, "to cause the volunteers of the battalion who already offered their services, to hold themselves in readiness for actual service, and to apply to the Quartermaster for such arms as are in his possession, to be used by the volunteers until others were got from Kingston. Capt. John McIntosh to take command, the other Captain will be J. W. Myers. Notice to be given at once, be it night or day, to meet on the Plains—and be drilled by the Sergt.-Major." Col. Bell received the letter at sunset on the 29th, by the hands of John Weaver. A postscript to the letter says "War is declared by the United States against Great Britain."

The militia of Hastings were hurried to Kingston, but after a few weeks when it was seen that Kingston would not be immediately attacked, they were ordered home. The next year the Northumberland Militia was ordered to York, and soon saw service.

In connection with Kingston were two events which may be alluded to, one was a hostile demonstration against Sacket's Harbour, which had for its object principally the destruction of a man-of-war there building; the other was an attempt, on the part of the Americans, to destroy the British frigate, Royal George, lying at Kingston.

It was in May, 1813, that Sir George Prevost and Sir James L. Yeo, arrived at Kingston, where were Capt. Barclay Pring and Furnis, preparing for service the few vessels stationed there; among them one lately launched, the Sir George Prevost. of 30 guns, greeted them with a salute from the vessels. The American fleet was at the head of the lake, bombarding Fort George. Under these circumstances it was resolved to make an attack upon Sackets Harbour, "About 1000 men were embarked on board the Wolfe of 24 guns, the Royal George of 24 guns, the Earl of Moira, of 18 guns, and four armed schooners each carrying from 10 to 12 guns, with a number of batteaux, so that no time might be lost in the debarkation. Two gun-boats were placed in readiness as a landing escort. The boats were under the direction of Capt. Mulcaster, of the Royal Navy, and the landing under the immediate superintendence of Sir George Prevost and Sir James Yeo. The following account is from A. O. Petrie, Esq., of Belleville, who was present as a volunteer, being then clerk to Capt. Gray, Assistant Quartermaster-General. So quickly was the expedition arranged that Petrie had no knowledge of it until about to start. By permission of Capt. Gray, Mr. Petrie formed one of the party, who, although forgetting to procure a red coat, did not forget his gun. "Was in a batteau with Capt. Gray the greater part of the night, which was crowded with men. Capt. Gray told Petrie that the object of the expedition was to burn the ship there building, and told him he might have a hand in it, Petrie said he would be there as soon as any one. They landed about four o'clock in the morni n g, and Mr. Petrie carried Capt. Gray on his back to the shore through the water. But before they had landed the Americans fired upon them; they were soon relieved however, by the gun-boat. They then advanced and was not far from the ship when the bugle sounded the retreat. When he regained the boat he found that his friend Capt. Gray had been killed.

There is abundant evidence that the retreat was unnecessary, that the enemy were fleeing; but one of those fearful mistakes occurred by which the British and Canadian troops lost a victory which had been won. This expedition exhibited the bravery of the militia men in the fullest degree, and had the mind of Prevost remained unclouded, due reward would have been secured. But the precipitate retreat of the Americans was misunderstood by Prevost, he thought it a trap set. Says a writer, "It was true that Fort Tomkins was about to fall into British hands. Already the officers in charge of Navy Point, agreeably to orders, and supposing the fort to be lost, had set on fire the naval magazine, containing all the stores captured at York. The hospital and barracks were illuminating the lake by their grand conflagration, and the frigate on the stocks had been set on fire only to be extinguished when Prevost's mind became unsettled as to the ulterior design of the enemy. In the very moment of fully accomplishing the purpose of the expedition, he ordered a retreat, and the troops reached Kingston in safety.

But, the following year an expedition left Kingston on the 4th May, which arrived at Oswego on the following day, and took the fort; but the stores had been removed.

About five miles from Kingston lies what is called Herkimer's Point. It was thought a thing not improbable that the Americans might land upon this point and endeavor to enter Kingston. Here was a telegraph signal, and two cannon had been planted there; afterward one, a very good one was removed, lest it should fall into the hands of the enemy. From this point a fair view of the Upper Gap was to be had. At last, one morning, the Yankee fleet composed of some 14 sail, large and small, appeared off the Upper Gap. A shot it is said was fired from the old windmill by some militia men there, which was replied to. A schooner, the Simcoe was chased, but escaped by running over a bar between some islands at Herkimer's Point. She received several shots, and subsequently sank when she had reached Kingston. The inhabitants along the coast were ordered into the interior with all their stock. The fleet passed along not far from the shore, and the field artillery moved along at an equal pace, and a firing was kept up between them. The writer's father was present on the occasion. He was Sergt. in Capt. Dorland's Company from Adolphustown, and was this morning on duty with his Company at Herkimer's Point. He was standing a short distance from the shore. The brass artillery sent a ball through one of the enemy's vessels, he saw her haul off from the rest. The fleet fired back, and he saw the first ball from them as it passed near him. The Governor's horse being held by a negro near by, while the Governor stood a little off, squatted to the earth and the ball passed over his back, the ball then struck the top rail of the fence, near by him, and went bounding and plowing up the ground. All this he remembers distinctly. The artillery and troops marched along opposite the fleet on their way to Kingston, and were there paraded in a concealed spot behind the jail. It was a general expectation that the enemy would attempt to land, and he fully anticipated going into action. He could see the balls flying over the buildings.

It was a natural expectation that the enemy would endeavour to possess themselves of Kingston with its garrison and naval depot, and dock yard. Every necessary step was taken to frustrate any designs that might be entertained by the Americans against the place. In the Gazette of Oct. 9, 1813, is the following:

"By all accounts we understand that the Americans are on the eve of attacking this place. It is our province to observe that their intentions have become completely anticipated, and every necessary preparation has been made to give them a warm reception. We are happy to announce the arrival of Lieutenant-Colonel Drummond, with the first detachment of the 104th Regiment, from Burlington Heights. This regiment the 49th, and the corps of the Voltigeurs, may be expected here in the course of to-day or to-morrow. These three gallant regiments, together with our brave militia, who are pouring in from all quarters, and have already assembled in considerable numbers, will be a sufficient reinforcement, and with our present respectable garrison will be able to repel any force which the enemy may bring against us. We are are glad to observe that every piece of artillery is most advantageously placed, and we must really congratulate our fellow citizens on the formidable appearance of every defensible portion in the vicinity of this town. It has been the general rumor for a few days past that six or seven of our small vessels have been taken on their way from the head of the lake to this place and sent into Sackets; which rumor we fear is too true."

The woods around Kingston, and upon Point Henry, were all cut down to prevent a surprise. The enemy, however, did not attack Kingston, but landed lower down the St. Lawrence. With what result the following notice will show, "*Kingston Gazette*, Saturday, November, 13, 1813.

"POSTCRIPT—HIGHLY IMPORTANT."

"The following important intelligence was received in town this morning by express."

CHRYSLERS, 11th November.

The enemy attacked us this morning, suppose from 3 to 4,000 men in number, and has been completely repulsed and defeated, with a very considerable loss, a number of prisoners, and one General taken by us; the loss of the enemy cannot be less than 4 or 5,000. Ours has been severe. The Americans were commanded by Generals Lears and Boyd.

(Signed) WILLIAM MORRISON,
Lieutenant Colonel 89th Regiment.

Kingston Gazette, Saturday, Nov. 20, 1813.

We are assured on good authority, that the loss of the enemy in the late action at Williamsburgh, exceeded 1,000 in killed, wounded, prisoners and deserters; their flight was precipitate during the remainder of the day and night after the action; on the morning of the 12th they regained their own shore in the greatest confusion, and in momentary expectation of being attacked. Several officers of distinction were killed and wounded. Major General Covender was dangerously wounded, and is since dead; Lieutenant-Colonel Preston, noted for his ridiculous and insulting proclamation at Fort Erie, inviting the inhabitants of Upper Canada to place themselves under his protection, was dangerously wounded. One six-pounder field piece was taken on the charge, and about 120 prisoners, 350 or 400 stand of arms were collected on and near the field of action.

"The Militia of Cornwall and the neighbouring townships have come forward in the most spirited and loyal manner, and are daily joining the troops, shewing a spirit worthy of their ancestors, and a noble example to their countrymen. We sincerely hope it will be followed, and if the inhabitants of Upper Canada are true to themselves, they can have no reason to fear all the efforts of the enemy." Thus ended the attack which had been made with the usual boastful spirit. According to an American writer in the *New York Herald*, at that time, the American Commander-in-Chief was "a contemptible wretch," guilty of "low ribaldry," a drunkard, having to take "two drinks of hot rum to enable him to go through the operation of shaving," and finally as given to singing

"I am now a going to Canada,
And there I will get money—
And there I'll kiss the pretty squaws
They are as sweet as honey."

Not alone did the Midland district supply its quota of men for the incorporated militia; but the rich soil along the borders of the bay gave abundantly to the commissariat department. During the first year of the war, there was a time when the troops at Kingston had no more than a week's provision. Under these circumstances the Commandant enquired of Colonel Cartwright if he knew of any one who could be depended upon to raise the required supplies which were known to exist in the district. Cartwright informed him that the required person could at once be obtained in the person of Captain Robert Wilkins. Captain Wilkins, who had raised a company in the beginning of the war, was accordingly sent for, and instructed to prepare to undertake, as chief commissary, the duty. He asked for written instructions and authority that he might not be hindered in his work—that Militia Colonels, and sub-officers should yield to his demands for men to act as batteaux men, or do any other required duty to impress conveyances, &c. He was asked if he would be ready to set out in a day or two. The reply was, I will start in half an hour. "The devil you will," said the Commandant, "so much the better," and Captain Wilkins quickly wrote his resignation as Captain to the company, settled his hotel bill, and was on his way up the bay toward Picton. Arrived there, he called upon Mr. Cummings, and desired him to act as agent, which request was acceded to. He then pushed on to the head of the bay, at the Carrying Place, and established an agency there, afterwards his head-quarters. Proceeding to Myers' Creek, he procured as agent the services of Simon McNabb.

In the vicinity of Picton, were a considerable number of Quakers, who, although not wanting in loyalty, would, not only, not take up arms, but conscientiously would not sell the produce of their farms and take in payment government bills, or "shin plasters," then in circulation. Of course, they could, without scruples, sell their grain to any one without asking questions, for gold or silver but to take ephemeral paper born of war, and its circulation recognizing a state of war, was another thing. They absolutely refused to take it. Colonel Wilkins believing in their sincerity, at once wrote to the Commandant at Kingston, for a certain sum of gold, which was promptly forwarded. Thus the granaries of the rich section of the county in Prince Edward were opened. But Wilkins had not waited for the gold; on his own responsibility he had bought the grain promising to pay them as they required, and Mr. Cummings had been diligently carrying out his orders.

Commissary Wilkins had other difficulties to contend with. In some sections there was a disposition to hold the produce until prices were better, although pork, for instance, was fetching $14 a barrel. They wished to get $20. The result of this was a "half martial law," by which provisions, wherever found, could be taken at a fair valuation. But Colonel Wilkins says that this had rarely to be done. By kind persuasion, showing the people that their duty should lead them to be satisfied with a fair price, he succeeded in getting all the supplies of provision he wanted.

The duties devolving upon him were numerous and onerous. He had to supervise the batteaux carrying provisions up and down the bay from a distance, and often would have to give orders for 3 or 400 men to be collected to propel the batteaux, or assist to transport articles across the Carrying Place.

The rate of pay given to an officer, acting as pilot, or conductor to batteaux, was 10s. per day. Privates impressed to carry or assist received 2s. 6d., with rations; but supplied themselves with blankets. They were paid immediately their work was done, by Wilkins. We have before us a requisition sent by Wilkins to Colonel Bell in April, 1814, for 40 privates, and officer to manage the King's batteaux, as there was a quantity of provisions to be conveyed to Queenston Heights.

Although the foe found no footing, and made no attempt to land along the bay, the inhabitants had the opportunity of seeing not a few of their would be conquerors, as they passed as prisoners of war on their way to Quebec. Many of the 1000 taken at Detroit had to march along the road the whole length of the Province. Some were taken in batteaux, and others were conveyed in vessels down the lake as far as Kingston. Many of those who walked went by the way of the Prince Edward Peninsula, by Wellington and Picton, crossing the bay at the Stone Mills, others went by way of Napanee, and thence to Kingston. One way was as convenient as the other, as there was no bridge across the River Trent. Persons are now living along the routes who recollect the crest-fallen appearance of these prisoners; the more so, because the people whom they had come to invade, and dispossess, shewed them acts of kindness, and gave them food to eat. One old lady, so old that she remembers the Revolutionary War in 1783, says she told them she had given the British troops all she had to eat, as they passed up to conquer them, and she now as gladly gave food to them. Those brought in batteaux were transported across the Carrying Place into the bay. No doubt they appreciated the beauty of the scenery along the route, and had their appetite affected for the land they coveted.

On the morning of August 29, 1812, there arrived at Kingston, His Majesty's ships Royal George, Earl of Moira, and Prince Regent, with 400 prisoners, and General Hull.

The most of the prisoners taken at the Niagara frontier were carried in batteaux, and by the bay, Colonel Scott among the rest.

At a later date, arrived the American prisoners, General Chandler and Waider, captured at Stoney Creek. And again, "Arrived at this place yesterday, March 1st, 1813, on their way to Quebec, whither they will proceed to-day, Brigadier-General James Winchester, Colonel William Lewis, and Major George Madison, attached to the American army, captured by General Proctor on the River Raisine." We copy the following:

"Quebec, November 2nd. On Friday and Saturday were escorted by a detachment of Major Bell's Cavalry, from their quarters, at Beauport, to the new gaol, twenty-three American officers, and on the latter day were also taken from the prison ships, and escorted by a detachment of the 103rd regiment to the same prison, a like number of non-commissioned officers, making in all forty-six conformable to the General Orders of the 27th October."

But other sights than prisoners of war were presented during the conflict. Owing to the exposed state of the Province in the west, after the taking of York, a large number of the wounded were removed from the Niagara region to Kingston, sometimes by ships, sometimes by batteau. Many of those wounded at Lundy's Lane were taken by schooner to York, and thence by batteau down the lake shore, across the Carrying Place, and along the bay. Among them was Sheriff Ruttan, who was left at his father's house, to the kind care of his family. In this connection it may be observed that Surgeon Dougall, of Prince Edward Militia, served nine months at Kingston, and Dr. Meacham, of Belleville, also served during the most of the war.

We will here give an extract from an obituary notice taken from the *Hastings Chronicle*.

"A VETERAN OF 1812.—"Of the Provincial troops, the Glengary regiment of Infantry took perhaps the most active part. At the age of fifteen, Jonathan Phillips enlisted in this corps, then being raised throughout Canada. The urgent necessity for recruits inducing the authorities to accept youths even of that tender age. The story will best be told, as nearly as may be, in the veteran's own words:—"I was born in Duchess County, State of New York, in the year 1796; my father came from Devonshire, England, and my mother from Edinburgh, Scotland. In 1809, my parents removed to Canada and settled in Fredericksburgh, County of Lennox and Addington. In January, 1812, I was working for Mr. Chapman, in Fredericksburgh, getting out square pine, oak, and staves; whilst thus employed, Captain Judkins, formerly of the 104th Regiment of the Line, asked me to enlist, and I joined the Glengary's, and in a few days after was sent to Kingston with about twenty other recruits from Fredericksburgh, Richmond, and Ernesttown. We remained in Kingston till navigation opened, when the recruits assembled at that place, about 200 in all, descended the St. Lawrence in batteaux to Three Rivers, where we received uniforms, arms, and accoutrements, and commenced to learn our drill. The corps now numbered about 800.

Towards autumn we were ordered to Quebec, in charge of about 1000 prisoners from General Hull's army, captured in the west. We remained at Quebec a month or six weeks. In October, 1812, we were ordered to the west, (the season is recalled from the recollection that as they marched from Quebec the farmers were busy cutting wheat on the hillsides, and the snow was falling at the time). The march was by the North Shore road to Montreal. Here we remained all winter, expecting the Americans to attack that city. In the month of March, before the sleighing was gone, the regiment was ordered to King-ton, taking with them several pieces of cannon, which were drawn by oxen. The men marched. The cattle that drew the cannon and baggage, were slaughtered at Kingston for provisions. We remained a month at Kingston, and then passed up the Bay of Quinté to the Carrying Place in batteaux. The baggage and batteaux were transported across the Isthmus into Lake Ontario, and we re-embarked for York. On our arrival at York we were forwarded with all despatch to Burlington Bay. We first met the Yankees at Stoney Creek, and then pushed on towards Fort George. We halted at the village of St. Davids, and encamped at the cross-roads. The Yankees held Fort George; when they discovered we were so near them they retreated upon Black Creek. We followed them up, and had a battle with them at Lundy's Lane, on 25th July, 1813. In this affair I was in the advance guard, or reconnoitering party. The enemy retreated upon Fort Erie, and we pursued them and had several skirmishes with them. They blew up the fort, and evacuated Canada. In the fall of the year we marched back to York; there we embarked in batteaux and came to the Carrying Place—thence we crossed into the Bay of Quinté, and thence to Kingston. From Kingston we marched to Adolphustown Court House, and were billeted upon the farmers in that vicinity during the ensuing winter. There were from eight to ten men in each house. Whilst here we assembled every day at the Court House, at ten a. m., for drill—we were at least 800 strong.

On the 23rd March, 1814, all the three years' men were paraded at the Court House, paid off, and discharged. Each man so discharged drew 100 acres of land in Upper Canada, farming utensils, and a year's provisions. The provisions were distributed every three months, at Robert Charles Wilkins' store, at the Carrying Place."

From the time of his discharge till his decease, Phillips resided in the County of Hastings, pursuing the usual occupation of the first settlers of this county. For many years he followed "lumbering" in winter, and farming in the summer seasons, but being trustworthy, intelligent, and of a kindly disposition, his services were frequently sought after for various purposes. Several years ago, the farm which he drew for his military service, and which, for many years, afforded him a home and a support, he sold for the sum of $1,900, thus enjoying in his old age the well earned reward of the loyalty and courage of his youth. He died at his home, in the second concession, Rawdon, on the 15th February, 1868.

THE MILITIAMAN'S REWARD.

General Brock, on his way to Detroit, assembled the Legislature, and amongst other Acts, one was passed for the organization of a battalion of "Incorporated Militia," a body distinct from the Sedentary Militia. It was an inducement held out for action; and to properly fitted persons, to raise companies and regiments for service during the war. According to Ruttan, any one enlisting five persons was entitled to an Ensigncy; ten, a Lieutenancy; twenty, a Captaincy; fifty, a Major; and forty a Lieutenant-Colonel. Subsequently, in 1814 and 15, the Legislature "voted the supplies necessary to fill up the incorporated regiments to 800 men. A service of plate, and a pension of £20 per annum for the wounded, or for the widows of the killed, as well as an address to His Majesty for an allowance of 100 acres of land for each man, whether belonging to the regiment of flank companies or the Sedentary Militia."

No truly patriotic and brave man will seek, or demand a promise of reward for defending, or fighting for the interests of his country. He requires no more than what comes from a consciousness of his duty done, and his country's honor maintained; the land of his birth, or choice, preserved from the desecration of an invader's foot. But when the deadly conflict has incapacitated the brave one for the ordinary avocations of life, and he is left, perhaps, with a family, unable to secure life's comforts; or when the torch of war—of the unchristian men, such as President Madison, and his cold-blooded servant, Colonel McClure, at Niagara,—leaves the homes of helpless women in ashes; or with wilful wantoness destroys for the mere pleasure of gratifying a worse than heathenish disposition, then the tried veteran has a right to be rewarded in a substantial manner. The Government of Canada, as well as that of Great Britain, has never been found remiss in affording suitable rewards to those who were truly and knowingly worthy.

The smoke of war in 1815 had barely cleared away, after the Americans had sought and obtained a peace, to them ignoble, ere the Canadian Government took steps to secure a just reward to all worthy men. And to this end the following general order appeared in the *Kingston Gazette*, 17th July, 1815, having reference to settlers.

"Military Secretary's Office, Kingston.

"Each soldier to receive 100 acres of land; officers entitled in the first instance to 200. To receive provisions for themselves and families for one year, that is those who had last or, who might require it on new land. Implements of husbandry, and tools to be supplied in sufficient quantities, and other comforts according to necessity to cultivate land. The land thus taken cannot be sold until after three year's cultivation. Supt. Alex. McDonnell, and Angus McDonnell, of Glengary Fencibles, to take charge of the settlers." The same date was issued as follows:

"Acting Military Secretary, William Gibson, issued a notice at Kingston, 29th July, 1815, proclaiming that Boards to examine claims for losses met with during the American war, should meet during August and September, at Amherstburgh, Fort George, York, Kingston, and Fort Wellington.

"All discharged soldiers, applying for lands are to give in their names to Edward Jones, late of the 9th Regiment, now residing in the old Barrack Square. (Signed)—F. P. Robinson, *Secretary*, July 31.

Again is found—"Lieutenant Governor's Office, York, Dec. 10, 1816.

His Excellency, the Lieutenant-Governor has been pleased to appoint Surgeon Anthony Marshall, of Kingston, to examine and grant certificates of disability to Militiamen disabled from wounds received on service in defence of the Province during the late war. (Signed)—Edward McMahon, *Assistant Secretary*.

Among the Militia General Orders issued from the Adjutant General's office, appeared the following:

"His Excellency, Sir Frederick P. Robinson, Major-General Commanding, and Provincial Lieutenant-Governor of the Province of Upper Canada, has great satisfaction in publishing to the Militia of that Province, the following extract of a letter from Earl Bathurst, one of His Majesty's Secretaries of State; addressed to His Excellency Sir Gordon Drummond, dated Downing-street, 13th June, 1815.

"I should have felt that I was acting unjustly towards you and the officers and men under your command, if I had forborne bringing under the notice of His Royal Highness the Prince Regent, the great meritorious exertions, so long and so successfully made by them for the preservation of the Uppor Province. I am commanded to assure you, that His Royal Highness has contemplated your efforts with the highest satisfaction, not more on account of the skill and valor uniformly displayed by His Majesty's Troops, in presence of the enemy, than of the patience with which the privations incident to the peculiar nature of the service were supported and finally overcome."

"You will not fail to convey to the Troops under your Com- "mand, the strongest expression of His Royal Highness's approba- "tion, and to accept for yourself and the army under your orders, "that testimony which His Royal Highness is so anxious to bear, "to the great service which you have rendered to your country."

"Nor is His Royal Highness insensible to the merits of the inhabitants of Upper Canada, or to the great assistance which the Militia of the Province afforded during the whole of the war. His Royal Highness trusts that you will express to them in adequate terms, the high sense which he entertains of their services, as having mainly contributed to the immediate preservation of the Province, and its future security." N. Coffin, *Adjutant General of Militia.*

In 1815 the Legislature granted £6,000, stg. £5,883 6s. 8d. to be applied as follows:—To the officers, non-commissioned officers, and privates of the incorporated militia, six months' pay, £4,594 15s. 2d. To the officers and non-commissioned officers of the line attached to the incorporated militia, the well pay of their respective ranks in the said corps, £1,000. To the officers and non-commissioned officers, and privates of the incorporated militia artillery, six months' pay, £288 11s. 6d. To the speaker of the House of Assembly, to purchase a sword to be presented to Colonel Robinson, late of the incoporated militia, 100 guineas.

CHAPTER LXIV.

CONTENTS—The Six Nations in 1812—American Animus—"Manifest Destiny"—Mohawk Indians—A right to defend their homes—Inconsistency—American Savages—Extract from Playter—Brock's proclamation—Indian character, conduct, eloquence—Deserters in 1812—Few of them—Court-martials—The attempts at conquest by the Americans—The numbers—Result of war—Canadians saved the country—And can do so—Fraternal kindness.

THE SIX NATIONS AS CANADIANS IN 1812.

Maintaining their wonted hostile attitude to the Mohawks, and continuing to charge, upon the British and Canadian Governments, an uncivilized procedure, the Americans have attempted to create a belief that we waged not a warfare according to civilized ideas. Civilization consists, in the minds of Americans, in just those views, theories, beliefs, and proceedings, which belong to the Great United States, and nothing can eminate from their government that is not in strict accordance with civilization,—their civilization. It so happens that one of their beliefs is that destiny manifestly intends that they shall possess all of North America. In 1812, a pretext was formed under the question of the right to search American vessels for deserters from British service, to declare war against England. This was regarded by Madison and the Government at Washington, a fitting opportunity to make the already cherished attempt to obtain the British Provinces. It was not in accordance with their ideas of liberty and civilization, to give the slightest heed to the wishes of the loyalists whom they had, years before, forced away, and who had already done much to convert the wilderness into a noble Province; the British subjects who had emigrated to America, and preferred the yet infant colony of Canada, to the more advanced, but distasteful, United States. And still more, the Mohawk Indians, whom they had so cruelly treated, who had found homes under a benign and fatherly government, were not only disregarded, but their very right to defend their homes was denied by the very civilized government which longed to get Canada. And hence we find attempts made to cast obloquy, upon the Canadians, in connection with the war of 1812. The people who strove, but vainly, to enlist the Mohawks in their service in 1776, with wonderful inconsistency, in 1812, issue proclamations that no quarter will be given to Indians, nor the Canadians who were found fighting side by side. Yet, in the same war they had all the Indians they could get to assist in their invasion of a peaceful Province, who actually assisted in the hellish work of plunder in the Niagara region. The Senecas took sides with them. The Indians who had found a home in Canada, had a right to defend their country, and willingly did they march to the field. They rendered important service at Detroit when the immortal Brock hurled back the braggart foe, took General Hull and his army prisoners, and conquered the territory of Michigan. They likewise did good service at Queenston Heights.

A few instances occured where individual Indians did lapse into the warfare nature had implanted into their breasts. But let it be distinctly and emphatically stated that they were exceptions. "But the savage conduct of the white United States troops, was worse than the employment of savages. In civilized wars, or the wars of Christian people with each other, (alas! that Christians and war should be associated!) the usual rule is to harm only those who aim to harm, and to pass by the peaceable and unarmed. Considering, too, that the Canadian people were not enemies, but had always friendly dispositions towards the United States, that the war was merely for remote and abstract questions, that the British Canadians never set the example, that maurading was not the rule of the British officers and armies (as evinced before the world in the wars with Bonaparte),—the United States Government selecting the province as a battle field, should have treated the inhabitants without arms as mere spectators of the conflict. Shame on President Madison, and his cabinet of Christian "(?)" gentlemen, for ordering their General, McClure (under the name and seal of John Armstrong, Secretary of War), to burn up the Town of Niagara, and turn 400 women and children into the snow and icy streets, on a December day of a rigid Canadian winter! Had the cruelty been accomplished by a tribe of Indians, no astonishment would have been felt; but for Christians thus to treat Christians, and for people of the same ancestry, to show such barbarity, shows that the bad passions of the human heart are the same in the civilized as in the savage. The war might have been carried on, so that friendship might soon be resumed; but the dreadful aggravation, left in the bosoms of the Canadian settlers, such hatred as remains to the present day. The writer has even heard women say, on the banks of the St. Lawrence, that if the Americans ever invaded Canada again, they would shoulder muskets with their husbands. The democracy of the United States, like the democracy of the French Revolution, proffered liberty with the left hand, and scattered the fire-brands of savage war with the right."—(Playtor.)

The invading general having issued a proclamation, declaring that Canadians found fighting beside the Indians should have no quarter. Major-General Brock, in an address, issued to the Canadians at Fort George, July 22nd, 1812, referring to this matter, says:—

"Be not dismayed at the unjustifiable threat of the Commander of the enemy's forces to refuse quarter, should an Indian appear in the ranks.

"The brave bands of the Aborigines which inhabit this colony were like His Majesty's other subjects punished for their zeal and fidelity, by the loss of their possesions in the late colonies, and rewarded by His Majesty with lands of superior value in the Province. The faith of the British Government has never yet been violated by the Indians, who feel that the soil they inherit is to them and their prosperity, protected from the base arts so frequently devised to over-reach their simplicity."

"By what new principle are they to be prohibited from defending their property? If their warfare from being different to that of the white people, be more terrific than that of the enemy, let him retrace his steps, they seek him not, and cannot expect to find women and children in an invading army.

"But they are men, and have equal rights with all other men to defend themselves and their property when invaded, more especially when they find in the enemy's camp a ferocious and mortal fee, using the same warfare which the American commander affects to reprobate."

"This inconsistent and unjustifiable threat of refusing quarter, for such a cause as being found in arms with a brother sufferer, in defense of invaded rights, must be exercised with the certain assurance of retaliation, not only in the limited operations of war in this part of the King's dominion, but in every quarter of the globe; for the national character of Britain is not less distinguished for humanity than strict retributive justice, which will consider the execution of this inhuman threat as deliberate murder, for which every subject of the offending power must make expiation."—(Signed, Isaac Brock.)

In concluding this subject, we will quote the language of one who rose to sublime eloquence in connection with another event.

Seeing the on-coming moment of the extinction among the Americans—vainly resisting the inevitable fate, but still lofty and noble. Thus spoke a Seneca chief:—"Who is it causes this river to rise in the high mountains, and to empty itself in the ocean? Who is it that causes to blow the loud winds of winter, and that calms them again in summer? Who is it that rears up the shade of those lofty forests, and blasts them with the quick lightning at his pleasure? The same spirit, who gave you a country on the other side of the waters, gave this land to us, and we will defend it."

We would fail in our whole task did we not refer to one more topic; that concerning Deserters. There were, during the time of war, a few instances of desertion. There is every reason to believe, that the wily Americans sent emmissaries into the country with the object of tampering with the Canadians. The following, while having a local reference, will explain the steps taken by Government to meet the requirements of the day in this respect:

President's Office, Upper Canada, Kingston, 24th March, 1814.

His Honor the President has been pleased to appoint by commission, bearing this date, the under-mentioned gentlemen to be commissioners, for carrying into effect the provisions of an Act passed in the last session of the Legislature of this Province, entitled "An Act to empower His Majesty, for a limited time, to secure and detain such persons as His Majesty shall suspect of treasonable adherence to the enemy, in the several districts of this Province respectively:—For *Midland District*—The Hon. K. Cartwright, Alexander McDonell, Alexander Fisher, Thomas Dorland, Timothy Thompson, Thomas Markland, Peter Smith, John Cumming, James McNabb, Ebenezer Washburn, Robert C. Wilkins, James Young, William Crawford.

In every war there will be some desertions, and during the war of 1812, there were found a few, and a few indeed, who were base enough to desert from the ranks of the Canadian Militia.

The several attempts at conquest of Canada were:—

1st	Invasion..	Gen.	Hull	at	Sandwich	with	3,000	men.
2nd	" ..	"	VanRansler	"	Wodworth	"	2,000	"
3rd	" ..	"	Smyth	"	Fort Erie	"	3,000	"
4th	" ..	"	Pike	"	York	"	2,500	"
5th	" ..	"	Dearborne	"	Fort George	"	3,000	"
6th	" ..	"	Winchester, for Montreal,	"	Chryslers Farm	"	3,000	"
7th	" ..	"	Hampden	"	Chateauguay R.	"	8,000	"
8th	" ..	"	Brown	"	Fort Erie	"	5,000	"
9th	" ..	"	"	"	Lundy's Lane	"	5,000	"
10th	" ..	"	Izzard	"	Fort Erie	"	8,000	"
11th	" ..	"	Wilkinson	"	Lacote Mills	"	2,500	"
			Total number of men				45,000.	

"The foregoing is an aggregate of the attempt to invade Canada by the United States forces when they sued for peace; and, when such was proclaimed, they did not find themselves in possession of one inch of Canadian Territory."—(Clark.)

This glorious result was due, in a great measure, to the loyalty and bravery of the Canadian Militia. The first year, the Militia alone saved the Province.

The close of the war left no unpleasant remembrance. Called to arms for the most noble purpose, that of defending their homes, they discharged their duty bravely, but without unnecessary violence. There were no acts of cruelty to be laid to their charge. It was only the unprincipled foe that could be guilty of deeds of barbaric darkness. It remained for the American General Harrison to burn, contrary to the rules of civilized warfare, a peaceful village, and for General McClure to apply the torch to the building which protected the wounded men, women, and children, from the piercing cold of a December night, an outrage only equalled by their firing on a British flag of truce, under General Ross, before the capital Washington. These acts of villany met a just retribution. The former by destroying the frontier settlements from Lewiston to Buffalo, the latter by the destruction of the Capital. Canadians—Britons can deal out just retribution, as well as they can defend their homes. And the Americans ought to know, and remember, that no acts of cowardly villany toward us will for ever go unpunished. They incited rebellion among us in 1837–8. They have encouraged Fenianism, and assisted them as a people to invade our territory, and kill our young men. For this will come a day of judgment. It may not be this century, but it will come. Let but one more attempt be made to secure a footing on our soil, and the Americans will learn that Canadians can, and will, retaliate. The hardy honest Canadian goaded to seek justice, will play the raider also. Ours is a frontier, over which they may come and do much mischief; but their's is equally lengthy, and exposed. A sheet of flame will burst along their frontier as well as ours, the destruction will not be all on side.

During the Crimean war, the Canadians took great pleasure in giving contributions for the relief of the soldiers, wives and children. But this was only returning a like kindness displayed by England at the time of the invasion and rapine in 1812. The wanton destruction of Canadian homes brought much distress. By the *Kingston Gazette* of 5th December, 1813, we see "that the total sum subscribed in the City of London for the relief of the sufferers in Canada (which has come to our knowledge), amounts to £10,419 10s. 0d." And the same year "The General Assembly of Nova Scotia gave to the distressed of Upper Canada £2,500." An act of fraternal kindness that Canadians have been ready to return during the last year.

DIVISION XI.

ADVANCE OF CIVILIZATION.

CHAPTER LXV.

CONTENTS—Canada's first step in civilization—Slavery in America—By whom introduced—False charge—Slavery in Canada—History—Imperial Acts—Legislation in Canada—The several clauses—In Lower Canada—Justice Osgood—Slavery at the Rebellion—Among the U. E. Loyalists—Those who held slaves—Descendants of the slaves—"A British slave"—"For sale"—"Indian slave"—Upper Canada's Record—Compared with the States—Liberty—Why the United States abolished slavery—Honor to whom honor is due.

SLAVERY.

We devote a chapter to the subject of slavery, which may be appropriately noticed under *advance of civilization*. There can be no greater indication of a truly civilized people than a successful attempt to emancipate those in bondage. In this respect Upper Canada was very far in advance of the United States, and even of England herself.

The Americans have not unfrequently essayed to fasten the ignominy of this domestic institution upon the British nation, by asserting that it was the English that first brought slaves to the American continent. Supposing this to be true, it was the most pitiable attempt at excuse for continuing the accursed thing, after Britain had spent millions to abolish slavery in all her broad realm, that can possibly be imagined. But it is all untrue that slaves were first brought by the English. It was the Dutch, who found sale for them in Virginia. This was in 1620. "Shortly after the New England States adopted the 'institution,' the colonists and merchants introducing and controlling the whole trade, Massachusetts leading the way." And with all the cry, for ever echoing in the North against the South, because of slavery; it was the Yankee owners of ships, sent out from Northern ports to engage in the world-condemned crime of the slave trade, that kept alive the worst feature of American slavery, until the celebrated military necessity of Lincoln, emancipated the Southern slaves.

The present generation of Canadians are almost ignorant of the fact that the "institution" of slavery once existed in Canada, both Lower and Upper. The proud and pleasing appellation, which Canada enjoyed for so many years, of a safe asylum for slaves, who had effected their escape from the United States, is in most cases alone known to have belonged to us. But the record of our young country is so honorable upon the question of slavery, that the fact that slaves did once breathe among us, casts no stigma upon the maple leaf, no single stain upon her virgin garments. The fact is, slavery could not live in Canada; much less grow. The leading principles which guided the settlers of the country were of too noble a nature to accept the monstrous system of human bondage as an appendage of the Colony. They felt the truthfulness of the words, not long before uttered by John Wesley, that slavery was the "sum of all villainies," and knew they would be villains of the deepest dye to encourage it.

The history of slavery from the time Joseph was sold by his brothers into Egypt, by which it may be inferred that persons were already held in bondage, up to the present, is of no little interest; but it forms no part of our task to give even a sketch of it, except in relation to its existence in Canada.

In the year 1732, an Act was passed in the Imperial Parliament "for the more easy recovery of debts in His Majesty's plantations and colonies in America," by which "lands, houses, negroes, and other hereditaments and real estate, shall be liable to be taken by due process of law for any indebtedness."

Another Imperial Act having reference to slavery in Canada, was passed so late as 1790. The Act is intituled "An Act for encouraging new settlers in His Majesty's colonies and plantations in America." Among other things it is provided that if any persons shall come to the West India Islands or the Province of Quebec, from United States, with the view of settling, it shall be lawful for such, having obtained a license from the Governor, to import among other things "any negroes" he may possess. Such was the law in all Canada when Upper Canada was erected into a distinct Province.

The first Session of Parliament in Upper Canada was naturally and necessarily occupied in arranging the machinery requisite for the government of the body public. The second Session witnessed legislation to secure defence of the country by organizing a militia body; and also upon two most important subjects having reference to moral principles, viz.: concerning marriages, and

"*An Act to prevent the further introduction of slaves, and to limit the term of contract for servitude within this Province.*"

"Whereas it is unjust that a people who enjoy freedom by law, should encourage the introduction of slaves, and whereas it is highly expedient to abolish slavery in this Province, so far as the same may gradually be done without violating private property; be it enacted by the King's Most Excellent Majesty, by and with the advice and consent of the Legislative Council and Assembly of the Province of Upper Canada," &c. It is enacted "that from and after the passing of this Act, so much of a certain Act of the Parliament of Great Britain, entitled "An Act for encouraging new settlers," &c., as may enable the Governor or Lieutenant-Governor of this Province, heretofore parcel of His Majesty's Province of Quebec, to grant a license for importing into the same, any negro or negroes, shall be, and the same is hereby repealed; and that from and after the passing of this Act, it shall not be lawful for the Governor to grant a license for the importation of any negro or other person to be subjected to the condition of a slave, or to a bounden involuntary service for life, in any part of this Province, nor shall any negro, or other person who shall come, or be brought into the Province after the passing of this Act, be subject to the condition of a slave, or to such service as aforesaid, within this Province, nor shall any voluntary contract of service or indentures that may be entered into by any parties within this Province, after the passing of this Act, be binding upon them or either of them for a longer term than a term of nine years."

The second clause provided that the owners of slaves, at the time within the Province, should be secured in their property and contracts already made should not be affected. But in the third clause it is declared that

"In order to prevent the continuation of slavery within this Province, be it enacted by the authority aforesaid, that immediately from and after the passing of this Act, every child that shall be born of a negro mother, or other woman subjected to such service as aforesaid, shall abide and remain with the master or mistress in whose service the mother shall be living at the time of such child's birth, (unless such mother and child shall leave such service, by and with the consent of such master or mistress)—and such master or mistress shall, and is hereby required to give proper nourishment and clothing to such child or children, and shall and may put such child or children to work, when he, she, or they shall be able so to do, and shall and may retain him or her in their service until every such child shall have obtained the age of 25 years, at which time shall be entitled to demand his or her discharge from, and shall be discharged by such master or mistress, from any further service. And to the end that the age of such child or children may be more easily ascertained, the master or mistress of the mother thereof, shall, and is hereby required, to cause the day of the birth of every such child as shall be born of a negro or other mother, subjected to the condition of a slave, in their service, as aforesaid, to be registered within three months after its birth, by the clerk of the parish, township or place wherein such master or mistress reside, which clerk shall be authorized to demand and receive the sum of one shilling for registering the same. And in case any master or mistress shall refuse or neglect to cause such register to be made within the time aforesaid, and shall be convicted thereof, either on his or her confession, or by the oath of one or more credible witnesses before any justice of the peace, he or she shall for such offence forfeit and pay the sum of £5 to the public stock of the district.

"And be it further enacted, that in case any master or mistress shall detain any such child born in their service, after the passing of this Act, under any pretence whatever, after such servant shall have attained the age of 25 years, except by virtue of a contract of service or indentures duly and voluntarily executed, after such discharge as aforesaid, it shall be for such servant to apply for a discharge to any justice of the peace," and the party accused may be summoned to show cause why the servant is not discharged. The master failing to prove the servant under age, the justice is to discharge the same, and it was "provided always that in case any issue shall be born of such children during their infant servitude or after, such issue shall be entitled to all the rights and privileges of free-born subjects."

"And be it further enacted, that whenever any master or mistress shall liberate or release any person subject to the condition of a slave from their service, they shall at the same time give good and sufficient security to the church or town wardens of the parish or township where they live, that the person so released by them shall not become chargeable to the same, or any other parish or township." This act which reflects so much glory upon the Upper Canadian Legislators, was passed July 9, 1793. We thought our readers would prefer to see the act complete than any synopsis we might prepare.

To Robert Gray, then Solicitor-General, is Upper Canada primarily indebted for the above act. He was an earnest friend of the African race. He was lost in thé schooner *Speedy*, on Lake Ontario.

SLAVERY IN LOWER CANADA.—According to Garneau, in the year 1689, it was proposed to introduce negroes to the colony of France. But it was thought the climate would prove unsuitable. That slavery was, not long after introduced, seems certain, and that it "was legally recognized in Canada, is plain, from an ordinance of intendant Hocquart, dated 1736, regulating the manner of emancipating slaves in Canada."—(Bell.)

There are extant several royal declarations respecting slaves in the colony, bearing dates, 1721, 1742, and 1745. At the Conquest there were slaves in the province; and slavery "then increased for an instant, only to disappear forever." Slavery having continued to exist in Canada until the first decade of the present century. By a stipulation in the treaty of Montreal, the colonists were "to be allowed to retain their slaves." Says Bell in Garneau's history, "Sir L. H. Lafontaine in 1859, investigated this matter," (respecting the existence of slaves in French Canada), and from the published reports of his enquiries, it appears that in 1799-1800, the citizens of Montreal presented requisitions to Parliament, tending to cause the Legislature to vindicate the rights of masters over their slaves. The applicants invoked in favor of their demand, an ordinance rendered by Jacques Roudat, 9th intendant, dated April 13, 1709, which edict was, they urged, in force when the definitive treaty of peace was signed, and by consequence formed part and parcel of the laws, usages, and customs, of Canada, recognized by the Act of Quebec. The bills, on the subject, were introduced, in 1800, 1801, and 1803; but none of them passed. Since that time no Local Legislation sanctioned this matter; and if the act of the Imperial Parliament of 1797, had the effect of abolishing slavery in the British plantations, these would, of course, include Canada." "But," says Bell, the act in question could have no such effect. It only enacted, that negroes could not be taken in execution as chattles, for the debts of their masters, as had previously been the case in His Majesty's American Colonies." It appears tolerably certain from the foregoing, that slaves were introduced by the French into Canada, about the beginning of the 16th century, and that at least in 1709 it was a recognized institution, by virtue of an edict issued by the intendant. And, when the country was conquered by Great Britain, the colonists were "allowed to retain their slaves." In 1784, when Upper Canada was first settled, the number of slaves in Lower Canada according to census was 304.

When Upper Canada, in 1793, took the lead in the whole of Britain's vast domain in legislating against slavery, Lower Canada continued to regard it without disfavour; and, even in Montreal, endeavoured to fix the chains of bondage more firmly upon the negro. But what the Provincial Legislature did not, although presented with the example set by Upper Canada, was done in a different way by Chief Justice Osgood, who in 1803, at Montreal, declared slavery inconsistent with the laws of the country, and gave freedom to the persons in that condition. And when the British Act of Emancipation was passed, in 1833, setting free the slaves in all parts of the Empire, there was no slaves in Canada, Upper or Lower. Thirty years previous had the evil been crushed in Lower Canada, and forty years before Upper Canada had declared that it was "highly expedient to abolish slavery," and had enacted laws to secure its abolition.

At the time of the rebellion of 1776—83, slavery was not limited to the Southern States.

There were a good many held by the old Knickerbocker families, both amongst the loyalists and rebels. When the families both of English and Dutch nationality, came as refugees to Canada, there accompanied them a number of slaves. In many cases these slaves came of their own accord, would not be separated from their masters, with whom they always lived; upon whose land they had been born. Indeed, the attachment between these faithful blacks and their owners was frequently of the most enduring nature, and, as we shall see, in some cases, although made free, they would not leave their old places as domestics.

The Rev. Mr. Stuart in his memoir, says, in speaking of his removal to Canada; "My negroes, being personal property, I take with me, one of which being a young man, and capable of bearing arms, I have to give £100 security to send back a white prisoner in his stead. Capt. Joseph Allan brought with him from New Jersey, after the war had ended, to Upper Canada, three slaves—Tom, Sam and Sal. The two men, some years after, ran away to Lower

Canada. Their owner pursued them to Montreal, and searched for them for ten days; but failed to get them. He sold the female, Sal, with her child, to Silas Hill. This boy was afterwards sold to Abram Barker, who kept him until he became twenty-one, when he became free. Freedom did not suit him, as he became a worthless fellow. Major VanAlstine had slaves, whom he treated with patriarchal kindness, and who lived in great comfort in the old-fashioned Dutch cellar kitchen, in his home, in Fourth Town. The Bogarts and John Huyck also had slaves. Capt. Myers had slaves; one, Black Bet, would never leave him, but continued until his death, under the care of her old master.

Cartwright, Herkimer, and Everitt, each was the owner of slaves. And Powles Claus, of the Mohawk settlement, had two slaves.

Col. Clark speaks, in his memoirs of his mother's death, in 1789, and of the funeral, when the negro Joe drove the favorite horses, Jolly and Bonny, before the sleigh, painted black. Again, Col. C. says: "After the Declaration of Independence, drovers used to come in with droves of horses, cattle, sheep and negroes, for the use of the troops, forts, and settlers in Canada, and my father purchased his four negroes, three males and one female, named Sue. In 1812, she gladly returned to our family, having become old and decrepid. She died in our house at Fifteen-mile Creek, in 1814.

Sheriff Ruttan says, "My uncle brought two negro servants with him, who were very faithful, hard working fellows." During the year of famine, they were sent from Adolphustown to Albany, "for four bushels of Indian corn; a dreadful hazardous journey through the forest, with no road, and the snow very deep. They executed this mission, and returned in safety."

These slaves were generally faithful, good natured, and occasionally mischievous. It was the custom, in the first years of Canada, to place the ovens in the yard upon stakes, and they could be lifted off them. It is related that sometimes they would carry off slyly, the oven when filled with good things.

Sheriff Sherwood says: "In answer to your letter of yesterday, as regards slaves, I only recollect two or three which settled in the District of Johnstown; one in particular, named Cæsar Congo, owned by Captain Justus Sherwood, who came with his family in the same brigade of boats that my father and family did, and located about two miles above Prescott. They were the very first actual settlers. Well I remember Cæsar Congo, then a stout, strong young man, and who often took the late Justice Sherwood, of Toronto, and myself on his back to assist us along, while the boats were drawn up the rapids. Cæsar was sold to a half-pay officer named Bottom, who settled about six miles above Prescott, who, after a year's service, gave Cæsar his freedom. Cæsar, soon after married suitably, and by his industry obtained a snug little place in the town of Brockville, where he lived many years, and died.

Daniel Jones, father of Sir Daniel Jones, of Brockville, had a female slave, and there were a few others residing in the district of which I have no personal knowledge.

Squire Bleeker, of the Trent, had a slave called Ham. Abraham Cronk, of Sophiasburgh, bought a female slave from Mrs. Simpson, of Myers' Creek, for $300. After a time, she returned to Mrs. Simpson, with whom she lived till her death. This female had a daughter, who grew up to be an unusually "smart girl."

Nicholas Lazier had slaves. One, named Sal, was noted for her attachment to Methodism, and would go long distances to attend meetings. As a female slave, Black Betty was one of the first congregation, to which the first Methodist preacher in America preached at New York, so this woman was one of the first Methodists at the Bay, and in Upper Canada. John Cronk and she were the only Methodists in the Township for a long time.

Pryne, who lived a short distance above Bath, had two slaves. Col. Thompson also had some, and Lieut. McGinness, of Amherst Isle, likewise possessed them. Capt. Trumpour, of Adolphustown, had two negroes. Leavens, of Belleville, bought a female slave of Wallbridge, for $100. A son of hers was purchased by Captain McIntosh.

The Hon. Peter Russell, when Receiver-General, had a man and his wife as slaves, with their son and two daughters.

Samuel Sherwood, writing to a person at Kingston, from Thurlow, in Oct. 1793, says, "My negro boy, and Canadian boy have absented themselves last night without leave. I send Jim and two Indians in pursuit of them. I beg, if you can give any assistance, you will do me that service. McLean's black woman is my boy's mother, he may call to see her."

We have before us the copy of an assignment made in 1824, by Eli Keeler, of Haldimand, Newcastle, to William Bell, of Thurlow, of a Mulatto boy, Tom, in which it is set forth, that the said boy has time unexpired to serve as the child of a female slave, namely, ten years, from the 29th Feb. 1824, according to the laws of the Province; for the sum of $75. Probably, this was the last slave in Canada whose service closed, 1835.

There are, at the present time, a good many of the descendants of the early Canadian slaves. Some of them have done badly, others again have made themselves respectable and happy. The Mink family are descended from an old slave that belonged to William Herkimer.

When made free, they, in many instances, preferred to remain in connection with their old masters, and even to this day, their children manifest a predilection for the name of their father's master. In and about Belleville, may yet be found such as spoken of. Most, or all of these are descendants of "Black Bess" who, at different times, was in possession of the Wallbridge's, Leaven's, and McLellan.

In the *Ottawa Citizen* of 1867, appeared the following:

A BRITISH SLAVE—An old negro appeared at the Court of Assize yesterday, in a case of Morris vs. Hennerson. He is 101 years of age, and was formerly a slave in Upper Canada, before the abolition of slavery in the British possessions. He fought through the American war in 1812, on the side of the British; was at the battles of Chippewa and Lundy's Lane, and was wounded at Sacket's Harbour. He is in full possession of all his faculties. He was born in New York State in 1766, and was the slave of a U. E. Loyalist, who brought him to Canada. He was brought to this city to prove the death of a person in 1803, and another in 1804.

It would seem odd enough at the present day to see the following advertisements in a Canadian journal. This appeared in the *Gazette*, Newark:

"FOR SALE.—A negro slave, 18 years of age, stout and healthy, has had the small pox, and is capable of service, either in house or out door. The terms will be made easy to the purchaser; and cash or new lands received in payment. Enquire of the Printer.

"Niagara, November 28th, 1802."

"INDIAN SLAVE.—All persons are forbidden harboring, employing, or concealing my Indian slave, called Sal, as I am determined to prosecute any offender, to the utmost extremity of the law; and persons who may suffer her to remain on their premises for the space of half an hour, without my written consent, will be taken as offending, and dealt with according to law.

(Signed) CHARLES FIELDS.

Niagara, August 28th, 1802."

"FOR SALE—The negro man and woman, the property of Mrs. (widow) Clement. They have been bred to the business of a farm; will be sold on highly advantageous terms, for cash or lands. Apply to Mrs. Clement. Niagara, January 9th, 1802."

We have seen that the record of Upper Canada with respect to the subject of human bondage is particularly bright and honorable. This Province, in its very infancy, took the lead in severing the fetters which a dark and penurious age had rivetted upon the bodies of the African. This blackest curse of the world, which the power of England assisted to create, and which her offspring, the United States, continued to perpetuate for so many years, was put aside by the young Province at the first; while, but a few years later, a Canadian Judge, of Lower Canada, declared slavery to be inconsistent with the laws of Canada. These are facts of which every Canadian may well be proud. It was no "military necessity" which caused the abolition of slavery in Canada. It was a question of right, which the Canadian Parliament experienced no difficulty in solving. How grand the spectacle! How noble the conduct, setting an example to the world! In striking contrast, behold the United States. Flaunting their flag of liberty before the gaze of the world, they cried "All men are born free and equal, with the right to pursue that course which will lead to happiness;" yet notwithstanding these principles, enunciated with so much boldness, and, year after year, proclaimed by wordy fourth of July orators; they continued, not only to hold slaves, but made the bonds tighter until oceans of blood had been shed, and the Union was almost destroyed—when it could not be saved with slavery, as Lincoln had declared he would wish to save it; when it became necessary to strike a blow, which the northern legions had been unable to deal the Southern Confederacy, then, and not until then, were the slaves declared to be free. Lincoln said he would save the Union with slavery, if he could, failing this, then he would enlist the African slave to assist in saving the Union, by giving them liberty. The Southern blacks owe their liberty to-day, to the almost superhuman courage of the people with whom they lived, who held them in bondage, not, it is true, because their masters wished to liberate them; but because they were unable to successfully combat the perfect flood of men that was poured against their northern border and which infested their sea-board with an unbroken circle of armed vessels, shutting them out from all means of carrying on the unequal combat. It was this heroic attitude that made it necessary for

Lincoln to issue the famous proclamation. Let the freedman thank the exigency which made necessary the step which broke the back of the Confederacy, and thereby gave efficiency to the proclamation. It cannot be doubted that the great body of abolitionists were from the commencement of the war, anxious to secure the abolition of slavery; but they were impotent, their councils to the President were unheeded, their desires disregarded. The great mass of the Northerners had no sympathy with the poor slave, they only cared for the Union; and many of them were even dissatisfied that Lincoln should resort to the plan of freeing them in order to save the Union. It is abundantly easy, now to declare that, from the first the Washington Government was determined to abolish slavery—that, from the first, it was a war for, and against the life of that institution; but reading the events of the war, carefully scanning each page of its history, examining each line, studying every word; looking with an unbiassed eye upon the whole gigantic drama, it is submitted there is no reason for believing that the *nation* desired to free the slave at all; but, always excepting the Abolitionist, submitted to the necessity of setting the negro free, rather than sacrifice the Union, or, rather than be conquered by the South.

All honor then, to the U. E. Loyalists, in Parliament assembled, at the young capital of Newark—the representatives of the devoted band of refugees, who had been made such by rebels, who pretended to fight for "liberty," who placed on record their interpretation of the word Freedom; that it meant not liberty to a certain class; but to all, irrespective of color. All honor to the noble Judge, who had the probity and moral courage to enunciate a doctrine that at once made every supposed slave in Lower Canada conscious of being a free man. This noble beginning in the Canadas was followed by events no less interesting. They became the asylum of the slave, who were not only sought after by their Southern masters, but who were chased to the very borders by Northerners themselves.

CHAPTER LXVI.

CONTENTS.—Returns to the Pioneer—Bay Region—Garden of Canada—Clogs—False views of settlers—Result—New blood—Good example—Anecdote—The "Family Compact"—Partiality—Origin of the *Compact*—Their conduct—The evil they did—A proposed Canadian Aristocracy—What it would have led to—What may come—"Peter Funks."

THE OBSTACLES TO ADVANCEMENT.

In the section devoted to the first years of Upper Canada there has much been said having reference to the growth and prosperity of the Province, and advance of civilization, but something remains to be told which requires particular notice, and without which our sketch would not be complete.

The privations endured, and hardships overcome by the pioneers, tended to make them careful and prudent, and no doubt led to the more permanent prosperity of their children. As years wore away, comforts began to reward their toil and patience. Acre after acre was brought under cultivation; the log house received an addition, not large, but so as to supply a second room, which a growing family of boys and girls seriously demanded. Stock began to accumulate, and the future brightened up before them. In considering the rate and degree of advancement, it must be remembered that many of the first settlers were disbanded soldiers, and understood as little about agriculture as about clearing the land. "Though in most instances, a man of intelligence, the U. E. Loyalist introduced but a primitive system of agriculture; and the facilities of acquiring lands in the western part of the Province, has in a measure prevented that admixture among them of the more scientific and educated agriculturist from the old countries, which has helped to improve other parts of Canada. It has been only of late years, and since the general establishment of agricultural societies, that the real capacities of the Midland District has begun to be developed, and improvements introduced, which have resulted in making, even in the neighbourhood of Kingston, where the soil was looked upon as comparatively unproductive, some of the best and handsomest farms that can be seen in the Province."—(Cooper).

The region about the Bay because of its central position, received the name of Midland District. This district embraced, and at the beginning of the present century was regarded as the most important and influential part of Canada. But times have changed. Upper Canada has grown to be the largest and wealthiest province in British America, and although improvements around the Bay have continued to increase, yet westward the bulk of the immigrants have found a home, so that this section no longer holds so important a position. Nevertheless, as in former years, so now, the Bay country may be regarded as the garden of Western Canada. Long since the wilderness has become a fruitful field, and the fertile land has returned to the toiler a full reward. To the tourist passing along the Bay the appearance of the lands is exceedingly beautiful, especially in the days of summer; in June when all things are clothed in the richest green, and some weeks later when the golden hues of harvest have gathered over the fields of grain. The substantial residences of the farmers tell of prosperity and advancement. The old log house around which clustered so many associations, made dear by the circumstances of pioneer life, has been superseded by the more pretending frame building, and this again has been removed to be followed by elegant, and often stately edifices. The work of improvement and of beautifying has gone on from year to year, and now the inhabitants of the Bay are in most cases living in affluence. But while we mark the advancement, it must not be forgotten that it ought to have been greater. While we give all credit to the soldier farmer, for achieving so much, it must be related that there were certain land-holders who were as clogs to the wheel of progress, who displayed not that enterprize, at an early day, which they ought to have done. Had the greedy few who hoarded up land, and grasped for more, and still more; who stood ready to buy up the land of every unfortunate one compelled to sell—had such made themselves acquainted with the improvements in the agriculture of the day; had they, instead of leaving the hard workers to make roads across their lands, opened them up and provided a passible way; had they endeavored to make their land productive, and by example to show the struggling farmers a better way, and how to increase and advance; then, instead of merely the prosperity which now exists, there would have been great wealth. The broad acres are old enough, the landscape charming enough, the ground productive enough, and had the proper spirit been abroad among the class mentioned, those who aspired to be landed aristocrats then, the Bay Quinté might have presented, not alone a beauty rivaling that of the Hudson, but also the palatial mansions which adorn its shores. No more suitable spot in the wide world can be found for ornamental residences, and it is to be hoped that many with capital and taste, will very shortly proceed to set examples, for the wealthy farmers in some degree, to imitate. It may be said it were better the farmers and their children should have humble ideas, and the fact may be adduced that not a few of the descendants of the first settlers have, by their excesses in dress, and by trying to imitate the habits of the dwellers of towns and cities, laid the foundation of their ruin, by getting into the books of the merchant, and ultimately becoming helpless in his hands, so that the fathers heritage passed away to the stranger. But it is forgotten that such was principally the case with those who, suddenly becoming well to do, thought, if they desired to associate with the aristocracy, they must dress in finer clothing, and have clean hands; that their daughters must cease spinning, and the wife no longer do housework, that it was a disgrace to be seen working. It was such feelings and views which creeping in, paved the way for the downfall of many a one, who had begun to get on in the world; whereas, had gentlemen by birth and education, and there were such among the first settlers, given their time to actual improvement, had shewn that they considered it honorable to work with their hands. Had they carried their refinement into the more rural parts and shewn that agriculture and gentility may go together, and that education is as important for the agriculturist as for any other, both in enabling him to till the soil with success, and in providing him with those superior means of enjoyment which a wise Providence desires us to possess, a most valuable service would have been rendered. It was because the farmer thought he must dress as they did in the city, in order to associate with them, and that labor was not honorable, that ruin came to many a household, and the names of the first owner of farms are not now there; who laid low the forest in the infancy of the country. There is no forgetfulness that those blamed had once been wealthy and occupied high positions in the old colonies, and owned broad acres. It was perhaps natural that such persons, exiled in the wilderness, and struggling with the stern realities of their existence, should aim to regain a position of similar power and affluence, and were determined that, although they might not see the return of those independent days, their children should; so they continued to bend every energy to secure it. But alas! how rarely was the dream realized! How few of the limited number who first ruled the country—how few of the Family Compact are now in the higher circle of independence.

Respecting the more common settler, it was to be expected that now and then one would fail to advance—would fall behind in the onward march of the country. The wonder is great that so few of the old soldiers made shipwreck of the liberal grants bestowed by a motherly government. "The sons of some of those men who have hewn out a home in the primitive forest, have, in some cases, through bad management or bad conduct, suffered their possessions to pass to the stranger: the speculating merchant has grasped their all under a mortgage, and indolence or dissipation has completed the ruin."—(Cooper). "These evils, however, are rapidly curing themselves or producing an equivalent or greater amount of good—the idle and shiftless sells out to the practical and industrious farmer, who introduces among his neighbours the latest improvements in agricultural skill, and implements of husbandry; new systems of drainage, new stock, or improved breeds occupy the attention and employ the capital of the father of a family, whilst his wife and daughters, though well able to compete with the gayest and grandest, readily forego, when necessary, the imported and costly silks sported by the family of a less enterprising neighbour, and set an example of neatness, taste and appropriateness, in attire."

Cooper, in his essay, relates the following: He says, "The ideas of enterprize and modern progress entertained by some, may be illustrated by the following anecdote: When a new road was proposed leading through some of the best portions of the counties (of Frontenac, Lennox and Addington), opening up others, and affording many and great advantages, the benefits of which in short were apparent to all, and the only question involved was how to raise the money, a very wealthy landholder, who had amassed his thousands in the City of Kingston, and part of whose possessions lay on the route, replied to an application to take stock, that the effect of the road would be to enable people to steal his timber, and he declined to subscribe! It is presumed that railroads and electric telegraphs were not in fashion when this gentleman made his money." It was a feeling indulged by many similar to what this person had, that from the first, assisted to retard the judicious development of the young country.

Reference has been made to the "Family Compact." In speaking of Bishop Strachan, the statement is made that he was honest in his convictions that Church and State would best serve the interest of Canada, that in the uneducated state of the people,

Government should reside altogether or principally in the hands of the Governor and Executive Council. But while the honesty of the late Bishop is thus freely admitted, it must at the same time be acknowledged that those in authority were not disinterested dispensers of the good things which always exist in connection with a Government; and which particularly were provided for the loyalist settlers of Upper Canada by the British Government. For instance, it is averred by McMullen, and sharply reiterated by Gourlay, that "the provisions, clothing, and farming utensils, granted by the British Government for the benefit of the poor loyalists, were in many cases handed over to favorites, in others allowed to become useless from negligence in the public stores."

It was not alone provisions, clothing, and farming utensils that were enjoyed by the favorites. Lands—choice lands, were to be had by them, by the choosing. Settlements in Upper Canada commenced at several points, in each settlement were a few leading men, half-pay officers, or those who had held important positions during the Revolutionary war, with a good sprinkling of personal friends and relatives. At the capital, those were in excess. These leading men throughout the Province were in the most cases closely united by consanguinity and marriage; and soon became even more closely identified in interest—forming a strong political body, which derived its life-blood from the Executive. Its members surrounded the gubernatorial throne, and had the ear of the Governor, they formed his Councillors, and managed to become his friends; and as such secured abundantly of the bounties. It was not enough that large blocks of land should be held in reserve for the Crown, the Clergy, and for the Indians, which last was right; but choice bits of land were granted to members of this strong family, compacted together, to help one another, and the land was left uncultivated, unimproved, until the energies of the pioneers around had made it more valuable.

With the departure of Simcoe commenced the manipulations of this *family*. That Governor had invited by proclamation, persons from the United States, who might wish to become Canadians, and promised them grants of land. But he was re-called, and his promises were not attended to, although many came to the Province on their strength. Government ignored them, and it is stated, with abundant show of plausibility, that the reason was; that the growing family might have the more land to choose from, and to leave for their children; and with some, that they might live in

England upon the rents derived from Canada, and so "men of capital and enterprise, who had come into the Province furnished with cattle and implements to commence the settlement of townships," were disappointed. Some of these persons, who desired to live under the British flag, returned to the States to become truly republicans, others remained to form an element in the party which was in time to rise in opposition to the Family Compact. Such, in brief was the origin of the *Family Compact.* They aspired not alone, to possess the best tracts of land; but to fill every post of honor and emolument, to hold the reins of Government exclusively, and to constitute a select circle of nobility, to act the part of Lords over vassals; and to this end desired to possess extensive lands upon which, and around which should grow the belongings to estated gentlemen. When eight schools were granted certain sums of money, and the teachers were nominated by the Governor, generally half-pay officers. For a long time they had everything pretty much their own way. If any dissented from them, he was accused of disloyalty. Did an honest farmer question their honesty, he was pointed out as one to be suspected—as seditious, and as one of the King's enemies, against whom it was thought necessary to legislate. Nor did the House of Assembly, in any respect, for a long time, interfere with the growth and prosperity of the Family Compact, for, generally speaking, a member of the *family* managed to get elected. The charge is not made that all of the members of the early Parliaments were of the Compact; but they were more or less under their influence.

A history of the Family Compact, would be a history of the political life of Canada for many years, including the rebellion of 1837-8. The attempt has not been made to cast unnecessary reproach upon the old tory party of Upper Canada. As one brought up a conservative, the writer is free to admit all mistakes committed by the party in early times—to acknowledge that too much exclusiveness existed among those, forming the leaders of the party, and occasionally a disregard of justice. And it is freely admitted, that great mistakes were made by them, mistakes from the effects of which the country has not yet recovered. But then, they were but mistakes, and who does not make them.

It may, then, be said, that in some respects the Family Compact retarded the advance of civilization. An aristocracy, or nobility cannot thrive in a new country and will certainly fail, and in its efforts to live be a drawback on improvements.

In the debate in the Imperial Parliament upon the constitution of Canada, Mr. Pitt expresses his desire to have established in Canada, an hereditary nobility. While never endorsing the extreme views of Gourlay, it is thought he spake the truth when he said that "nothing could have so exposed the absurdity, as actual trial and consequent ridicule. By this day we should have witnessed many a pleasant farce. We should have seen, perhaps, the Duke of Ontario leading in a cart of hay, my Lord Erie pitching; and Sir Peter Superior, making the rick; or perhaps, his Grace might now have been figuring as a petty-fogging lawyer, his Lordship as a pedlar, and, Sir Knight, as a poor parson, starving on 5,000 acres of Clergy Reserves."

If we allowed ourselves to speak of the future of our country, with respect to this question, we should hesitate to say that the idea of Pitt cannot be carried out. The repulsiveness of Republicanism is to Canadians so great that we almost entertain the belief that our Dominion may ultimately develope into a *nation* with a constitutional monarchy, with all its surroundings. It would certainly be infinitely preferable to the "Model Republic."

In strong contrast to the Family Compact, yet likewise obstructionists in the work of advancement, we now mention another class.

We have said that not a few came to Canada from the States to trade with the Canadians, to do work, and that some took up lands, and that of all these a good many became true subjects of the realm, showing their attachment by taking up arms in 1812. But while this fact is recognized, it cannot be forgotten, that Canada was often, is even to-day, plagued with a certain class, styled oftentimes speculators; but who are in reality of the Peter Funk order. The class to whom reference is made, is recognized by the honest Americans themselves. The *New York Tribune*, after the close of the Southern war, in speaking of the South, says thus: "We hear that many of the blacks, thoroughly distrusting their old masters, place all confidence in the Yankees, who have recently come among them, and will work for these on almost any terms. We regret this; for while many of these Yankees will justify their confidence, others will grossly abuse it. New England produces many of the best specimens of the human race, and along with these, some of the very meanest beings that ever stood on two legs—cunning, rapacious, hypocritical, ever ready to skin a flint with a borrowed knife, and make (for others) soup out of the peelings. This class soon became too well known at home—"run out," as the phrase is —when they wandered all over the earth, snuffling and swindling, to the injury of the land that bore them and cast them out. Now let it generally be presumed by the ignorant blacks of the South, that a Yankee, because a Yankee, is necessarily their friend, and this unclean brood will overspread the South like locusts, starting schools and prayer-meetings at every cross-road, getting hold of abandoned or confiscated plantations, and hiring laborers right and left, cutting timber here, frying out tar and turpentine there, and growing corn, cotton, rice, and sugar, which they will have sold at the earliest day and run away with the proceeds, leaving the negroes in rags and foodless, with winter just coming on."

It is unnecessary to say, that civilization was never much advanced by this class, many specimens of which, time after time, have visited Canada.

CHAPTER LXVII.

CONTENTS—Agriculture—Natural Products—Rice—Ginseng—Orchards—Plows—Reaping—Flax—Legislation—Agricultural Society organized by Simcoe—A Snuff Box—Fogies—Silver—Want of help—Midland District taking the lead—Societies—Legislative help—Prince Edward—Pearl Ashes—Factories—Tanneries—Breweries, Carding Machines—Paper—Lumber—First vehicles—Sleighs— Waggons— Home-made —Roads—First Public Conveyances—Stages—Fare—Building Greater—Sawing Mills introduced by the Dutch—First Brick Building—Myers' House—Its past history—Furniture from Albany — Currency — Paper Money—Banks — First Merchants—Barter—Pedlars—On the Bay.

AGRICULTURAL MATTERS—PRODUCTS.

While the dense forest everywhere yet covered the earth, the shores of the Bay yielded some natural productions. The wild plum was plentiful in some places; a fruit which, although in its natural state somewhat sour, has, under cultivation, much improved in size as well as quality; and constitutes to this day a valuable luxury; at the same time, it is exceedingly healthy. In some places also, at the proper seasons, was the delicious cranberries. These were often brought by the Indians, and exchanged for some article of the settlers. In some parts of the Bay, there grew wild rice, which was much prized by the Indians, and which was often used by the settlers. It is spoken of as an excellent article of diet, and when boiled with meat, very tasty as well. The grain is much smaller than the imported article; not unfrequently, the Indians would collect the grain and sell it to the settlers.

In the year 1716, a Jesuit discovered in the forests of Canada, the Ginseng plant, which grew also in China, where it was in much demand because of certain supposed virtues to which, however, it rightly has no claim. It is of the *genus Panax*. It "became a means of enriching the colony for a time, by its exportation to China. A pound weight of it worth two francs at Quebec, sold at Canton for twenty-five francs. Its price ultimately rose to eighty francs per pound. One year, there was sent thither, ginseng yielding a return of 500,000 francs. The high price it obtained set everybody at work to find it. The plant was not in proper condition till August or September; but with purblind avidity, the seekers gathered it in May. The fresh plants ought to have been slowly dried in the shade; the gatherers, anxious to get returns, dried them in ovens. They then became worthless in Chinese estimation; and the trade in it ceased almost as suddenly as it began." —(Garneau.) But, according to other authority, the trouble consisted in the actual destruction of the plant, from gathering it too early in the season, whereby the plant was killed, which seems a more likely thing. Some of the settlers of the Bay had knowledge of the value of the plant in Chinese estimation, as the following letter will show. It is addressed to Mr. Wm. Bell, of Thurlow, who was subsequently known as Col. Bell. "Fredericksburgh, 16th July, 1799. Sir—I have taken the liberty of enclosing to you an advertisement, as you will see—Respecting Ginseng roots, having in view to get all I can—and, thinking the Indians would be likely to collect considerable of a quantity, will thank you to acquaint them of it, or any of the white people you may see; and set up the advertisement in the most publick place about you.—And oblige, Your very humble servant, Eben'r Washburn."

Another letter, dated Aug. 27, 1799, says "I have to acknowledge the attention you have paid to mine of prior date, in respect of Ginseng. I will thank you to keep the refusal of the 500 lbs. you mention, if possible, and collect more if you can." Mr. Washburn says that he is about to set out for Montreal; and it was, most likely, to see what market he could make of the article in question.

One of the first considerations, after the settler had attained comparative comfort, at least secured what was requisite for life, was the planting of fruit trees. No doubt, the thoughts often reverted back to the old orchards which had been left behind, and although the pioneer, in the afternoon of life, could not expect to derive any personal return for planting orchards, he was anxious to leave them to his children. This same spirit—this regard for offspring, constituted a marked feature in the U. E. Loyalists. The earliest reference to apple trees we find, is in a letter, dated "Sydney, 22rd July, 1791," from John Ferguson, to William Bell, Kingston, requesting the latter to bring some to Sidney.

The implements of husbandry, like the utensils for household use, were, for a considerable time, of the rudest description. Among the articles granted by government, were but few to use in the tilling of land and the reaping of crops. Here and there was one who had come at a later date, who had fetched with them articles more essential for farm use; but the great majority had not such things as hoes, plows, pitch-forks, seythes, &c. Many of these were made by the settlers, and were of the rudest order, although generally strong enough, and therefore cumbersome enough. It was many years before these home-made implements were substituted by others made abroad. Gourlay informs us, writing, 1817, that most of the farmers made their own plows and harrows. The iron of the plow costing from nine to twelve dollars.

As the thickly covered ground, with stumps, materially interfered with the sowing of grain; so with gathering the products. For several years, they had only in use the sickle; but, in time, the Yankee pedlar, brought in the scythe, which ultimately took the place of the sickle.

It has been observed, in connection with the "clothing" of the early settlers, that they turned their attention to the growing of flax, and that it was made to afford comfortable and durable habiliments for both sexes. There was, as well, early attention given to the cultivation of hemp," "in pursuance of two several addresses of the House of Commons." In 1804, £1,000 was granted, and Commissioners appointed, to carry into effect the object thereof, cultivation and exportation. The following year, £45 was granted for the purchase of hemp seed. Another Act was passed in 1808, to encourage its cultivation and exportation. Again, there was legislation in 1810, and in 1812, when £1,000 was granted for the purchase, sale and exportation of hemp, purchase of seed, and for bounties. In 1822, it was enacted that £300 be appropriated to purchase machinery for dressing hemp, that the machinery should be imported free, the place for erection to be selected by the Governor, £50 was to be applied annually to keep it in repair. But, notwithstanding all this legislation, and substantial encouragement, the cultivation of hemp did not succeed. The object seems to have been to supply hemp for the British market, which derived it from Russia. But labor being cheaper in that country than in Canada, there was no chance for success. Gourlay says "This absurdity we must not wholly rest on the shoulders of the simple Canadians. They were simple indeed, to be voting away the public money; but it was a patriotic measure, and blindness may be allowable in matters so elevated and pure. No doubt they were spurred on by our home ministers, who should have known better. The failure produced more beneficial effects than would have waited on success."

Gov. Simcoe, who had the interest of the Province so much at heart, gave his patronage to, if indeed he did not inspire the organization of the first Agricultural Society, at Newark. Col. Clark, of Dalhousie says "I have a perfect remembrance of the first Agricultural Society patronized by Governor Simcoe, who subscribed his ten guineas a year cheerfully. My father was a member, and the monthly dinners were given by the members during the season, with the great silver snuff-box ornamented with the horn of plenty on its lid." The Col. remarks that this snuff-box was the property of the society, and was taken care of by the one who was next to furnish the dinner; and goes on to lament that it is lost, hoping it may be found, "that it may remain as an heir-loom to tell posterity at what an early period the progress of Agriculture was followed up and which has led to its present high state of perfection. Thus we see that in Niagara District, at the very commencement of the Government of Upper Canada, attention was given, even by the Governor, to agricultural matters. Although the settlers upon the Niagara frontier, established agricultural societies at an earlier date than any found in the Midland Districts, it may be presumed that it was in a great measure due to the impetus given to the settlement by the presence of the seat of Government, and the influence exerted by the Governor. And, although steps may not have been taken to secure their establishment along the Bay Quinté, yet, even so early as the beginning of the last decade of the last century, individuals were to be found who sought to introduce improvements in agriculture, and everything that would advance the art. At the same time it must be admitted that a vast number were content to follow in the footsteps of their fathers so long as food and enough were yielded by the soil. The land was plentiful, and productive. The course of events was even as a steady stream. The old men satisfied with the abundance of to-day, and drawing a contrast between the present and the past, when starvation was at the door, and in the cupboard, were quite content with the primitive system of agriculture, which his soldier father had adopted. He saw no other mode of tilling the soil, and with no reason sought not a change, so no innovations by scientific agriculturalists disturbed the quiet repose of many of the steady going plodders. Their sons rarely went abroad to learn the ways of others; and often what did come to their ears was regarded with great suspicion. They wanted no new-fangled notions. Hence, the farms were not fully cultivated for many a day, parts remaining in a waste state for want of drain. But the establishment of agricultural associations and the occasional coming of a new man upon an old farm gradually, and frequently very gradually, dispelled the old man's ideas.

The townships most contiguous to the town of Kingston, naturally were the first to experience prosperity, and gradually the adjacent townships also became productive, and means were created to transport the produce to the market.

We are told by Mrs. P——, daughter of John Ham, of Ernesttown, now upwards of seventy, that she remembers one occasion, about the beginning of the present century, that her father coming from Kingston, after selling produce, had a bag of silver dollars, as much as she could lift—$900. By this we learn that his farm was productive, his labor well directed, and that hard cash was paid for his produce by the Kingston merchants. It shows, moreover, that this was over and above the cost of what was required of merchandise by him for his family using.

One serious drawback with the farmers often was the want of assistants. If a farmer had not a son old enough to help, he was in great trouble oftentimes to secure the necessary help. Frenchmen were frequently employed, yet they could not be fully depended upon to remain during the whole season. At harvest time, when large wages would be offered, the hired man would often, without hesitation, leave his employer to go to another who would give for a while, larger wages. In the absence of men, the wife and daughters took hold of the fork, cradle, and rake.

If we may credit the statements of writers who had passed through Canada in the beginning of the present century, the Midland District took the lead in agricultural and social progress. Mr.

Talbot, whose opinion of the Canadians, as to their intelligence, education, morals, and religion, was anything but flattering, made a pedestrian tour from the west to Montreal, in 1823. He says of the inhabitants of Sidney, Thurlow, and Richmond, that they possessed more wealth than any other people in the Province. But Mr. Talbot passed only along the Kingston Road by Napanee, and saw not the townships of the lower part of the bay, or he would have seen even a more advanced state of prosperity and agricultural wealth.

The first formation of agricultural societies was initiated by an Act of Parliament, passed March 6, 1830. The object of this Act was to give encouragement to organize associations in the several districts, "For the purpose of importing live stock, grain, grass, seeds, useful implements, or whatever else might conduce to the improvement of agriculture." It was enacted that each society, having had subscribed to it £50, should, upon petitioning the Governor, receive the sum of £100. This Act was to remain in force four years.

This Act was promptly responded to by the inhabitant of the Midland District. So early as the 27th April following, a meeting of the inhabitants of the district was held at the Court House, Kingston, H. C. Thompson, Esq., Chairman, and H. Smyth, Esq., Secretary, and "A form of a constitution for an Agricultural Society was read and submitted to the meeting for approval. The following day, the adjourned meeting adopted a constitution for the Midland District Agricultural Society. The officers were to be a President, five Vice-Presidents, thirty Directors, a Treasurer, and a Secretary —One Vice-President, and six Directors to be elected from each of the five counties in the district. John McCaulay, Esq., was elected President; David J. Smith, Esq., Treasurer, and H. C. Thompson, Esq., Secretary of the Society. It was "*Resolved*" by the Society, "that Isaac Fraser, Esq., of Addington; Allan McPherson, Esq., of Lennox; Asa Worden, Esq., of Prince Edward; and William Bell, Esq., of Hastings, be requested to call meetings in their respective counties," and make returns as to whom had been elected for Vice-Presidents and Directors. The Vice-President for the County of Frontenac was John Marks, Esq.

In the *Hallowell Free Press* of May 31, 1831, we find that the "Annual Meeting of the Prince Edward Agricultural Association was held at Striker's Inn, in Hallowell, on the 26th instant. The following officers were chosen for the following year:—Stephen Miles,

President; James Colter, William Cunningham, and Paul Clapp, Vice-Presidents; S. P. McPherson, Secretary; B. Dougall, Assistant Secretary; David Smith, Treasurer." The Government having offered a bounty of £100 to every society which could raise £50; the Prince Edward Society raised the necessary amount. But judging from a communication, which subsequently appeared in the *Press*, the townships of Hallowell and Hillier, raised the most of the amount, £46; Marysburgh, Sophiasburgh, and Ameliasburgh, paying only £4.

In a General Report of Midland District, 1817, it is stated that "the assess roll gives about 3,600 horses above two years; 100 oxen above four years; 6,185 milch cows; 1,654 head of young cattle above two years."

The first great obstacle to agriculture in Upper Canada was the thickly standing trees, many of which were large and hard in substance. For the first years, with every one, destruction of the trees was the only consideration, not even the ashes were thought of. But after a time, their value for the manufacture of pot and pearl ashes was recognized. In July, 1801, an Act was passed to appoint Inspectors of flour, and pot and pearl ashes, in order to establish the credit of those articles in foreign markets, the fee for examining to be threepence per barrel of flour, and one shilling for every cask of pot ash.

The following appears in the *Kingston Gazette*, April 19, 1817, after stating that "a Pearl and Pot Barley Factory is to be established in Ernesttown. It is said this is the first establishment of the kind we recollect to have heard of in Upper Canada, we have seen some of the barley, and think it equal to that imported. Such domestic manufactories ought to be encouraged by the community."

AGRICULTURE—FACTORIES—MERCHANTS.

The first Brewery and Distillery established in Upper Canada, was built by John Finkle, of Ernesttown, on his own place. He also kept, for many years the only tavern between Kingston and York. Mr. Finkle also built the first Masonic Lodge of Upper Canada, at his own expense, upon the town plot of Fredericksburgh.

It is stated in Gourlay, that in 1817, there was in Kingston township "a machine for carding wool, at the rate of nine-pence per pound." In Ernesttown "there were two carding, and one fulling machines. One barley hulling mill, together with a blast furnace. Carding is nine-pence half-penny per pound, and fulling six-pence per yard." In Sophiasburgh there was one carding machine. In Hallowell, there was one carding, and one fulling machine. Thurlow had two carding machines, and two fulling mills. In the whole Midland District, there were twenty-four grist-mills and forty saw-mills.

John Morden, who came to the bay about 1790, "was a man well known in his day, being a manufacturer of general household goods, as chairs, spinning-wheels, flax-dressers, weaver's apparatus, and other things. In the house of mostly every descendant of a Quinté settler, may be found some ot his work, especially those who occupy the homesteads."

As an indication of the desire of Government to encourage home manufactures, we find that Parliament, in 1826, granted £125 as a premium to the first "who should set up a manufactory of paper," and bring it into successful operation.

The valuable timber that thickly covered the ground, was, at the first, indiscriminately destroyed, scarcely thinking of saving the ashes; but, in a few years, the majestic pine, oak, elm, and other trees of the forest were sought after by the lumber merchant. For many years, lumbering was carried on in the Bay Quinté, and rafted to Montreal, and was a source of no little profit.

The wilderness was trackless, and of course some time elapsed before vehicles of any kind could be used, except in winter, after the bays and rivers had frozen. Rude sleighs, made by inferior tools, were the first made. At first hand-sleighs; and then heavier ones, to be used with oxen and horses. But as the beasts of burden were scarce, there was but one here and there, who had occasion to make a vehicle of any kind, except what could be hauled by hand. The sleighs were often used in summer to haul in grain and hay from the field. Some constructed a sort of waggon by sawing a hard-wood tree, of suitable size across, making four pieces about a foot in length. Holes having been bored through the centre of the blocks, they constituted the wheels of the waggon. The axle-tree of hard-wood was then fashioned to suit the wheels, and in this way a rough, but serviceable vehicle was made, which proved of great use, especially in hauling grain and hay to the place of stacking. The account of one is given which would carry as much as 150 sheaves.

As years elapsed, and roads were cut and made passable, waggons were introduced. One of the first waggons brought into the Province was, it is said, by Jacob Cronk, of Sophiasburgh. It came from Duchess County, New York. The second one was brought by James Way. Possibly this is not true, but at least they were the first introduced into that township.

The first public conveyance by land between Kingston and Montreal, was made by Dickenson. He called on Judge Cartwright to consult him about opening a line of stage travel. Consequently, in 1808, a line was established. It ran all the year round, though not so regularly in summer as in winter. "Lumber gentlemen from Quebec traveled through by the stage."—(Finkle.)

It was not until the war of 1812, that a line of stages was commenced between Kingston and York. By an advertisement in the *Kingston Gazette*, it is learned that in June, 1817, "A stage was commenced running from Kingston to York, leaving Kingston every Monday morning at six o'clock, and York every Thursday morning, same hour." "Persons wishing for a passage will call at Mr. David Brown's Inn, Kingston, where the stage-books will be kept. From twenty to twenty-eight pounds baggage will be allowed to each passenger, over this they must be charged for. All baggage sent by the stage will be forwarded with care, and delivered with punctuality, and all favors acknowledged by the public's humble servant. (Signed), Samuel Purdy, Kingston, January 23, 1817. N.B. Stage fare, eighteen dollars."

The same year, Lieutenant Hull, traveling in Canada, writes that there is a stage waggon from Montreal to Prescott, which carries the mail. From thence to Kingston the mail is carried on horseback. The stage waggon, he remarks, is the roughest conveyance on either side of the Atlantic.

The first buildings were of logs, generally put up in their natural rough state; now and then, as the Government mill at Kingston, the logs were squared. There was only one way of procuring sawed lumber, and that was by the whip saw. But few of the settlers thought of spending the time and labor necessary to obtain what was not strictly necessary. Houses, barns, saw-mills, flouring-mills, even breweries and still-houses were all alike constructed of logs. Indeed, many a one had no barn for years; stacking his grain, and thrashing upon the ground, made smooth and hard. When, however, sawing-mills began to spring up here and there, sawed lumber became a more common article, and after several years, individuals, better off than others, began to put up framed buildings, both houses and barns, and so forth. Sawing-mills were introduced originally into America by the Dutch, and it was their descendants who introduced them into Canada. But it was slowly done. It required no little capital to procure even the small amount of machinery which was then used, and to have it brought so long a distance. Then, millwrights were not plentiful, and often inferior in skill. Indeed there was nothing at hand by which to erect sawing-mills, until after many years. In the meantime, the whip saw enabled them to construct something like a door for the house and log barn ; and rough sort of furniture was made for the house. But toward the close of the last century, sawing-mills became somewhat numerous. The demand for lumber was foreseen, and those who had a water privilege set about to get up a mill. Following the saw-mill came the grist-mill, which, though more needed than the former, because of its greater expense, was not built until a later period. It was about the first of 1800, that frame buildings began to appear in the first, second, and third townships particularly, to take the place of the log hut. Mr. George Finkle, of Ernesttown, says, his father Henry Finkle, who, during the war, had learned the use of carpenter's tools, in the Engineer Department, built, with his whip saw and cross-cut saw, the first frame house in the country. He also built the first school-house, and a dwelling house for the teacher on his own premises. Likewise, the first wharf along the bay.

We have made somewhat extensive enquiries, and believe we are correct in stating that the oldest brick building in Upper Canada is situated upon the brow of the hill at Belleville. We also entertain the belief that it was the first, certainly one of the very first brick buildings put up in the Province. It is known as Myers' House, having been built by Captain Myers about the year 1794. This quaint edifice, upon which the tooth of time is eating so peacefully, standing upon the brink of the hill was, when new, of most imposing appearance; and, no doubt, stood up grandly, overlooking the winding river, and the thickly set cedars at its base. The bricks were made in Sidney *at the Myers Place*, five miles east of Trenton. Captain Myers was a man of great hospitality, which was shared in by his estimable spouse, whose short stature and genial face is remembered by some yet living. They served visitors at the brick house always with an excellent board. Here, many a distinguished traveler between Kingston and York, Dr. Strachan among the number, found a welcome. Not less so was it with the farmers round about, who came long distances to get grists ground; all such were invited to the table and supplied with a bed until the grist was ground. The furniture for the house was procured at Albany.

In June, 1796, an Act was passed "for the better Regulation of certain Coins current in the Province;" and it was enacted that the British guinea, the Johannes of Portugal, the moidore of Portugal, the American eagle, the British crown, the British shilling, the Spanish milled dollar, the Spanish pistoreen, the French crown, and several other French pieces; the American dollar, should pass as legal tender at certain specified value.

The punishment for tendering "a counterfeit, knowingly," of any of the gold or silver coins of Great Britain, Portugal, the United States, Spain, or France, was to suffer one year's imprisonment, and be set in and upon the pillory for the space of one hour, in some conspicuous place, and upon a second conviction, he should be adjudged guilty of felony without benefit of clergy.

The first paper money issued in America, was by the Anglo-Americans in 1689, to pay the troops under Sir William Phipps, when he returned from the unsuccessful seige of Quebec. The value ranged from ten pounds to two shillings.

During the war of 1812, in 1813, an Act was passed "to facilitate the circulation within the Province, of Army Bills, issued by the authority of the Lower Province." It was to continue one year unless peace was declared.

The first Legislation in Upper Canada, with respect to banks, was in 1819, when the Bank of Kingston, or, as it was subsequently called Pretended Bank of Upper Canada, was incorporated; but, this was "forfeited by non-user," although the institution was in operation, under the title of "the President, Directors, and Company of the Bank of Upper Canada." Legislation was made in 1823, to settle the affairs of the "pretended bank." The commissioners were George Herkimer, Markland, John Kirby, and John Macaulay. Repeated Acts were necessary before the affairs of this company were fully settled.

In 1819, was also passed an Act to "form the Company of the Bank of Upper Canada." It was reserved for the assent of His Majesty, which was given and made known by proclamation in 1821. Among the names of those who petitioned for the Act of Incorporation, are those of Allan, Baldwin, Legge, Jackson, Ridout, Boulton, Robinson, Macaulay, Cameron, and Anderson. This bank, the failure of which so recently occurred, was, in its time, of great benefit to the Province, and it deserved a better fate.

A necessary attendant of civilization is a sufficient supply of such merchandize as is requisite to give comfort, and even luxuries.

The long distance of the first settlers of Upper Canada from the marts of commerce, with a barrier of forest, and the swift rapids of the St. Lawrence, kept out for many a day, many comforts, and all luxuries. But in time, persons engaged in the mercantile business, and articles of various kinds began to find their way into the wilderness-bound colony. The first merchants of the Province were engaged in the fur trade; but, as time passed away, they found customers among the settlers, who bought their produce, and, in return, brought to them goods.

Among the first, and the principal merchants of Upper Canada were Duncan, of Matilda; Cartwright, of Kingston; Hamilton, of Queenstown; and Robertson, of Sandwich. These gentlemen, we have seen, occupied conspicuous positions, and amassed no little wealth; unless we except Duncan, who removed. The Hon. Robert Hamilton, it is said, died, leaving an estate worth £200,000.

Colonel Clarke, of Dalhousie, speaks of his brothers Peter and James, who "turned merchants, having been supplied with an assortment of goods from Montreal. In 1790, they went into the Indian trade at Kingston, which had a great communication with the back lakes."

We also learn that Mr. Macaulay carried on business first at Carleton Island, and afterward at Kingston, with no little profit. One of the oldest settlers in Kingston was Joseph Forsyth. He became one of the first merchants in Kingston, and for many years conducted a lucrative business with the Indians and settlers. He "ever maintained the character of an upright and reputable merchant." He died 20th September, 1813, aged fifty-three.

A bartering trade commenced between the settlers in the township of Kingston, and the nearer townships, and some persons at Carleton Island; gradually the field of operation was transferred to Kingston. Many of the loyalists, who were constantly arriving, procured food and a few other things at these places.

In 1817, there were in the Township of Kingston "sixty-seven stores and shops, this includes the different denominations of shops kept by mechanics. In the whole of Midland District there were about eighty-eight merchants' shops: twenty-four store-houses. Mr. Gourlay says, at this time, that Kingston is the third place in the Canadas, Quebec and Montreal being first.

When want no longer rested upon the inhabitants, they began to look even for comforts and luxuries. They were supplied now and then with articles, both those essential to living, and those which may be called comforts, and luxuries, by itinerant merchants. These pedlars were generally from the States, and often managed to drive bargains in which the settler received not a fair return for the grain or other article he parted with. But some of the pedlars were honest, and ultimately became settlers and good loyal subjects. One of the first, probably the first, to visit the western extremity of the bay, was one Asa Walbridge, an old bachelor, somewhat eccentric, and withal shrewd, he not only turned an honest penny, but contributed very much to the welfare and comfort of the settlers. His head-quarters, when ashore, were at the mouth of Myers' Creek, where he was the first to erect a log house. It was he brought in many of the first fruit trees, which have rendered many of the old farms more valuable. He brought in the seeds from the States, and planted numbers here and there, often from motives of kindness alone. We have been told that all the old orchards in Prince Edward came from his planting. Some of the merchants in Kingston entrusted goods to local storekeepers by whom the settlers were also supplied with articles of different kinds.

Dr. Armstrong says, I ought not to omit the name of James Cummings, Esq., merchant, of the Port of Hallowell, now Picton. He was a man of sterling integrity, upright and just in all his dealings. He was greatly respected and esteemed, and died in the midst of his manhood, greatly lamented, about the year 1818. He was a younger brother of the late John Cummings, of Kingston.

CHAPTER LXVIII.

CONTENTS—Steam vessels—Crossing the Atlantic in 1791—First Steam Vessel—Hudson—The second on the St. Lawrence—First across the Atlantic—In Upper Canada—*Frontenac*—Built in Ernesttown—The Builders—Finkle's Point—Cost of Vessel—Dimensions—Launched—First Trip—Captain McKenzie—*Walk-in-the-Water*—*Queen Charlotte*—How Built—Upon Bay Quinté—Capt. Dennis—First year—Death of Dennis—Henry Gilderslieve—What he did—Other Steamboats—Canals—First in Upper Canada—Welland Canal—Desjardin—Rideau—Its object—Col. By—A proposed Canal—Railroads—The first in the world—Proposed Railway from Kingston to Toronto, 1846—In Prince Edward District—Increase of Population—Extract from Dr. Lillie—Comparison with the United States—Favorable to Canada—False Cries—The French—Midland District, 1818.

THE FIRST STEAM VESSELS—CANALS, RAILWAYS.

We have already, under "Traveling in early Times," spoken of the first vessels that floated upon the waters of the western world, and we design now to speak of those which advancing civilization brought, to a certain extent, to supersede the original boats used by the Indians and first European colonisers. At the present day Europe is brought into close relationship with us by the swiftly running steamer, while the two continents hold daily intercouse by means of the telegraph; yet, not a century ago, it required many months for the slow-sailing ship to traverse the breadth of the Atlantic. In 1789, mails with England was only twice a year. At the time Simcoe came to Canada, in 1791, there were only those merchant ships that made altogether eleven voyages in the year. "A Traveler," writes, that "regular packets across the Atlantic, first sailed in 1764. The Liverpool Packet Line began running in 1818."

The river Hudson, named after the navigator of that name, who ascended this splendid stream, called, by the native Indians, "The great River of Mountains," in 1609, has the honor of being the place whereon floated the first steamboat that existed in the world. The boat was launched in the year 1807, being named 'Clermont.' It was of 150 tons burden. The engine was procured from Birmingham. "Robert Fulton, of New York, though not the originator of steam power, was the first in America who directed it to the propelling of boats. Fulton, the pioneer in boats by steam, lived not long enough to see accomplished the grand end of propelling boats thus across the Atlantic. He died in 1815. The second steamboat built in America, was launched at Montreal, 3rd Nov., 1809, built by John Molson. It was called *Accommodation*, and plied between Montreal and Quebec. At the first trip it carried ten passengers from Montreal to Quebec, taking thirty-six hours. The whole city of Quebec came out to see her enter the harbor. The fare was eight dollars down, and nine up.

It is found stated that the first steamboat from America to England, was in 1819; and the first steamboat built in Great Britain was in 1812, by Henry Bell, of Glasgow. But the following is found in the Portland *Advertiser*:—"The first steamship which made the voyage, under steam throughout, across the Atlantic, was the *Royal William*, in 1833. This vessel was of 180 horse-power, and 1,000 tons burden, and built at a place called Three Rivers, on the St. Lawrence, in Canada. The voyage was made from Picton, Nova Scotia to Cowes, Isle of Wight."

The first steamboat on Lake Ontario, the *Frontenac*, was built upon the shores of the Bay, at Finkle's Point, Ernesttown, eighteen miles from Kingston, and within the corporation of Bath. She was commenced in October, 1815, and launched the following season. The three years of war had caused many changes in Upper Canada. On the whole, it may be said that the war materially benefitted the Province. After peace, things did not relapse into their former state. A spirit of enterprise was abroad, especially in the mercantile community. "The leading men of Kingston conceived the idea of forming a company to build a steamboat, to ply on Lake Ontario, and the navigable waters of the St. Lawrence. A company was consequently formed, composed of individuals belonging to Kingston, Niagara, Queenston, York, and Prescott. The shareholders of Kingston were Joseph Forsyth, Yeomans, Marsh, Lawrence Herkimer, John Kirby, Capt. Murney, William Mitchell, and, in fact, all of the principal men except the Cartwright family. Advertisements were issued for tenders to construct the boat. The advertisement was responded to by two parties; a Scotchman, by the name of Bruce, from Montreal, and Henry Teabout, from Sacket's Harbor. Bruce was several days at Kingston before the other person arrived, and he supposed he would get the contract. Mr. Finkle says Teabout came with a letter from Hooker and Crane to Johns and Finkle, informing them who Teabout was, and asking them to favor him with their influence in procuring the contract. The letter was shown to Mr. Kirby, of Kingston, who was one of the committee of the company. Mr. Kirby assured Finkle and Johns, that notwithstanding the prejudice which existed on account of the war, the tender of Teabout should receive every justice. No other tender being made, the committee met and decided, by a small majority, to accept Teabout's. All those who voted for Bruce "were either Scotch or of Scottish descent." Teabout having received the contract, at once, with Finkle, set about to find a place to build. After two day's examination of the coast, he selected Finkle's Point, in consequence of the gravelly nature of the shore, as thereby would be obviated the delay which frequently followed rains, where soils would not quickly dry. "The next consideration was to advance £5,000 to go to New York and procure a ship carpenter and other necessaries to commence operations. Accordingly, we (Johns and Finkle) became security, with the understanding that so soon as the boat should be so far advanced as to be considered worth the security, our bond would be returned. So satisfactorily did the work progress, that the bond was shortly handed to us by the Treasurer, who was William Mitchell. Here I will digress a short time. During the war of 1812, David Eckford, the Master ship-builder, of New York, was sent to Sacket's Harbour, to take charge of the ship building at that place, and brought with him his carpenters. Among them were three young men, Henry Teabout, James Chapman and William Smith. The last was born on Staten Island, the other two in New York. Teabout and Smith served their time with Eckford. Chapman was a block turner. At the close of the war, these three formed a co-partnership, and Teabout, in contracting for building the *Frontenac*, was acting for the company. Before building the steamboat, they had built for themselves at Sacket's Harbour, the *Kingston*, the only craft plying between Sacket's and Kingston, and a fine schooner for the Lake, called the *Woolsley*. Chapman was in charge of the *Kingston*, and was doing a more than ordinary profitable business. Bruce's friends wished to do something for him, and had him appointed, at a guinea a day, to inspect the timber (of the Frontenac). His study was to delay the building of the boat; there was a constant contest between him and Teabout."—(Finkle). The contract price of the wood work was £7,000. When the boat was almost ready for the machinery, the contractor's funds were expended. The engine cost £7,000. Before the vessel was completed, the cost reached nearly the sum of £20,000.

The Kingston *Gazette* informs us that "On Saturday, the 7th of September, 1816, the steamboat *Frontenac* was launched at the village of Ernesttown. A numerous concourse of people assembled on the occasion. But, in consequence of an approaching shower, a part of the spectators withdrew before the launch actually took place. The boat moved slowly from her place, and descended with majestic sweep into her proper element. The length of her keel is 150 feet; her deck, 170 feet; (the tonnage was about 700). Her proportions strike the eye very agreeably; and good judges have pronounced this to be the best piece of naval architecture of the kind yet produced in America. It reflects honor upon Messrs. Trebout and Chapman, the contractors, and their workmen; and also upon the proprietors, the greater part of whom are among the most respectable merchants and other inhabitants of the County of Frontenac, from which the name is derived. The machinery for this valuable boat was imported from England, and is said to be of an excellent structure. It is expected that she will be finished and ready for use in a few weeks. Steam navigation having succeeded to admiration in various rivers, the application of it to the waters of the Lakes is an interesting experiment. Every friend to public improvements must wish it all the success which is due to a spirit of useful enterprise." The *Gazette* adds: "A steamboat was lately launched at Sacket's Harbor. The opposite side of the Lake, which not long ago vied with each other in the building of ships of war, seem now to be equally emulous of commercial superiority." Gourlay says the boat at Sacket's Harbor was on a smaller scale, and less expensive. "She, the *Frontenac*, was estimated to cost £14,000; before she commenced her watery walk, her cost exceeded £20,000."—(Finkle). "The deck was 170 feet long and thirty-two feet wide, draws only eight feet when loaded. Two paddle-wheels, with about forty feet circumference; answers slowly to the helm."—(Howison).

The Kingston *Gazette*, of May 24, 1817, says, "Yesterday afternoon the steamboat left Mr. Kirby's wharf for the dock at Point Frederick. We are sorry to hear, that through some accident, the machinery of one of the wheels has been considerably damaged, notwithstanding which, however, she moved with majestic grandeur against a strong wind. We understand she has gone to the dock, it being a more convenient place for putting in a suction pipe." The same paper, of May 31, 1817, further says, "The steamboat *Frontenac*, after having completed the necessary work at the Naval Yard, left this port yesterday morning, for the purpose of taking in wood at the Bay Quinté. A fresh breeze was blowing into the harbor, against which she proceeded swiftly and steadily, to the admiration of a great number of spectators. We congratulate the managers and proprietors of this elegant boat, upon the prospects she affords of facilitating the navigation of Lake Ontario, by furnishing an expeditious and *certain mode* of conveyance to its various ports." "June 7th, 1817. The *Frontenac* left this port on Thursday (5th,) on her first trip for the head of the Lake." She was commanded by Capt. James McKenzie, of the Royal Navy, the first trip she made, who continued in command until she was no longer sea-worthy. The Purser was A. G. Petrie, of Belleville, now far advanced in years. The *Frontenac* made the trip up and down the Lake and River, to Prescott, once a week. Whether she went further west than York, at first, is uncertain. Capt. Jas. McKenzie "came to Canada with the first division of the Royal Navy, sent from England to serve on the Lakes during the war of 1812. At the conclusion of the war, he returned to England, and was placed on half pay; but his active habits led him to consider and study the powers of the steam engine, and he soon became acquainted with its complicated machinery. In 1816, he returned to Kingston, and assisted in fitting up the *Frontenac*, which he commanded till she was worn out. Since, he has commanded the *Alciope* on this Lake, and at the time of his death, (27th August, 1832, aged 50), was engaged in the construction of two other steamboats; one at the head of the Lake, and one at Lake Simcoe; and was, on most occasions, consulted respecting the management of steamboats, so that he may justly be called the father of steam navigation in Upper Canada—his death may be considered a great loss to society and to the country."

The first steamboat built to ply on Lake Erie was "Walk-in-the-Water," built at Buffalo at the same time the "Frontenac" was built, and commenced her watery walk about the same time.

Respecting the *Kingston*, built at Sacket's Harbor, we find it stated she was intended to ply between Lewiston and Ogdensburgh, but after a trial of a few months the undertaking was found to be either unprofitable or too much for the powers of the vessel to accomplish, and she afterwards employed ten days in making the round trip of 600 miles. She was 100 feet long and 24 feet wide, measuring 246 tons. The wheels were about 11 feet in diameter, and the capacity of the engine 21 horse power.

Almost immediately after the *Frontenac* was launched a second steamboat was commenced. The material which had been collected while building the *Frontenac* had not all been used, and went far in the construction of the "Queen Charlotte," which was destined to be the pioneer steamer upon the Bay Quinté and River St. Lawrence, in its upper waters. She was built by shares of £50 each. Johns and Finkle had nine shares. She was built, (Gilderslieve being the principal shipwright,) launched, and commenced running in the early part of 1818. The engine was furnished by Brothers Wards of Montreal, being made at their foundry. She was not long launched before she was ready to run. She made trips twice a week from Wilkins' wharf, at the Carrying Place, to Prescott. She was commanded a few of the first trips by an old veteran captain named Richardson, who lived then near Picton, and afterward to the close of the season, by a young man named Mosier. Of the number of passengers on the first trip we have no knowlege, but suppose them to be few, for Belleville, then the largest place above Kingston, was a mere hamlet—Trent, Hallowell, Adolphustown and Bath were the only stopping places from the head of the Bay to Kingston.

They were regulated in their course, the first summer by frequently heaving the lead, an old man-of-war's-man being on board for the purpose. (Collins reported in 1788 that vessels drawing only from eight to ten feet of water can go into the Bay Quinté). For two seasons she was commanded by Capt. Dennis; Mr. Gilderslieve was purser the second and third seasons; and the fourth commenced his captaincy, which lasted as long as the boat was seaworthy, a period of nearly twenty years; he was, at the building, a master shipwright, and became a stockholder.

Says Mrs. Carroll, "of the fare from place to place I have no knowledge, but from the head of the bay to Kingston, the first season it was five dollars, meals included."

The good old Charlotte was a very acceptable improvement in the navigation of the Bay. A few of the owners of sailing crafts, perhaps, suffered for a time; but the settlers regarded her as an unmixed blessing. During the first years she was so accommodating as to stop any where to pick up a passenger from a small boat, or let one off.

The old inhabitants of to-day speak of her with words of kindness. But the *Queen Charlotte* has passed away. The last remembered of her was her hull rotting away in the Cataraqui Bay above the bridge.

The steamer did not prove remunerative to the stock-holders until Gilderslieve became the commander. Of the second Captain, we produce the subjoined from a Toronto daily of 1867:

DEATH OF MR. DENNIS.—"We observe with much regret the death of Joseph Dennis, Esq., of Weston, and with it the severance of another link connecting us with the early history of this country. Mr. Dennis was born in New Brunswick in 1789, his father, the late John Dennis, having settled there after being driven out of the United States as a U. E. Loyalist. The family removed to Canada some three years later, Mr. John Dennis receiving a grant of land for his services and losses as a Loyalist. This land was selected on the Humber river, and on it he then settled and lived, till having been appointed Superintendent of the dock-yard, he removed to Kingston.

"Our recently deceased friend, Mr. Joseph Dennis, was brought up in the dock-yard to a thorough knowledge of shipbuilding, which occupation, however, he soon exchanged for a more congenial one—that of sailing. Owning a vessel on the lake at the outbreak of the American war of 1812, he placed himself and his vessel at the disposal of the Government, and was attached to the Provincial Marine. In one of the actions on Lake Ontario he lost his vessel, was captured, and retained a prisoner in the hands of the enemy for some fifteen months. He subsequently commanded, we believe, the first steamer on the waters of Lake Ontario, the *Princess Charlotte*, which plied, as regularly as could be expected from a steamer of fifty years back, between the Bay of Quinté, Kingston, and Prescott. For the last six and thirty years Mr. Dennis had retired from active pursuits, retaining, till within the last year, remarkable vigour, which, however, he taxed but little excepting to indulge his taste in fishing, of which he was an enthusiastic disciple. A man of genial and happy temperament, of unbending integrity, of simple tastes and methodical habits, he was a type of men fast passing out of this country."

The successor of the "Charlotte" was built by John G. Parker, called the "Kingston" commanded for a time by John Grass. She did not prove so serviceable as the "Charlotte." Then followed the "Sir James Kemp," which was built also at Finkle's Point.

A history of the first steamboats of the bay would be incomplete without particular reference to one individual, whose name is even yet associated with one of the steamboats which ply up and down the Bay.

Henry Gilderslieve came into Canada about a month before the Frontenac was launched, in August, 1816. He was the son of a ship-builder, who owned yards on the Connecticut river, and built vessels for the New York market. Being a skilful shipwright he assisted to finish off the Frontenac, and then as master ship-builder, assisted at the Charlotte. During this time Mr. Gilderslieve himself built a packet named the Minerva. In building this vessel he brought to his assistance the knowledge he had acquired in his father's yard. The result was, that when "she was taken to Kingston to receive her fittings out, Capt. Murney examined her inside and out, and particularly her mould, which exceeded anything he had seen, and declared her to be the best craft that ever floated in the harbour of Kingston, which afterward she proved herself to be, when plying two years as a packet between Toronto and Niagara.—(Finkle).

At a later date Mr. Gilderslieve superintended the building of the "Sir James Kemp," at Finkle's Point. This was the last built there, after which Mr. Gilderslieve commenced building at Kingston. Here were constructed the Barry, a lake boat, with two engines, which in its third year of running collided with the schooner Kingston, at night, and immediately sank, the passengers only being saved; the *Prince of Wales*, the *New Era*, and the *Bay of Quinté*. Thus it will be seen that Mr. Gilderslieve's name is associated with most of the steamers which have plowed the waters of the Bay, first as a skilful shipwright, then commander and shareholder, and finally as a successful proprietor of a ship-yard, and owner of vessels. Says one who knew him long: "Of Mr. Gilderslieve's business habits there are numerous evidences, for years it seemed that everything he touched turned to gold, hence the wealth he left behind him, and I can say, that during the many years I knew him, I never heard a want of honest integrity laid to his charge, he died in the fall of, I think, 1851, of cholera, much lamented and greatly missed."

The following we clip from a paper of 1842:

"In 1821 the new steamboat *Prince Edward*, built at Garden Island, and intended for the Bay of Quinté route, made her trial trip to Bath and back last week in three hours. She is beautifully finished, but being rather *crank* in the water, it will probably be necessary to give her false sides.

"The new steamboat *Prince of Wales*, built at the marine railway by Mr. Shea, and intended for the Bay, was also tried last week, and performed well. She has the engine of the *Sir James Kempt*."

CANALS.—The mighty water way from the Atlantic to the head water of the western lakes is interrupted in its course by numerous rapids down rock-strewed channels, and by the Falls of Niagara. These natural obstacles to navigation had to be overcome by artificial means, before the water road could become a highway. This has already been done for vessels of a certain tonnage, by constructing the St. Lawrence Canals—the Lachine Canal, Beauharnois, and Cornwall, which were completed in 1847; and the Welland Canal, across the Niagara District, to Lake Erie. The distance from this Lake to Montreal, is 367 miles. The total fall in this way, is 564 feet.

After the war of 1812, seeing the importance of inland navigation, beyond the easy reach of an enemy, the country was explored with the view of securing navigation between Montreal and Kingston. It was proposed to open a "new route up the Ottawa to the mouth of the Rideau, and up that river near to its head waters, thence by a short portage to Kingston Mill river, and down that stream to Kingston;" but the want of means for a time delayed the work, although, at the time mentioned, advertisements were made for estimates.

The Welland Canal Company was incorporated in 1824 by Act of Parliament. The projector and the most earnest worker securing this important work, was the late William Hamilton Merritt.

The first canal cut in Canada, was that between Burlington Bay and Lake Ontario. An Act to provide for this was passed in March, 1813.

In 1826, the Desjardin Canal Company was incorporated by Act of Parliament, in accordance with the petition of Peter Desjardin, and others, to make a canal between Burlington Bay and the village of "Coats' Paradise."

"At Kingston is the outlet of that stupendous work, the Rideau Canal, an immense military highway, connecting the Ottawa and St. Lawrence Rivers. The locks on this canal are amongst the grandest structures of the same nature in the world. The undertaking was commenced and carried out by the Imperial Government at an immense expenditure, chiefly for military purposes, as affording a safe channel for the conveyance of stores, arms, &c., when the frontiers might be exposed, and partly with a commercial view of avoiding the rapids of the St. Lawrence, at that time considered insurmountable, in the transit from the sea-board. This canal cost upwards of £1,000,000 sterling. It construction was expected to have great influence on the welfare of Kingston, and for some time such influence was doubtlessly beneficially felt, as it was necessary to trans-ship at that port as well the products of the west in their carriage to the seaboard, as the merchandize for Western Canada in its transportation westward, and to forward them by other crafts through the canal, or up the lake, thus creating a large source of labor, outlay and gain, and employment to numerous forwarders, agents, and workmen in the transhipment. The improved navigation of the St. Lawrence, by the construction of the St. Lawrence Canals, and the discovery of other and better channels than were known, to a great extent abolished that source of life and activity on the wharfs and in the harbours of the city."

"The canal was intended for the passage of barges, both down and up between Kingston and Bytown. Steamers, however, were soon made available in guiding barges down the rapids, which came with return cargoes up the canal. Now steam-tugs tow, through the course afforded by the St. Lawrence Canals, both schooners and barges up as well as down the stream, and where schooners are used, no transhipment necessarily takes place at Kingston. Of late, it has been found profitable to employ barges in the navigation of the St. Lawnence, or it has been found profitable for schooners to confine their trip to the open lake, which, with the facilities for the transhipment of grain afforded by an extensive steam elevator, has caused a renewed life in that branch of business."

"This important work unites, as we have stated, the waters of the St. Lawrence, with those of the Ottawa. It commences at Kingston, and pursues a north-eastern direction through a chain of lakes, with most of which it becomes identified in its course, until it intersects Rideau River, continuing its route along the banks, and sometimes in the bed of the river; it enters the Ottawa at Bytown, (now the City of Ottawa) in north latitude 45° 23"—Length from Kingston to Bytown, including the navigable courses, 126 miles, with 46 locks, each 33 feet wide, and 134 long. Ascent from Kingston to the Summit Pond by 15 locks, 162 feet. Decent from the Summit Pond to the Ottawa by 32 locks, 283 feet; total lockage, 455 feet, depression of the Ottawa below Lake Ontario, at Kingston 141 feet; general course, north, north-east. It was commenced in 1826, when the Duke of Wellington was in office, and it is understood that that great General had a voice in the designing of this mighty structure, which is not unworthy of his genius. Sir James Carmichael Smith, of the Engineer's Department, is said to have originated the idea of its construction. It was carried out under the superintendence of Colonel By, and the town at its junction with the Ottawa, was named after him. That name has since been changed, when Bytown was made a city. It was the only testimonial to his energy and skill, which deserved from the Province some better acknowledgment. This great work, together with the extensive lands along its line of route, held by the Imperial Government, have lately been transferred to the Province, and there is no doubt that its resources and revenue will be made the most of for the general benefit of the country. Already the local trade along its course is fast increasing, with the improvements and growth of the settlements in the neighborhood of the Ottawa. The transport of iron ore from the same section of the country to Kingston, also adds largely to it. Along the courses of the stream are valuable water privileges."—(Hooper.)

A vague story obtains, among some persons, that when the treaty of peace between the United States and England took place in 1815, the former agreed to pay £1,000,000, which the Duke of Wellington applied to this purpose.

Below is given a document, the importance of which is unquestioned, whether we consider the interests of those living along the bay, or the welfare of the whole Province.

REPORT OF THE SPECIAL COMMITTEE ON THE MURRAY CANAL.

"The Select Committee appointed to enquire into the expediency of constructing a Canal to connect the head waters of the Bay of Quinté with Lake Ontario, usually called the "Murray Canal," and also to enquire and report whether any money or lands are applicable to that purpose, and if so, what may be the amount or value thereof, beg leave to report:

"That it appears a grant of land was made for the above purpose as early as the year 1796, and that said grant, which was then ascertained to contain some six thousand acres, was afterwards repeatedly acknowledged and confirmed;

"That a reservation of sixty-four acres has been made between Presqu'isle Harbour and Bay of Quinté, on which said Canal was intended to be constructed;

"That the value of the original reservation of six thousand acres was estimated by the Crown Lands Department, in 1839, at three pounds per acre, or eighteen thousand pounds currency;

"That the construction of said Canal, in addition to the important commercial advantages which would be bestowed on the inhabitants of the counties adjacent to the Bay of Quinté, and the trade and navigation of the country generally, would afford most important facilities for the safe transport of men and munitions in time of war;

"That your Committee obtained the evidence of Colonel McDougal, Adjutant General of Militia, which is appended to this Report;

"That besides providing an admirable harbour of some seventy or eighty miles in length, capable of being made almost impregnable against attack, the great natural facilities for ship-building and for obtaining supplies of timber, would enable the Bay of Quinté to be used to great advantage for the repair or construction of ships of war;

"That on reference to the Journals of the Legislative Assembly of 1845, Your Committee found the record of a letter dated 7th January, 1840, signed by R. B. Sullivan, then Commissioner of Crown Lands, which was furnished as a report on the whole question of the Murray Canal, for the information of the House, in reply to an Address to His Excellency, under date 17th January, 1845.

"Your Committee have deemed it expedient to quote fully from this Report for the information of Your Honorable House.

"1st. *Extract.*—The suggestion of constructing the Canal by a grant of money instead of the appropriation of Crown Lands to that object, was adopted by the Legislative in an Address of the 16th

February, 1838, to His Excellency the Lieutenant Governor, on the subject, with the trust that in the estimation of amount to be granted in lieu of the reservation, due regard may be had to the increased value to which these lands may have attained. His Excellency, by answer of 26th February, was pleased to concur with the Address.

"*Extract No.* 2.—I would respectfully recommend to His Excellency to fix upon some specific sum which may be charged upon the Crown Reserve, and made payable out of its first disposable proceeds toward the completion of the Canal, and which, upon the cession of the Crown Revenue to the Legislature, will be considered a payment for which the faith of the Government is pledged and provided for in any Bill which may be passed for the granting a civil list in return for the cession of the Revenue.

"That Your Committee examined a work, composed in the year 1826, by Major General Sir James Carmichael-Smyth, Baronet, entitled, *Precis of the Wars in Canada from* 1755 *to the Treaty of Ghent in* 1814, the said work having been published for the first time in 1862, by Sir James Carmichael, Baronet, son of the author. That this work contains the following statements, which may fairly be quoted in favor of the construction of this Canal.

"In the dedication of this work to His Grace the Duke of Wellington, the author makes the following remarks:—

"The events of these wars afford, in my opinion, a demonstration as clear as that of any proposition in *Euclid*, of the impossibility (under Divine Providence) of these Provinces ever being wrested from under Her Majesty's authority by the Government of the United States, provided we avail ourselves of the military precautions in our power to adopt, by establishing those communications and occupying those points which posterity will one day learn with, if possible, increased respect for Your Grace's great name, were principally suggested by Your Grace."

At page 202 he writes as follows:—

"Our Harbour and Naval Establishment at Kingston are very good indeed, and infinitely beyond what the Americans possess at Sacket's Harbour. There cannot be a finer basin in the world than the Bay of Quinté. When Rideau Canal is completed there will be great facilities for forwarding stores to Kingston."

At page 203:—

"In the event of the Americans having the temporary command of the Lake (Ontario), York (now Toronto) would be useful for the protection of small craft and coasting vessels sailing from the Bay of Quinté with supplies for the Niagara Frontier."

In a Report published by the Board of Trade of the City of Montreal, for the year 1865, under the heading of "Improvement of Inland Navigation," Your Committee have found the following:

"AN IMPORTANT CUT-OFF.—"It was long ago proposed to connect Lake Ontario with the Western extremity of the Bay Quinté, by a short Canal. The land required for such a purpose is reserved by the Government. The distance to be cut through is less than two miles; some additional dredging being, of course, required in the Bay and Lake to perfect the communication. As no lockage is requisite, the expense of the work would be small, while the advantage would be great

"When it is remembered that the stretch between Presqu'isle Harbor and Kingston is the most hazardous on Lake Ontario, the advantages to be derived from such a cut-off will be evident, especially in the fall, when stormy weather is most prevalent. Had that little Canal existed last year, a number of marine disasters might have been avoided. Any one who examines the map may see at once how important the Bay of Quinté would thus become in the event of hostilities on the Lake."

"That under these circumstances Your Committee would recommend that a Survey be made of the neck of land lying between Lake Ontario and the Bay of Quinté, and also of the Harbours of Presqu'isle and Weller's Bay, for the purpose of ascertaining the cost and feasibility of said Canal, and that the Survey should be commenced with the least possible delay.

Respectfully submitted, JAMES L. BIGGAR, *Chairman*."

APPENDIX.—COMMITTEE ROOM, Tuesday, 24th July, 1866.

Colonel MACDOUGALL attended, and was examined as follows:

By the Hon. Mr. *Holton*:

Be pleased to state to the Committee your views of the importance, in a military point of view, of connecting the waters of Lake Ontario and the Bay of Quinté by a Canal, navigable for vessels of the largest class in use on Lake Ontario?—I am aware that the Defense Commission sent to Canada in 1862, to report on the general defenses of the Province, strongly recommend the formation of a Naval Station in the Bay of Quinté. The natural features of that bay render it, in my opinion, admirably adapted for such purpose. In the event of the Naval Station being formed in the Bay of Quinté, it would be of great importance to have a short and secure entrance direct from Lake Ontario to the head waters of the bay. This is especially the case in view of the fact that the stretch between Presqu'isle Harbour and Kingston is the most dangerous and difficult on the Lake. Judging by the map, and in ignorance of local peculiarities, it appears to me that the best means of obtaining such a short and secure communication as is above referred to, would be by cutting a Canal between the head waters of the Bay Quinté and Weller Bay. The mouth of the Canal would be covered and protected by the perfectly land-locked harbour of Weller Bay, the entrance to which, from Lake Ontario, is susceptible of being very easily defended against a hostile flotilla. If the case is considered of Canadian vessels running before a superior naval force of the enemy from the general direction of Toronto, it is obvious that if the first were obliged to weather the peninsula of Prince Edward, in certain winds they would run serious risks of being driven ashore or captured before they could make the entrance to the Bay of Quinté, whereas the same vessels, with the same wind as would expose them to destruction in the first supposed case, could enter the harbour of Weller Bay under full sail, and reach the head of Bay of Quinté without molestation. Even though it may not be in contemplation to establish a regular Naval Station in the Bay of Quinté, that bay would, in the case of war, afford an admirable harbour of refuge, which would be made perfectly secure in a military, or rather naval sense. Again, in case of war, the proposed Canal would supply the means of far safer communication by water, without the sacrifice of time between Kingston and Toronto, than could be afforded by the open Lake.

In the Hallowell *Free Press*, of February 1, 1831, is a communication from "A country lad," who says, "there are several new roads required, but the one of most essential benefit to the inhabitants would be that which would lead from Wellington Village, Hillier, across the peninsula to Belleville. But, while improvements of this description are in contemplation, it must not be forgotten that the period is not far distant when the East Lake in Hallowell must be cleared out, and a canal suitable for the passage of the Lake Ontario steamboats, cut from thence to Hallowell Village. Such an improvement as this, would, in our opinion, not only lessen the distance from Kingston to York, and make the navigation less dangerous, but would afford a safe and commodious harbour."

RAILWAYS.—At the present day Canada, in addition to the unsurpassed water ways through her vast extent, has the greatest number of miles of railway according to inhabitants in any part of the world. In 1832, the Liverpool and Manchester Railroad was completed, which was "the great precursor of all railroads." Fourteen years later, 1846, a movement was initiated at Kingston to build a road from Wolfe Island, through Kingston to Toronto, and a survey was ordered to be made. A part of the "Report of the Preliminary Survey of Wolfe Island, Kingston and Toronto Railroad," is now before us, signed by James Cull and Thomas Gore, Civil Engineers. In addition the engineering results of the Preliminary Survey, they give in an appendix, the grounds upon which they form their opinion as to the probable cost and revenue. It would be interesting to give their statements in full did space allow.

"*Another scheme.*—The Picton *Sun* is advocating the building of a railroad, running through the County of Prince Edward, and terminating at Long Point, whence freight and passengers could be shipped to the United States."

THE INCREASE OF POPULATION.

It is a common belief among the Americans, a belief which is shared in by the few Annexationists living in Canada, that increase of population, productiveness of the soil, and general advance of civilization, are very much greater in the several States of the Union than in Canada. Nothing can be farther from the truth. Upper Canada especially, has quite outstripped, even the most prosperous of all the original States of the Union. A comparison of the statistics of the two countries shows this to be undoubtedly the case. The following paragraph, taken from a valuable little work by Dr. Lillie, affords some idea of the relative progress of the two countries.

He says, "The rate at which Canada West is growing, and has been for the last twenty or thirty years, equals, if it does not more than equal the growth of the very best of the Western States. It will be seen from the United States census, that the three States of Ohio, Michigan, and Illinois, contained in 1830, 1,126,851. In 1850, they contained 355,000, a little over 320 per cent. in twenty years. Canada West contained in 1830, 210,473, in 1749, it contained 791,-000, which is over 275 per cent. of the same period of twenty years. So that increase in the three choice States was 55 per cent. less than that of Canada West during the same time."

And with respect to the products of the two countries, there is found the same proportion in favor of Canada. So also with regard to vessels, "in proportion to population the tonnage of Canada more than equals that of the United States." And if we look at the various internal improvements as to canals, railroads, we find that Canada stands pre-eminent in these things.

Yet, in the face of these facts we can find persons to say, and so believe that Canada is behind the States in enterprise.

If we regard Lower Canada, it is found that the growth of population is vastly greater than the States of Vermont and Maine, lying along her border. Taking Canada as a whole, it is seen "that as compared with the States, which in 1850 had a population as great as her own, the decimal rate of increase was greater than in any of those States, with one solitary exception.

"That in nine years to their ten, she lessened by two the number of States which in 1850 had a population exceeding hers.

"That she maintained a decimal rate of increase greater than that of the whole United States, not including the Western States and Territories, but including California and the other States and Territories on the Pacific.

"That Upper Canada maintained a decimal rate of increase greater by one-half than that of the whole United States and Territories—more than double that of all the United States, excluding the Western States—and only falling short of the increase in the Western States and Territories by 7 per cent.

"That in nine years to their ten, she passed four States of the Union, which in 1850, had a population exceeding hers, leaving at the date of the last census only five States which exceeded her in population.

The population of French Canada at the time of the revolution, did not much exceed 70,000. Since that time the increase of population in Lower Canada has been steady; not from immigration, so much as from early marriages. In the year 1783, there were by enumeration 113,000. In 1831, the French had increased 400,000. As we have said this was due to their social habits.

The loyalists and soldiers that settled in Western Canada in 1783-4-5, were estimated at 10,000. It has been stated that when Canada was divided into two Provinces in 1791, the inhabitants had increased to 50,000; but this is doubted by some. It is said that the number did not exceed 12,000. McMullen puts it at 20,000. The increase of population up to the time of the war of 1812, was by no means rapid, at that time they numbered about 70,000; 1822, 130,000; in 1837, 396,000. The number of inhabitants in 1852 was somewhere about 500,000.

Coming to the Midland Districts, the townships around the bay, it is found that here advancement was greater than elsewhere for many years.

Robert Gourlay sought information from the several townships of the Province in 1817, in response it is stated, among other things, that "the number of inhabited houses now is about 550; population about 2,850. This enumeration includes the town of Kingston, which contains 450 houses, and 2,250 souls. Thomas Markland says, 26th November, 1818, "The reports from this district (Midland) being few in proportion and several of these irregular, I cannot give an exact estimate of the population, but the following will not be far wrong:—Kingston, Ernesttown, Adolphustown, and Thurlow, contain 7,083. Fredericksburgh, Marysburgh, Hallowell, Ameliasburgh, and Sidney, 5,340. Pittsburgh, with Wolfe Island, Loborough, Portland, Camden, Richmond, and Rawdon, will not average above 300 each, a total of 1,800. In Huntington, I heard only of five settlers—say 24. Total white population 14,855; Indians 200. Total number of houses in Midland district was 900 Thomas Markland. A report before me made in October 1826, by John Portt, says the total number of white inhabitants of Tyendinagua is 27.

DIVISION XII.

THE UNITED EMPIRE LOYALISTS—THE FATHERS OF UPPER CANADA.

CHAPTER LXIX.

CONTENTS—Definition—A division—Their principles—Our position—Ancestry—Dutch—Puritans—Huguenots—New Rochelle—English writers—Talbot—Falsehoods—Canadian and English ancestry—Howison—Maligner—Gourlay's reply—Palatines—Old names.

ANCESTRY OF THE U. E. LOYALISTS.

Under this designation allusion is made to all who left, or were compelled to leave, the revolting colonies, and Independent States, and who sought a home in the wilderness of Canada. There is, however, a class which will be specially referred to, who, in subsequent years, were placed upon the "U. E. list," and who, by virtue thereof, secured important privileges to themselves and family.

The United Empire Loyalist, was one who advocated, or wished to have maintained, the *unity of the British empire*, who felt as much a Briton in the colony of America, as if he were in old England; who desired to perpetuate British rule in America; not blindly believing that no imperfections could exist in such rule, but desiring to seek reform in a conservative spirit. This class, we have seen, became, as the tide of rebellion gained strength and violence, exceedingly obnoxious to those in rebellion against their King and country. It will be convenient to divide them into three classes, viz., (1.) Those who were forced to leave during the contest, many of whom took part in the war; (2.) Those who were driven away after the war, because they were known or suspected to have sympathy with the the loyalist party, and (3.) Those who would not remain in the Republic, who voluntarily forsook the land of their birth or adoption, and removed to a country which acknowledged the sovereignty of the King of England. Many of this noble class relinquished comfortable homes, rather than live under an alien flag; they preferred, above all measure, to enter a wilderness and hew out a new home. They would live anywhere, endure any toil, undergo any privation, so long as they were in the King's dominion, and the good old flag waved over their head, and their families. It was oft declared that their bones should lie on the King's soil. These sentiments are taken, not from the imagination, but from the accumulated testimony of those who have supplied statements of family history. Elsewhere it has been shewn how cruel were the persecutions made against the "tories," how relentless the spirit of vengefulness. All this, it may be said by some, should be forgotten,—buried in the past, with the whigs and tories, both of whom committed errors and outrages. Under certain circumstances this would be the proper course—the course indicated by the great Ruler; but, regarding the United States in the light derived from the statesmen, orators, and the press, it cannot for a moment be allowed. Until the descendants of those who successfully rebelled in 1776, cease to vilify our fathers; until they can find other subject matter for their fourth of July orations, than foul abuse of our country; until they can produce school-books which are not stained by unjust and dishonest representations; and books of a religious nature which are not marred by unchristian, not to say untruthful, statements respecting Britain and her colonies. Until the "Great Republic" can rise above the petty course of perpetuating old feuds, we cannot—we whose fathers suffered, cannot be required to shut our mouths, and thereby seemingly acquiesce in their uncharitable and malignant charges against the U. E. Loyalists. Washington was a rebel as much as Jefferson Davis, and history will accord to the latter a character as honorable and distinguished as the former. Washington succeeded against a power that put not forth the gigantic efforts which the United States did to subjugate the States over which Jefferson Davis presided. By the events of the civil war in the United States, we, the descendants of those who occupied the same relative position in the American Revolution, feel it right to be guided.

The most of the loyalists were Americans by birth. Their feelings of attachment to the realm, preponderated over the attachments which bound them to the homes of their childhood and maturer years. The great majority of those who settled Upper Canada were from the Provinces of New York, Pensylvania, and the New England States. New York, originally a Dutch colony, had many loyal sons. Indeed this state was dragged into the rebellion. It follows that a goodly number of the settlers around the bay were of Dutch extraction, and possessed all the honesty and industry peculiar to that people. The U. E. list, and the larger list of refugees, include a large number of names unmistakably Dutch. But there came from this state as well, many a true son of England, Ireland, and Scotland, with a sprinkling of the Huguenots, and the Germans, the last of whom began to emigrate to America in 1710. Many of the settlers of Upper Canada may point with pride to their Dutch forefathers. Many Canadians have an equal right also to boast of their Puritan fathers. They more especially may point to the justice-loving ones who came to America with honest William Penn, whose son was also a refugee from the State his father founded, not by taking forceable possession, but by *buying* the land from the Indians.

Among the devoted band of firm adherents to the British Crown were not a few of the descendants of the Huguenots, whose fathers had been expatriated by the King of France, because they were Protestants, and who had found safe homes in England. So early as 1686, a number of Huguenots found their way to America. And from time to time, accessions were made to the number by emigration. They mostly settled in Westchester County, New-York, in 1689, where a tract of land was purchased for them by Jacob Leisler, of the Admiralty, and there founded a town called New Rochelle, after Rochelle in France, noted for the stand its inhabitants took against Roman Catholicism. In 1700, New Rochelle had become quite a place, and here was found, when the rebellion had commenced, "a vast number of Militia officers loyal to the backbone." —(Ruttan).

The ancestry of the U. E. Loyalists has been called in question, not by the rebels alone, but by British subjects. The few instances constitute, fortunately, but exceptions to a general rule. Travelers from Great Britain have repeatedly, perhaps we may say persistently, displayed an astonishing amount of ignorance of the people of Canada and its society. Allowance can be made for a certain amount of egotism, but downright bias is unworthy a high-minded writer. Incapable of examining any subject, except from a stand point exclusively English, they have found no difficulty in attributing the most unworthy and even scandalous causes to a state of society to them unusual, and seemingly abnormal. Perhaps no writer has so disgraced himself, in writing about Canada, as Talbot. Certainly no one more ignobly essayed to injure Canadian reputation in Great Britain than he. "Mr. Talbot has stated in his book that most of the Canadians are descended from private soldiers or settlers, or the illegitimate offspring of some gentlemen, or his servant." The writer had no scruples in publishing a falsehood. Full well he knew how noble had been the conduct of the U. E. Loyalists as a class; who relinquished property, homes,—everything for a cause dear to their heart. Private soldiers indeed! They thought it no disgrace to enter the ranks to help to suppress an unrighteous rebellion. And the descendants of the private soldiers feel it an honor to claim them for sires. Mr. Talbot, we are informed, came to Canada to speculate in lands; and his record does not justify him in casting a stigma upon the fathers of Canada. Could we accept a slanderous statement as true, yet the question might be raised:—Is not their origin as good as many of the great houses of Great Britain would be found, were we enabled to trace back their pedigree. Probably, at the present time, and perhaps at no time, did more than a few read the pages of Mr. Talbot's production. But lest there might come a time when the false statements should be reiterated, we felt it our duty to thus advert to the subject.

Another writer, to whom it may be well to refer, is one Dr. John Howison, who wrote *Sketches of Upper Canada*. His knowledge of Canada was pretty much confined to the Niagara district. Hear what the great (?) man said of the inhabitants. "They are still the untutored incorrigible beings that they probably were, when the ruffian remnant of a disbanded regiment, or the outlawed refuse of some European nation, they sought refuge in the wilds of Upper Canada, aware that they would neither find means of subsistance, nor be countenanced in any civilized country. Their original depravity has been confirmed and increased by the circumstances in which they are now placed." This is a pleasant picture that the accomplished doctor draws of our forefathers. The very flagrancy of the falsehood has rendered the above statement as harmless as the doctor's reputation is unknown. It is but too common a story for a stupid Englishman, with no other ideas than those derived from supreme egotism, to pass through our country, and after merely glancing at the outside of everything, proceed to give an account of the people of Canada. But this Howison was either guilty of drawing his views from Yankee sources, or of giving vent to some spiteful feeling. Robert Gourlay, who was no tory, referring to the above statement, speaks in this way:—"It is not true, it is not fair, it is not discreet. The first settlers of Upper Canada, in my opinion, were wrong-headed men as to politics; but they were far from being bad-hearted men, and anything but "the ruffian remnant of a disbanded regiment." They were soldiers who had done their duty: who had regarded with reverence their oath of allegiance; who had risked their lives a hundred times over a support of their principles; who had sacrificed all which the world in general holds dear, to maintain their loyalty and honor. They were anything but the "outlawed refuse of some European nation. They adhered to the laws of Britain; and for the laws of Britain they bled. They did not "seek refuge in the wilds of Upper Canada, aware they would neither find means of subsistence, nor be countenanced in any civilized country." It is a libel on the British Government to say they sought refuge, and a libel on common sense to say that men, who resolved to earn their bread by labour, under the worst circumstances in the world, could not find means of subsistence anywhere else. The whole passage is untrue, is shameful, and Dr. Howison should apologize for it in the public prints of this country. These very farmers whom he scandalizes so cruelly, stood up for British Government most noble during the late war, (1812), many of them lost their all at that time (in Niagara District), and to many of them the British Government is now deeply indebted. The mass of first settlers in Upper Canada were true men, and to this day there is a peculiar cast of goodness in their natures, which distinguishes them from their neighbours in the United States. There were among them ruffians of the very worst description. His Majesty's ministers needed spies, and horse stealers, and liars, and perjured villians; and America furnished such characters, just as England can furnish an Oliver and an Edward. Why should a whole people be slandered because of a few? Dr. Howison wrote in Canada only to trifle, and now we see the consummation, we see a book very well written; very readable as a romance—the tale of a weak man; but as it affects men, worse than trifling—scandalous. To say all the ill he could of Canada, and no good of it is unfair—is deceitful—after all, in his parting exclamations, he "spoke about the happy shores of Canada." The refined Dr. Howison, it would seem, remembered "many civilities" from the Canadians; but because he could not appreciate the nobility of nature when crowned by the rough circumstances of pioneer life, he must needs write a libel. No doubt his mind was influenced by Yankee tales of Butlers' Rangers, and perhaps his exquisite sensibility was wounded forsooth, because a Canadian would not touch his hat to him." Robert Gourlay was a friend to Canada, a friend to humanity; he was not always right; but he was far more correct while in Canada than those who persecuted him. He was a patient and close observer, and made himself thoroughly acquainted with Canada, and his statement in reply to Howison's utterances are fully satisfying. What was true of the settlers at Niagara, must remain true of the whole class of U. E. Loyalists. Notwithstanding the many adverse circumstances—the earnest contest for life, the daily struggle for food, their isolation from the influences of civilized life, the absence of regular ministers of the gospel, notwithstanding all, the old soldiers constituted a band of pioneers infinitely better than these who form the outer belt of settlers, at the present day, in the Western States.

As intimated, not a few of the U. E. Loyalists were descendants of those who had likewise been driven, by persecution, from their homes. There were not only the children of the noble old Huguenots, but a good many German Irishmen, called Palatines. They originally came from the Palatinate of the Rhine, once the possession of the House of Palatine. The Palatines were Protestants, and during the seventeenth century, were exposed to the most cruel barbarities. They fled in thousands to the friendly camp of the Duke of Marlborough, when commander of the allied armies. In 1709, Queen Anne sent a fleet to Rotterdam for the distressed Palatines, and carried about 7,000 to England. Of these, 3,000 were sent to New York, but finally found homes in Pennsylvania, among the Quakers. The names of some of these are before us, and it may be seen they are familiar ones, although some of them are somewhat altered.

Frantz Lucas, Deitrich Klein, Conrad Frederick, Ludwig Henrich Newkirk, Keiser, John Mortan, Casper Hartwig, Christoper Warner, Hermanus Hoffman, Rudolph Neff, Schmidt, Schumacher, Lenhard, John Peter Zenger, Philip Muller, Schaffer, Peter Wagner, Straale, Henrich Man, Eberhard, Kremer, Franke Ross, Peter Becker, Christian Meyer, Godfry Fidler, Weller, George Mathias, Christo, Hagedom, Fink, John William Dill, Barnard, Conradt, Bellinger.

"Of those who remained, five hundred families removed to Ireland, and settled, principally, in the County of Limerick." Among their names we find, Baker, Barham, Barrabier, Bennoser, Bethel, Bowen, Bowman, Bovinezer, Brethower, Cole, Coach, Corneil, Cronsberry, Dobe, Dulmage, Embury, Fizzle, Grunse, Grier, Heck, Hoffman, Hifle, Heavener, Ozier, (probably Lazier of our day), Lawrence, Lowes, Rhineheart, Rose, Rodenbucher, Ruckle, Switzer, Sparling, Stack, St. John, St. Ledger, Strongle, Sleeper, Shoemaker, Shier, Smeltzer, Shoultace, Shavewise, Tesby, (probably Detlor of our day), Tettler, Urshelbaugh, Williams, and Young.

A certain number of the Palatines settled at the German Flats, many of whom, being Loyalists, were obliged to leave; and become pioneers in Canada. Likewise, were there many from other parts of the State, and from Pennsylvania.

In the early history of New York State, may be found many names, generally Dutch-like, closely resembling those of the first settlers of Western Canada.

In a letter, dated "Albany, 30 July, 1689," we find the names of Capt. Bleeker and D. Myers.

At a convention at Albany, Oct. 24, 1669, was present, among others, Gert Ryerse, Jan Jense Bleeker.

"Proposals made to ye people, Albany, ye 5 day of November, 1689, by 40 inhabitants," among which is Jacob Vanden Bogaert.

"At a meeting, at Albany, 28th March, 1690," were present, Gert Ryersen, John Pietersen, Hendrick Hedgeman, (Hagerman).

At a meeting in Albany, after the massacre of Schenectady, February 9, 1690, to arrange for defending against the French and Indians, and to bury the dead; there were, among 60 others present, D. Wessels, Rector, J. Bleecker, Ald. Ryckman, Ens. Bennet.

In the list of those killed at Schenectady, are several of the Vroomans, Symon, Skemerhoorn. "Taken prisoners at Skinnechtady, and carried to Canada ye 9th day of February, 16[illegible]." "John Wemp, sonne of Myndt & 2 negroes, and 26 others."

In a list of officers in the Province of New York, 1693, members of Council—are found Phillips, Brook, Lawrence, Young, Marshall, Shaw, Evetts, (probably Everit), Handcock, Direk Wessels, Recorder at Albany; Beekman, Howell, Barker, Platt, Whitehead, Harrison, Hageman, Strycker, Willet. Among the militia officers, N. Yorrk, 1700, we find Booth, Moore, Wheler, Hubbs, Kechum, Frederick, Daniel Wright; Robert Coles; Lake, Hegemen, Evert, Bogardus, Hosbrooke, Rose.

List of inhabitants in County of Orange, 1702, we find—Geritssen, (Garrison); Reynerssen, (Ryerson), Ceniff, Mieyer, (Meyer,) Weller, Coeper, Merritt.

Freeholders of the city and county of Albany, 1720, Williams, Van Alen, Holland, Collins, VanDyke, several Bleeker's; Cornelius Boarghaert, Vandusen, Meebe, Weemp, (Wemp), Trueax, Van Valkenburgh, Huyck, Gardimer, Dingmans, VanAlstine, Coonradt, Ham, Luyke, Deeker, Esselstine, Fritts, Quackenboes, (Quackenbush) Van Rensalaer.

In the war of the Indians, at the battle of Point Pleasant, 1774, there was killed, among others, Ensign Candiff.

The following we take from the *Schenectady Evening Star:*

VALLEY OF THE MOHAWK IN OLDEN TIMES.—*Schoharie—The Vroomans.*—When the Schoharie settlements were invaded by the British, under Colonel Butler, in the year 1789, the following persons, among others, were murdered by the Indians: Tunis Vrooman, his wife and son, and on this occasion Ephraim Vrooman and his two sons, Bartholomew, Josias and John Vrooman, Bartholomew Vrooman, Jr., and his wife and son Jacob, were taken prisoners. The wife and daughter of Ephraim Vrooman was killed by an Indian named Seth Hendrick. Mr. E. Vrooman, while on his way to Canada, whither he was carried in captivity, was under the immediate charge of Seth Hendrick, who treated him with much kindness. There were two or three Indians who accompanied Seth. These before they arrived at their destination, grew tired of their prisoner, and proposed to despatch him. Mr. Vrooman overheard the conversation, which was conducted in a whisper, and repeated it to Hendrick. Hendrick assured him in the most positive manner, that "not a hair of his head should be touched," and gave his companions a severe reprimand for their ungenerous conspiracy. After the termination of the Revolutionary contest, Hendrick paid Mr. Vrooman a visit, and apologised for his conduct during the war, in the strong, metaphorical language of his nation: "The tomahawk," said he, "is used only in war; in time of peace it is buried; it cuts down the sturdy oak as well as the tender vine; but I (laying his hand on Mr. Vrooman's shoulder) saved the oak."

"EVA'S KILL.—The creek which runs through the village of Cranesville has, for the last ninety years, been known as Eva's Kill, or creek. It owes this name to the circumstance of a woman named Eva being murdered near its banks. In the year 1755 Mrs. Van Alstine, from Canojoharie, traveled through this place on her way to this city to visit her parents. She was on horseback, and had her daughter with her, a child about four years of age. A party of French and Indians had just arrived from Canada, and were prowling about with murderous designs on the defenceless inhabitants of the Mohawk Valley. Espying Mrs. Van Alstine, they marked her for their prey. They pounced upon, wounded and scalped her, left her as they supposed, dead on the margin of the creek which bears her name. Her daughter they took to Canada. After they had departed, Mrs. Van Alstine partially recovered, and mustered strength enough to crawl to the river, on the opposite shore of which she saw some men standing, to whom she beckoned. She feared to speak lest she should be overheard by her enemies who were still in the neighborhood. These men came over cautiously, and conveyed her safely to her agonised parents. She lingered nine or ten days in a state of extreme suffering, when she gave up the ghost. Her daughter's life was spared, and she, in time, was restored to her friends."

In 1750–60, are found the names of Jordan, Dunham, Grant, Harkamer, Spenser, Peterson, Wilson, Church, Devenport, Kemp, Gibson.

Census of New York, about 1703. Amongst others, Vanhorn, Larrance, Loukes, Vandewater, White, Hams, Wessels, Wm. Taylor, Johnston, Vesey, Bogert, Oastrom, Waldron, Davis, Marshall, Clapp.

Census of Long Island, 1673.—Jacobs, Carman, Symonds, Beedel, Allen, Williams, Valentyn, Ellesson, (probably Allison), Osborne, Hobbs, Soddard, Ellison, Foster, Mott, Applebe, Persell, Truax, Hoyt.

The Roll of those who have taken the oath of allegiance, September, 1687: Peter Stryker, native of the Province; Cornelis Pertise, (Peterson), native; Beakman, native; Gerrit Dorlant, native; Joseph Hagemen, (Hagerman), 37 years; Adrien Ryerse, 41 years. Living in Breucklyn (Brooklyn): Covert, native; Bogaert, 35 years; Jan Fredericks, 35 years; Pieter Corson native; Caspere, (Casper); Jacobus Vande Water, (Vandewater), native; Dirck Janse Waertman, (Wartman), 40 years; Van Clief, De Witt, Loyse, Waldron, Willensen, Badgely, Culver, Jessop, Rogers Diamond, Erle, Butler, Johnes (Jones), Whiting, Arnold, Washbourn, Way, Harton, Booth, Bradly, Goldsmith, Giles, Baily, Osmond, Carey, Case, Miller, Garitson.

CHAPTER LXX.

CONTENTS—Character—Hospitality—At home—Fireside—Visitors—Bees—Raisings Easter Eggs—Dancing—Hovingten House—Caste—Drinks—Horse-racing—Boxing—Amusements—La Crosse—Duels—Patriotism—Annexation—Freedom—Egotism—The Loyalists—Instances—Longevity—Climate of Canada A quotation—Long lived—The children—The present race—A nationality Comparison—"U.E. Loyalist"—Their Privileges—Order of Council—Dissatisfaction.

CHARACTER, CUSTOMS, AMUSEMENTS, PATRIOTISM, AGE AND DESCENDANTS OF THE U. E. LOYALISTS.

When we compare the motives which actuated all classes of those who adhered to the Crown with the rebels in their various grades, we feel to exult and express sincere thankfulness that the fathers of Upper Canada were honest, devoted, loyal, truthful, law-abiding, and actuated by the higher motives which spring from religion. The habits of the loyalists were simple, and comparatively free from immorality. Their love of order and adherence to law is noteworthy. No people in the world have been characterised by so firm and devoted adherence to the established laws than the U. E. Loyalists. Never deprived of that freedom which ennobles the man, they always abominated that monstrous offshoot of republican liberty which teaches a man to take the law in his own hands. In later years in Canada some strife has been witnessed between parties who have introduced their national feuds from the old country. But those who fought in the revolutionary war, and who mainly assisted to drive back the invading foe in 1812, have always been peace-loving citizens. Lynch Law, (a term derived from a man of that name living in South Carolina, who constituted himself the arbiter between any contestants, and to their satisfaction) has always been held in utter detestation.

The settlers were always hospitable. The circumstances of their life, in which they so often were cast upon the care and attention of others, made each experience the deep feeling of gladness to have a visitor, which belongs to a sense of kindness received. In this they differed widely from the people of the more Northern States. Strangers were never turned away, and a clergyman, no matter of what denomination, was received "right gladly." The Rev. Mr. Smart says that he was often up the Bay in his early days of ministerial labor, and he was ever treated by the inhabitants of all classes with great hospitality. And after a few years had worn away, carrying with them the burden of many heart sorrows, there came an occasional opportunity to exchange friendly hospitality. Visiting indeed became a regular "institution," to borrow a Yankee phrase. Near neighbours would of an evening call in, uninvited, to spend the evening, and talk over the times, present, past and coming. Sometimes visits were made to friends a long distance off, going by canoe or batteau, or perchance on horseback, by a bridle-path, with saddle-bags containing oats for the horse. But the winter visits were characterised more especially by genial hospitality. On such occasions the hostess brought forth things new and old. Choice viands, carefully stored away, were brought to the light. The first fruits of the soil were lavishly spread upon the unassuming board. The famine of 1787–8, and the subsequent lack of the necessaries of life, and the total absence of luxuries for many a year, had the effect of intensifying the value that might naturally be placed upon plenty and luxury. To be truly entertaining to guests, was to set before them a feast of good things. Hence it came in the later years of the country that the table of the well-to-do farmer always groaned with substantials and delicacies. On those occasions the old soldier recounted his deeds of warfare, and hair-breadth escapes, and his struggles in the wilderness. The blazing hearth became the centre of attractive conversation, and lit up the hardy faces of the pioneers, and the milder countenances of their wives and daughters, while in the back ground might be seen the bright eyes of the children, listening to the tales that were told. The younger ones had been ordered off to bed, but they lie wakeful in their bunks, which were in the same room, to catch the ever flowing talk. The conversation at these times did not always relate to those matters above stated, it often took a mysterious turn, and ghosts became the subject of their evening's talk. The above is not from imagination, but in substance from the lips of more than one, who remembers to have occupied the little bunk and listened upon many an evening to the conversations.

Family visiting was a common mode of exchanging civilities. It was necessary because of the widely separated houses. The evenings were times of the most pleasing reunions. Every log house possessed a large Dutch fireplace, into which was placed a back log of immense size, while upon the hand irons, or, as at first, large square stones was heaped light dry wood which sent forth a cheerful blaze. By the light thus made there would be in the fall and winter carried on various household duties, each family was to a great extent dependent upon themselves for almost every thing required upon a farm, or about a farm-house. The wife would be busy carding, or making clothes of home-made linen, or of cloth. The daughters would be employed in mending or darning. The farmer would be engaged in making or repairing harness, or boots, or "fixing" an implement of husbandry, while the son would be fashioning an axe-helve, or an ox-yoke, or whittling a whip handle. The simple meal, though of a homely fare, was satisfying, for their taste was not pampered by unnecessary luxuries when alone. But when company came everything was changed. The work was put aside, and they set themselves out to make their visitors enjoy themselves. They would encircle the wide and glowing fire, and indulge in the most amiable talk. There was no spirit of envy in their midst, but a quiet content and thankfulness that the wilderness was beginning to blossom. The triumphs of the past would be duly recounted, and the future looked forward to with highest hopes. Plans would be canvassed and laid for the children, while apples, cider and nuts would receive due attention by all. At these meetings were often the young folks—marriageable daughters and sons who had been preparing to go on the other farm, or back hundred acres where a log house was partially erected; before long the company would be divided into two distinct groups, the old and the young. Sometimes matters would be managed that the older ones would meet at one house and the young at another, by which means a more pleasing state of things was created. But courting, or sparking as it was termed, was generally done upon Sunday evening. The day of rest was the only one when the love-sick swain could get away. And even the most exemplary christians regarded "going to see the girls" on a Sunday night as quite allowable. Then, this practice favored the desire, so prevalent, to keep secret the intention of any two to get married.

Visits were made without invitations. To wait for an invitation was quite contrary to the primitive views of the settlers. The visit must be a voluntary action. Even to give a hint to one to make a visit by parties not related was considered as beneath proper respect. It was a species of independence. "I do'nt want one to come to my house if he do'nt want to," the phase went in that way. But there were occasions when invitations were sent out, and that was when some help was required; and to persons not familiar with the habits, it will seem strange that it was considered a compliment to get an invitation, and a slight to be neglected. Those invitations were to be present at bees, and help to do work. At the first these bees were common, to put up the log houses, and get a little clearing done, by a certain time. But afterwards, though less frequent, they were of a more pretentious nature. Raising Bees were in time, indications of prosperity. A frame barn or house showed that the farmer was progressing, and in accordance with the general expectation, treated "the hands" with the best he had. Then there were, beside the raising bees, the clearing bees, logging bees, and stone bees, and husking bees, and in later times apple bees; and there was the women's bee for quilting. All these meetings were of a more or less hilarious order.

The work was done, and done with a will; it was a sort of duty—a matter of principle that either the work should be done, or a proper effort made to that end. For many years spirituous liquors were dealt out, or set freely before the men, but in time, some, seeing the evil of drinking, and sometimes fearful of accidents, determined to discontinue the custom. Whether drinking was indulged in or not, all were treated to a glorious supper, generally of pot-pie and cakes, and pies of pumkin and apple. The women folks of course, required assistance, and the neighbours would come to help, so that at night there would be collected a goodly number of both sexes. Husking bees and apple bees took place at night, but they did not last so long that no time was allowed for amusement. And then commenced the play and the dance. At first these unions and plays were exceedingly harmless and indulged in with the utmost artlessness. The young of both sexes were well known to each other, and it was more like a family gathering than aught else. But now fortunately these bees and kissing-plays are no longer in vogue. They were natural enough in the days of primitive pioneer life; but with increasing inhabitants and the addition of people of other countries, they became unnatural.

The breaking up of winter brought to a termination for a time, all the social festivities. In connection with sugar making was here and there a jovial meeting to "sugar off."

Aside from the Sabbath there were but few holidays; and, with many, Christmas was imperfectly observed. Easter was remembered principally because of the feast of eggs on Sunday. At first, when hens were scarce, it was not every family that had eggs on that day, or had enough. So it came to pass that eggs would be preserved beforehand, not by the natural provider however. The boys regarded it as their prerogative to hide the eggs for some time before, and even when it was unnecessary, large numbers would be safely secreted by the young ones. This was generally done by the youngest, old enough; and he was to so hide them that no one could find them. The honor was lost if the eggs were found. The Easter morning consequently was one of anticipation, to see however many eggs had been preserved.

An old settler of Ameliasburgh discourses of Bees in this wise: "Bees were great institutions in those days, every settler was licensed to make two or three each year, provided he furnished a good "pot pie," and plenty of grog, and never made any objections to his guests fighting. Fighting might take place at any stage, but more generally occurred after work was done, before and after supper."

Dancing seems to have been particularly attractive to almost all. Almost every neighbourhood or concession had its fiddler, the only kind of instrumental music of the times. The fiddler was generally an old soldier, who had acquired some knowledge of the art of playing during his time of service.

A kind correspondent, (Morden), has supplied us pleasing information, obtained from an old resident of Sophiasburgh. This person came from Adolphustown, when a girl of fifteen, in the first year of the present century. We quote :—"She tells many funny stories of balls and private "sprees" that they used to have over in the Indian woods, at Capt. Isaac's (Hill), an Indian chief, who had a large house, which is still occupied, and which appears to have been the scene of numberless "hops," &c. They could have a civil dance at Captain Isaac's, and it would not cost much. The Sixth Town youngsters seem to have delighted in patronizing his house." This young woman married and became, with her husband, a pioneer of Ameliasburgh, in 1805. It seems that these new settlers of the Seventh Town considered themselves somewhat superior to the inhabitants generally, and would not join in their "frolickings," but would occasionally visit Sophiasburgh for the purpose of having a "spree." This feeling of caste was a marked feature in the several townships at an early date.

The Hovington House, situated about sixty rods above the bridge at Picton, was a place of no little fame. It was built by one Hovington who came with VanAlstine. It was a long narrow edifice forty or fifty feet deep, and about twenty feet broad, and not very high. It was divided into two portions by a log partition, the ends of which projected without. This public house was especially for the benefit of the settlers at East Lake, in their journeyings back and forth across the Carrying Place. To use the language of our informant, "it was a great place to dance and frolic." At stated times the bay settlers would come even from forty miles distance Fredericksburgh on the east, and the Carrying Place and Sidney on the west. But now the foundation of the old building which so often resounded to the sounds of mirth, the fiddle, and the tripping feet, can scarcely be traced.

As a general thing, the hard pinching circumstances of the new country brought all to a common level, excepting a few Govern ment officials. But in certain localities there existed a feeling of superciliousness, not very deep, but yet it was there. The places, and the inhabitants thereof, in time, became noted as being "big feeling" or stylish. For instance, the denizens of Kingston regarded the settlers up the bay as somewhat behind them; while the people of the Fourth Town spoke disparagingly of the Fifth Towners. By the settlers of the Sixth and Seventh Towns, the citizens of Sidney and Thurlow were looked upon as stylish. But the wheel of fortune turned with many a one.

Amusement, and diversions of different kinds, when properly used, are not only allowable, but even salutary to man's physical and mental state; but if uncontrolled by reason; if irrational from want of education, they may easily run into excess and immorality. To the educated man, who is cast away from all that can supply food for his mind, there is a terrible danger of seeking unholy and even vicious sources to allay the constant longing after mental food. There is likewise a danger of such seeking artificial excitement. To such the evil of intemperance too often comes with overwhelming waves steadily and certainly flowing. The first settlers of Upper Canada, when their circumstances are taken into consideration, and the usages of the times, it must be said, were not particularly addicted to the evil of intemperance. In after years, this evil did certainly increase; but at the first, although almost every one had liquor of some kind in the house, yet the great majority were guiltless of excess. In those early days, teetotalism and temperance societies were unknown; but it must be here mentioned that the first temperance society organized in Canada, was in Adolphustown. The drinking usages of the day among all classes led to the erection of distilleries and breweries at an early period. There was also an extensive traffic in rum, and it is known that many a one made himself rich by selling to buyers along the bay, and across the Carrying Place up the lake, even as far as York.

Perhaps the most common out-of-door amusement was horse-racing, after horses became more general among the settlers. It was looked upon as dancing was by all, as amusement of the most unobjectionable character, and it is said of a certain reverend individual, that he was accustomed to run horses on his way home after preaching. Probably this was true, as the same person became a reprobate. On the occasion of the annual training of the Militia, which took place for many a year, the 4th June, (and this comes within the writer's recollection) there was, at the different training places, more or less of horse racing. These races were made, not by horses trained specially for the purpose, but by such animals as were in daily use by the farmers, some of which, although ungainly in looks, and in indifferent condition, could get over the ground in a remarkably short time.

Kingston and Newark being military stations, were, from the presence of officers, who were always gentlemen by birth, more dignified in the ways of amusement. Not but gentlemen existed through the country, but not in sufficient numbers to regulate the modes of pleasure, and give tone to society. The officers were very fond of horse-racing, and would frequently spend field days, especially the King's Birthday in testing the mettle of their steeds. At these there would generally be a great entertainment by the ladies who, says Colonel Clarke, would be gorgeously clad in "brilliant dresses, with threads of silver forming the motto, *God save the King*."

A kind of amusement common at the close of the last century, and the beginning of the present, in America, and to a certain extent in Canada, was that of boxing—boxing that too often amounted to brutal fighting. There were a certain number in every township who availed themselves of training days to show their athletic qualifications. Gourlay says, 1817, that "pugilism, which once prevailed, is now declining." And at the present day, happily, it is confined to those of a brutish disposition. It is only the lowest who find amusement in engaging in, or witnessing pugilistic encounters.

As Upper Canada was, in a limited sense, an off-shoot of Lower Canada, so but a few of the peculiarities of Lower Canada were introduced to the Upper. One was that of *Charivariing*, which means a great noise with petty music. It was introduced from France. The custom is now almost obsolete among us, but time was when it was quite common. It generally was indulged in at second marriages, or when an unequal match and marriage took place; when a young girl married an old man for instance, or if either party were unpopular. The night of the wedding, instead of being passed in joyous in-door pleasures by the wedded ones, was made hideous by a crowd of masked persons, who with guns, tin-pans, pails, horns, horse-fiddles, and everything else that could be made to produce a discordant noise, disturbed the night until silenced by a treat, or money. Sometimes those meetings resulted in serious consequences to one or more of the party, by the bridegroom resorting to loaded firearms.

Sometimes the native Indians contributed to the general amusement, upon days when there was a public gathering. Now and then they engaged alone in certain sports which would be witnessed by the whites. Playing ball—bandy-ball, lacrosse, foot-races, and the war-dance, were occasionally engaged in. The present fashionable game of lacrosse is of Indian origin, and may well be remembered by every Canadian, and even American. After the conquest of Canada, when the Great Ottawa chief Pontiac had effected an alliance of all the western and northern tribes, to destroy the frontier forts of the British. There were several forts, originally French, along the upper lakes; two notably, one at Detroit, the other at Michilmacinac. Smaller forts had been attacked and taken, in most cases by treachery and Indian cunning. These two forts remained untaken. Pontiac devised the plan of pretending to wish for peace. With the ostensible intention of holding a council to make peace, the chiefs were to enter the forts; while the Indians, engaged in ball-playing along the ramparts, were to amuse those within the ramparts. The squaws were to be present, seemingly as spectators, but in reality to hold under their blankets, rifles, the ends of which had been cut off for concealment. At a given signal, the ball was to be knocked over the outer defence, and the Indians were to rush in as if to get it; but seizing their rifles from the women who had placed themselves conveniently, they were to rush in to slaughter the unsuspecting inmates. At Michilmacinac this proved successful, and the whole garrison was massacred, and Detroit barely escaped the same fate.

Duelling.—At the time when fierce encounters took place between organized forces in America, which resulted in the independence of the United States, and the settlement of Upper Canada, the practise of duelling obtained among the higher classes. Happily, this heinous crime, an outrage against humanity, is no longer tolerated where British laws and British principles of justice and freedom have force. But such was not the case seventy years ago. The early history of Canada witnessed a few personal engagements of honor. The first duel was between Peter Clark, Chief Clerk of the Legislative Council, and Captain Sutherland of the 25th regiment. The meeting took place at Kingston, and Mr. Clark fell fatally wounded. This occurred in the winter of 1795.

On the 22nd July, 1817, a duel was fought between S. P. Jarvis, Esq., and Mr. John Ridout. The latter received a wound in the chest and died in about an hour.

"DUEL.—On Friday the 11th inst., Alexander McMillan, Esquire, and Alexander Thom, Esquire, met in a field on the Brockville Road, to decide an affair of honor—the former attended by Mr. Radenhurst, and the latter by Mr. Cumming. After exchanging shots, the seconds interfered, and on mutual explanations being made, the matter terminated amicably. Doctor Thom received a contusion on the leg."

One of the latest instances in which a duel was fought in Upper Canada, occurred some forty years ago. The event resulted in the death of one of the combatants, the other, who was tried for his life, has now for some years adorned the bench of the Province.

PATRIOTISM.—In no country upon the face of the Globe, and at no period in the history of any country, has appeared a higher or purer order of patriotism, than is written upon the pages of the history of British America. British connection is to mostly every son of the land dearer even than life itself. At least it has been so in respect to those of whom we write, the U. E. Loyalists. Co-equal with the love they have to the British Crown, is the hearty aversion they bear to Republicanism. Neither the overtures of annexation, nor the direct and indirect attempts to coerce, has produced a momentary wavering on the part of the descendants of the ancient stock. Americans in our midst have vainly tried to inoculate the minds of the people with the principles of Republican Government; but the Canadian mind was too free, the body politic too healthy, the system too strong to imbibe any lasting feeling of desire to change the tried for the untried. The few annexationists who have, from time to time, existed, were but the fungoid offshoot of a healthy plant. From the time Franklin and his coadjutors vainly essayed to draw the French Canadian into their rebellious cause, until the present there has been a frequently manifested desire, on the part of the United States, to force us into the union. The contemptible duplicity of Webster, who concealed from Ashburton the existence of a second map, whereby he tricked Canada, Yankee like, out of a valuable portion of territory along the Atlantic coast, with a view of cutting us off from the ocean. The declaration of war in 1812, and the repeated but unsuccessful invasions of our Province. The proclamations issued to Canadians, by the would be conquerors, Hull, Wilkinson, and others. Their sympathy and aid to turbulent spirits in 1836–7. The attempts at bullying England when she was at war with Russia. The organization of the Fenian association, with the publicly avowed purpose of seizing some portion of our Province. The abrogation of the Reciprocity Treaty, the object of which was proclaimed by Consul Potter—all along the eighty years' history of the United States, is to be seen a disreputable attempt, by all possible means, to bully a weaker neighbor. All this does not become a great and honorable nation, a nation so extensive, whose people are so loud-tongued upon the principles of liberty—Liberty! The name with the United States is only synonomous with their government. They cannot discover that a people should be free to choose their own form of government, always excepting those who rebelled in 1776. Oh yes! we have liberty to choose; but then we must choose in accordance with Yankee ideas of liberty. Egotistic to the heart's core, they cannot understand how we entertain views dissimilar to their own. How applicable the words of the immortal Burns:—

> "O wad some power the giftie gie us,
> To see oursels as others see us:
> It wad frae monie a blunder free us
> An' foolish notion."

Without detracting from the well-known loyalty of the other sections of the Province, it may be safely said that the inhabitants of the Bay Quinté and St. Lawrence, and Niagara, have proved themselves devotedly attached to British institutions. The U. E. Loyalists have been as a barrier of rock, against which the waves of Republicanism have dashed in vain. It has been the refugee-settlers and their descendants, who prevented the Province from being engulfed in its dark waters. In 1812, in '37, and at all times, their loyalty has never wavered. It has been elsewhere stated, that settlers from the States came in at a later date. Those were found likwise truly loyal. Says McMullen, speaking of the war of 1812, "But comparatively few. Canadians joined the American standard in the war, and throughout which none were more gallant in rolling back the tide of unprincipled avarice than the emigrant from New England and New York, who aside from the U. E. Loyalist, had settled in the country." There were a few renegades who forsook the country, not so much to join the enemy as because they had no soul to fight. In this connection it will be desirable to refer to one notable case; that of "Bill Johnson."

The following will sufficiently shew how intense were the feelings of loyalty many years ago. The writer's father was present at a meeting, which was conducted by a minister lately from the United States, and who was unaccustomed to pray for the King.

The good man thought only of his allegiance to the King of Kings, and omitted, in the extemporaneous prayer, to pray for the King of England. Whereupon Mr. T. arose and requested the preacher either to pray for his Majesty, or leave his territories. The minister did not again forget so manifest a duty. In this connection, we cannot forbear inserting another instance of Canadian loyalty, which exhibited itself not long ago in the loyal city of Toronto.

"CANADIAN LOYALTY.—A very extraordinary manifestation of feeling took place on Thursday night last in Toronto, at the closing meeting of the Sabbath School Convention. A gentleman from New York delivered a parting address, on behalf of the American visitors who had attended the Convention; at the conclusion of which he referred to our Queen as a "model woman," and said that from the fulness of his heart he could say, 'Long live Her Majesty Queen Victoria!' When he gave expression to this sentiment there was such an outburst of enthusiastic loyalty that every one seemed carried completely away. The immense audience immediately commenced such a cheering, and clapping of hands, as is seldom seen, and kept it up till there was an accidental "change of exercise." Under the powerful excitement of the moment, a gentleman near the platform commenced singing "God Save the Queen," when the entire audience rose to their feet and joined in singing it through. That was singing with a will! Several persons were quite overpowered, and even wept freely. It was simply an unpremeditated expression of the warm devotion of the Canadian heart to the best Queen that ever sat on the Britise throne.

LONGEVITY.—The climate of Canada, even of Ontario, is by some considered very severe. The months of unpleasant weather which intervene between summer and winter, and again between winter and summer; and the snowy months of winter itself are not, it must be admitted, so agreeable as in other climates. And, occasionally, even the summer itself is comparatively cold. For instance, in 1817, snow fell at Kingston in the month of June. But, notwithstanding the occasional severity, and the general unpleasantness, (although all do not so consider it) the climate of Canada seems conducive to longevity. Both in Upper and Lower Canada, among the French and English may be found a great many instances of wonderfully extended age. There is a school of naturalists, who entertain the belief that the races of men are strictly indigenous; that if removed from the land of their birth, they will degenerate, and unless intermixed with constantly flowing recruits, will ultimately die out. They assert that the European races transplanted to America are doomed to degeneration and death so soon as emigration shall cease to maintain the vitality brought by the original settlers. To this view we have ventured to give very positive dissent, and have supported this position in another place with the following language: "In Canada are to be seen quite remote descendants of the most prominent people of Europe, the British and French, and, I am prepared to assert, with no marked signs of physical degeneration, the French of Lower Canada, even under many adverse circumstances, have fully maintained their ancient bodily vigor, and can compare favorably with the present inhabitants of old France, while their number has increased." "Yet their ancestors, many of them, emigrated two hundred years ago; and, since the colony became a part of Britain, no replenishment has been received from the old stock.

"Turning to Upper Canada, we find a fact no less important, and quite as antagonistic to the theory. In consequence of the American Revolutionary war, some twenty-five or thirty thousand United Empire Loyalists were forced, or induced, to seek a home in the Canadian wilderness. Many of those were descendants of those who had first peopled New Holland. A large number settled along the St. Lawrence and the Bay of Quinté. In the main, indeed, almost altogether, until very recently, these old settlers have intermarried. The great-grandchildren of those American pioneers now live on the old homestead, and are found scattered over the whole Province. And although I have no positive data upon which to base my assertion; yet, from careful observation, I have no hesitation in declaring that in physical development, in slight mortality among the children, in length of life, in powers of endurance, not to say in bravery and patriotism, they cannot be excelled by any class of emigrants."—(Principles of Surgery).

Since the above was written, we have become more intimately acquainted with regard to the longevity, both among the French and Anglo-Canadians; and the opinion then expressed has been greatly strengthened. Respecting the latter class, personal observation has aided us. In our frequent visits to different parts, made during the last few years, we have enjoyed the opportunity of conversing with many persons who had much over-ran the period allotted to man; and others who had exceeded their three score years and ten. Some of them have been spectators of the very scenes of the settlement of the country, and retain a vivid recollection of the events attending that trying period. Venerable, with hairs blossoming for the grave, and chastened by the long endured fire of affliction, they are happy in their old age. They connect the present with the past, and remind us how great the heritage they have secured to us from a vast, untrodden wilderness. Notwithstanding the toils, the privations in early life, ere the tender child had merged into the adult, when the food was limited, and often inferior in quality, they yet have had iron constitutions that in the earnest contingency of life served them well. Of course, the plain and regular habits of the settlers, with plenty of out-door exercise, assisted to promote long life, and give them a hardy nature. We have knowledge of a vast number who attained to a great age. Of those who lived to an old age, "A Traveler," writing in 1835 says of Upper Canada, "I often met the venerable in years."

The children and grand-children of the early settlers live, in many cases, to as great an age as their fathers.

DESCENDANTS.—While there were some among the first settlers of European birth, the majority were of American birth, and possessed the characteristics of the colonists of that day. But, separated from the people and the scenes intimate to them in their youth, and living in the profound shades of the interminable wilderness, they gradually lost many of their characteristic features and habits, and acquired others instead.

The Canadian immigrant, be he English, Irish, or Scotch, or even German or French, will, as time gives lines to his face, and gray hair to his head, insensibly loose many of the peculiarities of his race, and in the end sensibly approximate to the character and appearance of the people among whom he has settled. The children of the emigrant, no matter what pains the parents may take to preserve in their children what belongs to their own native country, will grow up quite unlike the parents. So much is this the case that any one on entering a mixed school, high or low, or by noticing the children at play, as he passes along the street, whose parents are both natives and foreigners, would find it quite impossible to point out one from the other, whether the child was of Canadian parentage, or whether its parents were of another country. The fact at which it is desired to get is that emigrants to Canada, no matter how heterogenous, are gradually moulded into a whole more or less homogenous. That this is observable somewhat in the emigrant himself, but decidedly so in the children. The fact being admitted that a transformation is slowly but certainly effected, it may be inquired by what influence it is accomplished. It cannot be due solely, to the climate, nor to dress, nor diet, nor the original habits of the people, although each has its influence. Must we not search for a more powerful cause of peculiarity as a people, in some other channel. A natural one seemingly presents itself. The growth of a nation, as the growth of a tree will be modified by its own intrinsic vitality, and at the same time by external circumstances. Upper Canada was planted by British heroes of the American Revolution. It arose out of that revolution. The first settlers were U. E. Loyalists. The majority of the original settlers were natives of America, and brought up in one or other of the provinces that rebelled. They were Americans in all respects, as much as those who took sides with the rebels, yet to-day the descendants of the U. E. Loyalists are as unlike the descendants of the rebels, as each is unlike a full blooded Englishman. The pure Yankee and the Canadian of the first water may trace their ancestors to a common parentage, and have the same name. As Canadians we are not afraid to institute a comparison between ourselves and the natives of New England or New York, or Pennsylvania. Let the comparison refer to any question whatever, either of the body or mind, of society or of government. The external influences which have operated have been elsewhere indicated. The circumstances of the U. E. Loyalists as settlers in a wilderness, were widely different from those of the States after the Independence was secured. Incessant toil and privations, without opportunities for acquiring education, on the one hand; on the other there was all the advantages of civilization. And so it continued for nearly half a century. It is to be desired that we had statistics to show the difference as to longevity, and general health. Suffice it to say that scientific men are debating the cause of gradual decline among the New Englanders, while Upper Canada overflows with native population. Another influence of an external nature, which must not be omitted as operating upon the loyalists, is that derived from the emigrants from Great Britain and the officers from the army and navy, and other gentlemen who became part of the first settlers. That they had a wholesome effect cannot be doubted, and gave a healthy tone to the provincial mind. From these internal and external influences the Upper Canadian has been developed into an individual singular in some respects, but yet constituting a middle link between the Englishman, and the "Englishman intensified," as the American has been called.

The difference in the character between the British American and those who have lived under Republican Government is a striking commentary upon the effects of social and political institutions.

Canadians may not have excelled in making wooden nutmegs, and basswood hams; but they have succeeded in converting a wilderness into a splendid Province. And although eighty years behind in commencing the race with those who robbed them of their homes, they have even now caught up in many respects, and to-day a young State with great breadth and resources presents itself at the threshold of nations. It has for a population a stable people. Canada has no long list of cruel charges against her for aggression. Her escutcheon is clean as the northern snow against which she rests, from the stains of blood—blood of the Indian, the African, the Mexican, or of a neighbor.

After all, notwithstanding this bright record of loyalty on the part of settlers and their descendants, yet the Bay of Quinté inhabitants were not permitted to receive the heir to the Crown of England, to support which, their sires suffered so much. They spilled their blood, they suffered starvation; and yet by the advice of one who held in higher consideration the Roman Catholic Church, than the grand-children of the U. E. Loyalists. The Prince of Wales passed up and down the bay without landing. They waited with burning enthusiasim to receive the Prince, but he passed and repassed without gratifying their desire. Notwithstanding this there were some who followed him to Toronto, determined to pay their respect to the Prince, notwithstanding the Duke of Newcastle."

"THE U. E. LIST."—It will be remembered that a certain number of Americans who had remained in the States, were induced to remove to Canada by a proclamation issued by Simcoe; many of these were always loyalists in heart, some had become tired of republicanism, and others were attracted by the offer of lands, free grants of which were offered upon paying fees of office, some $30. By this means a new element was added to the Province. At the same time the first settlers were to be placed in a position to which the new comers, however loyal, could never attain.

Distinct from the general class is here meant those whose names were entered upon a list ordered to be prepared by Government. "To put a mark of honor," as it was expressed in the orders of Council, "upon the families who had adhered to the unity of the empire and joined the royal standard in America, before the treaty of separation in the year 1783, to the end that their posterity might be discriminated from the then future settlers. From the initials of two emphatic words, the unity of the empire, it was styled the

"U. E. List," and they, whose names were entered on it, were distinguished as the U. E. Loyalists, a distinction of some consequence, for, in addition to the promise of such loyalty by themselves, it was declared that their children, as well as those born hereafter, as those already born, should, upon arriving at the age of twenty-one years, and females upon their marriage within that age, be entitled to grants of 200 acres each, free from all expense." Upon arriving at age, the descendant petitioned the Governor, stating the facts upon oath, and accompanied with the affidavit of one person. The order was issued, and land in one of the newer townships was duly allotted and the patent issued free of cost.

The following is the order of Council referring to the grants of land to the U. E. Loyalists:

"QUEBEC, Monday, 9th Nov. 1789."

Present, LORD DORCHESTER and thirteen Councillors.

"His Lordship intimated to the Council, that it remained a question upon the regulations for the disposition of the waste lands of the Crown, whether the board constituted for that purpose, were authorized to make locations to the sons of loyalists, on their arriving to full age, and that it was his wish to put a mark of honor upon the families who had adhered to the unity of the empire, and joined the Royal standard in America, before the treaty of separation in the year 1783."

"The Council concurring with his Lordship, it is accordingly ordered, that the several land boards take course for preserving a registry of the names of all persons falling under the description aforementioned, to the end that their posterity may be discriminated from future settlers, in the parish registers, and rolls of the militia of their respective districts, and other public remembrances of the Province, as proper objects, by their persevering in the fidelity and conduct so honorable to their ancestors, for distinguished benefits and privileges."

"And it is also ordered that the said land boards may, in every such case, provide not only for the sons of the loyalists, as they arrive at full age, but for their daughters also, of that age, or on their marriage, assigning to each a lot of 200 acres, more or less, provided, nevertheless, that they respectfully comply with the general regulations, and that it shall satisfactorily appear that there has been no default in the due cultivation and improvement of the lands already assigned to the head of the family of which they are members."

In the first days of the Upper Canadian Militia, instructions were given to the Captains in each battalion that in the roll of members, all of the U. E. Loyalists enrolled should have the capitals U. E. affixed to their names.

After the war of 1812, it became necessary for the applicant to present a certificate from a Clerk of the Peace that he retained his loyalty. The following is the order of the Executive Council:

YORK, 27th June, 1816.

"Public notice is hereby given by order of His Excellency Governor in Council, that no petition from sons and daughters of U. E. Loyalists will be hereafter received without a certificate from the Magistrate in Quarter Sessions, signed by the chairman and Clerk of the Peace, that the parent retained his loyalty during the late war, and was under no suspicion of aiding or assisting the enemy. And if a son then of age, that he also was loyal during the late war, and did his duty in defense of the Province. And if a daughter of an U. E. L. married, that her husband was loyal, and did his duty in defense of the Province." (Signed) JOHN SMALL, Clerk of the Executive Council.

The steps taken by Government to prevent persons not actually upon the U. E. List from enjoying the peculiar privileges operated sometimes against the U. E. Loyalists unpleasanty, which led to some agitation, as the following will show:

In the year 1832, a meeting was held at Bath. Referring to this meeting the Kingston *Herald*, of April 4, says:

The alleged injustice of the Government with regard to the sons and daughters of U. E. Loyalists has been a fruitful source of complaint by the grievance-mongers. At the late Bath meeting Mr. PERRY offered the following amendment to a resolution, which was negatived by a large majority,

"Resolved, That a free grant of 200 acres of the waste lands of the Crown, by His Majesty the King, to the U. E. Loyalists and their sons and daughters, was intended as a mark of His Majesty's Royal munificence towards those who had shown a devotedness to His Majesty's person and government during the sanguinary struggle at the late American Revolution, and that the settlement duty required of late to be performed by the above description of persons and others equally entitled to gratuitous grants, and also their not being allowed the privilege of locating in any, or all townships surveyed and open for location, appears to this meeting to be unjust, and ought therefore to be abolished."

CHAPTER LXXI.

CONTENTS—Notice of a Few—Booth—Brock—Burritt—Cotter—Cartwright—Conger—Cole—Dempsey—Detlor—Fraser—Finkle—Fisher—Fairfield—Grass—Gamble Hagerman—Johnson's—" Bill" Johnson—Macaulay—The Captive, Christian Moore—Parliament—Morden—Roblins—Simon—Van Alstine—Wallbridge—Chrysler—White—Wilkins—Stewart—Wilson—Metcalf—Jayne—McIntosh—Bird—Gerow—Vankleek—Perry—Sir William Johnson's children.

INDIVIDUAL NOTICES—CONCLUSION.

The noble band of Loyalists have now almost all passed away. Their bodies have long since been laid in the grave; their children also have almost all departed, and the grand-children are getting old. Their last resting places—resting from war, famine, and toil—are to be found upon beautiful eminences, overlooking the blue waters of the Bay and River and Lake. All along their shores may be seen the quiet burying-places of those who cleared the land and met the terrible realities of a pioneer life.

The present work cannot embrace a history of the many noble ones, deserving attention, who laid the foundation of the brightest colony of Great Britain. Yet it would be incomplete without giving the names of a few representative persons. They are such as we have been able to procure, and while there are others, not referred to, well worthy of a place in history, these are no less worthy. We have, under "The Combatants," referred to others of the first settlers, and would gladly have introduced the names of all, could they have been obtained.

BOOTH—"DIED—At Ernesttown, on Saturday, Oct. 31, 1813, very suddenly, Joshua Booth, Esq., aged 54 years. He was one of the oldest settlers in that place, and ever retained the character of a respectable citizen. Left a widow and ten children."

THE BROCK FAMILY.—William Brock was a native of Scotland; born in 1715. Was taken by a press-gang when eighteen, and forced upon a man-of-war. Served in the navy several years, when he was taken prisoner by the French. Afterward was exchanged at Boston. Being set at liberty from the service, he settled at Fishkill, New York, where he married, and became the father of a large family, two sons, Philip and John, by the first wife; and eight children by a second, named William, Ruth, Naomi, Isabel, Deborah, Catherine, Samuel, Garret, and Lucretia. In consequence of the rebellion, he became a refugee, and, at the close, settled in Adolphustown; lived for a short time near the Court House, upon his town lot, two of his neighbors gave him theirs, and he continued to live upon the three acres for some time. He drew land near the Lake on the Mountain, and in the west, to which his sons went when they grew old enough. One of them was Captain of Militia during the war of 1812. He received at that time a letter from Gen. Brock, who claimed relationship; the letter was written a few days before Gen. Brock fell. This letter still exists. The youngest of the children married Watterberry, and still lives, (1867) aged 82, with her daughter, Mrs. Morden, Ameliasburgh.

CARTWRIGHT.—One of the most noted of the refugees who settled at Kingston, was Richard Cartwright. He was a native of Albany, and was forced to leave his home because of his loyalty. He found an asylum with others at Carleton Island, or Fort Niagara. Some time after the conclusion of the war he was in partnership with Robert, afterward Honorable Hamilton, at Niagara. But sometime about 1790, he settled in Kingston, where, as a merchant he acquired extensive property. The Government mills at Napanee came into his possession. Those who remember his business capacity, say it was very great. He was a man of "liberal education and highly esteemed. Suffered at last calmly and patiently, and died at Montreal, 27th July, 1815, aged fifty years."

The estimation in which this gentleman was held is sufficiently attested by the following, which we take from the *Kingston Gazette*:

YORK, March 13, 1816.

A new township in the rear of Darlington, in the district of Newcastle, has been surveyed, and is now open for the location of the U. E. Loyalists and military claimants. We understand that His Excellency, the Lieutenant-Governor to testify in the most public manner the high sense which he entertained of the merit and services of the late Honorable Richard Cartwright, has been pleased to honor this township with the name of CARTWRIGHT, a name ever to be remembered in Canada with gratitude and respect. Dignified with a seat in the Legislative Council, and also with a high appointment in the militia of the Province, Mr. Cartwright discharged the duties incident to those situations, with skill, fidelity, and attention. Animated with the purest principle of loyalty, and with an ardent seal for the preservation of that noble constitution which we enjoy, he dedicated, when even struggling under great bodily infirmity, the remains of a well spent life to the service of his country. Nor was he less perspicuous for his exemplary behaviour in private life; obliging to his equals—kind to his friends—affectionate to his family, he passed through life, eminently distinguished for virtuous and dignified propriety of conduct, uniformly maintaining the exalted character of a true patriot, and of a great man."

He was a good type of the old school, a tall, robust man, with a stern countenance, and a high mind. He had sustained the loss of one eye, but the remaining one was sharp and piercing. As the first Judge of Mecklenburgh, he discharged his duties with great firmness, amounting, it is said, often to severity. As an officer of the militia, a position he held in 1812, he was a strict disciplinarian, and often forgot that the militiamen were respectable farmers. Mr. Cartwright left two sons, the late John S. Cartwright, and the Rev. Robert Cartwright. It is unnecessary to say that the descendants of Judge Cartwright are among the most respectable, influential and wealthy, living in the Midland District.

Mr. James Cotter, was by profession, a farmer, residing in Sophiasburgh in good circumstances. He was universally respected; decided, and well informed in political matters; and as a proof of the public confidence was elected M.P.P. In Parliament he served his constituents faithfully, and maintained a reputation for consistency and uprightness. In 1819, when party spirit animated the two political parties, he became a candidate for re-election, but after a close contest was defeated by James Wilson, Esq.

Conger—"At West Lake, Hallowell, on the 27th May, 1825, died Dengine Conger, in the 60th year of his age. He held a commission in the First Battalion of the Prince Edward Militia, during twenty-three years. He resided in Hallowell forty years, and lived a very exemplary life, and died regretted by all who knew him."

Cole.—In the history of Adolphustown, reference is made to Daniel Cole, the very first settler in that township. The writer in the summer of 1866, took dinner with John Cole, of Ameliasburgh, son of Daniel. John was then in his 92nd year. He has since, 1867, passed away. Born in Albany before the rebellion, he, with his family during the war, found their way as loyalists to the city of New York, where they remained until the leaving of Van Alstine's company. The old man could remember many of the events of that exciting period, being, when they came to Canada, about ten years old. The brigade of batteaux from Sorel, was under the supervision of Collins, he says: "Old Mother Cook kept tavern in Kingston, in a low flat hut, with two rooms. There were four or five houses altogether in the place. Landed in fourth township in June. Saw no clearings or buildings all the way up from Kingston, nor tents; a complete wilderness. Remembers an early settler in second township, named Cornelius Sharp, from the fact that he injured his knee, and that Dr. Dougall desired to amputate; but his father cured it. His mothers name was Sophia de Long, from Albany. She lost property. A hogshead of spirits was brought up from New York. The settlers were called together every morning and supplied with a little on account of the new climate. His father had been a spy and carried despatches in a thin steel box, which was placed between the soles of the boot. Before resorting to this mode he had been caught, and sentenced to be hanged immediately. The rope was around his neck, and the end thrown over the limb of a tree, when he suddenly gave a spring from their grasp, and ran, while shot after shot was leveled at his flying figure; but he escaped, "God Almighty would not let the balls hit him." Remembers the Indians when first came, were frequently about, would come in and look at the dinner table; but refused to eat bread at first; afterward would, and then brought game to them in abundance at times. Remembers landing at Adolphustown, he hauled the boat to a block oak tree, which overhung the water, his father built a wharf here afterwards. It was in the afternoon. They all went ashore. There were three tents of linen put up. His father brought a scythe with him, with which they cut marsh hay, or flags. This was used to cover the houses, and they kept out the rain well.

His father's family consisted of twelve persons, two died at Sorel. The settlers used to meet every Sunday to hear the Bible read, generally by Ferguson; sometimes had prayer. Remembers, Quarter Sessions met at his father's, Cartwright was Judge. The Grand Jury would go to the stable to converse. Says he once saved Chrys. Hagerman's life, who was bleeding at nose, after Drs. Dougall and Dunham had failed. His father lived to be 105; his sister died last year, aged 101. Remembers the man that was convicted of stealing a watch, and hanged. Has seen the gallows on Gallows Point, Captain Grass' farm. The gallows remained there a dozen years. The man it turned out, was innocent.

DIED.—"On Friday the 5th of August, at his residence in Adolphustown, Mr. Daniel Cole, at the very advanced age of 105 years, 1 month and 12 days. He was a native of Long Island, N. Y., and the oldest settler in this township; he was respected and beloved by all who knew him—having long performed his duty as a loyal subject, a faithful friend, a kind husband, an indulgent parent, and an obliging neighbor. Born in the fifth year of the reign of George II, he lived under four Sovereigns, and saw many changes both in the land of his birth, and this of his adoption. He has beheld the horrors of war, and has tasted of the blessings of peace; he has seen that which was once a wilderness, "blossom and flourish like the rose," where formerly was nothing to be seen but the dark shadow of the lofty pine, oak, and maple, here and there broken by the thin blue vapor curling above the Indian wigwam, he has seen comfortable dwellings arise; out of the superabundance of nature man has supplied his necessity. Beneath the untiring efforts of human industry, the dark woods have disappeared and waiving fields of grain have taken their place. Where once was seen nought but the light birch bark canoe of the "son of the forest," he has beheld the stately steamboats sweep majestically along—where formerly resounded the savage howl of the panther, the wolf and bear, he has seen towns and villages spring up, as it were by magic; in fact the very face of the country seems changed since he first sat down upwards of 52 years ago, as a settler on the place where he died.

"But after all he saw, he too is gone, his venerable age could not save him, for we are told "the old must die." The friends of his early days were all gone before him; he was becoming "a stranger among men," generations had arisen and passed away, still he remained like a patriarch of old, unbroken by the weight of years. After witnessing the fifth generation, he died universally lamented by all his acquaintances, leaving behind him 8 children, 75 grandchildren, 172 great-grandchildren and 13 great grandchildren's children; in all 268 descendants."

Adolphustown, August 9, 1836. T. D.

DEMPSEY.—"Mark Dempsey was sent out by the British Government as Secretary to General Schuyler. Married about 1746 to Miss Carroll. Thomas, their youngest son, was born in New Jersey, 9th January, 1762. His father died while he was young, and he was left in a part of the country which was held by the rebels, when he had attained to an age to be drafted, Thomas Dempsey did not like to fight in the rebel ranks, and consequently escaped and joined the loyalists. Was in the service when New York was evacuated. Married 1782 to Mary Lawson, whose father, Peter was imprisoned by the rebels, and his property all plundered and confiscated. Came to Canada by Oswego, 1788, accompanied by his wife and her parents. Tarried at Napanee till 1789, when they came to Ameliasburgh, and settled on lot 91, which had been purchased from John Finkle. Dempsey's worldly effects then consisted of a cow, which they brought with them, seven bushels of potatoes, and a French crown, and a half acre of wheat which Finkle had sowed. They drew land in Cramahe. During the first years they were in great distress. A tablespoonful of flour, with milk boiled, or grain shelled by hand, formed their daily meals. Their clothing consisted of blankets obtained of the Indians for the women, and buckskin pants and shirts for the men. Dempsey was the second settler in the township, Weese having settled two years before. Margaret Dempsey, born October 24, 1790, was the third child born in the township.

Detlors—.The Detlors are of the Palatine stock. Says G. H. Detlor, Esq., of the Customs Department, Kingston:

My grandfather, John V. Deltor, emigrated with my grandmother from Ireland, to New York; directly after his marriage in the City of New York, they removed to the town of Camden, where they resided with their family—and at the close of the rebellion (having joined the Royal standard)—he with two or three of his sons and sons-in-law came to Canada, and finally located on lands in the Township of Fredericksburgh, Lot No. 21, 6th concession, where he and his sons lived and died. My father removed to the town of York (now City of Toronto), in 1802, and at the invasion of that place by the Americans, in April, 1813, my father lost his life in defense of the place. There is now but one of my grandfather's children living, an aunt of mine, Mrs. Anne Dulmage, resides in the village of Sydenham, Township of Loughboro', County of Frontenac.

They sacrificed their lands, and suffered great privations. The Detlors have ever been universally esteemed, not alone in the Midland District, but in all parts of Canada, and have been found worthy occupants of many responsible positions.

Isaac Fraser.—"Among the prominent men who resided in Ernesttown, near the Bay of Quinté, was Isaac Fraser, Esq., for many years M.P.P. for the Counties of Lennox and Addington. Mr. Fraser was a man of great decision of character, and during the active part of his life, probably wielded a great influence, and his opinions always commanded great respect. In his political opinions, he was identified with the Conservative or Tory party; and when he arrived at a conclusion on any particular point, he adhered to it with all the tenacity which a clear conviction of its justice could inspire. With him there was no wavering, no vacillation. He was always reliable, and his friends always knew where to find him. There is no doubt, he acted from conscientious motives, and from a clear conviction of duty; and, so far as I know, no man ever charged him with acting corruptly. In his religious views, Mr. Fraser sympathized with the Presbyterians, and, if I mistake not, was a member of the church organized, and watched over by the late Rev. Robert McDowall, of Fredericksburgh."

FINKLE.—The late Geo. Finkle, of Ernesttown, says, "My grandfather, Dr. Geo. Finkle, left Germany when a young man; and bought two estates, one at Great, and one at Little Nine Partners. In adhering to the British, he had all his estates, which were valuable at Nine Partners, Duchess Co., confiscated to the Rebel Government. My father, Henry, made his way to Quebec shortly after the war began, being sixteen years old. Entered the Engineer's Department, where he learned the use of carpenter's tools. In settling, this knowledge was of great use to him, and he became the builder of the first framed building in Upper Canada. His wife was a sister of Capt. John Bleeker. He settled on the front of Ernesttown, lot six." Finkle's Point is well known.

The First court held in Upper Canada, it is said, was at Finkle's house, which being larger than any at Kingston, or elsewhere on the Bay, afforded the most convenience. Mr. Finkle records the trial of a negro for stealing a loaf of bread, who, being found guilty, received thirty-nine lashes. The basswood tree, to which he was tied, is still standing; Mr. Finkle had slaves and was the first to give them freedom. One of the brothers, of which there were three, John, George, and Henry, served seven years in Johnson's regiment.

Mr. Finkle wrote us, Dec. 11, 1865; he says, "Being in my 74th year, and in impaired health, I am unable to write more." The kind man soon thereafter was called away, at a good old age, like his father and grandfather.

Geo. Finkle, son of Henry, had three sons, Gordon William, Roland Robinson, and Henry. The Finkle's, as we have seen elsewhere, were actively engaged in the construction of the first steamboats the 'Frontenac' and 'Charlotte,' having had an interest in the 'Charlotte,' and his eldest son, Gordon, is now one of the oldest captains upon the Bay, being attached to the steamer 'Bay Quinté.' The old place granted to the grandfather, still belongs to the family, Roland R. still residing there, and the youngest, Henry, is Postmaster at Bath.

FISHER.—Judge Alexander Fisher, a name well known in the Midland District, was a native of Perthshire, Scotland, from whence his parents, with a numerous family, emigrated to New York, then a British province. At the time of the rebellion they had accumulated a considerable amount of both real and personal property; but at the defeat of Burgoyne, near the place of whose defeat they lived, the Fisher family, who would not abandon their loyalty, left their all, and endured great hardships in finding their way to Montreal. Alexander was subsequently employed in the Commissariat, under McLean, at Carleton Island; while his twin-brother obtained the charge of the High School at Montreal, which situation he held until his death, in the year 1819. At the close of the war the family obtained their grants of land as U. E. Loyalists.

Alex. Fisher was appointed the first District Judge and Chairman of Quarter Sessions for the Midland District, to the last of which he was elected by his brother magistrates. He was also for many years a Captain of Militia, which post he held during the war of 1812. The family took up their abode in Adolphustown, upon the shores of Hay Bay. A sister of Judge Fisher was married to Mr. Hagerman, and another to Mr. Stocker, who, for a time, lived on the front of Sidney. He was related, by marriage, to McDonnell, of Marysburgh. His parents lived with him at the farm in Adolphustown. They were buried here in the family vault, with a brother, and the Judge's only son.

Judge Fisher was short in stature, and somewhat stout, with a prominent nose. He was, as a judge, and as a private individual, universally esteemed. "He was a man of great discernment, and moral honesty governed his decisions."—(Allison.) He died in the year 1830, and was buried in the family vault. As an evidence of the high esteem in which he was held, there was scarcely a lawyer or magistrate in the whole District, from the Carrying Place to Gananoque, who did not attend his funeral, together with a great concourse of the settlers throughout the counties.

FAIRFIELD.—The Kingston *Gazette* tells the following:

"DIED.—At his house, in Ernesttown, on the 7th Feb. 1816, in the 47th year of his age, W. Fairfield. His funeral was attended by a numerous circle of relatives, friends and neighbors. He left a widow and seven children. The first link that was broken in a family chain of twelve brothers and three sisters, all married at years of maturity. His death was a loss to the district, as well as to his family. He was one of the commissioners for expending the public money on the roads. Formerly a member of the Provincial Parliament; many years in the commission of the Peace. As a magistrate and a man, he was characterised by intelligence, impartiality, independence of mind and liberality of sentiments."

GRASS.—Captain Michael Grass, the first settler of Kingston township, was a native of Germany. The period of his emigration to America is unknown. He was a saddler and harness-maker by trade, and for years plied his trade in Philadelphia. It would seem that he removed from Philadelphia to New York, for his son Peter was born in this city in 1770. According to the statement of his grandson who often heard the facts from his father, Peter Grass, soon after the commencement of the rebellion, Michael Grass was taken prisoner by the Indians, who were staying at Cataraqui. In this he is probably mistaken. We learn from another source that it was during the previous French war, which is more likely to be correct. It would seem that Grass and two other prisoners were not con fined in the fort, but held in durance by a tribe of Indians, who permitted them to hunt, fish, &c. They made an effort to escape, but were caught and brought back. Again they attempted, carrying with them provisions, which they had managed to collect, sufficient to last them a week. But it was nine weeks before they reached an English settlement, one having died by the way from hunger and exposure. It was the knowledge which Grass had acquired of the territory at Cataraqui, while a prisoner, which led to his appointment to the leadership of a band of refugees at the close of the war.—(See settlement of Kingston.)

It does not appear that Captain Grass occupied any office in the army during the war. His captaincy commenced upon his leaving New York with the seven vessels for Canada. By virtue of his captaincy, he was entitled to draw 3000 acres. Beside lot twenty-five in Kingston, he drew in fourth concession of Sidney nearly 2000 acres in one block.

Captain Grass had three sons, Peter, John, and Daniel, and three daughters. Daniel, some years after, went sailing and was never heard from. Peter and John settled in the Second Town and became the fathers respectively of families. The land drawn by the captain, and the 600 acres by each of his children, has proved a lasting source of wealth and comfort to his descendants.

Captain Grass naturally took a leading part at least during the first years of the settlement at Kingston. He was possessed of some education, and was a man of excellent character, with a strict sense of honor. Although opportunities presented themselves to accumulate property at the expense of others, he refused to avail himself of all such. He was appointed a magistrate at an early period, and as such performed many of the first marriages in Kingston. In religion, he was an adherent to the Church of England. Probably he had been brought up a Lutheran. His old "Dutch" Bible still is read by an old German in Ernesttown; but it seems a pity that although none of the Grass family can read its time worn pages, it should be allowed to remain in other hands than the descendants of the old captain.

In connection, it may be mentioned that some time before the war, a poor German, a baker by trade, came to New York. Michael Grass assisted him into business, and even gave him a suit of clothes. When the refugees came to Canada, this baker accompanied them. He settled in Quebec, where he amassed eventually great wealth, and the P—— family are not unknown to the public.

Gamble.—The subjoined somewhat lengthy notice is taken from the *Toronto Colonist*:—"Dr. Gamble and family were for many years residing at Kingston, and he was intimately associated with the first days of Upper Canada, as a Province, while his offspring as will be seen, form no indifferent element of the society of the Province," we therefore insert the notice *in extenso*. "Isabella Elizabeth Gamble, the third daughter of Dr. Joseph Clark and Elizabeth Alleyne, was born at Stratford, in Connecticut—then a colony of Great Britain—on the 24th October, 1767. In the year 1776, her father, faithful to his allegiance, repaired to the British army in New York, to which place his family followed him. At the peace of 1783, Dr. Clark removed with his family to New Brunswick (then known as the Province of Acadia) and took up his residence at Mangerville. There his daughter, the subject of this memoir, then in her seventeenth year, was married on the 18th of May, 1884, to Dr. John Gamble, the eldest son of William Gamble and Leah Tyrer, of Duross, near Enniskillen, Ireland. Mr. Gamble was born in 1755, studied physic and surgery at Edinburgh; emigrated to the British colony in 1779, and landed in New York in September of that year. Immediately on his arrival, he entered the King's service as Assistant-Surgeon to the General Hospital; subsequently he was attached to the "Old Queen's Rangers," and for some time did duty with that regiment as surgeon. At the peace of 1783, he, with other American Loyalists, went to New

Brunswick. After his marriage Dr. Gamble practised his profession at St. John's, and resided in New Brunswick until 1798, when having been appointed Assistant-Surgeon to the late regiment of Queen's Rangers, by General Simcoe, then Lieutenant-Governor of Upper Canada, he joined his regiment at Niagara, where it was then quartered, having left his wife and five daughters at Mangerville. Mrs. Gamble continued to reside with her father until 1798, when her husband, having in the meantime, been promoted to the surgeoncy of his regiment; she, with her five daughters, the eldest then but thirteen years of age, accompanied by her father and a sister (afterwards married to the Hon. Samuel Smith), ascended the river St. John in a bark canoe, crossed the portage by Temi conata to the Rivierie du Loup, came up the St. Lawrence, and joined Dr. Gamble then with his regiment in garrison at York.

"In 1802, the Queen's Rangers were disbanded, and Mrs. Gamble accompanied her husband and family to Kingston, where he practised his profession until his death, in the fifty-sixth year of his age, on the 1st December, 1811. She remained in Kingston till the year 1820, when with the portion of her family then at home, she removed to Toronto, and there remained surrounded by her offspring until her death on the 9th March, 1859.

"Mrs. Gamble had thirteen children, nine daughters and four sons; Isabella, the eldest, married to Robert Charles Home, Esq., Assistant-Surgeon, Glengary Light Infantry; Mary Ann, married to Colonel Sinclair, Royal Artillery; Sarah Hannah Boyes, to James Geddes, Esq., Assistant-Surgeon, Medical Staff; Leah Tyrer, to the Hon. William Allen; Catharine, who died unmarried; Jane, married to Benjamin Whitney, Esq.; Rachel Crookshank, to Sir James Buchannan Macaulay; Magdaline, to Thomas William Birchall, Esq.; and Mary Ann unmarried; John William, of Vaughan, William, of Milton, Etobicoke; Clarke, of Toronto, and Joseph who died in infancy; of these thirteen, six only survive, but Mrs. Gamble's descendants have already reached the large number of 204, and some of her children's children are now upwards of thirty years of age.

"The remarkable longevity of a large number of the American Loyalist emigrants who came to the British Provinces after the American Revolution, has been noticed by the Lord Bishop of New Brunswick, as a striking instance of the fulfilment of the promise contained in the fifth commandment, embracing, as that commandment unquestionably does, the duty of obedience to civil rulers. Mrs. Gamble may well be counted among that number, having, in October last, entered upon her ninety-second year."—*Colonist.*

Among the company of refugees which followed VanAlstine's lead to Canada, was Nicholas Hagerman.

He settled in the village of Adolphustown, almost in front of the U. E. burying ground. The point of land here between the Bay and the Creek is still known as Hagerman's Point. The whole of the land except the burying ground was cleared by Hagerman. His house was situated a short distance west of the road leading from the wharf up to the village. It was built near the water's edge. The short period which has elapsed since that building was erected has not only consigned the builder to a grave almost unknown, and the building to the destructive teeth of time, but the very land on which the house stood, where he and his family daily passed in and out, is now washed away by the ceaseless waves of the bay.

Mr. Hagerman was a man of some education, and it is said had studied law before leaving New York. At all events he became one of the first appointed lawyers in Upper Canada, probably at the time McLean, of Kingston, was appointed. He continued to live and practice law in Adolphustown until his death. "He was the first lawyer to plead at these Courts. He was a self-made man."—Allison.

The writer's parents lived at, and near the village of Adolphustown when young; they knew the Hagerman's well, and for many a day and year attended school with Nicholas Hagerman's children. There were at least two brothers, David and Christopher, and two daughters, Betsy and Maria. Daniel was a sedate person, but "Chris," was a saucy boy. They were both elected to Parliament at the same time, but Daniel died before the meeting of Parliament. Christopher studied law with his father at first, was a pupil of Dr. Strachan's, and completed his legal studies in McLean's office in Kingston. The father and son were sometimes employed by opposing clients; at one time in Kingston, the son won the suit, much to the annoyance of the father. The father exclaimed, "have I raised a son to put out my eyes." No, replied the son, "to open them father." At the commencement of the war in 1812, Christopher went as Lieutenant with a Company from Adolphustown to Kingston. Shortly after he was chosen Aide-de-Camp to the Governor General. Thenceforth his way to preferment was steady. At the close of the war he was appointed Collector of Customs at Kingston. The *Gazette* of 5th September, 1815, says that Christopher Alexander Hagerman, Esq., Barrister-at-Law, was appointed to His Majesty's Council in and for the Province of Upper Canada.

On the 26th March, 1817, he was married to Elizabeth, eldest daughter of James Macaulay, Esq., Kingston.

JOHNSONS—Henry Johnson was born at New Jersey, 1757, where he lived till the rebellion, when he removed to Poughkeepsie. In June, 1788, being a loyalist, he came with his brother Andrew to Canada, enduring many privations and hardships. He settled in Hallowell, where he lived until his death, which took place 28th May, 1829, being in his 73rd year. "He was noted for his hospitality—charitable to the poor without ostentation, a pious christian. For the last five years he suffered much."

ANDREW JOHNSON.—Among the combatants, we have given the name of James Johnson; here we design to give a place to some account of his two sons, Andrew and William, or "Bill," as he was commonly called, a name yet remembered by many.

Perhaps there is not now living a more interesting historic character than Andrew Johnson, residing in the vicinity of Belleville. A native of New York State, Gainesborough, he came in with his father at the first settlement of Upper Canada. He was an eye witness of the first days of Ernesttown, and Kingston. At the beginning of the present century he was known as an unusually rapid walker. Andrew was engaged in carrying the mail from Kingston to York. Mr. Stuart was his employer. His route was by the Bay shore to Adolphustown, across the Bay, at the Stone Mills, by Picton and Wellington, to the Carrying Place; and thence along the Lake shore, fording streams as best he could, often upon a fallen tree, or by swimming. He would spend five hours in York and then start back. These trips were generally made once a fortnight. He subsequently lived at Bath for forty years, where he kept a tavern, and strangely enough, as he avers, he never drank liquor in his life.

His father's log house was used by Rev. Mr. Stuart to preach in for three years, before the frame building was erected on the hill, which would hold thirty or forty persons. It was a story and a-half high. Andrew Johnson is now upwards of a hundred. Although his memory is somewhat defective, he retains a great deal of bodily vigor; and eats and sleeps well. He rarely converses unless spoken to. He is a man of somewhat low stature, small frame, with spare limbs. Mr. Lockwood, who has known him a long time, says, "He was remarkably quick in his movements. During the war, the two started to walk from Prescott to Kingston, but Lockwood says that Johnson could walk three miles to his one. His brother,

"Bill," had a fast horse, which could outrun anything. Andrew offered to bet a hundred dollars that he could travel to York quicker than the horse. Of course there was but an imperfect path, with no bridges. His offer was not accepted. Andrew was a loyal soldier in 1812, and belonged to the same companies as his brother. The old man is yet very quick in his movements, retaining that peculiar swinging gait by which he formerly so rapidly traveled long distances. His days are passing away in a quiet dream, tenderly cared for by his son, with his wife.

Bill Johnson.—William Johnson, brother of the foregoing, was one of six sons of James Johnson, born in Ernesttown. His youthful days were spent in the vicinity of what is now the village of Bath. About the time of the commencement of the war of 1812, he was engaged in Kingston, in trading, and had a store of general merchandize. When the first draft for men was made, Johnson was one of the conscripts. For a very short time, he did service, and then procured his brother (not Andrew) as a substitute. There was not at this time any doubt of his loyalty. It was natural he should desire to attend to his business in Kingston, which at this time was lucrative. And there does not appear that he employed his brother in other than good faith. But some time after his brother entered the service, he deserted to the United States' shore. Even now it does not appear that the authorities of Kingston suspected his loyalty, for they desired that he should take his place in the ranks which his brother had forsaken. This, however, "Bill" would not do. The result was that a file of soldiers commanded by Sergeant Lockwood, (our principal informant) was sent to arrest Johnson, by order of the captain, Matthew Clark of Ernesttown.

Upon the approach of the soldiers, Johnson shouted to Sergeant Lockwood, who had been his life long playmate, "I know what you are after; but you won't get me yet," and immediately shut the door and turned the key. Lockwood, without hesitation, raised his musket, and with the butt knocked the door open, in time to see Bill escaping by the back door. A close chase ensued into a back enclosure, and Lockwood succeeded in catching him by the leg as he was passing through a window. Johnson then submitted, and was conveyed a prisoner to the guard house within the jail. After being confined for sometime he escaped by breaking the jail; probably aided by sympathizers, for a good many thought he was badly treated.

Whatever may have been Johnson's feelings towards the British.

Government before, he now became a most determined enemy of his native country. He vowed he should "be a thorn in Great Britain's side;" and his goods and some property at Bath, a few town lots, being confiscated, he declared he would get back all he lost. The foregoing occurence took place sometime during the fall of 1812. It would appear that Bill Johnson set to work in a systematic manner to carry out his threats.

Being well acquainted with the country and people, and, withal, a bold, determined and fearless man, he did not hesitate to visit the Canadian shore, and was even seen at Bath in day light. He built several small boats, light and trim, and he would at times unhesitatingly voyage upon the broad lake in bold undertakings. His operations consisted in privateering, in inducing American sympathizers to accompany him to the States, and in acting as a spy. During the war there were frequently boat loads of goods, consisting of liquors and other valuable articles passing up the bay, and across the Carrying Place, thence to York. On one occasion Thomas Parker, who was engaged in the business, left Kingston with a batteau laden with valuables for York. Johnson, who watched such events, saw Parker depart. While the latter made his way up the bay, Johnson proceeded in his craft around by the lake, and awaited Parker off Presqu'isle. In due time the batteau was seized by Johnson and his comrades, and taken to the other side. Parker being landed on Point Traverse, off Marysburgh.

Another exploit was the seizure of Government despatches near Brighton. A company of Dragoons, Captain Stinson, were on duty to carry despatches between the River Trent and Smith's Creek, Port Hope. On a certain occasion when a dragoon, by the name of Gardner, was pursuing his way with despatches, he was suddenly seized by Johnson, who deliberately took him with his horse to the lake shore, where he shot the horse, placed the despatch bag in his boat, and then permitted the man to find his way on foot through the woods to report himself to his captain.

"Bill Johnson still lives at French Creek upon the American shore of the St. Lawrence. He was an active participant in the events of 1837, and it is supposed had much to do in recruiting for the army of sympathizers. There is so much of fiction to be found respecting him in connection with that time, that it is difficult to say what part he did take. It has been generally supposed that he was one of the few who escaped from the Windmill, but while, no doubt, he was engaged at the time, there is nothing to rest a decided statement upon. We suspect that "Bill," in his later days, was given to boasting a little, and took pleasure in catering to the taste of his Yankee friends, in relating what he and his daughter Kate did, (in imagination.)

MACAULAY, "the father of the Honorable John, and the Rev. William Macaulay, settled during the Revolutionary war on Carleton Island, then a British station and fortification, where he supplied the commissariat and garrison, and carried on business. In 1794, Mr. Macaulay removed to Kingston, where he amassed considerable property. When he removed to Kingston, he had rafted over from Carleton Island his log dwelling house, and placed it where it now stands at the corner of Princess snd Ontario Streets. It has since been clap-boarded over and added to, and having been kept painted and in good repair is still a very habitable building."—(Cooper.)

Mr. Macaulay had come to New York shortly before the commencement of the Colonial troubles, and as a loyalist had his house pillaged and burnt, by the rebels, and became a refugee at the military post at Carleton Island. About 1785, he settled at Kingston, where he married, and remained until his death, in September, 1800, being fifty-six years old. He was at no time connected with the service, but engaged his time in commercial business, and was on most intimate terms with those in authority, being a particular friend of the Duke of Albano. His sons continued his business and in time were called to occupy honorable and responsible situations under Government, as Legislative Councilor, Surveyor General, Provincial Secretary, Inspector General, Chaplain to Legislative Assembly, and Commissioners on various important matters.

THE CAPTIVE CHRISTIAN MOORE.

Upon the 19th March, 1867, the writer was privileged, through the kindness of the Rev. Mr. Anderson, to visit an individual who, of all others, possesses historic interest. About half a mile north of the Indian Church upon the old York road, Tyendinaga, lives Christian Moore. Beside the stove, in a low Indian chair, sat a woman whose shrunken and bent appearance made her appear no larger than a girl of sixteen. But the face, with its parchment-like skin—the deeply wrinkled features, bespoke the burden of many winters. Yet, the eye still flashed looks of intelligence, as the face was upturned from her hands on which she almost incessantly rested her head, as if the shoulders had wearied in their long life duty. Christian is about a hundred years old, during eighty of which she has remained a captive with the Mohawks. Although a white woman, she knows not a word of English. Long, long years ago, in becoming the wife of an Indian, and the mother of Indians, she became to all purposes one of themselves. She is a living relic of the American Revolution, as well as of the customs of the Mohawk Indians a hundred years ago.

In the first days of the rebellion, in an encounter between the Indians and a party of rebels in the Mohawk valley, one of the Indians, by the name of Green, was killed. The custom among the several tribes, or families, when one of their number had been lost in war, was to take the first captive they could, and adopt him or her, into the tribe, to keep up the number. A party of Indians, under John Green, a chief and brother of the one killed, called in after days Captain Green, in the course of their foray, caught a little girl about ten years of age. That little girl is the old person of whom we are speaking. The old woman yet recollects the fact that her father's family, on the approach of the Indians, made haste to escape; she by accident was left alone or behind. She remembers to have been running along the road, when she was taken. She says there were a good many Indians. After this there is a blank in her memory, until the period of the Indians leaving their homes to escape. This was the time when they buried their Communion Plate. Christian says she was carried upon an Indian's back, as they fled to Lachine. She recollects that they were staying three years at Lachine, when the tribe set out to take possession of the land which Government was to give them. It was about a year from the time they started from Lachine, until they, under Brant, reached their destination, the Grand River. Captain Green was with this party, and stayed with them at Grand River for six years, when, becoming dissatisfied, he, with his family, came to the Bay Quinté. Christian remembers all this. She was living with Captain Green's sister. They came in a batteau, down the north shore of the lake, and crossed at the Carrying Place at the head of the bay.

Christian in time became the wife of an Indian, by the name of Anthony Smart, who, she says, has been dead now thirty-eight years. They had but one child, a daughter, who was married to Abram Maricle. They had three children, one being a son. Christian's daughter has been dead many years, but the old lady now is surrounded by grand-children to the third generation.

Some time after the close of the Revolution, a person by the name of Moore, came with his family to Canada, and settled at Napanee. By some means he learned that there was a white woman among the Mohawks, and he visited them to see if it might be his long lost daughter. Such proved to be the case. He was Christian's father. She remembers the occasion, (it was about forty-five years ago,) her father was then a very old man. Of course, there was no resemblance between the woman in Indian garb before him, and his little girl of ten years. But there was a mark upon her arm, the result of a burn by which he was enabled to recognize his own flesh and blood. The scar, upon the left fore-arm, can yet be distinctly seen. Painful, indeed, must have been the feelings of the parent, to know she was his daughter, and yet knew not a syllable of her mother tongue. The natural channel by which parental and filial affection might have flowed was sealed. She says, she has a sister now living back of Napanee. She asked her father if she had been christened, and he informed her she had been. Upon our asking her the question, if she ever went to school, she says, "No;" that she was "always working hard." Asking her the question, if she did not think she had lived a long while, she replied, "I don't think I'll live very long." The Rev. Mr. Anderson informs us that she has ever maintained the character of a true Christian, and is always happy to partake of the Holy Communion. Christian's great-grandson, himself a father, acted as interpreter.

It is possible that this woman, who belonged to another century, may live yet several years. There is much of vigor in her movements and conversation. Although shrivelled and bent almost double with age, her body seems to be well nourished, and her arms possess considerable thickness. She always enjoyed good health, and now eats and sleeps in the most comfortable manner.

We are informed by a recent letter from Rev. Mr. Andersen, 1869, that the old woman continues quite well, and works in the garden in summer.

PARLIAMENT.—Mrs. Morden, of Sophiasburgh, was born upon the banks of the Hudson, forty miles from its mouth. Her birthday stretches back ninety-eight years. She came into Canada with her father, George Parliament, who was of German parentage, born upon the sea; and like the ocean, he was through out his brief life tossed up and down with scarcely a day of calm and sunshine. The family reached the Fourth Town, and only six weeks after her father's eyes were closed in death. Mrs. Morden has a distinct recollection of the rebellion. Her father was staunchly loyal, and she has heard him repeatedly declare that he would lay his bones in the King's domains. During the war he was imprisoned twice, at Goshen and Poughkeepsie. She was thirteen years old when they came to Canada, and remembers the many weary days of travel by Oneida Lake. Her father walked and drove the cattle all day, her mother would sit up till late at night over the camp-kettle preparing food for the party to use the following day, so that there would be no delay on the way. Having crossed from the States, the Skenectady boats landed at Little Catariqui. The father was down below on the St. Lawrence swimming the cattle across the stream. They found their flour was nearly done. She, with a little sister, went along the shore to the village of Kingston to buy flour, she had only enough money to buy a quarter of a hundred of second flour, which she carried from McAulay's store to the hungry company at the Little Catariqui, where they were wind-bound. She remembers the appearance of the shores as they journeyed along; the rude log cabins in the small clearings. The family of eleven children settled upon the north shore of Hay Bay. The eldest boy was nineteen years old. They now thought that they, in common with other settlers, would be permitted to work out a peaceful and happy future, but the arrow of death was already in the bended bow. The mournful occasion can hardly be appreciated, the father of eleven children in the wilderness suddenly cut down. Each of the neighbours had quite enough to do to care for his own family. All these terrible facts are fresh in the mind of the venerable lady. The events of later years are faded from her memory; but those are too deeply engraven upon her mind, by the pen of sorrow, to be erased while life lasts and mind sits enthroned. The subsequent events connected with the family for a time are no less distressing. They had one cow, the milk of which supplied them with their principal food. Fish was occasionally caught. But they often had to seek herbs and greens. For weeks they were in the greatest distress for the very necessaries of life. All of the family who were old enough went out to work. The following spring, and the subsequent ones, her mother made sugar, not to use in the family, "oh! no, that was too great a luxury." It was all carried and sold for flour. Mrs. Morden remembers it, for she carried much of the sap. She subsequently worked out, until after several years she found a kind supporter. Mrs. Morden, whom the writer saw nearly four years ago, (1865), was then, although so old, yet vigorous and sprightly, with a kindly face, and even a sharp eye. Of all the persons it has been our privilege to converse with, there are only a few who gave such clear and appropriate testimony, and afforded so much satisfaction. She confined her remarks strickly to the questions, and we learned much in a short hour. She spoke feelingly; and with Christian nobleness said she, "I have lived a long time and had many blessings, thanks be to God." Thus spoke the lips of one whose youth had been spent in another century.

ROBLINS.—The Roblin family is extensively and favorably known in Upper Canada, especially in the bay region. They, although numerous, have sprung from a common ancestry. Originally of English or Welsh nativity; at the commencement of the rebellion they were found dwelling in New York, and New Jersey. As a result of the Revolution, four branches of the Roblin family came into Canada, two of whom, John and Stephen, were brothers.

John Roblin lived in New Jersey, he took no part in the contest, but his sympathies were doubtless with the loyalists. One day, he was sitting in the door-way, when a scouting party fired upon the house as they approached. Some fourteen shots were fired. This was done without any warning, the house being inhabited by a private family. John Roblin was wounded in the knee. The party entered the house and completely ransacked it, searching for valuables; not satisfied with what they found, they demanded where the money was; John's brother, Stephen, was suspended by his thumbs to a tree with the view of forcing him to tell where the money was concealed. John, although wounded, was stripped almost naked. The ruffians, who did all this under the name of "Liberty," destroyed what they could not carry; and flour, furniture, everything in fact, was strewn about and broken. One of the party put his bayoneted musket to the breast of Mrs. Roblin, and dared her to call George her king. She fearlessly replied, he once was, why not now. The demon was pulling the trigger, when a more human comrade knocked the weapon aside. The rebels were near by under Washington, and this was a regular detailed foraging party. John Roblin was afterward placed in the rebel hospital, but the doctor was unnecessarily cruel, and so maltreated him, that he became a life-long cripple. The family came into the rebel camp, and Mrs. Roblin complained to General Washington of the conduct of his men. He had her look among the men, and promised to punish any she said had been among the party. But of course they kept out of the way.

The Roblins settled originally in Adolphustown, John Roblin died, and his widow, with the family, removed to Sophiasburgh, where she bought 100 acres of land for $25, and paid for it by weaving. She likewise cut down trees and made her hut.

Roblin, who settled in the third concession of Fourth Town, became a member of Parliament.

SIMON.—John Simon was born in Massachusetts, joined the Royal Standard when the rebellion commenced. At the close of the war, he settled at first near Montreal. He soon removed to Cataraqui, and finally to the Township of Flamborough West, County Westmeath, where he lived till his death. He had three sons, Titus, John, Walter. A daughter married Detlor, another James McNabb, one Dr. Meacham, one Thompson, the last three lived at Belleville. One of the sons, Titus, we believe, distinguished himself in 1812, at the battle of Lundy's Lane. He had been Commissary at Kingston, and moved to Toronto.

MAJOR VANALSTINE.—The life of this man we have been unable to trace in full; but sufficient remains known to supply the requisites for a short sketch. He must have come from the vicinity of Albany, for he was decidedly Dutch, and spoke the English language very imperfectly. He was a stout, robust man, with a dark complexion, not one of military bearing; and most likely, until the rebellion, had nothing to do with military matters. Among the first to settle in Adolphustown, he well knew the hardships of pioneer life. During the course of the rebellion he had suffered many privations. Naturally a kind-hearted man, he for many years afforded to the new comers much comfort and material aid. His house was ever open to the passing stranger—to the old soldier, to poor refugees. He was known to everybody in the whole settlement of the Bay. No matter who came, he would order up from his cellar kitchen—the old Dutch style—his negro servants—slaves he had brought in with him, and set before the traveler the necessary refreshments. The son of one who knew him well, says he was hospitable to a fault. His religion was Lutheran, and the Government granted him a pension for distinguished service.

THE WALLBRIDGE FAMILY—Are of English descent, and were among the first settlers of America. There were several families of the name existing in America at the breaking out of the rebellion, one of which had been residents of Bennington, and were known as the Bennington Wallbridge's. The rebellion led, as in many other instances, to a division among the sons; some sided with the rebels, others remained loyal. Elijah Wallbridge took part with the loyalists. His children never heard him speaking of the part he took; but it is learned through another source that he was one of a party who on one occasion made a gallant attack upon a military prison, and relieved the prisoners. His old musket may yet be seen. It is in possession of the Hon. Lewis Wallbridge. At the close of the war, he desired, like many other loyalists, to remain in the States, and indeed did for a time, but the spirit of intolerance was manifested toward him, so that he determined to settle in Canada. He consequently, at the beginning of the present century, came to the Bay and purchased the tract of land held in Ameliasburgh by the family.

Elijah Wallbridge married the daughter of a U. E. Loyalist, Capt. Robert Everett, of Kingston. Mr. Wallbridge, in making his visits to the front of Ernesttown, found it convenient to cross the Bay from Mississauga Point to Ox Point, and as a canoe was not available he often disrobed himself, tied his clothes in a bundle and managed to swim across, holding the bundle of clothes above the water.

WHITE.—The Cobourg *Star* recorded the death of Mrs. White of White's Mills, aged 82 years, as follows:

"Another old and respectable inhabitant has paid the debt of nature, whose memory will long be cherished by survivors. In 1792 Mrs. White was living with her family, the Chrysler's, at the homestead, Sidney, near Belleville, but removed after her marriage with Mr. White, to Cobourg, in the neighborhood of which she has remained ever since, beloved by her family and greatly respected by all the settlers around. Although she often remarked, they had to undergo many privations, yet they were the happiest days of her existence. She feared the present generation was launching out too much into the fashion of the world, to conduce to solid happiness.

The Chryslers were U. E. Loyalists, and among the first who made Upper Canada their home after the Revolution. Sorel at that period was a government station, and here in 1802, Mrs. White, then Catherine Chrysler, was born. In 1784, their house was unfortunately burned down, when the General made them a liberal grant of lands in Sidney, near Belleville. This was the first settlement in that locality, which was soon followed by many others, so that a neighborhood was soon formed as helpmates to one another. A few years afterward, Mr. White, being a lumber merchant, located in the neighborhood; an intimacy soon sprang up between the parties, which ended in a family union. Clergymen were scarce in those days, but Rev. Robert McDowell, of the reformed Dutch Church, who kept a horse and traveled through the wilderness, tendered his services. By that worthy pioneer, Mr. and Mrs. White were happily united in country simplicity. These primeval days were often referred to as affording more solid happiness than modern finery and ostentation. May the present generation never lose sight of those good old times. She fulfilled the declaration of that discerner of the human heart, Solomon, who says: "She looketh well to the ways of her household, and eateth not the bread of idleness. Her children rise up and call her blessed; her husband also, and he praiseth her."

Wilkins.—Col. Charles Wilkins, although not one of the old U. E. Loyalists, yet having come to Canada at an early date, and taken an active part in matters pertaining to the welfare of the country, respecting military matters, and especially in the history of the Bay, this work would not be complete without a special notice of this very worthy gentleman. The writer had the privilege of visiting him at his home, the Carrying Place, in the summer of 1866, and procured many valuable facts, which were imparted with a kindly courtesy. The winters of 83 years had left their impress upon the tall and once erect figure. But notwithstanding the wear and tear of life, with many cares, and the intractable disease which steadily advanced, his face beamed with a pleasant smile, while he recounted many events with which he had had to do. While relating matters of a general nature, he was most unwilling to speak of his own services, and the diffidence and humbleness of manner, with which he referred to himself was remarkable. We have made reference to Col. Wilkins elsewhere, and will here allude to some events in his life.

He came to Canada with his father in 1792, aged 10 years. At an early period he took up his abode at the Carrying Place and engaged in business; was married in 1804 to Miss Mary, daughter of Charles Smith, of Port Hope, who died in 1847. Elsewhere has been mentioned the part he took in the war of 1812, for which he received an official recognition. Mr. Wilkins had for several days, the late General Scott of the American army, when a prisoner in Canada. Mr. Wilkins' kindness to him was remembered in later years. In the trouble of 1836–8, the Government called upon Mr. W. to take command of the militia. He was appointed to many posts of honor and duty, and in 1840 was called to the Legislative Council. Mr. Wilkins was always exceedingly popular, not because he sought popularity, but because of his naturally kind and gentlemanly deportment to all classes, and his many sterling qualities. The very high estimation in which he was held was fully evidenced on the occasion of his death in 1867, when old friends came long distances in unpleasant weather, to see his remains deposited in their last earthly resting place.

STEWART.—"A traveler writing in 1835, says of Canada, "I often met the venerable in years," and "on March 8, 1833, died Mrs. J. Stewart, near St. David's, Niagara District, aged 109 years; her husband died a few years since at the age of 96, leaving children, now living, aged 80, and grand-children at 60." "Last year a woman by the name of *Metcalf*, residing near the capital of Upper Canada, bore a child when past her sixtieth year."

Among obituary notices we find the following: "At Hope Village, East Guilliamsbury, in 1829, much and generally regretted, *John Wilson, Esq.*, a native of the Province of New Jersey, aged 90 years, 14 days."

DEATH OF A PIONEER OF LONDON TOWNSHIP.—We have to record the decease of Mr. Joseph Jayne, which took place at his residence in London Township, 7th concession, lot 32, on Wednesday last, the 10th inst., at the advanced age of nearly 101 years. He was born on Long Island, N. Y., on June 13, 1764, some years before the State of New York had ceased to be a British Province. Deceased was revered and held in esteem by a large circle of friends, for whose entertainment he was ever fond of recounting his adventures in the revolutionary period, and who deeply regret his loss.—*London Free Press.*

MCINTOSH.—"On the 25th February last at his residence in Marysburgh, in the 93rd year of his age, respected by all his acquaintances, Mr. Donald McIntosh, who came to America in the 42nd Royal Highlanders, and arrived the day before the battle of Bunker's Hill, and was in that engagement. He was subsequently in the 84th, and was at Quebec, when Montgomery made his unsuccessful attempt on that stronghold, and during last war, was a Lieutenant in the 1st Regt. of Prince Edward Militia."

BIRD.—"At his residence in Marysburgh, Mr. Henry Bird, in the 90th year of his age. He appeared to be in good health till a few moments before the vital spark took its flight; he was well respected; he came to Canada in the 54th Regt."

GEROW.—"At Ameliasburgh, in the County of Prince Edward, on Wednesday, the 19th inst., Mary Gerow, aged 80 years. Deceased was one of the first settlers on the borders of the Bay of Quinte, where the greater part of her long life has been spent."

VANKLEECK.—"In Madoc, on Monday, the 9th of October, Simeon Vankleeck, Esq., in his 98th year, after a short illness, almost entirely free from pain. Old age seemed to claim its rights, and the system quietly gave way. Mr. Vankleeck was one of the earliest pioneers of this part of the country, having resided in Madoc forty-one years. He was well and favourably known throughout the county, and his immediate acquaintance bear testimony to his energy and firmness, which mingled at the same time with a kindness and suavity that won their hearts. His old age was remarkable for genial good temper and activity of mind and body. In his 94th year, he presided at a political meeting held by the Hon. Sidney Smith, at Hazzard's Corners, to which place he walked from his son's residence, a distance of seven miles. In politics he was noted for his strong conservative feeling—the side he chose when a young man—and adhered to it through his whole life, believing it to be, as he stated in his later years, the "Loyal Side."

The deceased was a descendant of a branch of the Vankleeck family, whose loyalty to the British Crown caused them to leave their ancient home in Duchess County, New York, during the American Revolution, and to settle in the wilds of Canada. He was several years connected with the British army During the Revolution. He leaves several sons, two of whom reside in this township.—*Mercury*.

PERRY.—Died at Ernesttown, the 12th of January instant, Jemima Perry, wife of Robert Perry, Senr., and sister of the late Ebenezer Washburn, Esq., of Hallowell, in the 76th year of her age. Her remains were interred on the 14th, with every mark of real but unostentatious grief and respect.

"In the beginning of last November, she was seized with a distressing asthmatic affectation, which finally terminated her life, and which she endured with Christian patience and resignation to the will of heaven.

"Mrs. Perry was born in the Province of Massachusetts, and came with her husband and family into this Province among its first settlers.

"She has left an aged partner, with whom she lived in conjugal union and affection fifty-eight years: seven children; a numerous train of grandchildren and great-grandchildren; and a large circle of friends and acquaintances. Her loss is extensively felt. In the various relations of life, as a wife, a mother, a sister, a neighbour, and a member of civil and Christian society, her exemplary conduct entitled her to the esteem of all who knew her."

"OLD MAN.—Old John Baker, residing at Cornwall, Ontario, was born in 1766, at Quebec. His mother was a slave, and he was brought by his master, Colonel Grey, at one time Solicitor-General for Upper Canada. Baker enlisted in the 104th regiment, and served at Waterloo, Lundy's Lane, Fort Erie, and Sackett's Harbor. He is a little rheumatic, and is lame from a wound in the leg, received in action; but his intellect is as fresh and clear as when a boy. He draws a pension of one shilling sterling a day, and seems good for some years yet," 1869.

In conclusion we may mention the descendants of Sir William Johnson, by Miss Molly, a sister of Joseph Brant. She came to Kingston at an early date, having probably been in Lower Canada during the war, where she lived until her death in 1804 or 5. One of her daughters married Captain Farley, of the 16th Regiment, another Lieutenant Lemoine, of the 24th Regiment; a third John Ferguson, of the Indian Department; a fourth Captain Earle, of the Provincial Navy, and another to Doctor Kerr, an eminent surgeon, who settled in Niagara.

APPENDIX.

ROLL OF THE 2ND BATTALION KING'S ROYAL REGIMENT, NEW YORK, 28TH FEB., 1784.

Jacob Weegar
Alexander Clark
Alexander Platto
Jacob Cobman
Jonas Simmons
James Rankins
Jonas Larranary
Richard Albery
Gabriel Brefsea
Christopher Brefsea
Bankes, John, Jr
Bankes, John, Sen
Brant, Franc
Baxter, Lawrence
Benedict, Benjamin
Coons, Jacob
Coons, David
Campbell, Matthews
Connrad, William
Coolcraft, Christian
Cook, Seth
Catchcatch, Christian
Drihell, Cornelius
Dewitt, Garton
Dyckman, Martines
Foster, Moses
Hopkinson, John
Haines, Barrast
Haines, Frederick
Haines, John
Haines, David
Hoyle, John
Hoyle, Peter
House, John
Huffman, Jacob
Henerham, Andrew
Hill, Timothy
Mordon, John
Morrison, James
Wher, John
Phillips, Michael
Phillips, Peter
Pember, Phillip
Priest, Jacob
Redding, Francis
Friar, Samuel
File, John
Franklin, John
Fend, Andrew
Gates, Thomas
Hart, Zachariah
Howell, Warren
Johnson, Henry
Rahall, John
Loukes, Jacob
Millross, Andrew
McCarty, William
Matthews, Pompey
Middelton, Ruben
Northrup, Eson
Reynold, William
Scot, Daniel
Shaw, William
Sholtes, John
Snartfager, Frederick
Sipperly, Phillip
Smith, Stephen
Smith, Jacob
Cornell, Patner
Shilliner, Christian
Wallan, Samuel
Wirst, John
Young, Daniel
Defororest, Abraham
Willoughby, William
William, Albert
Young, Peter
Young, Stephen
Deal, Peter
Bernus, Gother
Fletcher, John
Lount, John
Michael Roughnett
Alexander Grant
George Christie
John Bondish
David Lishsamblin
Peter Zenith
Nicholas Schyler
Atherson, Charles
Magle, Gottip
Badernach, John
Ross, Alexander
John Casscallion
Cornelius Pitcher
Peter Deal
John Litcher
Alexander McDougall
Luke Carscallion
John Berrn
George Sullivan
James V. Alstine
Berron, John
Huben, Peter
Barnhart, David
Cole, John
Calden, John
Coons, Simon
Coons, Peter
Cronkhite, John
Conelius, John
Curtis, John
Dych, Nicholas
Dych, Henry
Deal, Adam
Detlor, Valentine
Detlor, Jacob
Emerish, Henry
French, Andrew
Finkle, George
Cameron, Alexander
Cameron, Angus
Cameron, Donald
Davis, Peter
Earner, Peter
Eearhart, Simon
Eaverson, John
Foy, John
Fory, Daniel
Farlinger, John
Fike, Peter
Fairchild, Benjamin
Faish, Christian
Goose, Frederick
Hugh, John

Randal, Joseph
Snider, Jacob
Snider, Lidwich
Sills, John
Sills, Lawrence
Sills, George
Smith, Michael
Smith, Phillip
Swathager, John
Vszie, Joseph
Baltingal, Jacob
Baltingal, Samuel
Rauley, Jacob
Plant, Peter
Rollin, Thomas
Clark, Hugh
Chrisholm, Donald
Sutter, Isaac
Thomson, Thomas
Thom, William
Christie, George
Beedehee, John
Samuel Ashley
James McPherson
George Barnhart
George Dagetger
George Prest
George Fitzpatrick
James Titehert
Peter Young
Cain Young
Clute, John
Cooper, Thomas
Cook, Silas
Coomb, John
Coomb, Barnard
Donser, John
Dire, John
Davis, Henery
Dogstader, Adam
Dengandre, Garrett
Dogstader, Pompey
Edgar, John
Foy, Francis
Gilbert Luke
Thomas Graham
Grant, Peter
Gold, Edward
Gallingher, George
Heming, Henry
Hawley, Jacob
Helmer, Adam
Helse, Frederick
Hugh, Henry
Hendrick, Peter
Harbinger, John
Tarhoson, David
Kough, Peter
Kreem, John

Bailer, William
Bell, Johnson
Beitte Barnard
Barnhart, Nicholas
Barnhart, Jacob
Barnhart John
Brown, Nicholas
Burch, Jacob
Brown, James
Christian, John
Christian, Simion
Cameron, William
Medagh, John
Myers, John
Cugh, George
Culman, Frederick
Parsons, John
Rood, Mitchell
Ramsay, Adam
Sulivan, Cornelius
Shirley, John
Shellop, Henry
Winter, Jacob
Winter, Henry
Wilson, James
Kough, James
Connor, Christian
Wilinger, Michael
Smith, Jacob
Eamer, Phillip
Hawdord, Edward
Mure, John
John Miller
Fossern, Daniel
Latoch, Halburt
Elijah Sarrabe
George Murraoff
Luke Bourteal
Toil Hurd
Samuel Suckey
John Saver
John Teague
Barnhart, Charles
Beramy, William
Boner, Gasper
Boner, Adam
Bender, Samuel
Cox, Alexander
Crander, Anthony
John Crander
Crander, William
Cadman, William
Cadman, George
Coundouse, George
Dow, Thomas
Delong, John
Evans, Tony
Landras, Samuel
Logest, Andrew

Hamilton, Thomas
Henning, Andrew
House, Coonroot
Hedlar, Adam
Johnson, John
Hellen, John
Himmerly, Andrew
Ylline,
Law, Samuel
Heller, Henry
Noon, William
Battingal, Jacob
French, Albert
Flamsbury, William
Howard, William
Harding, Richard
Jones, Thomas
Johnson, William
Jones, John
Roughnet, John
Rentner, George
Knight, Benjamin
Koughnet, John
Lonhey, George
Lonhey, Henry
Lonhes, Abraham
Savanay, Alexander
Sambert, David
Sawyer, William
Loft, David
McGowen, Stephen
Murdoff, James
Murdoff, George
Moss, Simon
Critchert, Bartholomew
Rogers, John
Rambaugh, Jacob
Rambaugh, John
Rambaugh, Andrew
Rambaugh, William
Shellop, Christian
Smith, Daniel
Shuk, Christian
Tute, John
Kemdy, Robert
Church, Oliver
Hillinger, Abraham
Laryo, Matthew
Erwiny, Robert
Schnars, Frederick
John Howell
Francis Hoyb
Richard Cotter
Matthew Farrent
Jothan Hart
Joseph Clement
Henry Davis
John Windaker
Brant, John.

Borven, William, Senr
Baker, Henry
Borven, William, Junr.
Bush, Henry
Cameron, Archibald
Dodger, Thomas
McDonnell, John, Senr.
McDonnell, John, Junr.
McDonnell, Roderick
McDonald, Ronald
McPherson, Laughlin
Matthew, Jacob
Naramore, Esau
Penn, Matthew
Prentice, Daniel
Prichell, John
Phillips, Jacob
Porker, Isaac
Ross, Thomas, Senr.
Ross, Thomas, Junr.
Ross, John
Roaf, John
Ryan, Dennis
Rowland, Jervis
Tingorac, John
Starring, Jacob
Severn, Peter
Servus, Phillip
Smith, John
Hart, Nathaniel
Sherman, William
Tuniver, William
Valentine, Alexander
Warmly, Jacob
Cook, Robert
Rierman, Henry
Schilles, Henry
Henry Deal
John Servin
Andrew Embury
Thomas Clark
William Nicholson
John Dogstider
Allen Chrisholm
John Dervitt
Arginsinger, John
Bartley, Muherd
Bartley, Isaac
Chrisholm, Duncan
Cain, John
Coon, Jacob
Campbell, John
Cain, Barney
Cook, Joseph

Farling, John
Hough, George
Hight, Mathew
Johnson, Prince
Peacock, John
Kenton, John
Delorm, John
Donevan, Herener
Evans, Bolton
Eglon, Leonard
Estwood, John
Flanagan, James
Gardiner, John
Horon, Peter
Horon, Jacob
Hubbert, Jubilee
Hegle, John
Koughnet, William
Koliph, Henry
Toyer, David
Toyer, Richard
Martin, Robert
Murphy, Patrick
McGran, Owen
McGran, Dennis
McDonnell, Daniel
Nellinger, Abraham
Phillips, Elijah
Rapole, George
Shaver, Adam
Sample, Hugh
Street, Daniel
Staly, Tobias
Stering, George
Truax, Isaac
Turnburny, John
Woodcock, Abraham
Woodcock, Peter
Welsh, Morris
Argussiger, Phillip
Wilson, James
Thomas Cavan
John McIntyre
John Ham,
Abiah Christie
Donald McPherson
John Tower
Peter Winter
John Lambert
Albert Edward
Ball, Samuel
Crawford, William
Crumwell, Nicholas

Santnere, Jacob
Witts, Henry
Witts, John
McCardy, Jacob
Mirile, Jacob
Minse, John
Crawford, Bryan
Clark, Jacob
Clark, Adam
Clark, John
Chrisholm, Hugh
Faber, David
Fitzgerald, William
Furny, Rodolph
Furny, Adam
Gilbert, Nathaniel
Graham, William
Grant, Peter
Helmer, John
Horon, Joseph
Howard, Christian
Towar, Canrobert
Tarranay, Isaac
Tarranay, Abraham
Matthew, Nicholas
McKay, Stephen
McTaggart, James
McDonald, Duncan
Mitchell, John
McIntyre, Duncan
McLennon, John
Oxbury, John
Phillip, John
Rote, George
Reyers, William
Robertson, Daniel
Shaver, James
Smith, William
Smith, Peter
Sweeney, Daniel
Stewart, John
Teagin, Jacob
Vandregoo, Phillip
Abstric, Lambert
Wright, John
Walroda, Jacob
Wood, James
Wood, William
Weegar, Thomas
West, John
Toursset, Benjamin
Tealy, Adam
Deprender, George

THE GOVERNORS OF UPPER CANADA.

Subjoined is a list of the Governors, Presidents, and Administrators of Upper Canada, until the Union of the Provinces in 1841 :—

NAMES.	TITLES.	TIME OF ACCESSION.
Col. John Graves Simcoe	Lieutenant-Governor	July 8, 1792.
Hon. Peter Russell	President	July 21, 1796.
Lieut.-Gen. Peter Hunter	Lieutenant-Governor	August 17, 1799.
Hon. Alexander Grant	President	Septr. 11, 1805.
His Excellency Francis Gore	Lieutenant-Governor	August 25, 1806.
Maj.-Gen. Sir Isaac Brock	President	Septr. 30, 1811.
Maj.-Gen. Sir R. Halesheaff, Bart	President	October, 20, 1812.
Maj.-Gen. F. Baron de Rottenburgh	President	June 19, 1813.
Lieut.-Gen. Sir Gordon Drummond, G.C.B	Provincial Lieut.-Governor	Decr. 13, 1813.
Lieut.-Gen. Sir George Murray, Bt.	Provincial Lieut.-Governor	April 25, 1815.
Maj.-Gen. Sir Frederick Phipps Robinson, K.C.B	Provincial Lieut.-Governor	July 1, 1815.
His Excellency Francis Gore	Lieutenant-Governor	Septr. 25, 1815.
Hon. Samuel Smith	Administrator	June 11, 1817.
Maj.-Gen. Sir Peregrine Maitland, K.C.B.	Lieutenant-Governor	August 13, 1818.
Hon. Samuel Smith	Administrator	March 8, 1820.
Maj.-Gen. Sir P. Maitland, K.C.B.	Lieutenant-Governor	June 30, 1820.
Maj.-Gen. Sir John Colborne, K.C.B.	Lieutenant-Governor	Novr. 5, 1828.
Maj. Sir Francis Bond Head, K.C.B.	Lieutenant-Governor	Jany. 25, 1836.
Maj.-Gen. Sir John Colborne, K.C.B	Administrator	Feby. 27, 1838.
Maj.-Gen. Sir George Arthur, K.C.B. H.G.O.	Lieutenant-Governor	March 23, 1838.
Baron Sydenham and Toronto	Lower Canada. Governor General	October, 1839.
Do. do. do. do.	United do. do. do.	Feby. 10, 1841.

THE ABORIGINES OF NORTH AMERICA.

THE MISSISSAUGA.

The following Report, sent by Col. Bell, of Thurlow, to John Ferguson, Superintendent for Indian Affairs, Kingston, dated 3rd May, 1815, supplies a tolerably correct idea of the articles furnished by Government to the Indians :—

"Account of Indian goods, on the 7th March, 1815, remaining in store in the barn of Lieut.-Col. William Bell, at Thurlow, and forwarded on the 10th, 11th and 20th of the said month of March to the store of Captain W. McIntosh, at the mouth of the river Moira, viz :—

12 Bales Cloths,
9 do. do.,
7 do. do.,
1 do. Calicoes,
1 do. Scotch Sheetings,
1 do. Spotted Black Swanskin,
2 do. Serges,
2 do. Common Grey Coats,
11 do. Caddises,
5 Packs Deer Skins,
11 Bales Moltons,
6 Cases Saddles and Bridles,
1 do. Pistols,
26 do. Chiefs' and Common Guns,
5 Casks Tobacco,
20 Cases Shot and Ball,
7 do. Tomahawks,
4 do. Spears, &c.,
3 Bags Beef Saws,
22 Bales 3-feet Blankets,
27 do. 2½-feet do.,
7 do. 2-feet do.

"N.B.—The above Packages have been delivered into the Store of Captain John McIntosh, at the mouth of the river Moira, and his receipt taken for them and delivered to you at Kingston, and also the book in which all the marks and numbers were entered."

CPSIA information can be obtained
at www.ICGtesting.com
Printed in the USA
LVHW041540051222
734620LV00004B/105